I0562914

THE MYSTERIES of BERLIN.

TO BE COMPLETED

IN

TEN PARTS.

NEW YORK: WILLIAM H. COLYER, PUBLISHER.

THE

MYSTERIES OF BERLIN,

FROM

THE PAPERS OF A BERLIN CRIMINAL OFFICER.

TRANSLATED FROM THE GERMAN, BY

C. B. BURKHARDT, ESQ.

WITH ILLUSTRATIONS ON STEEL, BY P. HABELMANN.

NEW-YORK:

WILLIAM H. COLYER, No. 5 HAGUE-STREET.

1845.

Entered according to an Act of Congress,

BY WILLIAM H. COLYER,

In the Clerk's Office of the Southern District of New York, in the year 1845

TURNEY & LOCKWOOD, STEREOTYPERS,
16 Spruce Street, New York.

TRANSLATOR'S PREFACE.

A word with you, kind reader, before you read or cast aside the " Mysteries of Berlin."

The favour with which my former translations from the German, comprising works of *Spindler, Zschokke, Seatsfield, &c.*, have been received, though those works mostly appeared anonymously, or under other names, emboldens me to offer these volumes, with a few words of recommendation on my part.

Since the appearance of *M. Eugene Sue's* famous work, *Mysteries* of every town and village have multiplied to a most unheard of extent. After the Mysteries of London, Hamburg, New York, Boston, Lowell, and a hundred other places, with which the market of light reading has been glutted, had appeared, an enterprising Parisian dealer in ready made linen, availing himself of the popularity of the name, favoured the reading public with, " *Les Mystères de la Chemise,*" a capital " paying advertisement " of his shop.

Although there was unquestionably some merit in most of the first mentioned works, yet for the greater part, they were either servile imitations of M. Sue's work, or else trifles unworthy of notice.

The classes of society in Paris, which M. Sue depicts in his "Mysteries," are, by this time well known to most Novel-readers, as well as the same classes in London have become familiar by means of the powerful plan of Mr. Dickens. The object of M. Sue and Mr. Dickens in their works was nearly the same—exposure of abuses of the laws, protection to the lower and working classes, and *prevention* of crime, rather than *punishment.*

The operation of common law in France, England and America, is, in these respects nearly the same, as in all these countries there are trials by jury, open courts, &c., &c. All, however, is different in Prussia and most of the other German Sovereignties, where the Courts of Justice are held in private, where the mass of the people cannot witness the proceedings, and where lawyers must argue with the pen instead of the tongue ; and this is one of our principal reasons for thinking that these volumes will prove interesting and acceptable to the American reader.

The Author of the " Mysteries of Berlin," (*Criminal Actuary* F. Thiele,) from his high official position, and his eminent standing in the world of letters, is the only man who, in that Capital, could undertake and successfully produce such a work.

But even he could not escape prosecution. An exposure of the operations of Secret Tribunals, as they exist there, though favourably drawn, was sure to excite persecution from the Authorities, particularly as the characters of most of the nobility and high functionaries were so strongly and well depicted, as to be easily recognized by almost every *habitué* of Berlin.

According to report, the author was arrested, and dismissed from his office ; but he had antici-pated all this, and had, in his work remained within the limits which he knew to be allowed him by law, and consequently was shortly again liberated and reinstated in his original position.

This trial, however, answered another and different purpose, from the one intended—that of attracting the attention of the world to this work; and before the second book had appeared, the first had gone through four editions in Germany, and been translated into several other languages. Some of the leading English Periodicals, (the " Foreign Quarterly," and others,) in speaking of these facts, wondered that the work should not yet have found a translator into English, as it was certainly destined to be a most popular book among all novel-readers on both sides of the Atlantic.

Whether I have, in translating it, succeeded in making it so, time alone will show. I have endeavoured to render the English version as literal, as the difference of the language, and the great amount of Provincialisms and Slang, which naturally occurs in such a work, would admit.

With these few preliminary remarks, I beg leave to offer the work " with all its imperfections on its head," to the kind attention of the American public.

THE TRANSLATOR.

37 Mercer-street,
New York, January, 1845.

THE MYSTERIES OF BERLIN.

CHAPTER I.

THE CABIN.

IF any of our kind readers have had the fortune, or, as the case may be, the misfortune to be soldiers, they will know the picture presented by a Berlin guard-room on a cold winter's night. The immense fire which burns in the gigantic stove, and offers plain proof that it is not fed at the expense of those who warm by it, the scanty light, usually consisting of a single stump of tallow candle, and the devil-may-care sort of rest which is usually expressed in the appearance of the lounging musketeers, give to such a guard-room an air of exceeding snugness and comfort. On the other hand, the hard wooden berths, the full uniform of those resting on them with their arms by their side, and their constant listening for the call of the sentinel, create a most dejecting and gloomy contrast.

Such was the picture which presented itself in the guard-room of the Cologne Town-hall, on the night between the ninth and tenth of December, 18——.

The night was very cold and comfortless. A sharp Northeast wind whistled along Broad-street, threatening every moment to extinguish the entire row of gas flames, spite their bright glass cases. Solitary snow-flakes, which seemed rather to rise to than fall from the skies, obscured the air, and hit like as many needles the faces of several misanthropic watchmen. The lights of the private dwellings were mostly extinguished. Only at the castle a few solitary chandeliers, who had just had the honour to shed light on a brilliant assembly of her Excellency the Lady Castellan, were still flickering, and in the new saloon of d'Heureuse, the confectioner, the pretty hands of the fair chocolate girls were just busy turning off the gas of the last lights in the place.

In the guard-room there lay six or eight strong muscular forms, in lazy attitudes upon the oaken reclining board. The sergeant of the watch alone sat by the dim light of his farthing candle at the much-whittled table, reading the adventures of Rinaldo Rinaldini, which his sweet-heart, the privy counsellor's fat cook, had brought him late in the evening, together with an immense pot of coffee. What remained of the Extract of Mocca stood in silent company with the ink-stand and the half-finished watch-report before the military despot, whose features displayed the important consciousness of having the safety of the entire quarter of the city entrusted to his vigilance for the night.

A fellow covered with rags, and whose hair-clothed face resembled that of the Orang Outang more than the " human face divine," and who had surrendered to the united exertions of three watchmen, lay wrapped in sweet slumbers by the side of the red-hot stove, upon a large bundle of stiffly frozen linen, which he most probably had just stolen from some garret. He snored a gentle duo with a Polish musketeer, who that night had mounted his first guard, and whose head was slackly hanging over the edge of the broad reclining board. An immense piece of the coarsest kind of sausage, half a loaf of ammunition-bread, and a small flask of dingy whiskey, indicated the sources whence this noble youth drew his nourishment.

The only strange sounds which were audible in this abode of peace, were the steps of the outside sentinel, who, to warm himself, ran up and down before his sentry-box, hitting his cold hands against the butt of his musket to produce circulation of the blood, whilst his feet were performing various antics upon the broad side-walk.

This monotonous scene was suddenly interrupted by a young, well formed man, dressed in a gray cloak and red striped cap, whose brown features had, through the aid of an immense moustache, an almost martial appearance, and who entered the guard-room with the words :

" Where is the sergeant on guard ?"

Slowly and with dignity, that functionary turned upon his stool, haughtily withdrawing the long pipe from his lips, and asked peevishly for the stranger's wishes.

" l am W——., the Criminal Commissary," was the reply, " and l wish the assistance of two men from the guard for a police search."

" May I ask to see your authority," replied the sergeant, who now thought proper to rise, and salute the stranger more respectfully.

With a slow and quiet manner, the other shook the snow off his cloak, turned down the collar, and then produced from his left vest pocket a medal, which on one side bore the inscription,

Königl: Preuss: Polizei-Beamter,
(Royal Prussian Police Officer,)
and on the other the Prussian eagle, and held this important token before the eyes of the careful commander. The hasty glance of the sergeant recognized the authority, and he turned to the sleepers with the question :

" Which number does next mount guard ?"

" Number two," replied a deep voice from the oaken couch, and then recommenced snoring in the sweet consciousness of belonging to number one.

" Czoseck and Brunnenthal, take your muskets then, and get ready," commanded the sergeant, as he resumed his pipe, and prepared himself to return to the lecture in which he had been interrupted.

Those who had been called, rose most unwillingly from their hard bed, packed their few matters together, placed their czakko (military hat) upon the head, and mechanically took down their muskets, which, to guard against the damp, were hanging inside the room.

In a few minutes the little caravan was in motion, and the soldiers lazily followed the police officer, who, with long strides passsed through Broad-street, and then turned to the right toward the Long Bridge. Here they met two gensd'armes who had remained behind to find the watchman of the district, and also to make a few observations, the purport of which our readers shall soon know.

The careful officer to avoid all suspicion, told his men to step behind a little shanty, which is situated by the old Post Buildings at the Long Bridge, and is occupied as a turner's shop. Here he explained to them, that, for several nights past, he had observed an empty turf-boat which lay for the winter in Burg-street, behind the Cathedral, and that suspicious rabble had taken up their quarters in the cabin of said boat. The arrest of this party was to be the task for the night. To accomplish this, the experienced officer gave the following instructions: the boat was to be approached from different sides upon the ice which covered the Spree, and thus to be surrounded. The greatest precaution and particular silence was necessary. When the signal of a low whistle was heard from the leader of the expedition, a loud and horrible noise should be made on all sides, to give the robbers a sudden affright. The watchman with one musketeer was then to secure the back door, and the other musketeer with a gensd'arme the front door of the cabin. The commander himself would enter with the second gensd'arme, and effect the arrest of the suspected.

After having once more passed the flask around, the party moved on, and approached that part of the shore, opposite to which the boat lay, a dark indistinct mass. By a silent motion the officer directed the attention of his party to the fine streak of smoke, which arose, scarcely visible, from the chimney of the boat, and also pointed to a soft ray of light, which most suspiciously passed through a crack in the wood-work. These plain and evident marks left no doubt of the favourable result of the expedition.

With a gentle and careful step, the servants of Justice descended one of the stairs, which in many places in Burg-street lead to the water, and which are marked by the words: " Public wharf." With the same care the party approached the hostile boat. The Criminal Commissary and the gend'armes had even succeeded to mount the stern of the boat without being discovered. But one of the musketeers in trying to climb the bow of the vessel, most awkwardly dropped his musket, and thereby creating a considerable noise, forced the officer to give the signal sooner than he had intended.

When the noise and cries of the approaching party had ceased, a considerable rustling was heard in the boat, followed in a few seconds by grave-like silence, interrupted only by the howling of the storm, and the creaking of a neighbouring sign on its hinges, until the officer loudly, and with a few official oaths, demanded the opening of the cabin. No answer, however, was returned to his repeated demands, so that at last a few kicks had to effect an opening of the tottering door.

The interior of the cabin presented a most surprising appearance. The entire furniture consisted on the one side, of a berth filled with straw and a wooden bench in front of it. On the opposite side stood an old rusty ship's stove, by the side of a small cupboard.

The berth was occupied by a strong, young fellow, whose pale, yet bloated features at the first glance betrayed the habitual inmate of the prison. By his side lay a young girl of about twenty or twenty-two years, whose face presented a strange mixture of noble and vulgar features. Both were covered with an old officer's cloak, evidently the fruit of a theft. Beneath their head lay a bundle of new linen, seemingly of the same origin. Both had partly risen from their couch, and stared in terror upon the intruders, while the female uttered a loud shriek.

Upon the bench in front of the couch sat an older man, whose long, black whiskers and crooked nose betrayed the Jewish descent, and looked with indifference on the scene, drumming with the fingers of his right hand upon his knee. The practised villain knew well that all resistance would be useless, and with the greatest *sang froid* awaited his oft experienced fate of an arrest.

Before the stove, where a large fire was burning, (but which, to avoid all suspicious smoke, was fed by charcoal,) sat a dirty old woman. A pan filled with meat, and a wooden spoon which she held in her hand, indicated her capacity of cook to this patriarchal family. A basket full of filthy rags, which stood in the background of the cabin, and a stick with a small hook to its end, standing by its side, betrayed the old woman's daily occupation.

By the side of the cabin upon mighty wooden pegs hung two freshly butchered animals, prepared in a perfectly artistical style, and which at first sight seemed the bodies of a lamb and a hare. But upon close examination you could observe in the larger animal the melancholy features of a big, black poodle, and on the smaller one, the long chin-bristles of a well fed grimalkin. On comparing the contents of the frying pan in the old woman's hands with the appearance of the largest of the animals, no doubt remained of the old woman's intentions of treating her fair guests with a fresh roasted dog's joint. The coal gas, and the natural bad odour which prevaded the entire place was so oppressive, that the intruders hesitated for a moment at the threshold.

This was the moment the old woman tried to use and make an adroit escape. She suddenly jumped up, sent the boiling contents of her pan into the face of the nearest gensd'arme, tore open the back door, where the watchman quietly awaiting the result of the expedition, smoked his pipe, hit his face a blow with the sooty bottom of the pan which loosened every tooth in his mouth, and with such effect that his fat, sleek face at once looked like that of a freshly tattooed Indian.

This sudden surprise completely overthrew the watchman's presence of mind. He staggered back, dropped his weighty spear, and was unable to utter a sound save a low grumbling from his burned lips, which still retained the end of his pipe, while the remainder of it was trampled beneath the feet of the furious old woman.

She would certainly have effected her escape—for after she had with her long nails made a perfect map of the soldier's face who stood beside the watchman, he also lost the desire of engaging with her any farther—had not the active Criminal-Commissary, convinced that the back door was not sufficienty manned, been quick as thought upon the spot where he was most needed. The old woman had just stumbled over a beam, and the strong arm of the Commissary caught her, and brought her back into the cabin. The two gend'armes had meanwhile taken the rest of the party, and they were properly tied with ropes which had been brought along for the occasion. Even at this the old woman gave a great deal of trouble, for in her rage and fury she distorted her limbs in such a manner, and strained them to a degree, that she could not be bound without danger of a fracture.

But the guardian of the night, who had meanwhile recovered from his shock, and gathered the remnants of his pipe, when he saw the old woman without power to harm him, attacked her in so furious a manner with his fists, that her limbs soon recovered their former flexibility.

In a few minutes the inhabitants of the cabin stood fettered before it, and in company of the two soldiers and one gensd'arme began their journey to the city prison, where, by order of the Commissary, they were kept separate until their examination should take place.

As the clock of the Cathedral struck one, the watchman had to be dismissed to announce that fact to the sleepless inhabitants of his district.

The Commissary remained behind in the cabin with the other gensd'arme, as a more close examination of those precincts had yet to take place. This examination produced a most favourable result. Beneath the straw of the couch they found two large bunches of skeleton and hook-keys, each of which formed a "Gross-Clamoniss," as it is called in the slang of the Berlin thieves, namely, each bunch contained thirty keys of so multitudinous a variety that no lock could be found to resist them all. Besides these, there was a number of chisels of different shapes and sizes, (called in their slang, Schabber, or Gross-Purim,) and finally beneath the double floor of the cabin, they found a large iron crowbar, called Krumm-Kopf, by the thieves.

All these instruments proved that they were dealing with Schränkern* of the most dangerous kind.

Beside the above, they found divers purses, candlesticks, clothing, &c., evidently the fruits of former robberies. The evidences of want which they found everywhere, proved that the band had not taken any good prize for a long time.

CHAPTER II.

THE INTERMEZZO.

WE will leave the official functionaries at their pursuits, and follow the fate of the captive Schränkers. Too much taken by surprise at their sudden arrest, they walked in silence side by side, taking the well known road towards the Molkenmarket.

One of the musketeers walked in advance, followed by the two male prisoners, and behind them the gensd'arme and second soldier leading the two females between them.

Not until they had passed the Joachimsthal College, and were walking along Little-Burg-street towards the street of the Holy Ghost, the youngest Schränker said to the eldest in a whisper:

"I should not have thought it, Schmerles, that we would so soon have been verschütt, (arrested.) That Lambden (Police Officer) is a smart man."

"Be easy, Eeleye," replied the other, "we are not treife (nothing can be proved against us.) We make the Putz, that we have found the Cabache as it is, and the Balverschmai cannot hurt us, (we tell them that we found our night's quarter as it was, and the criminal judge cannot punish us.) I am only sorry for the beautiful Masematten, (theft,) that would have enriched us forever, after I have baldowert (reconnoitered) it for five nights, and which Long Schmuel and the Blonde Augustus will to-morrow lift alone."

"And I," replied the younger prisoner, "I only regret my beautiful Schrankzeug, and my Chonte, (sweetheart,) who is now taken with us."

"Let the Chonte be," replied the Jewish Schränker, "the Chonte will know how to make her Putz, (her excuse,) and the Chonte will then go to Long Schmuel, and he will have to share with us. For the Masematten belongs to us."

This conversation would have been continued for some time longer, had not the conducting gensd'arme interrupted it, with the words—

"How long is this chatting to continue here?" to which he added a few oaths, and some unmistakeable manual demonstrations.

After this interruption, deep silence again reigned among the fettered band, which was only

* Berlin professional thieves are divided into two classes, the Schranker and Torfdrucker. The latter only pick pockets and commit petty larcenies, called Schlamassen. The former devote themselves exclusively to burglary, called Masematten, which they accomplish by the use of various instruments, called Schrankzeug. They consider it beneath their dignity to pick pockets, and only resort to it when in great Schwindel. (angl. need.)

occasionally broken by a deep sigh of the old man, until the Chonte, with a rather good voice, began singing a low song, the obscenity of which was sufficient proof of the baseness of her character, while at the same time it contributed no little to the momentary cheering of her companions. If these had not felt bitter disappointment in their hearts, on account of that glorious Masematten, for which they had so long waited, and at last in the following night had hoped to accomplish, but which now was hopelessly gone—had it not been for this, they would joyously have met their fate.

But under existing circumstances they walked forward with dark, furious looks, and wildly gnashed their teeth ; when near to St. Nicholas' church, the high walls of the Police buildings met their eye.

Just at this place, however, their fortune was destined again to take a sudden, unexpected, and favourable turn. As the party was turning the corner, they met a man of gigantic stature, who suddenly blew the full volume of smoke of a large cigar directly into the face of the leading gensd'arme.

Those who know the nature of a Berlin gensd'arme, know, that for them there exists not a more hostile element than the smoke of a burning cigar. Wherever these two opposing elements meet, there usually arises a strife, which, though only for the sum of two Thalers,* or for "durance vile" of forty-eight hours, is, for earnest determination and obstinacy, seldom equalled by more important battles.

As usual, there arose immediately a warm dispute between our gensd'arme and the strange smoker, which, as the puffing gentleman was no ways inclined to obey the orders of the minion of Justice, finally changed into a regular fist-fight.

At this, however, the zealous officer of Police found an opponent who was by far his superior. For the stranger possessed such Herculean strength, and such wonderful agility, that in a few seconds the gensd'arme found himself covered with innumerable blows and cuffs, and senselessly prostrated upon a door-step near the scene of action. The musketeers who had come to the assistance of their unfortunate leader, fared no better. For the unknown caught one of their necks in each of his gigantic fists, and knocked their heads together with such irresistible force, that they produced a rattling noise similar to that of two hollow nutshells, while the owners of these skulls, for a few moments, lost the entire use of their senses.

The Chonte availed herself of this lucky moment to obtain liberty for herself and her companions.

Some minutes before, she had succeeded in loosening the ropes which tied her arms on her back, while the old rag-gatherer, (whose hands had been loosened from pity for her age,) had

approached her cautiously, and assisted her from time to time, when no eye was upon them.

By an extraordinary exertion of all her strength, the active woman slipped off her bands, thereby loosing part of the sleeve of her dress, and then produced a knife from a secret pocket, with which, quick as thought, she cut the cords that impeded the escape of her fellow prisoners.

The others were not backward in availing themselves of this favourable opportunity, and in a few seconds they were scattered in all directions.

When the musketeers awoke from their swoon, they were at first inclined to believe the adventures of the night to have been a bad dream, and were about to turn over to get a little quiet sleep. But the appearance of the wet pavement, which had transferred part of its mud to their habiliments, the cut cords of the prisoners which lay at their feet, and the groans of the gensd'arme, soon assured them of the reality of their mishap. A few minutes afterwards the musketeers arrived at the Police-room of the Town-hall, and instead of the arrested thieves they delivered the sick gensd'arme, who was not able to return to his own quarters till late the next morning.

CHAPTER III.

THE VOIGHTLAND.

BERLIN, properly speaking, is composed of two towns, a large one, the actual city, and a smaller, the *Voightland.*

The latter is usually only called the *Rosenthal Vorstadt,* (Rosenthal Suburb,) but the Voightland is more than a mere suburb, it is a town by itself. Its peculiar mode of building makes it such. While in the city and the other faubourgs only three and four story buildings, and finely paved streets with brilliant gas lamps may be seen, in the Voightland we can find only filthy oil-lamps, unpaved streets, in the mud of which armies might be lost, and small, one story houses, built beneath the level of the street and without cellars, into the garret windows of which any well grown man might peep without trouble.

The occupations, manners and customs of the inhabitants are also entirely different from those of the city. For the majority of the denizens of Voightland consists of Tinkers, Potters, Turf-carriers, Ragmen, Dog-traders, Farriers, Bone-collectors, Wood-choppers, Weavers, Clothes-scourers, Pickle-merchants, Fruiterers, Cobblers, Bird-fanciers, Bandbox-makers, Shoe-blacks, *et hic genii omnes.* The aristocracy of these manifold classes, are pensioned subalterns, needy widows, bankrupt proprietors, shopkeepers, and the officers of the district.

Weddings are not the fashion in the Voightland, for the cheapest wedding costs at least 1 Thaler 22 sgr. 6 pf. (about one dollar twenty-five cents,) for the ceremony, and this amount will buy oceans of the finest *Schnapps.** Many of the

---

* The amount of the fine for smoking in the streets of Berlin, of which the gensd'arme or policeman gets one half.

* Every kind of common cordial or spirits is called Schnapps.—*Translator.*

Voightlanders consequently live in a so-called Polish wedlock, by which the police is cheated in every imaginable way.

Suits of libel or slander are never known in Voightland, for there are scarcely two persons within its limits who have not, either by word or action, fought with each other. Consequently the Voightlander has a most peaceable character, forgetting injuries as quickly as he inflicts them, and embracing as a brother to day the man whom yesterday he persecuted as his most bitter enemy.

The principal food of the Voightlanders consists in spirits, coffee, bread, potatoes and lard.

The taxgatherers and excisemen are the natural enemies of the Voightlander, with whom he lives in constant strife.

On the other hand, the district Commissary of Police is the demigod of all the inhabitants. He must settle all disputes, has to appear as guardian angel at every brawl or fight, has to collect contributions and assistance for the poor, obtain releases and pardons—in short, he has the entire earthly fortune of the Voightlander in his hands. By reference to the Commissary, the Voightlander silences a dun or frightens a debtor; by reference to him he consoles complaining widows and begging orphans, and sings his own children to sleep. He himself retires at night with a proud self-sufficiency, if he has had the good fortune to press the hand of this mighty man.

But wo to the poor Police Officer, if the Voightlander has committed some crime, or if on some holiday, Schnapps has assumed full command over his senses.

> "When on a glorious spree,
> In mud up to his knee,
> He fancies himself free——"

Then, the united exertions of several guards, and a number of policemen, are often insufficient for a single Voightlander.

The Voightlander is equally dangerous if he happens to follow a natural impulse, and his earthly goods and chattels on his shoulders, leaves his domicile at dead of night to escape the claws of his avaricious landlord.

Wo to the poor watchman, who, induced by a *Viergroschenstück** of the landlord, attempts treacherously to stop his way. For then the Voightlander fights for his own fireside, for his sole and only attachment, and in this strife he is usually victorious But should he fail, he loses his all, and may then say with Schiller—

> "One look—towards the grave
> Of all that fortune gave,
> Takes Voightland's daring son—
> Then lightly cuts his stick !
> Whatever the landord's stern fury has taken,
> In one respect he has still saved his bacon,
> And he discovers it quick.
> His fair childrens' noses he's just counted o'er,
> And finds them none less, nor a single one more.†"

Then the Voightlander sinks from the position

* A small coin.
† Parody on a verse of Schiller's *Song of the Bell.*

2

of a free man down to that of a *Schlafbursche*, (sleeper-out.) In other words, he, who hitherto has entertained Schlafburschen himself, now becomes one at the domicile of a more aristocratic Voightlander. From this position of dependence he can scarcely ever rise again, as he can never save enough of his scanty earnings to begin housekeeping anew.

Education of children is never thought of in the Voightland, for the noble parents usually leave their home at dawn of day in pursuit of their occupations. The children remain behind, left to themselves, either locked up in the lonely garret, or roving about the dirty yards. The only slender attempt at training consists in this, that the father, on coming home on Saturday evening, his cash, and consequently his drunken-day, beats his wife and children all round in the most marked and effective manner. On these occasions he often uses the smallest of the children, or the nursling, as the instrument of flagellation. At the sixth or seventh year of his age, the Voightlander emancipates himself from parental power.

His first occupation then is the noble science of begging. After this, the boy as vagabondizing salesman, enters the shop of a Plaster of Paris figure-maker, or of a fruit-huckster. Besides this, he makes small attempts at picking pockets and shop-lifting, and enticed by the rich harvests of these occupations, he is soon a perfect artist in his way. He gradually attempts more daring enterprises, and then the prison and the Voightland become alternately his place of abode.

The girl begins her life in a similar manner.— With a small basket she strolls lazily through the streets, trading in roses and violets, or in matches. Soon her youthful bloom attracts the notice of some libertine, to whom she falls an easy victim, and after the loose veil of her chastity has once been torn, she begins a wild, obscene, and dissipated life, which conducts her, after manifold changes of fortune, usually to the brothel or hospital. At a more advanced age she returns thence, often disfigured in her person, the consort of some notorious companion, and again takes up her home in Voightland, unless she should be lucky enough to drive a more lucrative business in the city, as procuress, or as receiver of stolen goods.

The greatest art of the Voightlander consists in making the smallest amount of room answer all his wants for space. A single small garret-room, dimly lit, often serves a family of father, mother, a number of children, and some Schlafburschen, for a domicile.

The central point and real capital of the Voightland is formed by the so-called family houses. These large, barrack-like buildings are occupied by thousands of human beings, sufficient for the population of whole towns, who, for a trifling rent, find here a roof to cover them. From these precincts every morning whole armies of thieving rabble issue forth, and pass through the Hamburg gate into the city, where they spread like a plague in all directions. The reader, comfortably reclining and looking over these pages, can form no conception of the modes and habits prevailing in these nests, where the lowest dregs of society are packed closely together closer than herrings.

It is no fable or fancy, that single rooms are frequently by chalk-marks on the floor divided into quarters, each of which is inhabited by a numerous family. It is no fable that in winter-time hundreds of cats and dogs furnish food for the inhabitants, and that whole families perish of the most disgusting and filthy diseases. That in such a state of things, particularly in times of need or scarcity, the most terrible scenes often occur here—scenes when the most holy family ties are trampled under foot, and that human beings in these places frequently appear far beneath the brute creation—all this, we trust, will need no farther explanation.

We gave this feeble description of life in the Voightland, to make the reader somewhat acquainted with the localities and customs which we shall have occasion to refer to in the development of our story.

The outer boundary of Voightland is near a great number of single farm-yards and houses built in the open fields, and adjoining the neighbouring country roads and villages. In one of these houses, an unseemly cellar is occupied as a low hedge-tavern, which has long been the head-quarters of the most dangerous thieves and robbers. The host of this place was a small, limping and crippled fellow, whose mouse grey bleared eyes, expressed much bad and little good of character. This man's business, from the small number and poverty of his neighbors, was so trifling, that apparently he was reduced to the utmost want. He had been a widower for several years, and his small tavern was attended by a step-daughter—a daughter of his late wife by a former marriage.

This young girl seemed not at all suited for the situation in which she was placed. Her fine slender form, appeared, spite her poor scanty habiliment, in such a noble and graceful outline, her large blue eye expressed such a silent resignation and gentle suffering that none could observe her without interest, and the first glance of her would bring conviction, that her mind was the seat of deep and bitter sorrow.

The old hunchback appeared to care very little for this, for he treated the girl with marked coarseness and austerity, and his brutality seemed only to increase by her meek submission to his will. It was alone the fear that sometime she might betray his criminal mode of life which prevented him from the roughest ill treatment of her. His actual occupation consisted principally in furnishing strolling vagabonds a safe asylum, and in procuring sales for stolen valuables to safe persons, for which he obtained a rich per centage. In this manner he was connected with the most dangerous criminals of the vicinity. Whenever these were in danger, they were sure to find with him a ready asylum and credit. In all their plans and enterprises he assisted by his advice and acts, and at his house they always procured, when necessary, forged passports or false witnesses. Spite of the lively trade he had carried on, the cunning villain succeeded for a long time to escape the vigilance of the Police, and had grown so bold by success, that he arranged the cellars of his dwelling into regular dens for thieves.

A very small and dim lamp, which flickered at the window of his public room, was usually to the vagabonds of the neighbourhood a sign that they could approach without danger. Then they would slip lightly and swiftly into the subterranean store-room of their host, thence into his private dwelling room, and from this into a large, dark cellar, whence a long obscure passage led them into the vaults of the side building. Here was the rendezvous of these dangerous guests, who, spectre-like, cowed along the walls upon the straw, or practised gambling with a few dirty packs of cards.

On the night on which our narrative commences, the company in this place was particularly numerous, and the busy, restless manner of the host showed that this night was of great and especial interest to him.

Before, however, we introduce the company individually to our readers, we must more closely describe the locality of this den.

It consisted of a cellar-room about ten yards square, the ceiling of which was moderately arched. Two small square windows only helped to show that there was usually little difference within, between the brightness of day or the darkness of night. The floor was unboarded, but almost entirely covered with half rotten planks.

An old, severely battered stove admitted the possibility of necessary warmth. The only furniture consisted of a large wooden table, and several old casks, which served as seats. Around the stove the floor was covered with masses of filthy trampled straw, and in one corner of the den, beneath the window, lay several odd pieces of bedding and half decayed mattresses.

Reclining upon the latter was a long, lank man, whose pale, convulsive features, expressed much malice, but also betrayed traces of much passed misery and distress. The long grey beard of this man, and the wide, ample caftan which enveloped his lean but muscular limbs, proved him to be a strict follower of the Mosaic faith. His bald head rested thoughtfully on his left hand, displaying five lank fingers, which were long enough to span round his entire skull. This man, known among his comrades under the name of "Long Schmuel," was one of the most dangerous and cunning Schränkers, who restlessly roved through all Germany, and disappeared as quickly with his booty as he had suddenly appeared.

Before him lay a female, whose head rested upon a small bundle, which seemed to contain the luggage of Long Schmuel. At the first glance, her large, protruding lips, gave her a somewhat vulgar and low appearance, but her face possessed such a brilliant whiteness, and this whiteness was so advantageously relieved by the jetty blackness of her hair, her nose was so beautifully formed, and in her large dark eyes sparkled such a noble fire, that none could find fault with the taste of Long Schmuel.

Between the two rested a small child, whose curly hair and Hebrew appearance left no doubt of its being an offspring of Long Schmuel. The little creature, which could not yet partake of its parents crimes, played with a merry innocent face with the broad girdle which bound its father's robe. The child's dress, like that of its mother, consisted only of a few dirty rags, scarce sufficient guard against the frost.

The whole group had a most strange, romantic and picturesque appearance, which involuntarily reminded the beholder of the well-known, excellent pictures of; "the mourning Jews of Babylon," and "the suffering pilgrims of the desert."

Of entirely different appearance were three figures which lay upon the straw near the stove. These were real Berlin ruffians, with coarse, vulgar faces, without anything in them to interest the beholder.

One of these fellows had on a pair of old torn summer pants, but was otherwise perfectly naked, as he had thrown off the rest of his habiliments, since these, and their inmates, annoyed him in his siesta. This fellow was originally a sand-carter, and distinguished himself by his peculiar talents for whistling, which enabled him to imitate nearly every kind of instrument, and from which his comrades gave him the name of *Maulspitzer*, (mouth-pointer.)

After he one day lost his horse, and was without the means of procuring another like animal, he adopted the noble art of stealing—which before he had only practised as an amateur—for his profession.

The individual by his side was of a very similar description, differing materially only in the circumstance, that the lower part of his body was in a paradisiacal state of nudity, and the upper part covered with an old military jacket, while the reverse was the case with the first mentioned fellow.

The third member of this group was much younger than his comrades, and distinguished from them by his long, blonde hair, divided in front, which caused him to have the nickname of the *Blonde Augustus*. The entire dress of this young fellow indicated that he was not quite so far removed from the bane of society as his two comrades. But his wild, and low-cunning face, his scanty dress, which, spite the severe season of the year, consisted of a light overcoat and short tattered summer-pants, proved him to be a no less dangerous vagabond.

Two young girls who sat at the table near the centre of the den, and were most unceremoniously attending to the duties of their toilette, formed the gems of this fair company.

They were a couple of worthless, prostituted beings, such as crowd the lively streets of Berlin by hundreds every evening, following their vile vocation, to which they add that of theft. They tried to rival each other in coarse, obscene jests, and made themselves particularly merry at the shameless costume of their male companions.

While the family of Long Schmuel silently enjoyed their rest, and while particularly its head stared vacantly before him, absorbed in thought, the trio upon the straw entered into a lively conversation, at which the Blonde Augustus particularly took the word.

"Boys," he began boastingly, "to-day we yet lie here like dogs, with Jobs' vermin devouring us, but the day after to-morrow ye shall drink Champagne and eat Boulognas as much as you can carry. For to-morrow we will do a bit of work, such as no Schränker has done these ten years.*

"It will be nothing so wonderful," replied the sand-carter. "You will be satisfied, if you are able to buy a new coat at Schlesinger and some stuff for your Chonte. For the hunchback Jobs has you pretty well in chalk."

"And if Jobs had me down with 100 Thalers, I could even buy him out afterwards, for our business yields over 10,000, and all in blank cash, which prevents the *Schärfen-spieler* (receiver of stolen goods) from swallowing part of it."

"But I hear, you intend to do the work with the Eel-eye, the Long Schmuel, and the cunning Schmerles, and also bring in the Jewess, and won't all these want their share? What will you have left for yourself, to enable you to make offers of Champagne and Boulognas?" replied the carter with a sneer. In a whisper he continued: "I will make you a better proposal. Let us do the job to-night and alone, and then escape to Hamburg with the money. The others then may look after us with long noses and be satisfied, if you only wipe the chalk off the hunchback's door. I have fine Schrank-zeug buried at the Triangular Garden,† and for the use of it, you shall only give me one fourth of the booty. You see, my dear Augustus, how much I am in Schwindel, and you should not grudge me a good haul. Did not Schmerles and the Eel-eye make a good job only a short time ago, and does not the Long Schmuel own good property in Poland?"

"It won't do, my old friend," replied the blonde Augustus, "the affair cannot be done before to-morrow night. The old gentleman does not draw the money of his aunt's inheritance before to-morrow, and his chest is so difficult to

* As the Berlin thieves usually hold their conversation in their own slang, we should also, to give the scene faithfully, only use corresponding English slang, or even the German slang which we have already had recourse to. But not to fatigue our readers with continual explanations of unintelligible words, we shall in future, with but few exceptions, use the plain and proper vernacular.
† The *Triangular Garden*, is a hollow pass, between the Rosenthal and Schönhause gates. This spot is much used by the Berlin thieves to bury their stolen property.

break open, that we must have at least four men. And then, Schmerles has also very fine Schränkzeug, consequently you must remain behind and watch the house, unless the Long Schmuel——"

"Should first break thine infernal neck," suddenly screamed the just named individual, who having listened to every word of the sand-carter's proposal, suddenly jumped up from his couch, twined his long, thin fingers like net-work around the naked throat of the other, while he put his knee upon the fellow's breast. "I will teach thee, villain, to steal my Masemattens from me, and spoil my business—curses and plagues upon thee," cried the furious Jew, while he twisted his fingers still closer and tighter round the carter's neck, and spat into his face, which in a few minutes became swollen and livid blue—the sand-carter struggling impotently with hands and feet all the time.

The frantic Jew would doubtlessly have strangled the fellow, as all present were too much frightened at the sudden, terrible change of the scene, to assist the doomed man, had not unexpectedly a strong hand caught the Jew's shoulder and pulled him back. It was the hand of the Eel-eye, who had suddenly entered the den, together with the Chonte and Schmerles, to find an asylum there after their recent escape. A few minutes after them the old rag-gatherer also arrived.

"What in the devil's name is the cause of all this quarrel among you," cried the cunning Schmerles, while he endeavoured to assist the Eel-eye, who only with difficulty was able to manage the Long Schmuel.

This resistance made the Jew only more furious; all the muscles of his pale face swelling and trembling convulsively, and froth oozing from his blue lips, he cried wildly—

"May the crows feast on thy carrion, and the dogs trample upon thy dust, accursed beast! I will teach thee to brew treachery and deceit here. Is this religion, is this morality, for one Schränker to steal from the other?" he cried, still more furious, trying to free himself from the hands of his companions. The Jewess, who had also risen from her bed, finally succeeded in pacifying her husband.

But meanwhile the sand-carter had recovered his stunned senses. Furious at the indignity he had received, he jumped up from his filthy berth, quickly produced a large knife from his tattered trousers, and struck a terrible and quick blow at the Jew. He would certainly have stabbed him to the heart, had not the other had some large gold pieces sewn into the lining of his garment, from which the point of the knife glided off.

The arm of the Jewess, which convulsively encircled the carter, prevented his repeating the blow; but he retained strength enough to throw himself frantically upon his oponent, and bite his nose and cheek, until his brown lips and black teeth were dyed in the blood of the Jew. The exertions of his mediating comrades being again turned to the carter, Schmuel recovered liberty enough to twist the knife from the other's hand : but he had scarcely obtained possession, when the remaining Schränkers, who lost all patience, turned upon both combatants, and dealt such a multitude of blows on both, that at last they were forced to conclude an armistice.

The bitter malicious look of the Jew as he hid the murderous knife in his garment, showed plainly that he had not abandoned his revenge upon the sand-carter.

The relation of the old rag-gatherer and her companions about their arrest and unexpected liberation, in a short time restored a better humour, and before many minutes the whole company sat around the table, where a large can of Schnapps freely circulated to the health of the unknown cigar smoker, who had done such heroic deeds.

All were lost in guesses who the great unknown could possibly have been.

"There is but one man among ' Ours ' who could possess such strength to dash gensd'armes and musketeers down, as if they were flies," observed the cunning Schmerles.

"And that man is in prison on a *Barsel*, (chain,) and will never see day-light again. It is my own brother," added the Jew, grimly gnashing his teeth.

"Your brother is a child to this unknown," answered the rag gatherer, "for the gensd'arme whom he knocked down was the very same who managed your brother. I recognized him by his gigantic arms, and his long, black beard. No, the only man who could equal this stranger in strength, was my own father."

"Your father ?" replied the blonde Augustus, with a sneer, "why, you never had a father. The devil himself has thrown you out of hell, because you were too bad for him there. Who ever heard of your father ?"

"Then, villain, I will tell you about my father, and afterwards you, sap-faced, unbearded boy, shall confess to me that you are not worthy to loosen my father's shoe-strings !"

"Tell us, rag-gatherer, tell us," was the universal cry around the table; "you have seen much, and passed through many scenes in your life, so you may be well worth listening to."

And after the large can of Schnapps had once more circulated, and the rag-gatherer had put a large piece of black bread into her toothless mouth, she began as follows :

CHAPTER IV.

THE NARRATIVE OF THE RAG-GATHERER.

"I AM not a native of Berlin, but I was born in a small village of the Saxony Harz-mountains. My father was the son of a rich but dissipated farmer, and my mother was a fine, tall, and handsome woman, of very good family. After famine and war had robbed us of every thing, we left the village and went to Berlin, where my father listed as a soldier. But the miserable dog's-life which the soldiers then led in times of peace, and the hard treatment they received, little agreed with my father's temper.

"One morning he returned home covered with blood, shook my mother's hand, and exclaimed : 'Christine, we will never see each other again ; the corporal struck me, and I shot him down !' Then my father kissed me and my younger brother, and turned weeping towards the door.

"That moment, however, two grenadiers entered the room, caught my father, and bound him. At first, he suffered all as quietly as a lamb. But when one of the grenadiers struck him in the face, and called him murderer, my father's face became cherry brown—and even at this day, a cold chill comes over me, when I remember how terrible he then looked. With a single pull he tore the cords that bound him, as if they were spiders' webs, took his musket, which was leaning against the wall, and with the butt of it struck the insulter a blow which broke his skull to splinters, and splashed his brains into my father's face and over the ceiling. The man's eyes gaped wide open, as if they would burst out of his head, then he stared at me so terribly, that I lost all consciousness, reached his arms towards me, and fell dead at my feet.

"When I recovered, my father had fled, and my mother was busy in binding up the wounds in the head of the grenadier, but it was in vain, for the man was dead.

"For three weeks we remained locked up in our cottage, and only lived upon the gifts which our charitable neighbors brought to us ; but one day a peasant came, and brought a letter from my father, which informed us that he had safely escaped and waited for us on the frontier.

"The next morning my mother, who was daily expecting to give birth to a child, packed all our things into one large bundle, which she carried under her left arm. She took me by her right hand, packed my little brother into a large cloth, in which we used to dry Chamomile flowers for our neighbour the Apothecary, and carried him on her back, and thus equipped, we started one morning on our journey. On the way my mother was taken sick, and had to lie by the roadside, until a charitable flayer took her upon his cart, by the side of a dead horse. After three weeks' journeying we reached my father, and with him we went to the forests of Meckleburg, where he turned poacher.

"We lived in an old coal-burner's hut, which stood partly above and partly below the ground, and we had a terrible life of it. As often as a chase would take place in the vicinity, of which the boors, to whom my father sold the stolen game, always advised us in time, we had to leave our hut, so as not to be discovered in it, and then take up our residence for the time in a cavern of the rocks. Ofttimes when my father had not sufficient money to buy powder and lead, we suffered the most bitter hunger for days and weeks together, and endeavoured to subsist on wild berries and roots. My poor mother suffered all this misery with resignation, for she loved my father, and was most happy when her delicate fingers, often torn and bleeding from the thorns and briers of the forest, could stroke back the dark hair off his brown forehead.

"But the most terrible part of our misery was yet to come.

"One evening as I rested my head in my mother's lap, while the younger children slept upon a bed of moss in front of the bright fire, which spread light and gentle warmth through the hut, a large, strong man, in green uniform, and with a high plume, entered suddenly our hut. It was the chief forester, as I judged from the description I had often heard my father give of him.

"With his hand upon the trigger of his gun, he entered the door, but when he discovered that mother and children were alone at home, he lowered it again, and harshly approached us with the words :

"Well, at last I find ye, you gallows-breed. You shall bitterly pay for the damage you have done to the chase of his most Serene Royal Highness."

"My poor mother turned ghastly pale at these hard words, and instantly prostrated herself before the stranger, imploringly grasping his knees and hands, while she exclaimed ! 'Mercy, oh mercy, gracious sir, we are already so unspeakably miserable !'

"The fair form of my mother, that form still so noble and beautiful, her rich dark hair, the peculiar light shed upon her by the flickering pine fire, and which animated her pale features in a strange and effective manner, seemed to make a favourable impression upon the harsh intruder. For he suddenly became more friendly towards her, listened kindly to the recital of her misery, and put his arm around her waist. We children hid behind the piles of brushes which lay in our hut, and dared not, in our extreme fright, look upon the strange man.

"Suddenly we heard our mother cry for help, and to our horror we beheld her wildly struggling with that fearful man.

"We also began to weep and cry aloud, and that moment my father entered the hut. He had scarcely discovered what was passing, ere we heard the well known report of his gun, and the hut was filled with a dense smoke. But the unfortunate man had missed his mark. Whether it was that the bright reflection of the fire had misguided him, or, whether in the excitement of the moment his aim was uncertain, or, whether my mother had in her struggle made a fatal movement, enough, the ball had only grazed the cheek of the chief-forester, and had entered directly the heart of my poor mother, who now lay groaning in her death-struggle, while a warm stream of blood issued from her convulsed breast.

"The chief-forester, with the cry of : 'assassin :' rose from the corpse of my mother, and threw himself furiously upon my father, who for the moment overcome by the immensity of the misery he had caused, stood palsied and like a statue.

" But suddenly his face again became cherry-brown, as at the time when he had broken the skull of the strange soldier, and his eyes filled with blood. With a tremendous blow he hurled the robber of his honour to the other end of the hut, and then began a terrible struggle between them.

" But the forester was also a strong and most active man. Twice had he thrown my father to the ground, but still he rose again, and at last he pressed his opponent against one of the strong logs which supported the roof of our hut, while his right hand convulsively grasped the throat of the forester, and he was thus slowly strangling him.

" At this moment the large dog of the forester broke into the hut, and furiously attacked the legs of my father. Undoubtedly he must have fallen under this additional assault, had not Providence that moment inspired me with a sudden and happy thought. I took the rifle which the forester had brought and had carelessly laid down, put it to the dog's neck, and fired so luckily, that the dog fell howling and expiring at my feet. The effort, the report and all, was too much for me, and I fell to the ground in a swoon.

" When I awoke, I saw the body of the stranger lying upon the floor of our hut. His eyes were torn wide open, his face was of a dark blue colour, his tongue hung far from his fine white teeth, and his neck was covered with dark purple stripes, bearing the evident marks of the terrible avenging hand of my father.

" Before the dead body of my mother kneeled that unfortunate man, wiping the gore from her wound. His face was ashy pale, his eyes had sunk deep, deep into their sockets, and no tear wetted his burning cheek.

" When he saw that my mother would not return to life again, he pressed a long ardent kiss upon her pale lips, and madly rushed from the hut.

" Since that evening I have never beheld him again.—— —— ——

" When, on the following morning, I awoke from the sleep which had followed my swoon, the bright sun shone friendly through the open door of our hut, and a merry lark hopped about the outside, twittering her glad morning song. But within lay the dead body of our good mother in its gore, and she replied not to the friendly call of my poor little brothers, or to the warm pressure of my hand.

" For two days we remained by the corpse of our mother, but then the bad smell drove us thence. We wandered far, far through the forest, and at last reached a village, where no door would receive us, until finally a poor old woman took pity and shared her scanty mouthful of bread with us.

" Several weeks we remained with her. I made frequent attempts to return to the forest and again find our hut and my mother's corpse,

but in vain, the wilderness was too dense and pathless. We endeavoured to show our gratitude to our benefactress, by gathering manure upon the highway, and carrying it to her little field.

" One morning there was a great rush in the streets, and many people were out, as if for a holiday show; I then was told that a poacher, who had murdered his wife and the chief-forester, was to be quartered that day. The criminal was no other than my own father, who had surrendered himself to justice, after having strayed about in wild and mad despair, for some time.

" When the people returned from the execution, they related the most terrible things about it. My father had not quietly submitted to the murderous attacks of the executioner; but even upon the scaffold had begun a terrible death-struggle, and killed three of the executioner's assistants with an iron bar, which, with Herculean strength, he had wrenched from the railing of the scaffold, till at last the blow of an axe prostrated him. The ceremony of quartering was performed upon his dead body.——

" The day after this, the people drove us from the village, as they had discovered our origin, and now despised us.

" For several weeks we roved about without a roof to shelter us. We lived upon the fruits we stole from fields and gardens, and slept alternately in barns, stables, or in the open air. At last a shepherd took pity on our condition, gave us food and obtained some old clothes, which he begged for us in the village. In return we assisted him in tending his flock.

" One day a party of soldiers passed our hut, with bright arms and merry martial music.

" Attracted by this novelty, which seemed so charming, I ran after, and followed them the whole day, till I could no more find the way back. The troops halted and made their camp for the night in an open field.

" Here I remained with them, for an old sutler-woman took pity on me, and kept me with her. With her I made several campaigns, and assisted her in her trade.

" I would certainly have remained long with this good old woman, and afterwards have taken her place in the regiment, had I not (as I was now a grown-up girl) fallen in love with one of the soldiers, who persuaded me to rob my benefactress of all her earnings—a good round sum —and to run off with him. The villain brought me to Hamburg, where he left me, after taking all the money and the few articles I possessed.

" Without help or assistance I strayed for several days through the streets of Hamburg, too poor even to pay for a bed, when I met a friendly old woman, who offered me fine dresses, handsome things, good food and a merry life, if I would follow her.

" I must not have been a sutler-woman for years, and with a handsome, smooth face, not to have known what was meant by this offer. At first I resisted, but finally, urged by hunger, I consented, and entered one of those large houses to be found along the harbour of Hamburg, where sailors partake to excess of the luxuries and joys of life.

" My beauty and fine figure ere long obtained me a better position, and I removed to a house frequented by persons of a higher station in life. Here I soon saved a considerable sum, as I did not hesitate, now and then, to cause valuable trifles belonging to my guests to disappear, when these intoxicated by pleasure, forgot caution in my arms. But these manœuvres had unexpectedly attracted the attention of the Police.

" One evening as I was about to abstract the valuable snuff-box of a young man, who seemed perfectly intoxicated from the use of whiskey, then so much in vogue at Hamburg, he suddenly jumped up, and with the words, ' at last I have caught you, you wretch !' discovered himself as a police officer. At a great hazard I succeeded in making my escape, dashing a boiling bowl of punch, which stood before us, into the face of my opponent, with the same *sang froid* as I treated the thick-headed watchman to-night to a similar dose.

" For several days I found refuge on board a ship, the captain of which was intimate with me ; then, during his absence, I broke open the ship's cash-box, with the assistance of a sailor, who was an old acquaintance of mine, and made my way to Berlin.

" Arrived here, I applied to one of the *Verschickfrauen*,* whom I had become acquainted with at Hamburg. This woman immediately obtained for me a situation in the formerly celebrated house of the beautiful Madame Bernhard, in Frederic street. The days which I passed in that house belong to the most delightful of my existence, and all that is now called pleasure or joy is mere child's play compared to those times !

" There were about a dozen girls at Madame Bernhard's, and all chosen beauties. No princess could surpass us in the arts of the toilette. We wore only the finest dresses, satin shoes, and our food consisted in the most choice meats, delicacies and wines. Our attendance was princely, and our company consisted of the richest and most influential in the city.

" In those days no country gentleman could boast that he had been in Berlin, unless he had paid a visit to the *belle Bernard,* and had passed an evening with us at a bowl of the richest punch, amid merriment and joy. Each day we took pleasure rides, and dukes and counts disputed for the honour to be our gallants ; in short, no pleasure or amusement was so rare or expensive that we did not enjoy a surfeit of it.

" The mask balls which were publicly given at the theatres were not to be compared to the masquerades which we had in private, and the large sleighing-parties, which in those days took a first rank among amusements, were flat and stale without our presence.

" Yes, yes, children, you do not think that the old rag-gatherer, who now with rotten rags can scarcely cover her nakedness, once dressed in velvet and silks, and had dukes and counts kneeling at her feet !

" Nor do you discover in the appearance of the quiet unpretending little house in Frederick street, No. 63, with its five small windows and its three low stories, what power and splendour, what might and grandeur, what joy and merriment once prevailed through those rooms ! Many a time and often has the rich satin train of my dress swept over those three stone steps which now lead to a hardware store on one side, and to a millinery on the other.

" A short time ago, when, after the great theft at the bankers, I had taken too much *Wachholder*,* and could not find the way back, and when rascally boys ran after me, and threw mud upon me, then I sank exhausted upon those same steps. At first I knew not where I was, but when a malicious boy threw water into my face, from the fire-plug which stands near by, I recovered my consciousness, and recognised the localities.

" The remembrance was too much for me, and bitterly I began to weep ; I was rejoiced that at least *I could weep,* for my fount of tears had long seemed exhausted, and my old eyes appeared to have been dried up. The stupid boys mocked me, and cried—

" Look, look, the old witch cries for her mamma," and threw the more stones and mud at me ; but the mischievous urchins dreamed not what hellish pain and misery tore my soul——''

The rag-gatherer, entirely overcome by her emotions and remembrance, had to stop at these words. Her listeners also stared at her in silent astonishment, and the Jewess wiped her eyes, as if to hide a silent tear.

But the rag-gatherer soon again mastered her emotions. She took a hearty draught at the spirit-can, which the hunchbacked Jobs, who had meanwhile taken his seat at the table, handed her with friendly politeness, and then she continued :

" When the French were in Berlin our life attained its highest degree of splendour. Many of those piles of gold, which they had robbed from the whole world, were spent at the house of Madame Bernhard. And children, I may tell you in confidence, the Emperor himself has been there ! Never in my life shall I forget the night.

" In the evening a French officer appeared at our house, and withdrew with our mother—thus we called Madame Bernhard—to her room. A young girl from Switzerland—who afterwards poisoned herself, because her face became disfigured by a dreadful disease, and who lived in the same room with me—had overheard her con-

* *Verschickfrauen* are those women who make it their business—and a profitable one—to send fresh subjects to the keepers of brothels. They obtain their victims either among fallen females at home, or from foreign brothels. Sometimes they undertake distant journeys, particularly to Brunswick, Bavaria and Saxony, and there they entice inexperienced country girls.

* A species of Gin.

versation with the stranger. She related to me that he had told mother to take good care that no strange guest was in the house that night. She should arrange a small room in the upper story—the room to have no more than one door—and there have supper prepared for six persons. Of this supper, our mother and two of our most beautiful girls should partake. At midnight, or shortly after, a small man in a simple officer's overcoat, would appear accompanied by two persons. Whether this small man was recognized or not, he must not, by any one, be addressed otherwise than ' *mon General.*' He forbade her and all concerned, under severe punishment, ever to mention the visit of this mysterious guest. At the same time the officer had handed to mother two heavy rolls of gold, but told her also that she must not leave his side until the arrival of the little man.

" The orders of the officer were executed to the letter. At eleven o'clock precisely all strangers had to leave the house, and all we girls had to retire for the night. The Swiss girl and another, who at that time was celebrated by the name of the ' Fair Clotilde,' were selected as companions for the Emperor.

" At a quarter to one, the well known sound of our door bell announced the arrival of a guest, and I could not resist the temptation of peeping through the key-hole of my door. Three persons, conducted by our mother, crossed the rich carpet of our hall. The first, was a large, strong man, with an immense black moustache and in the dress of a Mameluke.* Behind him was a small man in a grey over coat, with broad, large shoulders. Was it that he heard the rustling of my dress, or was it accident, he certainly cast a look towards the door of my cabinet, which struck me like a ray of lightning through the key hole, and the fire of which I could not endure. Behind the small man followed a French officer in a rich uniform.

" After the strange guests had remained for some time in the room, I could no longer resist my curiosity, and I ventured to creep up the stairs which led to the third story of our house, hoping to get some slight glance of the mysterious chamber.

" But I might have paid dearly for my daring curiosity. Just as I was about to turn the corner of the stairs I observed that the Mameluke stood guard at the door of the cabinet, with a drawn sword in hand. The darkness, which covered the place where I stood, luckily hid me from the sight of the gigantic sentinel, and enabled me to make a safe retreat.

" During my residence in this house, I had totally lost my former habit of making an occasional daring attempt upon the pockets of my visitors. For, in the first place, we were too strictly guarded, and in the second, we had money in abundance ; but I spent all I received with as much carelessness and levity as I earned it.

" With the war ceased also my residence with Madame Bernhard, as an officer who was returning home had fallen madly in love with me, and never ceased his prayers and threats, until I depended for my existence only upon him.

" But I soon learned that my lover was without any means and lived upon debt, which he contracted in anticipation of a large inheritance. This hope, however, failed, as his uncle gave his entire property to a charitable institution, and the consequence of this philanthropy was, that my lover sent a bullet through his head on hearing it.

" Deprived of all means, and with a load of debt upon my shoulders, I found myself in a most distressing situation, which became perfectly hopeless in consequence of my carrying a pledge of my love beneath my bosom, and consequently could not return to my former position.

" After having sold every trifle which the creditors of my lover had left me, I had just time to find a place of refuge for my delivery in a *Charité.**

" The great mental and bodily exertions to which I had been latterly exposed, had shaken my constitution to such a degree, that I had almost paid the life of my child with my own, and my recovery was very slow and protracted. At last I had become well enough to be dismissed from the institution, and then I had to seek my own support.

" The day of my discharge was to me a most terrible one. Formerly, there was nothing to bind me to life, save my bare existence. I had neither treasures nor relations, for I never again have heard of my brothers, and I possessed no friends.

" Still, I had loved life as long as I could pass it in joy, dissipation and merriment. But now, deprived of all assistance, my beauty, the only treasure I had formerly possessed, destroyed by my long and severe sickness, and impeded in all undertakings by the care of my child—I suddenly found myself possessed of a treasure which I loved most dearly and which bound me with inflexible, iron chains to this world—my child !

" Upon that dreadful day when I crossed the Weidendamm bridge, and after a long absence once again beheld the splendour of the city, but at the same time looked upon my hopeless future, I can assure you that then, in my despair, I pressed my child convulsively to my breast until it screamed, and was several times upon the point of leaping into the stream with it.—— ——But the love of offspring prevented me, I crept on, and came into the town.—— —— ——

" My first walk was to Madame Bernhard, but she could do nothing for me, except giving me an alms, just sufficient to keep me from starvation for a few days.

" When I turned from the house of Madame Bernhard, dressed in my simple calico frock, with the unseemly little cap, to cover my scanty re-

---

* This companion of the Emperor could have been no other, than his celebrated Mameluke *Rustan,* who never, day or night, left the side of his master, and was his confidant in secrets of every description.

.* A lying-in hospital.

maining hair—my unfortunate child in my arms—when I thus left the house, in which a few months before I had bloomed in an abundance of raven tresses, and the freshness of youth—when the porter, who had received many a gold piece from my hands, now with a contemptuous smile opened the door for me—then I felt, as if the earth would sink beneath me, and my very soul seemed torn to atoms.

" I believe that if at that moment some one had taken pity upon me, I would have turned back from my former courses, and would have *worked*, ay, worked, until the blood had oozed from my nails, for the support of my child !

" Perhaps, if then a guardian angel had appeared to me, I would now be surrounded by happy grandchildren, would enjoy a peaceable and blessed age, while now I am prosecuted step by step by the minions of justice, exposed at each moment to the greatest misery, and bringing my child as your Chonte to your haunts.

" My after life is well known to you all. Dressed in scanty rags, I offered in the streets for a few groats, ay, sometimes for a piece of bread, that which dressed in silks and velvets had furnished me with masses of gold. Then I became procuress and shop-lifter, and at last nothing remained for me, but to search the rubbish piles in the streets for their treasures, and thus to protract my miserable existence. But this trade is so trifling that I would certainly starve, if I did not sometimes scent out a good job for you, boys, after which I can refresh this old body a little. Ofttimes I wish from my soul, to have my life back, that I might live it over again, on different principles; but that wish is vain, and I suppose I may as well finish as I began.

" My only consolation in my distress, still is *Schnapps;* when that warms and again strengthens these stiff, trembling limbs, when it turns every thing before my eyes in wild, whirling circles, and drowns my memory in the very whirlpool of the past, then, children, then I am most happy, and I drink, and drink, and still drink again, till consciousness leaves me, and I sink in a deep, iron sleep.

" Once, and only once more in my life, it seemed as if fortune would favor me again; but it was only to let me feel the weight of my misery the heavier.

" It is about fifteen years ago when I was pedling matches up and down every street in the city, which at that time was a profitable kind of trade for our class. I came to a small house in Krausen-street. Here, in a very elegantly furnished dwelling, an elderly lady opened the upper window, but quickly discharged me again, as she said she was not in want of my wares.

" I was not, however, so easily sent away, but continued to describe to her my misery in the blackest possible colours. Suddenly she became friendly, and promised me an entire change of fortune, if I did a service for her which would not at all be difficult.

" She told me that she had a married daughter

who, although she was very fond of children, could not have the good fortune to present her husband with an heir. She therefore wanted me to find some mother willing to let her child go to be brought up and educated by her daughter. But the child must not be more than a few weeks old.

" Mother and child would thereby make their fortunes, for the mother would receive a large present in money, and the child would receive a princely education, and become heir to much wealth. During the conversation, the lady requested me to enter, and in a second room she showed me a most beautiful lady, whom she designated as her daughter.

" The daughter was even more urgent in her entreaties than the mother, and made me still larger promises if I would execute their wishes. At the same time they set a magnificent breakfast before me, such as I had not tasted in a long time, but made me promise strict silence about their offer.

" When I left the rooms of these ladies, an old woman who seemed to be their landlady, entered into conversation with me, and annoyed me with all sorts of curious questions about what I had seen or done in their rooms. At the same time she told me that the two strangers had arrived there from a distant land, but a short time before, and seemed very aristocratic and wealthy. They lived in a most mysterious solitude, and permitted no person, not even the landlady, to cross their threshold. The letters which arrived for them were marked by no name, but merely by initials. Their registry at the police* the ladies had attended to themselves. The youngest in particular was never to be seen by any person, and it almost seemed as if she had committed some crime, the consequence of which had compelled this retreat.

" Of course it was not my place to satisfy the curiosity of the talkative old woman respecting my conversation with the two mysterious ladies, so I merely told her, that they had commissioned me to find them a good washerwoman.

" Although the whole manner and the offers of the ladies were most suspicious to me, still I concluded to yield to their request, particularly as I had an easy opportunity to comply with their wishes, and as, by obliging them, I only could be the gainer.

" In the miserable garret where I then lived with my child, who was at that time a half grown-up girl, there resided also a most unfortunate, heart-broken young woman, who, a few days before, had been delivered of a child in that wretched, scarce habitable garret. To judge from her fine linen and delicate hands, that girl appeared to be of good family, but also to be most unfortunate, for she was without any means whatever, and often lay in wild, terrible fever-deliriums, when bitterly disappointed hope, broken

* A necessary form of law, which all strangers in Berlin are subjected to. It is usually done by the landlord, or lodging-house keepers.—TRANSLATOR.

vows and betrayed love, were uttered in every sentence of her mad dreams. Our landlord kept the poor wretch more from pity than from gain, and we all felt most deeply for her, which however, in our position, was all we could do. We had at first tried to get her an admission into some hospital, but upon her knees, and in the most heart-rending prayers, she beseeched us not to take her there, and not to ask her who she was, whence she came, or whither she would go.

"When the unfortunate wretch had in some measure recovered, she often wept and lamented that she did not know what would become of her child, for there was nobody in the world who cared for her, or would provide for her poor babe.

"To this young woman, then, I made a proposition to accept the offer of the two ladies. At first she repulsed me in a burst of indignation, and wept bitterly at the bare idea that any person should propose to her to part from her child. But when I explained to her, that, situated as she then was, the child must perish in misery, but that, with these ladies, it would become rich and happy, and that consequently her conscience, her very love for it, must urge her, not to refuse the good fortune which so unexpectedly smiled upon her offspring, the poor girl became thoughtful, and at last warmly pressing my hand, accepted my proposition. But she made it a condition that she must see the two ladies herself, and hear their promises from their own lips.

"I immediately informed my friends in Krausen-street of the success of my exertions, and they were willing to agree to the young mothers' demand, if she would come to them in the evening, but on no condition in daytime.

"After a few days, when the mother's health permitted it, they sent a hackney coach late one evening, which conducted myself, the unhappy mother and her child, to the residence of the strangers. They received the girl in the most friendly manner, and by their very kind, affectionate conduct, even induced her to leave the child with them immediately. They told her that they resided in Italy, but promised often to come to Berlin and show the child to its mother. They also said that they would remain some weeks longer in Berlin, and that the mother might frequently come and visit her child.

"Late in the evening we left the ladies, delighted with their kindness and urbanity. The unfortunate mother found it hard to part from her babe, but at last she calmly yielded to her fate.

"At noon the following day, I unexpectedly received a large letter, in which the two strangers informed me that unforeseen circumstances had compelled them to leave Berlin. Enclosed in the letter were two hundred Thalers, of which one half was intended for me, and the other half for the child's mother. At the same time they repeated their assurances regarding the child. With great difficulty I calmed her, by telling her that the child's fortune was not changed by this early departure, and that, sooner or later, she was sure to see it again.

"These demonstrations finally prevailed, and I endeavoured to impress their truth more strongly upon her mind, by referring her to her share of the money. But though she had scarcely had a morsel of food for some days, she threw the money back to me, in a paroxysm of rage, telling me that she had not sold her child, and that in following my advice, and accepting the offer of the strangers, she had not sought her own advantage, but merely the fortune of her child.

"Thus I kept the whole money, and for a long while, led a happy and comfortable life. Even afterwards, I frequently received considerable sums of money from an unknown giver, but after about two years, they ceased.————

"Immediately on the receipt of the ominous letter, I had inquired for the writers at their former residence, but was told that they had left the same night, shortly after our visit, on their journey to Naples, as they said.

"The mother of the abducted child remained only a few days longer with me. A strange and mysterious change had taken place in her entire manner and appearance. In her usually mild, soft eyes, there burned a dark, lowering fire. Her pale features became rigid as marble, no smile ever played upon her lips, and her former gentle, quiet manner was changed to harsh, repulsive coldness. Even her voice was changed, and had become more hard, rough and masculine. After a few days she left us, and none knew whither she had gone, or what had become of her. I never afterwards heard of her again."

Here the rag-gatherer closed her narrative, which seemed to have excited her very much. A few minutes afterwards her loud snoring indicated that she fallen fast asleep upon her seat.*

CHAPTER V.

MARIANNE.

WE must now take our kind readers away from the den† of the hunchback Jobs, for a few minutes, to accompany us to his sitting-room. Here his eyes will meet a picture entirely different from the former. The furniture here is also poor, for it consists only of two beds, one table, a ricketty bureau, an old looking-glass, a broken

* We are here compelled to remark, that the rag-gatherer certainly did not use the same mode of expression in which we let her speak, but that it was absolutely necessary to refine her language. The intelligent reader will thank us for this. It is, however, an established truth that even the most depraved wretch, at certain moments becomes conscious of the full extent of his depravity, and in that consciousness frequently displays thoughts and reflections, the sublimity of which could never have been expected from him. Whoever, like ourselves, has had occasion to have intercourse with these wretches at such moments, will know the truth of this assertion. But in that celestial spark, which inhabits the breast even of the most degraded of human beings, perhaps the greatest curse of their crime may be found.

† The German word indicating the particular apartment in which the last scene is laid is *Spelunke*, but there is no word in English which will express the meaning better than *den* or *thieves'-den*.—TRANSLATOR.

easy chair, and a heavy oaken chest. But cleanliness and order prevail here to a degree that could not have been expected in this place. That part of the bright scoured floor over which the passage from the store-room of old Jobs to the cellars in the back crosses, is carefully covered with a very common carpet, to guard it against the soils of muddy feet.

The coverings of the beds are as white as newly fallen snow. Upon the table and chest not a grain of sand or dust can be discovered, and on the bureau, which is covered with an old, but very clean cloth, lies a neat work-basket, a few religious books, a small toilette-box, and an old clock-case—all, so to say, in perfect apple-pie order.

In short, every thing indicates that these rooms contain a benevolent ruling genius, a totally different being from the many impure spirits to be found in the den close by.

On the evening of which we spoke in our former chapters, that benevolent genius which reigned through these dominions was not far off. It was the landlord's step-daughter, the " unfortunate Marianne," who was compelled to pass her youth in these gloomy cells, far from the din, bustle, and merriment of happy and glad mankind, suffering under the spiteful, malicious scourge with which her step-father governed her. She was seated on a simple small stool before her neat, clean little bed. Her beautiful chestnut-brown hair fell in two rich, heavy braids over her fair shoulders, and greatly added in giving her pale, care-worn features, an expression of deep melancholy.

Her dress only consisted in a thin frock, and an old woolen shawl, which was tied in a large knot upon her back, but all bore the stamp of neatness, care and cleanliness, and showed her fine tall figure to great advantage.

Before her stood two small children, a boy of about six, and a girl of five years, whose coal-black, curly hair, and large lips, indicated that they belonged to the family of Schmuel.—They were his two eldest children.

With excited and grateful attention, which was expressed in every feature, they watched the busy hands of Marianne, who was just occupied in altering the pieces of an old dress into a new frock for the girl.

" Oh, how glad I shall be, my dear Manni,* when my new frock is done," exclaimed the little girl, joyfully clapping her hands.

" But the dress would have been much prettier, if Manni had made it of the variegated piece of stuff which I yesterday brought from town for you," saucily added the boy.

" Yes, and I would have preferred that pretty piece," sadly replied the girl; " but Manni would not receive it. She said to me that you had *stolen* that stuff, and that stealing was a great sin, and that she would rather cut up her own dress and make me a frock of it, than that I should wear

* Abbreviation of Marianne.

stolen goods. So, of course, I have to be satisfied with what Manni gives me."

" Manni is very foolish," answered the boy, apparently much annoyed at the speech of his sister; " she is very foolish to throw away that beautiful stuff, and patch up a frock for you from her old rags. I was so glad to be able to bring you that pretty goods, dear sister, that you might not freeze any longer, when you had a new frock, and father praised me so much when I took it from the shop. He said, I had done it so cleverly, that he himself could not do it better. He only wanted me in future to take something more valuable; for beneath the counter whence I took that stuff, while father was showing the strange gold pieces to the merchant, there lay many other pieces of fine goods, but I took this one, because it just looked like the dress which you admired so much, and I put it beneath the long coat of father's, into the large pocket which he has there for *Schottenfellen*.* And on going home, father kissed me, and said, I would become very clever by the time I was a man, and I would be an honour to him.

" Fy, fy," said Marianne, interrupting the boy, who was relating his exploit with proud self-sufficiency, " did I not teach you, only lately, the commandment: ' *Thou shalt not steal*,' and did I not tell you then, that God himself had given that law, and that you must follow it. Have you so soon forgotten it? And did I not farther explain to you what would become of this world, if we were to steal from one another, and that you ought to work bravely, and earn your bread honestly, if you expected to go Heaven?"

" Yes, yes, into Heaven," interrupted the little girl, " where the dear little angels are, with their pretty wings, and the bright stars and fair flowers, yes we must go there when we die, and therefore you must steal no more, dear brother. For I am told that people always weep when any thing is stolen from them, and that they complain to our good God of it. You see I did a great deal better the other day, and I will tell you. When father was last in town with me, he told me to go into a very large fine house, up two pair of stairs, and if any body came, I should say that my mother washed there, and then I should take a piece of wax and press it into the keyhole, and bring the impression down to father. But it must have been something wicked, for father whispered it all to me, and told me that I must be particularly careful and let nobody see what I did at the key-hole. Then I did not do it, but told father I could not find the door. And father whipt me, and said I was very stupid, and he would send you, for you would do it better; but I thought to myself, Brother Siegbert will not do it either, for Marianne has forbidden it. And I was about to tell father that he was doing

* Schottenfellen, in thieves'-slang, means the science of shop-lifting. To do this, several of them usually unite for the operation, and part of them endeavour to draw off or occupy the attention of the merchant or clerks. This accomplished, the goods quickly pass into this large pocket, which is hidden in the skirts of the coat.

wrong, but I was afraid, and mother has forbidden me to say any thing to him about the fine things which Manni teaches us in the evening."

"And have you told your mother of what I taught you?" asked Marianne in astonishment.

"Oh yes, I have told mother all about the child Jesus which was born in a stable, and about the holy three kings, who were guided there by a bright star, and about the blessed little angels who were with Jesus, and I have recited to her all the pretty prayers you have taught us, and the prayer which we are to say every evening, beginning:

' Gracious God, I pray to thee,
Make a pious child of me,'

And when I had told mother all this, she wept and kissed me, but forbade me to let father know of it."

"Did your mother do this?" hastily asked Marianne.

"Yes, she did it, and told me to be very obedient to you."

"Strange woman," murmured Marianne to herself, "she approves of my acts and words, yet she hates and persecutes me for ever!"

While this conversation had taken place between his sister and Marianne, the boy had stood by in abashed silence, and in his youthful mind had fought a severe struggle—a struggle which his experience was too young to compass.

In his actions he himself could see nothing to consider wrong, for since the first moment of his existence, he had heard theft called a virtue, and the praise which his father had given him, flattered his vanity; but a dark, indefinable feeling, which in older persons would have been called the voice of conscience, but which in so tender a child can only be designated as a divine instinct for good, told him that he had done wrong.

Suddenly he appeared to awake from his thoughtful mood, but with a clouded brow, which indicated that he believed he had found an egress from the labyrinth of his thoughts, yet was doubting, and addressed a question to Marianne, which certainly did honour to his mind and heart:

"How could I do wrong when my father had commanded me to act as I did, and you yourself have taught me, To honour and obey father and mother?"

This question came most unexpectedly upon Marianne, and it cost her no little trouble—for she was not a great logician—to determine upon the answer to give the child. She told him finally, that "if commanded to do bad, children need not obey their parents," but even to herself this maxim appeared most doubtful and impracticable, as a child could certainly not always distinguish good from evil. A deep sigh arose from her breast at the meditations, yet she found sweet consolation in them, as she exclaimed: "Great Heaven, how often have I murmured at the loss of father and mother, but now I thank thee, good God, for not giving me parents, such as these children have, for they are even more miserable than I!"

The little group had become thoughtful at these reflections, and for several minutes a deep silence prevailed, during which Marianne diligently continued at her work. As soon as this was finished, and the little girl caught a glimpse of herself dressed in her new warm frock in the little mirror, the children again became lively and merry, and jumped gladly about the room, never more thinking of their former conversation, which had left such a deep impression on the mind of poor Marianne.

After a few minutes the little girl ran out of the room to show her new dress to her parents; but soon returned, as she found them engaged in deep and earnest conversation with the host, and consequently disinclined to partake of her joy.

Assisted by little Siegbert, Marrianne had meanwhile put aside her work-box and other utensils, and had brought out her Bible, her only friend and consolation in her misery.

In these her religious inclinations, she almost went too far, as in every deed and action, her almost ostensible piety stood out in bold relief, and assumed an appearance of methodism. But this extreme of piety, so near akin to fanaticism, had been produced by the extreme of her miserable position. For a blind, constant and quiet submission to the will and guidance of divine Providence, which she saw in all her sufferings, was alone capable to give her that strength of soul, which was necessary to keep her still erect in the pool of vice, where she passed her life, and to guard her against sin.

Moreover, the mind of Marianne might naturally have been somewhat inclined to fanaticism, and this germ was nursed by the instructions of an old *devotee* shoemaker, who was formerly her father's neighbor, and had been her first religious instructer. For Marianne had only enjoyed very scanty instructions in school-or-religious matters, and had, after the wrong fashion of our time, been confirmed at an age, in which she was not yet capable properly to understand, appreciate or carry into practice the great religious truths. In this manner, the cultivation of Marianne's mind and heart could only be considered as the result of her natural and excellent abilities, and be admired as such.

The children of the Jew, who with their parents often passed a day and a night at the hunchbacked landlord's, had, by their pious, childish disposition, created at once a favourable impression upon Marianne. She, therefore, frequently occupied herself with them, and after she had observed with pleasure that the minds of these poor children were not spoiled by the bad example of their parents, she closed a strict species of friendship with them, and at last believed herself destined by Heaven to lead these children into the paths of religion and christianity, and to guard them from the temporal and eternal perdition to which the creed and the mode of life of their parents must inevitably lead them.

She therefore availed herself of every moment she was permitted to remain alone and unobserved with the children, to instruct them and make their minds accessible to the doctrines of christianity. This was the easier, as the children had received no religious instructions whatever, and consequently had no conception even of their own, the Mosaic religion. All they knew of that, consisted in the strange superstitious religious customs and ceremonies of their parents and their associates.

In this manner, through their love for Marianne, and by their good memory, they had pretty well advanced in the doctrines of Christianity, and took a great interest in the beautiful childish tales and parables of the Christian belief, which have such an irresistible charm for the young.

Thus, then, they were occupied on the night of our story, and would not rest until Marianne related to them, and read how Jesus said, " suffer little children to come unto me."

" Jesus must have been such a nice, good man," added little Susy, with naivete, to the narrative of her teacher, " to have loved little children as much as he did. And it was very wrong that the Jews should afterwards have tortured and murdered him, as you told us yesterday."

" Now I know why the boys in the streets often run after us, when I walk with father, and call us 'Jews,'" began the boy, half crying, " it was because the Jews have killed Jesus. But that was not our fault, for we were not present, no more was father."

" Little fool," interrupted Marianne, " do you not know that all this occurred more than a thousand years ago; how could any body think you had been present. And it is not for this that people mock you, but because your father looks and dresses different from other people, and because he does not believe in Jesus, but thinks he has been a bad man, and an impostor."

" No, father does not do that, I know he don't," interrupted the boy with passion; " Jesus has been so good, that he can't be a liar or an impostor, and is it not all written in the Bible, of which you tell us that it is the word of God ?"

" Do not trouble your head about this, dear Siegbert," replied Marianne to the hot headed boy, " let them mock you, for they know no better and are doing very wrong. And you need not cry about it. You are no worse than they are, for they also mock and call each other names, why should they not do so to you ? But you must not turn upon them, for they will outnumber and beat you, and moreover, the Bible says ' do good to those that hate thee.' "

After this conversation, sleep began to assume its ascendancy over the children, so Marianne advised them to go to rest, and made them repeat several prayers.

But even at the close of her noble endeavours, during which she had entirely forgotten the position in which she lived, she had yet to learn the most terrible part of it.

* * * * * * *

Suddenly she heard the praying children utter a scream of intense terror, and saw their looks directed to the door of the cabinet. Her eye involuntarily followed theirs, but full of horror she turned away again.——

The long Schmuel, the father of her pupils, stood close behind her, with a grinning and terribly distorted face, and was at the point of striking a treacherous blow at her with the knife of the sand-carter, crying furiously :

" Wait, thou infernal Christian beast, I will assist thee on thy way to thy Christian heaven ; but thou shalt leave my children behind."

But, as if suddenly palsied, the Jew's hand stopped the blow, for the two children had fallen upon Marianne, and covered her body so, that he could not strike without injuring them. The Jewess at the same time arrested his arm with the words: " Would you ruin all with the hunchback, and throw us into misery, by stabbing this girl ?"

Notwithstanding all this, the Jew had strength enough left to toss back the children, and give a terrible blow to poor Marianne, which felled her to the earth, and sent the blood streaming from her mouth and nose.

The Jew would undoubtedly have killed her, had not the remaining inhabitants of the den entered the room of the host, and taken the part of the ill-treated Marianne. The blonde Augustus was particularly valorous, and wrung the knife from the Jew's hands. The girls also took her part, as much as they all usually hated her, they now fought for her, to the best of their powers, as they attacked the Jew, who was running in mad fury about the room, with their long, sharp nails.

But even at these humane demonstrations these women could not hide their natural malice, as the Chonte sneeringly remarked : " The blonde Augustus plays the lover, and wants to make court to the devotee, so we must assist him a little."

The hunchback Jobs also took the part of his daughter, and said to the Jew : " For shame, Schmuel, you know how much depends upon the life of the girl, and you would take that support from me, and that after the many good deeds I have done for you ; strike her, whip her, as much as you like, if she crosses your path, but do not seek her life."

But all these exhortations could not quiet the Jew, until suddenly the bell, which was fastened to the door of the hunchback's shop, indicated the entrance of a stranger, which induced the secret guests to retreat to their den, while Jobs hurried to his store.

CHAPTER VI.

THE VIGILANT.*

THE hunchbacked Jobs found himself no little embarrassed when he entered his shop, and there

* This is the name given to those persons who are used as spies by the police. They are usually dangerous criminals themselves, as thieves can only be followed into their secret dens by thieves.

met an entirely strange young man, who, after a modest, diffident greeting, addressed him with the words: "Have I the honour to see Mr. Jobs, the host of this place?"

Jobs for some time hesitated with his answer, while he subjected the stranger to a close scrutiny.—He might be about thirty years of age, of a small but muscular figure. His dress could not well be judged, as he had enveloped his entire person in a large cloak; but as much as could be surmised from the shabby state of the cloak, or by the coarse and common features of the stranger, he belonged to a very low grade of the human society. A certain lowering, low cunning feature, which expressed itself in his pale beardless face, made it highly probable that the stranger was not far from being connected with the usual guests of hunchbacked Jobs.

It was, in particular, this feature which quieted the rising fears of the host, and at last produced the answer; "Yes, an it please you, I am Job, the host of this cellar."

"We will not enter into long compliments, my dear Mr. Jobs," replied the stranger, quietly, "but I will at once deliver a message to you, which must gain me your gratitude, and loosen your tongue a little, and I'll warrant that at parting we shall be better friends than we are now. But let me first ask one little question, to which I must request a strict answer. Is nobody within hearing of our conversation here? Many things might be said which ought not exactly to be proclaimed from the pulpit."

"If the gentleman has something to confide to me, he may depend that there is nobody present who would feel sufficiently interested to listen to our indifferent conversation," replied Jobs, still mistrusting."

"Well, then, my dear Mr. Jobs, I will tell you a little word, which will sound like a dead brother's voice from the grave: To the left of the mountain, about three ells deep, there lies a treasure, mostly in gold and silver. And a little box is there also, with thirteen divisions; who would take that treasure, must ask for it of a man who carries two hundred weights in one hand, and who has a yellow wart on the middle finger of his right hand."

These enigmatic, mysterious words operated like an electric shock upon our hunchbacked host, and his face, which at the first disclosures of the stranger, had assumed a most distrusting and thoughtful expression, suddenly beamed with joy, and warmly embracing the stranger, he exclaimed:

"You can come from no other person, brother, than from my old friend *Hanne Schmuel*, the brother of Long Schmuel, and unless I mistake much, you bring disclosures about the great Mascmatten, which that curious, farcical fellow, laid *Kabore*, the day before he was *verschütt*, instead of *verchärfen* it to me.* How does the good, old boy? He must fare very bad in prison! Has

he no chance or prospect of escape? On my honour, we will do all in our power to assist him, poor devil. He has thousands and thousands buried under ground, and must now live like a dog. Yes, yes, this is the way if they won't trust to their honest friends. If he had given me the money, I might have managed to have sent him many a Thaler. For, as I always say, every thing can be made possible with money."

"Well, my friend, did I not tell you that I could speak a word to you that would loosen your tongue," interrupted the stranger, with a cunning grin.

But the hunchback would not let him gain time to speak, but besieged him with the repeated question:

"My dear boy, did Hanne Schmuel properly designate the spot to you, where the money lies, so that we can find it without much trouble?"

The stranger seemed not to be over anxious to answer this question, for in reply, he slapped the hunchback's shoulder, and said: "That is a long, a very long story, my friend, for which we must take our time, and talk in day-light about it. It is an affair which won't spoil by keeping. Let me, in the first place, have a glass of Schnapps, for in the street it is devilish cold, and I have been running about all day without having anything warm either within or without. Luckily, a couple of hours ago, I met a drunken wood-chopper on the road, whose cloak seemed to be too heavy for him, so I relieved him of the burden."

"Well, my boy, and have you done no other little job, and have you no place to rest your weary body?" inquired the humane landlord, most affectionately.

"No, for to night you will have to keep me here, and perhaps also for a few days longer," quietly replied the stranger, as I have only yesterday been dismissed from the academy at Spandau,* and this morning have delivered the letter of recommendation, which the Commander gave me, at the Police office. The gentlemen there were most particularly polite to me, and would scarce let me go again, but absolutely wanted to keep me, as I could not show them the means by which roast meat and buttered bread should find their way to my mouth.—As to work, how could they expect such a thing of a fellow like me, and moreover, who could be found that would give me work!

"Luckily, at the right moment, I remembered the commission which my friend Hanne Schmuel had given me for you, so I told these gentlemen that I was engaged by you as an ostler. Consequently, I shall be compelled to play that part for a few days at least in your house."

"My dear boy, I am not exactly pleased that you have mixed me up with this affair, for I am not fond of seeing these gentlemen with red collars and bright buttons at my house. But I think

---

* The produce of the great theft, which the fellow buried the day before his arrest, instead of selling it to me.

* Spandau is the seat of the Prussian Penitentiary, jocularly called among thieves the "Academy, or the *Penzionate.*"—TRANSLATOR.

that through you I may earn a few dollars with Hanne Schmuel, so let it pass. But, my son, tell me, who you really are, and what branch of the business you are most fond of?"

" And is it a fact that you do not know me, my old hunchbacked friend?" replied the pseudo-ostler to his pseudo-master—"why, I am the *schlappe Anthony*, the son of *Black Henry*."

"Of Black Henry! God rest his soul, he was a fine fellow, one who understood his business thoroughly, and no chick in the egg was safe from him. Why, my boy, I have often had you in my arms, when your father was here at my place, and used to do business with me. The Lord rest him! but boy, why should we stand here in the cold? Come in with me, and I will introduce you to a first rate company, all honourable people, and all *chesse** boys. There are also a few pretty Chontes among them, the *Black Harriet*, the *Pearl-guste*, (pearly Augusta,) and the *Students-Clara*, all old acquaintances."

At these words the hunchback conducted the stranger into his parlour. The eyes of his guest here immediately fell upon the bleeding form of Marianne, who was still lying senseless on the floor, and he cried in horror, "My God! what is the matter with this female?"

"It is my daughter," replied the host, "a stupid, obstinate wench, who has for ever her prayer books before her nose, and has her head full of religious fancies. With her pretty face, she might be very useful in the business, and might soon make her fortune, but I can beat no sense into her. A little while ago, just before you came, she had a dispute with Long Schmuel, the brother of your friend Hanne Schmuel, and he beat her rather severely, that is all."

" Let us at least lay her upon the bed," replied the stranger, who seemed possessed of a little more humane feeling than the old hunchback, " and let us wipe off the blood."

" Why, yes, we may do that," replied the other, as he assisted the son of black Henry to carry Marianne to the bed. "I thought, she might of herself have had sense enough to get up again. But she will soon come to. I will send the old rag-gatherer to her, who understands this kind of thing."

During these words both had entered the den by way of the long dark passage which led to it from old Jobs' parlour.

The stranger was struck dumb when he first caught sight of the numerous inmates of the den, and even began to tremble violently; but soon recovered his self-possession, and offered a friendly " good-evening " to the companions of the hunchbacked Jobs.

The company also examined the stranger with close scrutiny, as the long absence of their host had caused them some disquietude. But when the blonde Augustus recognised the stranger as the schlappe Anthony, the friend of his youth,

and after the hunchback, as far as he considered it advisable, had communicated to them his conversation with the stranger, they again gathered in merry groups around the table, and the hunchbacked Jobs spread a very fair supper before the schlappe Anthony.

All now became merry, and even the Jew, who in consequence of the unfortunate scene with Marianne, still gnashing his teeth, sat in moody silence, and cast furious glances at his children who were already lost in sweet slumbers—even he became again serene, and almost merry, when he heard of his brother, and pressed the stranger with a thousand questions about him, which the other rather evaded than answered. The Jewess, whom the momentary fright of Anthony, and the embarrassment of his manners had not escaped, whispered to her husband: " Schmuel, all seems not to be right with that man, and I fear he is not chesse."

But the Long Schmuel seemed not at all inclined to listen to the warnings of his wife, as he answered her, " Jobs would then never have brought him here. No, no, that man is only wise, and won't speak yet, as he does not know us well enough. He is as cautious, and more so, than we are."

Suddenly and most unexpectedly this conversation was interrupted by a cry of horror, simultaneously uttered by all the inmates of the den. The Jew swiftly turned round, and to his horror he beheld the colossal figure of a man in their midst, entirely muffled up, but who, to judge by the red collar of his cloak, and a mass of documents which he held in his hand, must be an officer of police.

The Jewess now immediately whispered to her husband: " Did I not tell you that all was not right with this Anthony?" The Jew was on the point of catching Anthony—who was no less frightened than the rest—by the throat, when of a sudden, the stranger, with a loud horse-laugh, dropped his cloak, and exposed the grey linen dress, the livery of the inmates of the city prison, to the astonished guests.

" Why, this is the *stiff Gottlieb*, was now heard from every lip. " Where do you come from, you devil's imp, and how can you frighten us in this manner?"

" How I came here, children," he replied, " I can scarcely tell you myself. You can all easily discover that I am escaped, for I still wear the Royal Prussian epauletts.* I cannot really say that did *escape*, for the gentlemen of the court themselves opened the door for me, and dismissed me with many polite and humble bows. It is a story of witchcraft, children, such as you have never heard of before, and probably never will again. But ere I can tell it to you, you must give me a can of drink and something to eat, for I have passed the whole day in a new building, of which the windows and doors had been walled up, and

---

* Chesse, in thieve's jargon, indicates those initiated in the secrets of the craft, and those who will not betray another thief.

* The convicts wear a dress consisting of grey linen trousers and jacket, with a large yellow number on the shoulder.

you all know that, in the city prison, they have neither breweries, distilleries, or cookshops. I consequently am as hungry as a starved wolf.

At these words, and without farther ado, the new guest attacked the supper intended for An-thony, and without paying any attention to its rightful owner, hastily devoured it. The disap-pointed proprietor of the supper seemed not at all delighted at the arrival of his guest, and availed himself of the excitement to avoid the sight of the new comer as much as possible, and even tried quietly to leave the den.

This, however, was for the moment impossible, for the hunchbacked host, who had not yet re-covered from the fright which the arrival of stiff Gottlieb had caused him, stood like a statue just by the door. The schlappe Anthony had also observed that the Jewess watched most in-tently every one of his movements, and knew that a sudden departure must make him appear more suspicious.

After the stiff Gottlieb had in a measure sa-tisfied his ferocious appetite, he began the story of his escape as follows :

" You all probably know, that in the beginning of this winter, I had the ill-luck to be caught at picking a pocket in the Catholic church, and by a new Commissary of police, whom I never previously had the honour to become acquainted with. Thunder and the devil, how I was fright-ened and astonished, when the man suddenly showed me his silver visiting card,* and intro-duced me to two gensd'armes who seemed to have sprung like mushrooms from the ground.

" I had already been three times punished for thefts, had a number of witnesses against me, and consequently prepared myself to become matriculated for a dozen years at Spandau or Brandenburg. In this manner, then, I was this morning, or rather yesterday morning—for it is long past midnight now—sitting in my hole of a cell, and was telling to four other boys—poor fellows, they are sticking there yet—some of my military adventures, although I was in no parti-cular good humour to amuse any body, when of a sudden we heard the keys turned in the lock, and the door opened. The thick turnkey with black whiskers, who has played the *valet de chambre* to many of you, made his appearance to call me in for examination.

" If I had known that the good man would not conduct me back, I swear I would have given him a parting kiss, and would have jumped like a lamb after him. As it was, however, I follow-ed with a heavy heart, and with a most anxious mind entered the audience-room, into which he pushed me, while he remained outside.

" I had already put my face into the most sanctified wrinkles, and had a most polite " good morning, *Herr Justizrath*," and " your servant, *Herr Assessor*,"† upon the tip of my tongue—

for the thick *Criminalrath*, who was my inqui-sitor, does not like impolite people, and the long thin *Referendarius*, who writes for him, is twice as friendly, when he is called Herr Assessor—when I suddenly observed to my astonishment that I was entirely alone in the audience-room.

" An immense pile of documents lay on the little stand before the table, and upon it lay the large gold watch of the Criminalrath before an open document, most probably the record of my deeds.

" The cloak of the Herr Referendarius hung against the wall, and to judge by the red collar, said Referendarius must be lieutenant of Mili-tia ; the *caloshes* of the Justizrath stood there also, so that it was perfectly evident, that both had gone out for a moment, thinking that the turnkey would not bring me in so soon.

" At first this delay somewhat annoyed me, but suddenly a grand brilliant idea entered my head. The corridor which passes before the audience-chamber, was, in consequence of the murky weather of yesterday, rather dark, so that a person's face could not easily be recognised by another. Like lightning I leaped over the railing behind which these judiciary gentlemen usually sit, threw the cloak of the Referendarius around me, turned up the collar, put on the caloshes of the Justizrath, which fitted as if they were made for me, put the hat on, which laid upon the table, and took the documents of my own case under my arm, not forgetting of course the large gold watch and heavy chain.

" Thus equipped, I opened the door of the au-dience-chamber with immense and becoming dig-nity, and hurriedly passed along the corridor lead-ing to the door of the staircase. The turnkeys of course mistook me for the Referendarius, for they made most obsequious bows, and with the utmost courtesy opened the large door which leads down the stairs, politely wishing me a ' good morning !'

" I could not see any particular necessity for entering into conversation with such people as these, but grumbled a few unintelligible words between my teeth, hurried like a madman down the stairs and past the porter's lodge into the street. A closed cab was just stopping before the door of justice. Although I had not a penny about me, I jumped in, as in this manner I could soon-est find safety, and as my grey linen trousers, which peeped out under the cloak might easily create suspicion in the street, and also, as I wore the caloshes of the Justizrath over my bare stock-ings. I called to the cabman to drive towards the *Stralau-gate,* and soon we were under way.

" Arrived at the *Holzmarkt-street* I stopped be-fore a house, the court of which I knew led to the water, and told the driver to wait my return. Of course that did not take place, as I immedi-ately crossed on the ice to the opposite side of the Spree. Here, after crossing several wood-yards, I reached *Cöpnicker-street,* and thence the fields which stretch along the city walls as far as *Husar-street.* Not a soul had seen me, and with

---

* The silver medal carried as a sign of authority by Police officers in civic dress.
† Titles of legal functionaries, which have no equivalent terms in English.—TRANSLATOR.

the utmost comfort I hid myself in the cellar of a house, which is in progress of building in a new street there.

"The bundle of documents served me now as an excellent pillow, and for a few hours I slept like a rat, as the excitement of the whole affair had rather fatigued me. Had I failed in carrying it through, I would have caught no small amount of blows; they would have put me on a chain like a monkey, and the theft of that gold watch would have cost me very dear. Well, Providence was kind to me; for I am safe among you, have that splendid watch with me, and if the hunchback will give me five Thalers for it, he may have the legal documents in the bargain, which will be a first rate lot of cheese paper."

"But first we must have a little lark with these documents," observed the Sand-carter, "for it must certainly be an entertaining and instructive lecture for one of us, to see what these judiciary gentlemen think and write, when they send us into *Pension* for a few years, and how they go about it. Here is Eel-eye, who had a good school, and he would be the best fellow to entertain us with some extracts from these documents."

This proposition was accepted with general approbation, and Eel-eye began by reading the report of the arrest of Stiff Gottlieb, as follows:

"Most humble report concerning the arrest of Carl Friedrich Gottlieb, laborer——aged thirty-nine years, a native of Berlin, for picking a pocket.

"On the 10th inst. I repaired in my official capacity to the Catholic church, for the purpose of watching for pick-pockets, as repeated complaints had been lodged, that said offence had been frequently committed of late in said church. My attention was attracted by a man who was on his knees, apparently very devout, by the side of several ladies, and I observed him in the endeavour to slip a purse from the pocket of one of them. As soon as I noticed that the thief had gained possession of said purse, and was about to rise from his kneeling position, I arrested his person. In consequence of the great surrounding number of persons, the thief succeeded in transferring the purse to a young man who stood close by, and who immediately disappeared with it in great haste, so as to make his arrest impossible. I sent the thief to the proper place for criminal arrestants. When first taken he gave his name as Heinrich Schulz, but gens-d'arme G—— recognised him as the notorious pick-pocket Carl Friedrich Gottlieb, who, among his associates passes by the name of 'Stiff Gottlieb.' The witnesses of the theft were——, &c. &c. The stolen purse contained four Fredericd'or and seven Thaler Courant. X——

Criminal Commissary."

The thieves listened to the reading of this do-

4

cument with pleased attention, which changec into boisterous laughter when they heard tha. the confederate of the "stiff Gottlieb" had safely escaped with the booty. Their merriment increased, when from the subsequent examination-record they learned in what barefaced and impu· dent manner their companion had sought to hide his crime. The following is an extract of his defence on first examination:

"I cannot deny to have had my hand in the pocket of the lady mentioned, and also to have taken a purse therefrom, but I thereby intended no theft, but was brought to do so in the most innocent manner.

"On the 10th inst. I visited the Catholic church, as I had never before witnessed the ceremonies of the service there. I stood for some moments before an image of a saint, in front of which a number of people were kneeling, when suddenly two elegant looking ladies knelt down immediately before me, to their devotions. They had scarcely done so, when a gentleman came to me and said, that the younger of the ladies was his wife, and by mistake she had put his key into her purse and taken it along. In consequence of this, he found himself in a most terrible embarrassment, as he had to pay a draft, and could not open his safe. He begged me most earnestly to obtain that purse for him, as he dared not venture to interrupt his wife in her devotions. At the same time he gave me the Thaler which, on my arrest, was found in my pocket. As I suspected nothing, I knelt by the lady's side, and gently touched and pushed her several times. But she was so much absorbed in her prayer's, that she would take no notice of it. As I thought it very wrong to interrupt her any longer in her holy business, I slipped the purse gently from her pocket, and gave it to the gentleman. But he must, most probably have been a rogue, for he immediatly ran off with the purse, and I was arrested. I however feel myself entirely innocent, and consequently request an *honourable release*, as I became a victim of mere credulity and good nature."

"Lie and beat the devil at it," interrupted the cunning Schmerles, "that Putz* was really good. But harkye, brother Gottlieb, you must have been in a very bad pickle, to admit at all, that your diggets had really entered the lady's pocket. For when a *Torfdrucker* (pick-pocket) admits that once, his chance becomes a very poor one."

"Yes, my dear Schmerles," replied the other, "but what could I do? Should I deny, what unfortunately had been seen by three or four ,witnesses, and thereby increase the suspicion

* Putz, in thieves' jargon, means those circumstances by which the criminal would clear himself before his judge, or extenuate his guilt. The word is applied to any kind of excuse or plea of justification.

against me. No, no, children, deny as long as possible, that certainly is the best thing one of us can do; but to deny blankly what has been seen by witnesses, only makes the matter worse. Then it is advisable to admit as much as has been seen, but not lay one's pipe* even then, only arrange the Putz in a manner, to leave a place to creep out again."

While this conversation took place between the cunning Schmerles and the stiff Gottlieb, the blonde Augustus had recommenced his reading, and had read the depositions of the lady and of the witnesses, by which, of course, the entire justification and excuse of the accused were contradicted. These documents had less interest for the guests at the den, than the former, and they paid but little attention to them. But suddenly all rose of one accord, as if an electric shock had passed through them, the schlappe Anthony alone retaining his seat. Augustus on reading the report of the officer who had effected the arrest of stiff Gottlieb, read as follows:

"Most humble appendix to the report concerning the arrest of the laborer, &c. &c.

"I have succeeded in engaging as one of my Vigilants, a formerly most dangerous and notorious criminal, the pattern colourer, Anthony K——, who is known among his comrades by the nickname of Schlappe Anthony. A few weeks ago, on his dismissal from prison, he promised to begin a better course of life, and he seems to be in earnest, as he has already made some important disclosures. Among other things he has informed me, that the person by whose assistance the so-called stiff Gottlieb on the 10th inst., accomplished the theft at the Catholic church, is the former scrivener, Henry P——, who is known by the nickname of the "Syrupsnose." I have consequently caused the immediate arrest of the latter, and trust that he will be confronted with the witnesses. I have myself in said Henry P—— recognized, with certainty, the same person to whom the accused slipped the purse on that day. A search which I undertook with the assistance of the gensd'armes P— and L—, in the lodgings of Syrupsnose, throws suspicion of several other thefts upon him, and I am still employed at gathering additional facts."

The blonde Augustus read the latter part of this report with increased haste and under intense excitement. He then furiously tossed the documents aside, and threw himself upon the Schlappe Anthony, who, pale as a corpse, sat among his companions, and was so entirely paralyzed by his horror, that he even felt unable to attempt his escape.

The cry was: "Then you are a Slichner,† and have come here to sell us; but wait and I will silence your treacherous tongue——"

* To lay one's pipe—to pipe, means to make a full confession.
† Slichner means a spy, or a traitor.

But while the blonde Augustus with the latter words threatened the life of the Vigilant, that threat had already been fulfilled. For the Sandcarter, who after the scene with the unfortunate Marianne, had regained possession of his knife, had at the same moment that Augustus rose, sent the entire blade of the instrument into the breast of the Vigilant, and with such force, that the wound did not even bleed.

The female members of the company rose with a cry of horror, while the men exclaimed with one accord: "Served the scoundrel right, for trying to betray us. Let him now go and tell that!"

For a few moments the stabbed man remained immoveable upon the cask which had served him as a seat. Then his eyes assumed a glassy appearance, they opened wide as if they would burst from his head, and he stared with a deadly and steady gaze before him. After a few seconds his hand reached for the knife, which as soon as touched, slipped about an inch out of the wound.

The moment this was done, a bright stream of blood rushed from the wound as if from a fountain, and with such force as to sprinkle it over all the bystanders. Instantly the wounded man fell back upon the floor, and began a terrible convulsive struggle, wildly tossing about his hands and feet, while in the most terrible agony, he cried: "Good God! good God! my poor, poor mother, and my——my——my——Bertha——"

Gradually the convulsive motions of the dying man changed to a restless shaking of limbs, and a hollow rattle was heard in his breast, interrupted in the most terrible manner by a rumbling of single air-bubbles, which rose in the breast simultaneously with the blood. After a few moments the wound ceased to bleed, the corpse of the Vigilant lay lifelessly on the ground, and it appeared as if his earthly race was run. But for one moment again the departing strength of life assumed its supremacy. The murdered man suddenly raised the upper part of his body with a convulsive effort, stared with glaring eyes at all present, but as quickly fell back, stretched his every limb with a terrible effort, and——was dead.

During this dreadful death-struggle, a gloomy silence prevailed in the company, and even the hardened mind of the Jew was filled with horror, when the last rattle in the throat announced the end.

But this feeling of horror increased to the stupor of terror, when suddenly close below the window, they heard the rattling of a sabre, which evidently passed through the yard of their own den, and this rattling was soon followed by a perceptible whispering of many voices.

Involuntarily the Schränkers put their fingers to their lips, and with feverish attention watched for things to come. Their uncertainty was not of long duration. The little Siegbert, who had been awakened at the entrance of Stiff Gottlieb, and was upon the point of leaving the cellar for an instant, suddenly rushed back to the den, with the exclamation: "Father, father, the house is surrounded by gensd'armes and soldiers, and the whole yard is full of people."

At this intelligence, a panic of terror befell the company. The hunchbacked Jobs, particularly, ran like a madman about the den, tearing out the few hairs which covered his skull, wailing and crying: "My God, what have ye done! instead of murdering him, you should have fled as soon as you discovered a Vigilant. For you might easily have known that where a Vigilant is found, the gend'armes are not far off. Oh, what an unfortunate wretch I am! what now have I gained by all the anxiety and trouble, which I have suffered so many years! Now they will find you all here, and besides, that corpse, that corpse!!"

The stiff Gottlieb also found it very disagreeable to have to return to prison so soon, and not to be able to enjoy the result of his courage and presence of mind, for any length of time. But the greatest danger threatened the Sand-carter, who seemed perfectly aware of his ticklish position. He scratched his head most doubtingly, when his eye fell upon the dead body of the Vigilant, and he felt a peculiar and most fatal itching of the muscles of his neck.

The Jewess, however, presented the strangest and most wonderful phenomenon of all. During all the occurrences of the night she had preserved an immoveable quiet and self-possession, but the murder had so much filled her with horror, that she almost sank in a swoon when the Vigilant fell, and was only awakened from her stupor by the terrible message of little Siegbert. At that critical moment, however, all her strength and presence of mind returned. Whilst the men in stupid fright and horror were perfectly idle, that woman suddenly, with an inner fire lighting up her sparkling eyes, rose from her couch, and asked her son: "Siegbert, is it very dark outside?".

On being answered in the affirmative, with a powerful push of her foot, she rolled the body of the Vigilant to one side, pulled off his blood-stained cloak, put it around herself, took his cap upon her head, and with the words: "Perhaps I may yet succeed in saving you all," she left the den.

In silent astonishment the Schränkers looked after that wonderful woman, who slipped with unequalled agility through the dark passage into the hunchback's parlour. She there pressed an ardent and hasty kiss upon the trembling lips of Marianne, and, with the words: "Angel, pray for me, and that my enterprise may succeed," she disappeared through the outer door of the hunchback's shop.

Marianne, who had just awoke from her long swoon, uttered a trembling shriek when she saw that form in male attire approach her; but when she recognized the voice of the Jewess, and when the terrible scene which she had just passed, once more presented itself to her mind, her senses again became confused, and she fell into a wild feverish delirium.

CHAPTER VII.

THE GEHEIMERATH.[*]

WE must now leave for a while the den of the hunchbacked Jobs, and conduct our indulgent readers to a very fine and comfortable house in the *Friedrichstadt*,[†] consequently among an entirely different class of people. This house consists of only two stories, and has but six front windows to each, yet it contains an abundance of room for the single family which occupies it. Whatever part of this house we chance to examine, we discover traces of wealth and comfort. The stairs and corridors are covered with the richest kind of carpets, and the most choice flowers adorn the windows. The arched niches of the hall are inlaid with marble, and adorned by magnificent statues. A large full sized bronze statue of a Greek boy stands at the turning of the mahogany staircase, carrying a large torch in his right hand, which in the evening sheds brilliant rays of gas light.

The large and very cleanly court-yard of the building is the promenade ground of a large collection of choice poultry. Here you can find the fat Calcutta chicken, by the side of the magnificent peacock, and the gentle carrier-dove. In a large heavy wire cage, the proud bird of Jove reigns by the side of a pair of diminutive, droll monkeys. A slender deer, remarkable as well for his size as for his gentleness, completes the number of these strange inmates of a court-yard in the city.

A lattice, worked of bright brass wire-netting, supported by strong iron bars, divides the yard from a small, but most neat and tasteful garden. During summer, its beds were covered with a great variety of rose bushes, encircled by a garland of Box shrubs; but now, in the winter, they resemble a large white blanket. On one side of the garden stands a large, well arranged hot-house, which reaches across the court-yard, and is connected with the rooms of the dwelling-house by a long covered passage. This passage also serves a part of the feathered inhabitants of the yard as a shelter against cold during the winter. An ice cellar, which rises at the end of the garden in the shape of a moss covered hill, granting a pleasant resting place, as well as a delightful view over the adjoining gardens, must also be added to the embellishments of the place.

The family, which, as we have already remarked, occupied the whole of this house alone, consisted only of the Geheimerath Berthold, his

* We shall hereafter retain most of the titles in their original German, giving the translation as near as it is possible to render them into English, when they *first occur*. Those acquainted with the German language, must be aware, that the many complimentary and honourable titles in use, and particularly those given to all grades of public functionaries, are utterly intranslatable. *Geheimerath* means Privy Council, also Privy Counsellor.—TRANSLATOR.

† We must observe, for the benefit of our readers who are unacquainted with the localities of Berlin, that the *Friedrichstadt* is one of the finest quarters of Berlin, consequently the residence of the most wealthy and fashionable classes.

daughter, one man servant, a cook and a house-maid. The localities of the house were divided among these inhabitants in such a manner, that the Geheimerath occupied the lower story for his sitting rooms, his office and his library, but the rooms for company and those of his daughter were in the upper story. The servants' domicile consisted in two small attic rooms.

As the Geheimerath and his daughter will play a most important part in our narrative, our first duty now must be to make the reader somewhat acquainted with these two persons.

The Geheimerath was a long, lank man of a little over three-score years of age. Whatever he wanted in talents or acquirements of the mind was replaced by his wealth and natural adroitness. He had for many years been a widower, and this comparatively free estate favoured his peculiar devotion to the fair sex. This passion, after he had exhausted all the sources of luxury and en-joyment, which the refined civilization of our country offers to the man of wealth, alone re-mained the fount of all his pleasures; he lived and existed only in his devotions to the sex.

Although the Geheimerath in this manner could be called a voluptuary, a libertine, who had de-stroyed many a tender flower, who had under-mined the happiness of families, and blindly sa-crificed it at the shrine of his passions, yet to judge by his general conduct, and by the natural gene-rosity of his heart, he appeared a most amiable and good-natured man. To his daughter he was the most affectionate of fathers; he endeavoured to give her the best possible education, and evinced a most painful over-anxiety to keep her from any chance of seductive temptations, the dangers of which he knew only too well. He was a most conscientious officer, and attended to the duties of his station with the utmost punctuality. He was the kind and philanthropic patron of the poor and needy, and most liberal in his benevolent gifts. In short, he was one of the best men in the world.

But all these good qualities disappeared when some pretty face or fair form passed before his eye; then his passion awoke in its entire strength, and he used any and all means to satisfy it. No position then was too holy, no sacrifice too great, and what formerly his youth and amiability could gain, now was accomplished by his wealth and power. His operations were, consequently, usu-ally crowned with success. Be it that his wishes only moved among lower circles or those of easy access, and that ladies of more elevated positions timidly kept at a distance of him, or that he had gained by practice great celerity in the art of se-duction, or that particular fortune favoured him, enough, he had ever been triumphant.

In this manner the noble germ of the sex had always remained hidden from him. He had not the remotest idea of pure and virtuous love, no conception of the great admiration and respect which a really virtuous woman may inspire, but he looked upon the whole sex as a congregation of more or less veiled wantons, whose fictitious virtue could always in one or the other way be overthrown. The few instances which he met, and found exceptions to this rule, he considered stupid or fanatical.

He had not the slighest notion of the high and noble destiny of woman, to become by the ties of family the central point of all earthly bless-ing and happiness, but he rather considered her as a well formed kind of animal, which the crea-tor had placed in this world only for the pleasure of men, and for the propagation of the race.

A fine woman to him was consequently on a par with a fine horse, a good hound, or a well prepared *pâté de foi grâs*.

The only woman whom he loved or valued, and whose heart or mind had any worth for him, was his daughter. But she, to him, stood aloof from all her sex, and in her he loved not the no-ble mind and gentle heart of woman, but only *his daughter*. His late wife even, never had been able to instil higher opinions of her sex into his mind, for in reality he only looked upon her as a disguised wanton, who had possessed cunning enough to bring the Geheimerath in a position in which he could not help asking for her hand. Her death had just occurred at the right time to prevent a public separation, which had long be-fore taken place in private.

Mary, the daughter of the Geheimerath, was just at the happy age of sixteen; an age, when the joyousness of youth has not yet been touched by the bitter experience of after life, and when the world with all its treasures and hopes appears to the young, happy mind, as an open Paradise.

At such an age the natural inclinations of the young are not sufficiently developed to warrant us in taking a decided portrait of character, but it was easy to discover in the lively, sometimes even wild manners of Mary, that she was more strongly inclined to a noisy life, devoted to merri-ment and pleasure, than to one of quiet and re-tired domestic felicity. The tenderness of her father, or the obedience and submission of her do-mestics, had never been sufficient substitutes for the blissful influence which the wise love of an intelligent, and the noble example of a virtuous mother, may exercise upon a daughter's heart.

Thus Mary had not remained untouched by the poisonous breath which the vicious courses of her father threw around her, and already her actions often showed traces of a levity and ob-stinacy, which would fill the judicious observer with anxious fear for her future, as that future had no guide, no trusty and powerful guardian.

For the moment, these dangerous symptoms of Mary's character showed themselves in a most mild, even favourable light.

Her levity, beneath the veil of youthful inno-cence, appeared as childish playfulness, her obsti-nacy as amiable boldness and decision, and her whole, lively and merry manner, lent to her beau-tiful blooming person such unspeakable sweetness and charm that even thereby the dangers of her position were increased.

*   *   *   *   *   *

On the evening on which the scenes of terror passed in the cellars of the hunchbacked Jobs, the Geheimerath gave a grand soirée at his house, thereby celebrating the receipt of a large inheritance, which most unexpectedly had reverted to him from the estate of a distant relative. He had that day drawn the funds from the *Depositorio* of the *Kammergericht*.*

Among the guests of the Geheimerath were many persons of great distinction and high in office, as he himself, by his high official position and his great wealth, occupied an eminent situation, and could command his choice of company. The ladies of the company, also, belonged more or less to the great world, yet they were mostly those, who were not very strict in their views and judgments, and were consequently rather inclined to substitute the results of those modern philosophical deductions, which our age is so apt at inventing, for the austere and antiquadated opinions of female modesty, diffidence or timidity.

As this class of ladies generally embraces the most beautiful, witty and accomplished of the sex—for wit, talents and humour are the most dangerous enemies to female virtue—the entertainment and conversation was naturally most lively and interesting.

Around the charming vocalist *Amalie*, in particular, a large circle had formed, while its fair centre was warmly engaged with the *Baron von Pesth*, in a lively debate of the question, whether matrimony was productive of happiness or misery to the human race.

"What nonsense you do chat, dear Baron," said the charming artiste, with a merry peal of laughter, hitting her opponent's fingers playfully with her fan; "how can you talk of the happiness of matrimony? Would that be happiness to me, to be constantly fettered to one and the same person, to be bound and expected to love that person because I have him, although I may rather wish him a thousand miles away from me?"

"But, my dear, I beg you for the world's sake," cried the Baron in astonishment, "what is to become of mankind, when all married people can leave each other as soon as a third person pleases them better. Why, all decency and order would soon be at an end?"

"Just the contrary, Baron, for then, and only then, the happiness of the world would be firmly established; because then every one would be satisfied with his choice and his fate. Good matches would remain, and bad one's would be broken, and there would be little loss in them. And if a good match is accidentally broken by a misunderstanding, they will naturally come together again."

"But what in the world is to become of women when they get old, and are no longer able to find another husband?"

"If a woman is really loved by her husband, he will be sure to protect her in her age, and

* Treasury of Doctors Commons.

much rather of his own free accord than by being forced to it by the bonds of matrimony. If she is not loved, she should long have severed those bonds, which according to every principle, are sinful and unnatural if they are not hallowed by love and reciprocal free will, and should have altered her position."

"You, my fair friend, with your charming face, may easily argue, for you have no earthly difficulty in daily finding thousands of new connexions; but what are homely, sickly, or deformed women to do, who are utterly unable to charm any man by their mind or person?"

"I will pass over the sarcastic sting you were about to inflict upon me, and rather thank you for the delicate compliment which you use to cover the adder of your wit.—Homely women are not intended for marriage, but rather for work, education of children, &c., and the state must provide for the deformed and crippled."

"But, my dearest," interrupted the coarse voice of *Major von Steinfort*, "you are labouring under a great mistake, if you would measure the happiness of married life by the beauty of the woman. For, let me tell you, fair lady, that beautiful wives are usually not worth much. Now, my late wife, God rest her, was wofully ugly; upon my honour, her face was as pockmarked, as if the devil had been thrashing peas upon it, but no matter; I lived most happy with her, and I would to Heaven, she were still alive, for I would certainly prefer her by far to many a smooth handsome face, or to any young vain plaything."

"But, my dear Baron," resumed the fair Amalie, without being in the least disconcerted by the coarse remarks of the Major, "your words only prove the truth of my position. Had you not been married to your wife, would you not have lived fully as happy with her as you did under the so-called married state?"

"Oh no, no, if you will allow me, my dear, I will offer you a most excellent illustration of the contrary. You see my son yonder, the lieutenant, is just talking to that pretty coquette, that blonde danseuse, with the blue velvet dress, and I can tell you my story in confidence, so that the devil's boy wont hear it," continued the old warrior, taking a seat by the side of the contentious songstress.

"When I had only been married a few years, and had not yet become quite accustomed to my sainted wife, and could consequently not fully appreciate her many excellent qualities, I became acquainted with a very pretty young thing, who travelled through the world, and gave concerts. You see, my fair lady, when this little girl sat before me, shaking and roulading, my heart jumped into my throat, and before I was well aware of it, I was as mad as a March hare after the girl. I can assure you, my dear, and give you my word, if I could have done it as easily as you would have it, I should immediately have unmarried again, and left the blessed departed to look out for herself. And the young lady would have been sure to have taken me, for at that time I was a handsome young fellow, just like my devil's imp there, the lieutenant, and when an article like that, can pick up a Baron, and one who has not only the empty title, they generally do not hesitate very long. But I regained my reason at the right time, and most lucky it was for me. The fair songstress afterwards crazed the head of one of my comrades, and adorned that same head with as fine a pair of horns as ever I saw. He always afterwards reminded me of a Tyrolien chamois-buck, and I thanked God ever after, for having ridden me of this Megaera, at the cheap rate of a few thousand Thalers."

" But, my dear Major," replied Amalie, half in joke and half in earnest," you are only offering another proof of what I have just asserted. You found your own blessed wife again, and would have certainly done so, even had you not been previously married to her."

" No, no, excuse me, you little slippery witch, that point is not by any means proved. Who knows whether I would not rather have run after another, for a young fellow as I was, is not very fond of cool reasoning, and who knows, moreover, whether my poor departed wife would have accepted me again. For I can assure you, that with all my levity, I had honour and honesty about me, more perhaps than many others, and who knows whether in the interim some other man might not have become acquainted with my wife, and better appreciated her value than I did. And then, what would in the meanwhile have become of her, unless she happened accidentally to have some little money ?"

" Why, then, she would have worked, or if she could not have done so, the state would have taken care of her."

" No, my dear, you must certainly excuse me, but there is no use arguing, for nobody can come to a reasonable conclusion with you," replied the Major, rising somewhat ill-humouredly. " My poor departed wife was certainly never created to serve or work for any Tom fool, and she had received too good an education, had too noble a heart to feed in an hospital, and no one ever yet grew fat upon charity-soup. I wish that that fine voice and smooth pretty face of yours was lost for a little while, so that you might try personally the effect of your theory, and that after some time I might then have the opportunity of asking you: How goes it ? How do you find yourself ? Where are those bracelets, those brilliant earrings, those magnificent dresses ? No, my dear, it is no such easy matter, it is not practicable to throw so holy a subject as matrimony with indifference aside, and run after every petticoat. * * * Look well at each other before you marry; love in a virtuous Christian spirit, and if then you find that you entertain sincere affection for each other, prepare for the wedding, and afterwards remain honestly together. And even if all seems not to go right and sweet at first, in time you will get to know each other better, and the rough corners will smooth off by kind intercourse * * *

But please to tell me, my charming little professor, what, according to your method, you would do with the children; are we to kill them off, or are they to have the same chance of running to whatever parents may best suit their fancy ? The result would be a most perfect pandemonium throughout the world."

" No, Heaven forbid, my dear Major, I do not mean to imply anything of the kind. If the parents remain together, the children of course will know where they belong to; and if the parents should separate, the state must adopt them, and the state will naturally select the best immediately for its officers, no matter what parents they may come from.

" But only remember, we would then have the whole world full of orphan boys."

" Well, and what is the harm of that ?"

" I only pray you, look at a herd of our public orphans! do they look so very charming ? Have they not mostly all pale sickly faces, and would you have all our boys become so ? No, no, my dear, better leave things as they are ! You certainly had a mother who tenderly watched over you, and who would ask you—my daughter, are you sick ? my daughter, would you have one thing or another ? a mother, who affectionately watched and guided every one of your steps. But the state makes a very poor appearance as a child's-nurse. No, my fair friend, you do not know this, you don't understand what it is to a man to have a good honest wife by one's side, and a couple of hearty boys on one's knee—devil take me, the heart jumps for very joy. We know that man is but a frail, changeable being, and sometimes, if all goes not right, would send the whole world to the devil. Consequently it is not proper that we should always be allowed to follow our own humours; but these humours must by force be kept under proper restraint. A pretty time we should have of it, if we should discard all the good old fashions and customs of our forefathers, and follow the thrashy, twaddling schemes, these devilish novel-writers put into young people's heads."

" But, my dear Baron, we certainly must progress with the age, for all the world is different now to what it used to be. Does not the world, even the common people, daily learn that our deeds are not to be judged by their external appearance, but by the hidden meaning within ?"

" You call this progression, then, if we again rove like savages or like beasts through this world, and only care for our pleasure, not for anything higher, or more noble. No; let me tell you, that all the misery and crime of our day may be traced to the pernicious looseness of family ties. A divorce must sometimes occur, it is true, if one of the parties will not listen to reason; but in my time, an affair like that occurred perhaps once in twenty years, whilst now-a-days the *Judge* seems to have as much to do with matrimony as the *Parson*. In my time, thunder! a boy had every respect and obedience for his father, even if the boy was twenty years old; but now, these forward rascals, know everything better than their fathers, and they look in self-sufficient grandeur upon their parents. Now-a-days one of these weakly, pale-faced boys, stalks about, spectacles on nose, a fine watch with a heavy chain around the neck, thinking himself somebody, whilst formerly they used modestly to follow the father's periwig. You, see my dear, it is my opinion that we must unite the family ties more closely, give them again their former sanctity, and not try to loosen them still more."

This conversation had grown so warm that it would certainly have continued for some time longer, had it not been interrupted by the entrance of the beautiful Sidonie, the danseuse, who, the Ballet being over, had just arrived, and joined the party. The appearance of this young artiste was really delightful. Her tall, graceful form, possessed that ethereal sylph-like appearance peculiar to talented dancers, whilst she materially differed from the majority of them, in possessing a fresh blooming colour, and a most gentle soft and languid look, yet an eye whose power no one could easily withstand.

All these charms were much increased and elevated by a most artistical toilette.

The dark hair which was slightly fastened by a most valuable dart and a splendid diamond pin, fell in rich ringlets upon the soft and snowy neck, which peeped roguishly from beneath the airy folds of a Mouseline shawl. The glossy brilliancy of her bosom was favourably contrasted by a rich dress of ash-coloured satin, which fitted so closely, as to develope the beautiful outline of her form to the admiration of all beholders. A pair of tiny satin shoes enclosed the neatest foot, joined to the most delicate ankle imaginable. A hand so soft and transparent, as to be liable to be mistaken for wax rather than flesh and blood, closed the Cyclus of all these charms, the central point of which was formed by a rainbow-coloured velvet belt, which encircled the waist of the Sylphide. Soon as this charming apparition passed through the folding-doors of the saloon, she at once commanded the general attention of the company. All conversation stopped for some moments, all eyes were directed to the open door, and an involuntary expression of admiration was heard from the lips of all the gentlemen present.

Even the old mayor, whose conversation with the vocalist Amalie might have created just doubts of his gallantry, even he turned to his neighbour with the words:

"Hark ye, Doctor, that *is* a devilish fine woman." Even the old warrior could not take his eyes from the fair creature, though she did not by any means resemble his poor departed.

The Geheimerath who was just with his friend, the *Justiz-director Abelsberg*, upon the point of examining the merits of a bowl of Ananas punch, put down the goblet, and hastened to greet his fair guest. "Ah, my dearest, fairest, best, this is charming, charming indeed, to be honoured by your presence even at this late hour. You look a little *echauffée*, but I hope you are quite well?"

"Thank you, Herr Geheimerath, I am quite well, though this Ballet has tired me a little."

"But, my Heavens! dearest, then you should not have ventured out, and exposed yourself so soon to the cold night air. Such incautiousness creates colds, coughs, rheumatism, gout, hypochondry, melancholy, and whatever else may be the names of those entertaining guests of my leisure hours. You must permit me to put one of my daughter's warm shawls around you," hastily continued the Geheimerath, as he called upon nearly all the servants of his establishment to bring shawls, and some cups of hot tea.

During this amiable excitement, he bustled about his fair guest with every appearance of anxious hurried care, patted paternally her fair cheek and shoulders, and finally endeavoured to find a resting-place for his dried-up thin lips upon the lily hand of the Sylphide. But that hand was dexterously withdrawn from his caresses, and the little tapering fingers playfully struck the saucy lips that dared to approach them.

The fair one hurried toward the *Commerzien-rath Moritzfeld*, who had the good fortune to be generally supposed the most favoured lover of this fairy queen. The warm kiss which met him at her soft rosy lips, again secured him his accustomed and envied triumph.

But the fair Sidonie had sought in vain to escape the intrusive attentions of the Geheimerath, for at the very moment when she endeavoured to escape the hands of her favourite, she felt herself enveloped in a large woollen covering, put upon her shoulders by the emaciated hands of the Geheimerath.

As much as she struggled against it, nothing remained for her to do, but to remain for some time in this covering, and to swallow a cup of hot tea, which the Geheimerath presented to her, and insisted stoutly on her taking, whilst he quoted a dozen examples of the terrible consequences of incautiousness like hers. Finally, our friend the Geheimerath, in company of the *Justiz-director*, who by the way had succeeded in the application of a kiss upon the fair Sylph's hand, continued his studium of Punch, and the much-envied danseuse now gained an opportunity to salute several professional friends among the ladies of the company. These had been no little annoyed at the favourable impression which their much-feared rival Sidonie had created to their cost, and by many bitter and sarcastic remarks among themselves, endeavoured to vent their rage.

"My Heavens! that woman Sidonie is really the most unbearable coquette I ever beheld," whispered the little Antonie, with the blue velvet dress, to her female neighbour.

"Coquette, my dear, is far too good a word. It is downright vulgarity, to see that person permitting herself to be thus kissed publicly. Why, I never saw the like!"

"Oh, that is nothing new to her!" added the slender Ninon, most sarcastically. "I, for my part, cannot understand what people can see in such a skeleton of a woman."

"Oh! her being lean, is the least of her faults; only look at her badly formed feet!"

"And her pointed shoulders—"

"And her vulgar red face—"

"And her bad pronunciation—"

"Why, she cannot speak proper German—"

"Yesterday at rehearsal, she said three times *mir* instead of *mich.*"*

"And four times to day!"

"And day before yesterday always!"

"No, no, I shall never again come to the Geheimerath unless he omits this disagreeable guest."

Such were the opinions which her companions gave of the charming Sidonie. But their sour, long faces, were soon changed to a mirror of love and friendship, as the object of their conversation quietly approached and wished them "good evening."

"Oh, how glad I am, my dear Sidonie, that you have come at last," suddenly began little Minna, as she repeatedly kissed Sidonie, and most tenderly embraced her.

"We have waited very long for you," continued Amalie.

"You certainly are coming to the Commerzienraths to-morrow?" added the sweet Ninon.

Sidonie, however, soon gave another turn to the conversation, by telling them an incident of immense importance to their clique:

"Children," said she, "have you heard the news? It is all over with Betty and the Captain. That beautiful bracelet which she received of him as a Christmas present, she has pledged to pay a gaming debt for her blonde Lieutenant. She told the Captain that she had lost it, and he was just at the point of ordering her a new one, when accidentally he learned the whole story. He came very near a duel with the Lieutenant, but preferred to write a very coarse and insulting farewell letter to Betty. I am quite astonished that Betty is not yet here, for she was done after the first act of the Ballet, and might have come then."

"Serves her perfectly right, and I am glad the Captain has at last found out her tricks. She has certainly made a fool of him long enough," continued Ninon, in malicious joy.

"But I still pity the poor girl, for she will not easily get such another admirer. He would certainly have married her as soon as he had obtained his discharge," replied Emily.

"Oh, they will soon make peace again," added Ninon, in ill-humour, "for it is not the first time they have had those quarrels. Betty is sure always to be the gainer by a scene like that, and the Captain cannot keep from her. Some valuable trinket usually is the price of their re-union."

This opinion seemed to be founded on well established precedents. It had scarcely been pro-

* A grammatical error peculiar to the lower classes of Berlin. Although the error is about as *common* in Berlin as the omission of the letter *h* before a vowel is to the Cockneys in London, it is so glaringly bad grammar, as to be considered unpardonable in good society.—TRANSLATOR.

nounced, when Betty's large and colossal figure appeared at the door, with a most happy and pleased countenance.

The impression created by her entrance was materially different from that which the entrance of the charming Sidonie had caused. Betty could also be called handsome, and possessed a fine graceful manner, at least such was generally acknowledged. But her large, strong figure, bore a far more sensual, vulgar impress, than the delicate form of Sidonie, and her strongly marked features bordered almost on the grotesque, which was no little increased by a showy, overladen toilette.

Betty was dressed in a heavy, glaring and brilliant satin robe; and had just thrown a valuable Moirée shawl over her broad shoulders, which left them far too much free play-room. Every part of her person, wherever costume would possibly admit of ornament, was so overloaded with gold and jewelry, that she almost appeared a walking bijoutery-sign, and of course could not create so pleasing and delightful an impression as the simple, lovely and modest appearance of Sidonie.

The sensation on Betty's entrance was consequently far less than that excited by her predecessor. Most of the persons present were satisfied to greet her, with the simple and usual salutation of a plain "good evening," &c.

The *Referendarius von Birkheim* was the only one who paid her particular attention, kissing repeatedly her fleshy hand, and addressing her! "Betty, how very charming and pleased you look to-night! You certainly have played your friend the Captain another of your tricks!" And he gallantly conducted her to her friends, the other lady-artistes.

Betty would not give that party a chance of saying a word, or asking a single question, but still almost out of breath, as she was, began immediately the recital of her love adventure:

"Just imagine, children, that the Captain should have heard of that little affair with the blonde Lieutenant, and of course was all in flame and fury against me. Day before yesterday I received a letter from him, in which he forswore all allegiance to me, and formally declared that he would withdraw his hand and support from me for ever. At first I was somewhat annoyed at this, but soon consoled myself with the conviction that our quarrel would be over again in a few days, though I certainly would not take the first step towards a reconciliation. Of course, I had guessed aright.

"After the Captain had for two days purposely avoided me everywhere, and never deigned a look, save an indignant or a furious one towards me, and after he had not visited me for three days, he must have become tired of the affair. This evening I found him standing by the stage-door of the theatre, and he offered me his company home. Of course, I was at first very abrupt and rough to him, and told him, that he might go again to where he had been for three long

[Unmutilated and Only Genuine Edition.]

THIERS' LIFE OF NAPOLEON,

WITH SUPERB STEEL ENGRAVINGS,

FOR SEVENTY-FIVE CENTS,

[If paid in Advance.]

W. H. COLYER having been at great expense to procure a copy of this unrivalled work, now publishes

PART I.

OF THE

HISTORY OF THE CONSULATE AND THE EMPIRE

OF

FRANCE UNDER NAPOLEON,

By M. A. THIERS,

LATE PRIME MINISTER OF FRANCE.

WM. H. COLYER's edition of this splendid work, The Life of Napoleon, is decidedly the best in this country. It is printed on fine paper and new type, according to the design of the author, M. A. Thiers, and on comparison with other editions will be found far superior.

In Press.

THIERS' FRENCH REVOLUTION,

TO BE COMPLETED IN SIX PARTS, AT 12 1-2 CENTS EACH.

TO BE COMPLETED IN TEN NUMBERS.

THE MYSTERIES OF BERLIN,

FROM

THE PAPERS OF A BERLIN CRIMINAL OFFICER.

TRANSLATED FROM THE GERMAN

By C. B. BURKHARDT.

With Illustrations on Steel, by P. Habelmann.

This work in Europe has been universally pronounced far superior to M. Sue's celebrated "Mysteries of Paris," and we confidently predict that the popularity of this translation will be without a parallel in the history of light reading.

Part II.   Price 12½ cents.

THE MYSTERIES of BERLIN.

TO BE COMPLETED

IN

TEN PARTS.

NEW YORK: WILLIAM H. COLYER, PUBLISHER.

days. He was not, however, to be put off, but continued to walk with me, and load me with all kinds of reproaches, about my great ingratitude, and about being undeserving of his tender love, &c., &c.

"Well, one word gave the other, and at last I declared to him that I could not understand how he should dare, after having so deeply insulted me in his letter, to persecute me thus with his verbal reproaches. I did not even consider it worth my while to defend myself against them."

"Heavens!" he suddenly exclaimed, "if I thought that I had wronged you, I would be the most miserable wretch on earth."

"Captain," I replied calmly, "you cannot doubt that for a moment, when you learn all the circumstances. The Lieutenant has a poor unfortunate mother, whose whole joy, hope and consolation is her son. That son was upon the point of committing suicide, because he had contracted a debt on his word of honour, which he could not pay. Accidentally I learned the whole story. Now, tell me, was it so great an error to give my bracelet—which was so very dear to me, as it had been your gift—ay, to give it willingly, and save a whole family? Can you possibly believe that other motives than those of pure humanity should have excited me to favour the poor Lieutenant? Certainly, treacherous and slanderous tongues can make anything appear in a different light, and you are only too much inclined always to believe the worst of me, and to condemn me without a hearing.— —

"Enough, children, to make a long story short, the result was that the Captain earnestly begged my forgiveness, and immediately walked with me to Hossauer's, to buy this beautiful broach, which I have so long desired to obtain."

"But, my dear Betty, do not carry things too far with the Captain," interrupted Sidonie, entreatingly. "He has done so much for you already, he loves you as his own child, and sacrifices his whole fortune to you. You would certainly miss a great deal, if you were once to lose him, and he really is a very good man."

"Bah, bah! I did not ask him to come and court me," replied Betty with indifference, "and if he leaves me, the misfortune won't be so very great. For I have provided for a case like that, and three years ago made him secure me a proper income."

The old Major, who in company with Doctor Hellmold, had listened to the conversation of the ladies at some distance, was lost in astonishment at what he had just heard.

"My dear Doctor, a little while ago I had trouble enough in my argument with the little singer, but the young people here go beyond my horizon. So young, so pretty, so amiable, yet so full of intrigue."

"Why, yes, my dear Major, but you must not take all this so critically," replied the Doctor with indifference, "these are little affairs, such as daily occur in this world."

"Pretty *little* affairs, thus to trifle and play with the peace, quiet and love of others!"

"Love and fiddle-sticks! do you think, my dear Major, that the attachment of the Captain to Betty is real, pure, honest love? The old fellow only loves life and pleasure. He is amused to play the young lover in his old days, and the girl has only grown dear to him because she has cost him a great deal of money, and because we are always interested for that which costs most trouble or cash. This kind of attachment is nothing more than an essence concocted of desire, lust, and vanity, resembling love in its external appearance, but internally, far, immensely far different from it."

"Harkye, Doctor, I almost believe you are right. If the Captain really had possessed love for Betty, would he have degraded her to his mistress, would he have poisoned her youth and innocence? No, just the contrary; he would have endeavoured to elevate, to protect her, and would have married her at once. Now it serves him perfectly right, the old fool, that this young thing pulls his nose for him, and that after robbing her of all she possessed that could be of value to her, she should cheat him of his money. But still, Doctor, this is a sorry state of things, if we coolly look at them."

"My dear Major, I do not understand how you can be astonished at it. It cannot be otherwise. These young people must naturally have recourse to such means. Let me explain to you. Such a girl has honestly, at the utmost, an income of two or three hundred Thalers. With this she is expected to dress well and live respectably. Then she is frequently of low origin, has an old blind mother, a sickly sister, a dissipated brother, or something of that kind to support.

She cannot think or hope for earning anything by manual labour, as her profession occupies most of her time, and moreover, requires particularly good living on account of its severe exercise. What calm, great strength of soul would be required to remain virtuous under such circumstances, and not to be blinded by the glaring brillancy of wealth, which suddenly offers to surround the homely domicile of want? When a rich and noble gentleman comes to such a young and inexperienced girl, and leading her to the highest pinnacle of pleasure and joy, tells her: "All this is thine, if thou wilt fall down and worship me."—Let me tell you, my dear sir, there are few who are capable of resistance, and those who sink beneath this temptation are only to be pitied, not despised. But I can swear to you, Baron, that even in these circles, women sometimes can be found, who to judge from the elevation of their sentiments, their nobility of mind and character, certainly deserve a better fate, than that of being the football of the libertine and superannuated roué."

The Major seemed wholly and entirely to agree with the sentiments of the doctor, for he warmly and cordially pressed his hand, and said: "Doctor, you are the man for me, and perhaps we may yet be able, united, to do a great deal of good among these unhappy beings.

The Referendarius von Birkheim, however, who during Betty's narrative had left the circle of ladies, and had attentively listened to the conversation of the Major and the Doctor, burst into a loud laugh, when he observed that at the conclusion of his speech, the doctor had really become excited and enthusiastic.

"My dear Doctor," he exclaimed, "You are either crazed or in love. How the devil come you to moralize in this nonsensical manner? Have you forgotten our adventures with the divine Cecilia, the blonde Bertha, the sweet little Clara, and whatever else their names may have been, that you should so suddenly begin to play the Parson? What care we for the affairs of our ladies. Be merry and happy, when you are with them, and let them do what or how they like at all other times. When the present assortment is gone, there will be others, for, thank God, there is no want of fresh young growth.——

"No, no, Doctor, I know what all this means. That devil's girl, Sidonie, sticks in your head, and knowing that nothing can be gained of her in the ordinary way, and that she is strongly inclined to Romance and Fanaticism, you would try it another way. Upon my word, Doctor, you are a capital fellow, one who can suit himself to all emergencies."

"Let that be, my dear Max," replied the Doctor, somewhat out of humour, "you may believe me, that I was in earnest in what I said just now. I know we have played many a mad prank together, and done much mischief, but I can also assure you, that it has often sorely troubled my conscience when we so cruelly tricked one of these poor things. Now yesterday, in particular, I was much annoyed when I learned that the wedding of poor Bertha was broken off, only because she had been foolish enough to make a country party with you, whilst she was betrothed. Who knows, whether for the sake of satisfying a trifling fancy, you have not for ever ruined the prospects of the poor girl. I, for one, cannot make up my mind to look upon our fellow creatures merely as we do upon lemons, which we squeeze out, and then toss the peals out of the window."

"But tell me, Doctor, are you perfectly crazy to-night, with your everlasting Philosophy. What do I care for Bertha, or for the lemons? Why was she so foolish as to come to me? I see nothing in this to reproach myself with, for if it had not been done with me, she would have been taken by some one else, so the matter remains the same. The stupid fellow of a smith, who was about to marry her, might have been proud of the honour, to have received for his wife, a girl whom we had taken into such especial favour. But, my friend, be easy on that score, for that harm can soon be remedied. Our friend, the little Captain of Marine, who arrived here last week, seeks a connexion. Perhaps Bertha may please him, and it would be a fortune to her, for the Captain has plenty of money, and is a good-hearted, nice fellow, whom something can be done with."

The Major, who had only heard a part of the remarks of the Referendarius, but for whom that part was quite sufficient to fill him with the greatest dislike, was just about to vent his indignation on him, when he was interrupted by the entrance of a new guest, who made his appearance with so much bustle, that the attention of the entire company was necessarily drawn toward him.

This new guest was the *Rentier* * *Wertheim*, a man who formerly had been remarkably handsome and amiable, but who could not prevent time from causing him to grow old, though he laboured most ardently still to appear young.

Although his face, probably red by the continued use of generous wine, bore strong marks of his having lived with it in riot and fun through half a century, he still dressed in the style of the youngest beaux of the day. An immense wig of modern fashion covered his cranium, a white velvet vest enclosed his broad breast, and a brown riding-coat with large bright buttons added its share to the comic-fashionable appearance of the antiquated dandy. A pair of pantaloons encircled his lean shanks, according to the prevailing taste, to such a degree, that a burst or fracture was threatened at every movement. The base of this walking tailor's pattern was formed by a pair of patent doe-skin half-boots, and a heavy watch-chain, a large lorgnette, and rich breast-pin with a solitary large diamond, made him conspicuously visible at some distance.

Thus accoutred, the Rentier by means of an artistical *entrechat*, appeared suddenly in the middle of the saloon, with a gracious and would-be-graceful bend of the head scanned the company, and then dissolved in a number of well-studied compliments.

"Ah, good evening, *Messieurs et Mesdames!* good evening, my dear little Sidonie! servant, charming Ninon! beautiful, heavenly Minna, what a very charming velvet dress you have on! Your most obedient, fairest Amalie, on my honour you look, if possible, more lovely than usual, in these new ornaments; how do I find you, my most bewitching Betty?" With such exclamations as these, accompanied by a pleased and patronizing smile, the Rentier passed through the circle of the ladies, and then turned to salute with a most respectful bow, the *distingué* portion of the gentlemen present.

"Why, bless me, here is my most respected friend the *Herr Oberst-Wachtmeister*," he cried, addressing the Major; "is it possible that I find you once more in our circle. I thought you had become an entire misanthrope in the country. My gracious, it must be ten years since we had that delightful journey to the baths together. And here, why, here is your son, also; well that is right that you bring him out a little, and make him acquainted with these charming children we have here."

"Yes, my old friend, it is a long time since we

* *Rentier:* one who lives by his rents or interest. The term is applied to any private gentleman of wealth following no business.—TRANSLATOR.

have seen each other," replied the Major. "Business of various kinds has brought me into the city, and I want to see once again how the young people live, and make my son a little acquainted with the dangers of the great world. It is much better to let these young gentlemen see all with their own eyes, than to blindfold them, and run the risk of their being entirely blinded, if they accidentally should see the light by themselves. I only wish my papa had done so with me, for he then might have saved me many a bitter lesson."

The Rentier seemed little inclined to enter further on this subject, for he suddenly turned to the gentlemen who were seated round the whist-table, with the words: "I had almost forgotten to impart to you a most interesting piece of news, which will be particularly welcome to you, Herr Geheimerath.

"I just come from the Circus,* outside the Brandenburg-gate, where I attended the first representation of the lately arrived company of equestrians, for you know I am very fond of these exhibitions. I entertained but small anticipation, as the company had not been preceded by much fame, and as the exterior looked rather poverty-struck. But to tell you what I saw there ! ! ! Ladies, you are all pretty, very pretty, extraordinary so, but *parbleu*, I can swear to you, in this troupe I have seen a woman—a woman, whom I must unhesitatingly pronounce the most beautiful of all her sex ! She is not so ethereal as our charming Sidonie, not so *naïve* as our Minna, not so graceful as our Ninon, in short, in any one point, she is surpassed by some one of these ladies, but the *ensemble* impression which she creates, is so extraordinary, so bewitching, that I really became dizzy as I watched the daring leaps of this wonderful woman.

" Picture to yourself a large, beautiful figure, united with a strength and agility which makes her alternately resemble a giantess, or a snake, or an eel. Imagine farther, an arm so round, full, and yet so ethereal and soft, that the gods must envy a mortal's pleasure to be encircled by it.—

" And what shall I say of that face, of the beautiful proportions of that form? Never before have I beheld such beautiful, blooming cheeks, never such dark, burning eyes, never such full rosy lips, never such a high noble forehead, never such a perfect symmetry of outline, in short, it seems as if nature had lavished all her charms upon that woman.

" She certainly is no longer in the first bloom of her youth, but is perhaps past thirty; but that very ripeness of figure, that complete development of her form, give her appearance so majestic a charm, that one might easily lose his senses at the sight of this Venus. And what is the most wonderful, is, that her features never contract into that forced assumed smile, which is so customary to women of her profession, but her

* The circus or amphitheatre is situated outside the city, and in a fine large building mostly used for equestrian exhibitions.

face remains placid, immoveable as marble, while her brilliant eye shines upon the intoxicated spectator with a strange and gloomy glance, exercising an almost supernatural influence over every beholder.

" A hundred times did I look at my watch, and felt every time how very rude it was of me, to join the present charming company at so late an hour; yet I could not tear myself away, I was charmed to the spot as long as that divine woman was before me, and long, long after she was gone, my eye was fixed upon the door through which she had disappeared from my enchanted glance. And listen, when I loudly applauded her, so loud that my kids—on my word, they cost me ten Thalers a dozen, for they are of Rey's best—burst to pieces, and when her earnest, serene features on perceiving it, for a moment lit up, and smiled upon me — — then I became raving, and cried *bravo, bravo, capo, capo*, like a madman.— —

" Gentlemen, I can assure you, that woman has perfectly bewitched me, and my first care to-morrow must be to ascertain how, where, and in what condition she lives. But in the meanwhile may I beg to propose, that to-morrow we will all visit the place, with these ladies, for I can promise you an enjoyment which you will find far to exceed your anticipations."

The proposal of the Rentier met with universal approbation, although his description was generally considered a most exaggerated one. All adjourned in the best and merriest humour, and with many a joke at the Rentier's expense, to the supper-room, whither the company had just been summoned by the butler.

The Major, with the agility of a young beau, had managed to get a seat by the charming Sidonie, and attended to all her wishes with such marked and tender care, that the whole company soon playfully congratulated him on his new conquest, and drank a merry health to the new couple. The old warrior accepted this most readily, stroked complacently his grey beard, and managed, spite of her struggles, to imprint a kiss upon the lips of his fair neighbour.—

But soon the Major became the mark of universal raillery, when one of the servants announced, that a closely veiled lady had just arrived, who insisted on seeing him alone and immediately, and who could not be induced to give her name or expose her face.

" But, my friend, what wild pranks are these of yours in your old days, that veiled ladies should come after you," cried the Geheimerath with a merry laugh, after the Major, who, somewhat embarrassed, hurried from the door. The Geheimerath, then, to the general amusement of the company, proposed the health of the fair unknown, not dreaming at the time of the portentous meaning of this visit.

The Major must have had a most important interview with the unknown, for he took her to a distant room at the end of the corridor, conversed most earnestly and in whispers with her for some time, and then dismissed her with the assurance that he would follow her in a few minutes, while he continued impatiently and greatly excited to pace up and down the room.

A loud conversation in the adjoining room at last interrupted his reverie, and involuntarily induced him to listen. He immediately recognised the voice of the Referendarius von Birkheim, who had a little while before annoyed him so much by his libertine remarks, conversing with a person, whose soft, gentle voice, seemed to belong to a young girl.

"But, my dear, sweet Mary, what stupid thoughts are these you have to-night. You are usually fond of going to a ball; why will you deny yourself the pleasure to-night?" was heard from the voice of the Referendarius, interrupted by frequent and ardent kisses.

"I would be glad to go with you, dear Adolphus," replied the daughter of the Geheimerath, for that voice belonged to none else, "but it is really too dangerous to remain away all night. Just imagine, if my father were to discover our secret excursions, I would die with shame at the exposure."

"And it would be a great misfortune for me, I can assure you, for I have to thank your father for my entire present existence, and I hope that his hand will also help me on in my future career. But the old papa cannot find us out. He would have to be wiser than he is. And upon the whole, do you imagine that you commit so very great a wrong? Your father is below, merry and happy, and making court to those theatrical ladies, whilst he lets you sit here solitary and alone, like a little nun. No, no, my dear Mary, it would be right cruel, if I were not to take pity on you, and endeavour to enliven your youthful hours. I owe as much to your father, who mistakes your advantage and my gratitude. I will depend on it, then, at eleven o'clock. I shall expect you in the hot-house, you know the place. I have provided an excellent mask for you, as a female pilgrim of the Cross, and I shall go as your knight."

"I am very much frightened to-night. I hope that nothing ill will happen to us," whispered Mary, tenderly embracing her seducer. Suddenly she started up, however, like a frightened deer, and broke from him with the words: "Hark, hark, Adolphus, there is a rustling by the door! Oh, if somebody has listened!"

The old Major, who had become too much excited in his indignation, and had incautiously betrayed his presence by a careless movement, just gained time enough to retreat unobserved along the corridor.

After waiting a few moments at the other end, he hurried down the stairs, with the words: "Just wait, and I will teach you a severe lesson." Pretending the sudden and unexpected arrival of a relative, he hastily left the company.

CHAPTER VIII.

THE MASQUERADE.

ON the same evening on which the events related in the last chapter occurred, a large masquerade took place at the Colliseum.

This edifice, which has since come to such a tragical end,* was at that time in the zenith of its glory, and was a favourite place of amusement even among the highest classes, although even at that period many of the frequenters of the place were mere adventurers.

On the evening in question, the company there was most brilliant and numerous. An immense row of carriages stretched along Jacob-street, and at the entrance to the festal halls, a thick knot had formed, which the Police officers found no little difficulty to sever. The favourite, "Sie müssen hier zaruck," (You must stand back,) had escaped the bearded lips of the gensd'arme so often, that his voice had become perfectly hoarse.

At such moments the position of a Berlin executive Policeman becomes the most onerous, difficult, and disagreeable, and all merely through curiosity, that characteristic peculiarity of all the natives. For hours and hours together, will a Berlinian freeze, hunger and starve, simply to see the nose-tip of a bride, whose nose is not in the least different from that of any one else. Urged by this passion, he defies the threats of the usually so much feared gensd'armes with astonishing temerity, he even exposes his precious body to the danger of being trampled beneath horses' feet, or crushed by the wheels of a passing carriage, and all only to see the hired tunic of some poor counter-jumper, who is just conducting his master's seamstress proudly to the ball, although the same youth has perhaps an hour before, with a most humble smile, weighed a few ounces of sugar or coffee for our Berlinian.

As much as the peace-officer endeavours, according to received instructions, to keep the large, curious crowd at bay, still that mass is continually increased and strengthened by fresh arrivals, and every moment he sees the oft-repeated prohibition broken again. But, notwithstanding all this, he must not lose his patience, but oppose stoical composure to the annoyances of the daring multitude.

But curiosity is not the only enemy the officer has to contend with on occasions like this; crime also surrounds him on all sides, defying all his vigilance, activity and cunning. Pickpockets, above all others, use these occasions to reap a rich harvest by their adroitness. The arrest of these characters consequently is one of the principal and most important duties of the Police; but the discharge of it is most onerous and difficult, as the gentry of the swell-mob usually seek safety under an exceedingly elegant appearance, and a gentlemanly, easy behaviour. The best, and most experienced officer, is consequently liable to disagreeable mistakes, such as the one which we shall now communicate to our readers.

Among the masks which on this evening

* That splendid structure was destroyed by fire a few years ago, and if we remember rightly, some lives were lost with it.—TRANSLATOR.

streamed in masses to the Colliseum, there was a simple, plain domino, which seemed to cover a strong, manly figure. This person did not, as the others, proceed to the interior of the saloons, but remained posted at the entrance, where, leaning against a pillar, he closely scrutinized all who passed him.

For a long while he remained thus, and with such perseverance, that he finally attracted the notice of the Commissary of Police on duty, who earnestly requested him not to obstruct the entrance in this manner. As this request was totally disregarded by the stranger, the officer considered it his duty to demand him to unmask at once. The other obstinately refused to comply with this order, but endeavoured to frighten off the official, by a hasty answer of:

"I am *Prince de Prominsky*, and I think nobody is forbidden to stand in this place."

As this name was unknown to the Commissary, and as the appearance of the stranger, and the obstinacy of his retaining his position at such a place, seemed not suitably to agree with the rank of a Prince, the cautious officer became still more convinced that he had some notorious adventurer before him. He consequently requested him without farther ado to prove his claims to that title, and also to give his reason for so obstinately obstructing the entrance to the saloon

The Prince felt no little offended at this peremptory and insulting manner of the officer, and replied, by telling him, that he stood there under the protection of the Ambassador of his Sovereign, and of Major von Steinforth, whom he was waiting for. This somewhat startled the Commissary, who withdrew to a respectful distance, whence he could conveniently observe the other. When, a few moments afterwards, the Major arrived in the costume of a knight of the Cross, and respectfully and friendly saluted the stranger, the officer disappeared in the crowd.

The two masks immediately withdrew to the interior of the saloon, ordered champagne, and took seats at a little table in the so-called Orange-room, whence they could conveniently overlook the variegated throng of masks.

"You have certainly chosen a peculiar place for our rendezvous, Herr Major," began the Prince, "for scarcely arrived at Berlin, I have been in great danger of being arrested. I should, moreover, never have found my way to these halls of pleasure, had not the Jewess proved so excellent a guide. But explain, my dear sir, why, when a friend whose entire fate lies in your hands, and who, after a long journey is anxious to rush to your arms, you should appoint this peculiar costume, and meet him in such a place, and amid such a motley crowd."

"I think," replied the Major, "that your Serene Highness will perfectly justify this step, when I give you the assurance that here we can uninterruptedly hold our conference. Moreover, I expect at this very place an occurrence of considerable importance to you, and finally, I shall have to inflict a severe, and perhaps, very amusing punishment upon a most daring pair of masks. I preferred to make your Serene Highness participator of my Censorship, rather than postpone the long desired moment of meeting you, even for an instant, by this undelayable business."

"First of all, my dear friend," resumed the Prince, greatly excited, "tell me how stands my affair. Have you found the Jew, and can, or will he give you any information? I am all impatience to receive some intelligence, for you know my entire happiness is at stake. The thought of being unjustly in possession of my brother's estates, to live in splendour and abundance, while he, unacquainted with his rank, wealth or descent, is probably exposed to want and misery, that thought becomes more terrible every day."

"I certainly take the most lively and intense interest in the fate of your Serene Highness," answered the Major; "but you should not reproach yourself with things which were brought about by the faults of your ancestors, and not by your own. On the contrary, you may look forward to the guidance of Providence, with calmness and resignation.

"Now please to lend a friendly and attentive ear to my report: The day after your Highness had left my estate, the Jewess, with her children, started upon her journey to Berlin, to seek her husband here. What success has crowned the endeavours of that good and noble woman, your Highness can best learn by the letters which she has addressed to me on this affair."

At these words the Major handed to the Prince a number of papers, the contents of which were something like the following:

"Berlin, ——— 18——

"MOST KIND AND RESPECTED BENEFACTOR!

"After a severe and difficult journey, I at last, a few days ago, arrived in Berlin. It is impossible to describe the feelings which overwhelmed me on entering the city. Only a few months ago by the side of my husband, burthened with crime, I had fled from here in the deepest misery, and pursued by the police. I now returned to the city, enlightened by those instructions, for which I have to thank your humane and philanthropic exertions, and in the proud consciousness of serving no longer the evil one. This contemplation had the most salutary and beneficent effect upon me. On the other hand, it was most painful to me to return, even for a short time, to the dens of vice whence I had escaped by so wonderful a guidance of Providence. The thought of again exposing my children to the pernicious influence and authority of their father was most horrible. But I brought the sacrifice with a willing heart, as it was your wish, and as it may serve as a proof how much I appreciated all the benefits you have conferred upon me.

"But I will not fatigue you with details of my own feelings, but simply give you a report of the result of my inquiries and search.

"For several days I found it utterly impossible to obtain any clue of the whereabouts of my husband. A tradesman, to whom he had sold some valuable silver plate, gave me the positive assurance, that he was in *Berlin*, and must certainly have committed some great theft; but none of my husband's former hosts could inform me of his present quarters. At last, at one of my peregrinations through the city, I met an old woman—a rag-gatherer—whom I had formerly known as one of the thieving companions of my husband. This woman pointed out a hostlery in the so-called Voightland, as the present headquarters of him I sought.

"The first meeting between myself and my husband, was to me a scene of great fear and anxiety. He reproached me bitterly that I had not long before—even as he had done—found means to escape from your prison, and to join him with my children; but with all this he was almost unmanned at the joy of seeing me so suddenly before him, and at the first moment it caused me bitter pain to think of deceiving him so cruelly. But the unfortunate, bad character, which has even become worse since my separation from him, soon made my part more easy.

"I fear the measure of his crimes is almost full, and we must not delay, if we would not be anticipated by the Police. My husband has, of course, not the remotest suspicion of my conversion to Christianity. Should such be the case, my life would certainly be in great danger, as you, my respected benefactor, have learned yourself how much my husband hates all Christians, except those who belong to his associates. As difficult as it was for me, as contrary as it was to my nature, I was compelled again to assume the costume and manners of a Jewess.

"The mysterious trinket, which is of such immense importance to yourself and his Serene Highness, is still in my husband's possession; but I have not yet dared to make any farther inquiries about it, as his suspicions are very easily excited. In the course of a few weeks I expect to approximate closer to the accomplishment of my object, and to obtain the idol, for such I believe the blue stone to be. In this manner you will soonest gain your object, as the Prince has not himself seen the trinket, and as a mistake regarding it, is not only possible, but even probable. For my husband, as I have already informed you, is much too young to be one of those who abducted the brother of the Prince when a child."

Thus ended the first letter of the Jewess. The second was as follows:

"Berlin, —— 18——

"MY DEAREST BENEFACTOR!

"How miserable, how very wretched, vice makes its followers, and how very unfortunate it is, that we never can discover the full extent of its misery until after we have escaped its snares! At the present moment, the Police of Berlin is particularly active, and follows and pursues every step we take. By the assistance of some of our companions, which have been gained over,

they even penetrate our most secret hiding-places. But the thieves are not so easily frightened, as their own cunning and daring rather increases with the activity of their pursuers. They have mostly removed their quarters to the outside of the city, as there is not so much danger of exciting attention there.

"My husband, as I have informed you, in a former letter, mostly lives in a cellar of the so-called Voightland, which cellar is kept by one of the most dangerous receivers of stolen goods and thieves-hosts. The trade carried on in this place is so lively, bold and extensive, that in the most anxious fear I look every day for the destruction thereof. It is a severe task for me to be compelled to be a witness and often participator of the scenes which occur here, and it sometimes is only with the greatest difficulty that I suppress an outburst of my real sentiments. And yet I am forced, if possible, even to surpass my companions in apparent wickedness, in order to gain their perfect confidence.

"Of the late crimes of my husband, I have not been able to learn sufficiently, to frighten him or to force from him a confession of his former position, or anything respecting the mysterious trinket. We may possibly gain our object in another way.

"An old friend and associate of my husband, who is known by the name of the 'cunning Schmerles,' and who always showed a particular attachment for me, is now again in Berlin. Through him I hope to gain more positive information about the origin of my children's father, and I trust that in my next I may be enabled to furnish you with some of the much desired information."

The next letter of the Jewess contained the following:

"Our object, alas! is too well gained. For my husband, within the last few days, is not only a thief, but has become a murderer. There is a rumour abroad in town, that an old woman was robbed of all she possessed, and on offering some slight resistance was cruelly murdered.

"That murderer is no other than my husband. The night when it was committed he was not at home, but came only towards morning, greatly excited, his hands and caftan clotted with blood, and having a large sum of money about him. The associates of my husband at this deed are unknown to me, as they never come to the den where at present we stay.

"I must assure you, my dear benefactor, since that day, the task which I have undertaken has become more onerous still, and I sink daily more under its weight. But I will bear it, bear all as long as I can. Yet I pray and beseech you, soon to recall me from that mission, and to consider the salvation of my children, who must become criminals under their father's hand. It will cost years to overcome the effects of the dangerous influence of a few weeks of their present association. My oldest son has already been used by his father for several thefts, and I dared not reproach him for it, but had to praise him, else excite my husband against me. I can swear to you, my dear benefactor, no mortal ever was slave to a more severe necessity. It is terrible to be compelled to plant the poisoned arrow in the breast of your own child.

"I would never have been able to endure this task, had not the Almighty hand which guides our fate, suddenly sent a powerful guardian to my children, and to me a help and consolation, where I least expected it.

"With the host of my husband, who, among his associates, passes by the name of 'Hunchbacked Jobs,' there lives a young girl, whom he calls his daughter. But this certainly is not the case, for Jobs is a fiend in human form, a monster of malice and villany; and this girl is an angel of innocence and love. Never have I seen so pure and noble a heart, never so pious and innocent a mind, united to such determination and strength. Certainly, the life which I have led for the long time since I parted from my parents, has given me but little chance to know and associate with good, honest people—and there may be more of them in the world than I dream of—still Marianne is one of the best beings that have ever appeared upon earth.

What strength of mind and soul must be necessary to remain virtuous among such people! Such strength of soul, alas! was not mine, when my husband tore me from the hands of my unfortunate parents, who, after the daring entrance of the robbers into their peaceable dwelling, had to weep the loss of their daughter, as well as that of all their wealth.

"And I had received a good education! What strong germs of goodness and virtue must have laid in the soul of her who, even as a child, without a teacher or example, resisted so bravely the persecutions and allurements of vice. That Marianne with such principles is not loved, but most bitterly hated by her father and his associates, you, my kind benefactor, who so well has studied human hearts, need not be told. Burthened with the severest and most degrading labours, exposed to the scorn and contempt of all, the poor girl leads the most miserable, wretched existence. And yet, no complaint, no reproach, passes her lips, but she repays her father's ill-treatment by affectionate love, by faithful services, and is most happy, when she can meet the scorn of her tormentors by some friendly or kind service.

"When I enjoyed the good fortune of receiving the instructions of your kind Pastor, he frequently told me of martyrs, who had suffered the severest tortures for their Christian creed, but who bore them as a tribulation sent to them by Providence, in joy and glory. I would compare this heavenly girl to those martyrs, for her patience and resignation increases with her tortures.

"Ofttimes I am tempted, weepingly, to fall on her neck, and with bitter tears, beg her pardon for the many, many indignities which are inflicted upon her; ay, and tear with my very teeth those who dare to injure her. Yes, I could venerate her as a Saint, kiss the dust at her feet, since I have learned how much she loves my children. Even at the greatest personal risk and danger, she employs every leisure hour to teach them the doctrines of Christianity, and guard them against the lures of vice.—But I may not do it; I must, on the contrary, treat her with contempt and severity, and even try to excel my associates in malice toward her, as the object of my mission requires it.

"I have often tried to find an opportunity of telling her my real sentiments, and of uniting with her in confidential secret union, but in vain. And, moreover, I know not whether I may really confide in her, as she appears partly too honest and open-hearted to dissemble, and partly is too inexperienced. All that I have thus far been able to do was, to avert, as far as in my power, and under the mask of accident or of falsehood, dangers from her head, and to impress upon my children the necessity of keeping silence about her efforts.

"But whatever may be the result of our enterprise, I must beg you, my dear benefactor, for mercy' sake, to free the unfortunate girl from the terrible position in which she now is, and which she really never deserved.

"The Prince has promised me large rewards if his plans succeed; as far as I am concerned, I despise these rewards for myself; for what I am doing, is a holy duty, it is gratitude for received benefits, and for saving my poor soul from temporal and everlasting perdition. But with the most stingy avarice I would receive these benefits for my unfortunate protegée, and whatever you, or his Serene Highness intended to confer upon me, I beg, I beseech you, to confer upon the liberation and support of poor Marianne.

"Who she really is, I have not yet been able to discover; but she certainly is not the daughter of the Hunchbacked Jobs. This was plainly evident from an expression he used toward her, and a proposal he made to her a few days ago. How could a father behave so cruelly to his own child, or how could the same consanguinity produce such opposite characters?

"But in sympathy for my unfortunate protegée, I almost forgot the object of my letter.—

"By the information which I have gathered from the cunning Schmerles and the Rag-gatherer, about the former life and adventures of my husband, and through my own observations and experience, I am enabled to give you a pretty complete account of his early life, &c., which, however, does not bring us much nearer to our final object.

"My husband is descended from a Jewish tribe, who roamed after the manner of Gipseys, throughout the wildernesses of Russia and Poland. He was the son of a chief, and in early youth was held in high respect among his fellows, as none of them could equal him in daring, courage, or agility.

"After the fashion of his forefathers he was, early in life, married to a daughter of his tribe. He was attached to her with most devoted love, and she was said to be an affectionate, kind and faithful companion to him. But after very few years, their happiness was most cruelly destroyed.

" A detachment of Russian boors attacked his tribe, whom they suspected of having robbed a church, cruelly ill-treated his wife before his eyes, threw his children into the fire, and dragged him along, a prisoner, as they hoped by torture to gain some important confessions from him.

" After some terrible torments he was brought to Siberia, where he suffered in chains for some years. By a lucky accident, he succeeded in making his escape, and after unspeakable miseries and sufferings, reached Poland.

" Aided by internal convulsions which then prevailed, he gathered a mass of outlaws and robbers around him, and was soon at the head of a large band. With this band he crossed the Russian frontier to revenge himself upon his enemies, as he had sworn to do in a terrible oath, while writhing under their tortures.

"After a long and restless search, he at last found the hamlet, whose inhabitants had in so cruel a manner destroyed all the hope and happiness of his life. A desperate fight took place, but he was victorious, made them all prisoners, bound them together and locked them in a barn. He set fire to it, and watched his mortal foes slowly dying a terrible death.

" Since that day, the character of my husband has assumed that fiendish malice, which afterwards became so prominent a feature of all his actions.

" The mysterious trinket he cut after the fire from the neck of one of the roasted bodies, and transferred it to his own. The truth of these circumstances I can vouch for to a certainty, my dear benefactor, as the father of cunning Schmerles was present at the fire and discovered the trinket himself.

" Since that day it has never left my husband's neck even for a moment, and he is said to venerate it with almost superstitious devotion, regarding it as the Talisman of his fortune. There can be no doubt of its authenticity, as according to the account of cunning Schmerles, it really contains the mysterious characters which the Prince mentions in his description.

" As the hamlet, upon which my husband took such a terrible revenge, has disappeared from the face of the earth, leaving no trace behind, there would indeed be very little hope to receive any information of the brother of the Prince, had not the cunning Schmerles been informed by his father of a dark report, that my husband had formerly been in the possession of that trinket, and that it had been taken from him by the boors at their attack.

" According to this, it would certainly be possible that the brother of the Prince was abducted by the tribe to which my husband belonged. But I am sorry to say, that he alone is able to give any definite information on that point. Yet I daily despair more of being able to succeed in obtaining that information of him

by gentle means. Whenever I allude to the mysterious ornament around his neck, he invariably gets into a most feverish state of excitement, and repulses me with dark and furious looks. I must, consequently, now only endeavour to bring him into your power.

" The murder with which he has lately soiled his hands would offer a fair opportunity for doing this, if I could succeed in gathering sufficient evidence for his conviction, and if you would give me a secret promise not to drive matters to the utmost in that respect.

" But although my husband has ruined all my hopes for peace or happiness in this life, and though he is fallen to be one of the lowest of criminals, yet all the world should not induce me to consign him to a scaffold. He is still the father of my children, and a most unfortunate man, who, though sinning, has been heavily sinned against.

" Such a sacrifice, you, my kind benefactor, cannot and will not exact. I hope in my next letter to be able to design a certain and positive plan of action, but I must then beg that you will immediately come here, that I may be released of my most cruel and onerous office.

" Your son will fully inform you of the ways and means of finding me."

The last letter was as follows :

" Berlin, —— 18——

" RESPECTED SIR !

" Everything at this moment depends upon your immediate arrival here, with his Serene Highness, as the long wished for moment has at last come.

My husband intends shortly to commit a burglary at the house of Geheimerath Berthold. The purpose of this burglarly is to obtain a large sum of money, which the Geheimerath will receive in a few days from the estate of his deceased grand-uncle. The money will remain only a single night in the house, and is then to be deposited in bank. This single night is selected for the accomplishment of the crime. What particular night this will be, cannot, for the moment, be ascertained with any degree of certainty, but to judge from the preparations already made, it cannot be far off.

" An associate of my husband, who is known under the name of Eel-eye, has *baldowert* the Massematten, by engaging the old cook of the Geheimerath in an amour. This man, and cunning Schmerles, will assist my husband in the affair. I have so far regained the confidence of the latter, that he has communicated to me all his plans regarding this enterprise, and has even commissioned me to examine the localities of the place, which commission I will execute to-day.

" As the Geheimerath, according to the assertion of your son, is a relative of yourself, this burglary will offer an excellent opportunity for the accomplishment of our object, but it will also be the last chance we may have for a long time, as my husband intends to leave Berlin the very night after the theft.

"We must not, therefore, on any consideration, let this decisive moment pass by, and it would be a most severe blow, should you, by any chance, arrive too late in Berlin.

"Nothing would then remain for me to do, than to give the sleeping draught which I still carry about me, to my husband, and to bind and deliver him to you in that manner. For as soon as my husband recommences his vagabondizing mode of life, I shall want opportunities to continue our correspondence unobservedly, and even if I could find those opportunities, you would meet with great difficulties in receiving my communications."

*   *   *   *   *   *   *

The contents of these letters seemed to create a deep impression upon the Prince, for he devoured them with the most greedy haste and interest, while his face each moment changed colours.

"Now, my dear friend," he exclaimed, in the greatest anxiety, as he returned the communications to the Major, "how has the affair turned out? But, for mercy' sake, be brief and hasty, for I die of impatience and excitement."

"That also your Serene Highness shall learn immediately," replied the Major, without being at all discomposed by the excitement of the Prince. "In one word: This night is designated by the Jew for the burglary, and in a very few hours your fate may be decided.

"Immediately on the receipt of the last letter from the Jewess, I hastened per extra post to Berlin, and even on the evening of my arrival I succeeded in seeing the Jewess. The accomplishment of the theft was luckily postponed for a few days, by the delayed payment of the money, and I consequently arrived here in good time.

"The following day I hastened to Geheimerath Berthold, an old friend of my brother's, and found all the information of the Jewess fully confirmed. He has really inherited 10,000 Thalers from his grand-uncle, and the time of payment was this very day.

"At first I thought of initiating the Geheimerath into the secret, and to arrest the Jew in the rooms. But upon the urgent representations of the Jewess, I omitted this, as the Geheimerath is very cowardly and talkative, and we consequently had to fear that the Jew's suspicions might be aroused through the cook.

"We have, after due consideration, concluded to arrest the Jew after the committal of the burglary, and at the very moment when he leaves the house of the Geheimerath. But as the enterprise, which Heaven forefend, may fail, by some accident or chance, the Jew must not, by any means be allowed to obtain possession of the money, and the Jewess, to accomplish this, has thought of a very ingenious and peculiar plan.

"The money is in an iron safe in a room on the first story, which safe can only be broken open by means of an iron jack-screw. The Jewess, shortly before the committal of the theft, will withdraw the iron bolt from this instrument, and substitute a black painted wooden peg, so that the least application of force must make the jack-screw useless, and compel the Jew to retreat.

"I trust that your Serene Highness will join the expedition, at all events. Beside my son, we will have two confidential and well-armed servants with us. A carriage with my police agent will wait near by, to transport the Jew immediately after his arrest to a solitary house, which I have rented for the purpose.

"As the Jew knows that there is a feast this evening at the house of the Geheimerath, to celebrate the accession to his fortune, the burglary will not be attempted until toward morning. We shall be on the spot sometime before, and remain in an opposite house, until the Jew has entered the house of the Geheimerath, from the garden of a side building. Then we shall enter by the front-door, and creep along to the hot-house in the yard, which the Jew must pass on his retreat, and there we shall arrest him.

"The Jewess has received instructions from her husband to keep watch in the street, during the theft, and to give a preconcerted signal, if any danger approaches. She will consequently be in our immediate vicinity, and can advise us of everything that might unexpectedly occur.

"In order to prevent the possibility of the Jew's escape by the street, it would be advisable, if your Serene Highness would there put your secretary, who is fully acquainted with the whole affair, together with one of my servants, on guard. Four persons will certainly be fully sufficient to manage the Jew, as we intend to let his companions escape."

With these words the Major closed his report. The Prince, who had listened most anxiously, warmly pressed the Major's hand at its conclusion, and endeavoured to hide a tear that stole into his manly eye.

"Really, my dear friend, I could embrace you, and press the kiss of brotherly-love upon your cheek, for all the good you have done for me. Whether I ever find my brother again or not, this much is certain, that in you I have found a friend more valuable than all the treasures of earth, and such a treasure is certainly a great and rich reward."

"Do not speak thus," replied the Major, no less affected; "the person whom you have to thank most, is only——the Jewess. Without the endeavours of that excellent woman, we would never have gained our object. And the sacrifice which she has brought for us, is really an unspeakably great one. I must confess it openly to you, that I have read her letters with the deepest sympathy, and could never sufficiently admire the nobility of heart and the wisdom which characterizes that woman. Who, when my Police-agent brought the Jew and his ragged family before me, who would then have dreamed that we had such a wonderful couple of human beings before us, two such strange extremes of virtue and of vice, and who would have dreamed that the Jewess was destined to put us to the blush, as our benefactress. But if it should cost half my fortune, I will certainly reward her, as far as is in my power."

"I fear, my dear friend, we shall have to fight a severe battle of friendship," replied the Prince, "when the time arrives to pay this debt, and I think the Jewess will only be gainer by this strife. But, my dear friend, do not meanwhile forget or neglect her wishes. How is it with the unfortunate girl whom she so warmly refers to in her letters? Have you made farther inquiries about her? Can we not do something for that unfortunate girl immediately, and have we no means of getting her out of the hands of her inhuman father?"

"In this respect, I am sorry to say, I must complete my report by a sorrowful recital," replied the Major.

"The Jewess last night hurried to me, filled with consternation and terror, wrapped in a blood-stained man's-cloak, and related things to me which filled my mind with horror. The Jew accidentally became a witness how Marianne instructed his two eldest children in the doctrines of Christianity. This discovery so enraged him, that he made the instant attempt to murder Marianne. With the greatest difficulty the Jewess prevented him, but she was unable to save the poor girl from the cruel, and almost mortal ill-treatment of her husband.

"This scene of horror being scarcely over, the Jewess was again witness of a still more cruel and terrible outrage. A spy of the Police had entered the den of the Hunchbacked Jobs, for the purpose of betraying the inmates. By a mere accident he was discovered, and was instantly murdered before the eyes of the Jewess. Still occupied with the corpse of the murdered man, the murderers suddenly discovered the approach of the Police, and without this woman's wonderful presence of mind, all our labours and endeavours would at once have been made useless. For if the Jew falls into the hands of the Police, he can make no disclosures of his former life, without pronouncing his own sentence of death, and we shall lose the principal means by which we may hope to operate upon his mind—the promise of non-punishment.

"At the most critical moment, the Jewess well considered this, and adopted a most daring, venturous plan, but which succeeded even beyond expectation. Favoured by a lucky resemblance of size, stature and voice, as well as by darkness, she quickly put on the dress of the murdered man, assumed his part towards the Agents of Police, and induced them to leave the Hunchback's cellar, under the assurance that the persons whom they sought would only arrive an hour or two later, and that a visit too early would frighten them away. The good woman was so perfectly exhausted from excitement and fright, that she sank fainting at my feet, and was not able to return to her children till next morning.

"The unfortunate Marianne lies sick at her inhuman father's house, but under some pretence I shall send a physician to her to-morrow, and have her taken away and taken care of. A great part of this depends, of course, on the results of this night. For if we have once gained our object with the Jew, we must not delay a moment, but deliver the den of the Hunchbacked Jobs to the Police. Your Serene Highness is now in possession of all the circumstances of this important affair, and we may quietly and with the best of hopes look for the farther results.——

"Let us now for a few hours enjoy the general hilarity, and please to assist me in the execution of a joke, serious in many respects, and which induced me to meet your Highness in this place."

It was difficult to persuade the Prince to agree to the proposition of the Major, as he had become very seriously disposed by the communications he had received. The persuasive powers of his friend, and the magic force of champagne, finally succeeded in enlivening him, and drawing him into the whirlpool of masks which filled the room with the most grotesque groups. All classes of human society were here personated and represented in the most ludicrous medley.

Here the slippered centennarian danced with the blooming violet girl, yonder a stern knight of St. John whirled in a cotillion with a meek looking nun. Here the chaste Maid of Orleans flirted with jovial Falstaff, yonder a Priestess of Vesta was courted by a variegated Harlequin. Here a staunch-looking watchman was strolling arm in arm with a stiff Prelate, yonder emperor Nero was debating with a lamp-lighter. Charles the Great and Rinaldo Rinaldini were here drinking from the same glass, whilst yonder sat Mary of Stuart and King Lear at cards with a pair of Galley-slaves. An enormous bat was on one side speaking soft nonsense to a Sylphide, and on the other Nathan the Wise kissed an orange-girl. In short, all casts of rank, all difference of age, and all limits of time seemed annihilated by some magic power, and the Colliseum on this evening resembled Paradise.

But beneath the masks, also, the same motley variety prevailed. The knowing spectator here observed in one and the same saloon, ay, in one and the same quadrille, Privy-Counsellors and Under-secretaries, Counts and Jockeys, Students and Millers, Ambassadors and Penny-Postmen, Majors and Brewers, Philosophers and Tailors, Attorneys and Hatters, Assessors and Bakers, Justices and Distillers, Commissaries of Police and Pickpockets, Squires and Confectioners, Lieutenants and Cobblers, Booksellers and old clothesmen, Professors and Doctors and Tinkers and Farriers. Among the ladies in particular, there was a most wonderful and mysterious mixture, and many a one of the fair dancers would have instantly fainted of fright and horror, if she had known the exact set to which her next neighbor belonged.

Many a married man paid delighted attention to an old flame of his youth, while his better half, whom he believed to be solitary and quietly at home, was dancing past him, leaning upon the arm of the family physician. The liberty of masks allowed all these wonders.

"Your Serene Highness has often expressed the wish to become somewhat acquainted with all the mysteries of life in this city," began the Major, after he had taken a turn through the saloon with the Prince. "You have now an excellent opportunity to earn a rich harvest of the knowledge you desire. Unfortunately, I am not sufficiently acquainted with the present life of the city, to be a very a good Cicerone in this respect. But in yonder mask I have just discovered my friend X— , the Police Recorder, who will certainly be able to furnish interesting particulars of the personalities of many of these masks."

With these words the Major introduced the Prince to the mask he had named, and informed the other of the desire and rank of his guest.

"It gives me the greater pleasure to be of service to your Serene Highness," replied the Recorder, "as the department to which I have the honour to belong, owes you an apology. The Commissary on duty has just informed me that he had the misfortune to mistake your Serene Highness in a very unpleasant manner. He has requested me to ask your pardon, in his name, and I beg that you will accept his apologies."

"Far be it from me," answered the Prince, quickly interrupting him, "to cast the least reproach upon the officer. I have caused the misunderstanding by my own behaviour, and am fully convinced that the man did nothing but his duty. Let us, therefore, say nothing more about it, but begin our perambulation. Tell me first, who is that lady with blonde ringlets, whose splendid figure attracts the attention of all, and who is surrounded by a swarm of admirers, all of whom she seems superior to, in wit and humour. To judge from her appearance and manners she must belong to the upper classes."

"If that lady would unmask, you would discover a face in perfect accordance with the other charms of the fair owner. But she certainly does not belong to the upper classes, as it is only a few months since she has been dismissed from the work-house. She is the natural daughter of a chief-forester, and formerly was bar-maid in several restaurats. Then she eloped with the clerk of a shop-keeper who had robbed his employer's till. After her paramour had spent nearly all his money, she cheated him of the rest, and returned here. At present, the levity and wealth of a few young men, whom she entices into her lures, enables her to lead a most extravagant life. Sometimes she assists her most favoured lover, who sits at yonder card table by a glass of champagne, and who is mostly supported by her, in the execution of some cheating. This man is a professional cheat and gambler, and with the lady visits during the summer the most fashionable watering-places, when both, aided by their fair personal appearance, pass themselves for persons of high rank and wealth."

The face of the Prince during this recital had become very serious, and for the moment he was unable to answer anything but: "My Heavens, but this is terrible!" — — —

"Much more interesting," continued the Recorder with a smile, "is yonder small, neatly formed lady, whom you see chatting with that lean Harlequin. That lady speaks nearly every living language, can even comment well upon a Latin author, and possesses talents and education which would do honour to many a Professor; yet she is one of the most dangerous persons that ever existed in the world of crime. Under the mask of love and friendship she introduces herself into the most distinguished families, and by her intrigues, causes dissensions of every kind, which she usually knows how to turn to her own advantage.

"She understands particularly well how to assume the mask of the religious fanatic, and in this manner has crept into several fat legacies. On the other hand, she has succeeded only a few weeks ago, in obtaining a large amount of valuable presents from a distinguished stranger, as in his presence she played the satirical free-thinker. This stranger was so perfectly enchanted by the charms of this female Proteus, that he would very probably have placed a coronet upon her head, had not a lucky or unlucky accident interrupted it. Unfortunately, this active and intriguing woman, being perfectly acquainted with the use of the pen and the letter of the law, has usually so arranged her enterprises that the authorities never yet have been able to bring her to conviction. But I hope her measure will soon be filled, and she will not long escape her well merited punishment.*

"That large woman whom you see there, overladen with ornaments, presents also many interesting peculiarities.

"She is the daughter of a stevedore, and accumulated a considerable fortune as a priestess of Venus. For several misdemeanors in conducting her business, she was some years ago detained in the house of correction. Notwithstanding this, she succeeded in her advanced age to marry a bankrupt brewer, with whom she now carries on a lucrative business. Mother of two handsome daughters, each of whom will receive a rich dowry, in possession of a fine house and splendid carriage, that woman now stands in a respectable position, and even enjoys no small influence, as she plays a conspicious part in the family secrets of several distinguished houses. Results like these, bring the best proof, what an unfortunate influence the possession of money exercises over the judgments of men.

"That lady, with snowy white arms, who in the costume of Minerva, has just glided past your Serene Highness, and who was addressed '*gnädige Frau*,'† by her companion, is the daughter

* To quiet the apprehensions of our Berlin readers, and for general information we would remark, that the lady to whom we refer, is at present in prison, for forgery and theft.

† Equivalent to "your ladyship."

of a laborer, and formerly led a most degraded course of life in this city. Afterwards, in some watering place, she married some old Italian nobleman, from whom she inherited a considerable fortune, with which she entertains a swarm of lovers, and lives in the greatest extravagance."

The Recorder was about to point out several other persons to the Prince, but the latter interrupted him with the words :

"I pray and beg you, desist, and put not my preference for the fair sex upon too severe a trial, nor rob me of my fond belief in female virtue."

"I pray your Serene Highness," continued the Recorder, who seemed delighted at the surprise and indignation of the Prince, "not to direct your suspicion only to the fair sex, but believe me, that in many respects they are surpassed by the gentlemen you see present.

"Yonder dandy for instance, who struts about with a heavy gold chain, quizzing all the masks that pass him with a supercilious air, is a professional cheat and gambler. He has already brought many an inexperienced young man to ruin. Only lately he became the murderer of the son of a distinguished family. The unfortunate youth could not resist temptation, and after having lost all his own funds, spent those of his employers. Governed by a false sense of honour, he next preferred to send a bullet through his brain, to a candid confession to his parents. No serpent is more certain of entangling a little victim in its coil, than are such monsters in human form. Soon as they discover among their acquaintances a hot, inconsiderate youth, they let him win for weeks, ay, for months, to be the more secure of him afterwards.

"But then, the accident *which they rule*, suddenly turns the wheel of fortune. The poor victim ventures one stake after another, but instead of regaining what is lost, he still suffers new and heavier losses. Finally, driven to despair, he risks the whole of his fortune upon a single chance, and—sinks hopelessly into the abyss which has long yawned at his feet.

"That lean man yonder, who despite his tailor's science, labors under a great want of leg and calf, is descended from a very noble family. But from his childhood devoted to vicious courses, he was soon forced to leave an honourable and profitable post, and has since lead a vagabondizing course of life, as gambler, actor and pseudo-literateur. In the bosom of the old widow of his tailor, he at last found a resting place for a few years, until he was forced by her entire ruin to resume his former mode of life. For a long time he then protracted his existence as pettifogger, dog-trader or horse-jockey, till the death of his aunt again raised him from that position. He received a few thousand Thalers from her estate, but these were soon exhausted in champagne and fine horses. For some time afterwards he managed to live upon his newly gained credit, but that fair dream came also to an end, and a struggle with creditors and bailiffs ensued, which ended with a debtor's prison.

"At present the adventurer occupies the post of under-secretary to a Commissary of Justice, and is an ardent Methodist. He is a member of several benevolent institutions, and is particularly fond of assuming the *rôle* of a pious devotee. Only occasionally, when he believes himself unobserved, he ventures to return for the moment into the whirlpool of his former amusements, but I fear that we shall soon make some very surprising discoveries regarding him, as his means are far from sufficient for his present excesses.

"I might entertain your Highness with a mass of similar disclosures, but I partly fear to fatigue you, for, upon the whole, the courses of vice are still fundamentally the same, and partly as I am at present called off by duty, since I discover in yonder beau with blonde curls, one of our most dangerous pick-pockets."

"What ! that elegantly dressed young man a pick-pocket ?" exclaimed the Prince in astonishment.

"Yes, your Highness, he has already been thirteen times under criminal arrest, and has passed five years in prison. He has moreover, as a convict, received at least five hundred lashes on his bare back at different times." At these words the Recorder left them.

The astonishment of the Prince had continued to increase during the recital of his obliging companion, and at last he exclaimed : "By Heavens ! I do not envy the experience of this man, for it must be a terrible and cruel knowledge to be acquainted with our fellow men in this way." He then walked for a long time in silence by the side of the Major, who was no little discomposed at the long absence of the two masks he expected, until he suddenly saw them entering the door in the costumes of pilgrim, and knight of the Cross.

The two friends now arranged their plan of operation ; the Prince immediately approached the daughter of the Geheimerath, and addressed her in the most friendly manner with the words :

"Good evening, *Fräulein* Berthold;* why, this is really charming, that you are good enough to adorn the masquerade by your presence. I hope your papa is also here, or is he perhaps detained by the festivities of his house ?"

Mary was thunderstruck to find herself so quickly recognised on her first entrance into the ball-room, and could not utter a syllable for very shame and confusion.

Her companion finally took the word, and replied to the Prince :

"You must be mistaken, sir, that lady is not Fräulein Berthold."

"Ah ! is it you, Herr Referendarius von Birkheim, are you here also ?" answered the Prince, laughing ; "this is charming, to find all old friends and acquaintances. The Geheimerath very probably knows nothing of the friendly service you do his daughter in bringing her here, and that is the cause of your incognito."

Frightened, the Referendarius bit his lips,

* Fräulein—Miss of rank.

at finding himself so completely out-manœuvred, and answered abashed:

"My dear sir, I trust you will not be indiscreet. We are not those you take us to be. But above all things, I must beg to have your name?"

"That would be of very little consequence, and I am as little desirous of being recognised at this place as you are." And with these words the Prince disappeared among the crowd of masks.

"My God, Adolph! what have you done?" whispered Mary, weeping, to her companion; "let us hasten and return home as quick as possible."

"What! are you mad, child?" replied the Referendarius, "we would only make ourselves the more suspicious. Nobody can recognise us with certainty, and if your father should hear anything, we must deny it all. At the very worst, the misfortune has now happened, so let us at least be merry while we may."

With such words, the Referendarius quieted the fears of the timid girl. But they had scarcely crossed the half of the saloon, when the Major met them.

After scrutinizing the daughter of the Geheimerath for some time, he addressed the lovers in a disguised voice:

"Good-evening, Fräulein Berthold; good-evening, Herr Referendarius von Birkheim."

Before the parties he had addressed could recover from their new fright, the unwelcome speaker had already disappeared. Mary was very near fainting, and was compelled to seek a seat for a few moments.

Accidentally she seated herself at the table which the Major and Prince had occupied, and upon which their champagne still remained. The Prince immediately hastened there also, and urged the lady to drink. Mary was so perfectly overcome by her fright, and the Prince urged so warmly, that she drank a goblet of wine, and thereby gained fresh courage, although her unknown, mysterious friend still continued to address her "Fräulein Berthold."

The Referendarius tried in vain to induce the Prince to unmask; for the latter suddenly again disappeared in the motley crowd. The two lovers now believed themselves secure from any farther attacks, and somewhat reassured, they strolled through the saloon. Mary even became merry and lively, when the excellent orchestra suddenly played from the gallery the bewitching air of the favourite Scotch waltz.

But suddenly they observed to their terror, that a black monk followed every step they took like their shadow, and never left their heels for a moment. It was no other than the Major, who had meanwhile changed his mask at the public wardrobe.

The Referendarius who felt not in the least flattered by the company, endeavoured to get rid of it, by addressing the monk suddenly and harshly, with—

"Black mask, what would'st thou? Hence, away, Satanas!"

But in a hollow, unearthly voice, he received the mocking reply: "The fair Pilgrim here wishes to pray a Rosary with me, as atonement for her sinful elopement from her father. I go not hence, nor leave her, till penitent she has returned to his arms, for that is the rule of my order, and—wo, wo, thrice wo, to the seducer."

"Adolphus, I pray you, for Heaven's sake take me away from this place!" whispered the frightened maiden to her conductor. "I am nearly fainting, and can no longer endure this scorn."

Nothing remained for the Referendarius, but to lead the daughter of the Geheimerath from the room. In the corridor he again employed all his eloquence to induce her to stay.

He represented to the foolish girl, that the strange masks must be a couple of his own friends, who amused themselves with what they considered an innocent joke. They could easily escape their importunities by merely changing their costumes and masks for others. This would, moreover, be the best and easiest way of discovering who their tormentors were, and finding out their object.

Mary at last consented, and in the course of another half hour, both of them re-appeared in the ball-room, the one in the mask of a Jew, and the other in the mask and costume of a gardener's-girl. They were thus freed from farther annoyances, as the Major did not again recognize them in their present costume.

CHAPTER IX.

THE BURGLARY.

THE brilliant lights in the rooms of the Geheimerath were long since extinguished, and a deep universal silence prevailed, as the watchman calling the second hour, passed along the street. The tones of his voice had just died away, when a muscular, manly form passed up Frederic-street, and slipped gently into the house opposite that of the Geheimerath. A second, third and fourth figure followed the first, whilst several others walked toward Charlotten-street, and entered a coach which stood in waiting there.

Half an hour later, and a second group approached the house of the Geheimerath, consisting of the Jew, the Eel-eye, and the cunning Schmerles. The Jewess walked in advance to reconnoitre the grounds. As soon as she had arrived at the basement windows of the house next to that of the Geheimerath, she laid herself down on the pavement, and pretended to suffer of convulsions. The Jew and the cunning Schmerles now assumed the part of accidental passers, and appeared to assist the unfortunate suffering woman. These preparations merely took place for the purpose of deceiving the eye of an accidentally passing officer, or unseen spectator.

The Eel-eye, meanwhile, occupied himself with fastening a large rag, smeared with bird-lime, against the lower pane of the basement window. Soon as this operation was completed, the Eel-eye broke the glass with a forcible pressure of his thumb, but thereby did not create the least noise, as all the splinters of glass stuck to the rag. Eel-eye next passed his arm through the opening, withdrew the bolt, opened half of the window, and entered the basement. All this was the work of a moment, as frequent practice had made him perfect at it

Schmerles and the Jew, who carried a large bagful of different instruments, followed immediately after Eel-eye. The Jewess quickly rose again from the ground, re-shut the opened window, and passed to the opposite side of the street, where, like a sentinel, she walked up and down, or, as the Berlin thieves say, " stood *Schmiere.*"

Arrived in the lower room of the side building, the Schränkers immediately lit their business-lantern. This consisted of a glass cylinder encased in tin, containing a small light, behind which there was a concave mirror fastened, to reflect the light. Opposite the mirror, in the tin-cover, was a loose, sliding piece, by which a great or small stream of light, as circumstances required, could be thrown upon particular points, whilst all surrounding objects remained hidden in utter darkness.

Their next task was to enter the court-yard of the neighbouring building, so as thence to gain access to the premises of the Geheimerath. As the door toward the yard was locked, and could not be opened with any key of the bunch, and as there was no window on the side of the court, the thieves opened a door leading to the cellar with one of their keys, descended, and after breaking one of the little cellar-windows, climbed thence into the yard. Here, after surmounting the enclosure of the first garden, they entered the garden of the Geheimerath.

Arrived there, the Jew and cunning Schmerles rested a few moments in one of the arbours. The Eel-eye meanwhile went to the side of the hot-house toward the garden, lightly removed the boards which covered it, bent the leaden rods which held the glass panes, with a strong knife, and in this manner carefully removed one pane of glass after the other. He then tore the strips of lead which remained, and having made a good sized aperture, he crawled through it into the hot-house. His two companions followed his steps, and with him reached the door which led from the lower story of the dwelling to the hot-house.

This door, however, offered a much stronger barrier to the intruders than any they had yet passed. The Jew, by the ray of light which Eel-eye with the little lantern threw upon the lock, soon found a key which fitted, but at the same time made the discovery, that above the lock there was a strong bolt, which was not so easily opened. By slightly rattling at the door, Eel-eye discovered whereabouts the place of this bolt was, and with a species of auger, made about an inch-wide hole in the door. Through this aperture he passed a wire hook, and endeavoured to catch

and withdraw the bolt with that. But all his endeavours were in vain. Although Eel-eye made four more holes in the door, he did not succeed in hitting the right place of the bolt.

"We must cut out the whole piece, together with the accursed bolt," whispered the Jew to Eel-eye, who immediately began making a row of holes at the designated place. He next took a small pointed saw, and in this manner cut the solid wood between the holes. When he had come to the last hole, the Jew put a small gimblet into the piece he wanted taken out, so that he might take it out on opening the door, and prevent the noise which its falling would necessarily have caused.

After a few seconds, the Schränkers had entered the library of the Geheimerath. Here they only needed to turn the key which was in the lock to enter thence into the corridor. They next, in their stocking-feet stole up stairs, passed the chamber of Mary, and soon reached the door of the room which contained the iron safe.

The opening of this door cost them more than half an hour's labour, for within the lock there was a so-called *thorn*, which fitted exactly into the pipe of the key-hole. This prevented any key from entering, and it became absolutely necessary to remove it before they could hope to gain access.

To accomplish this, they took a strong string of sulphur, put it into the key-hole, and lit it. After this operation had been repeated several times, the soft metal with which the thorn had been soldered on, began to melt, and now, upon the application of a little pressure, fell out. The lock was now opened without any difficulty, but the door could not yet be moved an inch, as it was still fastened by two bolts. The Schränkers again endeavoured to bore a number of holes into the door, and withdraw the bolts with hooks, but their auger suddenly would not work, as the door had been strongly secured with sheet-iron around the lock and the bolts.

At this unexpected resistance, the Jew got into a terrible passion, and uttered the most bitter oaths and blasphemies. The cunning Schmerles, however, retained his coolness, and quietly whispered to Eel-eye:

"We must cut out the door-lining, and then the matter will be settled."

The Eel-eye immediately produced a long-handled strong knife, and leaning the butt-end against his shoulder, he began to split the thinner laths which held the iron facings. After a few minutes, this work was completed, and he now removed the door-lining with little difficulty. He next produced a small vial of blood, which he carried in his pocket, and daubed it upon several places of the door, whispering to Schmerles:

"This is what I always do at my work, so that the Criminal-Commissary may believe that I have cut my fingers at it. If he should afterwards catch me with uninjured fingers, he will have the less suspicion of me."

But as the Schränkers now attempted to creep

through the opening in the door, they found to their consternation that it was much too small—so small, indeed, that not even the slim and active Eel-eye could pass through it.

"Now we must either as quickly as possible steal a ladder somewhere, and by that means creep into the window from the court, or we must cut these bolts with the iron-saw," observed cunning Schmerles to the Jew.

The latter alternative seemed the most feasible; and after the Schränkers had bored a large hole above each of the bolts, Eel-eye, with a metal-saw, which had been well oiled, began at the upper, while Schmerles with a similar instrument began sawing at the lower bolt. In about half an hour, and by immense exertion, they had cut the bolts in two, scarcely creating any perceptible noise by their arduous work.

As the Schränkers had finally entered the room, their first care was to hang whatever pieces of blanket and carpets they could find about the premises over the windows, and to cover the holes in the door with paper, so as not to be betrayed by any glimmer of light. This precaution taken, they withdrew the tin cover from the lantern, which now spread sufficient light over every part of the room.

This room was only a small one, and seemed intended for the repository of all valuable and important documents and papers in the possession of the Geheimerath. It contained very little furniture other than a number of bookcases, drawers and chests, and particularly the large iron money safe, which was fastened to the floor by immense iron screws.

After the Schränkers had closely examined the safe from every side, they became convinced that they could never open it with a false key, but that they must endeavour to raise the lid with a jackscrew, so as to be able to see how the lock held it.

While the Jew began by screwing an immense iron bolt into the floor, so as to make this a resting place and hold for the jackscrew, the cunning Schmerles with chisels or keys, as the circumstances seemed to require, opened the remaining boxes and drawers, abstracting thence whatever he considered worth taking.

The Eel-eye meanwhile occupied himself by gently opening the window which looked into the yard, and fastening a strong cable, long enough to reach from the sill of the window to the ground, so that the Schränkers, if they were unexpectedly discovered, might have this road open for a sudden retreat.

After all these preparations were completed, the jackscrew was placed against the lid of the safe, and the Jew began with the full application of his strength to turn the crank. — — —

— — — — — —

We will now leave the Schränkers at their work, and follow the active Prince and his followers. The arrival of the thievish trio had not escaped them, and they had watched all their operations with the most particular attention.

About a quarter of an hour after the others had entered the windows, the Prince and his party also entered the house of the Geheimerath, but with a proper key, which the Major had found means to obtain. They also opened with the right key the door which lead from the yard into the hot-house, where they remained well hidden, as they knew from the Jewess that the Schränkers must come that way.

The position of the two friends and their followers in this place was most disagreeable and difficult. Without uttering a single sound, even without the least motion, they had to wait nearly an hour in a bent-up position, and in the most terrible tormenting excitement. Besides this, it was so uncomfortable in the place they stood, that the Major began to tremble with cold, and was scarcely able to retain his position.

Finally, when they had already despaired of the success of their undertaking, and were almost convinced that the Schränkers must have made their escape to the street, they heard a terrible crash in the upper rooms, and the cry of a female voice for help. Immediately after, again followed a deadly silence, so that the beating of the Prince's heart could almost be heard.

In a few minutes hasty steps were heard approaching from the interior of the house, the door which lead from the library of the Geheimerath into the hot-house moved upon its hinges, and—the form of the Jew stood in the midst of his persecutors.

To catch sight of that form, grasp hold of it, to muffle it with a cloth which had been held in readiness for the purpose, to drag or carry it to the street, throw it into the coach—all this was the work of a very few moments. The two servants of the Major took their seats by the side of the Jew in the carriage, which drove off at the most rapid pace.

The Major and his companions retired on foot, after he had whispered to the Jewess the words:

"We have succeeded! go and bring your children to the house of my father. The business in the den of the Hunchback has come to an end."

CHAPTER X.

CRUEL DISAPPOINTMENT.

THE Jew, by his sudden and unlooked for arrest, had been frightened to such a degree, that he lay in the carriage like a corpse, or in a fainting condition, and never uttered a sound. It seemed a perfectly unnecessary precaution that the servants of the Major tied a handkerchief over his eyes, to prevent his recognizing the place of their destination.

After many crossings and re-crossings, the carriage stopped at a house in *Gollnowgasse*, which stood solitary and alone, at some distance from the street, in a large garden. This house, during the warm season, served as the summer residence of the family of a friend of the Major, but at present it was lonely and deserted.

The Jew was carried to a chamber, prepared expressly for the purpose, and laid upon a sofa, after his fetters had been somewhat loosened, but not taken off. One of the two servants remained with him, whilst the other reported their arrival to the Major.

He found the Major and his companions in an old-fashioned saloon, which was tastefully decorated, a bright fire burning in its antiquated chimney.

The room was arranged as if for the session of a tribunal. Upon the large, green-covered table, spread with documents and papers of different kinds, and surrounded by high-backed leather-cushioned chairs, burned four large wax-lights, which spread a brilliant light through the room. A solemn serenity was expressed upon every face, and none of the company dared to utter a loud word. The Jew could not be the only person who was expected, for even after he had been brought to the house, the Prince impatiently walked up and down the room for a quarter of an hour, and at last uttered the words : " The Count lets us wait very long for him."

That moment, however, the rattling of carriage wheels was heard, the folding-doors opened wide, and the son of the Major entered, in company of a fine, stately-looking man—dressed in a simple officer's overcoat.

" It is a very peculiar request which I have made of you, my dear Count, to give me the honour of your presence at such an hour, and in so solitary and distant a location," were the words with which the Prince addressed the stranger ; " but the importance of the subject, which we must here discuss, will certainly justify me, and I give you my most heartfelt thanks for having so promptly answered my invitation."

" The confidence of your Serene Highness is so flattering, and my obligations to you are so very strong, that your Serene Highness may dispose of me at any and every hour. I trust that you shall be satisfied with me," replied the Count.

" Before I can communicate to you the object of our meeting, my dearest friend," replied the Prince, kindly taking the stranger's hand, " I must pray you most urgently and sincerely to inform no person in the world of the least circumstance that may transpire here, unless I should myself desire you to do so. Our object is by no means a dishonourable or criminal one, but merely concerns the discovery of an immensely important family secret, which requires these most extraordinary measures. It is very possible, that 1 may afterwards want a powerful mediator elsewhere, and I therefore, my honoured friend, wish to interest you for my affair, as I know the very great influence which you possess here."

" I pray you, my dear friend—if your Serene Highness will permit me to address you thus—inform me of your wishes, and you will in me find a servant who is devoted to you, body and soul, and is as silent as the grave. Take my hand and word upon this, and without farther preamble, let us proceed to the business."

" Then, in the first place, take your seat between me and our mutual friend, the good Major, and then lend me your ear for a tolerable long story, which will explain all our objects to you. During the last few years, you have often been struck with peculiarities in my conduct, and you have sometimes reproached me for them, I now hope, when you hear my story that you will judge me differently.

" It must be well known to you, Sir Count, that my family originally resided in the interior of Russia, and that only its late descendants have taken up their residence in Poland. From time immemorial my family has been in possession of a large blue stone, which represents a very curious figure, and is covered with several mysterious characters, the so-called *Runen*-characters. To judge from this inscription, the trinket is a relic from times of heathenism, and represents a deity. Afterwards having been baptized by the name of the Patron Saint of our family, it was then considered as a holy amulet, upon which depended all the fortune and power of our family. This trinket, consequently, was always inherited by the eldest son of our house, from his progenitor, and was held in high honour.

" All this is evident by the papers and documents upon the table before you, and among them you will also find an accurate drawing and description of the trinket, according to which it consists of a particularly large piece of the *lapis lazuli*, frequently found in Italy.

" About forty years ago my family was robbed of this amulet, and the eldest scion of the house abducted in a most peculiar manner. My father at the time, which was before my birth, was at a distant hunting-castle, with his only child, and surrounded by a few servants, when in the night the castle was suddenly attacked and plundered by a band of Gipseys. The inhabitants of the castle were all tied, partly murdered, and partly cruelly tortured, At last, the robbers set fire to the castle, expecting thus to destroy all traces of their crime. But the very light of the fire attracted a party of wood-choppers from the neighbourhood, just in time to save my good father from a cruel death in the flames. But his son had disappeared, and all the world believed that he had fallen a victim to the flames. The amulet also was missing, and my father had some dark recollection that it was cut from his neck by a large bearded man. The reality, of what might be considered the superstitious confidence which my family had in the power of this trinket, seemed now to become confirmed. For with the loss of that mysterious stone all success and good fortune fled for many years from our house.

War and robberies followed famine and destructive tempests, and our immense herds in a short time melted into a most diminutive handful. My mother presented her husband with another son, but he died shortly after his birth. Hatred and dissension entered our once peaceable family. The younger brother of my father had married a Polish lady of rank, a woman who in beauty, but also in quarrelsome ill-temper, surpassed all her sex, and who lived at constant strife with us all. This hostile and unfortunate position was increased by a strange dark report among the people, that my father's second son had been poisoned by this woman, in order to secure the possession of our estates to her own child.

"This report induced my father, when a few years afterward I was unexpectedly added to his family, and his hopes thereby were again renewed, to watch over me most closely and attentively, and even to remove me to a distant place, the location of which was kept a secret from every body. When I had grown up to be a strong boy, he sent me to Germany and to Paris, and there I received a most excellent and expensive education.

"Only when I was eighteen years of age, I returned to my father. When at home, I mostly enjoyed the pleasures of the chase, for which I had abundant opportunities upon the large domains belonging to my family. In my hunting tours I particularly attached myself to a confidential servant of our family, who was a Frenchman by birth, and passionately fond of the chase.

"As much as I felt attracted toward this man, something mysterious and gloomy was perceptible in his whole demeanour, which often in an inexplicable manner repulsed me, and made me somewhat mistrustful of him. I only too soon made the discovery how much I was justified in this feeling of dislike.

"One day we had scarcely left the castle of my parents to hunt through our Park for woodgrouse, a species of game then very plenty with us, when I suddenly heard the report of a gun behind me, and my companion uttering cries of intense anguish. His gun, accidentally catching against the root of a tree, had suddenly discharged and inflicted a wound on his shoulder. I hurried to his assistance, examined the wound, and consoled him with the assurance that the wound was only trifling, and that he would soon recover from his fright, and be able to reach the castle without farther assistance.

"Tremblingly he pressed my hand, looked at me for some moments with a wild confused stare, and then whispered to me:

"My Prince, I will never leave this place, but shall be a corpse in a very few minutes."

"At first I believed the man to be delirious, and endeavoured to console him, but suddenly he rose and uttered with a terrible coolness and a distinct voice, these important words:

"The ball is poisoned, and was destined for you. The lady, your aunt, has hired me to assassinate you, in order to gain the reign for her house. But God is just, and I fall the victim of my own guilt!"

"Even during this speech the features of the assassin had assumed a pale and peculiar hue, and his limbs became strangely convulsed, which caused him exhaustedly to fall to the ground.

7

After a few minutes he endeavoured again to rise, and tearing his hair in wild despair, he exclaimed:

"Oh God, my God! the poison begins to operate, in a few moments my race is run, and I must appear before the throne of my Maker. Wo, bitter wo, to that terrible woman, who has thus cast me into perdition! But I will repair as much as still remains in my power. Pardon, my Prince, pardon me! it is terrible to pronounce my own guilt, but do not curse me too bitterly.—Your eldest brother is not dead, but was carried off by a tribe of strolling vagabonds. The castle was fired by the machinations of the same terrible woman, and this, my own accursed hand, gave the poison to your second brother. That woman, your aunt, is the cause of all, she has bribed me, and sinfully pledged her love to me. Your eldest brother perhaps is still—" the villain could speak no farther, but sank to the ground, incoherently uttering the words—curse—woman—woman—love—lost for ever—ever—

"What a terrible impression this scene produced upon me, I need not describe to you, Sir Count. For a long time I stood aghast, and had placed my foot, unconsciously, upon the breast of the corpse, for I dared not touch it. At last I awoke to consciousness, undressed the body, which had meanwhile assumed a terrible bluish colour, and upon the breast I found a small parcel suspended by a silken ribbon.

"This parcel contained the miniature of my aunt, and several of her letters—all testifying to the terrible truth of the dying confession of the guilty man. Up to this moment a feeling of terror had retained possession of my mind; but now the pale sorrowful figure of my father, who still wept the loss of his first-born came before me, and as I pictured to myself all the sorrow and misery which that fiendish woman had brought upon my family, a feeling of intense rage overmastered me. Without speaking a word, I arrived at my father's castle, saddled a horse, and in a few hours had reached the place, and stood before the object of my revenge. I found her sitting alone by the window of her house, probably awaiting the message of my death, and the fulfilment of her wishes. She turned pale as marble, when, instead of the much expected messenger, she so suddenly saw me with a countenance displaying every appearance of rage and bitter hatred, stand before her. I should certainly have acted more wisely, if I had secured her person, and from her obtained farther disclosures of the fate of my brother; but passion and anger raged so within me, that I passed my sword through her body, and then retreated over the garden walls as unobservedly as I had come.

"No one ever discovered how my aunt and her sinful associate lost their lives. Even to my father, I never disclosed the secret of his terrible calamities, as this would only have increased his great sufferings. But silently and energetically I used all the means in my power to obtain tidings of the fate of my unfortunate brother. From the last of those letters, which I had found upon the Frenchman, I learned that my aunt had intended to take the life of my brother, but that accidentally he had survived, and most probably was still roving about with the tribe of his kidnappers.

"My aunt had no fears that my brother might again return and claim his hereditary rights, as almost every evidence of his birth had been taken from him, and as the chief of the band only knew his descent, and was solemnly bound, by a most terrible oath to eternal silence; but the artful woman still thought it more advisable entirely to destroy her victim, and consequently had commissioned the Frenchman to discover his whereabouts, but previously to despatch me to another world. The letter, however, contained no farther information which I could avail myself of, and consequently I had to trust to accident or fortune for the success of my endeavours.

"As long as my father was still alive, I was somewhat consoled for the loss of my brother; but when I afterwards gained possession of our dominions, that possession rested like a heavy judgment upon my conscience, and I considered myself only the administrator, not the successor of my brother. This feeling increased when, after a short time, I lost wife and daughter, and I as well as others, began to incline towards the superstition, that all fortune and blessing of our family had been lost with the mysterious trinket. Induced by this superstition, I roamed for many years, over the wilderneses of Poland and Russia. I sent confidential servants to all tribes and bands, which roved about those countries in multitudes, and even mixed personally with the lowest rabble, and became in disguise intimate with the coarsest ruffians—still hoping again to find my poor brother and our long lost happiness, but all in vain. Nowhere could I find the least trace of him, and my desire to attain the wished for end only increased with the many sacrifices I had already made.

"At last, a few months ago, I passed through a pretty, pleasant village in West-Prussia, but had the misfortune, or I should rather say, the fortune, to be upset by the awkwardness of my coachman, and to break my arm. Away from all relations and friends, without sufficient surgical attendance, and unable to pursue my journey, I found myself in a really disagreeable and vexatious position. The proprietor of the domains on which the accident happened, hearing of it, took pity upon me, and with the greatest love and kindness nursed me for weeks, and thus ere long effected my entire recovery.

"In the Major, here present, you see my kind benefactor, who since then has become my dearest friend. I was not only destined to gain a dear friend by that accident, but it likewise brought me nearer to the long sought object of my travels.

"At a promenade, which I one day undertook with my kind host, over part of his very extensive domains, I did not hesitate to recount to him the whole of my past history, with the same candour and fidelity as I have just related it to you. But I could not come to the conclusion of my narrative, for my friend suddenly rushed to my arms, exclaiming: 'Huzzah, huzzah, he is found, found, and I will assist you."

"At the first moment I was as much frightened as surprised, and for an instant even indulged in the sweet delusion that the Major himself might probably be my long lost brother. I even went so far, as to ascribe the affection I felt for him to a secret sympathy which naturally attracted me to my brother, and was delighted at the accident which, in so romantic a manner, led to finding him again. But a single glance at the grey hair of my friend, destroyed all the heavens of my dreams, by the conviction that our friend might possibly be my father, but could not be my brother. Yet the Major's communication sufficiently satisfied me for the moment, for I now had a trace, and a certain one.

"The Police man of the Major's estate had, as I was told, a few weeks previous arrested a Jewish family and delivered them to prison, as they could not give any account of their occupation and residence, and consequently were suspicious vagrants. The Major, who is ever kind to all the unfortunate under his care, paid some friendly attentions to this poor family, and made the surprising discovery, that the wife of the Jew possessed a cultivation of mind and a heart such as none of us could have believed her capable of possessing. She seemed to feel very unhappy in her position, and to find real consolation in the friendly solicitude with which she was treated.

"She particularly lent a willing ear to the endeavours and instructions of the minister, who sought to convert her to Christianity, and the Major concluded to assist her all in his power. This philanthropic resolution produced a most desirable result, the more so, as the Jew suddenly escaped the prison, and thus freed his family from the pernicious influence which hitherto he had exercised over it. A few months afterward, the Jewess amidst the cheers and acclamations of the multitude, became a christian. She, moreover, related some very wonderful things of the former life of her husband, and particularly referred to a peculiar blue stone which he carried upon his person. In short, there was the greatest probability that the Jew was in some way connected with the abduction of my brother, and that he was in the possession of the long sought trinket.

"But the Jewess could not by any means give us any definite information regarding this, to us so very important subject, as she had never thought it worth while to pay any attention to it, and as her husband had always showed toward her a demure and stern silence of character, regarding everything connected with his own affairs, or his former life.

"Nothing consequently remained for us, but to send the Jewess, who had meanwhile more and more gained our confidence, after her husband, and in this manner either again gain the

Jew into our power, or to obtain a free confession from him. As it was highly probable that he had gone to Berlin, the Jewess first went there, and was lucky enough to find her husband in a very short time. After many very difficult operations, we have this night succeeded in arresting him, just as he was occupied at the execution of a burglary in the house of Geheimerath Berthold, and silently and unobservedly to transport him to this place. Here, we will undertake a strict and close examination of him, and if possible induce him by the promise of liberty, to give us the much desired information. Should he, however, not comply with our wishes, the Major will claim him as an escaped criminal from his prisons, and thus take him back to his own domains. We will then leave no means untried to force the secret from him.

"You will be convinced, Sir Count, by this relation, that we are not engaged in an unjust or improper enterprise, but that, notwithstanding, we cannot avail ourselves of the force and strict form of law. I have consequently not dared to undertake the forthcoming examination of the Jew, without the presence of a high and responsible witness, and upon the whole, have held it advisable to confide the entire affair to your powerful protection, so as to be guarded, should things come to the worst, against the interference of authorities, and against other mishaps and annoyances, that might occur.

"And now, my dear sir, you have my whole history, and you can convince yourself, how very unfortunate I have hitherto been, and how full of importance is this hour to my fate! And you will please to tell me openly and candidly, whether you will be my coadjutor, or whether with a solemn promise of everlasting silence, you will withdraw from this dangerous affair?"

"I most frankly choose the first alternative," quickly interrupted the Count, and as I can conceive perfectly well, with what anxiety your Serene Highness looks for the examination of the Jew, I must beg that you will hasten it, and produce your prisoner without delay."

The Prince immediately agreed to this proposition. The documents upon the table were quickly arranged, the chairs placed, and the Prince then took his place between the Major and the Count. The other persons present stood behind their chairs. After all these preparations were completed, the Prince gave orders that the Jew should be brought in. After a few minutes, the folding-doors of the saloon opened, and the figure of the Jew, led by his two guardians, his face entirely muffled, tottered into the room.

"Let him sit down here, right before us," exclaimed the Prince, addressing the servants, as he pointed to a chair which stood in the middle of the room, and take off the bandage from his eyes, but only gradually, so that he may not be blinded by the glaring of the strong light. This order was most punctually obeyed.

The Jew took his place opposite to his judges, and the covering was loosened, and slowly fell from his eyes. But an intense and fearful cry of horror was uttered from every lip, and nearly every person in the assembly turned deadly pale, for before them, instead of the Jew——sat, the pale, trembling figure of——the Referendarius *von Birkheim*, who with a trembling voice begged for grace and mercy.

The Referendarius, after having changed his costume, had assumed the dress of a Jew, and conducted the daughter of the Geheimerath to her home, and had used the passage through the hot-house for an entrance.

An accident had detained him until the thieves had entered the dwelling. He had been a witness of their operations, but had not dared to call for assistance, as his own deeds would have been disclosed by the discovery of the Schränkers. But when the jack-screw had suddenly broken, and the noise caused by it resounded through the whole house, he had quickly taken to his heels, to call for help.

By his unfortunate disguise, the followers of the Major had been misled, and seized him—instead of the Jew.

END OF BOOK I.

BOOK II.

CHAPTER XI.

THE LADY-EQUESTRIAN.

It was a clear and beautiful day in December as the inhabitants of Berlin issued in motley throngs through the Brandenburg gate, to enjoy at the there situated circus, the performances of a lately arrived Company of Equestrians. It was especially the beauty of the artiste, whom Rentier Wertheim, at the soirée of the Geheimerath, had so passionately described, which thus operated like a magnet upon all the youth of Berlin. All the under-secretaries, officers, barbers, and clerks, spoke of nothing but the beautiful equestrian, and entered into the wildest speculations regarding her position and circumstances.

The one dreamed of a fallen princess, the other of a former Orange-girl, a third of a tailor's daughter, who had ran away, but none could assert anything with certainty. With this mystery, the interest all took in this wonderful novelty naturally increased, and the treasury of the manager reaped a rich harvest in consequence; for the house was daily crowded, and many anxious visiters had to return, unable to gain admission. The object of their worship seemed to gain very little advantage from the great excitement she caused.

None of her many admirers could boast of having received the slightest favour from her, nor could she by any means be persuaded to accept anything in the shape of a present. In this very circumstance, so rare among artistes of her class, lay the something which was so peculiarly *piquant* and attractive to the mass of her admirers.

On the evening in question, the crowd at the door of the circus was even greater than usual. The harlequin who had been placed there to attract the notice of passers-by, was scarcely able to protect himself against the elbowings of the multitude, and his continual struggle to free himself from the crowd, formed a strange contrast with the constant stereotyped speech, which he repeated without intermission : " Walk up, walk up, ladies and gentlemen ! you may here see the great and never-to-be-equalled company of equestrians ; you can see *Almansor*, the wonderful and well-trained Arabian horse, the greatest phenomenon in animal creation ! Walk up, walk up, only five *Silbergroschen* for the last place ! Money returned if you are not satisfied," &c., &c.

The comic situation and appearance of this herald, was much increased by the pale, ashy colour of his face, and his artificial moustache, the coal-black brillancy and enormous size of which, gave his natural Voightland-face an almost Chinese appearance. Dirty, flesh-coloured hose, beneath which a pair of thin legs trembled with cold ; a red, much worn jacket, whose tatters waved in the breeze ; a torn fanciful cap, upon which a turkey-plume was waving, made him an object of disgust more than of pity.

It needed but little physiognomical knowledge to recognize in him, at the first glance, a vagabond of the first water, who had here sought a temporary and needful asylum, and had only for a while changed the prison-dress for his present fantastical accoutrements. But his character is most clearly shown, by the following conversation, which, after the crowd had somewhat diminished, two well dressed and respectable looking strangers, held with him.

" My gracious, Ludwig !" began one of the strangers, " is it possible that you are again free from Spandau ?"

" Oh yes, I am already these four weeks at liberty ! They had sentenced me for three years, but I gammoned the minister of the prison most excellently ; I learned hymns, sang and prayed continually, and got myself off in that way. But just now i fare ill enough. For only five silbergroschen I have to bawl and crack jokes here all day, till my teeth rattle with cold and my stomach aches for very hunger."

" You infernal fool ! why do you make a monkey of yourself for such a trumpery sum ? A fellow who can work the keys as well as you, can make more, in a single night, than you make here in ten years. Look at us ! last week we done a little job, which partly failed, but still we live in joy and merriment, like gentlemen, and if our money is all gone, we will find another opportunity to make more."

" I can no longer do any business," replied the other, " for I have been thrice punished for larceny and once for burglary. Should I be caught, or get into difficulties again, it will be punishment for life, and I beg to be excused of that. I may do a little swindling, which is not punished so severely, but thieving is at an end with me. At the utmost, I may commit a small trifling theft, under five Thalers, for then my former offences don't count. But if I can otherwise do something for you here, I will, with the greatest pleasure, for I am fond of making a few shillings privately."

" You may probably have a chance, as we intend doing a little *Drücker* business in the crowd, and have, therefore, taken seats in the dress-circle. Should any accident happen, and we be pursued, be in readiness, so that we may pass the *Schürig*, (stolen goods,) into your hands, and clear ourselves. If, at the worst, something should be found upon you, you can get yourself clear, by saying that another had slipped those things into your pocket, and nobody will suspect you as the thief."

" Enough, brother, I agree ; but you must give me *Hellig*, (a proportionate share,) even in case you get off safely, for a good business may be done here."

" It is a bargain, upon ' *Lotscherehre*,' (the honour of a thief.")

The two strangers withdrew with these words. They were no others than the cunning Schmerles and the Eel-eye.

The booty which they had taken in the rooms of the Geheimerath, and had safely carried off, after the departure of the Major and his followers, had been, spite of the failure of their attempt upon the safe, so lucrative, that nearly all the thieves belonging to the band had exchanged their old ragged habiliments for the dress of fine modern dandies, and had, in every respect, improved their condition.

Although in the manners and movements of the pair of whom we are now speaking, there was much awkwardness and vulgarity perceptible, yet no one could suspect in their appearance, a couple of such dangerous thieves. The cunning Schmerles might rather have been mistaken for a travelling merchant, and Eel-eye for a student from the country, or for a merchant's clerk.

When they had entered the house, they carefully scrutinized the brilliant rows of spectators, for the purpose of seeking a seat, partly suited for their criminal intentions, and also one which would not too much expose them to the vigilant glances of the Police, who were present.

At last they decided upon a little bench in the first tier, which stood behind a pillar, and in front of which several rows of spectators ranged along. Among these spectators, there were two gentlemen in civic dress, who particularly attracted their attention.

Both seemed to be of high rank, and were particularly distinguished from the crowd which surrounded them, by their fine personal appearance. The one, who wore many orders, was rather advanced in years, whilst the other, much younger than the first, was only dressed in a simple over-coat. The reader will probably guess, that they were no others than the Prince and the Major, whom accident had brought here.

"Both of these seem to have *Moos,* (cash,) and to be strangers, so we must begin with them," whispered Eel-eye to the cunning Schmerles.

"That is just my opinion, and I shall push on till I am close behind them," was the reply. "Do you stay more to this side, and observe whereabout they carry their money. We shall then see, whether it will be best to take their watches or their purses. The oldest of the two carries a very thick pocket-book in the breast pocket of his coat. I shall induce him by some means to open that pocket-book, and if its contents seem to suit us, the thing is easily done in the crowd, on its way out."

Amidst this conversation, the two villains took their places behind their victims, and watched with indifference the performance which had just commenced.

The beginning of the exhibition consisted in gymnastic evolutions of the male members of the company, who were all dressed alike in their almost transparent, yet rather shabby hose and vests.

This part of the performance being over, the manager came forth, dressed in a rich uniform, and announced the appearance of *Giacomo,* the *Atleth of Gothland.*

Immediately after, the Atleth, dressed like his predecessors, with only some slight variation, issued from the door of the side-room, and commenced his performance by lifting several heavy weights between his teeth. The attention of the two thieves was at this moment diverted from the performance, for the Prince had just drawn from his pocket a fine and valuable watch, to compare its time with that of the Major's, and the appearance of these two watches was naturally of the greatest interest to the couple behind them. As soon, however, as their eyes again fell upon the stage, they exchanged intelligible glances at the sight of the Atleth, while their countenances betrayed a most pleasant surprise.

"Why, this is the unknown cigar-smoker!" whispered Schmerles to the Eel-eye, "who liberated us last week when we were arrested in the boat. Now I can understand how the fellow was capable to knock down a gensd'arme and two musketeers."

"Yes, you are right," replied the Eel-eye. "We must pay some attention to this man, for without him we would now be chained like dogs. We will let him have his share of our booty, for whoever works with us, must earn with us, and he would be a dishonourable thief who would not act in that way."

"You are a brave fellow, and a chap of honour," replied Schmerles with a friendly nod. "Come, let us hasten to the room of our liberator, and give him our thanks, and we can afterwards gain time enough to attend to our little business."

At these words, the two thieves withdrew from the Circus, and requested their friend, who to protect himself against cold, had meanwhile wrapped an old coach-man's cloak around him, and had withdrawn to the inside of the house, to show them the dressing-rooms of the equestrians. Here things looked wondrously wild.

Articles of dress of every imaginable kind lay scattered about in medley confusion, and among them moved a dozen or two of half naked figures, none of whom paid any particular regard to the modesty or immodesty of their appearance.

Here sat a gigantic form, devouring by large morsels, the substance of a *Groschenbrod,*[*] while his colleague occupied himself with mending an ill-looking rent in his dancing boot. Here a faded beauty endeavoured to restore the decayed roses of her cheeks, by the magic power of common rouge, while a pretty and very young thing by her side, endeavoured to create the appearance of a bosom by spoiling a large quantity of wadding. A third beauty completed the rows of her teeth by a set of new ones, just from the dentist's, while a dirty cabinet-maker's boy endeavoured, by the side of a foaming glue-pot, to fasten a pair of Sylphide-wings to her shoulders. A fourth, would not suffer the little fire to be all wasted on the glue-pot, but endeavoured with much care to warm thereby the contents of a broken coffee-can.

A couple of other ladies in this motley group, were far less advanced in their toilette, and did not seem likely soon to proceed with it; for they were engaged in a warm and wordy dispute, respecting the partnership use of divers pieces of linen, during which dispute they exposed several very unpleasant reminiscences of each other's life. These two were evidently the youngest and most beautiful of the company; particularly one of them, a lovely Blonde, who developed a fullness of charms, which almost dazzled the susceptible Eel-eye, and for some minutes arrested that worthy at the door of the room. But the cunning Schmerles, who had long since lost all taste for similar temptations, roughly dragged him into a side-chamber, which had been designated to them as the dressing-room of the Atleth, while he earnestly reminded him that they had no time to lose.

In this room, which might have been the so-called Green-room, as it served for the resting place of the artistes immediately before or after their appearance, they formed a still more strange and picturesque company, than in the former. In the next act, a mythological scene was to be represented, and they consequently found in this room all the gods and demigods of Olympus, in the most glorious and wild confusion.

Jupiter and Apollo regaled themselves with large draughts of Schnapps, inhaling their Olympic nectar from one and the same greasy tumbler.

Neptune amused himself by devouring a large hot garlic-sausage, and thereby bespattered the stiff muslin wings of Mercury, who was quietly discussing a ham-sandwich.

* A quartern-loaf.

Venus, clad in very light and transparent hose, but protected against cold by a brown cloth cloak, squatted upon a footstool, and darned her husband's socks, while Minerva was watching the process with a searching glance, meanwhile occupying her hands in pealing a bucket-full of potatoes for the supper of the gods.

Upon the whole, though the troupe was numerous and containing a variety of talent, yet it bore every appearance of misery and of great poverty. It was easily perceptible, in the wrinkled and furrowed faces of the men, that they must have arrived at their present course of life, by many sufferings and adventures; and the pale cheeks of the women were more disfigured than improved by the unnatural colour of their rouge.

There was only a single being among this company who could excite any real interest, but who also appeared like a queen among all her companions. This woman was between twenty and thirty years old, an age when we can no longer decide with certainty between maiden and woman-hood. Her whole appearance bore the stamp of singularity and eccentricity. Dressed in a light hunting-dress, she impatiently walked up and down the room, flourishing a neat riding whip in the air, while a mysterious fire sparkled in her dark, brilliant eyes, and her glances passed over the surrounding objects with a proud indifference. A delicious beauty of her features, a full, finely moulded arm, a bosom like alabaster, and a most graceful carriage, all helped to increase the interest which this woman excited in every beholder. It was the much praised principal artiste of the company, of whom we have spoken above.

When she observed the two thieves, she fixed a long and searching glance for some time upon Eel-eye, then suddenly approached him, and tapped him upon the shoulder with the words:

"Albert, I think, we should know each other?"

The other on hearing so suddenly and unexpectedly his real name pronounced, retreated a step or two, and replied in confusion:

"I do not remember to have the honour—"

"You may depend upon it, I know you perfectly well," was the answer. "Your name is Albert N——. Your father was an honest man, and schoolmaster in B——. I recognize you by the scar upon your forehead, which you received by falling upon a plough-share at the door of the land-holder, although you may scarcely recognize me again. It is many years since we have seen each other, and I don't know what you may follow now; but to judge from your appearance, you are not badly off."

The cunning Schmerles, who, at the commencement of this speech, had been at the point of retreating, as so close a biography of his associate seemed rather dangerous, returned at its conclusion, finding that there was nothing to fear from the fair equestrian, and whispered to his companion:

" *Schole* her out, whence she *Kneifet*." (Pump her, to discover whence she knows you.)

But the Eel-eye stood like a statue when he thus suddenly found the secrets of his youth laid open.

This sudden re-presentation of the innocent spring days of his life, arose before him like a mocking phantom, which at a moment's impulse springs from a cloud of vapours, and the spirits of his father and mother arose from their graves, and threatening and in anger, presented themselves to him. He again saw the friendly, pleasant school-house of his parents before him; he saw two snowy lambs playing upon the meadows; he saw the grey, venerable head of his father, and the mighty bunch of keys at the side of his mother, which so often had welcomely rattled for him, when he received his luncheon at her hands; he again heard the friendly bark of his father's house-dog, and saw the great family bible and the hymn-book open at his desk, and again heard devotional prayer and song ascend on high from that family circle; like a voice of thunder, he again heard the parting words, which his father had called after him, on leaving home for the wide world—

"Still practice truth and honesty,
'Till in thy grave thou'rt laid;"

and recognized in his mind's eye the white 'kerchief which fluttered in the breeze, and with which Kate had dried her tearful eyes when she cast the last glance of farewell to him. The inmost recesses of his soul were crushed, annihilated, and remorse, bitter remorse, suddenly seized him—but as sudden—he felt convulsively for his side pocket, and there he discovered the keys and Schränkzeug which he usually carried about him, and—again stood cool and collected before the equestrian. The phantoms of virtue and innocence had disappeared, and fear for his liberty and the consummation of other crimes only were before his eyes, and became his only object.

"You appear to me like a supernatural being," he replied with embarrassment, "as you refer to things which have long since escaped my memory, and as you seem to know me so well, whilst I have not the least recollection of your person. You must certainly be from the home of my childhood, yet I can only remember two ladies there, who might resemble you. The daughter of the land-holder, and the minister's daughter; the first was married far away from home, and the latter has been dead many years, as I myself have stood by her tomb-stone, when last I visited the graves of my parents."

On hearing these latter words, the equestrian slightly changed colour, her dark eyebrows contracted, and her eyes cast a threatening, fiery glance upon the embarrassed features of Eel-eye.

Thus she stood for some seconds without uttering a sound, when suddenly the Orchestra in front played a loud gallop, which was interrupted by the impatient neighing of horses. These sounds operated like magic upon the fair equestrian, for, flourishing her riding-whip, she hurried quickly from the door, as, in departing she cried to her guests:

"Hark! my horse is calling me."

A loud burst of applause welcomed the artiste, as soon as the audience perceived her appearance; but Eel-eye heard nothing of it, as he was still lost in deep meditation, and was too much excited by the peculiar and inexplicable emotions this interview had caused him. The appearance of the Atleth awoke him from his dreams, as that personage now entered and addressed the strangers with the words:

"Gentlemen, you have desired to speak to me."

"Just so," replied Schmerles; "but we desire a conversation without witnesses."

"You can very easily obtain that," was the reply, "as all who are here must leave in a few moments, and enter the ring to perform."

When the three men were alone, Eel-eye, with the greatest coolness, addressed him thus:

"First, one question, before we can enter into farther particulars. Do you know what is meant by the *Hellig of a Gannew?*"*

"I can answer that question, gentlemen, to your perfect satisfaction, as I have long been with a man who is *chess to the bone.*"†

"If that is the case, my dear friend, we need no farther compliments. You had the kindness, not long ago, to liberate us from a very disagreeable situation, when we were bound and on our way to the city prison. Without your powerful intervention, we would now be covered with rags and chained like dogs. You will, therefore, please receive our thanks for your kind endeavours, and accept this purse. It can be of no possible interest to you how we came by this money. Enjoy it at your pleasure, and permit us to retire, as other business is awaiting us."

At these words, the thieves were about to leave the room, but the Atleth called after them:

"Gentlemen, I do not object to your retiring so soon, when other business awaits you, but I should be sorry to have made your acquaintance for so short a time only. Please to visit me tomorrow at my hotel. I reside with the rest of the company, at the 'Green Elephant,' in X——street, and shall be most happy, if you accept my invitation."

"Well, well; we agree," replied Eel-eye; "to-morrow evening at seven o'clock; but first one word; who is that lady who left the room just before you entered? She wore a green hunting-habit, and has coal-black hair."

"She is our Prima Donna, and an excellent artiste in her line, who earns much money for our manager, and also for us. Who she really is, no one among us knows; she seems to be of good family—and is probably the victim of a youthful indiscretion. She possesses many accomplishments, and a good education, and this is the cause of the supposition, or report, that she is the daughter of a Count. We usually call her *Francisca*. Is it possible, that this devilish woman has set your head crazy, that you should make these inquiries about her? But beware of the little satan; wo to him who falls into her hands, for she has a bad heart, and delights in nothing more than in the torture of her admirers. I was once severely smitten with her myself, and followed her like her shadow. I have certainly since overcome that folly; but sometimes my passion awakes again in all its force, and then the woman may ask what she will of me. But she only yields to her admirers just sufficient to torture and enslave them. When you do me the honour to visit me to-morrow, gentlemen, you may very probably have sufficient opportunities of learning more of this strange and mysterious woman."

At these words, the Atleth, who from his exertions was perfectly bathed in perspiration, retired to change his dress. The two thieves returning to their former seats in the boxes.

After they were again settled in their places, they observed how the Major and the Prince, who still sat before them, were perfectly enraptured by the charming performance of Francisca. The Prince, particularly, joined loudly in the enthusiastic exclamations of the multitude, and at last rose with the Major from his seat, for the purpose of obtaining a better and less obstructed view of the daring equestrian, as in reality, the artiste offered a performance, and an appearance, which charmed every beholder.

She stood upon the back of her beautiful steed with a firmness, as if she were grown upon it, and in her motions and evolutions displayed a grace and agility, such as could rarely be found in an accomplished danseuse, even upon the firm footing of the stage of a theatre; and with all this grace she united a strength and daring, which made her the most perfect mistress of her horse, and forced the animal to slavish obedience. In wild and terrific circles she hurried round the course, quick as lightning she was seen now on this, now on the opposite side.

Now she stood, now lay, now kneeled upon the horse, and again she ran a few steps by its side, or moving in whirling circles, turned upon the broad saddle; then she stood like a fair statue upon its broad shoulders, and finally seemed suspended over it, and only to touch its back with the tip of her fairy foot.

But however gently and gracefully all these evolutions were done, their effect upon the spectators was rather like that produced by a fearful apparition than by an attractive and lovely woman. The beautiful and finely formed features of the artiste were rigid as marble, her full purple lips were not moved by any friendly smile, and the glances of her dark eyes fell gloomily upon the multitude.

---

* *Hellig of a Gannew* is the share of booty which one thief owes to another.

† *Chess to the bone*—A man upon whom a thief can depend, as he is initiated in all the secrets of the craft.

Thus she resembled, at one moment, a proud Amazonian queen, rushing through her wide kingdom in high and conscious majesty, and the next, a dark demon, endeavouring to rise above the earth, until suddenly the orchestra changed its wild strains to a gentle pastoral melody; she then reined in her horse, her features brightened, and with a friendly salute she guided the beautiful animal along the rows of spectators;—but soon the strains of the music again became more wild, the horse renewed its speed—still faster became his pace, and quicker the *tempo* of the orchestra, and in a few minutes the frantic woman flew in wild circles, like the bride of the winds, around the arena. Now she was here, now there, at last she seemed everywhere at once, her hair became disheveled, her hat and whip fell from her hand, and her steed was covered with foam.

The audience cheered loudly at the daring of the equestrian, and the house rang with applause from every side; but suddenly there was a universal cry of terror.

The wild horse-woman had fallen from her charger, and was dragged along through the arena. "Help, help! she's lost, she will be trampled upon!" was the cry from every side; but suddenly the noble form of Francisca arose again, quick as thought she had leaped upon the horse, and in safety and composure she stood upon its back, casting a contemptuous glance at the deceived multitude. In a few moments she and her well-tried steed had disappeared, and spite of the tumultuous call made for her, did not again appear.

The Prince and the Major had also been frightened at the apparent fall of the equestrian, and rising from their seats, had anxiously watched the wild progress of the horse. This was the moment which the two thieves used to abstract the purse of the Prince, and the pocket-book of the Major. Schmerles immediately withdrew from the Circus, but Eel-eye remained behind for some moments, in order not to excite suspicions by their hasty departure together.

When, a moment afterward, he observed that the robbed parties noticed their loss, he hastily retreated also. The Major, however, quickly suspected the two persons who had sat behind him, and followed Eel-eye, whom he perceived near the entrance of the theatre, crying lustily, "Stop thief!" For a moment Eel-eye was in no small danger. To gain his exit, he must yet pass several doors, and at the last of these stood a gensd'arme, who had already heard the cry in the building. Besides him, several officers and others were in readiness every where, to arrest the thief, who dared not even hurry, else he would increase the suspicions against him.

The herald in the red jacket, who had meanwhile entered the saloon, seized upon this critical moment to assist his friend. A glance which he exchanged with Eel-eye, and a hasty motion with the fingers, was sufficient for the pair to understand each other. He pounced upon Eel-eye, apparently very angry, and caught him by the shoulder with the words:

"Just wait, fellow, I shall know how to hold you!" By this attack, their bodies came close together; Eel-eye apparently repelled the red jacket, but by an expert slight-of-hand, slipped the purse into the other's vest, and was safe.

When he was afterwards searched, none of the stolen property could be found upon him. The Major was, moreover, compelled, most humbly to make an apology, as he feared a disagreeable suit for false arrest; but the purse, and the pocket book containing the letters of the Jewess, had disappeared.

CHAPTER XII.

A THIRD CLASS HOTEL.

THE hotel of the "Green Elephant," in X—— street, unquestionably belongs to the most benevolent institutions of the city; for whoever comes to Berlin, and is not especially blessed with the riches of this world, certainly does best to seek an asylum here. At this house he can find, according to his circumstances or his wants, for a few Louis d'ors, Thalers, Groschen or Pennies, a ready welcome and compliance with all his desires.

The soul and ruling spirit of this Institute is *Mistress Barbara*, the rodunt hostess. From early dawn to the latest hours of the night, her never-resting voice is heard through the wide halls of the hotel, endeavouring to keep the immense machinery of her servant-system in proper and regular order. It is she only, who by the most perfect utilitarian principles, can furnish her guests—usually Polish Jews, drovers, wool-dealers, &c.—for the small price of three and a half silbergroschen, with a most delicious bit of "roast," including et ceteras. It is she, who also subjects the offals of this splendid meal to a process or regeneration, which produces ragouts, stews, cotelettes, and fricassées innumerable, by which she can meet the wishes of the poorest of tramping artisans; for even these for one and a half Silbergroschen are enabled perfectly to satisfy their appetite there. If one of them has the good fortune to arrive upon the day when Mistress Barbara has pease for dinner, and is in a very good humour, a single Silbergroschen may be sufficient for his purpose.

Thus, the guests at Mistress Barbara's house, form only one great family, where the wealthy assist their poorer brethern in overcoming the expenses and difficulties of living in the city.

Porters or waiters cannot of course be expected at this house, but the old hunchbacked hostler, who possesses great knowledge of localities and persons, can satisfy all demands in that line, *for a consideration.* In this respect he is considered the factotum of X—— street, and is held in the highest respect among all the barbers, counter-jumpers, cab-drivers, and poor artists of the neighbourhood, as he exercises no small influence upon their welfare, since, as guests of Mistress Barbara, they are frequently compelled to confide to him their inmost secrets.

Should one of these, contrary to expectation, require some of the highest luxuries or enjoyments of life, *Herr August*, by the assistance of his worthy and highly respectable Mistress, can alone obtain them for him.

On the first floor of the house, there are even a few nicely tapestried and well furnished rooms, wherein many a time champagne-corks have popped, and fair lips have been refreshed, while the poor and weary traveller was regaling himself in the story below, with a crust of coarse black bread, and taking his rest upon the hard bench by the stove.

Mistress Barbara, spite her humble appearance and pretensions, enjoyed in consequence of the great number of her customers, a very fair income. She had even amassed a considerable fortune, as, besides the keeping of her hotel, she had two other, and very lucrative branches, of business.

She was, in the first place, rather leniently inclined towards young lovers, who had cause to withdraw from the close observation of strict parents, or ascetic guardians; and secondly, she kept a little magazine for the purchase and sale of articles, about the right ownership of which, she never questioned her customers too closely.

This kind of business could naturally not long remain a secret from the police, with whom, consequently, she lived in continual strife. However, she usually was victorious in these struggles; partly because her cunning and experience was equal to all the exertions of her persecutors, and partly, because she never hesitated in very critical moments to sacrifice some of her followers at the shrine of offended justice.

This then was the place which the new company of equestrians had chosen for an asylum, as all seemed best to suit them here. Mistress Barbara, to accommodate them, had even lowered her usually low charges, as she hoped, that this company might attract many guests from the city to her house; and in this she was not mistaken, for on every evening when the company gave their performance, her house presented a crowded and most lively scene, which brought her no small profit.

Her quiet and modest hotel even became for some time a place of rendezvous for many distinguished citizens, who were all urged thither by a desire to see the charming, beautiful Francisca, more closely than they could at the circus. But in this they were mistaken, for Francisca never appeared publicly in this place, and the mass of guests gradually diminished.

On the evening which followed the scenes described in the last chapter, there was much more than the usual amount of noise and merriment among the equestrians. It was the birthday of Francisca, and all the members of the company had arranged a grand feast on the occasion, which was held on the first-floor rooms, and at which

8

generous wine flowed in streams. The purse which Eel-eye had presented to the Atleth, contributed no little to increase the pleasures of the table, for this man was too good natured to withhold his treasures from the enjoyment of his companions.

The queen of the feast graced the head of the table by her own presence; and her features displayed a degree of hilarity, which her companions had seldom seen in her before. She even increased the merriment of the meal, by her wit and humor, and thereby displayed a quality of intellect and mind, which could never have been expected from one in her position.

The Atleth, who sat by her side, seemed perfectly enchanted by the charms of this woman; his eyes never left her beautiful, seductive features for one moment, and even to the slightest of her wishes he paid the greatest and most prompt attention. To the continual replenishing of her glass, especially, he was so indefatigably attentive, that the magic power of the sparkling champagne soon expressed itself in her burning cheek, and her hilarity increased with every glass.

The Atleth would not let this favourable moment pass, without availing himself of this opportunity, at last, to obtain the much desired disclosures, about her origin and former history. After the company had drank a toast to her health, which Francisca had received with much favour and kindness, the Atleth, with good-natured eloquence, urged his request.

He represented to her, that she had now been so long among them, that they had received much good, but also much evil at her hands, but that still, they were utterly in the dark, as to who or what she really was, and concluded by begging her to break through her perverse and obstinate silence, as she certainly could depend upon the utmost sympathy and discretion, on the part of her companions. When Francisca first heard this unexpected request, her brows lowered, and her serene features became dark; but when all present joined their prayers to that of the Atleth, she hastily swallowed another glass of champagne, and began her history, as follows:

"I am not, as many pretend to say, descended from Counts or Dukes, nor am I of entirely low origin, but I am the only daughter of an honest village parson. My father had a small parish, in a most beautiful part of the Thuringen forest. We lived some few miles from the highest points of the mountain, and thus our village enjoyed all the pleasures of a mountain home, without its disagreeables. The hills near my home were of but moderate height, they could easily be ascended, and the most beautiful views of the rich and fertile plains of Saxony could there be enjoyed.

"No dark pine or cedar forests are to be found in our neighbourhood, we only see oak and beach groves, which lend a fresh and blooming charm to the landscape. Nor have we any sandy wastes, but the country consists of heavy, healthy wheat ground, which yields its rich golden blessings to the land.

Under the care of the tenderest of mothers and the protection of the best of fathers, I grew up in this Paradise, a picture of innocence and peace, and became a tall, fine-looking girl. My beauty attracted general attention, and I was universally called the *beautiful Francisca*. My father, endeavouring to equal the beauty of my person by the cultivation of my mind, assisted me, by his tuition, in penetrating the deepest theological mysteries of all nations, and instructed me in the excess of his love and tenderness, in all possible arts and sciences.

" Greek and Latin classics remained no strangers to me, and I even learned to ride and fence, as the unfulfilled wish of my father, to possess a son, induced him to give me a semi-masculine education. The son of a neighbouring land-holder had, by general report, and by the mutual wish of our parents, been early intended for me, and I was pleased with this choice, for my lover was young, handsome and rich.

" Thus, filled with the fairest of hopes, I entered life, and saw naught but a bright, blooming future before me.

* * * *

" ' But the stern degrees of fate
Man cannot alleviate,
And misery comes quick.'

" War and misery caused the downfall of several bankers, and thereby ruined the fortune of my future husband's family, as also the hard earned little fortune of my father. At last the din of battle reached even our own district.

" The enemy's torch and sword destroyed some of our homes, and the rich harvest upon our fields, leaving nothing for the winter, but a prospect of want and misery. Many of our poor neighbours, who had vainly endeavoured to avert destruction from their peaceable firesides, fell victims of their humane endeavours, by the cruelty and the assassin's weapon of the enemy; among them was my lover, who in defending me from the insulting hand of a *chasseur*, was shot down by a comrade of the villain. Without the intervention of an officer, I would even then have fallen a victim of beastly passion. But the cup of my misery was not yet filled.

" The severe winter, aided by sickness and famine, carried off, first my father, and a few weeks afterward, my mother. There I was, the loved, the adored Francisca, a picture of the most intense misery and despair. Father, mother, lover, wealth—all, all had been taken from me, and a poor orphan I wept at the grave of my parents. None could assist me, for all had enough to do with their own misfortunes, nor would I accept charity, the thought of which, by the sudden change of my fortune, was unbearable.

" Oh, that I had then followed the desires and temptations, which beset my mind for days, and had leaped into the dark floods of the *Unstrut!* I would have saved myself much misery in after times. But I conquered the thoughts of suicide, and placed my hopes upon an aunt, who resided in a distant provincial town.

" It was a fine, beautiful day in spring, when I left the lovely village of my youth. The sun sent down its first warm rays upon the devastated ground, urging a few early spring flowers to raise their heads ; the lark merrily twittered her glad morning song, and the mountain springs again danced towards the silvery rivulet by our village ; peace and happiness seemed to prevail once more through nature, but my heart alone was torn by bitter, terrible wo.

" Once more I visited the favourite haunts of my childhood, once more I bade farewell to my playmates, and caressed again that horse, upon whose back I had so often roved carelessly through these scenes, but which now had been sold for a few Thalers to a neighbour, by whom it had almost been starved through the long winter. Once again I wept my fount of tears dry, by the grave of my parents and my lover, and once more I prayed devoutly at the desolate altar of the church where I had been baptized and confirmed. Then I ascended the steep path of the mountain, cast back a single glance upon the scenes of all my youthful innocence and happiness, and since that time—I never saw my village again. Nor will I ever visit it again, except as a corpse. It is my inmost, dearest wish, to rest when dead, in a quiet corner of that country grave-yard, not far from my dear parents, for their sinful, criminal daughter, may not aspire to a place by their side. I would fear the sacrilege of having my impure ashes laid too close to their hallowed remains. But I will not excite myself farther, else my feelings may overpower me, and prevent the conclusion of my narrative.

" After a long and toilsome journey, I arrived at the residence of my aunt. Enlivened by fresh hopes, I walked towards her dwelling. But, alas ! here also I found—a corpse. My aunt had died the day before, and I was just in time to attend her funeral.

" But even this misfortune was far from being the last of my sorrows. My aunt had willed her entire and large fortune to strangers, and the heartless heirs drove me from their threshold. Then, indeed, I was deserted of all hopes, deprived of all means, wretched and miserable in health and spirit. My beauty, however, had not suffered much in all these miseries and troubles, for it was still sufficient to attract towards me the attention of a young man, who was then Assessor in the little provincial town, and who had become acquainted with me at the funeral of my aunt. Beneath the mask of friendly care and sympathy, that villain ensnared me, poor and helpless girl as I was, and robbed me of the only treasure which had remained to me in my misfortunes, my innocence and honour.

" There are, no doubt, many among my lady-companions present—for usually it is misery which leads us to our present mode of life—who know the wretchedness of a fallen girl, who know the tortures which a heart must suffer in such a position, and who know that the honour and nobility of mind of the seducer, are the only dim rays of hope which can support her failing powers and strength.

"But fool that I was, how had I been deceived! Bitter scorn was my only reward, and my miserable seducer threatened me with the police. At that time I knew no other laws but those of honour, and nothing remained for me to do, but to leave the scene of my shame, and again wander into the wide world. The heirs of my aunt, glad to see me removed, gave me a tolerable rich travelling purse. I hated them, and cursed the fate that had led me to them; but had to take the money, for hunger pressed me, and I preferred to derive my support from the mercy of those strange, hard-hearted people, rather than from my seducer. After having madly roved about for some days, I turned toward the city of Berlin, where all who are wretched usually seek an asylum; but here, also, new misery and fresh misfortunes awaited me.

"My fate next threw me into the hands of an old woman, who offered me the kindest reception beneath the mask of christian love and philanthropic sympathy, but who in reality only counted in advance the wages of sin, which she hoped to earn by my shame and degradation. A young, pale looking girl, who lived with me at the house of this fiendish woman, and who had fallen the victim of her machinations long since, though I did not dream of it, at last opened my eyes to her intentions. The relation of my sufferings had moved this unfortunate girl, and she showed me the ways and means to save myself, which means she had become too weak and unnerved to use herself.

"But I only freed myself at a heavy sacrifice, and with bitter sorrow. In my sudden revolt against this devilish woman, I was incautious enough to betray the source of my unlooked for information. The consequence of my ill-advised action, was the most savage and cruel mal-treatment which my unfortunate guardian-angel had to suffer at her hands, and which pained me even more than if it had been inflicted upon myself.

"Towards me, she feigned redoubled care and tenderness, endeavouring to beguile me anew by her hypocritical, insincere cant. But when she became convinced that all her endeavours availed naught against my resolution, and that there were no means to secure the rich harvest, which she had hoped to gain by my degradation, she began to persecute me with the most fiendish cruelty. The most trifling service she had ever done me, was charged with thrice its equivalent in gold, and she established a demand against me, which was far beyond my means and powers of paying. Finally, she availed herself of the assistance of the police, and in the most wretched, miserable condition imaginable, deprived of all and every thing I had possessed, covered only with a few rags, she turned me into the streets.

"On the point of despair, and almost frantic, I roved about the city for an entire day, till I found one of those unfortunate girls, whom circumstances or levity of character had robbed of those feelings of shame and modesty, innate to the female heart.

"She was the daughter of a tax-collector, who had died in the discharge of his duties, but had only left her his debts as an inheritance, on which, of course, she could not subsist. The first inconsiderate action of her life had thrown her into the public city-hospital, casting her there into the deepest pool of vice, and her mind and soul became forever poisoned by its influence. Yet she possessed a kind, sympathizing heart, for she readily offered to share with me the sorrowful wages of her sin. When she saw that I shuddered at the thought of accepting this money, she proffered me a Thaler, which she carried about her person, carefully wrapt up and hidden, and swore to me that this was honestly earned, as that coin had been given her by her mother on the day of her confirmation.

"She told me that she had intended never to part with this money, but that she now believed she could not apply it better, than by devoting it to the alleviation of my misfortune. She only begged me, most earnestly and sincerely, to give her a single penny of the change which I would get for the Thaler, so that she might cherish that, in memory of her mother.

"Such generosity and nobility of soul overcame the scruples of my conscience; enraged at my own folly, I returned her the Thaler, and accepted part of the wages of *shame* which she had offered me at first. The bitterness of my sorrow was increased by the knowledge that they were the wages of the shame of my friend, of the only being in the world who sympathized with, or felt for me.

"For several nights I lived in company with this girl, in a damp cellar, where the water ran from the walls, and where we rested together upon a half-rotten bunch of straw; suddenly my benefactress did not return. In her peregrinations she had fallen into the hands of the Police, and had been sent to the work-house. I bitterly wept over her fate, and wanted to imitate her course, only to be united with her; but our experienced hostess told me that I had not yet been under arrest, and consequently could not be sent to the work-house. Moreover, my situation at this time, would not permit such treatment. And even if I should be sent there, it would depend greatly upon accident, whether I would gain my object, and be placed near to my guardian angel. The only chance I could have of seeing her, would be to visit her occasionally in her prison, and carry some little aid and support to her.

"But whence should I take those means of support, which alone would open her prison-doors to my visits? Despair then inspired me with the thought of a terrible alternative; I began to beg. I, the envied, adored, and beautiful Francisca, now in my most wretched and miserable condition—a condition which betrayed my shame to every beholder at the first glance, begged bread from door to door, among strangers. To ask alms for myself would have been impossible, but I begged for my friend, for my benefactress, and at noon on every Sunday—this is the hour when Police-prisoners may be seen and spoken to by their friends—I gladly brought her the mite I had received from charity.

"My gratitude made a deep and salutary impression upon my benefactress, and she swore to me that she would amend her ways, and become virtuous and industrious when the time of her imprisonment should have expired. We anticipated much pleasure and delight when that time should have arrived, and devised plans of working together, and leading a life of industry. But in a very few days my strength failed me. A rich, proud lady, with abuse and scorn spurned me from her door, and exhausted I sank upon the pavement.

"An old rag-gatherer took pity on me, seeing me thus, and carried me to a miserable garret; here I became a mother. I now thought that the measure of my misery was full, and that I had sufficiently atoned for my guilt. Gladly and happily I folded my child—it was a daughter—in my arms; in its innocent smile, I again beheld the heavens of my bliss; I again had a possession, and a possession which I loved most dearly, and once more I was reconciled to the world.

"In my mind's eye, I already saw myself and my friend seated at our work-table in an humble but cleanly little room, plying our needles with indefatigable industry;—had I not two strong arms, and had not my sainted mother taught me to work? My dear child was playing at our feet, and I again thought of my dear little village, and once more pictured to myself a happy home, like that of my childhood!! But fool that I was! my greatest crime, and my utmost misery was yet to come. I wanted to secure a bright future to my child, I desired to make it very happy, and suffered myself to be misled by the old woman and a young Italian lady, and—*sold* my child. But no, friends, no, no, no, do not believe this of me, I did not sell my child, *I was cheated of it!!*——

Francisca pronounced these last words in a wild, frantic tone of voice, as she suddenly started from her seat, threw the wine bottles near her upon the floor, and madly stamped upon the fragments. Then, like a maniac she paced up and down the room, casting wild and fearful looks upon all around her. Only after a great deal of persuasion from the Atleth and others, they succeeded in quieting the frantic woman, and in conducting her back to her seat.

"Where am I?" she exclaimed, as she looked distractedly around and pushed the flowing hair from her forehead. "Oh yes, yes, I was relating to you my history—but I saw my stolen child before me; I saw its image, pale as death, on yonder wall, and it cursed its unnatural mother, who had sold it. But no, no, I have already sworn it to you! No, I have not sold thee, my child, I was cheated of thee.—Still—still—now it is gone, and again I am composed."

At these words she sank exhausted into her chair, and closed her eyes for a few minutes. When she recovered from this apparent swoon, she had regained her former composure and determination, and continued her narrative:

"The loss of my child had wrought a terrible change in me, for now I stood entirely alone in the world; father, mother, lover, honour, and wealth, and at last even my child had been taken from me, not by misfortunes, but by the malice and villany of men. My formerly tender and gentle mind became hardened from that hour, and was filled with hatred and dislike against all mankind.

"I now knew no other destiny in this world, than that of seeking revenge for all the injuries which humanity had inflicted upon me. All mankind from that hour became my enemies.—Now, perhaps, you can explain to yourselves whence the demon comes, which inhabits my soul. Curses upon this fair mask, which has thrown me so deeply into misery! I could peel it, like a savage with a scalping knife, from my bones, were it not that it must still serve me to revenge myself on mankind and to ensnare my victims. Wo to him, who raises his eyes to me! I do not leave him, till I have ruined and annihilated him, as I have been ruined.

"I will only then rest in my demoniac task, and sink exhausted into my grave, when my reconciled child rests upon my bosom, and my seducer like a crushed serpent, winds at my feet. These are the only two joys which yet wait me in this world, the only wishes which I would gladly buy with my heart's blood. But even in this, the fiend of misfortune pursues me. I have already traversed with you half the world. I have sought, inquired, and searched among all classes and in every corner, but nowhere have I found a trace of my seducer or my child. Still I have not yet lost the hope, and least of all now, since I have again visited this city; for a dark presentiment tells me, that fearful disclosures, and terrible denouements, await me here.

"The conclusion of my history is very simple. I scarcely know what has passed over me since the loss of my child. I had left the garret of my hostess shortly afterward, in mad flight, and remember finding myself next in the public Hospital. I cannot tell what they wanted with me there, but I believe they thought me crazy, for they put me into a cell with a number of mad women.

"By a daring leap over the wall, I escaped from this prison; I reached the high road, and ran for many miles, until I fell down exhausted. There, as you all know, your troupe, then on its way to Magdeburg, found me. I became one of you, partly because I had no other choice left, and partly because I thought I would with you have the best chance of roving through the world, and finding my lost child again.

"Accustomed from my youth to ride on horseback, and rather seeking than fearing death, I made rapid progress in your art, and thus created for myself an independent and brilliant existence.

such as I had never hoped to attain. By many of you I have been treated with kindness and love, and under other circumstances, I might feel perfectly happy in my present position; but my heart is not susceptible to such blissful emotions, as it is gnawed by a secret demon, who destroys me."

With these words, the equestrian concluded her narrative. The passionate excitement which had gained possession of her, in the middle of her story, had entirely left her, and she had re-assumed her former coldness and determination. Meanwhile, the two thieves had entered, and upon the invitation of the Atleth, who introduced them to the company as his most particular friends, had taken seats at the table. It needed but little urging to induce them to partake of the joys of the feast, and soon they were as merry and noisy as the rest.

Eel-eye, however, had evidently eyes for no other object than the charms of Francisca, for step by step he gradually approached her seat, and finally entered into a long conversation with her, endeavouring thereby to appear as charming and amiable as he possibly could. At last, when the effects of wine became more and more visible by his excited manner, and when he accidentally had learned the object of the feast, he raised his glass in tumultuous delight, and noisily emptied it to the health and welfare of the fair Francisca.

Francisca received the toast and the accompanying pressure of her hand, in the most friendly manner, but seriously repulsed Eel-eye when he was about to proceed to further demonstrations of tenderness, and wanted to imprint a burning kiss upon her rosy lips.

"How dare you attempt such things, Albert," she said to him; "don't you remember how your father, the schoolmaster, whipped you, when you attempted to kiss the parson's maid, at the well, and how your mother scolded, and how the girl threw her pitcher of water into your face. Have you forgotten this so soon?"

"Stop," cried Albert in return to the equestrian, as he drew from his pocket a valuable miniature-case, containing the portrait of a young and beautiful girl, which trinket he had obtained at the theft at the Geheimerath's, "now you have betrayed yourself. You are no other than the daughter of our parson, for only she was present at the affair you have mentioned. Yesterday, at the sight of this miniature, it recalled your features to my memory, even from the time when we sat side by side at school, and now I recognize you with certainty, though you have most wonderfully changed."

The sight of the miniature operated like an electric shock upon the equestrian. Madly she snatched it from the hand of Eel-eye, stared long and with burning glances upon it, then jumping frantically from her seat, she danced wildly about the room, exclaiming:

"At last, at last, I have found a trace! This is the miniature the villain had made in remembrance of our betrothal." Then with a voice which filled Eel-eye with consternation and terror, she addressed him:

"Where, man, where, or of whom, did you obtain that picture? Ask of me whatever you will, but tell me, where did you get that picture?"

Eel-eye hesitated long with his answer, and was naturally little inclined to tell its right origin to the equestrian, yet her endearments, caresses, and promises, would without doubt have finally obtained a full confession from him, had not the cunning Schmerles quickly interfered, as he had long observed what a dangerous turn the conversation was taking, and how little mastery of his senses remained to Eel-eye. A few silent glances were sufficient for the two thieves to understand each other, and to disappoint Francisca's hope of obtaining the desired information. She received nothing but evasive answers, but possessed wisdom enough to perceive that greater urgency would only make her the more suspicious, and remove her still farther from the attainment of her object.

She finally determined, by all means and at any price, to separate the cunning Schmerles from his companion, as she then expected to have an easier game with the latter. The next chapter will show to our readers in what manner she attained her object.

CHAPTER XIV.

THE END OF A ROGUE.

THE night after the celebration of her birthday, Francisca enjoyed but little rest. Wild and strange fantasies moved before her eyes, and frightened her from her slumbers. All the pictures of terror and misfortune, which her eventful life had shown her, again passed in bold outline before her mind's eye, and ere the first rays of the morning sun had cast their purple lines upon the point of the steeple of St. Mary's church, which was visible from her windows, she was roaming with hasty steps through the rooms of the hotel.

Exhausted in mind and body, she sank upon the seat on which Eel-eye, the companion of her youth had sat; he, who so unexpectedly had given her the hope of throwing the much sought light upon the darkness of her soul. Her eye rested upon the spot of the white table-cloth, where she had again seen on last evening, that ominous portrait, and her wild fancy conjured the strangest phantoms upon that spot.

Now it appeared glaring with diamonds, now like a burning pile of coals—again it was red with blood, or appeared like a single drop; now it grew to a coal-black wall, from the surface of which rose her image, which was pursued and tortured by fiery fiends. At last she sank exhausted into the chair, and fell into a sound sleep.

When she awoke, Mistress Barbara stood by her side, gently tapping her on the shoulder:

"Francisca, my dear Mam'sel, you will catch

cold, if you thus expose yourself to the fresh morning air in your thin night dress. You'd better go to bed, for you look tired and wearied, and take more care of your pocket-book, than to leave it carelessly about the room."

At these words the hostess took a large pocket-book from the floor. It was the same which Schmerles had yesterday taken from the Major's pocket, and which the thief had lost in the evening, whilst in a state of intoxication. Francisca looked with astonishment at this pocket-book, and with indifference glanced over the letters of the Jewess which it contained. Almost the first word which met her eye, was the name of her seducer, the Geheimerath ——. She now perceived clearly, that this pocket-book came from no other than the companion of her early youth, whom she had so lately met. She therefore took it, and hastily retired to her room, saying to the hostess :

"Mistress Barbara, I must absolutely see you after breakfast, and alone, for I have to speak with you about important matters."

The equestrian devoured the contents of the letters she found with avidity, and learned from the dates, that the drama which was described in them, had not yet been played to the end. From the addresses of these letters she learned the names and residences of all the persons concerned. She even knew where to find her seducer, and determined to make great use of the unexpected information which she had thus suddenly acquired.

She would join the work of the Jewess and the Prince, and besides the part she there intended to play, satisfy her fell revenge. The most proper instruments for her purpose seemed the Jew himself, and the Eel-eye, about whose real character she now no longer was in doubt. But her next care must be to put the cunning Schmerles out of the way, that he might not obstruct the blind passion of her early companion, and thus counteract the power she must gain over him.

"Mistress Barbara," she said, addressing the hostess, who shortly after entered the room, "I have refused you many a request you made of me, as these requests did not suit my character. It may be possible that you will find me more obliging in future, if you will also serve me in what I shall require."

"My dear, good child, ask of me what you will. I will do anything and everything for you, my angel, if you will only lessen your pride a little, and not be so very cruel towards Mistress Barbara."

"Well, well, we will see what bargain we can make. But above all things, answer me now in plain, honest truth, all questions I shall address to you. Who were those two gentlemen who last evening came in with Giacomo? Their fine dress seemed not altogether to harmonize with their behaviour."

"My child, I will make no secret of it to you, but confess, that they were people against whom doors should always be secured, except when they are here. Here, my daughter, you are perfectly safe from them. You know, as hostess, I must have intercourse with all sorts of people."

"Then, Mistress Barbara, you will not find it difficult to comply with my wishes. One of these two men, the eldest of them, who wears a black beard and looks like a Jew, is in my way. I am greatly desirous that this man should be removed, you understand. Cause him to leave Berlin, deliver him into the hands of the Police, or arrange the matter in whatever way you think best. I observed yesterday that he was well acquainted with you, that you had a great deal of secret conversation with him, and in passing you, I heard him speak of jewels and plate. I think you will understand what I mean to say, and give me credit for some penetration. Under these circumstances, you cannot find it difficult, to ascertain all the connexions and circumstances of this man, and to use that knowledge for the attainment of our purpose."

"My child, my child, you say and insinuate very strange things about me, but I see you have peeped too deep into my cards, and I must even let you have your own will. But you really demand a great deal, for this man has brought many a Thaler to my pocket. Yet I think that you will oblige me in return. Listen then : the man with the black beard has as smooth a face as you or I ; that beard is a false one, and serves to hide its owner from the eyes of the police, who are in search of him. He must have done a very good bit of business lately, for he has shown me a mass of valuable things, which he wished me to buy of him, or sell for him. But I never buy those things myself, as it is apt to bring one into trouble, although the man with the beard has a pedlar's license, and nobody could say anything against my dealing with him, as I may buy of a pedlar whatever I like, or whatever he may have for sale. But I have promised to find him a purchaser for his things, who is to arrive here at noon this day. I will inform the Criminal Commissary of this, that same Commissary who lives opposite, and seems to have his eye so much upon me. In this manner I can kill two birds with one stone. I do you the service you so much desire, and make friends with the police, who will be leniently inclined towards me another time. The man then will be sure to be out of your way ; he will either be imprisoned, or else will not show himself for some time to come. But then, my dear child, you must have a care that he has no suspicion of me ; it must appear that I myself have been out-manœuvred, otherwise I shall lose my good name, and get into all sorts of misfortune."

"This will be captial fun," interrupted the equestrian, "and I will tell you how it must be done. The Criminal Commissary himself must be disguised as a Jew, and purchase these things of the pedlar, and I will give him the dress and all he needs for the purpose, from our wardrobe. I love such scenes, and I will watch the progress through the key-hole. How I shall be delighted, when suddenly the Commissary discloses his real character."

"But then I will also count upon you, my child. You know how much money I have lost by your foolish obstinacy, as you never would walk a step into my public room. Only yesterday there was again a rich gentleman with me, who offered a great deal of money, if I would only obtain him a single conversation with you; a large fine gentleman; but I had to send him back, as I knew your prudery. Now you will no longer be so obstinate, and the gentleman can come here to-morrow, and in this room take a cup of coffee with you?"

"Yes, I will now agree! let him come, and he shall find a merry companion in me, but only on condition, that we attain our object. Perhaps the man may even consent to take a part in the drama, which I intend shortly to perform."

A few hours after this conversation, the Criminal-Commissary, in company with the Referendarius von Birkheim and one gensd'arme, appeared in the room of Mistress Barbara, whither Francisca had followed them, full of curiosity.

After a short conversation the parties understood each other, and had agreed upon their *modus operandi*. The Criminal-Commissary would disguise himself as a Schärfenspieler, and close a mock bargain for the stolen goods with the cunning Schmerles, so as to make his conviction more secure. Only in a case of extreme necessity, the Commissary would disclose his office, but rather if possible remain incognito, be arrested with the cunning Schmerles, and for a few hours be imprisoned in the same cell with him, in order to elicit farther information from him regarding his connexions and crimes. Mistress Barbara determined to reap the utmost profit out of the sacrifice which she brought for Francisca, concluded the conversation with the words:

"So, Herr Commissarius, at all events I deliver the notorious Schmerles, whom you have so long sought for in vain, directly into your hands, and that *with all the sore yet warm*, (with all the freshly stolen goods,) but in return I count upon your favour.

"I trust that you will take good care that *Ottilie* is not sent to the work-house. The poor girl's constitution will suffer too much, if she has to do the work you give them there, for three long months, and then perhaps her Lieutenant will leave her altogether. How should I, poor woman that I am, then be able to get the money she owes me. I have a demand of thirty-two Thalers, for the new silk dress alone which she wore at the last ball in the Frederic-Hall, and there had it all ruined with oil-spots."

"Thirty-two Thalers for a silk dress! and of the kind you have, Mistress Barbara," replied the Commissary, laughing; "why, that is an enormous price. Such a dress costs you at the utmost eight or ten Thalers, for you never buy new goods. All that you need of that kind, you usually get from the maids of rich ladies, and you pay them just what you like."

"Yes, yes, that is the way! You may easily talk, Herr Commissary; but surely one wants to make something for the annoyance and trouble one has with these women, and consider what losses we have to cover by our profits. Only yesterday, the Polish Countess ran off with a satin cloak and fine velvet hat of mine, and I cannot hope to see those things again, until she is once more caught. Ottilie is a very good, honest girl, who has some respectability—she is the daughter of a Geheim-Secretary—but these good girls always must help to cover my losses by bad ones. So I depend upon you for the safety of this girl, and I will soon arrange my business with her."

"We will see what can be done for you; considering the very important service you are about to do for the Department, you may hope that the authorities will not be averse, if it is at all possible, to comply with your wishes. Now, you understand, in half an hour I shall be back, disguised as a real Schärfenspieler."

At these words, the Commissary withdrew, and Mistress Barbara occupied herself by emptying two large closets, for the purpose of there secreting the Referendarius and the gensd'arme, who should listen to the conversation of the Commissary and cunning Schmerles, and interrupt it at the right time. When all these preparations were completed, the Commissary himself returned.

Even Mistress Barbara could scarcely recognize him on his return. He wore a large caftan, and an immense black beard of most artistical construction, which gave him the perfect appearance of a Polish trading Jew. A black velvet cap which he had on, completed his disguise. Mistress Barbara once more endeavoured to initiate the pseudo-Jew into the manners and usages of Jewish dealers, so that he might not betray himself by any ignorance in these matters, and then retired to her kitchen, there to await the arrival of cunning Schmerles. He did not arrive, however, until after sundown.

"You come very late, Schmerles," began Mistress Barbara, "a full hour later than we had agreed upon; the man whom I appointed to meet you here, already began to be impatient and wanted to leave."

"You know, Mistress Barbara," replied the rogue, "that a Gannew rarely comes at the appointed hour, so that no one may follow him and discover his ways. Those who would do business with a Gannew, and make money by him, may afford to wait a few hours."

At these words both walked up stairs into the *boudoir* of Mistress Barbara. The cunning Schmerles had noticed the earnest reproof which Mistress Barbara had made him at his late appearance, and her peculiarly friendly manner had struck him with suspicion; he felt annoyed, afraid, and in very ill-humour all day, just as if he had a dark presentiment of what awaited him. Had he not been greatly in want of money, he would certainly have gone away again, but his need compelled his blind confidence in Mistress

Barbara. His sharp eye, however, searched every corner, and not the smallest trifle escaped his inquisitive glance. Upon the threshold of the room he first observed the marks of several broad, large footsteps, a circumstance which attracted his utmost attention, as he knew that Mistress Barbara rarely received any visitors in that room.

"You seem to have had a great many visitors to-day already, and to have entirely forgotten your usual excessive cleanliness," he said to Mistress Barbara, pointing to the foot marks, "and still even now to have disagreeable company," he continued with a grin, as he took up the czakko of the gend'arme who had carelessly left it behind in the room, as he withdrew to the closet.

Mistress Barbara quickly composed herself, as without changing her smiling friendly features, she replied with the utmost coolness and composure :

"You people must trouble yourself about every trifle." Then as she lightly approached close to him, she whispered in his ear : "For Heaven's sake, have the kindness and love for me, and do not appear as if you had ever in your life seen this czakko. Carry it as quickly as possible down to the yard, and throw it where no one can find it again, but be careful nobody sees you. Just think, those devilish boys, the *Stammerige* and the *Schielen* came here a little while ago, greatly excited and out of breath. Even while they were at work breaking into a house, some gens-d'armes attacked them, and they had a severe struggle with them, but at last made their escape, and that with the czakko of the long, thin gens-darme, who wears the blonde moustache, and whom you must know.

"Those fellows have become so daring and impudent, as to bring the stolen goods here, and the czakko along. Yonder lays the whole lump of it," she continued, as she pointed to the clothing which she had taken from the closets. "I shall die, if any body find these things here : you are the only man whom I can trust, so go quickly down stairs, and throw away that infernal czakko. When you have arranged your business with the gentleman yonder,"—pointing to the Commissary, who had put a pair of greasy spectacles upon his nose, and without seeming to listen to the cunning Schmerles or Mistress Barbara, was looking through his pocket-book and counting money—"You can assist me in carrying this *sore* out of the way."

The cunning Schmerles was so delighted at the adventure and heroic deeds which Mistress Barbara told of his friends the Stammerige and Schielen, and felt so flattered at the confidence with which seemingly he was honoured by her, that he entertained not the slightest doubt of the correctness of her statements, but hastily hurried down to the yard, and threw the czakko of the gensd'arme into a sink, with as much conscientiousness as if the fate of all the thieves of Germany had depended upon the issue.

The cunning manœuvre of Mistress Barbara so astonished the Criminal Commissary, that he could not contain himself, but burst into a loud peal of laughter.

"You certainly are the most shrewd woman I ever knew, Mistress Barbara, to carry such schemes in your head," he whispered to her, when he saw Schmerles hastily disappear through the door, "and I am no longer astonished that the police never yet could succeed in fastening any conviction upon you ; but what will the gensd'arme say, when he must go home bare-headed, or wear the old hat of your dead and gone husband to his green jacket ? Besides, there are some important papers in that czakko which I am loath to lose. But I think it may yet be recovered, so have a care that you find it again and return it to us."

"Don't trouble yourself, Herr Commissary," replied Mistress Barbara in the proud consciousness of her great deed. "The value of the things you will find upon cunning Schmerles is sufficient to buy a few hundred of such czakkos."

This conversation could not be continued any farther, as the object of it had already returned from the yard.

"Yonder is the man," whispered Mistress Barbara to him as he entered, pointing to the Commissary, "who will buy your things ; he seems to be engaged for the moment upon important business-matters, in which he cannot be interrupted ; be a little careful of him, for he is very fond of out-bargaining his costumers."

The Commissary meanwhile continued absorbed in writing and calculating over a large number of papers spread before him, which he had just a day before seized of a Polish Jew ; he also opened the passport belonging to the same Jew, as if by accident upon the table, so that its contents could easily be seen at a distance ; he continued again and again to count his money, as if he was trying to discover a mistake in his account. All these manœuvres were only intended to lull the other into greater security, and to excite his avarice. At last his business seemed to be concluded, he put his pocket book away, apparently murmuring a Hebrew prayer between his teeth, and turning ill-humoredly to Mistress Barbara, he said :

"Mistress Barbara, your friend stays a long time. I shall have to go away without making the trade, and I shall not pay you my bill, because you have uselessly retained me here, and made me neglect my business."

"Don't get angry so quick, Herr Sampson, the man who wishes to speak to you has been waiting for some time, but you stick to your papers and calculations till you are blind, and have eyes for nothing but your money and your accounts, and never even look round." At these words Mistress Barbara introduced the thief to the Criminal Commissary.

"You are welcome," began the latter, addressing Schmerles, as he pressed his hand in the most friendly manner, "sit down close by me, that we may soon conclude our business. I have

[Unmutilated and Only Genuine Edition.]

THIERS' LIFE OF NAPOLEON,

WITH SUPERB STEEL ENGRAVINGS,

FOR SEVENTY-FIVE CENTS,

[If paid in Advance.]

W. H. COLYER having been at great expense to procure a copy of this unrivalled work, now publishes

PART I.

OF THE

HISTORY OF THE CONSULATE AND THE EMPIRE

OF

FRANCE UNDER NAPOLEON,

By M. A. THIERS,

LATE PRIME MINISTER OF FRANCE.

WM. H. COLYER's edition of this splendid work, The Life of Napoleon, is decidedly the best in this country. It is printed on fine paper and new type, according to the design of the author, M. A. Thiers, and on comparison with other editions will be found far superior.

In Press.

THIERS' FRENCH REVOLUTION,

TO BE COMPLETED IN SIX PARTS, AT 12 1-2 CENTS EACH.

TO BE COMPLETED IN TEN NUMBERS.

THE MYSTERIES OF BERLIN,

FROM

THE PAPERS OF A BERLIN CRIMINAL OFFICER.

TRANSLATED FROM THE GERMAN.

By C. B. BURKHARDT.

With Illustrations on Steel, by P. Habelmann.

This work in Europe has been universally pronounced far superior to M. Sue's celebrated "Mysteries of Paris," and we confidently predict, that the popularity of this translation will be without a parallel in the history of light reading.

Part III. Price 12½ cents.

THE MYSTERIES of BERLIN.

TO BE COMPLETED

IN

TEN PARTS.

NEW YORK: WILLIAM H. COLYER, PUBLISHER.

often heard of you from my friend Moses, to whom you lately sold that gold snuff-box; you are said to be a good customer, and a man who understands his business."

"That may be true," replied the cunning Schmerles with a knowing grin. "I do not believe that this room would hold all I have stolen in my time, and I have taken more gold and silver than would balance my own weight. And yet, they have only had me twice on the Barsel, (twice in prison.) The first time I managed to clear myself, and the second time they gave me but two years. I am now so well initiated in all the secrets of the craft, and am so cunning, that I think they will never in this life catch me again."

"My dear son, do not boast of thy fortune," interrupted the Commissary, who could scarcely retain a secret laugh. "Jehovah often reverses our fate, and there are cunning people among these Christians. The most trifling circumstances have sometimes overthrown the greatest thieves. But don't let us spend our time in such useless talk, rather tell me at once what trade we can make with each other. Dry goods and clothing I do not buy; this I wish you to remember beforehand. I only deal in gold and silver which can be melted, and then all trace is gone forever, and no living man can recognize it again."

"You are just the man I want," replied cunning Schmerles, "for I have some good metal with me, a few spoons, some rings, and broken plate." At these words he produced an oblong package from his pocket, and presented it to the Criminal Commissary.

The officer examined the articles with the most careful scrutiny, produced a minute pair of scales from his pocket, and weighed them with great seeming exactness and attention. At the first glance, he recognized among them articles which had been obtained at the most daring burglary in the house of the Geheimerath, the report of which had since spread all over town. Only with great difficulty, he was enabled to hide his pleasure at this valuable recovery, and retain his former coolness and composure.

"All valuable goods," he said smirkingly to Schmerles; "but at the moment I cannot tell you their exact value, as I have to ascertain that in another way. But in the meanwhile, take this on account—with these words he handed him a ten Thaler bill—to-morrow at this hour you shall receive the remaining money in the same place I think we can easily make a bargain together, and you can have no doubt of my honesty, as Mistress Barbara will become security for me."

"That is all right," replied the thief; "take the things with you, in God's name; it will be your own loss if you attempt to cheat me, for you will lose many a nice bit of business in future by it. I have another affair before me this very week, where a pretty round sum may be made, and it will all be in gold and real jewels."

"Well, my dear fellow," began the Commis-

sary, who was delighted at this information, "then you must be sure not to forget me, and here, take these two Thalers in advance, upon that account. You see, I am only a poor man, and am very glad to make a little money; I have five children to take care of, and you do a good deed, if you can let me have the chance of earning something."

"If you treat me right well this time, and if you don't blab about it, I have no objection to do that business with you also. But tell me as near as you can, how much you give an ounce for good gold, and for fine silver?"

"Oh, I will give you whatever is right, and what is paid by all good Schärfenspielers; for an ounce of silver, ten gute Groschen, and for the gold, three Thalers."

"That is devilish little," replied Schmerles. The ounce of silver is worth twenty Groschen everywhere, and gold is eight Thaler, so you must just make fifty per cent. and more. But it is always so, and will be so; the thief remains a poor devil, whilst the Schärfenspieler grows a rich man. And when any misfortune happens, the Schärfenspieler can always manage to work himself out of the scrape, or at the utmost to get off with a few months once in a while, whilst the poor Gannew goes to the prison for the best part of his life."

"But, my dear boy," replied the Commissary, astonished at the truth contained in the speech of cunning Schmerles, "you must not take such foolish fancies into your head. Has not the Schärfenspieler also to suffer any amount of misery and anxiety, for the good, hard earned money, which he gives you? What is the use of riches, when we cannot enjoy them, but must travel through the world, from village to village, as a Schacher-jude, (peddling Jew.) But depend upon it, I shall deal fairly and honestly with you, and if you bring me good articles, you will not have occasion to be sorry for it. You very probably have a Jeweller's-shop upon the tapis. Not that of my friend in the Brüderstrasse, I hope?"

"Something like it at least. We intend to select the best pieces out of a collection of old rarities, belonging to a Count or Duke, under the Linden. The theft has been for some time preparing. When I was still an inmate of the prison, I heard this business spoken of there, but as yet no one has dared to accomplish it, as there is a large black dog in the yard; otherwise the affair can be easily done. I have now arranged everything, and the Masematten will shortly take place.

"For some time past, I have daily been in the yard, taking a slut with me. In this manner I have so quieted the house dog, that he is friendly and runs after me whenever I show myself, and consequently makes no noise. If I had sufficient keys, the thing could be done this very evening."

"If it is nothing else," replied the Commissary, producing from his pocket a large bunch of keys which he had only lately taken from a thief, "I can easily assist you. Take these keys, they are well worth four or five Thalers, but I will give them to you in the bargain, for the purchase I expect to make of you."

As shrewdly as the Commissary had hitherto behaved in his intercourse with the thief, all his further plans were nearly destroyed by his producing those keys, for the Jew suddenly started up, exclaiming:

"By heavens! these are my own keys, which I loaned the *bunte Robert*, and with which he was arrested the day before yesterday. *How came you by these keys?*"

"That is very possible," replied the Commissary, who quickly collected himself, although he involuntarily felt for his poignard, which he had hidden beneath his coat, "for only yesterday I bought them *sub rosa* from the thick, dark turnkey. You know that fellow always does a little private business of the kind, and frequently lets things disappear."

"Oh, yes; I know the fellow well, he has delivered many a little note for me, and frequently received a few pieces of gold; but it is an unheard-of piece of impudence, to steal the keys from among the documents."

"Yes, yes, you see what a man will do for the sake of money. Now this poor fellow has a large family of children, and so small a salary, that he can scarcely get enough to eat, and he must have recourse to such things. I have bought many a bunch of keys of him; it is always a long time before they are missed, and no one then knows what has become of them. But to return to our business, when do you think that this good Masematten will be done? I must be at the Frankfort fair in a few days, and therefore would rather see the matter settled to-day than to-morrow. If you should be in want of a *Caver*, (assistant at the theft,) I can get you one who is a good lock-smith."

"You need not trouble yourself about it," replied Schmerles smilingly, "I have a Caver, as good a one as I could wish. You must probably have heard of him; we usually call him Eel-eye among ourselves, and I contend that there is not a better thief in the country. There will not be much to lock or unlock in this case, for we shall climb into the windows from the grape trellises in the yard. You shall hear the remainder to-morrow, when we arrange our account. But first one more word with you: is it really not convenient for you to buy silk goods? I yesterday made a good haul, and have left three pieces of fine satin, with my former Schärfenspieler, the *thick Joel*, but he will not keep them as he has no opportunity for selling them. Come with me and take the goods, and you may have them cheap, at two Thalers a piece; but keep quiet towards the thick Joel about our other business, for I must not venture to offend the man."

Although the Commissary had long before this learned enough of cunning Schmerles to answer his purpose, yet he could not resist the temptation to out-manœuvre and catch also the thick Joel, and therefore prepared to accompany cunning Schmerles, as he confided sufficiently in his own personal strength, presence of mind, and determination to overmaster his victim at any place and at all times.

It was already quite dark, when these two men pursued their way through several streets of the regal city, till at last they stopped in front of a tall, gloomy looking house in the *Reezengasse*. The Crimminal Commissary had several times looked around to ascertain whether the gens-d'arme and the Referendarius were following him, but an unfortunate misunderstanding had detained them, and he alone in company of Schmerles, and in utter darkness, ascended three flights of crooked stairs, which were not even provided with railing, and caused him continually to make missteps. Even when nearly arrived at the top, he fell back several steps at the imminent risk of breaking his neck.

At last they stopped before a half rotten door, which hung loosely upon its hinges, and through many cracks showed small rays of a dim light within. Schmerles for some time sought for the latch, then struck the door three times with his foot, and rattled in a peculiar manner at the lock. This was the signal by which the thick Joel recognized his particular friends.

"Coming, coming, presently!" was heard from within, and after a great noise, as if several boxes were removed in great haste, the grinning face of the old Jew, whose hair was bleached by age and whose back was bent by the same cause, appeared at the door.

"It is me, old man," whispered Schmerles distinctly, "and I bring a chesse man with me, who can put you in the way of some good business."

"Then you are both welcome," growled the Schärfenspieler as he opened the door for his guests, "an old man always needs a little luck."

The domicile of the Jew consisted of a small garret. Old and decayed furniture adorned the walls, and household utensils of various kinds lay in wild disorder about the floor. Upon a massively worked table, which seemed to have seen more than half a century, and still bore traces of having once been gilded, lay a variety of valuables; old watch cases, broken seals, doubled-up spoons, valuable stones which had been taken from trinkets, and divers other similar objects, such as Schärfenspielers are in the habit of buying. Above all these things hung the most necessary object for this trade, a small pair of brass scales, which were fastened to a projecting iron rod.

A small adjoining room, which could be examined through the open door, only showed dirty lime-coloured and bare walls. It contained nothing but a motley pile of various garments, which were lying in a disordered heap in the corner.

The entire dwelling was most sparingly lighted by a small, greasy lamp, which burned so dimly, that it would scarcely have been possible to discern a single object, had it not been for an immense coal fire which burned in the wreck of a stove, and which the thick Joel endeavoured to increase by means of a small pair of bellows, for the purpose of melting the contents of two crucibles which he had placed over it.

"I must beg the gentlemen to excuse me for a moment, as I have to do a little work that admits of no delay," he said, addressing his visitors, while he motioned them to take seats upon two small stools.

The cunning Schmerles and the Commissary *en masque* seated themselves upon these uncomfortable resting places, and the former began rubbing his chilled hands; while the latter, from apparent mercantile curiosity, examined the articles, to ascertain whether he could not recognize some stolen property.

Absorbed in thought, the Jew stared for some minutes into the fire, the bright reflection of which illuminated his haggard features in a peculiar "Rembrandt" style; then he drew the crucibles towards him.

"The mass is already glowing, and the gold will be melted in a few minutes," he said, as at the same time, beside some other articles, he drew a finely worked golden cross from the sleeve of his caftan, and prepared to throw it into the crucible.

In this cross, the Criminal Commissary immediately recognized a valuable trinket, which had been stolen at a very great and extensive mail-robbery. Spite of the most extraordinary exertions of the police, the perpetrators of that robbery, or any traces of their goods, had not yet been found.

This discovery was of too great value to the officer, to let it pass, without availing himself of it. Moreover, as a young Commissary, and in his present function, it was of the greatest importance to him, to display his activity in the service.

Already he saw, in his mind's eye, letters of promotion, perhaps even an order. In an instant, cloak, beard, and spectacles had disappeared, and the old crooked Jew-pedlar was transformed into the fine and muscular person of a handsome and strong young man. A powerful kick against the crucible sent its contents into the protruding face of the Schärfenspieler, who was leaning over it. The old Jew fell howling with pain to the floor, while the police officer hastily gathered the valuables that were strewn about.

This sudden metamorphosis operated like an electric shock upon cunning Schmerles, who was so stupified by surprise, that he remained immovable upon his seat; in a few moments, however, he recovered his wonted presence of mind, and rushed in desperate haste towards the door, which rattled upon its hinges, from the fury of his attempts to burst it open. But this very haste became his ruin. Instead of pulling the door towards him, as it opened into the room, he pushed with all his strength against the lock. When he discovered his unfortunate mistake, he already felt the grasp of the muscular hand of the Commissary upon his shoulder.

"You'd better surrender, Schmerles," cried the latter, in a determined voice. "I am an officer of police, and all resistance will only make your position worse."

Cunning Schmerles on seeing himself thus outmanœuvred, roared in the excess of his rage, and with the strength of despair endeavoured to break away. But all his strength and agility were insufficient against the iron grasp which held him.

The fire in the stove had meanwhile become extinguished, a cold and sudden draught of wind had torn open one of the windows, and the shrill voice of the storm whistled through the narrow apartment, mingling with the wailings of the Jew, who still lay upon the floor, writhing in the most terrible agony.

Suddenly the thin and half-decayed door burst open, both wings of it were knocked aside, and the two men, in a terrible struggle, rolled outside into the dark and dirty entry. An active turn, had in their fall freed the right arm of the thief, which gave him a much more advantageous position.

Foaming with rage and despair, he cried to the Commissary: "Let me go, sir, or I shall throw you down stairs." These words had scarcely passed his lips, when both, with a terrible racket, tumbled down stairs, thus changing the scene of battle to the second story.

But here, also, the room was too small to retain them long, and they had scarcely gained their legs, when they again fell down the stairs, and still struggling, arrived on the first floor.

Until now, not unlike a pair of bull-dogs, the combatants had convulsively clung to each other, and had fairly divided the dangers of their unexpected descent. But upon this new field of battle, the Commissary struck his head so severely against the floor, that the force of the blow almost deprived him of his senses, and for the moment disabled him in his struggle.

The cunning Schmerles availed himself of the chance which this accident gave him with the most terrible coolness. He pressed his opponent to the ground, set his knee upon his breast, and with all his strength grasped his throat, thus slowly to strangle him. He would undoubtedly have gained his object, as the arms of the Commissary were already sinking helplessly by his side, had not the previous noise aroused all the inmates of the house. From every side, provided with lights, they now arrived at the scene of action.

This naturally again gave another aspect to things. Schmerles, however, by his deep cunning and presence of mind never at a loss, turned this scene to his own advantage, in a manner which did honour to his ingenuity and ready invention.

Without being in the least discomposed, he cried, even louder than the united voices of the approaching parties, and apparently in terrible agony:

"For Heaven's sake, take pity upon my poor unfortunate brother! He was intoxicated on coming home, has fallen down stairs, and is dying in my hands. Look, look, how his head is bleeding! help him but for one moment; I will run for a surgeon." With these words he had hurried to the stairs, leaped down in a single bound, opened the house-door, and rushed into the street.

At this moment the Commissary was in the greatest danger of losing the fruits of all his extraordinary endeavours. Perhaps he would even have lost much more, for an entrapped fox is not easily caught a second time.

Moreover, the momentary danger had not prevented cunning Schmerles from availing himself of the chance to practice his profession, and even in his haste he had snatched the watch and purse of the Commissary, and pocketed them, so as to pay himself for the danger and trouble of this struggle.

But in much less time than the thief had expected, the Commissary rose again from his momentary swoon. To the great astonishment of all the group around him, he also took one daring leap down the stairs, and with a stentorian cry of "stop thief!" quickly rushed into the street.

Whoever has resided for some time in Berlin, and has observed life in the streets, must certainly know the wonderful electric effects produced by the above cry. In an instant the entire street-population is in motion. Those who reside on the ground floors, rush through their rattling front doors; in the upper stories more heads than windows suddenly become visible, and everything else is for the moment entirely forgotten.

The mass in the streets soon begins to grow like an avalanche; no one knows whence comes the mass of pursuers, but there they are; they spring like mushrooms from the ground, and in a wild, mad race, run after their victim, echoing with hundreds of voices, the general cry of "stop thief!"

The latter rushes before them, like a chased wild boar, foaming, breathless, groaning, and in despair, kicking and striking blindly to the right and left;—the few who meet him, turn aside as if from a mad dog.

Thus they pursue their frantic course through a few streets. "Stop thief! stop thief!" The cry increases to hoarse roaring; children are overturned, horses break loose, until at last the pursued wretch succeeds in slipping into a house, and by the back-door to escape thence into another and safe street, or faint and exhausted, he sinks to the ground, a worn-out victim of this terrible, popular justice. It is lucky for him, if the guarding arm of Police is near him at that moment to protect him, otherwise the heartless multitude will soon raise him from the ground, and amidst abuse, maltreatment, and cruelty of every kind, drag him to the nearest District Commissary.

A scene, something like the above, was the one which now presented itself in the narrow Reezengasse, after the Criminal Commissary had given the well known and exciting cry of alarm. The deep darkness of the night, only broken by the dim light of a few solitary oil lamps, if possible, increased the general confusion.

Cunning Schmerles, who was about a hundred steps in advance of his pursuer, even then did not lose the cool presence of mind by which he had so much distinguished himself. He immediately availed himself of a means of safety usually successful under such circumstances, and which was made doubly available by the uncertain light of the street.

As soon as he heard the cry of the Commissary, he joined in it as loud as he could, transformign himself thus into the pursuer instead of the pursued. In this way he managed to misguide the multitude, and soon reached in successful safety a little cross street, into which he quickly rushed.

He already began to breathe more freely, but his lucky star had deserted him for the time, or rather even as the Criminal Commissary had warned him, he had too freely boasted of his fortune, which now left him, and he therefore could not escape his final destiny.

In that cross street, just at this moment, was the Referendarius von Birkheim and the two police gensd'armes, who, seeking the Commissary, had just directed their way towards the Reezengasse, and were attracted by the cry and general alarm. As they had met no one before, the cry of cunning Schmerles, as he usurped the appearance of a pursuer, naturally seemed suspicious to them.

They well knew the practice of thieves in assuming such a character in like cases, and therefore quickly stepped before him, so that he could not pass.

A single glance at his deranged toilette and lacerated face, convinced them that they were not mistaken in arresting him. Placed thus between two fires, disheartened by his endless misfortune, exhausted by his long, almost incredible exertions, nothing remained for the bold rogue but to surrender at discretion.

When the Criminal Commissary arrived at the spot, every thing was quickly explained, and the hour for the rogue had come at last. The little expedition immediately moved towards the safe prisons of the *Molken-market*, glad to have at last attained their object, after so much trouble and danger.

Raging and roaring, the rabble ran by their sides, but Schmerles walked quieter and more subdued than usual, for he was well enough acquainted with law, to know that according to the common course of things, his feet were for the last time pressing the side-walks of Berlin.

CHAPTER XIV.

THE POLICE SEARCH.

THE quickly succeeding incidents of this narrative have hitherto withdrawn from our observation a person, whose first appearance was in more than one respect calculated to enlist the sympathy of our readers.

We refer to the unfortunate Marianne, whose cause the Jewess had so warmly advocated in her letters to the Major von Heinfordt, who had already determined upon her delivery, and had united for that purpose with his friend Prince Prominki.

We will return to that night, when the Jewess, by her extraordinary presence of mind, disguised in the dress of the Vigilant, had succeeded in deceiving the officers of police, and by the assurance, that the arrests they intended could not be made till a later hour, had caused them to leave the cellar of hunchbacked Jobs. The Jewess was satisfied with informing the band of the result of her endeavours, and particularly her husband, for reasons which we already know.

She advised immediate flight; but then she immediately hurried, even in the blood-stained garments she had on, to Major von Heinfort, to bring him a full account of all the occurrences of that night. Our readers will remember that they learned all about these communications at the masquerade in the Colliseum.

Long Schmuel, who was not at all anxious to renew his acquaintance with the Police, did not suffer his wife twice to repeat her warnings. He quickly gathered his goods and chattels, took his three children, and hastily left the cellar of the hunchback. When, however, the rest of the company prepared, in wild haste and disorder to follow his example, and thereby showed that they intended to leave the dead body of the Vigilant to its fate, Jobs arose and proclaimed his solemn protest.

" You do not stir hence," he cried, planting his small, hunchbacked form before the entrance of the cellar, his grey blear eyes playing in a mysterious green colour, " until you find means to remove this carcass. You, Maulspitzer, have laid him cold, and now you must see what can be done with him.

The Sand-carter looked disconcertedly upon the corpse, and again felt the peculiar and fatal convulsions in the muscles of his neck. Imploringly he looked towards his friends, but none seemed disposed to give him assistance against Jobs, or help him to remove the corpse. The fear of their hunchbacked host still increased in consequence.

" Don't be all of you possessed of the foul fiend," cried Jobs, wringing his hands in agony, " and get this infernal corpse out of the place. The Lampen (officers of police) may be here every moment. I am an honest man, what shall I say, or how get out of the scrape ?"

The thieves still were irresolute, ready to help, but not willing to throw themselves into danger.

Jobs' despair rose to the utmost height. He cast himself to the ground, kicked with both his feet, and tore the few remaining hairs from his bald skull. Suddenly urged by a fresh resolution, he jumped up, and foaming with rage, he bawled:

" Well, well, just wait, ye villains, I will at least be revenged on you. I shall run to the Lampen myself, and tell them all about you, and they will be sure to secure me from punishment. But you, infernal scoundrels, I will bring ye all to the wheel and the gallows, as sure as my name is Jobs, and as sure as I stand here." At these words he turned to make his way out, and seemed fully determined to make good his words, and betray them all.

When they saw the turn things were taking, the rogues cried aloud in horror and rage. The stiff Gottlieb, however, like a tiger flew at the Hunchback, caught him by the back of the neck with his nervous fist, and two or three times sent the little misgrown figure in whirling circles around, till it appeared like an unshapen mass of flesh.

" What is this, you would do, you villain ?" he cried, kicking the Hunchback like a foot-ball, into a corner; " have we enriched thee for this, and given thee the greatest Hellig, (share,) which you always get from every thief."

" That's right, that's right !" they cried in chorus, as they all had at some time or other suffered by the malicious character of Jobs, and were now glad to have an opportunity of repaying him some of the injuries he had done them.

The stiff Gottlieb again took hold of his victim, and now encouraged by the general approbation, would perhaps have maltreated him much longer, had not, suddenly, the tall, graceful figure of Marianne entered upon the scene of action. Her face was covered with an ashy-pale hue, she looked like marble, and the blood which still showed traces of the brutal injuries she had lately received, increased her phantom-like appearance.

An expression of the most intense sorrow played around her beautifully shaped mouth, and her large, blue eyes, cast dim and tearful glances through the room. At the first noise in the den she had been aroused from her swoon, and had hurried to the rescue of her father, on hearing his cries for help. The quiet, imposing appearance of true innocence, did not miss its effect even upon the wild natures of these hardened villains. Powerless and abashed, they stood opposite the weak girl, though they had often stood boldly and impudently before their judge and the turnkeys of the prisons.

Marianne's first glance fell upon the corpse of the Vigilant, and at that terrible sight she almost fell into a new swoon. She crossed both arms over her breast, casting her eyes despairingly toward the ceiling of the room, as if she was there inquiring for the dark reason and origin of all she saw.

The groans of her father soon brought her to herself again. Full of pity and kindness, she stepped toward him, endeavoured gently to lift him up, and in sympathizing, filial love, to assist him and alleviate his misery. After a few moments of anxious care, he had so far recovered as to be able to rise, and supported by the arms of his daughter, to leave the robber's den, and await his recovery in his own dwelling-room.

In dignified silence as she had come, the maiden disappeared in the dark passage.

"Devil take me," grumbled the stiff Gottlieb, "that young girl possesses a pair of eyes, which burn more intensely than the cat's of the thick turnkey."

"What puts it into the foolish girl's head to nurse that old imp of darkness?" said the Student's-Clara, tying her stockings, which in the previous excitement had come down; "she ought to be glad to have a chance of paying him back for some of his abuses."

"Let her alone," replied the rag-gatherer, upon whose hardened mind even this event made some impression, "this Marianne is worth more than you, and black Harriet and Pearl-guste, and a score of Chontes put together."

The girls contemptuously curled their lips, but were silent, as the old woman knew how to use her stick and hook for other purposes besides picking rags out of the mud.

The thieves meanwhile had become convinced that their own interest required them not to destroy the good terms upon which they stood with their host. They became aware, that his demand to have the corpse of the Vigilant removed, was no more than just, and that their own interest required them to comply with his request. It was certain that the Police would return, and equally certain that if they found the corpse, the Hunchback would first be arrested, and the consequences to them all could scarcely be foreseen. For even then Jobs could fulfil his former threat.

In consequence of these considerations, the secret thieves-council finally concluded that the body of the Vigilant must be removed. The Sand-carter and the blonde Augustus were commissioned with the execution of this task, and declared themselves ready for it. They immediately took the body, which had not yet become quite cold, wrapped it into an old stolen cloak, put a cap upon its head, and thus muffled, carried it out of the den into the open air.

Trembling and shuddering, Marianne drew back when the terrible transport passed through her room; but Jobs, who had meanwhile recovered from his fright and bruises, readily offered them a Schnapps gratis, as they passed through his store, and grinningly wished them good luck upon their way. The remaining guests did not think it advisable to stay longer, and therefore in silence withdrew, and scattered in all directions over the city.

The Sand-carter and blonde Augustus assumed the appearance of carrying a sick or fainting man, as beneath such a mask they would be able to remove the body with less suspicion. By joining hands they formed a kind of bier, upon which they seated the body, whilst with the other hand they supported its back, and kept it in an upright position. In this manner they continued their way unmolested and unnoticed, but as soon as it could conveniently be done, they left the public road, and took their way through by-paths, over gardens and fields, towards the Upper Spree.

After a short but severe march, they reached the river shore. Here they laid down their burden, partly to recover breath, and partly to refresh themselves by a draught of Schnapps from the bottle they had brought with them.

After this, they filled the pockets of the Vigilant with a few stones, which with difficulty they found in the darkness of the night, and with more difficulty broke from the frozen ground. This being also done, they laid the corpse upon the ice, each of them took hold of a corner of the cloak, and they thus dragged it over the bright mirror of the frozen river toward the middle of the stream, where they hoped to find some openings in the ice, made by fishermen.

In this, also, fortune favoured them, and nothing now remained to do, but to sink the body to the deep, whence it would never rise again.

Just as they were about to do this, a kind of religious scruple arose in the breast of blonde Augustus, who generally distinguished himself from his comrades by a little more humane feeling than they possessed.

"Hark'ye, Maulspitzer," he began, addressing the Sand-carter, "it seems to me to be most decidedly wrong, that we should have despatched the Schlappe Anthony, and send him thus to eternity without prayer, confession or penitence. Just think, that towards us he has been guilty of *Slichnerei*, (of spying,) and how do you suppose he can possibly get along with the devil—who is sure to have him—with that sin upon his head?"

"What infernal nonsense," growled the Sand-carter, "what care we for his position with the devil. He wanted to betray us, and so we laid him cold; such is ancient usage and custom among honourable thieves. Now let us make haste and put him under ground, or rather under water, the night will soon pass, and it would not answer our purpose to be surprised here by daylight."

Blonde Augustus, however, was not so easily silenced. He represented to the sand-carter, that he had been the executioner, and consequently must take care of the body of the delinquent; he reminded him of the brave father of their victim, Black Henry, of whom, as we have heard, a chick was not safe in its shell, and thereby endeavoured to persuade him to take part in the funeral service of Schlappe Anthony. The Sand-carter finally agreed, but upon two conditions; first, that blonde Augustus would say the prayer, as he himself was not much accustomed to such things, and secondly, that the prayer should be as short as possible.

Devoutly kneeled the thief and murderer, side by side, with the dead body of the Police-spy upon the cold ice. The moon shed its silvery light upon this strange and peculiar scene, where superstition and stupidity mingled so strangely with moral depravity, producing the most lamentable perversion of the powers of the human mind.

The following was the prayer offered most devoutly by blonde Augustus.

" Good God, we pray thee, to be a kind and " lenient judge towards Schlappe Anthony He " became guilty of the greatest crime known on " earth, for he turned Slichner, (spy,) he has " brought Syrupsnose upon the Barsel, (chain,) " and would have brought us all into misery, for " which we judged him. But for many years " he has been a good thief, has done many brave " acts, and always kept *Lotscherehre*, (thieves- " honour,) and never cheated another of his " *Hellig*, (share.) For these virtues, Good God, " receive him in mercy, when he appears before " thy throne. This we pray Thee, the Maul " spitzer and the blonde Augustus, two honour- " able thieves, and honour and glory be to Thee. " Amen."

This task of love being accomplished, and the conscience of the thief satisfied, they hurriedly pushed the corpse through the opening of the ice, whence it would never rise again; then they hastily withdrew, to refresh their weary limbs by a long and quiet sleep. The clock upon the distant church spire just then announced the fifth hour of the morning.

After the thieves had left, a grave-like silence prevailed in the cellars of the hunchbacked Jobs, forming a strange contrast with the usual baccha- nalian noise of the place. No one, who now passed this silent, humble building, the wretched outlines of which seemed by the dim light of the moon, to contain naught but simple, honest pov- erty, could have dreamed that murder and robbery there had taken up their terrible abode.

The small unseemly lamp at the window, the certain landmark of safety to vagabonds, when they sought a retreat in the neighbourhood, was extinguished, and the cellar-door was fastened by a strong oaken block inside. Marianne, exhaust- ed by the bodily ill-treatment and the manifold wild, dreadful adventures of the night, had cast herself upon the bed, without undressing, and had sank into a kind of waking sleep. Jobs alone moved busily about, arranging everything for the expected visit of the Police, whom he now looked for every moment.

The cunning construction of his dwelling, which was admirably arranged for such emergen- cies, made this an easy task. He had only to be careful that in his own proper dwelling, not a piece of *treife goods*, (stolen goods,) remained by some chance behind in a corner, and thus fall into the hands of the officers. With the most busy attention, he therefore examined every nook and corner of his shop and parlour, to convince himself that the thieves had left nothing that might cause suspicion.

His small, grey, cat's-eyes sparkled with the brilliancy of a tiger, and it might be asserted that no examining custom-house officer could equal his penetrating glance. After he had, in this manner, gathered every article that might betray him, he removed all to the thieves-cavern, back of his store and dwelling. He then took hold of a large press, which he had expressly constructed to close the opening which led from the dwelling to the cellars. This press was nailed to the door itself, and entered the wall so far, that the whole appeared like a clothes-press built into the wall.

To open the door, a person would have to en- ter the press, and move three secret and well- constructed springs at the same moment. As no one but those acquainted with the secret could even think of this, an officer would naturally, if he had strong grounds for his suspicions, break the press to pieces, before he could gain his object. This system of locking was the ingenious inven- tion of a cunning thief, who had thus paid a very heavy debt which he had contracted with Jobs.

After the Hunchback had completed all these preparations, he again breathed more freely, and quietly seated himself upon an old and damaged arm-chair which stood opposite Marianne's bed. Now the Police-officers might come as soon as they liked, it would be impossible for them to find anything, and as usual they would have their trouble in vain.

His little grey eyes twinkled in malicious joy at the new triumph he expected to have, and no- thing at this moment would have been more dis- agreeable to him than if they had omitted the visitation. Thus he sat in his easy chair oppo- site the slumbering maiden, not unlike a dragon in a nursery tale, watching a valuable gem.

Fatigue at last closed his eyelids, and his dreams soon brought him into the midst of a con- flict with the natural opponents of thieves and vagabonds.

The section of police, who had already given such a fright to the inmates of the den, had mean- while, in the utmost patience, passed the whole night in a hiding place, whither the Jewess un- der the mask of the Vigilant had sent them. Hour after hour they awaited quietly for the pro- mised arrival of their liberator, who was to bring them the desired intelligence of the arrival of those persons whom they expected to arrest in old Jobs' place. Among these, the principal victims, were the long Schmuel and cunning Schmerles, who had latterly particularly distin- guished themselves by the boldness of their ma- nœuvres. Meanwhile the hours of the night pass- ed away, the clock struck seven in the morning, and the grey dawn of day appeared in the east, yet their spy did not return.

Lazily and weariedly, the gensd'armes were seated around a little table, in the miserable room of a small and poor cabin, which had frequently served them as head-quarters at their night-expe- ditions to the Voightland. The dim oil-lamp had become almost invisible in the thick atmosphere of the room, which by means of the smoke from many pipes, had assumed the appearance of a military guard-room.

The Criminal Commissary who accompanied the expedition, paced impatiently up and down, now producing his thick, silver watch to ascer- tain the time, and again opening the little window, and staring anxiously out into the cold and frosty night.

At last he said to his subordinates: " I consider it useless to wait longer, for day is dawning, and the birds must have flown from their nest ere now. I almost fear that we have been deceived by that infernal pattern-colourer; we will therefore at all events pay a visit to the Hunchback on our own account. If the Schlappe Anthony is still there, and contrary to expectation has been unable to get away, we cannot now come too soon, and if he has betrayed us, our appearance can do no harm. Perhaps we may even find a trace of the murder and robbery committed on the old woman a few days ago."

"At all events," added one of the gensd'armes, whose long and effective services had given him a sort of privilege to express his opinion to his superiors—"at all events we shall get out of this infernal hole."

The officer and gensd'armes arose from their seats to prepare for the march. The Criminal Commissary, however, having now but little confidence in the success of his plan, considered it useless to take them all along. He therefore only selected two men, and ordered the others to take the shortest way to their quarters.

The young rising day had just dispelled the last strip of grey dawn, when the officers of police arrived before the shop of hunchbacked Jobs. The host already risen from his short uneasy slumbers, and who had seen his expected guests approaching from a distance, placed himself at his door, assuming a weather-wise appearance, seeming carelessly to look upon the rising clouds on all sides of the horizon.

With a grinning smile he received the comers, bowed most humbly and almost to the ground, when the Commissary informed him that he should be compelled to institute a police-search of his premises.

"It is reported, that for some time past your house has been a shelter for thieves and vagabonds," observed the officer earnestly, as he closely watched the cunning face of the thieves-host. "This very night, we are told, there has been quite a large assemblage of bad characters collected here?"

"All slander and calumny, pure calumny, Herr Commissary," replied Jobs, as he bowed, and still bowing entered the cellar, inviting the Police to follow him. "I am known as an honest man. The Lord is my witness, it is very hard to earn one's bread now-a-days, you must be aware of that, Herr Commissary. If I happen, once in a while to have a few guests, who are a little merry, envy, sheer envy, will immediately construe it to murder and robbery. You must stoop a little, Herr Commissary, the door is rather low."

The officer, without noticing this politeness, or the pious look which the other endeavoured to assume—as he always did in similar situations—impatiently pushed the talkative Hunchback to one side, and with his followers entered the cellar. He closely examined the shop utensils, which were arranged in proper order along the wall, or neatly placed upon the long counter.

"May I take the liberty of offering you a little bitters, Herr Commissary?" asked Jobs politely, as he took his accustomed place behind the counter; "it is rather a cold morning."

"Don't trouble yourself," harshly replied the Commissary, without suffering himself to be interrupted in his examination.

"Or perhaps the Herren gensd'armes would like to take a dram?" again began the indefatigable host. "Here is real *Nordhäuserkorn*, or good *Danziger Gold Wasser*, or fine *Kümmel-offizier*, or *Parfait amour*."*

To all appearances these tempting offers would not have missed their effect upon two constitutionally thirsty throats, had not the Commissary ordered them immediately to continue their search in the store-room adjoining the shop, and see if they could discover anything suspicious there.

"Are there any guests in your next room?" inquired the officer, who, meanwhile, had left no box or jar unexamined.

"Oh, my Lord, no," quickly replied Jobs, "who should come so early to my poor, humble dwelling? Yes, yes, if my business was as good as that!"

"Well, well, these fellows may have remained from their last night's carousal," replied the other. "We must examine at all events."

Jobs' feelings were not quite delicate enough to be at all annoyed at this insulting suspicion. His malicious pleasure principally consisted in the useless endeavours of the officers, which he watched with growing self-confidence. Readily he opened the door leading to his parlour, certain of a fresh triumph to his well established innocence.

The men entered the low chamber stamping with annoyance, and the rattling of their spurs resounded loudly against the arched ceiling of the cellar room. The gensd'armes had not been able to discover anything in this room, and the entire failure and uselessness of their expedition made them doubly sensitive to the fatigues of their long and weary night-watch. It was physiologically a necessary consequence, that they were little inclined to hide their anger and annoyance.

In the room they entered, the unfortunate Marianne still rested in her bed. She had undressed herself, and sought an unrefreshing morning-slumber to strengthen her after the fatiguing and exciting adventures of the past night. Frightened, she started up at the noise the men made when they entered, but on perceiving the bearded faces of the gensd'armes, she modestly hid her head underneath the poor coverlet. The appearance of officers was nothing new to her, for often before this time had the dwelling of Jobs been subjected to a search, so that she well discerned the object of this visit, but never before had her sense of female modesty been so bitterly outraged.

The officers of Police, however, took little or no notice of these natural emotions. The poor and humble furniture was next subjected to a

* Different kinds of liquors in use at Berlin

search. The fragile bureau, the heavy oaken chest, even the mysterious clothes-press, all were opened; they crawled beneath the bedsteads, searched in every nook and corner, without finding anything in the least suspicious. At last, one of the two gensd'armes approached the Commissary and whispered something in his ear.

"Yes, yes, we might try it," replied the officer, nodding assent. "Halloa, you girl!" he cried, "just get up out of that bed. With rabble like you, one cannot be too careful, and we will just search the bed."

Amidst burning blushes, the maiden raised her head a little. "Oh, my dear sir," she cried, half choked with shame, "only retire one instant into the shop, that I may dress myself."

"Oh, ho!" cried the Commissary, laughing scornfully, "so as to give you an opportunity to put a few small matters out of the way. No, no! we understand these things. Stuff and humbug! You have, I dare say, often enough dressed yourself in the presence of men; so get out of the feathers, or these my ladies' maids must assist you."

"Ha, ha, ha!" was heard from the gensd'armes, who, as in duty bound, laughed loudly at the wit of their superior.

In the intense anguish of her soul, Marianne knew not what to do. Fearfully she looked around, but could not reach even the most necessary articles of her dress, as the chair whereon she had laid them had been removed. She burst into a flood of tears.

"Postpone your confounded crying until afterwards," said one of the gensd'armes; "we have no time now." At these words he tore the coverlet from the unfortunate girl, leaving her, merely clad in her night-dress, exposed to the ruthless stare of the men.

At this cruel treatment Marianne cried aloud in terror and despair, and was scarcely able to move. Her heart was torn as if a poisonous adder had assailed it, the most holy sanctuary of her maiden modesty had been ruthlessly attacked. She no longer had any tears; palsied and motionless she submitted to the monstrosity which for ever destroyed the virgin purity of her mind. Who can or dare designate for what determinations, plans and ideas the Evil One might now have found that crushed heart ripe, had the tempter approached her at this terrible moment? And where would we then have had to seek for the seed, which grew up into the monstrous tree of iniquity in that young heart?

Busily, the coarse hands of the gensd'armes rummaged through the spotless virgin-bed, pushing their gentle victim, now to one side, now to the other, without even noticing the immediate contact in which their rough hands frequently came, with the delicate body of the girl. Marianne spoke not a syllable, her spirit was crushed, and her poor devoted head, hung like a broken, withered lily upon her bosom. After the maiden innocence of her mind had been so hopelessly destroyed, it mattered little for that of the body.

After this scene had continued for some minutes,

10

amidst a torrent of gibes and jeers, such as could only have been expected from the coarse intruders, the gensd'armes suddenly burst into a triumphant shout, which even caused Jobs to shrink back in affright. One of them victoriously produced from the foot of the maiden's bed, hidden beneath the bed-clothes, a tolerably large piece of variegated calico. It was the same which little Siegbert, the son of Long Schmuel, had stolen at the merchant's, and brought hither, that Marianne might make a dress of it for his little sister. As we know, Marianne had refused the stuff, because it was stolen goods, and preferred to cut up her own dress for the little girl.

The entrance of Long Schmuel had interrupted the beautiful domestic scene which, as we remember, followed this refusal. When his furious attack upon Marianne had brought the remaining thieves into the room, little Siegbert fearing the loss of the stuff, had hidden it for security in Marianne's bed. In consequence of the exciting adventures which followed immediately after, particularly the departure of Long Schmuel and his children, it had remained there.

At this unexpected discovery the Criminal Commissary started up from the old fragile armchair, whence he had hitherto watched with indifference the progress of the search. He hastily reached into his coat-pocket and produced a pattern of the calico, which the merchant had left at the Police, for the purpose of identifying the stolen goods, and at the first glance he was convinced that this was the same article. The discovery was quite sufficient for the officer to change his entire manner and behaviour towards his host.

"Oh, ho, my old fox, at last we have caught you," he said, turning to Jobs, who became deadly pale, "confess now, you hypocritical rascal, whence got you this goods?"

"Sir," cried Jobs, in the utmost fright, "devil take me, and roast and fry me in butter, if I have the remotest idea from where this stuff comes. You wicked, outrageous wanton," he cried furiously to his daughter, "who gave you that calico, confess all, I will have nothing to do with you, you shameless, ungrateful hussy!"

"Silence! this moment," commanded the Commissary of the furious Hunchback, "you are the fence, the receiver, if not even the thief; but I will soon bring you where they will open that lying mouth of yours."

"Mercy, sir! oh, have pity," cried Jobs, wringing his hands, "I am an honest, innocent man! As sure as there is a God in heaven, I know nothing of this stolen goods."

"So much the better for yourself," replied the officer, "but meanwhile I must arrest and deliver you to the proper authorities; there you may make your defence as best you can. Well, m'amselle," he continued, turning to Marianne, "how much longer will you endeavour to wear the mask of virtuous innocence? Presto! quick out of the bed, and dress yourself; you also are arrested. Dankmann, hand her the clothes from that chair."

This second terrible occurrence, that of finding the stolen goods, awoke Marianne from the lethargy of the silent despair into which her former ill-treatment had thrown her. It was more than her gentle heart could endure! First to receive bodily ill-treatment, and then to be suspected as a common thief! In this position of things, modesty and diffidence could no longer influence her. Beside herself, in the intensity of her terror, she rushed from her bed, and even as she was, only covered by her simple night-gown, she cast herself at the feet of the Criminal Commissary.

Her fair, virgin bosom heaved and panted, in terrible anguish and emotion, and her beauteous hair fell in wild confusion over her tearful eyes, burning with feverish intensity. Even the icy heart of the officer, who had seen much misery and many tears, was softened, when he saw this fair marble image kneeling before him, praying for mercy; but his *duty* commanded, and he had to obey. He even had to console himself with the belief that the girl was a criminal, caught for the first time in the fact, for he did not dream of the true state of things, and Marianne, for the sake of her father, dared not make any revelations.

Meanwhile, time urged them to depart. The officer of Police put an end to the violent protestations of the Hunchback, and also brought a momentary certainty to the silent sorrow of the maiden, by the assurance, that all resistance would be in vain, and would only tend to make matters worse.

The Commissary next locked up the cellars, which were now deserted, took his prisoners with him, and conducted them to the city, towards the nearest guard house. Jobs continued to assert his innocence, asseverated that he knew nothing of the stolen goods, railed continually at his unnatural daughter, while at the same time he cast suspicious and fearful side long glances upon her; Marianne walked along, silent as a lamb which is led to slaughter. Of course the conduct of both was a matter of total indifference to their guards, who only experienced a kind of coarse satisfaction to find their efforts finally crowned with success.

The transport stopped before the guard-house, at the city gate. The Commissary entered the guard-room to write the order of arrest, and to obtain the necessary military escort to conduct the prisoners to the well known prisons of the *Stadtvoigtei*.* Four men of the guards, armed with muskets and side arms, soon after made their appearance, two of whom took the father, and the two others the daughter in their middle, and began their march towards the prisons, each party by a different route. The services of the police were for the present no more required.

In the motley, variegated and busy life in the streets of Berlin, an arrest and transport certainly are no rarities. Military escorts, who deliver police arrestants to the different prisons, are daily seen marching through the streets. As often and frequently however as this takes place, it never occurs without a noisy and more or less numerous crowd of the rabble following in its train.

This certainly is not a very pleasant sight for the more refined part of the public, but it is also of bad tendency to the very rabble who delight in it, as it is in the nature of things that such scenes should harden the mind against a feeling of delicacy, and frequently cause the most brutal excesses. These considerations increase in importance, if the position of the criminal himself is taken into account. If he is shameless and impudent, he sets a bad example; if he still has a spark of finer feeling and honour in his breast, that is hopelessly crushed.

And how will this finally operate in a case where the arrest afterwards proves to have been unjustifiably and rashly made, which is by no means of rare occurrence? The mass of the rabble has seen the unfortunate man when he was arrested, but did not see him dismissed or justified, and thus the onus of the arrest sticks to him, and he must be ruined for all futurity. These public exhibitions are, to say the least, nothing more or less than a mild repetition of the pillory, only that they are done without sentence or justice. For these and similar reasons it has latterly been urged as advisable, to conduct all arrestants in close wagons from the different guard houses to the prisons. This much is certain, that a great deal that now offends the more refined and moral portion of citizens, would thus be removed, and a great cause of mental depravity to the rising generation be abolished.

The unfortunate Marianne suffered all we have just mentioned. She had scarcely been separated from her father, and reached the corner of the next street with the gensd'armes who escorted her, of whom one walked before, and the other behind her, when the crowd began to collect around them. The day had already advanced towards noon, and the streets were filled with moving masses of people The interesting appearance of the young girl, in whose fine, transparent features, traces of blood still betrayed the brutal abuse of the night before, attracted universal attention, and in proportion to this attention the mass of her followers increased. Men, women, and children, all, in short, who could spare a moment from more urgent affairs, followed with the transport, and exhausted their mind in conjectures of the cause of her arrest.

" Harkye, Lude," cried a journeyman tailor to another, whose leather apron and blackened appearance betrayed him to be a smith, " harkye, this is a prostitute, who did not take out a license from the police, and wanted to cheat the treasury out of the tax her trade has to pay."*

" Oh! bless us, and save us from all temptation," croaked an old maid, of very doubtful appearance, " such an unrighteous, ungodly hussy!"

" You are all in the wrong," observed that

---

* The common city jail.

* Such is the municipal law in Berlin.

most remarkable of all Berlin denizens, a *Ecken-steher*,* (ticket porter,) as he fastened his number upon his arm, " that woman must have began a *Keilerei*, (fight,) else how could her nose have been bleeding ?"

" With your kind permission, ladies and gentlemen," interrupted a fourth, whose black, threadbare coat, dirty, white cravat, and " shocking bad" hat, seemed to denote him a public scrivener, " according to my well experienced and infallible judgment, considering the external indications and personal qualifications of the culprit before us, her offence is most probably a small, trifling, petty larceny, under five Thalers."

" In that case, she will receive no greater punishment, than imprisonment of no less than eight days or more than four weeks; I understand that," again quietly observed another member of the coterie, whose desolate appearance indicated practical experience in the matter which he described. "A merry trip to you! A lady cannot lose the national cockade by this !"

Scarce one of these, and many other brutal observations, escaped Marianne's ear. Her position was indeed a terrible one, and gratefully she would have kissed the hand which at this moment in mercy would have killed her. If she had accidentally passed a stream, without hesitation she would have leaped into it. But no such fortune awaited her; patiently she was compelled to endure, and in the midst of this jeering, unfeeling mass of the lowest rabble, pass on her way, through nearly the entire length of the city, until they reached the Molken-market.

Arrived here, the unfortunate girl was scarcely able to support herself any longer, her pulse beat feverishly, and consciousness threatened to leave her. One of the soldiers compassionately supported her steps, to conduct her through the rows of huckster-women, who are seated behind their baskets in this open square, until they arrived before the Stadtvoigtei-buildings.†

The youthful innocence of her appearance, again excited many a bitter jest, and a loud roar of laughter was heard, when the old haggard fruit-woman, whose seat, from time immemorial has been right in front of the Stadtvoigtei, on seeing poor Marianne, repeated her old standing joke: " Well, here is another, and a new guest, to the coffee-house No 1."‡

Much as Marianne had already suffered, whatever sorrows had already united to lacerate her poor and gentle heart, yet, not until now, when the ponderous buildings of the Stadtvoigtei, in their grey, dark outlines rose before her glance, did she feel the intensity of her despair, and pressed her hands before her dimmed eyes. With a stare, like that of a maniac, she looked up the long, dirty door-way; it seemed as if she were bidding farewell to all hopes of life. Hitherto she had at least been *free*, she could watch the dawn and the sunrise, listen to the warblings of the birds; one step, and rattling fell the heavy portal, which excluded her—who could say for how long— from all intercourse with virtuous and proper society.

For a moment, she had to lean against a pillar at the entrance way to recover her failing breath, and to regain endurance and strength. For the first time, in the midst of her mental torture, a refreshing tear visited her burning cheek, and soon two streams issued from her eyes, pursuing their burning course down that beautiful face.

Two elegantly dressed Referendariuses, with portfolios of documents under their arms, issued from the house.

" Devil take me, brother," began the one, on perceiving the just described scene, " a weeping wanton always excites a peculiar interest with me. What is your name, child ?"

Marianne looked up with dignity; her tall, graceful figure became so majestic, so imposing, that the young jurist stared at her, and shrunk back in astonishment. But suddenly he collected himself; he remembered better. Humanity had expelled this woman from the pale of society, she was a common criminal, away then, away, from the pollution of her presence ! Protection, only protection from this *terrible* world, ay, if it be behind bars and keys ! Marianne forcibly pressed her hands upon her breast, as if she would drive the terrible pain and anguish to the lowest depths of her soul. Quick as an arrow she then rushed along the door-way to the inner courtyard, so fast that the soldiers only with difficulty followed her. The rabble which was just dispersing, once more screamed in mad delight on watching this scene.

They now conducted her across the courtyard, and up a small stair-case, to deliver her at the office of the prison department. A heavy door creakingly turned on its hinges; and the newly arrived party entered a spacious, and high, but gloomy looking room. The whole length of this room was divided by a railing and trellise work, such as is usually found in court and police rooms, and thus formed two offices. One of them, the one which Marianne entered with the soldiers, was intended for the public, and besides the large black stove, was entirely vacant.

The other side, along which ran the windows in large, deep recesses, through which the eye fell immediately upon the steep, tall and gloomy looking prison wall, was the room for the officers and persons employed.

In this division, at proper intervals, near to the trellise work were three desks, whose object was sufficiently indicated by the tall office stools before them, and by the immense sand boxes and ink stands of black wood which stood upon each.

Unbroken silence prevailed when our party entered, and increased the unpleasant, painful im-

* *Eckensteher*, properly, a man who stands at corners. These, the public porters of Berlin, are celebrated for their witty and odd sayings, political discussions, laziness, and fondness of fighting and drinking.—TRANSLATOR.

† City Court building.

‡ The Berlin Criminal-prison is in Stadtvoigtei building, Molken-market, No. 1.

pression always felt by a novice on entering one of these halls of judgment, particularly if that novice belongs to the gentler sex. In the whole of this large office, there was not a soul to be seen beside the secretary on duty, and the fat, well conditioned turnkey, who had seated himself upon a wooden chair in a corner, and with his fleshy hands comfortably folded over his corpulent body, had fallen into a most gentle slumber.

The secretary, rather a young man, had a most peculiar appearance. The long, thin body, which supported a small, blonde, *à la brebis* dressed head, exceeded by far the usual size allotted to man. The nose had evidently assumed a disproportionate extension, and shaded not only the small mouth, but even pushed the little, cunning grey-blue eyes far into the back-ground. The ash-coloured hue of the face was framed by a red, flashy silk 'neckerchief and two immense collar points. A silver-grey surtout and Scotch plaid pantaloons completed the toilette. The entire figure appeared like a six foot high beanstalk, with a small pumpkin stuck on top.

This officer sat, or rather hung, in evident ill-humour upon his high office stool. In his left hand he held a quill, upon which he indefatigably whittled with his right, whilst the open snuff-box before him, indicated a third occupation. By the hurried motions with which he attended to all these different employments, he betrayed the inner excitement of his mind.

His ill-humour was quite pardonable. Last evening at a *Boston*-party in the *Ressource*,* to the general delight of his companions, he had lost a game of ten point *Grandissimo*. This unheard-of ill fortune had haunted his mind during the whole night, and the peace and quiet of the court-room now again brought it to his memory.

After manifold calculations and speculations, he had arrived at the positive certainty, that he could not have lost his game, if he had lead a Diamond instead of a Heart. This conviction, which was not sufficient to cover a heavy deficiency in his cash account, had put him in the worst possible humour just as the persons of our story entered the room.

One of the soldiers approached the desk, and handed him the order of arrest, which the Criminal Commissary had made out and given to him at the Guard-house. Quickly the Secretary cast his eyes over the paper, then, in the same silence with which he had received the order, he wrote the necessary certificate of receipt of the prisoner, and dismissed the two valiant defenders of their country.

Marianne was now left alone with the Officer of Justice. She was quiet and composed. After all the ill-treatment she had received, after the great disgrace and cruelty she had endured ever since last evening, she did not believe that there could be anything left to injure her still more severely. On the contrary, she rejoiced at the prospect of partaking, separated from all the world, behind locks and bars, of a quiet, though

*A well known Club Room.

gloomy and miserable solitude. Poor, poor, unfortunate girl! she knew nothing of the terrible sufferings and tortures of a German criminal prison.

The secretary took up a large book of records, which lay by his side, turned over the leaves, cast a quick glance upon the fair prisoner, whilst between his teeth he muttered something about receivers of stolen goods, moral depravity of the times, &c., then dipping his pen into the enormous ink-stand, he asked:

"Your name?"

Hitherto, the wretched girl had stood by the door, quietly and with bent down looks. Frightened at the harsh tone of this address, which resounded in the large empty room, she started up. Quickly, however, she recovered her self possession, and replied with a soft, gentle voice:

"Marianne Jobs?"

"Occupation?"

"What do you mean, Herr Referendarius?" modestly inquired the maiden, who could not understand the exact meaning of this detached question.

"Open your ears, when questions are asked of you! I inquired for your occupation, I wish to know what you are?"

"Why, dear sir, I am nothing, nothing at all but a poor girl."

The secretary in very ill-humour hit his desk with the palm of his hand, whereupon a cloud of dust arose from the green cloth, and Marianne again frightened, shrunk back. "In the devil's name; I am quite sure, that you will not tell me *what* you *really* are; but what do you follow, how do you profess to support yourself? Your assumed stupidity is of no use here, and will help you nothing; we know these things long ago."

The poor girl suppressed a deep sigh. "I live with my father," she replied.

"What is your father?"

"A grocery keeper."

"His name?"

"Jobs."

"He resides?"

"In the Voightland."

"Age?"

"I think about fifty years."

The secretary burst into a loud fit of laughter. "You must answer to *this* order of arrest," he cried; "what care I for all this stuff about your father, unless he also takes up his quarters with us. I asked for *your* age?"

"Eighteen years, sir."

The secretary, who appeared to be fashionably short-sighted, at these words quickly drew a small square lorgnette which was fastened by a black string, from his pocket, and stuck it before his right eye. Placing his head upon his hand, he stared impudently for some minutes upon the maiden, then, without giving any external sign of satisfaction or dislike, he returned to his occupation.

"Religion?" he inquired, continuing his examination.

Marianne had already become so intimidated, that she scarcely dared to answer a question for fear of again giving a wrong reply; to guard against this, she asked timidly, " do you mean my father's, or mine ?"

The secretary now believed himself justified in losing his patience.

Full of rage he started up, resting both feet upon the front board of his office-stool, thus exhibiting the whole length of his lank figure.

" Harkye," he cried, " are you making fun of me, you impertinent hussy. We have here divers sorts of instruments which may bring you to reason; or do you perhaps think, that I can spend my time with your examination and come too late to my dinner ? I ask for *your* religion, if you have any, or at all believe in God ?"

The religious inclination of her mind, which we have already observed in Marianne, made her feel the reproach contained in this question with double bitterness, more bitterly indeed than all former insults. With a mien expressive of the intense sorrow which her soul felt, she uttered, in a scarcely audible tone, the words:

" Evangelic-Lutheran."

The officer wrote a few more words into his book, and then turned to the corner which was occupied by the sleepy prison-turnkey. At the beginning of the above scene, that individual had roused himself a little, but afterwards, as he knew well the result of the examination, and felt no interest in it, he had again fallen into a gentle doze.

" *Wicchman*," cried the secretary—" why, that fellow snores all the day long—Halloa, Wiechman, what number ?"

The other, awaking slowly, rose leisurely from his seat, and rubbed his sleepy eyes. He next unbuttoned the large white buttons of his official coat, took a couple of dirty, crumbled sheets of paper from his pocket, and replied with undisturbed quietness, " No. 36."

No 36 !! These words pronounced with so much *sang froid*, with such utter indifference, perhaps decided irrevocably the whole future destiny of this unfortunate girl. That number designated the prison room, and at the same time the prison-associates with whom she had to live. The influence which in this respect is usually experienced over a mind, perhaps innocent, or not yet totally lost, belongs to the darkest and most disagreeable spots of the German criminal code.

" Evil associates corrupt good manners." This well known, popular and trivial proverb, here becomes a rich inexhaustible source of nameless misery. It is incredible to those not intimately acquainted with the workings of prison machinery, how many have entered those cells, slightly guilty, and left them as accomplished criminals, having profited by the pernicious lessons taught them in this high school of crime, by their fellow prisoners.

If we consider that some youth, as it very frequently occurs, is innocently imprisoned, that before his judge his innocence is easily established, but that the infectious influence of his co-prisoner's society has destroyed the purity of his soul, the terrible revolting effects of this system will be easily recognised and understood. Perhaps very soon after his dismissal, the unfortunate wretch returns to the same prison as a real criminal, and now re-imparts the lessons he has received and digested, to other novices, and thus under the influence, and I may say, co-operation of the laws, a *school for criminals* is established, which must and will continue as long as the circumstances and laws exist which called it into life.

It is here philanthropy can find a large field for operations; this is a subject against which the press must again and again raise its voice, until we shall have succeeded in finding the remedy for this crying evil, for this pernicious nursery of crime. We shall hereafter find opportunity to show in what manner Marianne was affected by it.

The turnkey knew by long practice that the last question addressed to him, closed the examination; he rose from his corner, approached Marianne, and opening the door, said the brief laconic words :

" Come along."

Both entered a long, narrow, and dimly lighted corridor. Along the sides of this passage ranged door upon door, constructed of thick oaken planks, and secured by immense locks and thick iron bolts. This sight had something very gloomy and terrible, which was in no way lessened by the low whispers of turnkeys, who were stationed at intervals along the passage.

Trembling with fear and horror, Marianne had reached nearly to the end of the corridor, when she was met by Jobs and his military escort, who had been detained by an accident upon their way, and only now reached the halls of justice. Jobs looked with dull and careless indifference upon the scene around him. He had never yet been imprisoned; but from the frequent narratives of his guests, he was perfectly well acquainted with the localities. The circumstance, that the stolen goods had evidently been left behind by one of his guests, and that nothing could be proved against him, quieted his apprehensions, and he felt convinced, that he would soon again be at liberty.

Marianne had never felt much affection for her step-father, and still less, ever experienced from him any sign of parental attachment. The terrors of her present situation, however, caused her to forget all her repugnance—to forgive all that she had suffered at his hands. She would now have been delighted to have encountered even Long Schmuel. Beside herself with the excitement of the moment, and with the cry, " my father, oh, my poor father !" she was about to rush to the arms of the Hunchback, as the coarse hand of the prison turnkey roughly pulled her back; " Silence, silence !" he commanded, " we must have no scenes here; the Hunchback and you have nothing to do with each other."

In dark, unfeeling silence, Jobs passed his daughter, who, spite the strength of her conductor, had involuntarily opened her arms for his embrace. The malicious villain could even then not withstand the temptation of attempting, while passing her, to kick the poor girl, for which one of the soldiers immediately repaid him, with a thrust from the butt of his musket.

The prison turnkey, an old, large and muscular man, was not quite as bad as he appeared to be. He had formerly been a *Garde du Corps,* and had received his present situation as a reward for the long and good services he had done to his country in the field of battle; but like all old soldiers, he was rough, yet good hearted. "You infernal scoundrel," he cried, when he observed the malicious movement of the Hunchback, "only wait, and look out, when I get you once upon *the Fox.*"*

At these words he stopped before the above named room, No. 36, and rattled the keys which he carried in his hand, in the heavy door. Creaking, the springs of the lock gave way, the bolts were withdrawn, and the door opened to them.

Marianne turned deadly pale with fright, and almost swooned, as she breathlessly stared into the interior of the room, in which she discovered three shameless, bold, half-naked women, who had pressed towards the door on hearing the noise.

"Good day, father Wiechmann," they exclaimed all three, "ah, a new customer; well, that is fine!"

"For Heaven's sake," screamed Marianne in wild terror, as convulsively she grasped the arm of the turnkey, "kill me, kill me, if you will, only do not lock me in there!"

The old turnkey, upon whom the unaffected terror of the maiden really had made an impression, endeavoured to console her in his rough coarse manner. "Do not be afraid, my daughter," he said, "you will not find it so bad with us, you shall have good company."

Marianne could make no reply; with growing terror and disgust she watched the shameless manners and movements of these women, who in the dim light of the room, appeared to her bewildered eye like terrible fiendish phantoms. The rough man who conducted her, felt more and more pity for the unfortunate victim; heavy drops of perspiration, produced by the anxiety he felt for the girl and the difficulty of his own situation, appeared on his forehead. Suddenly he heard the heavy and well known steps of his superior officer, and he dared no longer lose time.

Gently he raised the unfortunate maiden in his arms, placed her, like a doll incapable of self-will or motion, on the inside of the threshold, and hastily locked the door upon her.

The heavy steps approached nearer: "Good day, Wiechmann."

'Good day, *Herr Criminalrath.*"

"Whom had you there?"

"I have just received a new prisoner, a girl; I believe a receiver of stolen goods."

* The bench upon which Criminals are whipped.

"Aha, nothing else?" And with indifference the Criminalrath left the corridor.

CHAPTER XV.

THE SCHMUEL FAMILY.

AFTER the den of the hunchback Jobs had been closed by order of the authorities, nothing remained for the old band of thieves and robbers, but to seek other shelters and other homes. To a few of them, this was no small difficulty; but most of the villains easily found accommodations, as they were always provided with several head-quarters. Regard for their own personal safety had before compelled them, to escape the lynx-eye of the police, repeatedly to change their abodes.

Long Schmuel, of course, belonged to the latter. In that eventful night, when he was compelled with his children hastily to leave the hunchback's, he had immediately repaired to a fellow-Jew in K— street, and for the present, had taken up his residence there.

K— street is a small, narrow, filthy, and bad smelling lane in the *Königstadt;* containing a superabundance of children, and is formed by irregular, bad looking one and two story houses. It is mostly inhabited by Jews; a class of them, however, who generally earn an honest, though scanty support, by traffic and easy trades. Most of them keep small shops, wherein they sell cotton goods, ribbons, buttons, thread, needles, &c. The mother of the family, assisted by her daughters, form the shop-keepers and clerks, while fathers and sons, as so-called "*Packjuden,*" (Jews with bundles,) peddle through the country.

The host of long Schmuel owned one of the houses in this street, wherein he kept a Hebrew Restaurat. In his youth he had also been a notorious thief, but after having accumulated a small fortune, had turned *gedinn,* (honest,) and retired from the scenes and localities of his former misdeeds. He now pursued his civic occupation with such industry and energy, that he had long since established a comparatively flourishing and lucrative business.

Although nearly seventy years of age, he still appeared a strong, undersized figure, with a shrewd, cunning, and strongly marked face, and a white, but full, almost rich head of hair. The rotundity of his person had obtained him the nick name of "*dicke Itzig,*" (*angl.* thick Isaac,) and among the thieves with whom his former occupations had brought him in connexion, he was universally known by that name.

This acquaintance with bad characters, was now, in his present position, the only source of real annoyance he had. It was a matter of no rare occurrence that thieves, who knew his former position, visited him, and were malicious and selfish enough, to use the knowledge they possessed of him, to their own pecuniary advantage. In other words, the villains, by the threat of exposing crimes he had formerly committed, but which had never been discovered, compelled him frequently to give them money, and do them many other favours.

This, in the language of the thieves, is called *brennen*, (to burn,) and as Itzig, as a renegade member, could no longer, according to the rules and laws of thieving, claim protection and mercy from the craft, nothing remained for him but to comply with their frequent requests. His only hope was, that the number of old practitioners at the trade, who still remembered him, was daily diminishing, while he remained unknown to the young, rising generation of thieves.

We are compelled, in justice to long Schmuel to state, that hitherto he had despised to operate in the above named manner upon the fear of his former associate. But latterly, since his manifold crimes had made him an object of especial vigilance to the police, even before the catastrophe at the cellar of the hunchback, he had been compelled for his own security to force thick Itzig to grant him an asylum, if necessary. This, of course, was done by means of brennen, and Schmuel gained his end, in so far, that the restaurateur gave him a small, well hidden garret in his own house as a place of refuge. For several weeks previously, the thief had frequently resorted there with his family, but since he had learned that old Jobs' cellar was effectually closed, he had made this his constant residence.

The many and divers preparations for the intended burglary at the house of the Geheimerath, which was to take place that night, had so occupied long Schmuel and his wife—though, as we know, in different ways—during the day after the murder of the Vigilant, that they had not received the least advice of the arrest of their hunchbacked host and his daughter.

When Major von Steinfort, in the mistaken belief that he had arrested long Schmuel, told the Jewess in the street before the house of the Geheimerath, to go and fetch her children, and then added the words, " the business in the den of the hunchback has come to an end," neither the Major himself, or the poor woman, had the least suspicion, that this had already taken place, though in quite a different manner from the one they intended.

The first thought of the Jewess, next to her children, had been of poor Marianne, whom she loved with all her heart, and would have saved at the risk of her life. She rejoiced at the thought, that the Major was now able to fulfil his promise, of sending the next day a physician to the poor sick girl, with less danger to either party.

The confederate of the old warrior hurried straightway, through many dark streets, towards the house of thick Itzig, whence she expected to bring her children to the house of the Major. Her mind was excited by emotions of joy and sorrow; after her long sufferings, the goal of her hopes was at last in view. She certainly had been compelled for some time to deceive her husband, but as a reward, she already saw him and her innocent children saved from the pool of temporal and eternal perdition.

In her mind's eye she already fancied herself installed in a quiet, clean and humble dwelling, upon the domain of the Major, a trusty companion and nurse to her husband, educating her children to become worthy and honest members of society. Her husband had returned from his wild, dishonest and dissolute courses, his crimes could no longer cause his arrest, the Major had given him honest employment, and by his upright course of life he atoned for his many former misdeeds; everything appeared pleasant and peaceable to her.

Without this richly promising future, the Jewess would certainly never have lent herself to the betrayal of her husband, for spite of his great crimes, she loved him with all that intensity of warm affection, which is so frequently found among Jewesses of the lower class. It is upon the whole a psychological fact, attested by many startling testimonials upon the records of our criminal courts, that in no other sphere of life, examples of greater affection and fidelity can be found, than the examples offered by the wives of these Hebrew thieves, even when they do not partake of the heinous trade of their husbands.

If the men are arrested, or if they are sent to the state prisons for their crimes, these women, of their own free will, and urged only by affection, undertake the longest and most wearisome journeys on foot, only to see the prisoner for a moment, or to bring him some small consolation or comfort. All which they can gain by a little petty trade or peddling, they gather together, only to alleviate the hard lot of the prisoner in some way, even if their gift or the produce of their labour should consist in nothing but a box of snuff.

This is a beautiful example of the innate goodness of the human heart; the primitive virtue of the soul will issue forth even through the strongest panoply of vice, crime and misery. Hence the well established truism : man is good by nature.

Thus, all the crimes long Schmuel had committed, as deeply as the Jewess abhorred them, could not smother in her heart the love she had once sworn to him. Never, never would she have consented to the plans of the Major and the Prince, spite of all the obligations she owed them, had she not therein discovered the sole means of bringing her unfortunate husband to a better life. Love, the purest and most intense love, was the only motive of her course of action.

Carefully feeling her way, the Jewess entered the cold, damp garret-chamber. An old oil lamp which she had just lit, spread as much light as barely sufficed to recognise her three children, who had soundly and quietly gone to sleep upon a few bunches of straw, beneath the cover of an old blanket, some tattered clothes, furs and similar things. The mother turned her lamp so as to cast a ray of light upon their blooming faces, the innocent smiles of which bore no impress of the terrible curse of their future lives.

The pride of a mother's joy, and bitter sorrow at the possible future of her darlings, moved the breast of the Jewess in feverish excitement; more lively than ever she felt the holy duty to become a saving, a guardian angel to these innocent victims.

Looking at them intensely she bent her head over the pallet of the little ones. The reflection of the lamp fell upon Siegbert's eyes; he awoke. "Let me sleep yet, dear mother," he begged, turning to the other side, "it is so very cold; to-day at noon I go with father to the jeweller's, and I will steal something right pretty for you."

At this terrible speech of her son, the poor mother was deeply affected. She set down the boy, and cast herself upon her knees in warm and fervent prayer to the Maker of the Universe, imploring him to grant the fulfilment of her plans and hopes. Long and intensely did she pray; it was the quiet penitence and humiliation of her soul, previous to the time, when with her darlings, she would leave this place of horror, and enter with them on a new and more promising path of life.

Suddenly, wild manly steps hurried up the stairs. Frightened, the Jewess started up; it sounded almost like her husband's foot; yet he used to walk more cautiously, moreover, he was a prisoner!—She listened attentively—the steps approached, they became still more familiar, her breath almost stopped, choked her, then — the door flew open, and long Schmuel furiously rushed into the room. Uttering a low scream of terror, the woman sank down upon the couch.

"The *Miszemeschunne* (consumption) take the accursed Maulspitzer," he cried, "for none other than his foul hand has spoiled my jackscrew. I might have imagined it last night at the hunch-back's, that the scoundrel would attempt treachery. A man who would try to steal from his fellow-Schranker has no religion in him, and is fit for any villany. The whole matter was arranged by the scoundrel; it was not without cause, that the blonde Augustus stayed away from the Masematten. The infernal villains! As if they would not have got their Hellig. But wait, if I get hold of the Maulspitzer, he is my *kapare* (sacrifice)! Still the business has not turned out so bad as the scoundrels thought it would. Even though we could not open the iron safe, there were plenty of other chests and drawers to empty. But a *Ruech* (curse) may fall upon my *Tate's* (father's) head, if I will give as much as a bad Groschen to any of them."

In this manner the Jew raged for a long time, venting his fury in short broken sentences and curses, while at the same time he busied himself with producing from his pockets sundry and divers things which he had brought from the dwelling of the Geheimerath, and putting them away in some places appropriated for the purpose.

The children had all been awakened, without daring, from fear of their enraged father, to let it be noticed. But when the long Schmuel rattled a well filled purse, little Siegbert in his curiosity could not resist the temptation to raise his head, and look at the movements of his father.

Quickly the long Schmuel observed this motion. "Hah, will yo go to sleep," he cried furiously and distrustfully, "would you cheat your Tate also? I shall break your neck, you little scoundrel!"

Hitherto the Jewess had also been too much frightened, even to utter a syllable. The care of her child, however, restored her speech, hoping thereby to give another direction to the current of her husband's thoughts.

At the same time she expected to get some explanation of the mysterious and incomprehensible result of the expedition. The Major had distinctly told her, that every thing had succeeded; how then was it possible that long Schmuel was at liberty, nay, to all appearances, had not even come in contact with the Major?

"Speak then, and tell me," she said, beginning her inquiries, "what is the cause of all this rage of yours? As yet I know and understand nothing of your speeches. When you had entered the window of the side building along with Eel-eye and Schmerles, I withdrew, so as not to excite any suspicion among the neighbours. What happened then? I thought all was so arranged that it must go right."

"And all would have gone right," growled the Jew, "if the devil had not had his hand in the game. Who can tell how a thing may turn out! I never had so much labour with a Masematten, but all in vain; devil may take me, if there is justice upon earth."

"Speak out then, and explain," said the Jewess to her husband, whose fury rose as he spoke, "I do not understand you yet."

"Don't I tell you," cried the Jew, "the Maulspitzer, that accursed scoundrel, has spoiled the jackscrew for me. But I will compose myself, speak quietly, and tell you all. With the greatest difficulty, and after breaking several doors, we finally reached the room in which stood the iron safe containing the amount of the great inheritance.

"Schmerles put the jackscrew to the lid, we began to turn, the top already began to raise, I anxiously awaited the moment when my soul should be rejoiced at the sight of the 10,000 Thalers—when suddenly—the jackscrew burst with a noise as if a whole battery had exploded. At the same moment, not far from us, we heard a female voice calling for help, and a man's steps rushing down the stairs. We thought we were betrayed, in a great hurry we gathered our tools, and what else we could find of any value, and climbed down a rope, which Eel-eye had cautiously fastened to the window-frame, thus making our escape through the yard.

"This was lucky for us, for in the hot-house we observed a great commotion, as if several men were struggling there. Immediately afterwards these men came out, through the front door of the house, hurriedly entered a carriage, and drove off.

"This was a strange and remarkable circumstance. Quietly we crept along the wall, climbed back into the next yard, and after waiting here some little time, we regained the street by the way we had come. We again met behind the *Kurfürstenbrücke* near the water, each took his Hellig of the booty, and we next examined the jackscrew. I thought I should have gone distracted with fright and fury; the iron bolt had been withdrawn, and a black painted wooden peg had been put in its place.

"Now, you see, no one but the Maulspitzer has done this, for he envied me the Masematten of 10,000 Thalers; I am a ruined man. A thousand curses upon his head!"

All the Jewess could gather from this narrative was, that some unfortunate exchange must have taken place; but how, in what manner? Spite of all thought and deliberation, she could not imagine how this could have occurred. Anxiously she awaited the dawn of day, hoping to have the mystery solved by the Major. She was glad when the long Schmuel, fatigued from the labour and excitement of the night, finally cast himself down, and declared his intention to endeavour to get a little sleep.

The family might have been asleep a couple of hours, when the Jewess was again awakened by a noise at the door. She rose from her pallet; it seemed to be near break of day. In quiet innocence her three children slept upon the straw beside her; upon a wooden bench, one of the few articles of furniture in the room, lay long Schmuel, in a restless, disturbed sleep. The dim burning oil lamp cast a melancholy light over this scene, where night and morning seemed to struggle for supremacy.

Three distinct knocks upon the door were heard, while the slight scraping of a foot against the threshold was also audible. With a gentle and silent push, the Jewess awakened her husband. Again the same noise was heard. By this Schmuel recognised the signal of his friends, and carelessly opened the door.

His host, the thick Itzig, stood before him, to deliver a letter, which a *chesse* man from Poland had left with him the evening before. Putting his finger to his lips, Itzig cautiously entered the room, after having carefully locked the door behind him.

"I have important news," he began; "yesterday morning the hunchbacked Jobs and his daughter were arrested by the Police."

The Jewess, who had meanwhile laid down again, turned deadly pale. She held it advisable, however, to appear fast asleep.

"What! Jobs?" asked Schmuel, to whom this news seemed not at all agreeable, with an expression of terror and surprise.

"Jobs, hunchbacked Jobs, I tell you;" replied Itzig; "I had a good deal of company in the house last evening, and several of my guests, who themselves had seen the prisoners conducted through the streets, told me all the circumstances."

Frowningly, but in silence, long Schmuel stared before him.

"I thought I would communicate this matter," said Itzig, "as it may be of importance to you. You may now take whatever course you think best."

At these words, the host withdrew as noiselessly as he had come.

"Well, well; misery, pestilence and misfortune, all come at once upon me," cried Schmuel in great rage, after the thick host had left him; "wife, we must leave this city this very day, if possible."

The Jewess did not stir; she seemed fast asleep.

Schmuel's glance next fell upon the letter he held in his hand. "What may be the contents of this?" he muttered; "some new Jobs-message? Well, 'tis immaterial! I must know what it is."

The Jew seated himself by the small window, through which the glimmer of the grey dawn of day made his pale features appear of a still more ashy hue. Carefully he broke the seal, and stared upon the handwriting.

The longer he stared, the more lively and vehement became his movements, till at last, driven by the Oriental, passionate susceptibility of his mind, he burst out into words, and began reading the letter aloud to himself.

"—The Prince, as I know from positive advices, is at present on a journey through Germany, most probably is even in Berlin, to continue his search and inquiry. As I hear, he is in close connexion with a certain Major von Steinfort, the same who arrested thee upon his domains.

"From divers reasons, I think it not at all improbable, that thy steps are watched; be careful and prudent my son, that this accursed people of *Gojim*, (christians,) may not out-manœuvre thee.—The moment of revenge has not yet come. The Prince Prominsky must also fall, even as his wife and child before him have been swept from our path. When with him the last scion of the house has disappeared, then and only then, can we safely produce the abducted Prince, and claim the succession of the throne for him.

"Though at present, the Prince Prominsky searches the world for his brother, for the purpose, it is said, of resigning the reins of government to the first-born, he would be compelled to think better of it, if he discovered his long lost brother to be a *thief*.

"Our influence over him, however, would certainly be cut off. We must therefore have free play, that our revenge and our advantage may go hand in hand, and that we may gain our end without obstruction. But this can only be accomplished by elevating him, whom we made one of us, whom we have cast into the lowest abyss of misery, upon whose back the lash of the Police has left its marks, to the rank of princely master over these *Gojims*, and thus compel him to have mercy upon our own people

"Then, Schmuel, and only then, can we take revenge upon this entire race, which murdered thy wife and butchered thy children, which slayed my poor father, and chased me with bloodhounds; which persecuted and prescribed us, even from our cradle, upon all our ways and steps. Let them scorn us then, because we are descended from foreign blood; we have shown them in their own accursed blood, that their most elevated and high-born race, is no better than the lowest, meanest of the children of Israel.

"To day, the very day I write this, is the anniversary of thy wife's death, and of that of thy children, for whom thou hast probably just said *Kadisch* (a Hebrew prayer for the souls of departed relatives.) Remember, then, and let me remind thee of that oath, which thou hast sworn to me, upon thy *cheilik l'aulim habbe*, (share of eternal salvation,) to assist me indefatigably, in our great work of revenge.

"Arise, then! I call upon thee, Schmuel, to arise! Seek everywhere for the Prince, and shouldst thou find him, have a care that he is soon swept from our path. My hand is trembling, and my eye is growing dim, but before I can leave this world, I must experience one more joy—the feeling of satisfied revenge.

"Thou knowest that, in one respect, I am but half a Jew, for gold gives no joy to my soul; but thou also knowest that, in another point, I am thrice a Jew, for I must have revenge upon my mortal ememy.

"*Masel and Broche* (Fortune and blessings) upon thee. May the God of our forefathers guide thee on thy ways. Farewell.

"Thy friend,
"MANASSE."

When he had read to the end, the long Schmuel, pale as death, rested his head upon his hand. Terrible remembrances, like demoniac apparitions, had risen before him, and he seemed lost in his thoughts.

Suddenly he started wildly up, and cast a penetrating glance towards the pallet where lay his wife. She slept quietly and soundly. "I was incautious," he muttered to himself, "but she has heard nothing. Yet I remember just now, she was a *long* time in the power of the Major; her cunning might have enabled her to make her escape much sooner!"

Again the thief cast a furious, revengeful glance towards the couch of his wife. "Woman," he growled in a hollow tone of voice to himself, "woman, excite not my suspicions! Do not intrude in my great work of revenge, or I shall forget thou art the mother of my children."

He took up the letter, which in his excitement he had dropped upon the floor, and tore it to small atoms, which he carefully burned by the still glimmering oil-lamp. He then believed himself perfectly secure, took his hat, and, without casting another look upon his family, disappeared through the door.

His morning prayers, which he never neglect-ed, called him to the Synagogue; this time he intended to offer an extra prayer, that his plans of revenge against the Prince might succeed. Immediately after prayers, he intended to be upon his road, and discover, if possible, where the Prince could be found.

Trembling in every limb, the Jewess arose from her pallet. After the entrance of Itzig she had feigned to be asleep, without exactly knowing why she did so. Instinctively she had expected that in this manner, she would learn something of importance, and she was not mistaken.

A terrible light had dawned upon her. Her husband had always appeared to her much too young to be one of those who had abducted the Prince in his early youth. Yet it became evident now, that he knew of the existence of the Prince, that he was deeply interested in his fate, and that he entertained terrible plans for the future. The elder Prince was a *thief*—the life of Prince Prominsky was sought after—her own life seemed in danger—the poor woman almost lost her senses with unspeakable terror.

For a long time, she endeavoured to devise a way or a plan to counteract these terrible machinations. But she was utterly at a loss. One plan seemed still more impracticable than the other. At last she concluded, at any and every risk, to go to her friends, the Major and the Prince, and to inform them of all she knew. Besides this, she was anxious to obtain an explanation of the strange result of last night's expedition.

She gently kissed her slumbering children, carefully covered them with a few more clothes, cast one more look of the most intense maternal love upon her offspring, and left the garret.

CHAPTER XVI.

THE GAMING PARTY.

THE Referendarius von Birkheim was a man, such as are often produced by the fashionable city life of Berlin—men, who live respectably, elegantly, nay, even in a brilliant and luxurious style, while the world knows not whence they draw the means to support their extravagance. He was a distant relative of Geheimerath Berthold, to whom, as we have already heard him confess, he owed his present position, as he had lost his parents at an early age, and had been left without any means.

The assistance of the Geheimerath, however, was by no means sufficiently great to support him in his extravagant mode of life, which fact seemed well known to most of his friends.

He occupied a large dwelling in *Behren-street*, which was very handsomely furnished; he dressed with remarkable elegance, attended every public amusement, and even gave the so-called *Garcon-soirees,** which have lately become

* Bachelor's parties, though, as we shall find, ladies were admitted to them.—TRANSLATOR.

fashionable, and at which extravagance is carried to a great degree.

Notwithstanding the circumstance that he depended upon foreign support, Herr von Birkheim had never been particularly industrious in the pursuit of his career, or the establishment of a higher position. He was already thirty odd years of age, without having advanced above the rank of Referendarius of the royal *Kammergericht*. But upon the same principles of ultra politeness or humanity, which in society usually invest the *Auscultator* with the title of Referendarius, and thereby most delicately decree that Auscultator is not a very respectable office or title, our Referendarius had long since been politely honoured with the title of *Assessor*.*

This courtesy seemed the more necessary, as a person of delicate feeling would naturally hesitate at addressing a man of a certain age, and who began to incline somewhat to embonpoint and rotund respectability, by a title which many a youth around him had already obtained for himself.—What an excellent, accommodating thing *bon ton* and elegant fashionable politeness is!

The previous occurrences of this narrative have already thrown some light upon the philosophical views and maxims which governed our friend's life. He was a modern *roué*, in every sense of the word, namely, obliging, smooth, flattering, of prepossessing exterior, but also lascivious, frivolous, faithless and immoral. Without being naturally inclined to do wrong, nay, being even good natured to a certain degree, he neither regarded persons, principles, or circumstances, when his passions or his interests were in question.

Whatever he may have wanted in scientific or literary acquirements, he replaced by his social accomplishments, in which, with good natural gifts, he had attained such a degree of excellence, that his reputation made him a welcome guest in all the most distinguished private circles. Those, in fact, were his only proper and natural sphere, for here the sole object was to make the most of a fleeting hour, and to exchange hollow formalities and compliments for the same commodity.

On the evening of our story, one of the above named *garçon soirées*, attended by both sexes, was to take place at the house of Herr von Birkheim.

During the forenoon he was busy in making the necessary preparations in his rooms, at which labour he was assisted by two hired waiters in black, rather threadbare frocks, loose pantaloons, and faded cravats, the stereotype appearance of these figures in Berlin.

In a small side room stood a *Büffet*, upon which the host, dressed in a velvet morning gown and richly embroidered slippers, was arranging his assortment of wine bottles. The green necks of the Moselle, the yellow and red ones of the French wines, intermixed with the silvery tops of sparkling Hock and Champagne, formed a battery, whose destruction promised much pleasure and revelry.

The confectioner had just sent in his sweet, many-coloured productions, and his two assistants, in white aprons, were busy arranging these in fanciful pyramids on the centre of the Büffet, and forming a Babylonian tower of wines and confectionary. Upon the side-tables stood little baskets, cups, sugar-bowls, and other useful appurtenances of the tea-table. Glasses, plates, and dinner utensils, still remained unpacked in the baskets, in which they had been received. They had been sent from one of those magazines, whose owners hire such things for the occasion, at a certain, very heavy premium.

In the centre rooms and parlours, the hired footmen were busy at their work. One of them had just arranged tables and chairs, obliterated small traces of disorder and unnecessary reminiscences of a bachelor's home, and was busy putting the waxlights into the heavy silver candelabras, which, by particular favour, the Geheimerath Berthold had loaned to increase the splendour of the whole. The other footman, assisted by two men, was fastening a massive bronze chandelier to the ceiling. The Inspector of the theatre, contrary to the orders of the Intendant,* had loaned this chandelier to his friend, the Referendarius, for *a certain pecuniary* consideration. The noise, oaths, and disputes usually accompanying such work, were of course not wanting.

Finally, in the front room, nearest the hall, was that unique being, usually denominated *Scheuerfrau*, (scouring woman), who had been engaged to give additional lustre to the polished floor. The right foot placed upon the brush, both arms tightly braced to her sides, this well known figure, (to Berlinians at least,) danced her peculiar *entrechats* and "double shuffles," over the floor, whilst heavy drops of perspiration rolled from her haggard face.

All these manifold preparations, which were to lend additional lustre and a higher degree of splendour to these elegant apartments, had more or less been brought to an end, when the doorbell was heard to ring with a rapid and authoritative peal. The lady of the brush, who was nearest the entrance, opened it, and a tall, well-formed man, of about the same age as the Referendarius, entered the house.

He was very fashionably, but also tastefully dressed. His greyish blue eyes, and his faded, ash-coloured features, betrayed years of wild dissipation, which most probably had also affected his blonde, and very short "*au mecontent*" cut hair. The face, however, was agreeably relieved, by a strong, particularly handsome moustache, which was also blonde, and covered the entire mouth and very white teeth.

Fastening his lorgnette to his right eye, and

---

* The reader will perceive that *Auscultator, Referendarius* and *Assessor*, are titles of different civil officers, ranking both in honour and emolument one still higher than the other.—TRANSLATOR.

* The Intendant and Inspector of the Royal Theatres, as well as all others employed in theatres, are appointed by the crown, and are considered public officers.—TRANSLATOR.

hastily glancing with a sarcastic smile over the arrangements, the new comer passed without stopping through the suit of rooms, until he arrived at the furthest, the private room of Herr von Birkheim. The latter had just completed his part of the work, and was engaged in giving to the porters of the different articles, the usual *douceur*. Without taking notice of this, the stranger slightly nodded to the master of the house, threw himself upon a sofa, and stretched his spurred feet out at length, whilst he amused himself by playing with and flourishing the elegant little riding-whip which he carried.

The new comer, who thus, in the most *nonchalant*, almost arrogant manner, made his appearance at the house of the Referendarius von Birkheim, was a person who has hitherto remained unknown in our story, *Herr Fischergraf*. We will soon show in what position he stood to the Referendarius, and thereby explain the impolite freedom of his manner.

He was originally the son of a plain citizen, who had followed a simple business, and by industry, perseverance and success, had accumulated considerable wealth. At the early death of his parents, these riches fell into the son's hands, who had, despite their good example, even in his youth, contracted bad habits and morals, and did not inherit any of his parents' virtues.

He now believed himself rich enough, without continuing the honest and simple business of his father; he followed his inclination for gaming and other vices, and in a few years succeeded in spending the very large inheritance which had partly consisted in valuable property, and partly in ready cash. Accustomed to a comfortable, idle and lazy life, without talent and without energy to attempt the earning of a proper livelihood, but one pursuit remained for him, which he understood and passionately loved, namely, gambling. He became a gambler by profession, and gained his subsistence by ruining others, even as he had been ruined himself.

As far as regards his external appearance, we have already alluded to his peculiar talent of making a tasteful toilette, but beyond this, his manners, though these were not quite rustic, yet they could never become patterns of good breeding or politeness. He moved awkwardly, without grace or ease, and conducted himself vulgarly, regardless of persons or positions.

In mental culture he was even more lamentably deficient than in manners. Scarcely possessing the most necessary elementary knowledge, coarse and selfish to excess, accustomed only to such scenes as are presented on wild and dissipated nights of gambling in the lowest circles, he had not even that external tact of manner, which helps to hide ordinary vulgarity. He was particularly remarkable for his broad, real Berlinian vulgar dialect; he mixed and perverted *mir* and *mich** in the most shocking manner. We think

* We have before alluded to the common usage of this perversion of grammar among the lower classes of Berlin.—TRANSLATOR.

that our readers will thank us, if, as far as possible, we translate his slang into better language.

"Well, my little Assessor," began Fischergraf, after the people had left the room, and the door had been carefully closed; "as I see, things remain as we have arranged them for to-night—that's all right! now tell me, is the old fellow sure to come?"

"I suppose you mean Geheimerath Berthold?" inquired the Referendarius, evidently piqued at the unceremonious manner and the insolent familiarity with which the other took a seat by his side, on the sofa; "he has at least promised."

"Then he will keep his word, depend upon it," continued Fischergraf, without taking notice of the other's irritability; "why, he can no more keep away from the *monkey trap*, (Faro box,) than a cat can leave a milk-bowl alone."

"You will please excuse me," replied Birkheim ill-humouredly, "but I really have a great deal left to arrange for to-night."

"Come, come, none of your airs, Master Assessor, as if we were not old and intimate friends. My time is also rather too valuable for chattering it away here, and I did not come to chat. I have brought fresh tools in my pockets, to operate* upon the old miser to-night. You must learn the application of these. Now pay every attention and don't be supercilious."

The Referendarius von Birkheim bit his lips, and thought it advisable to say nothing. Herr Fischergraf produced two small parcels from his coat pocket, and opened them very carefully. They were two packs of apparently new cards, from which he withdrew single cards, and began to spread them before him on the table. After this labour had been completed with great seriousness, attention and silence, the owner picked up single cards and brought them to the light.

"You must take care, my little Assessor," he began, "that the old fellow, as he is in the habit of doing, lets his passion have its course, and takes the Bank. Then you must be careful that these cards are put into his hands; as I have told you yesterday, I have marked them on a system of my own, and consequently a failure of our plan is impossible. The marks are most simple and distinct—just pay attention. The back of the Aces has a dark point at each corner, just in the centre of the blue square. The Kings have a horozintal, the Queens an upright, and the Knaves an angular stroke in the same place; the Tens are marked by an imperceptibly rounded corner at each end. Thus we are sure of twenty cards in the game; to avoid all suspicion, I would go no farther into the lower cards, for this at all events is quite enough. I hope you have understood all?"

"Perfectly," replied the Referendarius, rubbing his hands with joy. His eyes glistened with avarice; at the present turn the conversation had taken, he seemed to feel attachment

* To operate, *verarbeiten*, in German, is a technical term used by Berlin gamblers for false playing.—TRANSLATOR.

enough for his friend, and to forget all his former displeasure.

"You see now; I knew perfectly well that you would soon lose all your ill-humour," continued Fischergraf, "but now remember a few words of advice, which I must give you. In the first place, do not bring out the cards until the game is ready to commence; then have a couple of lamps so placed that the light falls direct upon the hands of the Geheimerath, so that we may easily recognize the backs of his cards; if it is at all possible or practicable, we must both sit directly opposite to him, placing the table lengthways, of course; but again, it would be well to have the remaining players as far as possible away from his right and left. You will easily be able to manage this, by saying that the room at his side is needed by the servants to hand refreshments around. You can do this, I suppose?"

"Oh, certainly," replied Birkheim, who had already gone heart and soul with the gambler.

"So far, so good! Now listen further. At first, we must let the game lightly take its course; the *Freier* (the cheated party) must always be drawn out gently at first, that he may not become shy. Besides this, we must be careful that the *witschen Pointeure* (the uninitiated players) take no particular notice of our fortune, follow our cards, and thus help to "thin the Freier," (pluck the pigeon,) on their own account. Finally, it will be advisable, now and then, to bet on uncertain cards, and if these lose, always to make considerable noise about it. The best mode of doing it, is this: we lose, if possible, on two cards; the third must win a double amount, and this double amount with a paroli is again wagered upon the fourth card, and thus imperceptibly the whole and more is won. I must positively win a great deal of money this night, for that girl *Augusta* costs me a mass of cash. The little nymph has troubled me for a new shawl for a week past, and I have not yet paid for the last costly dress I gave her."

"I fully appreciate your admirable qualities and talents, my dear Herr Fischergraf," said Herr von Birkheim, interrupting the course of the conversation, not without considerable embarrassment, "and I should not wish to be misunderstood by you, if I make a remark, which our mutual interest forces me to make. As you know, I have had the honour of making your first acquaintance at *Fuchsen's* Cafè by the *Reitbahn*, and learned with pleasure that in the saloons of that neighbourhood, you play a most distinguished part. But all different circles have different manners and costumes."

"At the last soirée at the house of the *General-Landschaftsdirektor** von Teichwitz, where I introduced you, and where I presented you to Geheimerath Berthold as *Count Pippi* of *Vienna*, I overheard many remarks about your manners,

your expressions, and particularly about your remarkable Berlin dialect, which disquieted me not a little. I do not know whether you will be able to overcome a few habits, trifling in themselves, but in society regarded as matters of importance, and therefore I would give you my friendly advice, not to arrive here till very late, if possible after eleven, when playing commences, and then to enter as little as possible into conversation. As a count and a stranger, this will not be noticed much; at the utmost, they will believe it eccentricity, which will make you appear the more interesting."

During this long and hesitating speech, Herr Fischergraf had been biting his nails, now in scorn and again in evident annoyance. With a passionate movement he now pushed his hat down upon his forehead. "Harkye, Assessor," he began, "you might have told me all this much more briefly, if you fear that I might drink too much of your Champagne, or destroy too much meat. May the devil take you, with your *bon ton;* if I did not need the money, I would much rather take my girl and go to *Villa Bella*, than to come here. Ten of your much praised and talked about *soirées*, are not worth half as much as a single Grisette-ball."

At these words the gambler started up, and spite of the mitigating exclamations of his friend, hurried angrily away.

That evening, punctual to the hour, we find in the brilliant rooms of the Referendarius von Birkheim, very nearly the same company, which we have already become acquainted with at the house of Geheimerath Berthold.

Above all, we see the Geheimerath himself, the most honoured guest of the feast, surrounded by his female friends, the light-footed children of the dance, the sylph-like Sidonie, the round luxurious Betty, the pert Ninon, the little Antonie, who seemed to own only her single blue velvet dress, Minna, Emily, and whatever else were the names of these fair priestesses of merriment. Besides these, among the invited guests, were the vocalist Amalie, and her opponent, the Baron von Pesth, moreover, the Major von Steinfort and his son the Lieutenant, the Prince Prominsky, whose acquaintance the Referendarius had made in such a peculiar manner, the foppish *Rentier* Wertheim, the serious Doctor Hellmold, and a mass of other persons, whom we are not yet acquainted with.

The usual busy hum, rattling of cups, moving of chairs, running about, laughter, talk, whispering, and all the other customary accompaniments of a large party, as every one of our readers may have witnessed them, prevailed through the rooms.

"Then the Equestrian has positively promised you, my dear Birkheim?" inquired the Geheimerath of his *protegée*. He seemed by this question to continue a conversation in which he was busily engaged with several gentlemen in one corner, who all appeared deeply interested in it.

---

* Another honorary title, as meaningless as it is intranslatable.—*Translator*.

"Certainly, my dear cousin; only yesterday I waited upon her at her hotel, and received the most positive promise from her own lips. She inquired particularly whether you would be of the party, and when I assured her that you would, she consented with an evident, peculiar, and almost fearful joy."

The Geheimerath seemed greatly flattered at this; he took it for granted that his fame as a distinguished patron of the fair sex, had reached the ears of the Equestrian, or that he had perhaps attracted her attention even when he visited the circus.

The Rentier Wertheim burst forth in exclamations of surprise. "How is this? my dear Birkheim! What? this artiste receives you, ay, lets you visit her? I thought that no mortal had yet been thus favoured? The hostess of the green Elephant has sent me off three times already, and I certainly do not look like a beggar." Herr Wertheim here tossed up his head, in his usual way, and mustered in the mirror opposite his remarkably foppish toilet, with a satisfactory blinking and twinkling of the eyes.

"Console yourself, Herr Wertheim," smilingly replied the Referendarius, "to my certain knowledge the lady receives no visits from any gentleman; my good fortune was brought about less from any merit of my own, than through other co-operating circumstances. May I relate the occurrences my dear cousin?" inquired the flatterer of the Geheimerath, certain of the answer he would receive, and adroitly attacking his cousin's weak points.

"Why—I almost fear that it would weary these gentlemen," replied the Geheimerath with hesitation, who, evidently vain and pleased, thought proper to attempt the part of blushing modesty.

The exact meaning of his speech was something like the following: "I do not expect that any body will be wearied or annoyed at it," and this meaning seemed to be the one most universally adopted, for a large number of the party present crowded around the Referendarius, showing the greatest curiosity, and begging him to tell the story.

"It is not very long since," began Herr von Birkheim, "when one evening after dark I left the house of the Herr Geheimerath to go to the theatre. On leaving the door, I observed a small, poorly dressed boy of perhaps six years of age, whose curly, coal-black hair, broad lips and aquiline nose, even by the light of the gas lamp, betrayed his being a descendant of the chosen people of God. After closely examining me for awhile, the boy approached and asked me whether the Geheimerath Berthold lived in the house I had left?"

"I answered him hastily and with indifference in the affirmative, believing that I had some little beggar boy before me. But the urchin followed, and began a perfect cross-examination of me. He asked if I could tell him whether the Geheimerath could be seen privately? what time he would go out? whether he was married, had children, was rich or not? and many more such questions.

"This, at last, attracted my attention, for as you know, a burglary was committed at the house of my cousin not long since,"—at these words the Referendarius blushed slightly, as his eye fell upon the attentive features of Major von Steinfort and Prince Prominsky—"a burglary, as I said, has been committed, and I began to fear that I had a new spy before me.

"You must recollect, my worthy guests, that we find in our tribunals daily examples, where the most experienced thieves use small children, who appear the least suspicious, as spies, to seek out their chances and opportunities for burglaries. I therefore endeavoured to come close to the boy, who had hitherto kept at a certain measured distance; but he still most adroitly kept out of my reach, and then renewed his questions. Thus we manœuvered down one street, and up another, whilst each of us endeavoured to accomplish his object in silence, and without letting the other suspect it.

"At last, just as we turned a corner, a court equipage drove up from the other side, and the suddenness of its approach forced the boy to come close to me. I availed myself of this lucky chance, bounced upon him, and caught him by the coat-collar; but in an instant he had slipped out of his coat, and stood on the opposite side of the street, whilst I held the coat in my hand."

"Thunder!" exclaimed Major von Steinfort, as he turned in his usual blunt manner to Prince Prominsky. "I will wager my life, your Highness, that this was no other than that smooth, adroit rascal, little Siegbert!"

"Why, why, Major, and have you connexions and acquaintances among little, suspicious beggar boys?" cried the fair vocalist Amalie, who, as we know, was fond of disputing with the rough old warrior.

The Major was too much interested in the result of this narrative; the exclamation had carelessly escaped his lips in a moment of surprise, and he preferred not to take up the proferred gauntlet of dispute which his fair antagonist had thrown. He was content, smilingly to threaten her with his finger, and begged the Referendarius to continue his story, and not to notice this interruption.

"I could not, of course, think of pursuing my swift-footed little questioner," continued Herr von Birkheim, "and consequently prepared to keep the little old coat, and walk away with it. But now the boy ran after me, and begged most humbly for the return of his garment, as the intense cold weather most probably tortured him severely. I promised to give him the coat, if he would tell me whence he came, and why he asked all those questions about Geheimerath Berthold.

"After a great deal of useless parley, he finally confessed that a lady, who lived in X—— street, had commissioned him to gain all the necessary replies to the questions he had asked, and had promised him a Thaler reward, if he executed his commission.

" This information still more excited my curiosity ; I thought that I had discovered some new gallant adventure of my cousin, and not only returned his garment to the boy, but, urged by a pardonable curiosity, I promised him double the sum, if he would lead me directly to the lady herself. The boy seemed particularly well pleased with this proposition, told me to follow him, and started off before me to the ' Green Elephant.'

" Arrived at this hotel, he asked me, whether I was willing to give to the lady herself the necessary replies to his questions, and on my promising to do so, he disappeared in the dark entry. Shortly afterwards, he returned, asked for his promised reward, conducted me up stairs, opened a room door, and with the joyous exclamation, ' Now I have earned three Thalers !' he hurried off.

" I entered a comfortably warmed chamber, wherein a lamp threw a brilliant light upon a most artistical confusion, and—imagine if you can, my astonishment—Francisca, our much admired Equestrian, met me."

A universal ah ! of astonishment was heard from the whole company, whilst the Geheimerath smilingly rubbed his hands, and with internal satisfaction observed the envy that was expressed in the features of a number of the gentlemen present.

" Geheimerath !" again exclaimed the old copper-nosed Rentier Wertheim, as he rubbed his immense fashionably curled wig, " Geheimerath, will you never cease to make conquests, and at last allow younger people to have some chances ?"

" Wonder if he counts himself among the younger people ?" inquired the arch Ninon of one of her friends, loud enough to be overheard.

After the auditors had in some measure again relapsed into silence, the Referendarius, at the earnest request of the Prince Prominsky, who had now become his most attentive listener, continued his story.

" I must confess, that this most unexpected of all appearances caused me some confusion. The artiste, however, met me without hesitation, begged me to take a seat, and requested me at the same time, not to consider her wishes as a freak of womanish humour, much less as a species of stupid and shameless importunateness, such as ladies of her rank and station were frequently guilty of. After asking me briefly and concisely about my connexion with the Berthold family, she told me a very long story about a certain Mr. Berthold who, in former, more prosperous times, had stood in intimate connexion with her family, and by many and important services rendered to them, had established an everlasting claim upon her gratitude. In the course of her narrative, she mentioned names and circumstances which had never reached my ears before, and of which my cousin also knows nothing.

" The origin of all this must consequently be a real and most mysterious and strange mistake, or the whole story is an invention, serving merely as a mask for becoming acquainted with Geheimerath Berthold, of whose well known gallantry and liberality the lady may have heard. Be this, however, as it may, Francisca showed a great desire to become personally known to my cousin, and praised her good fortune which by a lucky accident had introduced her to me, as according to her story, no other means had remained for her, but to send a boy belonging to the circus company, and induce him by a promised reward, to endeavour to learn something about the object of her anxiety.

" As the Geheimerath," he continued smiling, " had no objection to renew an interesting acquaintance, or most probably to make a new one, I have invited the Equestrian here to night, and received her promise to come. I can assure you, my worthy friends, that this really magnificent woman loses on nearer acquaintance, nothing of the great interest she excites when seen on horseback. She converses well, is intelligent, and what is perhaps the most remarkable for a lady in her position, she knows how to assume such a serene dignity in her demeanor, that any bold approach would immediately be coldly and seriously repelled."

The latter part of this report created new excitement in the company. The ladies looked at each other with sarcastic smiles, and re-arranged their toilette before the mirrors, so as not to be thrown too far into the background by a rival, who was evidently not a little dangerous. The gentlemen formed small chatting and joking groups, and frequently consulted their watches, to ascertain how long the much-expected fair one would yet let them wait.

" In reality, you are a man greatly to be envied," observed the sweet Baron von Pesth : " wherever you wander, wherever you go, the fair sex pursues you ; for who is there among us old practitioners, who can doubt your having made a conquest from your box-seat at the circus, a conquest too, of a lady who resorts to the most refined intrigues, only to give herself to you ?"

" That is, to draw occasionally upon his long purse," whispered little Minna, rising upon her toes to reach the ear of her tall neighbour. " I believe, Betty, that this woman may come most inopportune to all of us, and I really wish we were rid of her again."

" Well, well, all that can be managed," replied the other, with great self-sufficiency, " let us first see how she will conduct herself."

" Yes, yes," cried all the rest of the little conspirators in one voice, " we must soon get rid of her again."

" In reality, my dear Major," resumed the Prince Prominsky an interrupted conversation in another part of the room, " I am positively anxious to become acquainted with this lady. She certainly did not appear to me like a wanton. In that forehead so proud, so nobly formed, other and deeper plans are hidden. Mark my words, she has to carry out some other object with this foolish, amorous old fop."

"We shall see, your Highness," replied the gray warrior; "I certainly will not deny that the wild horsewoman has excited the greatest interest even in an old grey soldier as myself."

"No, no!" whispered *Commerzienrath Moritzfeld* to *Justiz-director von Derking*, "that old sexagenarian has immense luck. I tell you, in his younger days he has had as many amours as I have lost points at Faro, and that, you know, says no little. But not satisfied with this, even now, women pursue him as one of the most desirable of men. All the pretensions of the male part of our city's youth to wealth and beauty, are of no avail, and these women actually scorn the devotions of others, to throw themselves into his arms. Ridiculous, is it not?"

"It is so," answered the other, as he hid his faded, meaningless face still deeper behind his white, shining cravat, and the two immense points of his collar, "that story of eternal gratitude towards the Geheimerath sounds most ridiculous; people now-a-days are not so particularly grateful, least of all, a handsome circus-rider. The cunning, intriguing woman has learned that the old sinner is easily gulled and bleeds freely, and Birkheim, who knows perfectly well how he can ingratiate himself with his old cousin, earns something as a go-between. *Voilà tout.* But all my limbs are tired out, from this long standing and listening, so if you please, we will take a seat near that punch-bowl yonder."

Thus, the most contradictory judgments and opinions were formed, yet nearly all, more or less, agreed in that *one* position, which must appear as the hardest, the most unkind and unjust. When we observe the acts and movements of the so-called good society—and who is there of our readers, that is totally unacquainted with them?—we must almost arrive at the direct opposite of our formerly expressed opinion, namely, that man is bad by nature. Not one of all these gaudily dressed ladies and titled gentlemen had the remotest suspicion of that which brought the Equestrian to their gay saloon, with a bitter, bleeding heart. None of them knew, what our readers must have long since surmised, namely, that he, who once breathed the first poisonous breath of pestilence into her innermost soul, was now the most respected, honoured, and brilliant guest of their party!

The Geheimerath Berthold revelled in a sea of delight. We know that woman was his Alpha and his Omega, that lascivious triumphs over female hearts were the only font of all his pleasure. The nobler germ of woman's soul still remained unknown to him, nor did he dream of moral or virtuous feelings or sentiments in any woman's breast. Thus, he also believed, as we have above indicated, and believed firmly, that the communication of the Equestrian to the Referendarius was utterly groundless. His opinion was nearly the same, as that generally believed by the rest of the company, with the exception,

that he was vain enough to attribute a great part of his success to his own personal attractions, and not merely to his money. Apparently, however, he seemed to think that the object was only some more or less indifferent acquaintance, who might have played a part in former, now forgotten occurrences of his life, or that the whole adventure merely rested upon a mistake. Under the mask of this harmless and indifferent view, he enjoyed the more highly the consciousness of a quiet gratification and of a highly satisfied vanity.

Meanwhile the hour of tea had passed, and the enervating product of China, with its rattling cups, had disappeared. The productions of Stehely and Jostey's,* upon small glass plates, went the round of the rooms in company of delicious Ananas punch, thus filling up the interim between tea and supper, according to the inviolable laws of fashionable kitchen regulations. Still the Equestrian had not arrived, and already all kind of anxious cares were uttered by one party, whilst another slightly began to show malicious satisfaction. It was particularly the Geheimerath and the Prince, who inwardly felt greatly disquieted, though as we well know, from very different motives and inward feelings. At last—

A carriage rattled up to the house, almost at the same moment the door bell was violently rung, and a strong, well sounding female voice asked the servant who opened, loud enough for the greater part of the company to hear: "Does Herr Referendarius von Birkheim reside here?"

The new comer could not have been long occupied by taking off her hat or cloak, for immediately upon the affirmative answer of the servant, the doors flew open, and the tall, majestic figure of Francisca, the Equestrian, entered the room.

It is difficult to describe the impression produced by her sudden appearance. That imperial figure which had already ripened from the gentle blossom of the maiden into the graceful perfection of womanhood, overlooked proudly and commandingly, the whole array of women. A pair of dark black eyes burned beneath a marble forehead; regularly formed cheeks, momentarily overspread, as if by sudden excitement, with a dark incarnate hue, bloomed by the side of full fresh lips, and a brilliant, nobly formed neck moved easily and gracefully upon a full, snowy bosom. The glossy black hair flowed in rich locks freely around the entire head, and was only restrained upon the forehead by a small golden clasp. The latter was the only ornament which the artiste wore, who proved her exquisite taste by dispensing with the ornaments of earthly metals. Her most perfect form was covered by a valuable, but very simple robe of dark velvet, which beautifully displayed the brilliant whiteness of the neck, and the finely shaped arms, whilst it fitted closely enough to show the faultless symmetry of her graceful figure.

* Celebrated confectioners at Berlin.

Thus she entered with the grace and majesty of an Empress, a rich, full, blooming beauty. And yet, the sensation which she created was one, more of silent, astonished admiration, than of pure attractiveness. A dark, fearful fire burned in those eyes, upon that forehead was the impress of power and masculine spirit, and scorn and inexpressible contempt for the whole human race played about the corners of that well shaped mouth. This was not a woman for love; it was an Amazon-queen, created only to master the foaming horse, by her wild, daring courage.

The artiste had advanced a few steps with easy grace towards the centre of the saloon, when she stopped, and her earnest glance searched through the rooms. Her wild, boldly pencilled eyebrows rolled darkly, as if in anger at her tardy reception.

The deep silence that ensued on her arrival, had, however, attracted the attention of the host, who thought that something new must have occurred. He now observed the just arrived guest, and quickly hastened towards her, to present her to his company. The gentlemen all pressed *en masse* after him, and around the beauteous guest, who scarcely deigned to bestow a glance or passing notice upon all these devoted admirers, but apprently anxious, asked for Geheimerath Berthold.

Herr von Birkheim hastened to comply with her wishes, and conducted her to the middle room, where that gentleman then was. The Geheimerath met her with all the amiable affability of a refined and worldly man; in a well set and polished speech, he expressed his pleasure at making her personal acquaintance, although he doubted that he had ever before experienced the happy feeling of her presence or personal acquaintance, as he could never have forgotten or could forget so great a pleasure.

At the sight of her seducer, for that was the Geheimerath Berthold, the strong, masculine woman had turned deadly pale; his last words, however, brought the dark red hue of rage again upon her face. She seemed to fight a terrible internal struggle, and to endeavour to quiet wild remembrances by the power of her determined will. At last, her presence of mind and determination gained mastery over the storm of passion, which, of course, had been observed by several, but which by some was believed to be assumed, and by none rightly understood.

"Yet," she began with the seductive smile of a Calypso, "I must necessarily have seen you somewhere, even if you have never lived in L—— as your cousin Herr von Birkheim assures me, and consequently could not be the former benefactor of my family, who lived there. Were you not once, in former years, Assessor in the small town of B—— ?"

"In B——? Certainly!" replied the Geheimerath, not without some astonishment.

"You see then I must still know you. You there had an acquaintance with a young girl, who had come to the place to seek an aunt, but only came in time to follow her to her grave."

"Yes, yes, I remember," began the old Fawn with a smile, which meant to be very expressive. "she afterwards suddenly disappeared from the place."

A dark cloud overspread Francisca's face, and her teeth convulsively bit her lips. But it was not a second, before she again stood before him, with her most enchanting smile, which rose like an April sun through a heavy passing cloud.

"All sorts of things were at that time said about you, Herr Geheimerath," she observed in a merry humour, playing as it were, with the very tortures of her own soul.

"Slanders, all slanders, my dearest," replied Berthold laughingly, but in a tone which was meant to indicate directly the opposite. "But just tell me, how you came to know all this so well, for I really do not remember ever to have seen you?"

Another dark cloud overspread Francisca's handsome face. "At the time, when the just-mentioned affair was the great subject of town gossip, I was for a few days at B——, on a visit to an intimate school-friend, who was married and resided there, and at that time, I also saw you once at a public ball. As your name had important connexions with my family, though these connexions are, as I find, unknown to you, and have reference to a different person, still the circumstances remained impressed on my memory. Perhaps the tragical conclusion of the affair may have contributed no little to impress it on my memory, for as I learned, that young girl had shortly afterwards, by some cause, been driven to despair, and had sought relief in a watery grave."

Francisca had given a peculiar intonation to her last words. Bold, commanding, and majestic, she stood before the Geheimerath, whose eyes, before the burning fire of her glances, sought abashed the ground. A deep silence prevailed through the company; painfully embarrassed, all looked upon the Equestrian, who proudly folded her arms, and like an angry avenging angel, with mocking coldness observed the effects of her words.

But in one moment that wonderful and terrible woman was again changed. Her arms fell languidly by her side, and an indescribable loveliness suddenly overspread her blooming face. Approaching nearer to the victim of her humour, she gently placed her hand upon his shoulder, as looking into his faded, pale face, with soft liquid glances, she gently said: "I would not awaken dim and unpleasant remembrances in your heart, nor thereby lessen to myself the pleasure of an acquaintance which I have only just gained through a happy similarity of names. Excuse me, the judgment of the million is so often wrong and unjust."

The Geheimerath was in extacies at this language, and frivolous voluptuary as he was, the artiste soon, by these her well calculated proceedings, had entangled him in her nets. With the most attentive gallantry he conducted her to the *Büffet* close by, to drink a bumper, to a happy continuance of the happily begun acquaintance. With a most expressive and meaning smile the Equestrian pledged him in this toast.

Prince Prominsky had observed all the just related occurrences with a fixed and immoveable eye. Not a syllable, not a movement of Francisca had escaped him.

His keen intellect and his well-practised knowledge of the world had soon convinced him, that no common wanton stood before him, and that beneath the mask of the usual arts and lures of women, the artiste was playing another and a deeper game. It was certain that she knew a great deal of the Geheimerath, much more perhaps than was good or safe for that gentleman to have known. The great interest which the daring Equestrian had already at the circus excited in the mind of the fiery Pole, was in no small measure increased by these new discoveries. A supernatural and inexplicable something attracted him towards this wonderful woman, who was adored and admired by the men, and whose appearance even compelled the scandalous tongues of the women to remain silent. He could not believe that this marble bosom should be without a heart, and he fancied, that through the dark glances of that eye he could penetrate to the bottom of a soul, and there discover a much abused, and consequently peevish and fretful, but highly gifted mind.

Who could blame the Prince for thus reasoning? do not flames draw even the *Nachtfalter** into their devouring glow! And the Prince was not a capricious being, but a strong minded, thinking man, nay, what he thought, might fundamentally have been an incontrovertible truth.

The Prince was a handsome, well made person, in the very bloom of manhood. His aquiline nose, high rounded forehead, and splendid beard, gave a most noble and *distingué* appearance to his browned features, which gained no little interest by the peculiarly enthusiastic looks of the *high born Pole*.

His tall figure moved easy and gracefully, uniting knightly pride with attentive and cavalierly gallantry. He was a Prince, richly endowed in mind and wealth, handsome, and a bachelor—what more could there be necessary to engage the hearts of women in his favour. Certainly nothing! The prince had made many conquests, had enjoyed plenty of triumphs, and many a brilliant eye met his with most friendly and inviting glances to-night; but his looks met all with indifference, and in astonishment at himself, he confessed to his own heart, that he had never been so deeply affected as he was now, by the appearance of the Juno-like figure of this, according to aristocratic conception, vulgar, low, circus rider.

As soon as politeness and convenience permitted him, he endeavoured to reach the vicinity

* A large nocturnal butterfly.

of the Equestrian, for the purpose of being presented to her by the Referendarius von Birkheim.

The interest he took in her seemed suddenly to have become reciprocal, for the artiste, who before, had with marked indifference overlooked the distinguished person of the Prince as well as that of all the other guests, at the mention of his name changed colour, and a slight tremour passed over her. A ray of joy overspread her features, and showed that a pleasant and much desired chord had been touched in her bosom.

She quickly entered into a most lively conversation, such as she had not seemed capable of before, and by her brilliancy of spirit at first, produced upon the Prince a state of speechless astonishment, then a feeling of increasing delight. Both parties soon seemed to have forgotten all the rest of the company around them, which pleased many of the observers, but none more than the Rentier Wertheim, who secretly prophesied to himself, that that old fool, the Geheimerath, was completely " cut out."

The hour for supper had meanwhile arrived, and the company disposed itself, without much ceremony, around the different tables, which had quickly been arranged by the hired servants in attendance. We must confess that the Referendarius had gone to no small expense; the most costly and delicate viands were served, and the finest wines sparkled on the board. With the most perfect ease and *abandon*, which is sometimes found in these circles in Berlin as well as in the provinces, the company enjoyed the pleasures of the table; all the attendants were kept busily employed in replacing the empty dishes by fresh ones, and waiting on all the guests. The most lively of all the parties was around the large table which was placed in the centre of the room, beneath the large borrowed chandelier.

Here the Geheimerath Berthold, Prince Prominsky, Major Steinfort, Rentier Wertheim, and a few others, had taken their seats around the Equestrian, who entered with all of them simultaneously into a lively dispute, and by her lively wit and sarcasm as often wounded as delighted these gentlemen. The lively spirit of the reigning star soon diffused itself to every nook and corner of the room, where the young ladies began to recover from their first fright, and were urged to increased liveliness and merriment by the foaming and sparkling wines. Already many jokes began to be heard on all sides; toasts and unsuccessful speeches gave place to songs, sentiments and anecdotes; glasses were broken, laughter, mirth,—in short, a degree of merriment prevailed, that could not have been more perfect or hearty, even at the nuptials of Canaan.

Suddenly the joys of the table were interrupted by a noisy dispute in the entry, where a footman had been placed for the reception and watching of the wardrobe.

The Referendarius von Birkheim, who might have suspected the cause, hastened out and found his honourable friend, Herr Fischergraf, in actual altercation with the footman. Fischergraf had worshipped too devoutly at the shrine of Bacchus, which was very evident, and partly by this, partly by his particularly late arrival, had given the footman sufficient reason to doubt whether he belonged to the number of invited guests. These doubts were increased when Fischergraf obstinately insisted in the uncivil request of being admitted into the saloon in his cloak, alleging as a reason, that only a short time previous, another cloak of his, had been stolen from a wardrobe. Moreover, the footman had obstinately refused to admit a female companion of Fischergraf, whose character he knew from his former position as waiter at *Villa bella*, and whom he consequently, according to his simple judgment, considered as a person totally inadmissible to the present aristocratic company.

Both parties were warmly arguing this important point of difference with hand and mouth, when the third party, the Referendarius, made his appearance.

"Bravo! good! my little Assessor, that you came yourself," cried Fischergraf; "this scoundrel here will not believe that I come so late to save your champagne; the stupid rascal would even send me back; just oblige me and send the blockhead to the devil."

The unsteady movements, the flushed face and uncertain speech of his friend, soon told the Referendarius the position of things. This placed him in no small embarrassment, and he could plainly perceive that gentle means were the only ones he dared trust himself to apply.

"My dear Fischergraf," he began in the most friendly tone, at the same time motioning his servant to be quiet, "you are excited. This is most probably a misunderstanding, so have the kindness to lay off your cloak, follow me, and join the company, who are already expecting you."

"What is this!" cried Fischergraf noisily, "you, too, wish me to lay off my cloak? No, no, I won't do that, for it is quite a new one, and only last week my other was stolen out of the wardrobe in the "*König-street*." Do you want me to lose this also?"

Herr von Birkheim knew well, that his friend in his present state of intoxication would not bear contradiction, and he reluctantly found himself forced to yield the point, let him have his will, and thus avoid further altercation and uproar. He was just in the act of taking Herr Fischergraf by the arm, so as to give him if possible an upright position, when his eye fell upon the abovenamed lady, who had remained cloaked and bonnetted by the side of the door, and had watched the whole scene with a certain degree of mischievous pleasure.

"Who is the woman yonder?" he inquired of the ward-robe keeper, believing that it was most probably a servant who had arrived to take her mistress home.

"That is my *Augusta*," cried Fischergraf, again growing furious, "a devilish fine girl,

whom that rascal wanted to send off also. You know her now, Assessor, and she shall come along, for she has been with me all the evening. Thunder! what could the fellow mean, by refusing to admit such a capital girl! Come here, my dear, and kiss me."

The Referendarius thought he would sink to the ground with terror. This was too bad; the drunken plebeian had brought a common Grisette, and requested her admission into his select, aristocratic circle.

"My dear friend," he remonstrated, "yes, I know Augusta, and I know she is a most charming girl; but only think of it, her toilette, her appearance, and her manners! What will they say in the saloon?"

"What will they say?" cried Fischergraf even louder and more furious than before, "why nothing. They dare say nothing, or I will teach them better. Her manners? They are good enough, she needs not to alter them, and as to toilette, harkye, Assessor, she has a better toilette than all of them in there."

At these words, Fischergraf pulled the cloak from the girl, and Herr von Birkheim observed, with some degree of satisfaction, that she wore a very elegant silk dress, which looked remarkably well upon the fresh, full and fair figure of the handsome girl.

"Now look," bawled Fischergraf, "and if you are not satisfied now, we will both go away again, and you may alone operate on the old fellow. I shall go to Fuchs's Coffee-house, for there also is some play to-night; but first you will have to give up my cards."

Terror striken, Birkheim looked around, to observe if any one had overheard the latter part of his worthy friend's speech. The increasing drunkenness and excitement of the gambler made him now fear an exposure of their most important secrets, and he consequently concluded as the wisest plan, to submit to everything. He therefore merely reminded the furious gambler, that his name here was *Count Pippi*, and then, with the most desperate resignation, led him and his Augusta into the saloon.

The entrance of the strangers, which, particularly on the part of Herr Fischergraf, was made with considerable noise, attracted the general attention of the assembled company. The gentlemen raised their lorgnetts, to stare at the remarkable pretty Grisette, and the ladies tittered at the eccentric idea of the stranger entering among them in a large fur cloak.

Birkheim, however, quickly endeavoured to cut short all these reflections, by the loud announcement of "The Count Pippi and the Countess, his sister, from Vienna." By this introduction he of course obtained an immediate acknowledgment from his guests of the equal or superior rank and station of the new comers, with their own. He perfectly well knew, that this announcement would have a better effect than anything else he could do, since in personages of such rank, matters would easily be overlooked, which would be considered unpardonable crimes in those of lower station.

And in reality, the acknowledgment of equal birth proved to be absolutely necessary to save the host's and guest's character, as the latter immediately threw his cloak upon a chair, thereby upsetting and breaking a dozen glasses, whilst Augusta, placing her arms akimbo, burst into a loud fit of laughter at her pseudo-brother's awkwardness. Under all circumstances, it was most fortunate for the uncouth, vulgar pair, that the champagne had in a great measure dimmed the powers of observation and judgment of most of the guests, who could only discover, that Count Pippi might be a very amiable, as he was a very handsome *roué*, and that his sister must be a fascinating, lively lady; had the company been perfectly sober, these conclusions would probably have been widely different. To avoid, however, all further danger of exposure, Herr von Birkheim gave the signal to rise from supper, by which movement the company must again be mixed, and form into different small groups.

Shortly after supper the play was to commence. This was the regular finale of the parties, which these persons, particularly the Geheimerath, visited, as nearly all of them were passionately fond of *Faro*, and the Geheimerath, who considered himself an accomplished player, was at all times a ready and willing banker. The preparations for gaming now began to be made, by the removal of all the smaller tables, and arranging a single and large one for the play.

Herr Fischergraf possessed that very remarkable and peculiar faculty, which nearly all professional gamesters share with him, namely, to pass from a state of great inebriety to a certain degree of sober gravity, as soon as cards made their appearance at a table. The greater and ruling passion for play then awoke, and, as it were, conquered all minor inclinations, which were only allowed to gain supremacy in leisure moments. Certainly, the fact, that gaming was his only, his sole profession and means of existence, gave to this psychological phenomenon an additional support. It was easily to observe, though the present company failed to notice it, that though somewhat exalted and awkward, he conducted himself with quietness, and the very peculiarity of this contradiction, was finally looked upon as wit and spirit by these wine-heated heads. Herr von Birkheim, who, being the host, had remained the most sober, and, consequently, was the closest observer, gradually felt a heavy anxiety leave his mind, and began to breathe more free.

"It gives me great pleasure to meet you again, Count Pippi;" began the Geheimerath with a smile to the gambler, "from the last party we played together, you still owe me a heavy *revenge*."

"Well, well, be not backward then, and take it,' replied the pseudo-count rather bluntly.

"Yes, yes, Sir Count, be careful," interrupted the *Kammerjunker* von Stölzel*, "you have one of our best players to deal with."

Herr Fischergraf seemed to consider this remark exceedingly droll. He stroked his moustache with an air of pleasant indifference, and burst into a loud horse-laugh, when he observed, that the Geheimerath received this compliment with a friendly, self-sufficient nod.

"After all, this fellow is an uncouth ruffian," grumbled the Kammerjunker, as he withdrew with a fiery red face.

The table was now ready for play, covered with the usual green cloth, and sufficiently lighted with lamps. The gentlemen began to take their seats around it, and with earnest faces to sort the cards they held in their hands. Behind their chairs and partly leaning upon them, the ladies had ranged themselves, some to bet occasionally on a card themselves, and others in the expectation of seeing this done by their several admirers, from whose winnings they expected to draw their share.

Soon the heavy purses lay upon the table, and already the gold glimmered temptingly upon the dark ground,—*King Faro* was about to assume his terrible reign, the supremacy of unfettered and wild passion!

After everything had been thus far arranged, Herr von Birkheim, as if suddenly remembering something he had before forgotten, hurried to the sideroom to bring the ominous packs of cards, which Herr Fischergraf had given him. With a friendly "good luck," he handed them to his cousin, and then took his seat directly opposite, and by the side of his most worthy partner.

Slowly and carefully the Geheimerath turned back the cuffs of his coat and shirt-wrists, stretched out both arms at full length, as if to loosen the muscles, and took up one of the packs, offering it to his neighbour to cut. A deep silence ensued, and nothing but the monotonous, technical phrases were now heard through the room.

"*Le roi en bas*," cried the banker, turning the pack he held in his hand, and holding the bottom card to the light.

"*Faites vôtre jeu.*" Quickly the cards of the several players were laid on the table, and covered with gold, silver and paper-money.

"*Le jeu est fait.*"

"*Rien ne va plus.*"

The players hurried to lay their last cards down upon the table, and cover them here and there with more gold.

The banker now loudly proclaiming the names of the cards he turned up, and then began to play to the right and to the left before him: "*Dix et trois; Huit et valet.*"

"*Valet a gagné!*" observed a voice at the other side of the table.

The Geheimerath cast a glance to the place, and without losing another word, sent two Frederic d'or by an expert toss of the right hand to the place.

---

* *Kammerjunker*, another unmeaning title.—Transl.

"*Dix et Madame*," continued the same monotonous voice.

"*Dix a perdu*," cried another person, pushing his gold, with a very slight, subdued malediction, towards the Geheimerath, who drew it in with the same *sang froid* as before.

"*Roi et onze.*"

"*Deux et quatre, cinq et as*," continued the same indefatigable voice.

Suddenly, Fischergraf, who had hitherto, leaning both elbows upon the table, followed with lynx eyes the motions of the banker's hands, jumped up. "*Attention!*" he cried, "stop an instant, I shall make a game." Quickly he selected the King from the cards he held in his hands, placed it before him, and pointing to it with the first finger of his right hand, he exclaimed: "Twenty Frederic d'or on the King."

The banker continued to turn: "*Valet et —— roi.*"

"The King has won," cried Fischergraf, exultingly, without taking his eye off the cards, "go ahead, sir, I will *paroli* this time."

The Geheimerath continued:

"*As et neuf, Madame et —— roi.*"

"That's it, hand it over," said Fischergraf, as he pulled the sixty gold pieces towards himself.

At the same moment, the Referendarius puts ten Frederic d'or upon the Knave.

The banker continued to turn: *Cinq et —— valet.*" The Knave had won.

"But, gentlemen, you do play with the most wonderful luck against me," observed the Geheimerath with a forced smile, as he paid out the gold, and at the same time swallowed a glass of champagne. "If this continues to go on so, my bank will be broken in a very short time."

Behind the chair of the Geheimerath stood the Equestrian. At the last words of the Geheimerath she fixed her burning glance upon the Referendarius, as if she would penetrate to the very bottom of his soul. Trembling and abashed he drew the money towards himself. He felt that the mysterious stranger had observed his villainy. In vain he sought to escape the burning eye which the lady steadily, but in silence, had fixed upon his hand. He dared not again attempt to play a card, and Fischergraf had the field all to himself.

Among all the gentlemen present, there was but one, Lieutenant von Steinfort, son of Major von Steinfort, who had taken no share or interest in the play. Whether his father disliked it, or whether he was not in funds, or not in a playing humour, in short, he would not play, and had passed his time with the ladies, which certainly was not a very difficult task for so handsome, well-bred and intelligent a young man as he was. He was now leisurely strolling about the furthest rooms, somewhat annoyed and ill-humoured from want of amusement, when his eye fell upon the so called Countess Pippi, who had sunk into a gentle slumber upon the sofa. The Lieutenant began to feel a great interest in

that fresh, finely formed brunette, with cheeks as blooming as he had not often found them in the saloons of Berlin. To awake her, he endeavoured to make an accidental noise, and soon his efforts met with success.

The Countess yawned, stretched herself, rose up and stared at the Lieutenant in stupified astonishment.

"Pardon me, gracious Countess, if I disturb you," began the Lieutenant. "You are a stranger here, and may find this tedious. Will you allow me to endeavour and entertain you a little?"

The Countess opened her eyes still further, but instead of an answer, placed her handkerchief before her face and burst into loud laughter.

Lieutenant Steinfort felt not a little embarrassed at this very strange behaviour. He was unable to discover any reason for it, and felt very much inclined to show that he was offended.

"Will you please to inform me of the cause of your sudden and remarkable merriment, most gracious Countess?" he inquired, rather abruptly.

The lady withdrew her head from her pocket handkerchief, looked stealthily at him sideways, and burst into renewed peals of laughter.

The young Lieutenant now grew really angry; he believed that the stranger thought proper to make fun of him, and rose to take his departure. The Countess then called after him the following speech, the dialect and pronunciation of which was neither that of Vienna, nor a courtly or aristocratic one:

"Pray, where are you running to? Why don't you remain with me? do remain, for I am almost afraid to be here alone."

Steinfort turned back in the greatest astonishment, which must have been so plainly expressed in his features, that it could not escape his companion's observation. At least she quickly and satisfactorily solved the riddle.

"Stuff and nonsense, all this about Countess Pippi," she began, laughingly. "I have never in my life been a Countess from Vienna, so don't let them make a fool of you. I am a Berlinian to the backbone, go out sewing through the day, and amuse myself in the evening as best I can, with my *Pousseur* (lover)."

The lieutenant could scarcely recover from his astonishment. The natural beauty, freshness, and candid honesty of the girl, appeared quite attractive in his eyes.

"You are no Countess from Vienna?" he asked again, still doubting his ears, "and your brother, most probably, is not from Vienna, nor a Count either?"

"Brother!" cried the seamstress, merrily clapping her hands. "Oh, you mean that gambling devil in the other room? Why, that is my Pousseur, and as true a native of Berlin as myself; Fischergraf is his name and not Count Pippi. He has not the remotest idea of setting up for a Count, he is merely a private sporting gentleman."

"But how did you come to be introduced into

this circle, my dear child?" again inquired the Lieutenant, who, spite of the difference of rank, began to feel quite interested in his newly made acquaintance.

"I'll swear, I cannot exactly tell you, myself. This evening, Fischergraf came to my lodgings in the *Rosenthaler-street*, told me to dress myself in my best, and said he would take me out with him. We then visited some three or four places, until very late, we arrived here. I have never been here before, but Fischergraf told me it was all right, and that we were invited to a party in this house. The footman at first would not admit us, until Fischergraf, who was tolerably drunk, began making such a row, as to bring the master of the house to the door. My Pousseur knew him very well, and he received us, perhaps only from fear, but when he took us into the room he gave us those aristocratic names, you have heard. As for myself, I know nothing about gaming, and did not like the ladies, so I came here to rest myself, and fell asleep."

"But will you tell me what is your real name?" inquired the Lieutenant.

"*Augusta Strass*," was the reply.

"And you live in the *Rosenthaler-street?*"

"No. 142, up three pair of stairs."

"Will you allow me to pay you a visit?"

"I cannot promise that, exactly," replied the roguish Grisette with hesitation; "unless you come in the forenoon, for afterwards I always go out to my work, and in the evening my Pousseur comes to see me."

"You love your Pousseur then?"

"Why, why I cannot exactly say that I love him, for he is rough and coarse towards me, and I can feel a slight or an insult as well as any other lady of a higher rank; but then I like him very well, for he gives me many presents, and I expect, that sometime or other he will marry me. A ruffian is still better than no husband at all; and after all, women will in the end have their own way and rule these men.—But be quiet now, for I believe he is just coming."

And in reality the playing had just concluded, and Count Pippi, who had 'operated' to his heart's content upon his Freier, as he called the Geheimerath, entered with a most pleasant and joyous face.

Francisca, in her impenetrable humour, had thought proper to favour him more than the Referendarius. She had continually filled the goblet for the Geheimerath, and thereby made him more passionate and blind, till at last, unable to observe the game any longer, he had to withdraw with an enormous loss. In his heart, Fischergraf warmly thanked the Equestrian for her assistance, but what totally escaped his short-sightedness, was that fiendlike, sarcastic satisfaction, with which the artiste saw one sum after another disappear from the hands of the Gehei-merath. Some feature, so demoniac and wild, had during this time overspread her handsome face, that the Prince who had watched her with intense attention, felt a cold shudder creep over him. But despite of his will and endeavour this shudder did not leave him, but helped to chain him closer and closer to that mysterious woman.

The watchman was proclaiming the third hour of the morning, when weary, ill-humoured and exhausted, the brillant company separated.

The sweet hours of enjoyment and excitement had quickly passed away, but what those hours had produced, and the germ which had then been sown, was destined to be lasting, ominous, and important.

CHAPTER XVII.

THE MYSTERIES OF A HOFRATH.*

LET us now, kind reader, pass over the oc-currences of a few days of our story, and go to *Dorothee* street, to make the acquaintance of a man, whom the inexplicable degrees of fate destin-ed to be connected with the results of our narrative.

This important personage is *Herr Theophil Balthasar Christoph Christianus*, Royal Hof-rath in the Cabinet, possessor of the war-medal, husband, and father of two hopeful offsprings, a daughter of sweet eighteen, and a son of twenty-one years of age.

Herr Hofrath Christianus, at the commence-ment of our story, was somewhere about forty years old. He was a lank figure, of middling height, and of a most military air. His dress, once and forever, consisted in a pair of brightly-polished boots, large, dark blue cloth pantaloons without straps, a coat of the same, but some-what lighter colour with bright buttons, a vest of white Marseilles, ditto shirt-front, and a very stiff cravat, whose artificial and elaborate tie was fastened by a large solitair.

This regular, snowy-white frame, gave to the milky tint of his long face, a doubly inexpressive appearance, and corresponded with the dough-coloured hair, which already began to be more scarce upon the crown of the head than at the temples. The entire impression which this head might have produced upon looking at it, was the direct opposite of genius, spirit, wit, reason, or other qualities of the mind, which would cer-tainly have been more dangerous than whole-some in a subaltern officer of the Ministry. That head, at all events, never could have served as a model to Praxiteles.

In this figure and dress, and with the soft, noiseless step which he had acquired in the cabinet of the Minister, the Hofrath paced up and down over the rich, soft carpet of an elegant and fashionably arranged chamber.

This chamber he called his library, or office, and had endeavoured to give some justification to the name of office or study, by having a large mahogany writing-table placed in the centre, up-on which legal documents and legislative pam-phlets were arranged in the most admired and

* *Horath*, an honorary title, verbally Court-Council lor.—TRANSLATOR.

artistical disorder. Upon the whole, however, the title was misapplied, and neither justified by the just named arrangement, nor yet by a small library, situated above the narrow sofa, which contained all the latest and most fashionable novels, and which belonged to his daughter.

For in reality the Hofrath never had anything to do at home; his was the all important office, to copy all the articles the minister had written, as our Hofrath alone was fortunate enough to possess the necessary talent of deciphering the absolutely illegible hand-writing of his Excellency. Although the colleagues of the worthy officer were malicious enough, from this fact to draw the conclusion, that in reality he was nothing more or less than a common scrivener or copyist, the self-sufficiency and dignity of the Hofrath was far above noticing such expressions of envy, and he had considered it proper, and in accordance with his position and elevated station, to arrange his library, which at the same time was his reception room, as much as possible after the taste of his superior.

To be just, we must confess, that a reception room, such as this, was absolutely necessary for him, for there was constantly a mass of people, who thought that they could never gain anything of the Minister, without having first applied to the " all powerful Herr Hofrath," who was in daily intercourse with his Excellency, and consequently—certainly a most daring conclusion—must be the right hand of the Minister.

It is most natural, that, for his part, the Herr Hofrath had not the slightest objection to this conclusion; he rather considered it as an unquestionable guarantee of his merits, those merits, which had already obtained him the title of Hofrath, and, as he hoped, would help to promote him still further. Certain it is, that nothing could equal the dignity and grace, with which in his own reception room, he gave to petitioners his assurances of protection, except, perhaps, the earnest, business-like and dignified serenity, which overspread his features, when, leaving the cabinet of the Minister, and finding perhaps a few persons unknown to him, seeking an audience, he assured them that " His Excellency was not visible to anybody."

We must here observe, as it assists greatly in explaining the present position of the Hofrath, that slanderous tongues among the public did say, that he was bound to the Ministerial Cabinet by more bonds than those of business, and that he owed his title and office as Hofrath, more to these bonds than to his art of deciphering.

These ties or bonds, then, were frequently more closely explained; principally from the positive and established fact, that the Hofrath had received his present " better half " from the hands of his chief, and, it was now said, that the Hofrath had made sundry concessions on that occasion. But we must protest against all these slanders, as the honourable purity of his character seems to be fully established, by a retrospect of the former life of our friend.

As a collegian of eighteen, the Hofrath had fought through the so-called Liberation-wars, (Befreiungs Kriege,) had, during the peace, passed his time at the different Universities, with the intention of studying, had turned demagogue, practised gymnastics, fought, in short had been an irreproachable German youth of the olden time, with large embroidered shirt collar, and flowing hair.* In consequence of these free, noble and strengthening, but time losing qualities and passions, he could not pass his examination at the end of his student years. This miss of an examination, however, proved a lucky hit for him, for the difficulties in which he found himself, made him begin to reflect on his position.

Assisted by a few recommendations, he applied to the minister, who received him graciously, promoted him to the office of Court-Secretary, and he passed the great Demagogue-examinations unharmed and unsuspected. Gradually, he then rose higher and higher in office, and, at last, beside the hand of his wife, received the patent of Hofrath from his patron the minister. Evidently there was nothing wrong in all this; Herr Christianus had unquestionably by his own merits earned both distinctions, for as he never thought himself, he never wrote wrong, and consequently was the most valuable officer in the whole department.

As we said above, this Herr Hofrath Christoph Christianus, the main pillar of the cabinet, although it was scarce nine o'clock in the morning, already walked up and down full dressed in his study and reception room. His hands were crossed upon his back, his eyes were half closed, and a pleasant smile played about his lips. For once in his life, the man looked remarkably thoughtful; great ideas evidently crossed his mind. He remembered that yesterday, on passing through the cabinet, his Excellency had saluted him exceedingly friendly, and had told him in a whisper that he had a great joy in preparation for him.

Now what else could this be, but the consummation of the only, the highest object of all his wishes and endeavours, the " Geheime." For thus the Hofrath designated the title of Geheime Hofrath, which, beside his daughter, filled his whole soul. " Herr Geheime Rath !" That sounded noble, grand; that alone must put all his enemies down at once. At this thought, the Hofrath took a grand leap across the room, and with a most grateful expression of countenance, he stopped short before the full length portrait of his chief which adorned the wall.

During this elevating, heart-strengthening play of thought, a servant girl entered the room, and announced that madame and the young lady were ready, and that Johann also must be back shortly. This announcement brought the Hof-

---

* This sentence, in the original, is an excellent description of a German student of 30 or 35 years ago. It is impossible to translate it closely, the German description however, is—" hatte demagogisirt, geturnt, gewartburgt, kurzum war ein untadlicher altdeutscher Jungling gewesen," &c. &c.—TRANSLATOR.

rath to himself again ; he quickly pulled on his wadded overcoat, took his hat and cane, and retired to the sitting-room of his family.

Here he found all the members of his family collected, namely, mother, daughter and son ; all were dressed in walking costume, and moreover, as it seemed, determined upon one and the same excursion.

Let us examine them more closely.

Madame Christianus presented an imposing, or rather, we may say, a colossal appearance. In height she measured a little above five feet, and her breadth and circumference fully corresponded with this height. Her blooming—we had almost said blossoming—face, had attained that copper-coloured hue, which we frequently find with ladies of a certain age. Her exceedingly well fed cheeks, had driven the large round blear-eyes, of indescribable colour, into some remote depths; but her mouth with its strong thrown-up lips had been fully and richly developed, and when opened, displayed two rows of sound, large and brown teeth.

As we already know, the gentle partner of the joys and sorrows of the Hofrath had formerly been chambermaid to her Excellency. During the period she was thus engaged, she had also pursued her studies of elegance and refinement, and consequently was still even now endeavouring to make her Excellency, the minister's lady, the prototype of her views, demeanor and manners, even as the Hofrath did the same by his chief.

These endeavours, however, could not prevent her from retaining her original chambermaid's manners, which by the overbearing and proud behaviour of the " *Frau Hofräthin*," (the Lady Hofrath) showed themselves in the most vulgar and disagreeable colours ; yet blind to this, she endeavoured to keep up appearances as best she could. Thus, for instance, as soon as she learned that the Lady Minister had joined a Ladies' Society for the support of infant orphans, she immediately became a member of the same association. It constantly was a matter of the utmost importance to her, to ascertain what stuff her Excellency had chosen for a new dress, or how she had liked and judged the last new opera.

The youthful offsprings of this excellent couple had grown up, as might have been expected from these circumstances.

Fräulein Christianus was a remarkably handsome blonde, and decidedly the favourite of her father. Naturally endowed with sound sense and penetration, it was an easy matter for her to discover the humours and weak sides of her parents, and to use them to her own advantage. With only a superficial education, she knew no higher aim than the pleasures of society, and for this reason, at all risks, desired a rich husband, who as soon as possible might place her in an independent position, and furnish her the means of satisfying her love of pleasure. This was the great aim and end of her life, and just at present she thought its accomplishment nearer than ever, as she had succeeded in interesting the young Lieutenant Steinfort so far in her sweet self, that she daily looked for a formal declaration.

It would be wrong, if, in consequence of this, we were to call her a heartless coquette; she really possessed a great deal of heart and soul, but she was another example of those unfortunate results of the education of our age, which the wrong and stupid principle of the so-called good society, produce in such great abundance.

Endowed with that dangerous spirit, which so very easily proves perilous to the virtue of a woman, spoiled by the stupid, injudicious love of her father, disgusted at the vulgarity of her mother, she knew nothing of more consequence than her own will, which showed her nothing more disagreeable or wearisome than the parental roof. All the better feelings of childish attachment and love were lost in this, and the more she laughed at and scorned the silly, stupid vanity of her parents of imitating ministerial grandeur, the more she desired to be freed from them, and from her present position.

Knowing the dangerous points, which her natural propensities gave to her character, her parents should have treated her with the utmost care, instead of which, faults were heaped upon faults—and vices which grew the faster as they found a more congenial ground to grow upon.

The brother of this young lady, stood much further removed from the good graces and the heart of his father, than his sister, for in his views, his son was a most useless member of society. If here we only speak of the sympathies or antipathies of the father, and never mention the mother, it is for the reason, that the latter loved or hated none of her children, but looked upon them both with the utmost indifference.

The son, as we said above, was, in the eyes of his father, considered a most useless person. This son, already twenty-one years of age, was a handsome, well-made man for his years, possessed of a fine, fresh, and blooming appearance, and a small, just sprouting moustache. He had obstinately rejected all his father's endeavours to bring him into subaltern ministerial service, instead of which, the Hofrath said, he had entered the ranks of authors. This, doubtless, was a crime, but what was a still greater offence, was that the spoiled, graceless son, had so far partaken of the present political excitement, as to write and even publish a few political pamphlets, advocating liberal principles.

The conservative Hofrath would most willingly have rejected and abandoned his own flesh and blood, but to such a step he lacked the necessary energy ; prayers and remonstrances were the only available means he had, and these were of no effect. Tremblingly he looked forward to the time when his Excellency would send for him, and seriously reproach him with the behaviour of his son. Despairingly he had often asked that worthy son what answer he should

[Unmutilated and Only Genuine Edition.]

THIERS' LIFE OF NAPOLEON,

WITH SUPERB STEEL ENGRAVINGS.

FOR SEVENTY-FIVE CENTS,

[If paid in Advance.]

W. H. COLYER having been at great expense to procure a copy of this unrivalled work, now publishes

PART I.

OF THE

HISTORY OF THE CONSULATE AND THE EMPIRE

OF

FRANCE UNDER NAPOLEON,

By M. A. THIERS,

LATE PRIME MINISTER OF FRANCE.

WM. H. COLYER's edition of this splendid work, The Life of Napoleon, is decidedly the best in this country. It is printed on fine paper and new type, according to the design of the author, M. A. Thiers, and on comparison with other editions will be found far superior.

In Press.

THIERS' FRENCH REVOLUTION,

TO BE COMPLETED IN SIX PARTS, AT 12 1-2 CENTS EACH.

TO BE COMPLETED IN TEN NUMBERS.

THE MYSTERIES OF BERLIN,

FROM

THE PAPERS OF A BERLIN CRIMINAL OFFICER.

TRANSLATED FROM THE GERMAN

By C. B. BURKHARDT.

With Illustrations on Steel, by P. Habelmann.

This work in Europe has been universally pronounced far superior to M. Sue's celebrated "Mysteries of Paris," and we confidantly predict that the popularity of this translation will be without a parallel in the history of light reading.

Part IV.

Price 12½ cents.

THE MYSTERIES of BERLIN.

TO BE COMPLETED

IN

TEN PARTS.

NEW YORK: WILLIAM H. COLYER, PUBLISHER.

make the Minister in such a case; but the son —another of the results of a wrong education— would shrug his shoulders, whistle, and leave the room. Our readers may imagine the sorrows of a *Royal Ministerial Hofrath*, who expects daily to be promoted to "*Geheimer*," yet feels that such a liberal son, like an incubus, hanging at his heels!

Among this trio, then, the Herr Hofrath entered, after the chamber-maid had driven him out of his brown study into his brown over-coat.

As we have already observed, he found all his family in marching order; mother and daughter were dressed in heavy silk cloaks, the former with a velvet hat and a high plume, the latter in a more simple head-dress. The son had wrapped a small Spanish cloak around him, which was of but little service against the cold, but which showed his well formed feet and legs to more advantage.

"Well," began the Hofrath, as he entered the room, "are you all ready, children?"

"My dear Hofrath," replied his *cara sposa*, who, seated on the sofa, had passed the time she waited for him in looking over one of the last annuals, "do not for ever ask such stupid questions, when you know that we are always ready much sooner than yourself."

"Well, well, don't be angry, my dear Hofräthin," replied the husband, in a pacifying tone, "it was merely a habitual question. Has Johann come back?"

"I don't see him yet," replied the daughter, who was leaning from the window, and looking out upon the street.

"I hope the rascal will not delay and lose time," said the Hofrath, anxiously, "that would be doubly annoying to me this time, children."

"Not to me," grumbled the pamphleteer, half aloud, as he hastily looked over a newspaper, and made a few notes in his memorandum book.

"Just think, my dear Hofräthin," continued the Hofrath, as he seated himself in a very confidential manner by the side of his wife upon the sofa, "I have now certain expectations shortly to be 'Geheimer.' Yesterday, on passing through the cabinet, his Excellency whispered to me *en passant*, that he would shortly prepare a great joy for me, which I am certain can be nothing more or less than the title of 'Geheime.' Ah, my dear wife!" he sighed, almost tenderly, "then I shall no longer call you *Hof*, but *Geheimeräthin*, and you will always address me, 'dear Geheimer.'—My dear Matilda, do you hear?" cried the Geheime *in spe*, to his daughter, who was still leaning from the window.

"What is your wish, dear father?"

"Come hither, child, very near, and look at me closely; don't I look different from usual?"

"No, my dear father, I don't observe any change."

"Adolph, do you come here and look at me, my son; don't I look much altered?"

"No, my dear father. As usual you have put on a blue coat and a white cravat," replied the dutiful son, without glancing up from his paper.

"Children, do not mock your parent; there is something grand, something very grand, in the title of Geheimerath. Harkye, Matilda, just stand here in the middle of the room, make a low curtesy, and say: 'Good morning, Herr Geheimerath.' I would like to hear how it sounds."

"Yes, my dear papa," replied Matilda, determined to make hay while the sun shone, "but if I do this to please you, what will you give me?"

"Well, well," replied the father, smirking, "we will first see how you acquit yourself."

Matilda walked seriously to the centre of the room, made a very low curtesy, and said: "Good morning, Herr Geheimer Hofrath."

"Stop, stop," cried the father suddenly, with a disappointed smile, "this won't do, it is not the right title. You must leave off the Hofrath, by all means. That is the great advantage of the 'Geheime,' that the subaltern ranges equal with the Rath of any class; all are called Geheimerath. The title of Geheimerath in Prussia makes us all free and equal. So try it once more, my dear child."

Matilda made another curtesy, and said: "Good morning, Herr Geheimerath."

"That will do, now you are right," cried the Hofrath clapping his hands, "now whether I am a *Geheimer Hofrath*, or a *Geheimer Regierungsrath*, or a *Geheimer Ober-Regierungsrath*, or an *acting Geheimer Ober-Regierungsrath*, is all the same, I am a *Geheimerath*, as well as all the others."[*]

"Well then, papa, what will you give me now?"

"You shall have a velvet hat like your mother's, which I have hitherto refused to purchase for you," replied the delighted father.

At this moment the door opened, Johann entered and announced that: "His Excellency's carriage had just gone to the Cathedral."

"Then be in a hurry, children," commanded the head of the family, "the Cathedral is usually very full, and we have a long walk to get there. His Excellency must see us there to-day at any risk."

To enable the reader to understand these movements, we must here observe, that on every Sunday morning the servant of the Hofrath's family was regularly sent to the palace of the Minister, to watch until the carriage of his Excellency should drive up. It was then his duty to observe and ascertain to what church the coachman was ordered to drive, and immediately after, return home, to bring the result of his spying to the Hofrath. During his absence all the

* Ridiculous as all these distinctions may appear to the American reader, they are nevertheless correct, as all these titles are given to different ranks, and their distinctive grades are closely observed. Such characters as our Hofrath are by no means rarely seen in the different German States. Titles are everything, hence the multiplicity of them and the nice distinction observed.—TRANSLATOR.

family would dress and prepare for a start, so as, immediately on hearing the news, to be in readiness to follow to the same church, and then, if possible, to obtain a seat near the pew of his Excellency.

This regular Sunday custom had, of course, been observed to-day, and this had caused the early toilette of the family, as well as the report of Johann.

After Madame had quickly looked through the Annual, and the son had finished reading his paper—a number of the proscribed Manheim-Gazette, as the father observed with a sigh—the whole family began to move off. All four were provided with immense gilt Hymn-books, and walked slowly and humbly through the streets, towards the Cathedral.

The church was already well filled, and but few seats vacant; but after some endeavour, they succeeded in obtaining a pew, which brought the whole family directly in view of his Excellency. This was managed by a "*Viergroschenstück*," (a coin,) to the sexton. Herr Christianus was fully repaid for this, when, after some little while, the eyes of the minister caught his, and his Excellency replied to his low bow by a gracious inclination of the head.

The Hymn books were now opened, and all eyes devoutly directed to the pages. This, however, did not prevent Miss Matilda from looking with envy at the toilette of a lady whom she knew, in the choir, nor prevent the young literati from quizzing a few handsome ladies through his lorgnette. Mamma commenced gently to nod her head downwards, and Papa began carefully to examine whether his Excellency would observe it, if he threw a hard silver Thaler into the contribution bag.

If we overlook the loud snoring of the Frau Hofräthin, from which she was repeatedly awakened by forcible pushes from her better half, the church service passed without any remarkable occurrences to the Christianus family. The verse after the sermon had been scarce half sung, when papa gave the sign for departure, and hurried, with his family, towards the church door.

Here the whole group had to march up in rank and file, papa and mamma in the fore rank, and the two offsprings in the back ground. In this position the family waited each Sunday with a most earnest face until his Excellency had passed, and had once more graciously acknowledged their salutation. The Herr Hofrath had arranged it thus, and insisted upon this performance, although his children, who feared to be laughed at by their acquaintance, regularly protested against it.

His Excellency let them wait long on this occasion, as His Excellency, on going out, was engaged in conversation with two other Excellencies. Fräulein Christianus already stamped her neat little foot most impatiently, and the author grumbled a few words about servile hypocrisy, so loud that the Hofrath looked round in mute horror. At last, the happy moment arrived! His Excellency approached; but, oh Heaven! His Excellency actually passed by the Hofrath, who, by repeated and low bows, endeavoured to show his devotion, without even deigning to cast a glance towards his humble servant, entered a carriage and drove off.

This was a most severe blow. The Hofrath scarcely dared to trust his own eyes. Tremblingly he pulled the hat over his pale face, and had to rest upon his better half, to enable him only to make a few steps towards the street.

"Hofräthin, did you observe this?" he exclaimed, "what was it? No look, no smile, no notice as usual! Hofräthin, I cannot survive this."

"Pshaw, don't cry it aloud here in the street," replied his wife; "what should it have been? the Minister had his mind occupied with important affairs of state; had, perhaps, just received unexpected news, and could not think of you."

"Oh, wife, wife, I hope you may speak true," groaned the Geheime in *spe*, "he always used to smile from the left corner of his mouth; but to-day, he appeared in a state of most perfect, most terrible seriousness. As usual, I gave a hard Thaler into the contribution bag; he saw it, I am certain;—but yesterday he was so friendly, and to-day—Children, children, only think of the title of Geheimerath."

Suddenly the Hofrath stopped short in the middle of a street; a terrible thought seemed to have crossed his mind.

"Boy," he cried, looking furiously at his son, "boy, have you again been guilty of some mischief? I tell you, I shall cast you from my sight, out of my house! I shall withdraw my hand from you, with your accursed book-making! Can you not earn your bread honestly, by legal writing, as other people do? But no, you must—"

The good Hofrath once started upon the subject, had talked himself into a rage, and most probably would have railed for hours longer against book-making, if his wife had not seriously interrupted him. Upon the natural principles of reaction, she had taken the son's part, only because the father spoiled the daughter. Moreover, on this occasion, she feared scandal, as in his rage and anxiety, the worthy officer of state did not observe that several church-goers had stopped and were anxiously listening.

"Hofrath," she said, impressively, "now be quiet; would you raise a town talk? Why do you always attack Adolph? Just please to let the boy alone, and do not eternally annoy him and quarrel with him."

This was the time when the son thought he might "make hay whilst," &c., just as the daughter had done in the morning.

"My dear mother," he said, affectionately, "perhaps you have your purse with you, and I have forgotten mine. I would like to go to *Stehely's* and read the paper before dinner."

"Oh yes, my son," replied the Hofräthin, who now also was anxious to make a demonstration of her affection. "Here, take my purse; it is pretty full, and you may return me the rest."

"He will not be in a hurry to do that," said Matilda, laughing, as her brother hastily left the party. "He will not return so very soon, and you may at least save one dinner to-day."

"Hofräthin, you are acting very wrong," began the husband, boldly, "in supporting that boy in his wicked, outrageous ways; what does he want with papers at Stehely's? He can daily see *Voss's* paper at home, and that contains all he needs to know."

"Hofrath, I act according to my pleasure, just as you do when you buy velvet hats for Matilda which she does not want. Don't trouble yourself about my affairs. But we must ride home; my feet hurt me. Ho, cab there! cab, just stop."

"But my dear Hofräthin, we are almost at home."

"My dear Hofrath, I choose to have it so, and I will have it so."

And the family entered the cab to ride a few hundred steps to their house, and spend six groschen for the amusement.

"Major and Lieutenant von Steinfort are within, waiting your return," announced Johann, as he opened the cab door to the family of Hofraths.

"Ah!" cried Matilda, almost involuntarily, as she cast a triumphant glance towards the windows of the house. With affected coquetry she leaned upon Johann's arm, leaped lightly from the cab, and danced affectedly into the house. Papa and mamma followed with becoming dignity.

"Good morning, old comrade," cried Major von Steinfort, as the family entered. "What! been from home so early? Frau Hofräthin, allow me to kiss your hand; Fräulein, I hope you will give yours to my son."

The young lady bowed modestly, and cast her eyes to the ground with a blush, as if she did not, or dared not to understand the *double entendre* of the words addressed to her.

"Well, well, don't be so bashful, Fräulein," cried the old soldier, heartily shaking her by the hand; "I think we shall soon become better acquainted with each other. Lieutenant, come forward into rank and file, and don't stand back there, like a mummy."

Upon this order, the Lieutenant left his position by the pianoforte, made a low bow to the young lady, and again stopped, hesitating and uncertain.

"No, no, my friends," recommenced the Major, "this mode of action will never do, for if we would gain the fortress, we must first open the outworks. My dear Christianus, do me the favour to conduct me and your wife to your own room, for I have some serious matters to talk over. I hope, however, that these matters will tend more and more to fix our ancient friendship. Meanwhile we will leave these young people to themselves, and they may then, perhaps, easier come to a mutual understanding."

The old people left the room with the Major, and the young pair was left alone.

The Lieutenant had resumed his position by the pianoforte. In the left hand he held his military hat, and with his right he picked at the plume.

The young lady had placed herself at the other end of the room, by a corner-table, and played with a green parrot, who chattered and screamed whilst he rocked in his brass cage.

An embarrassed silence prevailed.

"Don't you think, Herr von Steinfort," at last began Matilda, "that my parrot is a most charming creature?"

"Very charming, Fräulein," replied the Lieutenant, as he plucked at his plume with an earnestness, as if a Captain's commission depended on the issue.

Another pause and embarrassment.

Herr von Steinfort, I must say, that I find you very dull to day," Matilda at last began anew, as she cast a side glance, half earnest and half smiling at the young officer.

The Lieutenant had approached near to the parrot's cage, and playfully held out his finger to him. As the bird put his head forward, the gentleman, who was evidently absorbed in unpleasant thoughts, hit him with his glove, so that the poor parrot retreated in fright, and hopped back upon his ring. "Rascal! rascal!" screamed the bird; Matilda bit her lips in anger, but made no further remark.

At last Steinfort, who seemed to have gained fresh courage through this by-play, said: "Fräulein, I would, or rather I should speak to you about something, if you will be kind enough to listen to me for a moment?"

"Certainly, Herr von Steinfort," replied Matilda, who believed that she already knew what was coming, and in consideration thereof, had even determined to forget and forgive the ill usage her parrot had received. "But let us be seated," she continued, as she took a place on the sofa, and motioned to the Lieutenant to seat himself upon a chair by her side.

The Lieutenant obeyed. He evidently was at a loss for a beginning, and thus began a third pause, filled only by the noise and screams of the parrot, who continued to cry "rascal! rascal!"

At last the young lady seemed to find this scene rather dull and monotonous; she had already changed her position, and that of her hands and arms a dozen times, and was just suppressing a yawn with some difficulty. The officer observed this movement; a blush passed quickly over his handsome manly face, and without farther hesitation he began his speech.

"You know, Fräulein, that it is the long cherished wish of our parents, to find in our union a new security for that friendship which has existed between our fathers since the time of the liberation wars. My father at this moment is in the library of yours, to conclude final and definite arrangements with your parents for that purpose, and it has become my duty meanwhile to come to an understanding with you."

The Lieutenant here made a momentary pause, whilst Matilda's head had sunk so low towards her bosom, that it was impossible to recognize her features. He then continued.

"For my own part I have hitherto entertained no objections to the wish of my father, to which I had gradually become accustomed. Your personal and mental attractions did not escape me, nay, I hoped, almost with certainty, to look forward to a happy and pleasant married state, as you also were not unacquainted with the wishes of our parents, and—if I am not greatly mistaken—seemed not much averse to compliance with those wishes.

Thus matters remained until last evening, when my father declared to me his determination of coming here to day, to take a definite step in this matter. I had not the courage to annihilate at one blow the hopes and long cherished wishes of the good old man; but I became suddenly convinced, that we are not born for each other, and that I can never become your husband. Allow me to speak candidly and openly to you! My heart has for some time past belonged to another; I love only with that full ardour, which my passionate mind is capable of; but for that same reason I cannot deceive you. I have rather considered it my duty to make a full and open confession to you, so as to have the matter ended at once, and that neither you nor myself shall be any longer tortured by the wishes of our parents, which can never be fulfilled."

Uttering a low scream, on hearing these words, Matilda sunk fainting into the corner of the sofa.

Frightened, the Lieutenant rose up to pull the bell-rope, but in doing so, he observed in the opposite mirror, that Matilda quickly opened her eyes to watch his movements, and as quickly closed them again.

It might perchance have happened, that penitently he would have returned and cast himself at her feet, as she lacked neither in personal nor mental attractions, and both had hitherto dazzled and enchanted the Lieutenant. But this last discovery at once severed all these bonds. Steinfort remembered the simple, natural and unaided charms of the grisette, whom he had seen at Birkheim's soirée—we scarcely need tell our readers that it was her who had charmed him so—and a deep disgust at the comedy which the daughter of the Hofrath played with him, overmastered him.

Suddenly he became fully convinced of a fact, which had frequently before obtruded itself on his mind, namely, that she only sought his wealth, his rank, and that she merely wanted him to give her an independent and grand position in society, and—he believed himself too good for that.

Beside himself in his fury, he took the bell-rope, and pulled as if he would call the whole town together. The rope broke at the ceiling, and his hand struck the parrot cage underneath, tossing cage and bird right between his legs. He stumbled, fell over it, and lay sprawling at full length on the floor at the very moment when the opposite door opened, and the parents expecting to find their children engaged and united at a friendly *tête-à-tête*, entered the room with pleasant and smiling faces.

It would have been a subject worthy of the pencil of the immortal *Hogarth* to pourtray the utter astonishment of the newly arrived group. We will, in a few words, state the result of this scene.

The Lieutenant hastily rose from the floor, snatched up his plumed hat, and without saying a word, rushed through the door.

Matilda thought it best and most proper to put an end to her fainting. With a deeply tragical face and position, and with the exclamation of: "my heart, my poor heart is broken," she rushed to the arms of her father.

The Hofrath, perfectly stupified, assumed a most dull, inexpressive sheep's face.

His wife, the Hofräthin, quietly went to work, and endeavoured to restore the parrot and his dwelling to their original position.

The Major swore military oaths enough to move a regiment of dragoons or huzzars, and then, urged by parental care and anxiety, rushed after his son at the top of his speed.

In the midst of this confusion, Johann made his appearance, and announced the rich banker, *Herr von N——*.

"Don't reject him, dear father," said Matilda, perfectly recovered; "perhaps he might be the man for me. He certainly may dine with us to-day, instead of Lieutenant Steinfort.

END OF PART SECOND.

PART III.

CHAPTER XVIII.

FURTHER CONSEQUENCES.

AFTER Lieutenant von Steinfort had reached the street, his great excitement gradually began to diminish. He now congratulated himself on having thus escaped the snares and traps of this accomplished coquette. He was perfectly well aware, that now there could be no hope of reestablishing their former position towards each other, and delighted in that knowledge, as it convinced him that the end of another of those unfortunate arrangements had come, by which anything but the happiness of a married couple is established.

Steinfort immediately proceeded to his home, as he was in no humour or condition to meet or have intercourse with any person.

His servant opened the door for him.

"Herr Lieutenant," he said, "a lady has been here, who wished to see you; she has left this letter."

"A letter! give it me; quick!—But first take off my uniform, and bring me my morning gown. Give me a pipe, if you have one filled? Very well!—Now, a light.—This will do; and now, you can leave me."

The Lieutenant stretched himself comfortably upon the sofa, began smoking his meershaum with the utmost composure, and then opened the letter, which was written on very common paper, and had by no means the appearance of a *billet d'amour*.

"If you will visit me for an hour this evening, you shall be welcome at seven o'clock. We can then have a chat without interruption; I shall be all alone, for Fischergraf is invited out to a playing party. I believe, I like you very well, for you are not so rude and coarse as my Pousseur. I certainly am but an humble girl, but I can appreciate the difference of your manners from those of Fischergraf. I shall come to your lodgings myself, and leave these lines, if I should not find you. I am very anxious to know how things look about you. Is not that a funny idea? I wish I would not find you in, that I might examine things at my leisure. Be sure to come to-night, else—I shall be very sad.

"AUGUSTA."

Postscript—"You must not again stay so long as the last time, else the neighbours might talk about it."

The Lieutenant read the letter two or three times over; it certainly was not as orthographically correct as we have given it, but after having read it, he rubbed his hands in delight.

"This is *the* girl;" he said to himself, "all nature, candour, and honesty; I'll swear she will never have any comedy-faints as the daughter of the Hofrath."

Heavy steps and the rattling of spurs was heard in the outer-chamber.

"Is the Lieutenant within?" inquired a rough, well known voice.

"At your service, Herr Major," was the servant's reply.

The Lieutenant quickly put the letter into the wide pocket of his morning gown.

The door was torn open, and the old Major rushed into the room. His face betrayed a mixture of manifold and very powerful emotions. But when he observed his son lying on the sofa, and in all comfort and ease smoking his pipe, just as if nothing had occurred, paternal anxiety disappeared to make room for the stronger feeling of irritated passion. The old gentleman fully believed that his son had taken the liberty of playing a wild, frivolous, and practical joke. "*Tausend sapperlotter*,"* he exclaimed, and his face became red with anger, "what an infernal trouble is this you have caused in the house of my early and valued friend? Did you try to make fools of us all?—May the old Harry take you if you have really dared to attempt it. There you lay stretching yourself at full length and smoking your pipe, just as if nothing had happened. Do you intend shortly to open your mouth, and

* A meaningless, big sounding oath, very much in use in Germany.—TRANSLATOR.

give me an explanation? Why was that girl weeping? Why did you run from the house like a madman?—Thunder and the devil, why don't you speak?"

"I will speak with pleasure, dear father, as soon as you will give me a chance of saying a word. I cannot marry the young lady."

"And why not?" cried the old man furiously, "is she not the daughter of my early friend, and a beautiful, amiable girl?"

"She is all that, my dear father, but I cannot determine to marry her, if I do not love her."

"So, so? and why did you not tell me so before?"

"Because," replied the Lieutenant hesitatingly; "because I did not before know my own feelings upon the subject; because I did not know that she was an artful coquette who falls into artificial swoons, because—"

"Stop there," said the Major seriously, "why did she fall into an artificial swoon? You must have said something severe and afflicting to her; not so?"

"Why, sir," continued the Lieutenant, "I simply told her that I could not marry her."

"And what reason did you give her for that," inquired the Major anew, "for I hope, that at least you did give some grounds or reasons to the lady, to polish over your sudden change of mind?"

"Why—I—I," stammered the Lieutenant.

"Well—I—I," mocked the Major after his son, with his most penetrating look fixed upon him.

Suddenly the Lieutenant jumped up from the sofa. "Father," he cried, "I will confess it to you at once. I love another girl who loves me in return, and I would be undeserving of that girl's love, if I were coward enough to deny it. This is the simple reason why I cannot marry the Hofrath's daughter."

"Well, well, I thought so," replied the Major, with a shrug of his shoulder, by which he endeavoured to justify his assumed calmness; "an amour, nothing more, I suppose. I have for several days past observed some affair of this kind in your manner. And pray, who is the object of this very sudden love?"

"This object of my sudden love," replied the Lieutenant, who now also began to grow excited, and took pride in speaking freely, "is a seamstress."

"A what?" cried the Major, as he endeavoured to hide his rising anger by a very loud laugh, "what! a seamstress? and you are not ashamed to confess it to me? Lieutenant, I really believe you are drunk; I shall have to put you under arrest, and give you a little time to get sober."

This scorn excited the Lieutenant still more.

"Father," he cried with incautious warmth, "father, I give you my word of honour, that I will never marry that Hofrath's daughter; and that you may fully know my mind, I shall marry the seamstress, and if I should have to bring her down from the moon."

For awhile the Major stood in mute astonishment, as if he could not comprehend the sense of this speech. Then a terrible passion overspread his browned face, the large vein upon his forehead distended, and his eyes flashed with fury.

"You vagabond," he finally burst out in a voice that made the windows rattle, "is this your language to your father? After you have for months and years been talking amorous nonsense to a respectable girl, after turning her head with this stuff, you would leave her, to marry a mere grisette? This is acting like a villain, not like an officer or a man of honour. I ask you once more, will you retract the declaration you have just made?"

"My dear father," replied the Lieutenant, who had again become calm, "your passion drives you too far. I have ever treated Fräulein Christianus with politeness and friendship, but never have I spoken to her of more serious connections. If she herself has taken such an idea into her mind, she certainly has not done it from any love she felt for me. I shall not relinquish or abandon the girl I have chosen. But you ought at least to know her, before you condemn her."

"Nonsense, accursed nonsense!" now cried the Major, perfectly foaming with rage, "what do you take me for? I certainly am not proud, but I have some respect for position and circumstances; it is not at all necessary that I should become acquainted with a seamstress. You are insane; do whatever you like; but come not before my sight. I shall leave the city to-day, that I may at least avoid meeting my friend Christianus, and being compelled to confess my shame to him."

At these words the Major rushed furiously from the room, without listening to the further remonstrances and prayers of his son.

The Lieutenant cast himself upon the sofa, and pressed both hands before his burning eyes. The anger and fury of his father touched him to the quick, but he could not resign the girl to whom his heart had so suddenly and inseparably attached itself.

A strange arm, after a while, gently withdrew the hands from his burning face, and roused him from his bitter broodings.

It was the Referendarius von Birkheim, who had unobservedly entered the room, and had approached the sofa.

"Steinfort, good Heavens! what ails you?" he asked affectionately, as he observed two large tear-drops upon the cheeks of his friend.

The necessity of speaking, opening his heart, and if possible, obtaining some consolation, in friendly confidence, was too deeply felt by the Lieutenant, to permit him to remain silent. He told his friend all his troubles, and openly related to him the whole conversation he had with his father, suppressing, however, the name of the parties.

"But are you not independent enough, through the fortune left you by your mother," inquired the Referendarius after hearing his friend's story to the end, "to marry the girl, and live respectably, even without the support of your father? What is to prevent you from having your own will, spite of your father's consent?"

"The Major will never be persuaded to give his consent to this union," replied the Lieutenant, most despondingly. "Even now he was perfectly furious, and what will he say, if he should be informed of the former position and life of this girl!"

"Pshaw! And is this all your trouble?" exclaimed the Referendarius, "stuff and nonsense! What would be the use of my having studied *jura*, if I could not manage so easy a matter as this. Come, come. I will soon find a way to arrange things. Come, put on your hat, and let us take a promenade in the open air. This bright, glorious winter day, will be most beneficial to you, and I will inform you of my plan, as we walk along."

Arm and arm the two friends left the house. Birkheim in all probability had very good and sufficient reasons, though perhaps, not disinterested ones, to lay the rich, young Lieutenant under obligations to himself.

CHAPTER XIX.

THE PRISON.

FROM the elegant and fashionable *Boudoirs* of the aristocratic world, we will now conduct our readers to a place where dwelt nothing but misery, shame and crime. Behind the desolate walls of this place, virtue abashed hides her head, no sound of joy is heard, except the joy expressed at the accomplishment of a misdeed, and the laughter is the laughter of despair or of malice.

We are speaking of the Criminal-prison, where, at the present time, three characters of our story were incarcerated, the hunchbacked Jobs, cunning Schmerles, and Marianne.

Let us first look after the unfortunate girl whom the turnkey, as we know, had to put almost by manual force into her present cell.

This cell is a high, white-washed little room, in size about twelve feet square. It has two windows, which are close to the ceiling, and are on the inside guarded by a strong railing, and on the outside by a tin box, which permits the light to penetrate into the apartment through an opening of a few inches at the top. This arrangement creates a continual twilight, which, particularly in the present winter weather, can scarcely be distinguished from actual darkness.

The walls of the prison, which by long use have become grey and dirty, are perfectly bare; only a few wooden pegs are fastened here and there, and serve to hang clothes upon.

The furniture consists in a rough, unpainted,

square table of pine-wood, and four stools of the same description. In one corner stands a large wooden pitcher with fresh water, and by its side a wooden goblet. In another corner stands a wash basin of a similar description.

In the middle of the room, and upon the bare floor, lay four straw mattresses in a row; upon these we find four prisoners, who have wrapped their white woolen blankets around them.

It is past midnight.

The moon throws its light directly upon the windows, and its pale rays fall upon the pallid faces of the four sleepers.

Let us examine these more closely.

Nearest to the stove lies a woman whose features still betray traces of what once was remarkable beauty. The destroying hand of vice has too early given to these features the appearance of faded age. The cheeks are sunken, and deep blue circles are drawn around the eyes. Her head is covered with a white cap, from beneath which the dark hair falls loosely upon her temples. Forehead, nose and mouth are well and nobly formed. Her strong, well built body is closely wrapped in her blanket, and she has moved her mattress as near as possible to the stove, to guard against the cold morning air.

This is the well-known and notorious *Rüthmann*, one of the most celebrated procuresses in Berlin, but formerly an equally celebrated grisette.

She descended from a respectable tradesman's family. A noble *roué* had seduced, and left her to her fate, after she had been rejected by her parents on his account. Thus, by want and misery, she had been forced to cast herself into an abyss of vice, and soon she was sunk so low, that no hope remained of her being again retrieved and restored to society.

When her fading beauty seemed no longer to possess the power of attracting inconstant lovers, she resorted to one of the usual and most common means of securing her existence, by becoming procuress, and favouring and permitting the immorality of others in her own dwelling. Her house then became one of the most fashionable and best known of the kind in *Kranich*-street, and many wealthy and aristocratic voluptuaries were her constant visitors.

After awhile, however, the punishing arm of justice reached her, and the severe penalty of a long imprisonment made her reflect upon her mode of life. In prison then—a most rare exception—she learned true penitence of her former courses; after her liberation she returned to Berlin, with the best and most virtuous intentions. For a length of time, she now honestly supported herself, partly by the work of her hands and partly by the assistance of her brother, a civil officer in good circumstances.

Unfortunately, however, the police again interfered with her position; proofs of her means of subsistence were demanded of her, and she designated her brother, as the person to whom she partly owed her support. The police now in-stituted further inquiries at her brother's house, by which that brother's wife became acquainted with her husband's liberality to his sister. This woman possessed power enough over her weak husband, to induce him to withdraw the support which he had hitherto given to her, as his wife told him that the wretch had fully deserved her misery, by her bad course of life.

Thus, the unfortunate woman again was thrown into want and wretchedness. Spite of all, she sought to support herself honestly for some time. She embroidered for a millinary establishment, and thereby earned daily five *Silbergroschen*,* suffering hunger and deprivation. Want and misery destroyed her weakened system, she became sick, and now, deserted by all the world, she existed only a prey to despair.

In this terrible and heart-rending situation, those despised and prostituted girls whom she had formerly assisted in their vile ways, were the only beings who were grateful to her, the only ones who took pity on the sick woman, shared their miserable earnings with her; who nursed and who finally restored her. But now the procuress again belonged to them; partly the continued want and poverty, and partly gratitude to her nurses, led her back to her former profession. She had come to the conviction, that, spite of her will or endeavours, society would not again receive her within its pale. She knew that her best intentions, all her efforts must be wrecked upon the shoals of society, as it is at present constituted, and therefore again resorted to crime, which at least kept her from starvation.

And that course had caused her present new imprisonment; but this time, there was so little proof against her, that she had a certain expectation of regaining her liberty in a very short time.

We almost think it unnecessary to explain, or point out, in how many ways our present social system, our regulations of society, caused the ruin of this woman. If the state had provided a mode or an arrangement, by which after her dismissal from prison, she might have been enabled to follow an honest occupation, if even the Police, satisfied with her present honest course, had not troubled itself to ascertain her exact means of existence; had the unfortunate wretch been provided in her sickness, instead of being left entirely to her fate—the state would have saved a soul from vice and perdition, an honest useful member of society would have been gained, instead of which, government only obtained a new candidate for its prisons.

It is just, it is necessary, that the state should provide for the punishment of the guilty; but it is equally important, equally just and necessary, that government should also reward the good, assist virtue in its honest intentions, and rulers should not satisfy their consciences by building prisons, they should also award civic crowns to worth. The state, as things stand at present, is only the severe, punishing judge of its citizens,

* The amount of about twelve and a half cents, American currency.

but it should become a praising, approving, and rewarding power.

By the side of the procuress, upon another mattress, lay the unfortunate Marianne. During the early part of her confinement, she had timidly and despairingly kept aloof from the others, and passed the day in silence in a corner of her cell. There she sat, indifferent of everything that passed around her, wringing her hands in tearful despair, or in perfect stupefaction, staring on the ground before her.

This was an excellent and wished for opportunity to the other two prisoners, to make the unfortunate girl the mark of their pastime, the playball of their humour. They mocked, derided and scoffed her, used the most coarse, vulgar, and offensive language to her, and mockingly asked her, how she liked her winter quarters. In this new misery, Mrs. Rüthmann, whose particular attention had been attracted by poor Marianne, when she first beheld her, declared herself the protectress of the unfortunate girl, and threatened the women with personal chastisement, unless they altered their behaviour to her protegé. This had the desired effect, for Mrs. Rüthmann was a strong, powerful woman, and much feared by the others. They, moreover, did not think it advisable to break with her, as she frequently had eatables, &c., sent to her from without, and invariably shared them with her fellow prisoners.

Gratitude induced Marianne to attach herself more closely to the procuress, and she shortly after, in confidence, made her acquainted with her entire position, as well as with the circumstances which had led to her present imprisonment. This confidence and closer connexion, were the reasons why she had laid her bed as near as possible by the side of her protectress, whose manners towards her became more kind, obliging and flattering every day.

The other two prisoners, whom we have already alluded to, slept a little further towards the window. The two women, one rather elderly, the other younger, had coarse, vulgar and dissolute faces. Their hair hung wildly and roughly about their necks; the first had her tresses somewhat held together by a dirty pocket handkerchief, the other had them fastened with a few hair pins. The few rags which formed their habiliments, but which left bosom and feet exposed in a most disgusting manner, were protruding here and there from beneath the blankets.

These were a pair of thieves of the most common, the lowest class; the one had been caught picking a pocket upon the market, and the other was accused of shoplifting. These miserable wretches had been born and had grown up in misery and sin; for three generations they descended from thieves-families, and they knew of no other destiny in life, than theft and crime.

Their occupations had for years past made them frequent inmates of prisons, and imprisonment had no longer any effect upon them; they were content, nay, even merry. Their principal amusement consisted in making indecent, vulgar jokes, laughing loudly at them, in boasting of crime and relating stories of thefts and robberies in which they had played a part.

Before the arrival of Marianne, Mrs. Rüthmann had frequently joined them in their low conversations and indecent jokes, but since then, as we have already observed, she had thought best to keep somewhat aloof from them, and to take the part of Marianne.

The clock of the prison in four shrill sounds, announced that hour after midnight.

Restlessly Marianne tossed about upon her hard couch. A deep, involuntary sigh betrayed that she was not asleep.

"What! are you awake already, my child?" inquired Mrs. Rüthmann, who had also just awoke.

"Oh Heavens, yes, and have been this hour past," replied the poor girl with a sigh; "my old thoughts and sorrows trouble me."

"Do not be so foolish, child," answered the other, "and let me convince you at last. We must take every thing as it comes, and try to help ourselves as best we can."

"I cannot quiet my conscience," continued Marianne. "If I should relate to the judge what things occurred in our house, my father will be lost; and if I do not tell it, I must speak false, and lie. Good God! I have never yet been able to tell a lie."

"How often have I already explained it to you," resumed the procuress emphatically, "that it is the duty of an honest child to save her father if possible. What duty do you owe to the Judge? Certainly none. He is a person whom you don't know, who will snarl at you, and be glad when he has done with you; so you can do him that favour, and for once speak an untruth. You will learn that soon enough. And then you positively assert even to me, that you know not how the stuff came into your bed?"

"No, by Heaven, I know not," cried Marianne, with great earnestness.

"Well then, tell the plain, simple truth at first. Say that you did not know how the calico came into your bed, but that most probably one of your father's guests had hidden it there and had forgotten it. Then you may slightly deviate from the path of truth, and speak to the Judge of the simple, honest cellar-business at your house, that you know nothing of all these thieves, and thereby you will not only save your father, but also help yourself. If you confess all, no one will believe your solitary innocence. They will sum up all the little facts you may tell them, and spite of all your assertions and protestations of innocence, they will condemn you as well as your father to the state prison."

Marianne heaved a deep, heart-rending sigh.

"Follow my advice," continued the procuress, urgently, "and you will soon be free again. Nothing can be proved against you, and most likely we will both be liberated at about the same time. Child, consider your father! he is old and not very strong," she added, impressively.

"Yes, yes, perhaps, after all, you may be right," replied Marianne, hesitatingly, after a pause, during which varied emotions had struggled for supremacy in her troubled mind; "you have so much more experience than myself."

"Yes, child, I have indeed. Even if your father behaved ill towards you, still you must save him, such is commanded by Christianity. But let me tell you this also; you need not return to his house, if he ill-treats you so cruelly; that is not required by Christianity."

"I myself have already thought of it," replied Marianne, "whether it would not be better for us both, if I did not return to the cellar. With the best will and spite of all endeavours I cannot please or satisfy my father, and he is angry and furious all day long; a stranger will certainly suit him better than I. And if he should get sick or weak, he can easily send for me again."

"That is right, my child," said the procuress; but watching like a cat for her prey, she added: "and what do you propose doing, after you are liberated?"

"Why, I shall endeavour to find service in some family," replied Marianne artlessly.

The procuress laughed aloud.

"What! find service? Well! you may seek a long time. Who do you suppose will take a young woman just liberated from the *Stadtvoigtei*, into service? You little fool, how can you think of it? such is not the custom of the world, who cares little or nothing for your honest intentions. People would slam the doors in your face, shrug their shoulders, or would even call you a vagabond strumpet."

Marianne burst into a flood of tears. "Oh, good Heavens," she cried, weeping, "then I must again return to my father's cellar."

"I would not advise that either;" resumed the other; "would you again expose yourself to the danger of being arrested, and spite of all your innocence be convicted and condemned at last? or do you think that your father will change his business and his mode of life?"

Despairingly, Marianne rung her hands, having no reply to give, but her incessant tears.

"I will make a proposition to you," now began the procuress, "come with me; I have learned to love you, and I will give you a home."

"Ah, how can I expect that, or how could I ever repay you?" cried Marianne, getting incautious and confiding in her childish innocence and inexperience.

"Alas, I know how a person feels in such troubles as yours," continued the procuress in a kind tone, "and therefore I would help and assist you; I will just tell you the story of my life, and the trials I have had to undergo."

The artful woman now related, as far as she thought it advisable, a great part of her history, with which we are already acquainted. She took care, however, to depict in strong colours the horrible and desperate position of a former crimi-nal, or even of an innocent person who has been once accused, when such a person is placed in juxtaposition with so called virtuous society.

At these revelations, Marianne's frantic despair again overpowered her. She saw her entire future annihilated, as she could not bring herself to a determination of passing her life idly, and existing upon the support of the procuress; of course she had not the remotest suspicion of that woman's trade, and in accepting her offer could only see a hope for a quiet, undisturbed life.

Weeping and wailing, she raised her hands to Heaven, and addressed the throne of Grace, in a warm prayer, that God might take her from a world where no choice remained her, between misery and crime.

At this moment the clock struck five; the turnkey entered with a light in his hand, to make his usual morning round among the prisoners.

Suddenly a most consoling thought occurred to Marianne. She petitioned the jailor to obtain her as soon as possible an interview with the prison minister. Here she hoped to have all doubts solved, which now tormented her soul; here she hoped to have the dim veil of the future raised to her consolation. The anointed minister of the Lord must have a balm for the wounds of her heart, and he certainly could tell her how far she ought to obey the advice and instruction of her protectress.

The two female thieves, on hearing her request, burst into a low laugh, which they suppressed from fear of Mrs. Rüthmann. Even the latter assumed a smile, without, however, making any further remark.

With the same stolid and unchanged face, which marked his entire demeanour, the turnkey promised to attend immediately to her request, and retired after examining and finding everything right and in order.

In the pious emotions of her soul, Marianne found a long desired consolation. She wrapped her blanket closer around her, and fell into an hour's quiet and undisturbed slumber.

CHAPTER XX.

THE MINISTER OF THE PRISON.

THE forenoon was far advanced when Wiechmann opened the door of the cell, to conduct Marianne to the Minister, as she had desired.

She followed him through the long corridor to a small room, into which the officer requested her to enter, while he remained outside.

The room had but one window, and was white-washed with the same ashy white colour as all the other rooms of the building. In the middle of the apartment was a small round table, upon which stood a crucifix of black metal by the side of a bible. Near the window stood a small sofa and a chair.

This was the entire furniture.

The pastor was seated upon the sofa, and read in a prayer-book. On the entrance of Marianne he closed the book, took his spectacles which he had on reading laid aside, placed them before his eyes, and walked towards the girl.

He was a large strong built man, with blooming, well fed and rounded cheeks, and a rather rotund body. His blonde hair was divided in the centre, and hung glossy and smooth down over both temples; a small, blonde pair of curly whiskers peeped out beneath his rounded cheeks.

The gentleman's dress consisted of a black cloth over-coat, and similar pantaloons, somewhat threadbare, and showing divers grease-spots. His shirt-bosom and neckcloth, both consisting of white materials, looked equally unclean. The boots showed much mud and many patches.

The reverend father, as it seemed, despised the vanities of this world.

He approached close to Marianne, and without saying a word, gazed at her long and intently through his spectacles.

Abashed, the maiden cast her eyes to the ground. Anxiously she awaited the moment, when the servant of the Lord would open his mouth, would address a word of consolation to her, would help, comfort, and advise her in her doubts and perplexities.

"Thou hast deserted the path of virtue, and art wandering upon the road of everlasting perdition," at length began the minister in a consoling, sonorous and well-sounding voice; "what is thy request of me?"

Marianne was silent; she really knew not how to express that which tortured and tore her heart, and knew still less, how to cloth it in a definite request.

"The wages of sin are death," continued the reverend speaker, "therefore repent of thine evil ways and mortify thy flesh and all its lusts and desires."

"Alas, most reverent sir," replied Marianne, and her tears flowed freely, "believe me, I have committed no crimes, but I fear—"

"What?" cried the other with angry voice, interrupting the weeping maiden, "what dost thou say? thou hast committed no crimes? Oh, how thy heart is obdurate, bad and hardened! I tell thee, that even wert thou not imprisoned here for a culpable, criminal offence, thou wouldst still be a worthless, reprobate creature, for we are all sinners, and wanting the glory which we should have before God."

"Alas, reverend sir," replied the maiden, "I know and feel this, and therefore I come to seek the consolations of our holy religion."

"Consolations?" inquired the preacher, in a tone of much severity, "there are no consolations for such as thou, as long as thou lovest the king of this world, which is the devil, and art fallen into accursed blindness. I proclaim unto thee the wrath of thy God! Before him, cast thyself to the dust, scourge thy heart, feel the thousand-fold tortures of thy conscience, and above all, pray for the faith which thou hast not."

"Oh, sir," cried Marianne enthusiastically, and with sparkling eyes, for the deepest feelings of her devout soul had been aroused, "I have the faith, the belief in an everlasting love."

"Miserable wretch," now thundered the minister, "there is no everlasting love for thee, but eternal punishment, and the bottomless pit with all its tortures awaits thee. Hardened sinner, pray to God, that he may enlighten thee by his great mercy, that he may guide thee to the recognition of the everlasting perdition, to which thou hast already devoted thy body and thine immortal soul."

Marianne cast a painful glance at the fantastical zealot, who must have, (if we remember her religious inclinations,) wounded her very soul and mind much more deeply than he was probably aware of.

"Go hence," now commanded the preacher, with earnestness, "that I may now bestow my time on more worthy objects. After thou hast done penitence, thou mayest return to me, but have a care that I may not again have cause to pronounce the curse of the church upon thee, instead of its blessing."

The minister folded his hands, and made a slight inclination with his head. Then with a bell he gave a sign, whereupon Wiechmann opened the door, and told the maiden to come out.

In silent despair the wretched girl tottered back to her prison.

This then was the consolation of the church upon which she had counted so much, which she hoped would give her courage and strength in her bitter sorrows! The minister of the Lord had not even listened to her, and all her questions, all her scruples of conscience, remained as torturing upon her mind as before! Alas! much more torturing, for the minister had not strengthened her faith, he had rather shaken it.

He had made her doubt her own religious convictions, made her doubt the main pillar on which these rested, the existence of eternal love. But, in proportion as her veneration for the ministers of religion was great and enthusiastic, even so could not penetration enough be expected from her, to appreciate rightly the blind zeal of this man, and the struggle of her soul became still more terrible.

How much good could the minister have effected, if, instead of obeying the impulses of pietistical fanaticism, he had kindly and humanely met the girl, had entered into her ideas, had consoled her, enlightened and instructed her upon her duties? He might have saved the poor sufferer—civilly and morally saved her; he might have assisted her judge in the discovery of innocence as well as in the punishment of guilt. What he did effect instead of this—what a germ of perdition he had sown, by casting the unfortunate maiden from him, instead of meeting her in love and kindness, according to the doctrine of his church, all this, the events of this story may perhaps yet bring to light.

Truly a heavy and important responsibility rests upon those who are entrusted with the keys of the kingdom of heaven; wo, wo unto them, if they mistake their trust!

The wildly disturbed appearance which Marianne presented on her return to the prison, was so affecting, that even her fellow prisoners were moved by it, and the two women, the thieves, suspended the mockeries with which they had determined to salute her return.

Without uttering a word, Marianne tottered to her corner. Pale as death she seated herself upon a stool, and like a lifeless bust, she stared upon the bare wall.

Her maiden modesty had been outraged, insulted, and bitterly wounded, by the rough official treatment at her arrest in the cellar of hunch-backed Jobs; her religious confidence was now equally destroyed; where, upon the storm-tossed ocean of her life was there a resting place? What should she believe? Where could she place her trust, when even the consolation of prayer was in a measure withdrawn from her? Or could she still in child-like confidence pray to the Deity, who, by the mouth of his servant, had been represented as a revengeful, punishing God? In her pious simplicity, she had never fancied to herself the servant of the Lord as such a person.

The holiest bonds, which had hitherto united Marianne to society, the bonds of modesty and religion, were now as good as severed. The ties of family she had never known;—*she now stood outside the pale of civilized society!*

It did not escape the observation of the cunning Mrs. Rüthmann, that Marianne had not found the consolations she so much sought, so much needed and hoped for. She patiently waited awhile, until the first very strong emotions had passed off; and when Marianne's behaviour showed such to be the case, she approached her with a friendly smile, and inquired after her adventures.

Marianne concealed nothing. It was a bitter consolation to relate her sorrows, and in her flowing tears, to find momentary relief.

The procuress, who considered it of great importance to bring this pretty girl out of prison at the same time when she should leave it herself, did not fail to avail herself of the advantage of the sudden and cruel change which had taken place in Marianne's mind. With glowing colours she painted to her the hopeless future that was before her, if she should again happen to fall into the hands of the zealous divine, who, on his part, would now be certain to inquire after her.

The necessity of an early release from this prison most naturally followed upon this, and that release could only be obtained, if Marianne, when confronted with her judge, followed strictly all the instructions and advice Mrs. Rüthmann had given her, and in all things obey her protectress.

Marianne had no longer any will of her own, to contradict or earnestly oppose the urgency of her friend's request. After having just now gained such disheartening experience, the views of the procuress seemed doubly well founded, and she was almost convinced that she would never succeed in proving her own innocence even by confessing the perfect truth, as no judge would believe, that, surrounded by crime and criminals of all kinds, she had still remained pure and virtuous.

And finally, her thoughts again turned upon her father, whom the procuress cunningly placed in the foreground, thus endeavouring and succeeding in putting an end to the doubt and hesitation of the girl. Marianne found unspeakable satisfaction in the thought of saving at least one person from the clutches of those tormentors, who had made her so very miserable.

The girl was determined to tell the Judge a falsehood, or at least not to make him acquainted with the truth. It was the first deviation from truth she had ever been guilty of—a deviation, moreover, which partly originated in the most noble motives, but one which she would never have been guilty of, had it not been for the occurrences which had taken place since her imprisonment. Her pious mind, and her sound sense, would even here have pointed to the right way; even in the heavy struggle with her duty as a child, and upon the risk of not amending her position with her father, she would have acted rightly.

Almost as if fate had intended that Marianne's present state of mind should undergo no change, and that the late instructions of the procuress should be fresh upon her, it was predestined so to happen, that upon this very day the term of her examination had been fixed.

Marianne and the procuress were still engaged in conversation, when father Wiechmann put his head into the room, and called out in his official tone: "*Marianne Jobs, unmarried!*"

The procuress, who well understood the meaning and import of this call, just found time enough to whisper to the girl: "child, now do not forget what I have told you, for your fate depends upon it."

With weak and tottering steps Marianne left the room.

CHAPTER XXI.

THE EXAMINATION.

THE pale appearance of the unfortunate girl, which was more strongly shown by the brighter light of the corridor, even excited the pity of old Wiechmann, whose rough exterior as we know, covered a sound and good heart.

"Come along, daughter," he said consolingly, "and be not afraid; they want to examine you. All will go right with you. If you are innocent, they will soon let you off. It is not half as bad here as it appears."

These friendly words made a deep impression upon the girl's mind; they were the first signs of real kindness she had experienced at this place. And so easily does tenderness or kindness awaken the better feelings of our nature, that Marianne had almost resolved, candidly and openly to confess her father's and her own position to the judge.

But suddenly she again remembered, that by such a course she would bring the decrepid old man to a prison for life, and she resolved to carry out the plan of duplicity she had conceived that morning.

The turnkey conducted Marianne through the long narrow corridors, throughout which a deep, anxious and fearful silence prevailed. Arrived at a heavy, iron-bound door, which divided the prisons from the court-rooms, he told the girl to enter another corridor, at the opposite end of which she would find the room for examination.

He now gave her a piece of paper, adding mechanically the words:

"This you will bring back again."

He then conducted her a few steps further along the corridor, and left her, saying:

"Go up that small staircase in the middle of the passage, then turn to the right, and go straight forward until you arrive before the last door, No. 17, where you will stop."

In fear and trembling Marianne continued a few steps farther along the gloomy passage. She knew not whether to stand still or go on. She looked upon the paper she held in her hand; nothing was written upon it but these words: "Marianne Jobs, unmarried, from 36 to 17," and below this there was some illegible scribbling, which most probably was intended for a signature.

At last she takes courage and walks onward. Just before reaching the staircase she passes a table, before which two men are seated, who stare at her silently and indifferently. She ascends the steps, and turns around the corner. Suddenly she hears one of the men behind her knocking three times upon the table with a wooden hammer; at the end of the corridor which she has now entered, three similar knocks are heard upon another table. These signals which announce the delivery and receipt of the prisoner, by the two parties upon guard. Marianne tremblingly shrinks back; all is strange to her, every thing increases the horror she feels, she fears every person she sees, and even those who pass without noticing her.

She has now reached the end of the corridor, and stops hesitatingly. Several doors are before her; she knows not where to find No 17, and does not think of looking upwards, where the number is painted in large figures.

The *Nuntius*, whose place is at this end of the corridor, and who had just frightened her by his knocks, observes her embarrassment. He knows from long practice what is the matter, and in an unaltered, careless manner, he asks the single word: "Whither?"

Startled and frightened afresh by the sound of his voice, the timid girl replies with trembling tones: "to No 17."

"Go in there," was the laconic reply, accompanied by a wink with his finger.

Whoever is accustomed to the social, pleasant and agreeable forms of domestic life, and looks upon them as matters of course, can scarcely conceive or understand how deep and severely wounding was the impression caused by this rough, rude and friendless manner upon the already sore and smitten heart of the poor girl. Those little words, friendly and kindly spoken, would have raised her heavenward, but the cold, repulsive and unkind manners of these men, almost crushed her.

Modestly she knocked at the door that had been designated; nobody answered from within. But the harsh authoritative tone of the Nuntius was again heard: "Enter!"

Tremblingly she turned the lock, and suddenly found herself in the examination-room.

The room looked, in many respects, like the one in which her first examination on her arrival in prison, had taken place.

It was a long, high chamber, divided as the other had been, by a barrier into two unequal parts, the smaller of which, that nearest the entrance, was intended for the public, and the larger, nearest the windows, for the judicial functionaries. In the latter part of the room stood an immense table, covered with green cloth, and the gigantic inkstands and sand-boxes upon it, sufficiently indicated its use. Several chairs were placed around it in picturesque disorder.

Two of these chairs, situated at the lower end of the table nearest the barrier, were occupied by a pair of male personages. These were the officers whose duty it was to examine Marianne.

The eldest of the two might be some twenty odd years of age. He had seated himself sideways by the table so that he might look towards the barrier by merely slightly turning his head. He was a remarkably small man, and this circumstance may have been the cause of his carrying his head in a position customary among astronomers.

The activity of his small limbs, the strong black hair of his head, the strongly marked brows, and the peculiar colour of his skin, proved him at once to be a descendant of one of the tribes of Israel. With this people he still seemed to share an affection for precious metals, for his puny body was actually laden with them. He wore a pair of silver spectacles upon his nose, two large gold chains crossed upon his breast, one intended for his lorgnette, the other for the watch, and between them shone a large brooch, corresponding in make and appearance with a couple of rings upon his fingers. His friends usually called him: "the walking show-case of oriental splendour."

This Herr, or rather, not to abuse the genius

of our language, this *Herrlein*,* was Referendarius *Genadi*, who was to-day the appointed Inquisitor of the unfortunate Marianne. Being only a Referendarius, he had yet to pass the third state-examination, at which all his labours in his present capacity would be brought up and scanned. He consequently considered Marianne merely as an instrument by whose assistance he this day expected to prepare another document which to submit at his examination. If all else but this was totally indifferent to him, it only proved that he had not lost the spirit of speculation natural to his people, a spirit which always provides only for self-interest.

The other person, who sat at the lower end of the table, his back turned to the barrier, and his face towards the Inquisitor, might have been about twenty years of age. It was a young, a very young Auscultator, who had only just left the university, and whose fresh, blooming features, bore every mark of innocence and harmlessness. He was now inspired with an unmistakeable degree of importance, for he had the honour to assist in the important business of document-making, in the capacity of Recorder.

The Inquisitor had doubled his left knee upon his chair, braced both his elbows upon the table, and supported his cheeks by his closed fists. In this position, which was more comfortable than plastically or gracefully becoming to his little figure, he studied with official and ambitious earnestness, the report of the Commissary of Police who had arrested Marianne.

The Recorder arranged his papers, mended a few pens with a very dull knife, and occasionally cast a glance of wonder and admiration at the Referendarius.

The latter now suddenly arouses from his absorbing study, his knee, notwithstanding, remains resting upon the chair, and he retains his sitting position. This movement, however, makes him appear somewhat taller, as the upper part of his body is disproportionately large when compared to his legs. He casts a hasty, severe glance upon the prisoner, and exclaims, with a snarling voice, " come nearer !"

Fearfully and tremblingly the poor girl approaches closer to the barrier; she scarcely knows what she is doing.

The Inquisitor casts his head back into his neck even further than usual, examines her for some minutes from head to foot, but without uttering a word or changing a feature. Herr Genadi has invented a new and peculiar system of psychology, and considered this manœuvre of great importance : partly to put the *inquisitees* into a proper fright, and partly to obtain, by observing their features, some glimpses of the probable state of their minds.

The Auscultator quickly availed himself of these momentary psychological studies of his superior, for the purpose of turning round and seeing the prisoner, although from his position

he had partly to rise in his chair in accomplishing this. He then seated himself again, as he already knew the course which would now be pursued, dipped his pen into ink, and awaited the golden words of the Inquisitor, which he had to record.

After a pause, the Referendarius turned his satisfied glance from the girl, and with a polite motion of the head, said : " May I beg, Herr Colleague ?"

Flattered at this dignified, yet cordial address, the Auscultator bowed, and again dipping his pen into the massive inkstand, prepared to write.

With a screeching voice, the Inquisitor dictated as follows :

Actum, Berlin, 25th January, 18—

" On this day, the prisoner, *Marianne Jobs, unmarried*, was brought up for examination, and the following answers were elicited. She was properly admonished to confess the truth and the whole truth, and was fully made acquainted with the advantages which would arise to her from an open confession, as also with the punishments attendant upon wilful, false, or perverted statements in court.

" Upon the question : wherefore she was at present imprisoned, Marianne Jobs replied :"

After the other had written all down thus far, the little Inquisitor again turned his head towards the prisoner, and he now began to display a degree of eloquence, which did no small honour to his Hebrew descent.

Raising both his hands high into the air, he demonstrated to her, how she would find it best openly to confess all her misdemeanours, as her punishment, in consideration of her youth and her open confession would then be very lenient; but if she endeavoured to hide or deny her crime, she would not alone prolong her present imprisonment for examination, but would also increase the severity of her punishment by her own obstinacy. The latter was the more certain, as she could not hope to get her liberation by falsehood, as he, the Inquisitor, would, under all and any circumstances, sift out and discover the exact amount of her crimes.

The Referendarius availed himself of this opportunity to introduce a large number of terrible criminal anecdotes, all showing how often he had brought the most hardened sinners to confession. He then continued in the regular prescribed speech, and descanted upon her moral obligations; he spoke eloquently of the sinfulness of untruth, as well as of the blessing of actual repentance and reform.

The Auscultator listened to the Referendarius in silent astonishment, and still remembering his scarcely passed student years, he said to himself, " what a famous *Pauke** he does make."

The accused had nothing to repent before her earthly judge, and yet she could not free herself from the suspicion which rested upon her. The eloquent words of the Referendarius had really

---

* *Herrlein*. The syllable *lein* is added to *Herr*, to express diminutiveness.—TRANSLATOR.

* To make a "*famose Pauke*" in student slang, means making an elegant or verbose speech.

made an impression upon her. Once more she began to doubt and to hesitate; but the precepts of Mrs. Rüthmann worked upon her distracted mind, and she remained firm to the resolution she had taken.

Marianne replied word for word as the procuress had instructed her. The old and terrible maxim, that persons often enter our prisons less guilty than they leave them, was again verified in this instance. Marianne had fallen a victim to her fellow-prisoners.

The Inquisitor now turned to the Recorder with the question: " the last words, if you please ?"

The Auscultator read from his record: " Upon the question, wherefore she was at present imprisoned, Marianne Jobs replied:"

" Please to continue writing," said the Referendarius as he brought the replies of the accused into a legal style after the following manner :

" I was imprisoned, because the police in my bed found a piece of calico, said to be stolen. I do not know whom said calico belongs to, nor how it came into my bed. It is very probable that one of the guests who frequent our cellar has put it into that place without my knowledge and consent."

Having dictated thus far, the Inquisitor added, the closing words: " read, approved and signed." He then pulled his Bandanna handkerchief from his pocket, wiped his forehead after the accomplishment of this difficult task, and with indifference turned to some other documents.

Now began the important part of the office of the Recorder. With great dignity he rises from his place, walks before Marianne, and reads the record to her. This is done in such a hasty, unintelligible manner, that the girl can scarcely understand a syllable of all that is said, and that, for all practical purposes, the Recorder might as well have read arabic or chaldaic to the girl.

Next the Auscultator places the document upon the barrier, and offers his pen to the accused, to sign her statement. But quickly he recollects himself, and draws back his arm: the accused is " a thing unclean," and might even contaminate his pen. Among the stumps of pens which lie about the table for this purpose, he selects another and hands it to the girl, who must sign the document with that.

None of these movements escaped the sensitive and delicate Marianne, and a ray of the deepest, bitterest sorrow overcast her features.

All the world repulsed her, and even her innocent hand was considered contaminating; this moment was not the first that she wished herself ten thousand fathoms beneath the ground.

And can we now deny, that it was the present state of society and the operation of its laws which systematically dragged her to perdition ? Can we deny that our laws, costumes, &c. were the only causes *   *   *   *   *
*   *   *   *   *   *   *
*   *   *   *   *   *   *
*   *   *   *   *   *   *

Could virtue and honesty be expected from a heart that was cast off by the world, torn and trampled down in its endeavours to follow the paths of virtue ?   *   *   *   *   *
*   *   *   *   *   *   *

What patient is there who, in the delirium of a fever, could be held accountable for his actions ?

After Marianne had signed the document with a trembling hand, the Referendarius rose with gravity, and pulled the green woolen bell-rope by his side.

A Nuntius appears at the door.

The Referendarius points his finger upon Marianne, and coolly utters the laconic words:

" That woman goes back."

At this last humiliation the poor girl left the examination-chamber, and in the same manner as she had come, she is conducted back to her cell.

The old Wiechmann closed the prison-door, and the outer world again ceased to exist for her.

Overpowered by various emotions, Marianne fell in a swoon upon her hard couch.

———

CHAPTER XXII.

THE BREACH OF DISCIPLINE AND ITS PUNISHMENT.

THE state of mind in which the unfortunate girl found herself on being reconducted to the prison, may be easier imagined than described.

Her mind was in a continual state of feverish excitement. For the first time in her life, she had told a falsehood, told it before her judge, before the tribunal which her bible had taught her, was instituted by God himself. Often, when in his regular rounds, the turnkey entered her cell, she was upon the point of asking him to conduct her back to her Inquisitor, as she there wanted to make a full confession.

That ominous request frequently hung upon her lips, but then again she felt the unspeakable miseries which even now embittered her innocent life, and it was a secret consolation, to use even the weapons of untruth and of duplicity in her revenge. The lie she told became the sting of the worm which pricks the footsoles of his tormentor.

This struggle in Marianne's mind did not escape the lynx-eye of the cunning Mrs. Rüthmann, who made it a particular point to strengthen the girl in her former resolves. She, as it were, was the demoniac spirit, who watched at all times and every where, to shake the foundation of good, wherever there was a chance to attack, and if possible, to open the way for the entrance of the Evil one into Marianne's heart.

An interlude of a very peculiar kind, which interrupted the sameness of the prison life, now occurred, and was not without its further evil consequences for the spiritual life of the maiden.

The younger of the two female thieves, had made the discovery that directly below her prison, another female criminal, and an old friend of hers, was incarcerated. The desire to see this old friend, and have some communication with her, overcame the fear of punishment, and induced her to break through one of the strictest laws of prison discipline.

Some few days after the examination of Marianne had taken place, this woman had left her couch at the earliest dawn of the morning. She placed the several stools on top of each other, and having thus reached the window, she endeavoured by calling to attract the attention of her friend. The other answered, and the two prisoners had a short conversation through their tin boxes.

Spite of every precaution, the sentry in the prison-yard observed this conversation, and on being relieved, reported, as in duty bound, that a prisoner, in number 36, had spoken with another through the window. As we have observed above, this is strictly forbidden, this measure being necessary to avoid all collusions between the criminals, and its transgression is severely punished. The usual punishment in such a case is to chain the offender to the wall for a few days, and even to put him or her, for a few hours into the *Zwangstuhl*, (forcing chair,) which consists in a box formed like a chair wherein they must sit, without having the power of moving a limb.

All this appears very severe, yet order could not possibly be kept without such measures. It is only necessary to apply them with justice and discrimination.

In the prison, the consequences were well known. The soldier had called to the woman to be quiet, and with all her experience in prison-life, she could not be doubtful of her fate, if she was discovered to be the guilty party.

She had, however, no fears of being betrayed by her two elder fellow prisoners, for both had been sufficiently initiated into the laws and customs of prisons, to know, and to regard it a sacred point of honour, "that a prisoner must never assist the authorities in their investigations."

This will prove how deeply in human nature that principle is rooted, which tells us, to defend, cherish, and keep under all circumstances, that which our free conviction has acknowledged as right. The same criminals, who scorned and laughed at all civil laws, who trampled them under foot, who lived in eternal warfare with the constituted authorities, these same people have their own laws, which they hold so dear and holy, that they prefer voluntarily to suffer punishment, rather than transgress them.

The procuress knew as well as the two thieves, that all three must suffer a severe punishment for the breach of discipline which had been committed, unless they chose to betray the guilty party; but they preferred to suffer this penalty, unjust and unmerited as they considered it, rather than act contrary to their conviction or conscience, and betray their cell-mate.

The woman, consequently, only feared Marianne's inexperience; she did not believe that Marianne would positively and willingly betray her—for educated as she was, she did not think such a thing possible—yet she thought it most likely that the poor girl would be frightened at the harsh manner and words of the Inspector, and tell the truth.

Being aware of the great influence which Mrs. Rüthmann exercised over the girl, she took the procuress to one side, and solicited her to use her influence and bind Marianne to secrecy.

Upon the whole, it was of little consequence to the procuress whether the other was punished or not, although she would not herself betray her under any circumstances. But she availed herself of this favourable opportunity to bind Marianne closer to evil, by another, and in this case, a united falsehood, and thus to add to the evil seed which she had already began to sow in the pure and virtuous bosom of the maiden. Only by this system of leading her gradually from the paths of virtue and religion, could she hope to execute plans which she had conceived at the first sight of the beautiful and unfortunate girl.

For these reasons the procuress informed Marianne of all that might shortly be expected to take place in the prison.

She explained to her all the inviolable laws of the world of criminals; she informed her that all four were partners in misery, that all four had been more or less ill-used and scorned by all the world without; that for these reasons they lived at a struggle with that world, and were bound in duty to assist each other in life and death.

She could think of nothing more unwise, and at the same time more dishonourable, than the betrayal of each other to a common enemy, as they would only increase each other's sufferings; situated as they were, they must assist one another, come what may.

Marianne, of course, struggled warmly against the proposition of committing another falsehood; but in the first instance pity and regard for her father had been the arguments of the procuress, and in the present, regard for her fellow prisoners, was an equally effective argument.

That woman painted the position of things in such horrible colours, much stronger really than the reality, and, moreover, knew so well to interweave truth with falsehood, that Marianne, perfectly entangled and blinded in the nets and by the sophistry of the adroit woman, soon believed it to be a demand of justice as well as sympathy, to assist in waging war against law and order.

Marianne had already accustomed herself to look no longer upon rights and laws as things holy and necessary, but as instruments of persecution and oppression to the unfortunate.

It was scarcely day, when the much-feared Inspector, in company of the turnkey, Wiechmann, made his appearance.

The Inspector was a tall, fine looking man, of

military demeanour, which he had assumed during his former years of service. His appearance was more one commanding respect, than creating repulsive feelings; his entire manner was cold and measured.

"Which of you spoke from the windows very early this morning?" he inquired with serious dignity.

Nobody replied.

"I call upon the one who has done it to come forward and confess of her own accord, else all of you will be punished," he said again, in a quiet tone.

All were silent as before.

The Inspector remained perfectly quiet. Before asking the question, he knew perfectly well that none would announce herself, and in his questions, he only observed the prescribed form.

For the same reason he finally directed the question, whether she was guilty, separately, to each prisoner.

Each answered no, and at the same time denied any knowledge of the offender.

At last Marianne's turn came also; she no longer betrayed any signs of hesitation or fear; she replied calmly what Mrs. Rüthmann had taught her, namely, that she had slept very sound towards morning.

The Inspector turning to the jailor Wiechmann, commanded in the same even and quiet tone: "Number 36, for three days without mattresses," and without turning back, quietly marched out of the cell.

The turnkey followed him, not even casting a look towards the tender person of his favourite.

The mattresses were taken away, and for three cold, long nights the prisoners had to sleep upon the hard floor. They did so, without complaint, without even casting a word of reproach upon the guilty party.

This circumstance created a wonderful revolution in Marianne's soul. The instructions of the procuress had already taken effect, so far, that she no longer considered her falsehoods as sinful or criminal. She therefore suffered a punishment, which, according to her own conviction, she had not deserved; an injustice had been done to her, for she believed that she had only fulfilled a duty of humanity towards her fellow prisoners.

This unfortunate conviction strengthened in Marianne's bosom the belief, that the authorities punished deeds, which in reality were not wrong, and that therefore she acted rightly, in opposing the state and its laws.

This idea became the declaration of war against civil order, after, as we have seen before, the religious and modest elements in the soul of the maiden had received so severe a shock, as almost to put her beyond the pale of society.

That she had justly merited this punishment; that this punishment was absolutely necessary, as a means of preserving order, and consequently supporting the first object of criminal justice—

all this she had forgotten. The idea of self-sacrifice to save her fellow prisoner reigned now supreme in her mind, and even to herself she appeared as a noble, high-minded heroine in her sphere.

CHAPTER XXIII.

THE SENTENCE.

It may easily be supposed, that in her present state of mind, Marianne was deaf to all further questions of her Inquisitor. The thought of telling to her judge the truth, of even assisting him in eliciting it, never recurred to her again.

The little Referendarius worked very hard, and tried all means to disclose the crime. He carried on the examination with a most terrible minuteness; Marianne had to undergo cross-questionings for hours and hours together, and the youthful recorder had to fill whole reams of paper with the results.

Then followed the hearing of the merchant who had been robbed, and of all his employees. But all was in vain! Marianne remained firm in her first statement, and not one of the witnesses could fix any definite suspicion upon her, as a great many people had been in the magazine, at the time the theft took place.

A single hope at last only remained to the votary of justice. A number of the witnesses had unanimously deposed on their examination, that on the day of the theft, a strange girl had come into their magazine, and had purchased some trifle.

It was now necessary to confront these witnesses with the accused, and thus to ascertain whether these people would recognize the purchaser in the person of the unfortunate Marianne.

The Referendarius now named a day, the last of the term, on which all these witnesses should be cited to appear in the examination-room. He was in a state of intense excitement, for upon the result of this day depended the fate of his favourite legal document. If the witnesses did not recognize the accused, all his labour had been in vain; he could then elicit no proof of crime sufficient for committal, and had before him the most unsatisfactory result of an examination, a provisionary discharge.

An entire or honourable discharge, or a regular committal—only one or the other, no matter which—was all he could possibly desire, for in either case, his inquisitorial talents were fully established, and his reputation safe.

With immense strides the little Referendarius paced up and down the examination-room. He had arrayed the witnesses inside the barrier in rank and file *a la militaire*, and all faces turned towards the door, that they might immediately on her entrance, obtain a full view of the prisoner. The excitement of that moment had given a dark red hue to his face, and the delay of Marianne's appearance, seemed almost unbearable to him.

The Auscultator also had grown so impatient, that he whittled half a pack of quills to pieces. The witnesses alone, waited with that abashed diffidence, which is so natural to persons unaccustomed to appear before the officers of justice, on their debut at a tribunal.

At last the door opens and the accused enters. In order to give the witnesses a chance of examining her more closely, the Referendarius places himself behind a chair, and there begins a most magnificent grandiloquent appeal to the accused, urging her once more to confess the truth. The Auscultator again remembered the " famose Pauke " of his student years.

The accused remained quiet, simply repeating her former statements, and is led away again.

" Well, gentlemen," now began the small functionary, as he anxiously passed his hand through his thick oriental hair, " how is it ? Am I right ? You recognize her again ? I knew you would ; no doubt of it! she must be guilty. Yes, yes! we have some experience in cross questioning."

The witnesses declared unanimously, that the person they had just seen was an utter stranger to them ; the Auscultator quickly hides his head in his pocket handkerchief, as if he was suddenly seized with a fit of coughing ; with a most disconsolate face the Referendarius looks around him, and says : " Hm! Hm !"

Another and a single anchor of hope remained to the Referendarius wherewith to save this case ; weak as that anchor seemed, it must be tried.

The hunchbacked Jobs might be the guilty party. The examination against him had been conducted in precisely the same manner as against his daughter ; but without first needing the instructions of his fellow prisoners, he had denied everything in a far more decided tone than Marianne.

We already know, that he most probably was unacquainted with the theft of this particular piece of goods.

Upon an order of the Referendarius, he was now also brought in for examination.

Bold and unabashed the old sinner approached the barrier. With his cunning, grey, blear-eyes he stared at all present so quietly, so impudently, that it almost appeared as if they were the culprits and he the judge or a witness. He resembled a wild tiger or cat, which is locked into a cage, and only thereby prevented from tearing everything to pieces.

This time the Inquisitor made no speech. The psychological system which he had adopted, told him, that in this case his labour would be in vain, and his eloquence lost.

After the hunchbacked Jobs had been stared at for a few minutes, he was lead away as he had been brought in without a word.

The witnesses also declare that they don't know him. All the hopes of the Referendarius, for the production of a document fit for examination, all these fond hopes are now destroyed! With a deep sigh, he dismisses the witnesses, and casts a last sorrowful look upon the pile of documents, which have thus been all written in vain.

The Auscultator showed more indifference. His examination for Assessorship is as yet very far in the perspective ; to him, it is immaterial what he does or how his cases succeed, as long as he only produces documents.

With his last failure the official energy of the Referendarius has cooled down, and he now wishes to dispose of the case as soon as he possibly can.

The same morning Marianne is brought up again, to be heard for the last time.

The Inquisitor asks the question, whether she had anything else to state ? upon her replying in the negative, he dictates with a heavy heart the following ominous words to his recorder :

" On her final hearing, Marianne Jobs declares :

" I have nothing further to say in the affair or in my defence. I once more protest my entire innocence, and pray for a discharge and immediate liberation."

And now the documents were all packed together and sent to the higher tribunal, which had to pronounce judgment in the case.

Marianne again passed eight long days in her prison, and then was once more recalled to the examination-room.

Herr Referendarius Genadi was there seated upon his official-stool, and cast dark glances at the unfortunate girl, as she entered.

" Your sentence has come," he said, " and you have escaped much more leniently than you deserve. It is to be hoped, that the leniency shown to you will induce you in future to lead a more virtuous and moral life.—Colleague, will you be kind enough to read her sentence to the accused ?"

The Auscultator rose from his seat, took up one of the many large sheets that lay before him, and read with an audible voice :

" After close judicial examination and upon all the collected evidences of the case, the Royal-Criminal-Tribunal (*Königliche Kriminal Gericht*) decides as follows :

" That the accused, Marianne Jobs, be *provisionally* declared *not* guilty of the theft charged against her."

Marianne listened to the reading of this decision, without having even the remotest conception of its real meaning. She still less knew what was meant, when the Inquisitor again taking the word, addressed her thus :

" You are now informed that the right of a further defence against this decision is still at your disposal, should you think proper to avail yourself of that right."

She stared at the Referendarius with a silent and puzzled mien, and she most probably presumed, that something which she could be able to understand would be added to this unintelligible speech.

The Referendarius, however, was silent, and after a short pause he added in very bad humour :

8

"Well, are you going to honour me with your answer?"

We remember the anxiety and fear which the poor girl suffered, when on her arrival in the office of the prison she misunderstood the questions of the secretary; now that female diffidence and bashfulness, that brilliant diadem of her maiden modesty, had almost entirely disappeared, sorrow, trouble, and fear, had made her firm and had given her assurance. Without hesitation she replied: "I have understood nothing of what you said, Herr Referendarius."

The small Inquisitor was on the point of venting his anger in a volley of abuse, and thus obtain some little satisfaction for the bad result of the trial; but he suddenly remembered that he had really spoken unintelligibly, that is to say, juristically.

He then began to explain to her, that the provisional discharge meant simply this: she was still suspected of the theft of the calico, but the court did not consider the evidence against her as sufficiently clear to condemn her. But if she herself thought that in such a decision, she had suffered injustice, and if she actually believed herself entirely free from guilt, the way of redress was still open to her. The documents then would be sent to the "*Kammergericht*,"* where the case would undergo another examination, and a second judgment would then be pronounced.

Although Marianne as yet knew, and could know nothing of the real consequences of a provisional discharge, still she understood that the court only liberated her as a suspected thief, and that she was still looked upon as such. Her honour and position in society as an honest member of it, was lost, and a stain was forever fixed upon her person.

This thought made a terrible impression upon a mind which knew itself free from all guilt. But on the other hand, the knowledge of the falsehoods which during her prison-life she had been guilty of, crushed her, and this knowledge prevented her from bearing her misfortune with the strength of soul of real virtuous innocence. She was innocent, yet guilty; guiltless she had been punished, and guilty she had escaped punishment.

It may easily be understood that all these counteracting positions only helped to confuse still more Marianne's views of right and wrong, particularly as her pure, religiously ardent mind was very susceptible of enthusiastic or fanatical impressions, but was incapable of clear reasoning and thought.

Gloomily and absorbed, she stared before her, without even having the power of saying a word in reply. Her account-book with society was laid before her as closed, why should she have the reckonings once more examined? The further proof of her innocence, moreover, seemed utterly unattainable; from the dark recesses and dens of her father's dwelling, only further matter for accusations could be brought.

* A higher tribunal.

At last she answered mechanically: "upon the whole, I am perfectly indifferent what turn matters may take; so I will let the case rest as it is."

The Inquisitor assentingly nodded his head; he was pleased and satisfied to have so bad a case brought to a definite conclusion.

He quickly dictated:

"Marianne Jobs declared that she would relinquish the right of a further defence, and abide by the first decision."

For the last time, Marianne had to sign a document, and was then led back to prison.

CHAPTER XXIV.

THE DISMISSAL.

ALTHOUGH Marianne had been innocently accused, had been as innocently sentenced, still we must confess that the judgment pronounced upon her was perfectly justifiable under the existing laws.

The simple circumstance that a piece of stolen goods was found within her bed, and, moreover, in a house of very bad repute, was quite enough to justify suspicions. These suspicions were not sufficiently strong to justify a full committal, and the tribunal was consequently compelled to pronounce the most unsatisfactory of all sentences, a conditional discharge.

At first, Marianne only felt morally the consequences of this sentence, by the suspicion of theft being thus fixed upon her. Of the terrible civic consequences of such a sentence, she had not the remotest conception.

These consequences consist in the institution of *surveillance by the Police*, and in the dangerous obstacles which are thereby thrown in the way of honest labour and respectable support.

On her return to prison, the poor girl informed Mrs. Rüthmann faithfully of all that had occurred, and learned from her that after such a result, she would undoubtedly be dismissed this very day, perhaps even in a very few hours.

"It is a great pity," continued the procuress, "that my liberation, for which I look day after day, has not yet taken place; I should in that case have provided a home for you upon your discharge."

"You are very kind," replied Marianne, with a grateful look, "but as it is, alas, you cannot help me."

"I would, after all, advise you," continued the other, after a thoughtful pause, "to return for the present to your father. I have not the least doubt, but that his sentence has turned out similar to your own; and to-day he will also be liberated. You shall certainly not have to remain long in his clutches, for as soon as I am liberated, I will come and take you away. We can then consider what is is next to be done."

The procuress had made all her calculations

when she gave this advice. She would thus know precisely where to seek Marianne, and could easily obtain the pretty girl into her power.

Marianne easily consented to this proposition, as that woman already exercised an almost unlimited authority over the poor girl's mind, although in assenting, she experienced an inner sense of dislike to this plan, and a certain fearful foreboding.

We must here observe, that since the occurrence of the punishment for breach of discipline, the conduct of the two other inmates of the cell towards Marianne had undergone a material change. It had evidently astonished them, that a girl, whom they had treated with scorn and abuse, should suffer punishment for other's offences without even uttering a word of reproach or complaint.

The youngest of the two thieves especially, she for whose fault Marianne had suffered, showed now a particular attachment to the poor girl. As much as it was in her power, she endeavoured to show Marianne little favours and attentions, which the latter received with friendly gratitude. By these means a greater intimacy had began to exist among all the inmates of the prison, and the attention of the two women seemed particularly to be drawn to the position of Marianne towards Mrs. Rüthmann.

For some days past the youngest of the thieves had shown great signs of trouble and restlessness. She often whispered with her friend, observed and watched Marianne with a fixed gaze, particularly when the latter conversed with the procuress about her hopes and views for the future; she did not, however, express any thing definite. It seemed as if she wanted to say something, yet had some particular reason for not daring to say it. One evening she had even, (what she had never done before,) placed her matrass by the side of Marianne's, but Mrs. Rüthmann proposed to the latter to lie close to the stove, and placed herself between the two.

This morning, however, when the final arrangements between Marianne and Mrs. Rüthmann seemed to have been made, the other, the younger thief, namely, became so excited, that she ran her head against the prison wall, and the blood suddenly rushed from her nose. Crying and grumbling she remained in a corner, her face turned to the wall, apparently endeavouring to stop the flow of blood. Thus she remained for some time.

Towards noon, as the procuress had predicted, old Wiechmann entered the prison.

His face was beaming with joy, and his stern old features assumed a serio-comic, pleased expression.

Still, in the presence of the other prisoners, he considered it his duty to preserve his official dignity; walking to the centre of the cell, he stood erect, and in a formal tone said:

"Marianne Jobs, unmarried, I announce your liberation, and have come to conduct you down."

The fellow-prisoners of the poor girl again crowded round her, as at the time when Marianne was brought among them; their sympathy this time, however, was more honest, more heartfelt.

"Fare you well," said the procuress, "I hope shortly to see you again, and in a more merry place."

At these words the youngest of the other women left the corner in which she had hitherto remained. She cast a dark look upon the speaker, and cordially offered her hand to Marianne.

"May you be happier," she said, "than I can ever expect to be, and do not think of me in anger."

At these words she slipped some soft rags into Marianne's hand, gave her a significant wink, and walked slowly back.

Wiechmann opened the door, and Marianne walked out.

"Well, you see, my child," he said, with hearty kindness, as he shook her hand until her whole body trembled, "you find it just as I told you. You will now soon again be outside of these walls, but be careful not to come back to us."

Marianne silently and pensively walked down the long corridor, without having the power of uttering a word in reply.

Old Wiechmann conducted her back to the office which she had at first been taken to, and where her discharge was now finally recorded. He then followed her down into the yard, pressed her hand once more, and added:

"Good bye, good bye, my child, but don't you come back again."

At these words he left her to her fate, and turned to attend to his other duties.

Marianne was *free*—free, after having passed long weeks between those damp and gloomy prison-walls. But she was incapable of enjoying the glorious feeling of liberty, she only felt an oppressive fear, which convulsively grasped her very soul.

She felt that she did not leave the prison as she had entered it;—the innocence of her heart, her peace of soul were gone, were lost forever. She had been looked upon as a criminal, and she had become a criminal.

For a long time she remained upon the spot, where old Wiechmann had left her. There she stood immoveable, her tearful eye fixed upon the ground.

She dared not to pass into the street by the large portal; she believed that every one who saw her, must know whence she came, ay, and that children would point their fingers at her. All the terrible scenes through which she had passed on her way to prison again appeared before her heated fancy.

And whither was she to turn, where to go at this moment? She knew not whether her father had yet been liberated or not. She dared not alone go and reside at the cellar, and even if she dared, she knew not who would open the doors for her.

Hopelessly she looked upon the high, gloomy

prison-walls that surrounded her. Her eyes rested upon the number thirty-six, which was painted on a board below the tin box of the window of her former cell, to denominate its location to the sentinels in the yard. She even wished herself back to the quiet solitude of that prison, where her fellow-prisoners spoke kindly to her; among the rest of humankind, she had become an outcast and a stranger.

On looking up to the window, Marianne suddenly remembered, that the youngest of the two thieves had secretly given something into her hand, which, from fear of Wiechmann's observing it, she had put into her pocket without examining it. She now took it out; it was a small rag of coarse dirty linen, evidently torn from part of a dress.

By means of a bit of wood and with blood, the following words were traced upon it, almost illegible and all misspelled.

"Mrs. Rüthmann is a bad, worthless woman, who would work your ruin; for Heaven's sake, avoid her as you would an infernal fiend."

With much trouble Marianne deciphered these words, and after reading them, was cast upon a fresh tide of doubts and painful fears.

Mrs. Rüthmann, the only being who had ever been kind to her, who had seemed to sympathize with her, who had promised her advice and help, upon whom her whole future seemed to depend, she was said to be false to her, to desire her ruin? Impossible! And yet what object could the other woman have in creating groundless suspicions in her mind? The thief who advised her thus, had, during the latter time of her imprisonment, been kind to her, had even abstained from all her former coarseness and vulgarity.

Marianne now remembered that that woman had often approached her during the last few days of her confinement, just as if she wanted to communicate something to her, but had as often retreated at the sight of Mrs. Rüthmann. Again the poor girl felt a decided aversion to return to the cellar of her father, and by going back now, she would only be following strictly the advice of her friend. She had, so to say, an instinctive presentiment, that she had already become too much depraved by her prison life, to return safely into this pool of crime and vulgarity; a pure spotless conscience was no longer her defence against sin and temptation.

Looking at her position in all these lights, the heart of the girl still struggled against the thought of condemning the procuress upon a bare accusation, which was not in any way substantiated.

With a tortured heart, Marianne proceeded a few steps, and now again stood in the gateway through which she had once sought and found safety against the scorn of the people, even in the prison itself.

She could not gather sufficient strength to proceed. And whither should she go? She would not return to the cellar. She felt unable to find her way out of the labyrinth of doubts which beset her on all sides when thinking of her late friends; but at least she had learned something, she had learned to be cautious. The warning of the thief had made her thus circumspect, and this warning corresponded with a truth that Marianne now felt more than ever—namely, that she must hopelessly be lost if she returned to her father's den.

But here again the old question pressed itself upon her mind: whither should she go? Where was the place which would hospitably receive the unfortunate girl? Where was the hand which would give her bread only until Mrs. Rüthmann should be discharged? She then might openly tell her of the accusations brought against her, as she still entertained a silent hope that some misunderstanding was the foundation of it.

Exhausted and faint, Marianne seated herself upon a large stone which protects a projecting pillar of the gate, and burst into bitter tears. She was unspeakably miserable and deserted.

An elderly gentleman came from the interior of the building and walked past the girl.

Moved by her appearance, he stopped for a moment to look at the weeping maiden.

The man was of a well-formed, noble figure, dressed in plain and neat citizen's dress. Long silvery hair fell around his face, which seemed a mirror of health, kindness, and good-will towards all men.

The gentleman wore a long over-coat of fine brown cloth, from beneath which, upon a black dress coat, an order was slightly protruding. A simple black hat covered his head, and in his hand he carried a cane with a large silver knob.

With a friendly, consoling smile, he looked at the girl, and then asked kindly:

"Why do you weep, child?"

Marianne looked up; the kind, smiling look of the elderly gentleman, was a balm to her wounded breast.

She told him that she was a dismissed prisoner, and knew not whither to turn her steps.

The simple story of the maiden seemed to make a deep impression upon the stranger.

"Good God!" he cried, "so young in years, and already so much sorrow!"

He asked a few more questions of the girl, then told her to wait his return, and re-entered the prison-yard.

After a while he returned and said: "I am glad to find that you have told me the truth in all things; come with me, child, and I will see what can be done for you."

Almost reconciled to her fate, Marianne followed the kind old man.

For the present we will leave her with her new friend.

CHAPTER XXV.

THE BOUDOIR.

It was a splendid and bright morning in February.

Masses of fresh fallen snow covered streets and houses with its virginal whiteness. The newly born sun illumined the smooth, brilliant plains with a new hue, until the sinful earth appeared transfigured in its glorious rays.

A busy and active multitude enlivened the streets.

House-keepers hurried to clear the snow from their doorsteps and the sidewalks in front of their dwellings, and behind them municipal officers sought to discover a fineable spot: any little spot where the snow had been left.

The cooks with their baskets hurried to the bakers to prepare the breakfast for their masters who would soon awake; on their way they disputed with the slow milkman whom they met with his dog-cart, and who ought to have delivered the milk for said breakfast somewhat earlier.

A cab drove slowly along, dividing the disputants, on its way to the regular cab and carriage stand at the end of the street.

Behind the cab followed a couple of lively seamstresses, who worked at some milliner shops at the *Schlossfreiheit*,* and who in great haste related to each other their adventures and the scandal of last night's ball.

Blushingly the one at the right nodded to the supernumerary *Registratur-vize-assistant*,† who only waited for a suitable promotion to offer her his hand and heart, and who now passed her on his way to his office, and acknowledged her courtesy by raising his very shabby hat.

A loud noise is heard at the corner of the next street. A troup of ragged and dirty street boys are on their way to work at some manufactory, and the newly fallen snow furnishes them material for exercise, fun and mischief. They have just attacked an *Eckensteher*, whom they observe staggering along the streets before them. Though it is yet early, that numbered and labelled individual, has already been paying his devotion at the shrine of Bacchus.

A gensd'arme, the *perpetuum mobile* of Berlin streets, arrives and soon restores the peace.

Gradually the streets assume a still more lively appearance.

Butchers in cleanly aprons, carrying trays filled with meat upon their shoulders; barbers with their unclean razor-bags, and their air of business; boot-blacks with dirty hands, laden with newly polished boots and shoes, sand-carters with their ear-piercing cries, cabs, carriages, horses, pedestrians—all now wildly mix through other, noisily proceeding to their daily occupations.

Whilst thus life and tumult in the streets has commenced, most of the shutters and curtains of windows are still closed, particularly those of the *Belle-Etage;* for the fashionable world of Berlin, no less than elsewhere, claims the prerogative of late sleeping.

In the most fashionable part of the city, in the *Wilhelms*-street, we observe a solitary exception.

* A locality in Berlin.
† Title of an inferior assistant in the Registry.

The appearance of the first story of a proud and splendid house, betrays that its occupants are already awake. The shutters are open and the curtains have all been drawn up; two chambermaids seem busily arranging the rooms. In the corner room we observe a tall, well formed lady, who lazily resting upon a soft *Fauteuil*, looks thoughtfully out upon the street.

The beautiful head, encircled by glossy raven locks, which still remain in the picturesque disorder of the night, rests upon a soft hand, and a snowy, well formed arm and elbow. The luxurious bosom, scarce hidden by the light elegant morning dress, heaves up and down as with internal emotion; a tear, which now and then escaped the brilliant dark eye, drops and seeks a hiding place in that breast.

The small room is a perfect picture of united comfort and elegance.

A pleasant, aromatic warmth pervades its atmosphere. Soft and rich carpets cover the floor. Near the window stands an elegant well furnished toilette-table; opposite, a soft swelling ottoman. A marble Cupid leaning upon a bronze clock of curious workmanship, is constantly sharpening his arrows by means of artificial wheelwork. A splendid *Trumeaux* reflects back this gem of ingenious workmanship. Before it stands a magnificent pedal harp, richly decorated with gold and purple velvet. The walls are hung with the most valuable, choice pictures, which are advantageously set off by the dark green and gold background of tapestry. Behind the pale red silk curtains at the window, a row of choice and rare flowers bloom and fill the air with fragrant odours.

The whole produces at a first glance, an impression of luxury, ease and voluptuousness.

The lady whom we find surrounded by so much splendour and elegance, is Francisca, the Equestrian.

Her present changed position she owed to the extravagant liberality of Geheimerath Berthold. She had succeeded in entangling the vain, amorous fop entirely in her nets, and in consequence of his repeated and earnest entreaties, she had exchanged the Hotel of the Green Elephant in X—— street, for handsome apartments in Wilhelm-street.

In this manner the Geheimerath had gained the chance of boasting to his friends of his intimacy with the beautiful artiste, and of her favours. In fact, he fairly insinuated that she was his mistress, and fed his vanity on the jealous despair of his acquaintances.

This, of course, was the only return he gained for his expensive extravagance, for Francisca had certainly listened to, but never granted any of his prayers, and our readers are well aware that he could never hope for further success.

The Equestrian had forced her way to his acquaintance, as she felt a burning impulse to be revenged upon him for her ruined, dishonoured youth. Indefatigably, though still unsuccessfully, she had sought for him year after year—

at last she had found him, but not found him to please him by hours of loving nonsense.

She meditated upon, and sought for a terrible, a peculiar mode of revenge, revenge that would seem to her sufficient, not alone upon her seducer, but upon all society, all civilized society, from which she found herself ejected and thrown among the Paria of humanity.

Often, when the Geheimerath lay at her feet, and did not hesitate to disgrace his grey hair by vows of love and faith, her bleeding heart trembled in convulsed anger. Glances of the deepest, most unspeakable contempt shot from her large fiery eyes, down upon the long, lank figure before her; but in an instant she regained mastery over herself, and a pleasant, kind smile of mixed encouragement and refusal played upon her purple lips.

She must still wait, 'bide her time for her revenge, prepare it quietly, and upon slow and certain plans; the prostrate form breathing vows before her, was only the May-fly which the boy suffers to play, fly and shrill around him, whilst its leg is held captive by the string in the urchin's hand.

By this well-managed game, the Geheimerath was, day after day, drawn deeper into the snares of this modern Calypso. At first it had only flattered his vanity to have so celebrated an artiste attached to him, but gradually he felt himself consuming by fierce sensual desires.

The more she opposed his importunities, the more ardent became his passions, and already Francisca was forced to confess to herself, that she exercised some of the pleasures of retribution, in the burning, unsatisfied passion which she had kindled, and which consumed her victim.

But to the fiery, passionate mind of this revengeful woman, this was but a small satisfaction. She still sought for another balm to her burning wounds.

Yet whilst the Equestrian pursued her dark and bloody plans of revenge, her heart had not been entirely dead to the more gentle feelings of womanhood. And this was the most wonderful transformation which had occurred during the whole of this eventful period; for since the infidelity of the Assessor many years ago, she had remained a stranger to such feelings, and only remembered them with scornful, bitter, and terrible coldness.

We already know that the pocket-book of the Major, which had been stolen and been afterwards lost by Schmerles at the feast of the Equestrian, into whose hands it had fallen, had informed her of all the particulars of the affairs of Prince Prominsky.

At the same time she had learned where her seducer was to be found, and determined to mix herself into the affair of the Jewess and the Prince, and to unite her own work of revenge with the part she there intended to play. Subsequent occurrences, as we know, made this plan in some measure superfluous.

As we have already related, by a fortunate accident she had succeeded in being introduced to the long sought person of her victim, through the mediation of Referendarius von Birkheim. But at the same time and place she had accidentally become personally acquainted with the Prince Prominsky, and the lively interest which she soon felt for the Prince, induced her to continue keeping a lively watch upon his affairs.

This interest had not diminished, but was still on the increase, and if we are to judge by the anxiety with which the Prince sought her society, the interest seemed to be mutual.

As we know, the Prince was a very handsome man, rich and amiable. More than all this, Francisca had been attracted by the elegant cavalierly attention he paid her, and by a respectful reserve towards her, such as she did not observe in any of her other rich admirers. It seemed to her that this man bore a warm feeling heart within his breast, and though her own soul had been hardened by many countless injuries and sorrows, yet this observation did not fail to make a deep impression upon her. And it is also possible that the sombre melancholy expression which not unfrequently dwelt upon the noble forehead of the Prince, and which Francisca justly believed herself acquainted with the cause, (from her knowledge of his family affairs, as she had learned them from the documents in the pocket book,) increased the interest she felt; sorrow ever converses confidingly with a sorrowful heart.

Whether she really loved the Prince, she scarcely knew herself; she certainly had never asked herself the question. On the contrary she seemed with the utmost anxiety to avoid calling her own heart to account upon this point. But her interest for the fate of the noble Prominsky, had already risen high enough to create the most lively desire of rendering actual service to him.

She secretly nursed the hope of appearing before him as a saving angel, who without being personally visible, would guide him to his long lost brother. The hope of gaining by such a course claims upon his respect and gratitude, was a sufficient reward for her.

With these views her mind again reverted to the Jew and Eel-eye, whom she had once before selected as instruments in her plans, but whom she had lost sight of, since the period when she had entered into closer connexion with her victim the Geheimerath.

By the assistance of Giacomo, the Atleth, she had, after many vain endeavours finally succeeded in finding the Eel-eye.

To be undisturbed, she had requested the thief to come to her house very early, and we find her now seated in her Boudoir, awaiting his momentary arrival.

Upon a handsome little table before her, lay the pocket-book of the Major.

The outlines of her position and plans which we have just attempted to give, will perhaps be sufficient to tell the reader, what manifold feelings and emotions at this moment possessed the breast of the beautiful artiste.

Was it thirst for revenge, or sad, bitter remembrance just awakened by the expected arrival of an early friend, or was it the more gentle feeling of unexplained attachment, which now moved her heart?

We know not which; but her cold marble features had assumed a soft, plaintive expression, and pearly tears chased each other down those blooming cheeks.

CHAPTER XXVI.

THE VISIT.

FRANCISCA was startled in her meditations by the approach of footsteps.

Quickly she rose from her seat, endeavoured with her handkerchief to obliterate the last traces of tears, and walked towards the door.

Eel-eye, who, according to her request, had entered unannounced, met her in the antechamber.

The villain had made an elegant toilette. No one would have supposed the fashionably, nay, tastefully dressed young man, to be one of the most dangerous thieves of Berlin. His exterior seemed that of a harmless, innocent and polite fop.

"Good-day, *Fränzel*,"* he said, looking pleasantly around the room, "as I live, you must have caught a rich pousseur. Why, Francisca, you live like a Princess: who would have looked for this in the once simple parson's daughter."

A dark cloud of sorrow and displeasure overspread Francisca's forehead.

"Let the past rest in oblivion, Albert," she said gloomily; "Your words are sacrilegious to its memory. I have forgotten the past—I must not remember it," she added in an under tone.

We already know the wonderful, chameleon-like powers of this woman. Lightly passing her hand accross her forehead she had obliterated all traces of her late excitement from her face, and with the most friendly smile, she invited the thief to a seat by her side on the sofa.

A pull of the bell-rope brought her waiting-maid into the room. She sent her to the cellar, richly stored by the bounty of the Geheimerath, for a bottle of fiery, sparkling, southern wine.

In brilliant pearls the noble product of Syracusian grapes flowed into the rich crystal goblet, which the artiste offered to her early companion with her most inviting smile.

At a single draught the thief poured down the contents of the glass, and smacked his lips after the manner of a *connoisseur* in wines.

Francisca filled a second and a third glass, all of which quickly shared the fate of the first.

"By Jove, you are a splendid girl," now exclaimed the rogue, as his lascivious glances fell upon the charms of the beauteous woman: "I

* Abbreviation of Francisca.

would like to marry you; I would soon gather enough by stealing, to enable us to live in joy and plenty."

At these words he approached closer to the Equestrian, seemingly determined to display more of his affection.

Smilingly, Francisca pushed him back.

"Albert, Albert," she said, threatening with her finger, "if your girl should hear of this; the hostess of the Green Elephant has told me, how jealous she is of you."

"Pshaw, what care I for the girl!" replied the other passionately. "I would give ten like her for you alone; may the devil take all other women, if I can get you for a wife."

The wine increased the excited passions of the bandit, and made the many charms of Francisca appear to him in a still more tempting light.

Overcome by excitement, he put his arm around her well-formed waist, and endeavoured to impress a kiss upon her cheek.

The Equestrian pushed him back, forcibly enough to send him to the other end of the sofa.

"Woman," cried the thief, whose every passion was now heated and excited, "I love you; *you shall and must be mine*; ay, and if you were chained to Heaven, I would have you!"

Beside himself, with passionate excitement, he grasped the Equestrian. His cheeks burned like fiery coals, his pulse trembled feverishly, and his heart beat in sensual paroxysm.

His muscular arms grasped tightly the fair form of Francisca; in her incautious haste she seemed to have sacrificed herself to his ardent, wild excitement.

At the same moment, however, her morning-dress tore open at the neck; her snowy, swelling bosom was exposed to the greedy eyes of the voluptuary, and— a bright dagger, freed from its scabbard, glistened in the hand of Francisca.

"Back, sir, back," she cried, her eyes flashing fire: "or by Heavens I will send this steel to your heart; you know me!"

The arms of the robber sank down relaxed; in terror he withdrew from that Juno-like figure.

The Equestrian had jumped up; with angry, furious mien, she stood before the pale, trembling sinner.

When she found herself out of danger, she coolly returned the dagger to its morocco case, quietly restored the case to its place near her heart, and resumed her former seat.

"Now you will quit your mad pranks, Albert, for you see, they avail you naught," she said scornfully; "but come, you have lost all the colour from your face; drink another glass of wine."

The proud woman knew her unbounded power so well, that she hesitated not a moment to challenge the passions of this unruly man, even by giving him more stimulants.

She filled the goblet again to its brim, and offered it with a quiet, steady hand.

The other sat sulking in a corner of the sofa,

staring gloomily on the ground before him; shame and anger struggled in his mind.

"Well, Albert, why don't you drink?" said the fair siren, in sweet flattering tones, as she placed her hand in innocent confidence upon his shoulders, "are you angry with the playmate of your childhood?"

The villain looked up and met the brilliant eye of the Equestrian, which was directed upon him with every expression of gentle and kind prayer.

"On my *Lotscherehre*," (thieves-honour,) he cried, rising passionately, "woman, you make a silly beardless boy of me."

And greedily he emptied the offered cup.

A slight ray of scorn, like a flash of distant lightning, trembled around Francisca's lips.

"Now see, Albert," she continued soothingly, "ever since we celebrated my birth-day, when so unexpectedly I met you again, I had a great desire to speak with you. Far, far away from home, I wanted once more to have a confidential chat with one whom I had known as a child; but it was difficult, very difficult to find you, and you did not come of your own accord."

"Yes, yes," replied the other, "you, no doubt, are fully aware what kind of business mine is, and that it is necessary to be on one's guard. I can no longer feel safe in the Green Elephant. The *Lambden* (Policemen) have caught even the cunning Schmerles; and of course, I feared also, to go *verschütt* also, (be caught and imprisoned.) Poor fellow! poor Schmerles! his measure is full; he will never be liberated again in his life."

"It must be an interesting life, this thieves' life," said Francisca with apparent curiosity, "if it were not so very dangerous."

"Pshaw, nonsense," replied the thief boastingly, "we must be cunning and cautious; Schmerles brought it all on himself; to be caught by an officer in disguise, it is ridiculous! Thunder! I am knowing enough, and can steal that ring from your finger without being caught. Three times have I been under examination already, and each time they had to liberate me for want of sufficient proof."

"Well, well," replied the other, "then you certainly know an old Jew, who is said to be here in Berlin, and whom I have often heard spoken of as one of the most daring and most dangerous of robbers? Stop, let me try and remember his name—the hostess of the Green Elephant often spoke of him to me. I think it was Schmiel or Schmuel?"

"Know him?" replied Eel-eye, with evident delight, "know him? Why, you mean long Schmuel, my trusty and honest partner. Yes, yes, he is the only man whom I acknowledge as my superior; he can steal the white out of your eye."

Francisca had purposely excited all the passions of Eel-eye, in order to make him first submissive, then confiding. She had hitherto not been quite certain of his being a perfect, accomplished, and graduated rascal, and if the latter were the case, she particularly wanted to ascertain whether he knew the Jew.

Neither of these doubts she could have hoped to solve in the ordinary way, if the man, as she rightly supposed, was an accomplished thief. His character would then be too cunning and cautious to disclose these points, and therefore she excited his passions, to train him into submission and confidence.

Her plan had been fully successful. She now knew that her early friend stood in intimate connexion with the old Jew, and upon this she built her further plans. Without, however, betraying in any way the object of her request, she merely, in a tone of easy indifference, expressed a wish of becoming acquainted with some of his thieving comrades; she disliked her present company and associates; "they are all a proud, aristocratic set," she said, "who only look down upon me, and are overbearing. I should much like a change."

Francisca found a quicker and more eager compliance with her desire than she herself could have hoped for. The industrial spirit of the thief, quickly caught at her wish with egotistical views.

"I will, with pleasure, let you have your wish," he replied readily, "they are all first rate people to whom I can bring you. All *chesse* boys. Upon the whole, I think you might attach yourself more closely to us, Francisca; it might be of great advantage to you."

"How do you mean? In what way?" inquired the Equestrian, appearing perfectly artless.

"Why, I'll tell you," replied the other. "Your present life may certainly be a very pleasant and delightful one; but how long do you think this will last? Therefore, it would be well for you, to provide something for the future. You cannot save much in the manner you live now; if a few years are past, you must go begging, just like the old rag-gatherer, the mother of our *chonte*. Now I will make a proposition to you. Your present life and associations introduce you into the houses of many rich and noble people. What think you, if in your occasional visits among those people, you were to *ausbaldower* (spy) opportunities to good *massemattens*, and then inform the *chawrusse* (company) of them? If our plans succeed, a considerable Hellig always falls to your share. You have nothing to fear or to risk, and gradually you can save a good sum of money for yourself."

"You mean, if I can rightly understand this jargon of yours; that I am to inform you of opportunities for thefts and robberies, and if these villanies are successful I am to receive a share of the proceeds?" inquired the Equestrian, with difficulty hiding a dark and angry frown that rose on her forehead.

"Yes, that is it," quietly replied the thief.

"That proposition is not so bad," answered the artiste, after a pause of consideration, during which her features assumed their former calm expression, " I believe, I might in the end agree to it."

" That would just now happen right," continued the greedy and industrious villain, " for we shall need your assistance immediately. Several days ago, long Schmuel proposed a robbery of the apartments of a foreign prince, who is at present in Berlin, and stays at the *Hotel de Rome, under den Linden.* Schmuel knows that this prince has lately drawn large sums of money from his banker. We cannot, however, accomplish our object without somebody's assistance, as we dare not venture to ascertain the localities ourselves. Now it would be very desirable, if you could find an opportunity, under some pretext or other, to gain access to this prince, and then gather and remember all the necessary local information."

Francisca's heart beat almost audibly in her excited breast; the prince thus threatened, was Prince Prominsky, *her* prince, if she dared call him so. Fate itself laid it within her power to hold a protecting shield over his head.

At the moment she certainly had no presentiment to how great an extent she was destined to do this. With difficulty she mastered the wild storm of her feelings, excited by the fear, anger, love and disgust she experienced. Under all circumstances, she considered it advisable, to enter further into the subject.

" But of what, in executing such a commission, must I take particular notice?" she inquired, with an assenting tone.

The villain was delighted on hearing this well chosen question. He thought at once that he had a pupil before him, whose willingness was only equalled by her docility.

Entirely in his element, he now explained to the Equestrian, that the most necessary things she must note on her first visit, were the entrance, situation of rooms, and the neighbourhood.

Next she must closely observe the nature of the locks, particularly whether they were patent, *Dorn,* or common locks, and, if possible, get a wax impression of the key-holes. In the room itself, she must induce the prince to get out some money, so that she might by this opportunity observe where he kept it.

The situation and appearance of the sleeping apartments must engage her most particular attention, as Schmuel had determined to execute the theft at night, by breaking into the house. She must, therefore, be sure to ascertain whether the sleeping apartment was in any close connexion with any of the sitting-rooms or parlours, whether the Prince had servants with him, or whether any one slept near him.

" Very well," said Francisca, " I agree to every thing, but first I must see and speak with the Jew myself; I must know whether every thing is just as you told me, and how it is about my share of the proceeds. Otherwise you might leave me to look after it when you have taken all, or at least a lion's share, yourself."

" Upon the whole, I like your caution extremely well," replied the thief, very seriously, " for it is a guarantee of your carefulness. But concerning your Hellig, (share,) you may rest perfectly secure. *Lotscherehre* guarantees that to you, and there is not an honest scoundrel living, who would not rather deliver himself to the *Lambden,* than to cheat you of the value of a pin."

The last request of the Equestrian, which a regular thief would find perfectly natural in a layman, although to him, acquainted with the customs and laws of thievery, it appeared perfectly superfluous, convinced Albert fully that he had made a most valuable acquisition to his band in the person of Francisca. He therefore willingly assented to her demand to bring her into immediate intercourse with the Jew, although he knew that the reserved manner of the latter, which partly arose from caution, and partly from misanthropy, would somewhat retard the execution of his intentions.

This last circumstance caused the thief to ask her for a short delay, in order to allow him to prepare the Jew for the meeting, and agree with him upon the time when it was to take place.

Albert now remembered that another affair called him away, and he left the Equestrian with the promise to bring her an answer as soon as possible.

The result of this meeting was most satisfactory to both parties.

The villain thought he had found a most valuable acquisition to his band; the Equestrian found herself advanced in her hopes of furthering the objects of the Prince, by her promised acquaintance with the Jew, and at the same time found herself placed in a position in which she could avert great dangers from his head.

Francisca withdrew the Major's pocket-book from her pocket, where she had carefully hidden it on the entrance of Albert, and long and sadly looked at it. Then she carefully locked it up in a drawer, and folded her hands in prayer, casting, for the first time in many years, a thankful look towards Heaven.

CHAPTER XXVII.

THE TETE-A-TETE.

AND now the scene changed. Francisca had to prepare for another drama.

She approached her toilette, and from a secret drawer therein, withdrew her own miniature which Albert had stolen at the house of the Geheimerath Berthold, and which had fallen into her hands.

A fearful, almost fury-like expression overspread her noble face as she looked upon the youthful, innocent features of that portrait. A dark purple hue of anger suddenly overshadowed her forehead, her right hand clenched tightly, and her lips trembled in convulsive fury.

Madly she cast the miniature away, and it rolled along the soft carpet. In wild vehemence she again drew the dagger from her bosom, and with terrific looks she stared upon it. Unintelligibly murmured words escaped her foaming lips.

Her passion overpowered her to such a degree that she drew back in terror when her eye, on looking up, caught her own terrific face in the opposite mirror.

At this moment of the most desperate excitement, she heard the sound of the door-bell.

To pick up the miniature from the floor, to hide the dagger in her bosom, to force her face into an appearance of serene happiness—all this was the work of a moment.

With her most enchanting smile, the mistress received the Geheimerath, who had come to pay his usual morning visit.

The tall and lank *bon vivant* was dressed with a care and elegance quite unbecoming to his years. All his clothes lay stiff and straight around his body, and gave it the appearance of a mere skeleton artistically dressed up by a tailor and valet.

The very thin, grey mixed hair, was laid in small neat ringlets around the forehead.

With a quick, juvenile bow, the long figure entered the room, threw his heavy cloak gracefully upon the nearest chair, and with fiery ardour pressed the hand of the artist to his faded, meagre lips.

" Your most obedient servant, my sweet child ; I hope you have rested well. How do you find yourself after yesterday's sleigh-ride ?"

" I thank you, Herr Geheimerath," replied the Equestrian with a modest curtesy, " when you are near me, I feel always well."

" But Francisca," continued the Geheimerath entreatingly, " why will you insist on these formalities ; how often must I beg of you, to call me simply, *Carl* and *thou*."

" Herr Geheimerath, this would ill become so poor a girl as I am, if people should hear it."

" Are we not alone in our sweet solitude," asked the Geheimerath most tenderly.

" You see ? You admit yourself that it would not be suitable *out of doors*," replied Francisca in a voice of unmistakeable scorn.

" I care little for the world, or its opinion," replied the Cicisbeo somewhat embarrassed.

" Ah yes, the world, its opinions," repeated the girl as her eye sparkled with a mysterious and gloomy fire, " yes, yes, I am only an ordinary Equestrian, in whom familiarities would not seem proper."

" Ah, Francisca ; how very cruel you are to me !" whispered the Geheimerath with a languishing glance.

" Carl !" said Francisca, in a tone of sad reproach, as she fixed her black eye with an incomparable loveliness upon his faded features.

" No, no, my own Francisca," cried the Geheimerath in a sea of delight, " do not get angry ! You are my deity, my angel, ay, and if you refuse me everything."

" Refuse ?" again repeated the Equestrian mischievously, as she seated herself laughingly upon the sofa, and without a word of thanks began pealing an orange which the Geheimerath had brought her as a rarity of the season : " why, what should a poor girl like myself have to give away ?"

" How can you torture and mock me so, dearest Francisca ! What have you to give away ? royal, imperial treasures, your love, your favour."

" And do you desire my love ?" again asked Francisca, as she unperceivedly cast a glance to one side, which if the Geheimerath had seen might have frozen the blood in his veins.

Berthold was almost beside himself.

" Dearest, most heavenly creature," he cried, " how, how can you ask me ! Do I not worship you—ay, upon my knees if you will ?"

" And do I not reward you with my gratitude ?" said Francisca smiling.

" A loving heart desires more than gratitude," pleaded the ardent lover.

Francisca's dark eye sought the ground. " Who knows," she said lowly and with an abashed smile after a well calculated pause, " perhaps the time may yet come, when the mere gratitude must change."

At these words, she involuntarily bent her beautiful head down to her admirer. Berthold, far from suspecting the terrible double meaning of her speech, in an ecstasy of delight, impressed a warm kiss upon that fair forehead. Never before had Francisca let him hope so much.

True to the character of an artful woman, the Equestrian now purposely gave another and more quiet turn to the conversation.

" Have you not a daughter, Herr Geheimerath ?" she inquired evasively.

This question was asked maliciously enough.

The Geheimerath never spoke of his daughter. He did this, partly because such conversation always was a disagreeable remembrancer of his own age, but partly also—and to his honour be it said—because he wanted to keep the girl also from the circles wherein he moved."

The friends of the Geheimerath had informed the Equestrian of the existence of Marie—informed her of it, in the true malicious spirit of society, for the purpose of counteracting the first motive of her father for secrecy.

For a moment, Berthold was silent and painfully embarrassed. It was doubly disagreeable to him to appear as the father of a grown up lady, in the presence of one whom he desired to make a conquest of. But he could see no method of getting out of his embarrassing situation.

" Oh, yes, yes," he replied with a lengthened face ; yes, I have a daughter, a very dear, good child. A daughter of sixteen. Yes, yes, I thought you knew that long ago. I love her most tenderly. She is almost as big as you ; but no, no, not quite so large. I never take her into society."

With internal satisfaction Francisca observed the painful embarrassment of the Geheimerath, which he was not capable of disguising in his disagreeable confession. After every sentence he made a short pause, in the hope that Francisca would interrupt his communication. But with malicious obstinacy she remained silent, and he himself had to recommence, as he dared not farther expose his mortifying perplexity by an interruption of the conversation.

The embarrassment which we feel, always increases when we know that it proceeds from our own folly; this is an observation we can make by our daily experience in society.

The Equestrian seemed not disposed to drop the subject of the discourse.

"If I were in your place, I would get the girl well married off," she continued, seemingly much interested.

"Perhaps," replied the Geheimerath, scarce knowing what he said.

"My proposition is not without its good reasons," continued the Equestrian : "You have no longer a wife, and it must be inconvenient and troublesome for you to watch over a grown daughter. Get her married off, and you will again be a free man, and at liberty to do as you please."

Silently the Geheimerath nodded his head.

"Now, for instance, there is Referendarius von Birkheim ; I believe he would make a very good son-in-law."

Francisca seemed to have predetermined to torment, and put the Geheimerath entirely out of temper. At this last proposition he wildly started up, and even destroyed the artificial ringlet arrangement of his head, by an impetuous movement of his hand.

"What next ?" he cried, really angry, and at the same time glad to have a subject whereon to vent his ill-humour. "Would you have me throw my child and my money into the hands of a swindler ? I support him, because he belongs to my family, and am on pretty fair terms with him, because the laws of society and politeness require it, and because he is a good companion ; but I beg you not to mention him as my son-in-law."

We cannot at present investigate the motive of the artiste, for becoming the advocate of a man so utterly indifferent to her as the Referendarius, nor can we just now ascertain, how she became at all acquainted with the attachment existing between the two young people. But she seemed determined to pursue this object still farther.

"Without wishing to contradict you," she continued with great calmness, as she began eating the orange which she had pealed and sugared, "I must assure you, that this young man seemed very agreeable to me."

"I am very willing to believe that," said Berthold, not without some degree of jealousy, "but this does not qualify him for my son-in-law. How does he expect to live ? He has nothing ! is a beggar and can pass no examination. Am I to hear my daughter called by such a title as the Lady Referendarius ?"

"Oh no, no, I don't mean that," explained the lady. "Let him quit office, and buy him some country property or something of that sort. I should think, that what I have told you just now of your personal liberty, deserved some attention also."

At these words the Equestrian cast a most speaking glance at her antiquated lover, which the other might construe in a thousand ways favourable to the interest of his suit.

The Geheimerath, however, was too warmly attached to his daughter, and had still too much honest principle to make the girl against his better conviction fall a sacrifice to mere egotism.

"No, no, my dearest Francisca," he replied with firmness, "even though my daughter is in my way, I can never condescend to make her a sacrifice to selfish motives. And I should be guilty of doing this, were I to obey your well meant proposition. I am perfectly well aware that Herr von Birkheim pays her most flattering and earnest attentions ; but she looks upon them with the utmost indifference, as he certainly only has my money for his object. So, if you please, we will let the matter rest."

Perhaps Francisca believed that nothing further could be accomplished at present; at least she was silent, and her purple lips closed with an expression of subdued, silent anger.

"But I should really like to become acquainted with your daughter," she began again, after a pause.

"That prayer I am also loath to grant," answered the Geheimerath with an expression of annoyance ; "she is much too young to visit our company. She is naturally not fond of society, and prefers quiet and retirement."

This, as we already know, was a falsehood ; still it was much to his credit, that the Geheimerath endeavoured to guard his daughter from the dangerous and slippery paths in which he wandered himself, by keeping her in quiet and retirement.

The Equestrian, however, only grew more and more impatient.

"Go, go," she said poutingly, as she left the sofa, and sought a seat by the window and away from her lover, "if you will refuse me every request, at least do not tell me that you love me."

The warm, enamoured mind of the Geheimerath was not proof against this artful manœuvre.

"My dearest Francisca, do not be angry," cried the weak voluptuary ; "I will obey you, if you absolutely will have it so. In a few days you shall become acquainted with Marie."

"But it must take place at some little soirée, or other festivity," insisted the Equestrian, "otherwise the matter will be too dull for me."

"You shall have your will in that also," promised the Geheimerath with a suppressed sigh.

"And very soon ?" asked Francisca, still delaying by the window, with her face averted.

"Very soon," replied the paternal lover, with a voice of sorrowful anxiety.

"Well, then, I am again your friend," cried the artiste, offering her cheek for a kiss from the Geheimerath.

"You are a charming girl," cried the other, embracing the tempter in an ecstasy of delight.

At this happy moment, the door was opened by the waiting maid, who announced the Referendarius von Birkheim.

Greatly annoyed, the interrupted lover started up, and doubly surprised by this disagreeable announcement, cast an inquiring glance upon his lady-love.

Instead of any answer, the latter exchanged a quick glance with the maid, which most probably served as an instruction. At least the girl immediately added: "he inquires for the Herr Geheimerath Berthold."

"Beg him to walk in," replied her mistress.

A few seconds after, Birkheim appeared, and made a hasty apology for his interruption. He then turned to the Geheimerath.

"For some time past I have been seeking you, my dear cousin," he began; "there is a stranger at your house, who anxiously desires to speak with you. By accident I also happened to come there, and the gentleman entreated me so earnestly to seek you, if possible, that I could not refuse him the service."

"This appears strange," said the Geheimerath, "then I must needs go and see who it is. Excuse me, my dearest Francisca; I shall see you again to-day.—Birkheim, will you accompany me?" he inquired, waiting for the Referendarius.

"Certainly I will," replied the other most obediently, as he easily understood the meaning of the question. "I am entirely at your service."

Arm in arm these two gentlemen left the boudoir.

The Equestrian, with a sarcastic smile at the apparently improvisato excuse of the Referendarius, looked after them till they were out of sight.

CHAPTER XXVIII.

PERNICIOUS PLANS.

An hour after this, the Referendarius returned to the Equestrian.

"You have caused me great embarrassment by your early arrival," she said ill-humouredly. "Why did you not keep the hour which I had appointed for your visit? You know the suspicious, jealous nature of your uncle, and I would give him no superfluous cause, as his jealousy would be roused in the present instance."

The Equestrian pronounced these latter words with an almost contemptuous expression of countenance, and in an unmistakeably sneering tone.

"You will pardon me, dear lady," replied the Referendarius humbly, "when I assure you, that the object of calling for my uncle brought me so early to your house."

"How? I thought this was a subterfuge suggested by my maid, to repair the fault of your incautious arrival."

"Not at all," answered Birkheim; "there really is a stranger at the house of my uncle, who so earnestly and so ardently begged me to endeavour immediately to find the latter, that I could not well refuse his prayer, and therefore came straightway here to fulfil his commission."

"Well, and how did you separate from your uncle?"

"I accompanied him to his house, and then parted from him, under pretence of having important business to attend to, and then I delayed so long upon a promenade through the streets, until the hour arrived which called me to your presence."

"You seem to have made an open confession," said the Equestrian, "and I will consequently let the matter rest; moreover, I wish to speak with you upon other points. Tell me, who is this Count Pippi, whom I saw at your house on the evening when you introduced me to the Geheimerath?"

"Count Pippi!" repeated the Referendarius with hesitation, as he looked sideways towards the lady; "Count Pippi is an Austrian nobleman, whom I became acquainted with here in Berlin."

"And here in Berlin, you most probably became also acquainted with his sister?" continued Francisca, pointedly.

"Certainly," replied Birkheim, with ill-assumed astonishment at the question, which made him feel anything but comfortable.

"The Count seems passionately fond of play?"

"I believe—yes."

"You also are a passionate player?"

"Now and then, I am fond of a game."

"Do you always play with such luck as you did on that night?"

"Not just always; fortune often turns her back to me."

"Why, you certainly should know how to prevent that!"

"In reality, I do not understand you. You speak very strangely, fairest Francisca."

The Referendarius had continued this conversation with evidently increasing embarrassment. He felt like a man whose bad conscience shows him terrible and dangerous phantoms. The latter words he only pronounced with a broken, uncertain voice.

The Equestrian had put all these questions with that icy coldness which she knew so well to assume when she placed a victim upon the rack.

But now, suddenly, a dark scarlet overspread her entire face; her eye flashed, and her voice trembled. Like an avenging angel, she stood before her trembling victim.

"Miserable liar!" she cried, with passion, "you understand me only too well. Must I first inform you that Count Pippi is an adventurer and a gambler, who lives by false play, and that you are his faithful partner?"

"Ha! this insult!" exclaimed Birkheim, starting up in his last attempt at defiance, "you shall answer me for that."

"We will immediately settle that matter," said Francisca, quietly, as she had again become perfectly calm. "Count Pippi's real name is Fischergraf, and his pseudo-sister is his sweetheart, and a common Berlin seamstress. In partnership with that swindler, you have robbed your uncle in your own house, and have made me a witness of your disgraceful villainy. Do you want me to answer you still further for my assertions?"

The Referendarius dared not to answer. He sat in silence, and with pallid countenance.

"In my unfortunate course of life it has been a part of sad my experience, to learn what false play means," continued the Equestrian, with sorrowful bitterness, "and therefore I understood the game you and your partner were playing, even long before I accidentally, through the members of our company, learned the name and occupation of your honourable friend. I thought that a single look I gave you, had, even at your own table, told you that I observed what you were doing."

In silent despair the Referendarius wrung his hands.

"And am I still to look on in silence? am I to permit you to rob, in the most villainous manner, a man who has heaped benefits upon you?"

"Mercy, oh mercy!" now cried the Referendarius, casting himself at the feet of the Equestrian, and presenting a most deplorable picture. "Do with me as you like, only for Heaven's sake, do not betray me to the Geheimerath, else I am entirely lost."

"The world perhaps would lose nothing by it," answered Francisca, with scornful indifference; "but rise; as you seek the hand of Fräulein Berthold, no one shall find you at my feet."

Frightened, the Referendarius rose to his feet: "How is this? do you know all, every thing? Who has told you of Mary Berthold, or of my love to her,"

"This letter," quietly replied the lady, as she produced a paper from her pocket and held it before him.

Birkheim struck his forehead with his hand; "this is the very letter," he cried, "which I was incautious enough to lose."

The letter certainly was an important one, for it had been written immediately after the night when the Referendarius had been arrested instead of the Jew.

Birkheim, in this communication, had informed the young lady of all the occurrences of that night, had tried to quiet her fears of the consequences, and had spoken of many things that dared not be further known.

"Now if I were to give this letter, together with my notes of your gambling qualifications, into the hands of the Geheimerath, would I do any injustice?" inquired Francisca, in calm seriousness.

"My weal and wo is in your power," said Birkheim, gloomily; "but before you condemn me, listen to my history."

"I am a descendant of an ancient and noble family. My father, as all fortuneless noblemen usually do, became a soldier, and, as a somewhat distinguished officer, he died for his father-land upon the field of battle during the last war. I was then still small and helpless.

"My mother was now forced to live upon her pension, fully sufficient for our wants, but which she entirely spent upon my education. She would make that education as brilliant as possible, as brilliant as her last penny would allow her. Too proud, to let me take to a plain civic trade or profession, she never offered me a choice between the army and civil service; painting my future prospects in either career, in the most brilliant colours.

"What was still a greater error of her system, was the fact that she always secreted from me the scanty state of our fortune, nay, on the contrary, withheld from herself the most necessary comforts of life for the purpose of giving me a position in accordance with my rank, not my fortune. Thus she instilled a belief of my own great riches in my breast.

"Her foolish, false pride went so far, that to appear grand in the eyes of the world, she inhabited splendid lodgings, whilst she had barely salt and bread for dinner. As I could never come home from school, but was there visited once a year by my mother, all these follies escaped my observation.

"Meanwhile I felt little or no inclination to become a soldier, so nothing finally remained for me to do, but to continue my studies. Just as I had entered the university, my mother died, and the same post which informed me of her death, also gave me the information that she had died without any property whatever; all that she possessed on the day of her death, had been barely sufficient to give her a respectable funeral.

"These communications made a most deep and terrible impression upon my mind. On the one hand I was overpowered by the love and kindness of my mother, whilst on the other hand I had reason to condemn her vanity, which had now placed me in such a desperate predicament. I was accustomed to live extravagantly, and as a rich cavalier, and now I knew not whence to obtain bread for the next hour.

"In order not to be compelled to abandon the studies I had began, I turned with a sad and heavy heart to my rich cousin, begging him to lend me his aid and support. He granted my prayer, and though at first I found it a bitter and sad task to accept his bounty, I had to stoop to its acceptance. This it was, that worked my mental ruin! My cousin often treated me harsh and unkindly; I felt that I was a burden to him; but the wrong education my mother had given me, had made me too weak and dependent, to enable me to take the weight of my support upon my own shoulders.

"Had I been a man, I might have become a wood-chopper or a porter, to enable me to eat my own bread!

"At last my studies were concluded; I became Auscultator, and as I now really worked and endeavoured to rise, I soon was made Referendarius. But now the time of my Referendariusship seemed to lie without end before me; I would have to work, and to work without hope of early promotion or pecuniary advantage. During this time, the strictness and severity of the great examination was much increased, and the end of my sorrows placed still further beyond my reach.

"At last the whole affair grew disgusting to me; the continual humiliation of living upon foreign bounty, had already taken all energy and ambition from my naturally weak character; more than this, I fell into bad company, and let things take their own way. This certainly was the worst course I could pursue, for I soon was overburthened with such a load of debts, that I could not hope to discharge them in any ordinary way.

"I did not dare to tell my difficulties to the Geheimerath, as I feared to have my request briefly and most justly refused.

"I then took to playing, and by the instructions of my associates, I soon attained in this the degree of perfection which you have discovered. *I finally became a false player.* Thus, for a long time I have worked my way, sometimes in good and sometimes in bad company.

"I have now grown too old to learn much more, or enough to enable me to pass the examination; so I think no more of that. My only hope remains in the daughter of my cousin. That girl loves me, she is the only daughter of a rich father, and a connexion with her would deliver me from all my difficulties. Only one obstacle is still in my way, and I fear will prove an insurmountable one; I fear that I can never gain the consent of the Geheimerath."

During these open confessions Francisca had listened with marked and excited attention. Her inner feelings had in quick succession expressed themselves in her features. At first sympathy, then sorrow, then contempt when she saw the narrator sink into unmanly weakness, and finally, bitter scorn, when she heard the intentions he had upon the daughter of his cousin.

"Then the girl is to be sacrificed for you, to enable you to continue the idle, worthless course of life you have hitherto led?" she inquired in a sarcastic tone.

"Oh! I would change, I would become another, better and more honest man," replied Birkheim.

"Because you would receive money," exclaimed the Equestrian with a most bitter, scornful expression; "I believe it; money is the password of the day. Whoever has money, is virtuous and respected!"

She remained silent for a moment, and placed her hand upon her bosom, as if to press the miniature which was secreted there. When her hand touched the spot, a ray of fury crossed her features. Then, with an entirely changed mien, and in a quiet, almost flattering tone, she said:

"I believe that you would be an honest and honourable man; believing this, and in consequence of having read your letter, I have become mediator between you and the Geheimerath, and have sought to obtain for you the hand of his daughter."

"Well, and—?" inquired Birkheim, bending forward and listening with the utmost attention.

"The Geheimerath can never be persuaded to comply with your wishes," said Francisca, watching the other closely. "He called you a gambler, a worthless spendthrift, who was an insufferable burden to him, and whom he only countenanced on account of his relationship and for the world's sake. He declared that he would rather put his daughter under lock and key for life, than give her to a vagabond, who only sought his money, and who deserved to be delivered to the beadle."

Foaming with rage and fury, his face ashy pale, the Referendarius cried:

"Stop, stop, for Heaven's sake, go no farther! Did he really say all that?"

"Verbally as I tell you," replied the artiste, with unchanged appearance.

Speechless the Referendarius sunk upon a chair, striking his forehead with both fists. But his fury had only been a passing attack. The imbecile worldling was already too powerless, to let a feeling of revenge really ripen in his heart, or systematically to pursue it.

"You must be a great coward," said Francisca contemptuously, "if now you can find nothing better to do, than to wail like a child."

Birkheim remained as before.

"After all, what is it?" she continued, addressing him. "You are now aware that the Geheimerath will not willingly give you his daughter, and you have known that long ago; I can see no reason for despair, in all this."

"But I had hopes! Oh, I thought that paternal love might decide him!" continued Birkheim still in despair. "After such language all must be lost."

"Nothing is lost," replied the Equestrian proudly, "as long as you do not lose yourself. You hoped? Very well then, hope no longer, but begin to act."

Birkheim still cast his eyes despairingly on the ground.

"I believe, you do not understand me. Or are you really simple enough not to observe, that there is a *sure* way, by which the hand of a daughter may be obtained from the father, if you are only loved by the daughter?"

The Equestrian had approached close to the Referendarius, had placed her hand upon his shoulder, and looked sharply into his face, as she pronounced these words.

For a moment the Referendarius stupidly stared at her, then he suddenly started up.

"Ha, what a thought; you are right! Oh, what a fool I was! He will not, then he *must*."

In this wild state of excitement, and without bidding farewell, the Referendarius rushed from the house.

With an attentive look Francisca followed his steps.

"It works well," she whispered to herself with a malicious smile. "One way or another, that is immaterial; one villain must ruin another. —And the unfortunate victim?—Pshaw? who took pity on me, when I fell a sacrifice to the vile arts and desires of the seducer?"

CHAPTER XXIX.

POLIZEIRATH X———.*

On the day preceding the scenes which we have just witnessed in the Boudoir of the Equestrian, Polizeirath X— was seated in his cabinet, absorbed in a brown study. It was about ten o'clock in the forenoon.

This officer, with whom we have already made a slight acquaintance at the masquerade at the Colliseum, resided in an elegant house in *Dönhofs-place*.

He was a thickset, broad-shouldered man, of middling height, with a full blooming and friendly face. His small blue eyes twinkled with harmless good nature; strong blonde hair, and short blonde whiskers adorned his round head.

His friends know him as a kind, pleasant and obliging man; his entire manner shows a great deal of bonhommie. He could even make a sacrifice for a third party;—but all this only as long as his ruling passion was not awakened.

This passion possesses such entire mastery over him, that on its awaking all else in the world ceases to exist for him. He no longer knows his friends—it tears him from the midst of joys, ay, he even flies the home of his family for that passion.

This all-ruling passion is one which is a rich blessing to society in general, and to the denizens of Berlin in particular; it is the rare and peculiar passion, of—*catching thieves.*

In grateful acknowledgment of his merits in preserving the security of property and wealth, Polizeirath X— was universally and most justly called, "the greatest-thief-catcher of his age."

If he scented a rogue any where—and he had a remarkably fine nose—that fellow was lost, for X— would not rest, night or day, until he had taken him.

The track or scent of a thief is his world, his ideal, his every thing; the most passionate huntsman could not follow the track of game more

attentively than X— followed that of thieves. He needs thieves for his existence as the fish needs water. In this manner he divides the entire world into two classes, thieves, and such as are not thieves; with the one he lives, among the others he exists.

In his study, as we happen to find him now, the just named passion had attained the entire mastery over him. He had pushed back his office-chair, and stretched his legs at full length before him. His good-natured face bore the impress of deep, dark, and intense thought.

He is altogether in an ill-humour. The theft at the house of the Geheimerath occupies his mind.

Without intermission he had for days past been occupied with the task of discovering the perpetrators, without being able to get upon their trail.

By the peculiar style and manner in which the theft had been accomplished, he had come to the conviction, that it had not been committed by Berlin thieves, at least not exclusively by such. The enormous power and application of strength which had been necessary to its accomplishment; the daring impudence which was requisite even to conceive the plan of its execution, all this brought the conviction to his mind, that strange thieves, and most probably Jewish thieves, must have been the perpetrators, certainly the originators of the burglary.

It is a well-established and psychologically wonderful fact, that Berlin thieves rarely if ever, commit a theft more daring than such as can be accomplished by false keys. A theft by means of house-breaking, seems a heinous crime among them.

Strange as it may sound, we may say, that the latter are too dangerous for them; they really lack the courage to commit them.

For the same reason, they will never undertake a larceny, the execution of which requires bodily strength. A life in the capital, with its hunger and its excesses, has unnerved them in their earliest youth, and dissipation of all kinds has destroyed their muscles, and eaten the very marrow in their bones. A Berlin rogue, consequently, will never excite that sympathy which we are too apt to accord to courage and determination even in criminals.

In Berlin thieves, we only find the lowest, filthiest vulgarity, at the utmost united with cunning and falsehood. They are lazy, weak and cowardly.

But on the opposite, it is an equally remarkable fact, that Jews, who have once taken to the profession of thieving, entirely lose the character of cowardice, pusillanimity and fear, which is usually considered characteristics of their nation. On the contrary, in all their criminal undertakings, they distinguish themselves by indescribable audaciousness and daring intrepidity. Instead of their usual smoothness and calmness, they then display cruelty, fury and a desire for blood.

Their intrepidity and assurance never leaves

---

* In the second part of this work, when the name of *Polizeirath X* occurred, we had, by mistake, given him the title of *Police Recorder*. We give this explanation, to prevent the reader from mistaking this worthy officer for some other individual.—TRANSLATOR.

them even before their civil judge. The Hebrew thief usually distinguishes himself from his Christian confrères, by never confessing his crimes. He will daringly and bluntly deny the most convincing, self-evident proof of guilt.

Polizeirath X——. was of course well acquainted with all these circumstances. His experience in such matters, as we have above observed, soon brought him to the conviction, that some of the Jew thieves, then in Berlin, must be the leaders of this burglary.

His mind was next occupied in trying to ascertain, whether among these Jews, there was any one person, whom he already knew, and upon whom he could justly fix his suspicions of having been the perpetrator. Very soon he arrived, we might say instinctively, at the result, that no one else but the long Schmuel could have been so bold or daring; the next person who might be guilty, was cunning Schmerles, but he knew that the latter individual was safe under lock and key. But this result was far from solving all his difficulties.

He was fully aware that the long Schmuel was then in Berlin, and knew equally well the present hiding-place of that distinguished individual; he was, however, very careful not to attempt his arrest, until he had sufficient proof of his being the perpetrator of the crime of which he suspected him. A premature arrest would even retard the much-desired discovery and conviction of the real criminals, for in the case of non-conviction or partial proof, he must content himself by sending the Jew over the frontier and towards his home. The question, consequently, was, how to obtain those necessary proofs?

The Polizeirath again relapsed into a study.

A sudden, unexpected visit into the Jew's hiding-place?

No: this would certainly turn out a failure, for as an old practitioner he knew full well, that Hebrew thieves immediately dispose of stolen property, or, at any rate, never keep a trace of it in their own dwelling.

Should he institute a search among fripperers and pawn-brokers, to see whether any part of the stolen property was sold or pledged?

This seemed too circumstantial, had partly been tried, and finally could not avail much at the examination of so cunning and accomplished a thief, certainly could not lead to a full conviction.

Impatiently the Polizeirath jumped from his seat, and with short, quick steps paced hastily up and down the room. The criminal *must* be discovered; his honour and reputation as thief-catcher depended on the issue. He had lately met the Geheimerath in company, and had to pocket the most disagreeable insinuations. His well-established ability of catching rogues was even doubted, since he, the omniscient, could not discover the least trace of so daring a burglar.

Heated by wine, and to put an end to the laughter at his expense, and to this mockery, he had pledged his honour, nay, taken a vow, that within less than a month's time, he would be upon the track of the right criminal.

His word and his pledged honour he must now redeem.

Suddenly he stopped in the middle of the room. He now seemed at once to have found a way.

Quickly he approached the table, rang a bell that stood upon it, and quietly seated himself in his office-chair.

———

CHAPTER XXX.

THE BODY-GENSD'ARME.

THE door opens. His head bent forward, a gensd'arme, measuring above six feet, enters the room. This gensd'arme is regularly in attendance about the person of the Polizeirath, who consequently denominates him his Body-Gensd'arme.

He presents a long, thin figure, with stony, immoveable features, and an ash-coloured face.

He now stands stiff and erect. Beneath his leather Czakko, short cut, light, dough-coloured hair is visible, and a thin and uneven moustache of a similar colour covers his upper lip.

In his usual slow and drawling tone the old warrior announces himself; "At your service, Herr Polizeirath."

The Polizeirath had selected this particular gensd'arme for his own especial service, for in consequence of his phlegmatic nature, he was always calm, quiet and collected, but still, whenever it seemed necessary, cunning and cautious. Having formerly been a subaltern officer, he was accustomed to silent and punctual obedience.

The success of a police-officer's duties often depends on such assistants, who are either mere machines, or independent and active instruments in the hands of their superiors.

"Do you know where the Maulspitzer keeps his sleeping quarters at present?" inquired the Polizeirath of the gensd'arme.

"No sir, I know not," replied the other touching his hat *a la militaire*, "but I will ask the *Match-Mary*; he is her lover, and she must know where he stays."

"Do you know then where *Match-Mary* is to be found?" again inquired the officer.

"No sir, I know not," was again the other's careful answer, "but the *Turf-Rieke* can give information, for yesterday evening the two women were together in the Parisian saloon, and the *squinting Gottlieb* told me, that the two intended to-morrow to take lodgings together."

"Then do you know where *Turf-Rieke* keeps herself?"

"No sir, I do not know," again replied the gensd'arme with the same quiet calmness, "but I will go the *Silberladen*, and I shall most probably find her. She is in the regular habit of

[Unmutilated and Only Genuine Edition.]

THIERS' LIFE OF NAPOLEON,

WITH SUPERB STEEL ENGRAVINGS.

FOR SEVENTY-FIVE CENTS,

[If paid in Advance.]

W. H. COLYER having been at great expense to procure a copy of this unrivalled work, now publishes

PART I.

OF THE

HISTORY OF THE CONSULATE AND THE EMPIRE

OF

FRANCE UNDER NAPOLEON,

By M. A. THIERS,

LATE PRIME MINISTER OF FRANCE.

Wm. H. Colyer's edition of this splendid work, The Life of Napoleon, is decidedly the best in this country. It is printed on fine paper and new type, according to the design of the author, M. A. Thiers, and on comparison with other editions will be found far superior.

In Press.

THIERS' FRENCH REVOLUTION,

TO BE COMPLETED IN SIX PARTS, AT 12 1-2 CENTS EACH.

TO BE COMPLETED IN TEN NUMBERS.

THE MYSTERIES OF BERLIN,

FROM

THE PAPERS OF A BERLIN CRIMINAL OFFICER,

TRANSLATED FROM THE GERMAN

By C. B. BURKHARDT.

With Illustrations on Steel, by P. Habelmann.

This work in Europe has been universally pronounced far superior to M. Sue's celebrated "Mysteries of Paris," and we confidently predict that the popularity of this translation will be without a parallel in the history of light reading.

THE MYSTERIES of BERLIN.

TO BE COMPLETED

IN

TEN PARTS.

NEW YORK: WILLIAM H. COLYER, PUBLISHER.

coming there in the morning with her present lover and drinking a glass of Schnapps."

"Very well," concluded the Polizeirath, as he winked his dismissal to the other, "you will immediately go to the *Silberladen*, and endeavour to bring the Maulspitzer here to me as soon as possible."

"At your service, Herr Polizeirath." And in the same stiff military manner as he had entered, the gensd'arme took his departure.

This comical, almost ridiculous circumstantiality with which the gensd'arme designated the way of his proposed search for a criminal, had its sufficient reasons. It was a well conceived precaution of the Polizeirath, which was already known to all his inferior functionaries, that in all cases, he must be strictly informed in what manner they intended to execute his commissions. He must ascertain this, to assure himself that his plans and modes of operation would not be crossed by some incautious or premature measure, or that they might not be discovered or betrayed before the proper time.

The plan which the Polizeireth had now conceived, was no other than to send a vigilant after the long Schmuel. This vigilant must, in the best manner he could, obtain from the Jew such proofs as must necessarily lead to his conviction, and report his regular progress at head-quarters.

He had long considered, who among all his people would be the most suitable to undertake such a commission, and had finally remembered the person of the Sand-carter, whom we already know, by his nickname, that of Maulspitzer.

A few days before, he had seen that individual very well dressed and in company of several other convicted criminals, promenading a public walk.

As he had frequently had him under his hands already, and had punished him, these facts were quite sufficient, therein to find the means of forcing the compliance of the Maulspitzer to his will.

Upon the whole, the Polizeirath X— was not in the habit of standing greatly upon ceremony in these respects; whoever was once caught among thieves and vagabonds, no longer was his own master, but belonged to him. This was not only the case when criminals had once been caught in the fact, but often before, and always after.

X— loved to boast that he reigned over the entire community of thieves, and had them all at his disposal, even when he was not required to deliver them to the hand of avenging justice.

CHAPTER XXXI.

THE EXPEDITION.

THE long body-gensd'arme, whose name was *Koftry*, quickly started upon his road. Passing with gigantic steps over the *Hausvoigtei-place*,

and by the *Schleusen-bridge*, near the castle, he soon reached *King-street*, and the Silberladen. Upon the steps, in front of the door, sat *Turf-Rieke*, in company of her lover and the *Flower-Caroline*, engaged in emptying a bottle of *Kümmel*, and devouring a piece of hard bread.

Accidentally she knew the present quarters of the Maulspitzer, and Koftry saved himself the trouble of having first to seek the Match-Mary.

The sleeping-quarter of the Maulspitzer was in the *Schindel-alley*, with *Greif*, the weaver, who lived in a cellar, back of the yard.

The dwelling of this weaver consisted in a damp, unhealthy cellar-room, which was reached from without by descending a few half-rotten steps. His room has two windows, but is, notwithstanding, very dark, as part of the window-panes consist of paper, and the remainder are covered with mud, as they are situated on a level with the ground.

The walls are low, black, full of holes, and consequently open to all the inclemencies of the seasons. Furniture is wanting. The eye discovers nothing but a weaver's loom and an old rickety bedstead, before which stands an old chair, which serves alternately as a table and a chair. Against the wall, by its side, hang a few poor, filthy, and ragged articles of clothing.

On the bedstead, nothing is seen but an old matrass of coarse linen. The straw is protruding from its torn corners.

A still young, but consumptive-looking woman lay upon this; by her side is a little two year old boy, pale and emaciated. Another child, an infant, rests upon her breast. The trio is most scantily covered with a few rags.

There is no fire in the room; upon this hard couch, the unfortunate wretches seek protection against the cold, which penetrates all the corners of the room. The damp ceiling and walls are frozen and chrystalized.

The weaver sits at his loom and works. He presents a lank, emaciated figure, with faded cheeks and a hectic cough. Sometimes he casts a sorrowful glance towards his wife, whose exhaustion and hunger have thrown her into a sleep. Then he turns again to his loom, and continues indefatigably at his work, only stopping occasionally to warm his frozen hands with his breath.

The boy awakens. "Father, I am very hungry," he cries; "give me a bit of bread."

"Soon, my boy, very soon," replied the weaver with a sigh; "be patient for a little while longer; this piece of linen will shortly be done, and then, when I get money, I will buy you a piece of sweet white bread."

"Father, you have told me so all day yesterday; I can bear this hunger no longer."

The poor weaver thinks that his heart will break; he works and works, until the blood mounts to his finger-tops.

"My dear husband, I am very thirsty; give me a little water," begins his wife.

The weaver rises to get the pitcher; he finds

it broken, in a corner; the water has run out, and is frozen on the ground.

"Oh! our pitcher is broken," cried the husband, despairingly, on seeing the pieces.

"Father, I broke it," said the boy. "Mother sometimes soaks bread-crusts in it for my little brother when he cries very much; last evening, when I was alone at home, hunger pained me so much, that I thought I would see if I could find some crumbs in it, and in doing so, I broke the pitcher."

In bitter distress, the weaver stared upon the fragments.

"Oh Heavens, how my tongue burns! For mercy's sake, give me a drop of water," cried the wife.

The weaver broke a piece of ice from the floor, and brought it to his sick wife, who greedily put it to her mouth.

"But, dear father, you don't work," again began the boy, "do be industrious and quick, that I may soon get bread."

"Father of Heaven!" cried the weaver, as he tore his hair with both hands, "this is enough to make me frantic. I will go and steal, to obtain bread for you."

"Husband, dear husband," sighed the sick wife, "think or speak not in so impious and sinful a manner; I shall grow more sick if you do."

The weaver had rushed towards the door; at these words of his wife he returned to his loom, wiped a silent tear from his eye, and recommenced his work.

A knock is heard.

The weaver rises and opens the door; Koftry enters, wishes the family good morning, and pointing his finger towards the door of the adjoining cabinet, he inquires briefly:

"Is he within?"

Upon this question, Greif nods a silent affirmative, and continues at his work.

Neither the weaver nor his wife were particularly excited by the entrance of the gensd'arme. To them it is a matter of indifference what the officer of justice may want, their misery has made them dull and indifferent to all external events.

Nay, in his own mind, the weaver thinks how lucky the chance would be, if the gensd'arme were to arrest him and his family. They would then at least have a warm room and sufficient food. If the Maulspitzer is arrested, it is a fresh misfortune to them; whence is the weaver to get another *Schlafbursche* (lodger) who will assist him in paying his heavy rent? He even envies the Maulspitzer, who, under arrest, will be so much better off than himself.

The gensd'arme enters the cabinet. Properly speaking, it is only a hole, which by a very small window receives the necessary light. Nothing is within but a couch, similar to the one in the other room. Upon this, partly undressed and wrapped in a woollen blanket lies the Maulspitzer. He has besides covered himself with his coat.

He had not arrived home till towards morning, and, consequently, still lies in restless sleep.

His muscular, bony form rolls disturbedly about the bed; the low, vulgar, ruffian's face, is even more disfigured by fearful dreams.

Without further ado, Koftry gives him a hearty push between his ribs with the hilt of his sword. He awakes, sees the most feared of all the gensd'armes stand by his bedside, and his face turns paler than the lime upon the wall. A murder rests upon his conscience; in his terror he believes himself discovered.

In the wild confusion of his first fright he does not even wait to ascertain what Koftry wants of him, but exclaims:

"What do you want with me? why do you arrest me? I have committed no crime!"

The gensd'arme replies to none of these questions, but briefly and laconically commands him to rise and dress himself.

Slowly and hesitatingly the Maulspitzer obeys, but still full of fear.

Whilst he puts on his coat, he watches his opportunity to take quickly a bunch of false keys from the pocket, and to hide them in the bed.

The lynx-eyes of the gensd'arme have well observed that movement, but he seems not to have seen it, as he knows what object the Polizeirath has with the thief at present.

The Maulspitzer being dressed, the gensd'arme accompanies him through the room into the street.

The family of weaver Greif is too much occupied with its own misery, to pay much attention to these movements. The weaver himself only casts a disconsolate look after the Maulspitzer, who, as he believes, goes to prison, where warm rooms and sufficient food is to be had. And then he wonders how he will henceforth be able to raise the amount of rent all by himself? He owed already for two months, and his children are starving in the straw!

Arrived in the street, the apprehensions of the Maulspitzer are somewhat lessened. He knows enough of police practice, to be perfectly aware, that if he had been arrested at his lodging-place for any crime he had lately committed, he would not have been lead away, without being subjected to a strict search beforehand.

In the same proportion as his apprehensions left him, his curiosity increased.

Quietly the two men pass along the streets; the Maulspitzer going before and the gensd'arme following after him.

The thief scarcely inquires for their place of destination, as he is sufficiently acquainted with that already. Koftry, mute and disciplined as usual, sees no occasion to say a word, but in silence pursues his way.

Thus they pass through the city, until they reach the Silberladen in King-street. Maulspitzer casts a glance towards the crowd of drinkers that are gathered around the door, and says:

"I am very cold, and have not yet broken my fast; I should much like to take a Schnapps.

Minna in there gives an excellent glass of *Danzic*, which would warm me very soon."

"Very well," answered the gensd'arme, "I have no particular objection; we will go in, and you can get a glass of Danzic from Minna."

Maulspitzer still felt very doubtful of the result of this mysterious expedition. Although, under all the present circumstances, he felt no particular desire to drink Schnapps, yet he made this proposition to the gensd'arme, in order that he might judge by his answer what were the intentions towards him.

The ready consent of his conductor, lifted a heavy burden from his heart, for he now knew that they did not intended to imprison him; had the latter been the case, Koftry would never have permitted him to stop anywhere on the road.

Both entered the Silberladen, (silver store,) which received its name from the rich silver bronze which adorns its walls and ceiling.

In front of the long counter was a large crowd of people of divers ranks and station. Here were students, subalterns, lieutenants in undress uniform, merchants-clerks, mechanics, labourers, down to that class called *Eckensteher* (ticket-porters.) All formed a motley crowd, which filled the entire room to the front steps. They were talking, drinking, laughing, playing and quarrelling.

Behind the counter stood the pretty bar-maids, four in number, all busily employed in dispensing liquids, and satisfying the wishes of the thirsty mass from the variegated liquor bottles along the wall. Many tender words and glances were exchanged, and many a soft pressure of the hand given along with the payment for the liquor to these Hebes.

Harmless and innocent as one of these places appears at first sight, (and these kind of *Laden* (shops) seem to be peculiar to Berlin,) a great deal that is objectionable in a moral point of view may be urged against them. These Berlin liquor-shops may be looked upon as the most pernicious and dangerous establishments in the city, for the morality of the lower classes of the people.

And we cannot discover what good they do? Perhaps they help to increase the revenue of the state by taxes. If so, that is all. But then they are an everlasting temptation to spend money and time, and are of the most dangerous consequences to the bodily health of the classes who frequent them.

Let any one observe, and he will find that every one of these places has its so-called standing guests, who daily pass a part, if not the greatest part of their time in these shops. At the best, these people are idle during this time, and chat with the bar-maids, who wisely encourage their visits by other artful temptations; or else they become intoxicated, get into quarrels and fights, while at home their wife and children are often in want. The lower officers of police can tell best how often their services are required to restore peace or make arrests at these places.

But besides all this, these liquors, with their filthy ingredients, even when taken in moderation, are most dangerous to the health. They cause excitement, nervousness, indigestion, loss of appetite, and help the partaker, to transfer all the elements of a decrepid body and mind to a coming generation.

By the side of these shops, we would place the small confectionaries, which we find scattered over many parts of the city, and which regulary offer other matters of temptation, besides unhealthy confectionary.

Maulspitzer now asked the handsome Minna for his glass of Danzic, and drank it with the greatest gusto, while he began to say soft and flattering things to the lively bar-maid, who seemed inclined to listen to him. He endeavoured, if possible, to repair by excessive merriment what he had just suffered with fright.

In all probability, Koftry would also have liked to drink a glass of liquor, at least he was not usually an enemy to Schnapps. But at present he seemed to hold it beneath his dignity, to make a drinking companion of an individual like Maulspitzer Phlegmatically he looked around and watched the tumult among the guests, thanked with a stiff dignity, when many of the drinkers respectfully bowed to him, and finally commanded Maulspitzer to put end to his love-making, and to continue his march.

At this moment, Maulspitzer felt how very disagreeable it was to be under the regular supervision of the Police. In the first place, he should have liked to chat for an hour with Minna, and in the next place, there seemed here to be such an excellent opportunity of trying his skill in emptying strange pockets.

By his side stood a couple of cattle-dealers from the provinces, both, to all appearance, weighty men. But Koftry would suffer no contradiction, as the Sandcarter knew from their former intercourse, and he found himself reluctantly compelled to obey orders.

They soon reached the dwelling of the Polizeirath.

Although the Maulspitzer was tolerably well assured that no great danger was immediately before him, he could not prevent an anxious shudder and a trembling that befell him when he approached the domicil of the most dreaded foe of all thieves and vagabonds.

They ascended the stairs to the *Belle-Etage.* The Body-Gend'arme made a halt before the office-door of the Polizeirath. Noiselessly, he pushed his companion through the half-open door into the cabinet, as remaining outside, he pronounced the words: " Herr Polizeirath, here I bring the Maulspitzer."

CHAPTER XXXII.

THE ENLISTMENT.

THE Polizeirath X— sat by his secretary, deeply engaged in studying an immense legal document, and occasionally taking pencil-notes therefrom in his pocket-book.

The Maulspitzer remained standing by the door which the gend'arme had closed behind him.

Thus passed a long while, during which nothing was heard but the noisy melody of a canary, whose cage hung directly over the head of the Polizeirath.

The former Sandcarter finally grew impatient; he coughed, noisily changed his position once or twice, and fumbled with the old, shabby hat he held in his hand, turning it round and round, as if it had been a top.

The Polizeirath was not to be interrupted. He quietly continued at his work, looking up occasionally to examine the villain, or to cast a patronizing look towards him.

Maulspitzer, however, did not find these attentions to his taste; he would have preferred to murder his friendly host, if he had only known how to pass by the long Koftry, on his way out.

At last, the Polizeirath concluded his studies. He pushed the documents away from him, and carelessly leaned back in his chair.

"Well, Maulspitzer," he began, with the most harmless face in the world, "how do you get along now?"

From his former experience, the Maulspitzer knew well that it was not advisable to talk too much before a Police magistrate. Silence had never yet brought him into trouble, though unadvised speeches had done so. He therefore contented himself, in this instance, to reply in the most laconic manner the word "good."

"Ha!" continued the Polizeirath, friendly and confidingly; "Well, I am glad to hear it. You see I have only sent for you to ascertain how you really make your living. Now, for instance, at present, what do you live by?"

"By my labour," replied the other, with the same laconic briefness.

"By your labour? Well, that is right; you should be industrious and gain an honest living; it is a much wiser plan than to steal. But tell me, what is it you work at?"

At these words, the Polizeirath took a pinch of snuff and looked most kind and friendly, like a charming, pleasant man.

"Why, sir," said the Maulspitzer, determined to have every word forced from him, "I work at divers things."

"What, for instance?"

"I chop wood, help at unloading boats, look out at stage-offices for parcels to carry; I am now here, now there, as all other poor men who look about for work."

"Are you able to give me the names of some of the people with whom you have lately worked?"

"No, sir, I cannot do that," replied the Maulspitzer somewhat annoyed; "I did not ask the names of persons who employed me to work. Such is not the fashion among labourers."

"Well, my boy," continued the officer with a very pleasant smile, "that makes things very bad for you. If you cannot prove that you have work, I must send you to the work-house, for your class of people is not to be believed on mere assertion."

"Work-house?" repeated the other in a saucy tone, trying to give himself courage, "you cannot send me there. I have committed no crime, and have worked for an honest living."

"Whether I can do it or not, we shall soon see, Maulspitzer. At present you will please to tell me what you were doing yesterday afternoon before the Circus?"

"Why—why, I only took a little promenade. I'm sure I may do that."

The Polizeirath only smiled good-naturedly.

"Yes, yes, just tell me whether I may not do that?" repeated the thief saucily, who, after all, began to feel somewhat uneasy at this friendly conversation, and who now believed himself upon safe ground.

"Oh yes, why not? but you must not be in company of convicted criminals, such as Eel-eye and Blonde Augustus. I cannot permit that."

"Oh, you mean those scoundrels," said Maulspitzer, trying to appear very indignant. "I met them by mere accident, and we remained together."

"That's all very well, but this accident is rather unlucky for you, for I shall now have to send you to the work-house, for strolling the streets with vagabonds and convicted thieves, as well as for showing no means of subsistence."

Now the Maulspitzer began to lose his artificial courage, for after this explanation of cause and effect, he actually became afraid that the Polizeirath might be in real earnest. At this particular moment it was of the utmost importance to him not to lose his liberty.

In the first place he had baldowert an excellent Massematten, and had already invited the assistance of his companions; his arrest might easily take all the profit from his hands. In the next place the guilt of the murder committed on the Pattern-colourer, and of which he alone would have to bear the punishment, lay heavily upon his conscience; it was necessary that he should be in a position to make his immediate escape whenever a discovery threatened him. He therefore thought best to resort to prayers, and if possible to get out of his disagreeable situation by kind words and begging.

For a long time, the Polizeirath let him display his eloquence in vain, until at last he observed: "This vagabondizing I cannot permit, but I do know an employment for you, in which you could make yourself useful. If you will undertake this, I may perhaps once more show leniency towards you."

Maulspitzer of course was immediately ready to place his services in any way he should wish them at his disposal.

This was all the Polizeirath wanted of him.

"Do you know long Schmuel?" he inquired.

The Maulspitzer considers a long while.

His penetration immediately tells him what is the object of the Geheimerath, and he begins to consider in his own mind, whether he will agree to the affair.

To become a vigilant, seems to him a dangerous and dishonourable office; but then how is he to escape the Polizeirath, unless he does comply with his will? Shall he suffer himself to be locked up in the work-house, whence he may probably be carried to the scaffold? And after all, he is at liberty to promise what he pleases, and having escaped immediate danger, he could do as he thought best.

After Maulspitzer had arrived at this result, he replied, just as if he had only then remembered the person: "Oh yes, yes, sir," and then added the question: "Do you seek the Jew?"

"Long Schmuel," replied the Polizeirath, "has committed a very extensive robbery at the house of a Geheimerath in the *Frederic-stadt.* If within three days you can bring me proofs which will lead to his conviction, I will let you off, and you shall earn a round sum of money besides."

"Hm," said the thief, "what robbery was that? You must first tell me all the particulars of the affair."

The Polizeirath granted his wish, and related to him all the details of the burglary.

"Very well," finally began the Maulspitzer, who had been a most attentive listener, "I think the affair might be done. I shall try and find long Schmuel, and if I cannot ascertain anything positive of him concerning this robbery, there is no doubt but he will soon have another on the tapis, at which I will endeavour to become his partner. By these means he will be sure to run into the trap. But three days is much too short a time."

"Then I will double it, and say six days," said the Polizeirath, after some consideration.

"Even that is too little," answered the other, "I must have at least fourteen days."

"You are a fool," said the Polizeirath laughing, "or perhaps you think that you can make one of me? no, no, this won't do. I have told you six days, and now I give you fair warning to keep your word, else you might fare ill."

At these words the Polizeirath rose from his chair, opened the door, and called out to the gend'arme in the ante-chamber: "Koftry, show the Maulspitzer out of the house."

With the same friendly and kind face as he had received him, the Polizeirath pushed the Maulspitzer out of the room.

When the thief had reached the street, he stopped for a moment thoughtful and hesitating. He wavered between faithfulness and treachery.

He was well aware that this burglary was the same, on account of which the Jew had almost murdered him at the den of hunchbacked Jobs. Since that time he had conceived a deep, deadly, and silent hatred against the Schränker, by whose interference he then not only had lost the great profit of the theft, for he could easily have persuaded the blonde Augustus to let him share it, but who had also inflicted bodily ill treatment upon him, who had even spat in his face, whilst it was out of his power to take immediate vengeance.

A vigilant of course appeared to him as the most villainous and dishonourable of scoundrels, and he himself had fulfilled, what he considered a just punishment upon the Pattern-colourer for the same offence. But in the present instance, circumstances seemed to alter the case.

His own welfare, the necessity of making a friend of the Polizeirath, as thereby he might hope to avoid all suspicion falling upon him, in case the murder of the vigilant should be discovered, all these were powerful motives for compliance. Moreover, his victim would only be an accursed Jew, about whose welfare an honest Christian (as he considered himself) need not be so very regardful.

As he thought of all this, his fists involuntarily clenched in his pockets.

He was fully determined to avenge himself, yet his conscience told him with a voice of thunder, that an honest Schränker should never become a traitor.

He finally solved his difficulties like a true philosopher.

Above all things, he said to himself, nothing will prevent me of entering into a good Massematten with the long Schmuel. Circumstances will then decide what my next movements shall be.

CHAPTER XXXIII.

SCHABBES-EVENING.*

In the same manner as the unfortunate Marianne, the hunchbacked Jobs had also received his provisional discharge, and a short time after her liberation, he also left the prison. Of course he returned to his cellar, and quietly resumed his former course of life.

Marianne, as our readers have already learned, had not returned to him, and he did not know where, at this moment, she might be. That she had been liberated, he had accidentally learned, before leaving the prison.

His paternal mind, however, was not in the least distress about her. What position or situation his daughter at present might be in, was of very little consequence to him.

It was not altogether agreeable to have to dispense with her services, yet the thought of instituting inquiries about her, never once occurred to him. He contented himself with hiring a woman from the neighbourhood, who, for a trifling remuneration, assisted him during the day, in his cellar business. At night, he endeavoured, as best he could, to do all himself,

* Sabbath evening.

since it was not advisable to employ a strange, uninitiated person to wait upon the mysterious guests, who then honoured him with their company.

All the consequences of Jobs' imprisonment to himself, consisted in the redoubled caution and circumspection with which he continued his business.

A few days after the re-opening of his old establishment, he might be seen, towards evening, limping up and down the street in front of his dwelling, evidently awaiting the arrival of some guests.

His small, hunchbacked figure had become even smaller and more decrepid by the prison life he had led for a few weeks; his pallid cheeks had assumed a dirty grey colour, in consequence of his late confinement.

His small, mouse-coloured blear-eyes searched through the approaching darkness of the night, and betrayed particular attention when a distant, bright uniform indicated the possibility of the approach of a gensd'arme, or a Police officer. But he was again quieted, when he found that the comers were only plain recruits or soldiers from a neighbouring garrison, who happened to pass this way on their business or pleasure.

Absorbed in these intense observations, he did not, perhaps, even notice that his neighbours who returned from their daily labour, carefully avoided passing too near him, or that they occasionally here and there pointed their fingers at him, and whispering, put their heads together. Only now and then, when such words as " thieves," " prison," " robbers' den," &c. distinctly reached his ear, he turned his head and measured his opponent with a look of deep, revengeful malice.

At last, the objects who had caused this long observation, appeared to approach.

Two figures, a male and a female, who began to be plainly distinguishable in the dark of the evening, seemed to take their way directly to his cellar.

On seeing them, the hunchbacked Jobs quickly retreated, descended the steps leading to his den, and extinguished the tallow-candle that had been burning upon his counter.

Immediately after, the bell at the outer door announced that the strangers had entered. It had already become quite dark. One of the approaching persons, whose footsteps betrayed him to be a man, struck his foot against a stick of wood that lay in the way.

" Thunder and the devil !" exclaimed a voice which was easily recognized as that of the Eel-eye; " did the old miser want to save his candles, to let his guests break their legs here in the dark ?"

" What ! candles ?" inquired the hunchback, grumblingly, as he hobbled out from behind the counter, and opened the door of his sitting-room, far enough to let a ray of light from a dim oil-lamp pass through the crack of the door from the sitting-room where it burned. " I would rather save my neck and my liberty which your daring carelessness will yet deprive me of. Why could you not come later than this ?"

" Because it did not suit us, old wild-cat," replied the thief, angrily, as he rubbed his wounded leg ; " I must yet speak with long Schmuel this evening, and to-night I have another business before me."

" At least don't bawl loud enough for people in the street to hear our conversation," grumbled Jobs fearfully, " else you might bring an innocent man a second time into prison."

" Hem !" answered the other, " your innocence is not so particularly pure and remarkable ; moreover, I think that whatever danger it is in, the amount we are obliged to pay to you affords a sufficient remuneration."

At these words the thief had entered the sitting room, which we already know well, and from which the passage led to the back rooms where the thieves transacted their nefarious business.

The oil lamp shed a scanty, dim light upon the surrounding objects. By its glimmer we discover that the companion of Eel-eye was no other than the Equestrian. Her tall figure was wrapped in a long cloak, making her fine form appear even more imposing than usual. A simple black hat, over which was spread a long veil, covered her features. Silently she had entered the cellar after her conductor, silently she had followed him into the room.

" Is the Jew within ?" inquired Eel-eye, pointing towards the clothes press, through which was the entrance to the robbers' den, but which at present was carefully closed.

" The whole day already," was Jobs reply, " he keeps his *Schabbes ;* for to-day is Saturday, so you must even have patience for a little while. In half an hour it will be six o'clock, and until then he will not suffer himself to be interrupted by anybody."

" Stuff and nonsense !" cried Eel-eye, ill-humouredly, " I have no time for delay ; I have more to do than to spend my valuable time here in your den. The Jew can finish his prayer to-morrow. Give me the key to the clothes-press."

" Let me advise you," remonstrated the hunchback, " you know long Schmuel when he is excited. I dare not give you the key, for he has strictly forbidden it. Stiff Gottlieb and blonde Augustus had also to leave this afternoon without seeing him, and only brought me unnecessarily into danger."

" Thunder and the devil," now cried Eel-eye, really angry, " is your chatting ever to come to an end ; give me the key or I'll break your neck, you hunchbacked rascal. Trouble yourself about your own affairs, and not about the Jew or myself.—Now, give me the key."

The hunchback no longer dared to oppose this imperative demand. He withdrew the key from his pocket, offered it to the thief, who opened the clothes-press. Knowing the secret mechanism of the entrance, he very soon approached the back den.

"Come, Francisca," he cried from the clothes-press, in a tone of satisfaction, " all obstacles are now removed. The long Schmuel on my earnest prayer, has at last graciously consented to give you an audience; and if you will permit me, I will now present you to him."

Until now, Francisca had stood in silence and indifference, without betraying a sign of either fear or astonishment. Calmly she had followed Eel-eye to the cellar, and had taken no part or interest in his conversation with the hunchback.

As he now requested her to follow him through the very peculiar door-way, and as the mouth of the narrow, dark corridor opened gloomily before her, she involuntarily halted. The cold, damp draught of air, which rose from the den as from a sepulchre, struck her cheek unpleasantly. But a second later she seemed ashamed of her childish fear, and with a determined step she entered the clothes press, to follow her conductor to the end of their journey.

She had scarcely entered the dark passage, when the wall again noisily closed behind her; at the same time she heard Jobs locking the outer side of the clothes-press again.

A total darkness prevailed where she now was. Nothing could be heard but the disagreeable noise made by the rats, who ran to and fro on the damp ground.

Francisca's hand sought her bosom to ascertain whether her dagger was still in its place. She then took the arm of her companion, who slowly felt his way along the damp wall.

After groping a little way further, the passage widened, and the actual den of the murderers opened before them.

From former scenes which we have witnessed here, we already know this locality, and are aware that there is little attractive in its appearance. Francisca drew back with a shudder as she overlooked this pool of vice, where nothing prevailed but filth, stench, and everything repulsive to the senses.

Strangely opposed to the general appearance of the place, was the tableaux presented at this moment by the family of the Schmuels.

The large wooden table had been drawn as near as possible to the old iron stove, in which a small dismal looking fire was glimmering. A fine white tablecloth was covered over this old table, upon which burned two wax lights in silver candlesticks.—All this, of course, was stolen goods.

Around the table the empty barrels and casks had been placed, and, as usual, served for seats to Schmuel, his wife and children. These were dressed in their best holiday rags, and with solemn and serious faces were gathered around the table.

It was still Schabbes. The Jew, on this day, thinks of nothing but the solemnity of the Sabbath.

With dignified composure he is seated at the upper end of the table, reading aloud from a Hebrew book of prayer. The children listen attentively, or at least appear to do so; they fear the fanatic anger of their father, although they understand little or nothing of what he reads to them. The unfortunate Jewess is absorbed in deep thought. She has already become a Christian, yet must externally assume the appearance of a Jewess; her mind, in consequence of this hypocrisy, is torn by bitter pangs of conscience.

The monotonous voice of the Jew resounds mournfully through the vacant space of the arched cellar.

The small company seated around the white table, the brilliant lights on which gave a doubly dim and gloomy aspect to the faint burning oil lamp, which was suspended from the ceiling, struck the beholder by its spiritual, supernatural appearance, until it seemed like a ghost's family in a nursery tale.

Francisca's heart beat aloud at this strange and remarkable picture; exhausted, she sunk into an old chair, to rest for a moment from her long, fatiguing walk.

Eel-eye for some moments remained a silent, ironical spectator. The end of the prayer, however, seemed too far off for his eager impatience; with noiseless steps he approached long Schmuel, whose back was still turned towards him. He lightly tapped him upon the shoulder, and in a half loud voice, whispered to his ear:

" The *Baldowerin* is here, and would speak with you."

In an instant the Jew started furiously from his seat, caught the thief by the throat, and with his herculean power hurled him to the other end of the den, where he fell half stunned and stupified upon a bed of rags and straw. He would probably have broken some of his limbs had he not received this comparatively soft fall.

" Accursed *Goi*," cried the Jew furiously, " do not interrupt me! Did not old Jobs tell you that this is Schabbes? After it is over we will speak of Massematten."

At these words long Schmuel resumed his seat upon the barrel, and quietly continued reading his prayers.

Eel-eye was too greatly frightened, to be able to answer a single word.

He had become tame and obedient, in the same measure as he had before been bold and imperative to Jobs.

The scene continued uninterruptedly, until the clock of a neighbouring steeple announced the sixth hour, and the end of the Sabbath had arrived.

Schmuel now closed his prayer book. From the folds of the large, wide caftan he wore, he produced the *Psohm-box*, which is a silver box shaped like a tower, and which contains spices. Holding this box in his hand, he prayed the *Hawdole*, (the evening prayer of the Sabbath) then looked at his finger nails, and offered the box to his wife and children, who followed his example, and smelled of it. He then pronounced a blessing, and the prescribed ceremony of sabbath celebration was concluded.

With the end of his Schabbes, the Jew again became transformed into another person. The Schabbes, a day strictly consecrated to rest, had closed. For four-and-twenty hours all his ruling passions, revenge, thirst of money, envy, all had rested; they now returned with renewed ardour.

The pious, devoted Hebrew, so strictly attentive to his religious ceremonies, now again was metamorphosed into the most feared and dangerous of all the robbers in Berlin.

CHAPTER XXXIV.

THE LONG SCHMUEL AND THE EQUESTRIAN.

In proportion as the thieves-nature of long Schmuel returned to him, a secret regret awoke in his breast, at having ill-treated so good and useful a partner as Eel-eye only on account of the Schabbes.

As he no longer owed any duty to his Schabbes, he would willingly have cursed its rest and quiet, if that curse would have given satisfaction to his insulted colleague.

As friendly as the pale distracted features of his face permitted him, he approached the other, who was still lying upon the bed of rags, and said:

"Well, Eel-eye, now the Shabbes is over, and we can speak about business."

Eel-eye did not think it advisable to show great resentment. He therefore only replied: "I wish you would in future receive your friends more peaceably, else they will not long be fit for any business. I have brought the Baldowerin with me."

"Very well," replied Schmuel, "bring her here; you will vouch for her."

"I will vouch for her honesty," exclaimed Eel-eye warmly, "she no longer can hope for anything among the *witsche* (honest) people, so she will come to us, and see how she can fare among us. I know the whole of her history; she is rejected by society, and therefore belongs entirely to us."

"Stop one moment," suddenly exclaimed the Jew, thoughtfully.

"Wife," he said, turning towards the unfortunate mother of his children, who had been engaged in taking the sabbath fineries from the table, and sat idly upon a cask, "wife, take the children with you, and go immediately to our lodgings at the house of the *dicke-Itzig*, for in this place we are no longer safe in the evening. There is no necessity of running into useless danger."

"*Tate* I want to remain wherever you do," cried the little black-headed Siegbert, "I am not afraid of the Lambden."

"Bravo, my boy," replied the father approvingly, "but this time you must go; I have a little business to attend to, and then I will follow you."

"A little business, Tate? I want to help you to do business."

"Thunder, boy," cried the Jew, who was growing impatient, "don't stop here, when I order you away; forward, march."

Come, Siegbert, don't interrupt your father, said the Jewess, who quickly observed that something particular was in the wind, and who well knew that the hasty temper of her husband would bear no contradiction.

With a dissatisfied air, the boy took the hand of his mother, who carried her youngest child in her arms. The little girl held on by her dress. Thus the family disappeared through the dark passage.

Carefully long Schmuel crept after them, watching until he was convinced by a well-known signal from their host, that they had disappeared through the clothes-press.

"Now we are all right," he murmured to himself, as he re-entered the den, "I no longer can trust to that woman; and least of all in *this* affair."

Francisca meanwhile had struggled with very peculiar conflicting sentiments. She had overheard the speech of Eel-eye, and could not dispute its truth. Yet it had never entered into her mind to make common cause with these thieves. She would take revenge upon society, but not after the manner of Schmuel and Eel-eye.

Only the most peculiar and wonderful concatenation of circumstances and adventures had, for the moment, introduced her into the companionship of thieves and murderers. It needed the most determined, iron will, to overcome the moral opposition to her present course, which she felt within her breast; at this struggle the memory of the person most in danger, Prince Prominsky, to whom she brought this whole sacrifice, assisted her not a little.

"Where is the Baldowerin?" now inquired the Jew, who had returned to the interior of the den.

The Equestrian quickly rose from her seat, and emerged from the dark corner of the cellar, where she had hitherto remained. Spite of the storm and excitement that prevailed in her mind, she had watched the entire behaviour and manner of the Jew with the most searching attention.

"Eel-eye has spoken rightly," she began, "I am your's for ever. I would dispense with all promises and assurances; for I think you will believe me, Schmuel, as soon as he shall have told you my entire history."

The Jew made no reply. Quietly he raised the veil that had hidden her face, and for some moments fixed his searching intense gaze upon her.

Quietly and firmly Francisca met his eye, without betraying the least emotion.

"You place much incautious confidence in us," said Schmuel, shrugging his shoulders. "I know from the Eel-eye that your house is richly and expensively stored; what would you do, if we were to confine or murder you here, and make the beginning of our business connexion in your own house."

Quickly Francisca drew back a step.

"If you dare to lay a hand upon me," she cried with firmness and determination, as her dagger glistened in her hand, "you will pay dearly for it. The Equestrian neither lacks strength nor courage."

The Jew cast a glance of satisfaction upon the daring, picturesque position of Francisca, and then said:

"I did not mean it so bad as that; you have passed a necessary ordeal, and I will believe you. But now let us not lose words or time, but proceed to our business."

Long Schmuel now invited his two friends to take seats with him at the wooden table. He then produced from a dirty bag, a bottle of liquor, and a small glass, to drink a welcome to the new member.—The Equestrian readily pledged him.

"This much, then, is agreed upon," now began the Jew, "that in partnership we endeavour to accomplish a burglary at the apartments of the foreign Prince in the *Hotel de Paris, under den Linden,* and you, Francisca, are commissioned to *ausbaldower* the opportunity as soon as possible, and in the best manner."

"Stop a moment," interrupted Francisca, "above all things I must know what I can gain by this affair, and who is to pay me my share?"

"That question is natural enough and properly asked," answered the Jew, nodding smilingly his assent, "a real Gannew must always be careful; I will, however, give you full satisfaction.

"By the rules of our *Chawrusse* (company,) the *Baldowerer* as well as any active participator of a *Massematten,* receives a full *Hellig,* (share.) The amount of the Hellig depends upon the quantity of goods stolen, and the number of participators, consequently, that cannot be determined beforehand. I have reason to believe, however, that this Massematten at the Prince's, will be a valuable one, and that we shall be fully repaid for our trouble.

"The division of spoils always takes place immediately after the theft; if one of the parties should not be present, his Hellig is honestly laid aside and kept for him. This, in all my undertakings, I guarantee upon my *Lotscherehre,* and no one can yet say that I have suffered him to be cheated of a penny in any transaction where I was concerned."

At these words, Long Schmuel cast a triumphant look—expressing the proud consciousness of an honest man—towards Eel-eye, as if appealing to him as a witness of his integrity.

"All this, then, seems to be right and in order," answered Francisca, with a satisfied look, "now tell me, how I can best arrange my plan of operation; I am, as you know, inexperienced in these matters, and will feel greatly obliged to you, for your kind instructions."

Again the Jew nodded a pleased assent, and showed by a passing smile, that he felt greatly flattered by the compliment.

He now repeated to the Equestrian the same instructions which she had already received from Eel-eye. He was, however, much more careful in explaining particulars. He described all the localities with a nicety, which proved that he himself had already subjected them to a close examination.

Francisca now assumed the appearance of sudden surprise, and it seemed as if this description had unexpectedly led her to a well known locality.

"Why, Schmuel," she cried with well feigned astonishment, "I have hitherto not inquired nor cared who was the person whom you wanted to rob, but now to judge from your description, it must be Prince Prominsky, whom this visit is intended for?"

"Exactly so," interrupted Eel-eye, "that is his name; I could not remember the confounded name."

"Certainly," said the Jew, fixing a searching look upon the Equestrian, "that is the man; perhaps you know him already?"

"Know him? Why, certainly I do," replied Francisca with a roguish smile, "this is an excellent chance. He is one of my principal would-be-lovers; and has even visited me once already."

"Well, then, we are all right at once," continued the Jew, "then you already know where he lives, and the principal arrangements about his house. It will consequently be an easy matter for you to find an excuse for paying him a visit, when you can soon learn all else that is necessary to know."

"Oh, certainly," answered the Equestrian, "I have already the necessary excuse; in a few days my benefit takes place at the Circus, and I can go to him immediately under pretence of asking him to purchase some tickets."

"Excellent, capital!" exclaimed the Jew, whose good humour rose in proportion as circumstances seemed to accommodate themselves to his plans, "then we must not delay the matter. Procrastination is the thief of time, and I have often seen the best of Massemattens ruined by unnecessary delay. To-morrow forenoon Francisca can go and visit the Prince, and in the evening we will again meet here. If the reports are favourable, we will immediately go to work, say in the night between Sunday and Monday.—The necessary tools I hope, are in good order?"

"Everything in excellent order," replied Eel-eye, with evident pride, "everything as a tip-top Schränker ought to have it."

"I am satisfied," observed Francisca, "and to-morrow evening at about this time, I shall be with you at all events.—And I shall greatly rejoice if the matter fully succeeds," she added, rubbing her hands, and affecting a malignant smile; "I think I can already see the Prince entering my apartments to tell me of his misfortune. He is a proud, overbearing man, who comes to court me, only to have an hour's pastime with me, and afterwards to boast of my favours, and scorn me. Perhaps we may be able to learn by the same opportunity, what is the real object of his stay here, for he must have important business here. He is always so very mysterious, that I could almost burst sometimes with curiosity."

Francisca made the last observation in the easy, confiding, and chatting tone of female curiosity, whilst her eye was directed with apparent carelessness upon the features of the Jew. But her heart trembled and her pulses beat high, for she endeavoured to ascertain whether the Jew knew something further about Prince Prominsky, or whether he would betray any particular interest about his person.

That such an interest existed, was plainly evident to her when she observed how closely the Jew was already acquainted with the domestic arrangements of the Prince, although she could not ascertain in what manner long Schmuel should have become acquainted with the circumstance, that the Prince had drawn certain large amounts of money from his banker, which fact, Eel-eye had already informed her of. This operation on her part was certainly somewhat instinctive, for the grounds which originated the real interest of the Jew, and by which the very character of this interest was designated, those, of course, she was unacquainted with, and could not even suspect.

The apparently careless words of the Equestrian made a deep and visible impression upon the Jew; his pale face grew much paler, his lips pressed closely together, and his eye stared wildly upon the table.

He looked like a hyena who is on the point of pouncing upon its prey.

The Equestrian tremblingly drew back. She was frightened at these horrible features, not for herself, but for the Prince, without actually knowing why or wherefore.

After a short pause the Jew quickly roused himself. With a mixture of embarrassment and suspicion he looked upon the other two, and at last, with a severe effort to assume calmness, he said :

"I have been considering with myself, whether it would not be advisable to let a third *Chawer* (companion) participate in this business. We absolutely must have another person to *stand Schmiere* (be on the lookout,) whilst Eel-eye and myself attempt the burglary. What a pity that poor Schmerles is no longer at liberty, for he would just be the man for us. As it is, I think we ought to select the Maulspitzer?"

"Hm," replied Eel-eye discontentedly, "then there is again another person to come in for a share; I should think that Francisca might undertake that commission."

"What are you thinking of, Albert," exclaimed the Equestrian, "you must be losing your senses, to expect me to stand alone in the street in the dead of night? No, I am too much afraid and too inexperienced for that, I insist on having the Maulspitzer."

Eel-eye had finally to consent to the proposition of his two partners, and Schmuel himself undertook the task of informing the Sandcarter

of their intentions, before the next evening, and also to invite him to become a participator in the enterprise.

Thus, then, the contract was looked upon as closed, and the *modus operandi* partly arranged.

The Eel-eye retired with the Equestrian, to conduct her safely back to her residence.

Immediately after they were gone, Schmuel seated himself by the rickety old table, produced a small ink bottle and a sheet of crumbled letter paper from his caftan, and quickly wrote the following words in Hebrew characters.

"My dear Manasse!—Undoubtedly thou hast received my full and explicit answer to thy letter long ere this. I must now only tell thee, in a few lines, that I have not been idle since then.

Thanks to thy instructions, I have at last succeeded in finding the residence of Prince Prominsky in this city. The coming night, I have arranged with two of my most trustworthy friends, for the time to commit a burglary at his apartments. We shall break into his house, and I hope then to find an opportunity of clearing him from our path. In order to make all this as sure as possible, I have gone to work with the utmost precaution, and have told no one of my principal object.

As soon as our plan has succeeded, I will send thee further advice. Until then, farewell. Pray for the success of my great work of revenge upon the accursed *Goi.*"

Masel and Broche upon thy head.

Thy friend,   Schmuel.

CHAPTER XXXV.

PATERNAL SORROWS.

The Sunday morning seemed to promise a bright and clear winter's day to the Berlinians; just such a day as they need, to enjoy the pleasure of the ice upon the meadows near *Moabit*, or to make an afternoon's promenade through the clean swept walks of the *Thier garten*, (Zoological Gardens.)

It might be about nine o'clock ; solemnly resounded the bells of the cathedral, calling believers to their devotions with their deep and heavy peals.

A light built open barouche, drawn by two light brown, high-mettled coursers, rattled swiftly along the *Charlottenburg Chaussee*, (Turnpike.) A single gentleman, wrapped so closely in his cloak that his face could not be recognized, was the sole occupant of this vehicle. Upon the box sat a coachman and a footman in plain livery.

Notwithstanding the early hour of the morning, the travellers seemed already to have made a long and hurried tour; for the noble, full blooded steeds foamed with heat, and the coldness of the morning had covered the habiliments and hair of the persons with a white frost.

Nevertheless, the speed seemed not quite to satisfy the gentleman within, for frequently he protruded a red heated face from the fur collar of his cloak, to urge the coachman to still greater speed. Obedient to his master's orders, but casting a pitying glance at his wearied horses, he would again swing and crack the long whip about their ears.

Rattlingly, the vehicle passed through one of the passages of the beautiful *Brandenburg-gate*, crossed over the *Pariser-Place*, and took the road along the *Linden*.

At last it stopped before the *Hotel de Paris*.

Upon the ringing of the *Portier's* bell, half a dozen well dressed waiters issued from the house, to assist the new-comer to alight. The stranger, however, despite a certain corpulence, alights quickly and easily from his vehicle, pushed the attentive and obtrusive waiters impatiently aside, and quickly hurries up the stairs of the hotel.

Arrived at the hall, he hastily asks the richly decorated *Portier* the hurried question: "Is Prince Prominsky at home?" and upon receiving a reply in the affirmative, he hastens without loss of time, up stairs, towards the *Belle-Etage*.

In the antechamber stood the *Leibyæger*, staring lazily out upon the street.

"Announce me quickly to his Highness," said the stranger, in a commanding tone, as he threw back the collar of his cloak.

The *Leibyæger* disappeared through the door.

A moment afterwards he returned, quickly disencumbered the stranger of his cloak, and conducted him through three rooms, into a small, elegantly arranged, and pleasantly warmed library.

"Good morning, my dear Major," cried the Prince, rising from the sofa, and warmly pressing the hand of Major von Steinfort, "what in the world brings you, to my great pleasure, so suddenly into town? I thought you were frozen in or snowed in at your country seat?"

"God bless your Highness," replied the old warrior, with a most serious face; "I almost wish myself that I were frozen in or snowed in, but my confounded rascal of a son, the Lieutenant, devil take him, has so warmed me up, that I believe an ice-house would have been too hot to hold me."

"How is this, my dear friend?" inquired the Prince affectionately. "You appear to be very greatly excited; compose yourself, and tell me afterwards what causes all this agitation."

"I will, your Highness, I will; and then you shall give me your advice. We always see things that concern ourselves in the worst light. This affair, however, presses, and I have travelled half the night, for the purpose of being here early this morning."

"Will you not first partake of some refreshment, or at least drink a glass of wine?" inquired the Prince, going towards the bell rope.

"No, your Highness, no, I thank you, I neither desire meat or drink; but alone and uninterrupted, I would be with you."

The Prince opened the door and called out; "I am at home to nobody."

The two friends then took their seats upon the sofa.

"Now we are alone and need fear no interruption," began the Prince, "relate to me what oppresses you? I am under so many obligations to you, that it would really give me the utmost pleasure to be of some little service to you in return."

"You remember, your Highness," began the Major, "that I have once before told you, that my son had commenced an amour with a citizen girl, and had in consequence of it broken off a good and proper match, which I wanted him to make with the daughter of an early friend of mine. That affair greatly annoyed me at the time, for every thing had already been arranged, the match had been settled between myself and the girl's father for years, and the stupid, obstinate refusal of my boy, compromised an entire, and highly respectable family.

"At that time, I immediately departed from the city, that I might hear or see nothing more of this infernal and disagreeable affair. But the worst was yet to come. The day before yesterday I received a letter from the rascal, wherein he informs me straightways, that he had determined upon marrying his sweetheart. He tells me, that the girl is much better than any of the rich or aristocratic coquettes in the city; because she had a heart, a heart for him as he had never before found one. But the end is the best of all — I pray you don't look at me, your Highness. Thunder and the devil! that I should have to be ashamed to lift up my grey head."

The Major stopped for a moment, and passed his hand across his burning forehead. It was plain to see, that the old warrior struggled convulsively to suppress the feelings which threatened to choke him.

The Prince looked at him with deep compassion, but without endeavouring to say a word of consolation. Partly because he did not understand or suspect what would be the end of the matter, and also because he was sufficient judge of human nature to know, that very deep and oppressive sorrow, such as his friend seemed to experience, will find all consolation flat and stale, and that such sorrow will only stop when it exhausts its own resources.

After a pause the Major continued;

"Excuse me, Highness; it was necessary that I should first compose myself a little; the matter, in reality, is so absurdly ridiculous, and withal so confoundedly exciting. Well then, the Lieutenant writes to me, that he considers it his duty, to confess to me openly, that the girl of his choice was formerly—formerly—well, can I not pronounce the word?—in fact that she was formerly a—grisette—no, thunder! let me call the thing by the right name—that she formerly was a woman of ill fame, a depraved, wanton wretch!

"You see, my friend, this is what he dares to write to me; a Lieutenant, in the service of his Majesty the King of Prussia, writes this to his father, a veteran Major. This is what the world has come to! I have had many a bullet flying about my ears, have been in many a hard fought battle, but never have I experienced anything that made me feel so hot, never was my mind in such a state, as it was when I read that infernal letter."

Absorbed in thought the Prince stared silently before him.

"These are now-a-days their ideas of soldiers' honour and of love," continued the Major, greatly excited, "all are matters of indifference to them, position, honour, innocence, wealth or rank; but the difference of education, those of family cannot be so easily eradicated, and the consequence is nothing but misery and wretchedness. I believe my scoundrel of a son has become a thorough radical; such a fellow, a reformer, a socialist, or whatever they are called; if they once become that, they care no longer for appearances, virtue or honesty.

"But what is still worse, the rascal paints the matter in such a virtuous, sentimental light. He says that the girl has fallen a victim to unfortunate circumstances; her mental innocence had remained untainted, and this was what he looked upon as the principal point. He therefore considered it his duty to rescue the poor girl, in whatever way was in his power, from her unfortunate position, and much as he honoured his father, this was one point on which he must break the obedience he owed him. He therefore requests my paternal consent, and in case of refusal, he would marry the girl without it—

"Thunder and the devil! You see, your Highness, this is the long and the short of the matter! Is it not enough to set one crazy at all the nonsense, at all these sentimental, confounded and infernal notions. Even if we could for a moment imagine, that this stupid thought would actually be carried out in earnest, and end in matrimony, the girl would crown him with a pair of horns such as no Peruvian goat ever carried, and laugh in her sleeve, whilst the fool would believe himself a hero of virtue, a knightly champion of innocence, and a safeguard against social vices. It is enough to make one lose his senses."

Through exhaustion, the Major became silent, leaned back on the sofa, and fixed the glance of his dark eye upon the ceiling.

"Well, what conclusion have you come to, my poor friend?" inquired the Prince after a momentary silence, during which he had also remained absorbed in thought.

"That is just what I have come to get your advice about," answered the Major. "According to my judgment it will be best to take the boy and carry him immediately to my country seat, by force if necessary. His commander, who is an old friend of mine, (we fought together in the last war,) can be of very great assistance to me in this. When I get him home, I shall lock him up until he has grown reasonable. Thunder and the devil! an old Major who has seen so much service as I have, ought to be able to bring a beardless young lieutenant to reason!"

"In matters of service, certainly," observed the Prince, shaking his head, "but whether in affairs of the heart, is quite another question. You must not forget, my worthy friend, that though you have but a young man to deal with, he is not a minor, but is full grown. Do you know the girl at all?"

"How should I know her?" answered the Major pettishly; "excuse me, Highness, but I keep no intercourse with, nor have I any acquaintances among, wantons."

"Under the present circumstances," replied the Prince with a smile, "you might without injuring your own reputation, see the girl for once at least."

With great astonishment at these words, the Major turned around.

"Your Highness, I do not understand you; would you speak a good word for my profligate son?"

"Oh, not that," replied the Prince evasively, "only I do not wish you to bring about an exposure by forcible measures. Everything depends on our gaining time. Meanwhile, you may still refuse your consent to your son."

"I have already informed your Highness that he threatens to marry the girl without my consent," continued the Major angrily. "Unfortunately he is independent of me, by the property of his mother, so we cannot let things go to extremes."

"Excuse me, dear friend," interrupted the Prince, "but I must quiet you on that point. Your son is a soldier, and as such bound to the state; you must be aware that no clergyman can marry him without your own consent."

"Thunder! that is a fact," said the Major, "and in my excitement I have entirely forgotten that circumstance."

"Under these circumstances," continued the Prince, "I would advise you not to have an interview with your son for the present, and thus excite him still more by any violent scenes that might occur. Treat his annoying, disrespectful letter at all events with perfect silence; if I know his mind rightly, I think that your silence will make the deepest impression upon him. I shall then make it my business shortly to speak further with him, about this matter—of course without betraying your commission to me—and perhaps I may succeed in preventing him from taking that hasty, ill-advised step—perhaps I may even arrange the entire matter to the satisfaction of all parties.

"Very well," said the Major after a short consideration, "I agree to your proposition; you are more calm, more collected than I am. But then you will immediately inform me of the result of your mediation?"

"Certainly, friend, certainly," said the Prince, pressing his hand, "I should never forgive myself, if I would let you remain in uncertainty, even for an instant, in an affair of such momentous importance."

"Well, then," said the Major rising from his seat, "then I will immediately go home again. This infernal city life is enough to send me to the mad-house; I feel better in body and mind, when I am at home among my horses, cows and cattle."

"But you ought to devote a few hours at least to rest and refreshment," said the Prince kindly and anxiously. "You certainly can remain here with me a short time."

"Pshaw! rest! refreshment! No, my friend, I am too excited for that. A father takes no rest, no refreshment, when the temporal and eternal welfare of his son is at stake."

Silenced by the very bitterness of this reply, the Prince bowed in mute sympathy.

"Once more, then," recommenced the Major, "I depend upon your kindness, Highness. You know me; I do not care a fig for all the titles of ragged nobility in the world, nor for any other similar prejudices; let the boy marry whom he likes; if the girl be as poor as a church-mouse, let her only be honest and of good repute. And now, before we part, one more question; a question which I properly ought to have asked on my entrance: how do your own affairs stand?"

"I am sorry to say, still badly," replied the Prince; "I have not advanced a step. Since the Jewess made those mysterious and unexplained communications to us, those which she had caught from her husband at an unwatched moment, the affair rests upon the old point. I am still in uninterrupted communication with that excellent woman, and my only hope at present is, that a lucky accident must, in the course of time, drive the Jew into my hands. As soon as any thing worthy of note happens, I shall instantly inform you, and beg for your assistance."

"Very well, we must help each other, then," replied the Major. He warmly pressed the hand of his friend, and took his leave.

CHAPTER XXXVI.

REFLECTIONS.

As the Prince, on his return to his cabinet, passed through his ante-chamber, his yaeger handed him a billet, which he said had a short time before been left by a strange girl, who was still waiting for an answer.

The Prince examined the note. It was neatly folded, and to judge from the fine and finished hand-writing, was written by a lady.

With some degree of curiosity, the Prince broke the seal, and was still more astonished at its contents.

It was from the Equestrian, who communicated to him that she must immediately see him, and that privately, on an affair of the utmost importance. The girl would wait to hear whether he was at home, alone, and disengaged, and if so, she would immediately call upon him.

The Prince hastily wrote an affirmative reply, and gave it to the girl for delivery.

He found himself in a peculiarly excited state of mind, excited even more than usual by the occurrences of this morning.

The intentions of Lieutenant von Steinfort; his own sorrows, newly awakened by the inquiries of his friend, the Major, this mysterious request and announcement of Francisca; all these circumstances were sufficient food for excitement and reflection.

The troubles and sorrows which he had suffered for years past, again began to oppress him: the memory of his long lost brother, and the possible injustice by which he held that brother's possessions. He reproached himself deeply with not having been sufficiently eager and active in his researches of late, although his own consciousness told him on the other hand, that he had in no instance missed an opportunity that seemed, in any way, to lead to a favourable result.

He often enough had held consultations with the Jewess, and from her had obtained the most important communications concerning the intelligence she had gained, when she listened to her husband's letter, on the morning of its receipt, in the house of *Dicke Itzig*. The positive fact which he had thus become acquainted with, namely, that his princely brother had grown up to be a thief, had almost driven him to despair, yet he was fully determined not to relinquish his plans in consequence.

The other intelligence which he had received at the same time, namely, that his own life was sought after by the Jew, made but very little impression upon his daring and chivalric mind; the less so, as despite of all reasoning and thought, he could not discover the ground or cause for this prosecution. In trying to connect this intelligence with the former fate of his family, his mind finally fixed upon the idea, that perhaps some other vows had to be fulfilled, which his revengeful aunt might have imposed upon the instruments of her plans. Under all these circumstances, he was still less inclined to abandon his search, as it was more than ever possible that the present position of things might lead to developments of the fate of his brother; he would even have proceeded more energetically, if the Jewess had dared to obtain him the opportunity of an interview with her husband.

But regarding this, the good woman had to go most cautiously to work, as in case of a discovery, she had to fear everything for her own safety and that of her children, and, moreover, would not incautiously expose the person of the Prince to any danger. The Prince himself had to consent to this reasoning, as he was already aware of the loss of the Major's pocket-book, which, of itself, was a most threatening circumstance. How easily was it possible, that the thief who had picked the pocket of the Major, might in some way be connected or acquainted with long Schmuel, and put these important letters into his hands. Then his long cherished plan must forever be annihilated, and the unfortunate Jewess would have prepared for herself, as a reward for her fidelity, a terrible, indescribably wretched fate.

As these thoughts presented themselves to his mind, the Prince experienced the most cruel pangs of conscience at the incautiousness with which he had guarded those important papers. Even though he had not lost them himself, still the affair was his, and he should have prevented the Major from carrying them carelessly about his person. He meditated long and deeply, whether he might not, in some way, be able to learn something of the fate of that pocket-book. Existing circumstances, of course, prevented him from having resort to the assistance of police. He would willingly have assumed a disguise, and put himself in connexion with the Berlin thieves, if he could only have found some person to act as mediator between him and them. But this mediator was entirely wanting, as he could not, and would not, induce the Jewess to undertake that office.

And still he knew, that among that band, perhaps even in Berlin, was his brother, the only blood relation that remained him in the whole world. It was a terrible feeling, to be compelled to confess to himself, that his own brother, the heir of immense possessions, the rightful owner of a high and illustrious name, must in misery and crime, daily proceed step by step nearer to a prison, to an ignominious death.

The Prince put his hand to his burning forehead, and uttered a deep sigh.

These sad and sorrowful thoughts were somewhat pleasantly relieved by the picture of the Equestrian, and the Prince could not avoid feeling great anxiety and interest in the communication she seemed to have to make to him. This interest greatly increased by the remembrance, that single observations, which she had made at the soirée of the Referendarius von Birkheim, led him to believe, that in some way or other, she must be more or less acquainted with his history. Her female sagacity had certainly avoided all questions which he afterwards directed to her, regarding the hints she had thus carelessly thrown out; but this unaccountable, mysterious circumstance had only helped to increase and heighten the interest he had felt on her appearance. The beauty of her person, the nobility of her entire demeanour, had made a deep impression upon him.

Although he discovered, or rather suspected instantly, that she must be a fallen woman, yet he arrived at the certain conclusion, that she could only have become in early life the victim of a vile and villanous seduction, and that she had afterwards been crushed by the bad tendency of our social system. Her intelligence, refinement, and the elegance of her demeanour, indi-

cated at once, and established beyond a doubt, the respectability of her origin, and entitled her to a better position.

Her position to the Geheimerath, even secured her his respect, as he at once and easily perceived, that she had not suffered herself to fall a sacrifice to the admiration of that grey-headed sinner, but that she had only granted an ear to his urgent importunities, for the purpose of avoiding the coarse, disgraceful influence of the society she had heretofore been compelled to keep. This view of the matter certainly was a correct one, although the plans of revenge which Francisca nourished, had been the main-spring of her action; of these, however, the Prince could have no suspicion. He luxuriated in the thought of perhaps being permitted to devote a part of his immense riches to her salvation; he hoped to restore her to society, and to put her into a position equivalent with her birth, mind, and education. If he persuaded himself that by doing so, he was only playing the part of a noble and humane philanthropist, he could not discover, much less did he confess it to himself, that the dark brilliant eyes of Francisca had already become the secret compass by which the wavering bark of his heart and his wishes was guided.

Amidst all these contrary, indistinct and unaccountable emotions, the communications of the Major had strangely excited the heart of the Prince. The heroic resolve of the Lieutenant appeared by no means so thoroughly repulsive to the romantic mind of Prince Prominsky, nay, he could not deny to himself, that here was a case in many respects similar to his own position with the Equestrian. The Lieutenant had only taken a more bold and decided step than himself, and although the Prince at the moment did not know, whether he would have the courage to take a step of such consequence, still he was candid enough to award to the strength of mind and decision of character shown by another, his entire esteem and respect. With such sentiments, it was natural that he should feel a painful uncertainty how to proceed in the fulfilment of his promise to the Major. He felt that from his peculiar position, that excellent man was entirely in the right; moreover, he had too great a veneration for the open, honourable character of his friend, independent of the many obligations under which he was to him, to think himself capable, even for a moment, of deceiveing his veteran friend. On the contrary, he was fully determined strictly to execute the will of the Major, and to try all the means in his power to change the Lieutenant's resolution.

But, on the other hand, a certain indefinable something which he could not explain, urged him to tenderness and kindness towards the latter. He simply asked himself the question; Why should not this young man marry this girl, when that, which to others would be an important condition of happy wedlock, may be perfectly valueless and indifferent to him? Why will the world strenuously insist on the well established past virtue of his wife, the existence of which seems to him who is most concerned, no guarantee for his future happiness? Our conception of innocence is at best only in a relative point of view. A person may be very innocent physically, yet mentally very guilty; and again the reverse may be the case. The first case never gives cause for hesitation, when matches are made, why then should the second absolutely do so? Must we not at least look upon body and soul in equal lights? Now the Lieutenant places the soul, the mind, higher than the body. Why should we find fault with this? He is pleased with this girl, he loves her, he believes that he will find happiness in her arms—is not that sufficient. Whether it is possible, that this happiness should be in accordance with the ideas of a third party, that is a question, the solution of which, does not seem to trouble him. Why will the third party force their own solution upon him? To speak in the words of a great king: "*Let every one seek happiness after his own, peculiar fashion.*"

CHAPTER XXXVII.

IMPORTANT COMMUNICATIONS.

FRANCISCA, fully equipped for a walk, was at her room, awaiting the return of her maid. She did not think, nor would she think of the possibility that her step would be misinterpreted. She felt herself far above trifling obstacles of this kind, when duty or necessity required her to act.

But withal, her entire soul and body was in a state of peculiar excitement. Her dark eye sparkled more brilliantly than usual, and a blush of inward excitement flushed her cheek.

Restlessly she walked up and down her boudoir, trying to fix her attention now upon one, then upon another object.

Her harp stood in a corner. Involuntarily she approached it, and her hand swept across the strings. The sound it produced only reminded her of what she was doing. Shrugging her fair shoulders, she replaced the instrument, walked towards the window, and looked out upon the street.

Her little boudoir became too narrow for her; she hurried to the adjoining saloon, and greedily breathed the fresh and pure air of this large, cold room.

Thoughtfully she stopped before a splendid marble bust of Apollo, which the liberality of the Geheimerath had placed in this room. That bust had become of great value to her, as she believed that in the features of the head she discovered a resemblance to those of Prince Prominsky. Her imagination was now occupied in tracing that resemblance still further.

A sweet, silent, and strange longing, such as she had not felt for many years, now began to fill her breast. Involuntarily she placed her hand upon her heart, as if endeavouring to subdue the rising passion there

Suddenly, a terrible thought flashed across her mind: "How, if the Prince would refuse to receive her? If he were little-minded enough to misunderstand or misconstrue my behaviour, and were to repulse me with cold pride?"

The mere thought put Francisca into a feverish excitement. Tremblingly she stood before the bust, looking upon it with dimmed, almost imploring looks. The proud, daring woman had melted into a tender, powerless child.

"No, no, that is impossible!" she cried aloud, "he will listen to me, he *must* listen to me, if he carries a heart within his breast. Ah, and I know it," she whispered, as if ashamed of her own confession, " he has a heart; a warm, enthusiastic, ardent heart, such as few mortals have."

She approached the bust closely, and imprinted a long, burning kiss upon the cold marble face.

Her maid entered the room, and brought the answer of the Prince.

Hastily Francisca tore the seal; her burning looks quickly perused the lines, and she then hid the paper in the snowy depths of her bosom.

Without losing a syllable, she left the house, and with hasty steps proceeded on her way towards the *Hotel de Paris.*

As she approached the Hotel, she observed the friend of her early youth, who was elegantly dressed, and promenading up and down on the opposite side of the street, looking carelessly, and like a fashionable fop, at the houses and the passers-by.

Of course she quickly perceived that his business was no other than to watch whether she really would go to the Prince. She could easily conceive that the distrustful Jew would consider this usual precaution particularly necessary in this case, when a new member of his company was entrusted with such an important office.

Arrived at the door, she therefore turned round once more, and quickly nodded her head to Eeleye, giving him, as it were, the signal that she was about to fulfil her commission. The thief replied with a glance of satisfactory recognition, and then, quieted about the further events, he quickly disappeared in a side street. Here he observed by a clock, that the hour for the close of divine service at the Cathedral, was close at hand; he hastened his steps for the purpose of practising his pickpocket propensities among the crowd of worshippers who were about to leave the temple.

Francisca's heart beat audibly as she ascended the broad, carpeted stairs of the hotel, which Major von Steinfort had just descended with somewhat similar feelings, though excited by a different cause.

Prince Prominsky received her with that respectful and kind attention which usually affected her heart so deeply, and which, probably, had been the first and great cause, by which the scorned, degraded, and despised Equestrian had felt herself attracted towards him.

As she had originally received an excellent education, as she certainly did not lack in intellectual qualities of head and heart, she felt the more deeply and bitterly the slights and insults of others who were so much her inferiors.

"I hope," at last began Francisca, after she had recovered her usual calmness with some difficulty, "I hope that your Highness will not misinterpret the strangeness of my present position and request. Should I, however, be mistaken in this hope, you will please to accept these self-evident excuses for my hasty step,"

At these words she produced the pocket-book of the Major from her pocket, and placed it upon the table.

"I pre-suppose," she continued, "that the loss of this very important pocket-book must already have caused you some anxiety. But I hope that you will find the contents all restored to you in good order; and I beg that your Highness will convince yourself of that fact."

The Prince stared at the Equestrian in mute astonishment.

He had just reproached himself bitterly with the loss of this pocket-book, and had in vain endeavoured to think of ways or means, by which he might regain the much-sought possession of it. Now it was suddenly offered to him, offered to him too, from a source, the very last he could possibly have thought of. What strange, mysterious connexions might here exist! The Equestrian returns to him a pocket-book, which he knows that a thief has taken!

These thoughts passed with lightning speed through his mind, and formed themselves into the most strange ideal monsters. It was perfectly natural, that such a result should take place, when we consider the sudden and strange request of the Equestrian for an audience, her immediate appearance as soon as it is granted, and the wonderful object of her mission. His surprise was so great, that he could scarcely experience any joy at being thus relieved of a heavy anxiety. It was only after Francisca had repeatedly offered him the pocket-book, that he took it, and hastily glanced over the papers it contained.

He found all the well-known letters of the Jewess, placed in the same order as he himself had read them at the Masquerade, and not one was missing.

"Certainly," began the Prince after a while, as his astonishment had somewhat subsided, "you are perfectly right. The loss of this pocket-book was neither unobserved, nor was it indifferent to me. It contains important papers, by which a third party might be dangerously compromised. Its safe return places me under the utmost obligations to you. But I am equally anxious, and excited by an excusable curiosity to ascertain how you came into possession of this pocket-book."

"Your Highness will pardon me, if I must decline answering that question," said Francisca, entreatingly. "I have to thank some fortunate circumstance for the pleasure of thus becoming useful to you; nothing farther I suppose, is actually necessary for you to know."

"That pocket-book," continued the Prince, "was withdrawn from the pocket of a particular friend of mine, in the most dishonourable manner, or rather, as I should say, was stolen from him. Perhaps your testimony might help to bring the criminal to the punishment he merits."

"And if such were the case," replied Francisca, "I doubt whether I would have a right to betray the person whom accident put into my power. Your Highness now is satisfied. Let the rest remain as it is; I ask this as a reward for the service I have rendered to you."

The Equestrian pronounced these last words in a half smiling, yet withal, so determined tone of voice, that the Prince could no longer contradict her. But he could not help shaking his head in thoughtful wonder.

His astonishment, however, was soon to be still more increased.

"My mission to you, however," continued the Equestrian, "is not yet concluded, for I have to impart to your Highness another piece of news, which, perhaps, may interest you as much, if not more, than even the recovery of the pocket-book. This news is the following: the Jew mentioned in your letters, and who is known by the name of long Schmuel, has determined to break into your house, and the night after this, is fixed upon for the consummation of this crime."

"How?" cried the Prince, with an expression of great wonder and astonishment, as he jumped up from his seat and closely approached the speaker.

The Equestrian took no notice of this excitement, which must appear very natural to her, but quietly continued her speech.

"I know already from the letters contained in the pocket-book, the reading of which you will not, I hope, look upon as an indiscretion on my part, how much it is an object to you to obtain the person of the Jew. It seems to me that an excellent opportunity now offers itself, to obtain possession of his person. Your Highness must only make the necessary preparations in your own rooms. If then, you catch the Jew in the fact, it will be a very easy matter for you to obtain all the necessary information from him, by simply threatening to deliver him to the proper tribunals."

Silently the Prince stared before him.

"And to-morrow night that burglary is to be committed?" he finally inquired.

The Equestrian answered affirmatively

"And the object is to rob me?"

"Certainly," answered Francisca.

"Wonderful and mysterious being," now began the Prince, "how can I ever reward you? Let me tell you then, as I suppose you do not know it, that you protect me against more than robbers, that you save more than my property, you save my life."

Francisca uttered a low scream of terror.

"If the Jew intends to break into my house at night, his object is not alone to obtain my property. His own wife, who is the author of those letters, has informed me of his determination to take my life, and there can be no doubt, that at this burglary he would make an attempt to accomplish his object."

Francisca's eyes grew alternately dim and brilliant, as different feelings obtained mastery over her mind, terror, rage and love. She had not the least doubt of the correctness of the suspicions of the Prince, for supposing that opinion to be correct, many things in the Jew's behaviour, which had before appeared remarkable, now were easily accounted for. No doubt remained in her own mind, of her having herself been deceived by the Jew.

An unspeakable degree of happiness filled her breast at the thought of having become a guarding, a saving angel to Prince Prominsky.

The Prince had walked towards the window, ardently struggling to regain that composure and calmness which these important communications had, for a moment, taken from him.

He had escaped the most threatening danger, and at the same moment, the fulfilment of his warmest wishes, of the object of his life, had approached nearer than ever. The Jew himself would come to him, to his own house, and he need but close his hand to have him a safe prisoner. How easy it would then be to get every necessary, every important information from him. All this he owed to the Equestrian, to that wonderful woman, whose appearance at first sight had so deeply affected him.

The excitable, enthusiastic mind of the noble Pole now looked upon the woman who saved his life, as a being of a higher sphere, sent into the world to guard his path of life as a saving and protecting angel.

"Tell me," he began, interrupting the mutual silence, as he took Francisca's hand within his own, "what do you ask of me? Nothing that is in my power to give will be too high a price, if I can thereby pay a small part of the heavy debt of gratitude which I owe you!"

Francisca's hand trembled convulsively within that of the Prince.

With an herculean effort she mastered her emotions, and said: "I have a request at hand, and your last words let me hope that you will easily grant it. As I have told you, the Jew will have two assistants at this robbery of your apartments; promise me, sir, that these two shall go free. Neither of them will finally escape his judge, but I would not appear as their accuser, as my object in this case is only to deliver the Jew into your hands."

A natural feeling of fairness had urged Francisca to make this request, as she remembered, that to a certain extent she had obtained the secrets of her early friend by superior cunning; she would not, therefore, consent to let him fall a sacrifice to his confidence in her.

The Prince most readily agreed to grant this prayer, for as we know, its object was for his own interest. If he would not deliver the Jew to his civil judge, he could not well pursue the same plan with the Jew's companions. To keep them privately imprisoned would have been a useless and troublesome task.

This petition, however, seemed to remind the Prince of his former questions, for on giving his consent, he added:

"But in this case also, will you not satisfy my curiosity, and make me acquainted with the source of your information?"

"I cannot, your Highness," quickly replied Francisca. "As I have already observed to you, I can betray nothing further. It was an accident that assisted me, and," she hesitated somewhat—"perhaps my own acuteness and ingenuity. Your Highness cannot have the least advantage from any communication I could make, as you neither can nor wish to call the assistance of the police. It is wiser in you to bless the lucky accident which has hitherto assisted us."

A slight cloud of displeasure overspread the features of the Prince.

"Your Highness will not think wrong of me in consequence of this," began the Equestrian, whose quick eye had observed the cloud upon the other's brow. "Only by keeping my secret entirely to myself, can I hope to become still further useful to you. And—it is part of the pleasure of my existence to be able to do that."

The intriguing character of the Equestrian renders it necessary that we should observe that the last few words were not uttered for external effect merely. These words really were the open and real sentiments of her heart, expressed through the painful consciousness of having most probably excited the displeasure of the Prince.

For this very reason her words contained an impress of veracity, which, with victorious certainty touched the heart of the Prince. At the same moment his glance fell upon the Equestrian, and the fire and ardour expressed in his eye, caused the black silken lashes of her large eyes, abashed, to sink to the ground.

This it is that makes love ever appear as the pure, real diamond; the light of that jewel is seen clear and brilliant, no matter what garb may enclose it.

We might be asked why the Equestrian was so reserved in communicating any of her secrets to the Prince; for after all, she must be able to perceive, that in her peculiar position, such a reserve would easily, to suspicious and ignoble minds, give sufficient foundation upon which to build the most remarkable suspicions and accusations. How, if she were guiltless, did she come into connexion with thieves and robbers, which enabled her to make these disclosures, and render this assistance to the Prince?

Perhaps the Equestrian did not fear to be thus misunderstood or misjudged, because in her own conscience, she felt herself elevated above such vile suspicions; perhaps also because she believed that she knew enough of the high-mindedness of the Prince, to think him incapable of such suspicions. Besides these reasons, however, there was a regard, an anxiety for the safety of her early friend, which induced her to remain silent; and she felt a fear, that on giving disclosures on the present points, she must naturally be led into giving disclosures of her own former history, which not alone might reach the ears of the Geheimerath, but which also she felt herself involuntarily urged to keep secret from the Prince.

"You display a most active interest in the strange and peculiar history of my life," said the Prince, continuing the conversation, "which gives me the right, and makes it my duty, if possible, to return your favours in the same way. Be open towards me; are there not many things in your present position which you would wish to have changed, and may it not be in my power to bring about that change? Remember, that I also would consider myself fortunate to be of service to you, after the very great and important services you have rendered to me."

Silently the Equestrian shook her head.

"Perhaps," continued the Prince more urgently, "there might be a possibility of my fulfilling one or the other of your wishes, if you gave me an opportunity of knowing something of your fate or history."

Francisca still remained silent.

"It is not curiosity," said the Prince warmly, "which induces me to inquire for your secrets. Accident has made you intimately acquainted with the most secret and important parts of my history, and I bless that accident for it. Perhaps I might urge even this as a claim to your confidence, but I have only one desire, which is, that you may tell me, how in any way I can deserve an expression of thanks from your lips."

"The kind, noble offer of your Highness commands my entire gratitude," Francisca replied at last; "but withal, though grateful for it, I must decline it. The world has dealt very severely with me; I must remain in it as I am, that I may at last square accounts with it."

This reply strengthened in the Prince's mind his former conviction, that the Equestrian pursued other objects than those which her external life seemed to indicate. And he would have her abandon those objects, without himself really knowing why or wherefore. He felt that these objects could not be good ones. The resistance of the Equestrian only urged him to further exertions upon that point.

"I will not deny it," he said openly, "that I feel a most lively interest in yourself and your fate. If you will agree, I will bear you away from these scenes. I am rich, noble and high-born; if I take you to my home, it will be easy for me to offer you a quiet, peaceable and respected position."

Francisca raised her head, and cast a happy, delighted and grateful look towards the Prince.

For a moment she luxuriated in a dream of peace and happiness. Whom would she rather have thanked for this than the Prince?

The Prince, who did not fail to observe her emotions, endeavoured to avail himself of them.

"Accept my proposition and I shall be happy," he said in a kind tone, offering his hand to the Equestrian.

Francisca raised her hand; her guardian angel stood invisibly by her side, to reconcile her with the past.

But the wild demons of vengeance again rose and assumed their supremacy.

"I cannot be helped," she said gloomily, as her arm slowly fell by her side. "Do not ask me, do not inquire for my fate; it is black and terrible. I am ejected from the civilized world; my destiny and the object of my life is to take revenge for myself and my thousand sisters in sufferance upon our mocking destroyers. Perhaps the time may come, when you will hear terrible things of me; then you will remember this hour, and instead of a curse, bestow a tear to the memory of the *dishonoured maiden*."

Francisca pronounced this word with a fearful and terrible bitterness.

The Prince shuddered, as he saw the speaker stand before him like an ancient Goddess of vengeance in her terrible beauty.

She looked to him almost like an evil sorceress. He endeavoured to free himself from her influence, and felt himself still more attracted toward her.

Was it gratitude, was it love, or was it hatred that moved him, when he was again alone and lonely in his cabinet? but earnestly and immoveably his silent looks were fixed upon the chair which had supported the beautiful Francisca.

END OF PART THREE.

PART IV.

CHAPTER XXXVIII.

HOW POLIZEIRATH X—— IS DUPED.

At about the same hour, in which the Equestrian made those important disclosures to the Prince, there sat in a victualling cellar at the corner of *Jerusalem-street* and *Dönhof-place*, a solitary, plain looking individual.

He had ordered a small bottle of *Weissbier* (light Ale,) which stood untouched upon the brightly scoured table before him. The host had taken his seat in the corner behind the stove, and had gently fallen into the arms of Morpheus.

The stranger was attired in the simple dress of a labourer. Early and quiet as it was in the city, being a Sunday morning, he was the only guest in the room.

He seemed to be absorbed in serious reflections; at least his exterior seemed to indicate a man deeply lost in thoughts and calculations.

This man was Maulspitzer, whom the Jew had last night invited to participate in the burglary of the Prince's apartments, and who now was consulting within himself, whether he should use this opportunity, to betray his comrade to Polizeirath X—.

Maulspitzer had already determined on such a course, and had been on his way to the house of the Polizeirath. But on arriving near the residence of the latter, his conscience had reproached him, and he had sat down here for a moment, to gain time for new reflections.

After a short pause his resolution was formed. Quickly he rose from his seat, emptied his glass at a single draught, and left the room so noisily, that he frightened the sleepy host, who started up from his slumbers.

Almost fearing, that his new resolution might again be shaken, he quickly started on his way. With long strides he crossed *Dönhofs-place*, reached the house of the Polizeirath, and pulled the door-bell so rapidly and anxiously, that the inmates of the house thought it meant an alarm of fire.

Koftry, the long gensd'arme, opened the door, and expressed no small astonishment at finding a notorious vagabond entering the house of a high police officer, with so disrespectful a noise. As he knew perfectly well, however, though from mere guessing, what was the object of the present visit, he immediately conducted Maulspitzer to the Polizeirath.

After long arguments with himself for and against the measure, he had finally determined so far to comply with the request of the Polizeirath as to deliver the Jew into his power. But he could not persuade himself to act treacherously to Eel-eye. The Jew had treated him badly, nay, had almost murdered him; therefore, according to his mode of reasoning he was justified in taking revenge. Another reason by which he excused his treachery to Schmuel, was, that the latter was only a Jew, to whom an honest christian, after all, need not consider himself so strictly and honourably bound.

Immediately on entering the cabinet of the Polizeirath, he made the latter acquainted with all the plans which the Jew had projected for that night, but informed him at the same time, that he himself had agreed to become a partner of this burglary. Knowing, however, that the Polizeirath was sufficiently acquainted with the usual system of thievery, to be fully aware, that the Jew dared not undertake such a burglary with him alone, but that there must unquestionably be a third party engaged, he endeavoured to prevent any disagreeable inquiries for the latter, by closing his report with the information, that beside himself and the Jew, there was a third party concerned in this affair, but that this third party would not show itself or be known, to him, before the evening of the theft.

The Polizeirath had very quietly listened to this report.

When the thief had concluded, he inquired: "Well, and what about this burglary at the house of the Geheimerath of which I told you?"

"I have not been able to learn anything about that," replied the villain evasively, "but I thought if I only delivered the Jew into your hands at some other opportunity, that would be sufficient, and that, having him once in your hands, you would easily worm out all that you wanted to know of him."

"So, so, this then was your opinion?" resumed the Polizeirath, again assuming a pleasant, harmless smile; "well, I approve your activity. But to return to your report; you say you don't know as yet, who is to be the third partner?"

"No, Herr Polizeirath."

"Just try and remember, friend; think very hard. You surely have not been so incautious, as to enter into an enterprise without knowing who were all the parties concerned?"

"And why not? Since in this instance it was only make-believe," replied Maulspitzer with a cunning look, for he thought he had now fully satisfied the Polizeirath.

"Only make-believe?" repeated the Polizeirath; "that is true; but would not the Jew, who knows that you are a cautious, cunning rascal, have thought it very suspicious and remarkable if you had not inquired, or seemed to care, who was to be your partner?"

"He may have thought that I would leave everything to his own well-established cunning and precaution," answered Maulspitzer.

"Hm?—Well, my friend, you must know torerably well, that I have a little experience among people of your class, and that I know how to take them; so you would act wisely by not throwing difficulties in my way. Now I will just tell you how the matter stands: from what I know of your manners, laws and customs, the Jew never thought of having any secrets from you, regarding anything concerning this burglary. As a matter of course, he has told you the names of all the participators, and you will also tell them to me immediately."

Spite of the friendly smile that still played upon the face of the Polizeirath, he pronounced these words in a most firm and decided tone of voice.

Nothing now remained for the Maulspitzer to do, than simply to deny any further knowledge of the affair, and to insist upon his utter ignorance of the third party.

"If you don't obey me," now continued the Polizeirath, "I shall have to proceed to the measures I threatened to you."

The villain was still in hopes that this remark had only been made to intimidate him, and swore heavy oaths, that he knew nothing further of the affair, than what he had already told.

The Polizeirath quietly approached the table and rang the bell. The long and fearful figure of Koftry immediately appeared at the door.

"Now, you may decide," said the officer, "otherwise I shall instantly send you to prison."

The Maulspitzer found himself in a most desperate position. He would not lose his liberty, nor yet betray his friend Eel-eye. In the utmost distress he alternately looked upon the fearful body-gensd'arme, who watched him with great indifference, and upon the Polizeirath, who observed him with some anxiety.

Suddenly his mind caught upon an idea which seemed available.

"Let the gensd'arme leave the room, Herr Polizeirath," he said, "and I will inform you of something else."

Upon a wink from his officer, the gensd'arme withdrew.

"What I have told you, Herr Polizeirath," continued the thief, "is nothing but the truth; as I was not in earnest about the affair, I did not trouble myself about the third partner, and perhaps from sheer accident, the Jew has not named him. But to convince you, that I am willing to give you all the information I can, upon the subject, I will tell you, that the *Baldowerin* of this robbery is a woman. The Jew has told me that she is well acquainted with the Prince, and that she could fully describe all the localities. I have not yet seen the person alluded to."

By this unasked-for confession, the thief, as he had intended, really made the Polizeirath believe, that he had been candid and honest in his former information.

The officer now directed a few more questions to Maulspitzer, concerning this woman, as also concerning their proposed mode of proceeding in the accomplishment of the burglary, and then dismissed him, with the command to use all his endeavours to accomplish the burglary on the evening designated.

With the comfortable consciousness of having safely escaped a threatening danger by his tact and cunning, the Maulspitzer left the house of his arch-enemy, Polizeirath X—.

Nothing now remained for him to do, but to arrange matters with his partners in such a manner, that he himself should enter the house with the Jew, whilst Eel-eye should *stand Schmiere* in the street. He was then convinced by the well-known cunning and activity of the latter, that he would make his timely escape, as from the street he must soon perceive that the burglary had failed.

Maulspitzer determined to arrange all this in the evening, and therefore would go to the den of hunchbacked Jobs at as early an hour as possible.

Internally satisfied, in thus having sacrificed the Jew to the Polizeirath, without betraying Eel-eye, he walked merrily along.

Besides this, it was no small satisfaction to him, to have made a dupe, at least in one point, of the much-feared Polizeirath X—.

CHAPTER XXXIX.

FATAL INTERRUPTION.

THE Prince had not remained idle during the day.

In careful silence he had made all necessary preparations, to secure the person of the Jew, this time, without fail.

His intention was immediately to leave Berlin with long Schmuel, and to bring him in all haste, to the domain of the Major. Once arrived there, he hoped by the threat of delivering him to the criminal tribunals, to elicit from him the long-sought information about the fate of his brother.

For this purpose he had already sent an express to Major von Steinfort, and the domestics of his household had all received orders to have everything prepared on the following night, for an immediate departure from Berlin. Only one confidential valet was in the real secret, and the Prince had made him fully acquainted with all his plans and expectations.

It was his intention to keep himself hidden in the dark, and silently watch where and from which side of the room the burglary would be attempted. The doors of all the different rooms were for this purpose to be left open. Both then would suddenly and unexpectedly rush forth, secure the person of the Jew, but suffer the other thieves to escape.

The Prince counted upon the certainty, that the latter, instead of thinking of resistance, would only be anxious to seek safety in flight. With the Jew alone, he could easily hope to accomplish his object, as both himself and the valet whom he employed, were remarkable for their personal strength.

Thus the Prince indulged in the fond and well-founded hope of seeing the dearest wish of his life near an accomplishment. The peace and happiness of his entire existence depended upon the issue; for only, after he had restored to the hand of his brother all the wealth of which he held unjust possession—after he had delivered that brother from the terrible associations, and from the pit of vice into which he had been thrown, he believed that the curse which his fiendish aunt had cast upon his unfortunate family, would be ended and atoned. He then might again hope to enjoy peaceful and happy days.

The Prince was an elegant and experienced man of the world, and knew how to hide the emotions of his soul from the eyes of observers; but beneath that formal exterior there lay a warm, feeling heart, which urged him restlessly to pursue his plans.

The evening had arrived. He found himself in a state of the utmost excitement. The approaching, decisive hour made him anxious, nervous and fearful.

He knew the power of an unforeseen accident. After years of vain and useless search he had once before believed himself near the accomplishment of his object, and had failed in the most annoying manner. His hopes and plans might again be wrecked.

The hands of his watch, which he had already consulted fifty times at least, pointed towards the hour of ten. The time seemed to-night to pass much more slowly than usual. He could not expect the thieves before midnight. He seated himself in his cabinet, to endeavour and pass the time by arranging some papers.

Thoughtfully he was looking over a manuscript which might have some connexion with the fate and history of his family, when a servant entered and announced that there was a stranger without who desired to speak with his Highness. This strange gentleman would not give his name, nor would he leave on being told that his Highness desired to be uninterrupted, but insisted on seeing the Prince immediately.

Annoyed at this interruption, Prince Prominsky rose to go into the adjoining room, determined to dismiss his obstinate visiter as soon as possible.

In the ante-chamber he found Polizeirath X—, who was plainly dressed in black coat and pantaloons, whilst the ribbon of the *order of the red eagle, fourth class*, was fastened into a button-hole of his coat.

The Polizeirath bowed most politely, begged to be excused for having thus unceremoniously interrupted him, at the same time expressing a hope that his Highness might still remember his person, from a short acquaintance they had formed at a masquerade in the Colosseum. He then added that it gave him much pleasure to have an occasion of being of service to his Highness, and that this was the only object why, at this unseasonable hour, he had forced his visit upon him.

This introduction, which was most verbosely and eloquently given, left no choice to the Prince but politely to receive his visiter, and to invite him to a seat. He hoped, however, that the Polizeirath would, as soon as possible, take his leave again, and inwardly determined, if necessary, to throw out hints to that purpose, as broad and decided as he could possibly give them, without deviating from the rules of politeness and good breeding.

With the same circumstantiality which had marked his introduction, the Polizeirath proceeded step by step with his disclosures.

He cast a retrospective glance at his past activity in his office, related several instances where he had delivered the state of the most dangerous criminals by his acute penetration, and his untiring activity. Nothing, however, pleased him more than the prospect which now presented itself to him, that of catching one of the most daring, bold and dangerous thieves, in the very act of committing a burglary; particularly as he had long and uselessly sought to catch this same cunning rogue.

The Prince, who had already began to be wearied by the circumstantiality of his friend's speech, suddenly became very attentive. He was greatly frightened, for he began to suspect what was coming.

Elated with pride and pleasure, the Polizeirath continued his statement, by telling the other how he had obtained the information that this same dangerous robber, who was a Polish Jew, together with some others, intended to break into the apartments of the Prince, for the purpose of robbing him.

The thieves would from the street climb over a high wall into the yard, and thence they would reach the back rooms by means of a ladder, and by extracting a few panes of glass from a window, enter those rooms. Thence they would turn to that apartment in which the Prince kept his money and valuables. The information about the localities, they had obtained from a female who was acquainted with the Prince, and had access to his rooms. Who this female could be, he had not found means of ascertaining, but under existing circumstances, he hoped that the Prince would grant his request, and, if possible, give him some further information on that point.

These disclosures placed the Prince in a state of the most painful embarrassment. He could no longer entertain any doubt of the Polizeirath's being acquainted with the intentions of the Jew, and that he would endeavour to arrest him on the premises. Reflecting on the interest of his long lost brother, he must endeavour, by all means, to prevent this. Moreover, he began to fear that Francisca might fall a victim of her noble energy, as in case the thieves were arrested, she would, most probably, be betrayed.

This thought became still more painful to him, when, led by the disclosures of the Polizeirath, he began to surmise, with a degree of certainty, that the Equestrian had originated the entire plan of this robbery for the purpose of delivering the Jew into his hands. How that mysterious and wonderful woman should have come into connexion with the thieves, that certainly remained unexplained ; but the fact of her being connected with them would only make her arrest the more certain. And it did not escape the close observation of the Prince, that Francisca's character and position must make such an exposure appear in a light which was as unmerited as it was dubious.

In his embarrassment, the Prince endeavoured to save himself and her, by listening to this part of the communication with an incredulous smile, and by positively denying ever having seen or admitted a female into his chambers.

The Polizeirath thought that he could easily perceive the Prince's reason for this denial, and obligingly observed that it was very possible that one of the large body of servants in the employ of his Highness, might stand in some connexion with the woman, and might even have received her here during his master's absence. It was not, however, advisable just at present, to seek any further information on that point, as such a course might easily interfere with, or betray their plans. His present object was to obtain permission from the Prince to introduce two gensd'armes dressed in civic dress, and who were waiting without. With these he intended to await the arrival of the thieves. One of them must find a hiding-place somewhere in the back rooms, whence he could give a signal in case the thieves should meet some unforeseen obstacle, and determine upon an early retreat. With the other gensd'arme he himself intended to remain in the ante-chamber, so as to receive the gentlemen on their arrival there, and secure their persons.

This unexpected interruption almost brought the Prince to despair, and it needed all his self-possession, not to expose the real state of things to the Polizeirath.

He cursed the unfortunate official activity of this thief-catcher, and would have been glad to begin the arrests with the person of the Polizeirath and his gensd'armes.

Again so near the accomplishment of his object, and again everything lost! And more than all this; for if the Jew fell into the hands of justice, all his hopes for the future must be cut off. Once in prison, and it could not be expected that the Jew, who already displayed such a bitter hatred to the Prince, could be persuaded to make any disclosures or confessions. And what was to become of Francisca, who must, of course, be compromised?

The Prince had almost determined to make a full and explicit confession of his position to the Polizeirath; but then he remembered that the official position and duty of the latter, would not allow him to relinquish his object, even if he should overcome his well-known and arduous passion of catching thieves.

The Prince would have given thousands to any one, who could have shown him ways or means, to get rid of the police, in a quiet, unsuspected manner.

However, he had no time for consideration. The Polizeirath observed the mute and embarrassed position of the Prince, with considerable astonishment, and then very politely repeated his request to let the gensd'armes enter the room.

Mechanically the Prince gave his consent; spite of thought and reflection, he saw no means of refusal.

The gensd'armes entered. One of them, as had been agreed upon, was hidden in the back-room, behind a stove screen. This screen luckily was placed in such a way, that the glimmer of a lantern which might fall upon it, would not betray the presence of any person behind. The other gensd'arme remained by the side of the Polizeirath, who repeatedly and very politely begged the Prince, to pardon their intrusion, and also begged him, whether he wished to go out or not, not to suffer himself to be disturbed or interrupted by their proceedings.

The Prince made but very few replies to these efforts of politeness; in a state of great mental excitement he walked up and down the room, fully convinced that nothing but a miracle could now alter his fate for the future.

The Polizeirath construed the behaviour of the Prince as an inexplicable displeasure at the annoyance and disturbance the whole accident caused him.

The hour of midnight was rapidly approaching.

Most politely, the Polizeirath requests to have all the lights put out, that the thieves might not be frightened away, or detained by their glimmer.

Biting his lips with rage and excitement the Prince suffers this to be done.

All are now seated in silent expectation in the dark rooms.

CHAPTER XL.

AUGUSTA STRASS.

The little *brunette* seamstress, Augusta Strass, resided in the *Rosenthaler-street*, Number 142, up three pair of stairs.

She inhabited a very narrow little room, but within, all was order and cleanliness.

The low little windows were covered with a pair of graceful, neat white curtains. A few flower-pots containing roses, cactus, ivy and other domestic flowers and plants, adorned the window-sills.

The wall between the windows lacked its customary mirror, but in its stead, there was a chest of drawers covered with clean white linen, upon which glasses and many coloured cups were arranged in neat and fanciful order.

To the right of the window stood a little bed, covered by a snowy counterpane of common material. To the left stood a small stove, and at each side of it, a couple of straw bottomed chairs.

By the side of the door stood a clothes-press of painted beach wood; its upper shelf was the repository of a few household utensils, and also of a little store of provisions. Opposite to this was a work-table, upon which stood a large bird cage, wherein a pair of green-finches merrily hopped about.

The walls of the room were plainly white-washed, and the bare floor brightly scoured.

It was four o'clock on the Sunday afternoon.

A pleasant warmth pervaded through the apartment.

The work-table has been moved from the middle of the room towards the windows, and Augusta is seated by its side. Her usual occupation she has at present laid aside. The birds have had to leave the table, and are now twittering in their cage upon the floor. In front of Augusta, upon the work-table lies a sheet of paper, which she has just produced from a handsome small writing apparatus—a present of Lieutenant Steinfort. She is about to begin to write.

She rests upon her right elbow, and the hand wherein she holds her pen is supporting her forehead. She is absorbed in thought, and her fresh blooming face has suddenly assumed a very serious expression. She is evidently cogitating upon the subject of her literary effusions.

At last, dictating aloud to herself, she begins to write.

"Yesterday I was *going promenading in the Thiergarden*."*

Suddenly she stops again, as she says aloud to herself; "no, no, that is not right, not grammatical; now I don't know, whether it is *in the Thiergarden* or *at the Thiergarden?*"

Again she stops to consider.

After a while she ill-humouredly shakes her head and lays down her pen.

"Oh dear, oh dear! *Carl* has told me this so often already, and still I cannot remember which is right; now if he comes and I give him this stupid specimen of my writing, he will again find such a lot of mistakes, and then he will scold me. Oh, I would be so glad to learn something, only it is so very difficult. In reality, I don't understand why Carl always troubles me with these things; he certainly knows what I mean just as well, whether I say *mir* or *mich*, and if other people laugh when I speak incorrectly, it is immaterial to me in the end. For what do I care for other people, as long as I am sure he loves me?"

Ill-humouredly and pettishly the little brunette takes up her pen, and carelessly scribbles a mass of strange and fanciful figures upon a little bit of paper by her side.

After a few minutes she again resumes her former reflections.

"But he certainly ought to know better than a simple, silly girl like myself. He wishes it done so, and that is enough for me. I do with pleasure everything he demands of me, though it is hard enough sometimes."

Eagerly she continues writing. This was to be a letter to Carl, which he had himself told her to write.

As we already know, the Lieutenant's intentions towards the girl were honest; he was fully determined to marry her. But first she must obtain the education and knowledge necessary on making her appearance in a world to which she had hitherto been a stranger.

Above all, it seemed to him necessary to instruct her in the grammar of her native language, as he knew well, that errors of grammar and pronunciation would be the first observed, and would first tend to make her and himself appear ridiculous in refined society He himself was her instructor, and had made it her task, each day to write a letter to him, upon some occurrence of her own life. In the evening, when he visited her, he would overlook her manuscript with her, and point out and correct all the errors he met with.

This then was at present her occupation. She had commenced the letter and had just come to a doubtful passage, at which she in vain tried to ascertain whether it would be grammatically correct to write *in the*, or *at the Thiergarden.*

After she had concluded the letter, she once more took it up to read it over again. She seemed not to be pleased with it, for with a dissatisfied air she shook her little head, and again laid the sheet down upon the table.

"I am really angry," she said after a while, endeavouring to look displeased. "Fischergraf never did trouble me with such things."

Suddenly she stopped, as if frightened at her own words.

"How very unjust I am," she continued her soliloquy, "Carl loves me, and certainly does everything for the best; Fischergraf used to drag me about with him, as he did many others. He gave me a great many presents, because it happened to be fashionable to give presents; he treated me occasionally good and again very ill, just as his humour happened to be. Otherwise, how could I have forgotten him so quickly?— And after all I sometimes still think of him; in his peculiar way he always had a liking for me. But certainly—to love him—to love him as I love my Carl—no, no—I could not love him.

"He used to beat me, yes, and call me bad names! Good Lord! and how often did he make me feel most bitterly what I really am. But Carl raised me up again—he it was who told me, *that a maiden might be innocent, even though she were fallen.* And I feel it; my love to him has already made me so much better than I was. Oh yes, yes, Carl is my life, my sole happiness, my world, my all; I wish that I could die for him!"

Augusta placed both her hands before her face, and closed her eyes, as if she would not suffer the unspeakable happiness she felt within, to be desecrated by any contact with the outer world.

Quick footsteps, which she heard upon the stairs, interrupted her meditations. The steps sounded like those of Lieutenant von Steinfort, although he was not in the habit of coming at this hour.

Her eyes beaming with joy she hurried towards the door. The Lieutenant met her.

"My Carl," cried the girl joyously, rushing abruptly into his arms, "how good of you to come just now; I was just thinking of you, and felt a great desire to see you."

"I wanted to surprise you for once, my dearest," replied the Lieutenant, imprinting a tender kiss upon her luscious lips. "I hope you will not take it amiss."

"Don't plague me, dear Carl," replied Augusta in a tone of gentle reproach, as she carried away her bird to place a chair where the cage had stood. "To tell you the truth, you come too soon, for my letter did not turn out good this time, and I was about to write another. But you know when once you are here, everything else has to be laid aside for you. I can then only exist by your side, and my letter-writing must stop for another opportunity. It is, at all times, very difficult work to write them."

* It is almost impossible to translate and preserve the ludicrous effect of the bad grammar in this sentence and the following.—*Translator.*

"Don't lose your courage my dear child," said the Lieutenant; "you see you must learn something, and as you progress you will find it much easier. Now as a reward of your attention and industry, I am going to prepare a great pleasure for you to-night. This evening, there is a *family* ball at the 'French-house.' I have purchased two tickets, and I will take you with me and introduce you there. You are fond of dancing, I suppose ?"

"Oh yes, yes, I am very, very fond of it," cried the girl, her eyes sparkling with joy, "and in your company I should be doubly happy—but—"

"Well, Augusta—but ?"

"Is not that place too fine for me ?" she inquired in a low tone of voice. "Will not the great people who will be there, look scornfully and suspiciously upon the poor seamstress ?—You see, my dear Carl, I know perfectly well, that I am much better than all those finely dressed ladies, because there is not one among them who can love you so truly, faithfully and honestly, as I love you; they only know how to appear grand, proud and indignant, and will make fun of me and scorn me, if I cannot do the same. When I had to go with Fischergraf to that soirée at the house of a Referendarius, I know that I must have appeared very ridiculous; but that was indifferent to me, for I had no business there, I did not belong there. But when I appear with you, it is quite another matter; I must do credit to you, not disgrace you, and I fear I could not do everything in the way it should be done."

"Let me take care of that, my child," replied the Lieutenant, who was evidently affected by the delicate scruples of the girl, "I shall have a care, that no one annoys or insults you. If I present you as my future wife, as you soon shall be, all these scoffing and insolent tongues will be silenced, and no one will dare to make any disrespectful observations about you."

"Oh, my dear Carl," said Augusta, leaning her head upon his breast, "I consider myself last of all. But do you think that I could bear it, if I were to observe others shrugging their shoulders at you ? And they will be sure to do that.

Warmly and affectionately the Lieutenant embraced the poor, loving and devoted girl.

"Oh, how I hate this aristocratic fashionable world !" he cried. "How much more candid and honest, simply unsophisticated truth is uttered from your lips ? But I must insist, my dear, that you visit the ball with me; we will show to the smooth, flattering, purse-proud world, that we have no reason to fear it."

Obstinately Augusta refused to comply with the wishes of her lover; in her mind she felt, and felt justly, that he might be placed under some embarrassment, or subjected to annoyance by having her with him. But he was as fully determined not to abandon his original intentions, the more so, as he thought that the loss of this ball would be a cause of silent mortification to the poor girl, who was finally forced to yield to his urgent request.

Steinfort was thus obstinate, because he believed himself morally strong enough to bid defiance to all prejudices, and because he lived in hopes, that the beauty of Augusta, as well as her open, kind and artless manners must not alone silence all abuse, but even gain for her every heart.

He moreover considered it necessary to bring her gradually into those circles, which were not too far removed from those still higher ones, wherein as his future wife she would be destined to appear. A ball at the "French house," although it was a public one, was usually visited by the better class of society, and he thought this a good primary school to instruct her in the customs of social intercourse among the more refined classes.

All these matters were fully and candidly explained to the girl by the Lieutenant, who thereby sought to convince her of the utility, besides the pleasure of her attendance at such a ball.

Augusta listened with great attention. She thought that she felt, that in reality, he was taking a wrong position, but as it was not in her power to ascertain wherein consisted the errors of his reasoning, she again returned to another question, a question which frequently before had caused her severe pangs of conscience, namely, whether in her particular position, she was not acting most wrongfully, by thus chaining her much loved Carl, more and more to herself, or by yielding to his desire of making her his wife ?

It was the immense difference in their social culture and position, which like a dark, threatening shadow appeared before her soul, and which warned her back from the merry mazes of the ball, with the same threatening finger which warned her from the indissoluble ties of matrimony.

Without being able to define its outlines, she saw in her mind's eye an abyss before her, across which the Lieutenant would daringly attempt to leap. She seemed to anticipate, that the lover of her choice, must become miserable by a union with her. Often she had opened her heart to him, had told him of all these heavy troubles, but still his reasoning had again quieted and silenced those pangs of conscience for a while.

Such then were again the ideas which oppressed her. For a long time she seemed lost in a thoughtful struggle with herself, at last she said :

"Alas ! Carl, I still fear that I am committing a sin, by yielding my assent to your wishes and desires for the future. You are a rich, high-born man, and I am not only a poor—that would matter but little—*but I am also an outcast girl*, one who, as your wife, would prepare naught but unfading shame for you, in the eyes of the world.

"Let me finish," she continued, gently placing her hand upon her lover's mouth, as he was about to interrupt her; "I have something upon my heart, for which I must absolutely find words. You are not yet acquainted with my former history; you have never even asked for it; let me now tell it to you, and listen to it quietly and attentively. If after hearing it you will still continue in your resolution, I will relinquish my doubts and objections."

" Well, tell me then, my dear, honest little girl," said the Lieutenant, with great difficulty suppressing his deeply excited emotions.

CHAPTER XLI.

THE CONFESSIONS OF A GRISETTE.

AUGUSTA carried the birds to one side, in order to place another of her straw-covered chairs near to the little table, where the cage had stood. After her lover, whom in her tender care, she had hitherto detained near the warm stove, had taken a seat by her side, she began her history.

" I shall be as brief and concise as possible, my dear Carl, for fear that I might weary you. My parents were of a very low class, and extremely poor. My father worked a common labourer in one of our manufactories, and earned about three thalers per week; upon this slender income he had to support a wife and three children, of whom I was the oldest.

" I had scarcely reached my seventh year, when I also had to take a part of the labour. I walked daily to the cotton-manufactory where I was employed in folding calicoes, for which I received twenty Groschen per week. But I had to work from early morning to a late hour of the night, and had moreover to walk great distances every day, as we lived in the *Stern-street* outside of the *Hamburg-gate*, while the manufactory was in *Köpenicker-street*. My dinner usually consisted in a piece of bread and butter, and a small can of coffee, which my mother always tied up in a handkerchief before I left home in the morning. I warmed the coffee in the manufactory, which I was not allowed to leave a moment throughout the day. Only in the evening, on my return home, I would sometimes get a somewhat more substantial meal, which usually consisted in boiled potatoes, or if I was very fortunate, in a bread or flour pudding.

The merry, happy plays of childhood I have never enjoyed. Even in midsummer, when in the evening I returned from my work, I never could enjoy any recreation; I was too tired and had to go to bed, to be enabled to rise again early on the next morning. Often did I look with tearful eyes upon happy, merry children; I would have so gladly joined their sports. The manufactory adjoined a beautiful garden, belonging to my employer, who had four children, two boys and two girls. These I often saw merrily dancing and jumping about their garden, and plucking flowers, while I only dared to cast a stolen, furtive look upon their happiness.

" Nothing, however, excited my longing, and I had almost said envy, so much as a small pet lamb, which they led about by a blue ribbon. When I saw that lamb, I would leave my work to look after it, although I knew that I would afterwards be severely punished for my negligence. Heaven knows, my offence was trifling and pardonable ! I had not even a Sunday to myself, that day when other children in our neighbourhood put on their best clothes, and scorned me, because I was always poorly dressed. On that day I must necessarily learn to read and write, and as I grew older, my mother, who was a very industrious woman, compelled me to mend my clothes, after I had, in a Sunday-school, been somewhat instructed in sewing.

" You see, my dear Carl, such a miserable childhood—a childhood such as you can scarcely imagine, was the one which I passed. When I had reached my fourteenth year, both of my parents died, one shortly after the other, of the Cholera. My younger brother and sister were taken to the Orphan Asylum; but I was already too old to be received. Thus I stood alone in the world, depending entirely upon my own power and resources; not a soul was there in God's wide world who would take the least interest in me.

" The hard lot of having been from earliest childhood compelled to earn my own bread, now became a fortune to me. I had early become dependent upon my own labours, and thus I had strength to support myself, else I might have starved in the first few weeks. I laboured honestly and contentedly, now in this, then in another manufactory, and thus gained a scanty livelihood; but I remained honest and uncorrupted. If often I had nothing but dry bread to eat, I cared not, I was used to want ever since infancy; misery and want were my surest friends, and had grown up with me.

" After many and divers other employments, at last, no longer than about two years ago, I came to the wool-sorting establishment of the Jewish wool-dealer, *Goldpinx*, in the *König-street*. The wages offered here, were so much higher than those I had hitherto received, that I undertook the work, though it was much more severe than my former employment. In the summer I could earn three thalers, and in the winter about two and a half; this, compared with my former earnings, was a large sum. I could now have regularly a warm dinner, which had formerly been a scarcity to me, and in consideration thereof, I willingly stood from morning till night exposed to the wintry air in a cold garret, and picked wool.

" There were about twenty girls, all similarly employed, in this place. Herr Goldpinx came daily once or twice up to the garret, to look after our work. He was a very young, exceedingly fashionably dressed gentleman, with long blonde hair, blue eyes, blooming colour, and a smooth, almost girlish face. I soon observed that he often found some excuse to be near me, that he scrutinized my work less severely than that of other girls, and that he even occasionally said a few friendly words to me.

"One very cold evening—as cold as this—I was retiring from my labour in a very distressed state of mind. It was only six o'clock, and I knew not where to pass the few intervening hours until bed time. I would not associate with the other working girls, for I did not like their coarse, vulgar, and uncouth behaviour. The place where I slept was too cold and dark to think of staying there. I had usually passed my evenings in the room of the people with whom I lodged, and who allowed me to sit there and do whatever repairs were necessary to my scanty wardrobe. But before I had gone out that morning, these good people had told me, that they would be absent to work the whole day, and that the room would therefore not be warmed. I had no money of my own to buy wood, for it was already Friday, and my week's wages had been spent, all but two groschen, which I would need the next day for the purchase of my dinner."

"Two groschen?" exclaimed the Lieutenant, interrupting her, in a tone of utter astonishment, "and could you satisfy your hunger for that sum? The cigars I smoke after my dinner, cost even more than that."

"I can readily believe that, my dear Carl," replied Augusta, with a sad smile, "but you are no wool-sorting girl. Yet listen further. I had just come from my work in the garret, and was weeping bitterly, as Herr Goldpinx met me in the entry. In his peculiar, good-natured manner, he asked me for the cause of my troubles. I candidly told him all, and he invited me to enter his counting-room with him, saying, that he would give me something. At first I refused, for I feared to be alone with him; I felt a presentiment of evil. But meanwhile I was nearly frozen, as I had worked all day in a bitter-cold place, and Goldpinx described the pleasant warmth of his counting room in such attractive colours, and spoke so kindly, that he finally overcame my fears.

"I accepted his invitation, and followed him. A warm, pleasant current of air met me on my entrance into the counting-room, and I soon succeeded in warming my almost frozen limbs by the side of the stove. After about half an hour, during which Goldpinx had been looking through his books and papers, I thought that it was time to go. I expressed my thanks for his kindness, and was about to walk towards the door. There he stopped me, and without further hesitation, made dishonourable proposals to me. I could hardly understand him at first, but when his demands became more intelligible to me, I could scarcely support myself with fright and horror. I was unable to reply, but burst into tears, and cried aloud for mercy. Goldpinx laughed, and asked me scornfully why I had come into the counting-room, if I intended afterwards to play the prude? I answered simply and honestly, that I had only come in by his invitation, to warm myself a little. On hearing this answer, he laughed still more, and replied by taking liberties. I struggled hard, but he only became more insulting.

"At last I threw myself on my knees before him, and begged and prayed him to let me peaceably go out; I told him that I was a poor, but honest and virtuous girl, and begged him not to rob me of the only treasure I possessed, my innocence.

"'What!' he exclaimed, 'a wool-sorting girl and innocent? and do you think that you can persuade me of that?' As I assured him by all the vows which my despair could give utterance to, that I had spoken the truth, as I repeated upon my knees all that I had said before, calling upon Heaven to witness my veracity, my innocent appearance, my earnestness and anxiety may have convinced him, that what I stated was the truth. But now he changed his language, and another, a most terrible light began to dawn upon me. He told me that if I really was innocent, all the world looked upon me as a fallen girl. It was considered a moral impossibility that a pretty wool-sorting girl, who only earned about two dollars a week, should be entirely innocent. I was thunderstruck. *Because I was poor, I must also be debased as a necessary consequence!* Alas! it is too true. Wo unto you, ye rich people, who make poverty actually criminal, by reasoning from such propositions! My moral power of resistance was broken; why should I not be dishonourable, when the world believed me to be dishonoured? Goldpinx became more urgent; the cold without was terrible—yet I feared that man—I feared myself—all mankind—and—I sought safety in guilt."

"What further happened to me I need not tell you, my dear Carl; I soon learned to make money out of vice. I was determined if ruined, at least to live in plenty and in luxury, and you know how you found me."

Augusta stopped and covered her face with both her hands. She now awaited the decision of the Lieutenant, which she expected with mingled emotions of fear, doubt, and hope.

Steinfort had listened attentively.

By her narrative, the girl had involuntarily only strengthened his former determination, not shaken it. Upon the whole, she had told him nothing new; if his former suspicions had now become certainties, his mind was too great, too noble to reject her on that account. On the contrary, he only loved her the more, for it seemed to him, as if through these sad and sorrowful confessions, and despite the desolate life at which she had hinted, he could discover the brilliant germ of an originally pure and good heart. He felt it his duty to restore that germ to its right position among human beings. He who was rich, would atone to poverty for the injuries wealth had done to it. He felt himself possessed of sufficient moral strength, to bid defiance to all prejudices, and even believed himself capable of forcing society to the acknowledgment of that which he himself had become convinced of.

With great tenderness he embraced the girl: "I have suffered you to finish your story, my poor child," he said, "and in your confession I have found more true love for me, than you could have expressed in a thousand vows and protestations. Now for my answer: at nine o'clock I will call for you to take you to the ball; hold yourself in readiness by that time."

Augusta had many more things to speak about, and much yet to object to. But the Lieutenant closed her mouth with a kiss, and left the room.

CHAPTER XLII.

LIGHT AND SHADE.

THE hours had quickly fled during Augusta's conversation with Lieutenant Steinfort; she had now to make all haste to be prepared, according to the wishes of her lover, at the proper time.

The clothes-press was opened, and a clean, white ball dress, adorned with pink trimmings, laid upon the bed.

This dress was one of the many presents of Fischergraf; a young mantua-maker, a friend of Augusta's, had cut it, and she herself had sewed and trimmed it.

We must take this occasion to remark, that our heroine, after having left the heavy work of the manufactories, as she no longer needed that income, had devoted herself to sewing, as it was not in her nature to lead an idle life. This was so much more to her credit, as her lovers, especially Fischergraf, provided so plentifully for her, that she needed not to labour for any thing she desired to have. But she found great pleasure in working, and soon attained by constant practice, a great deal of facility and skill as a seamstress, an occupation which she had ever been very fond of even as a child.

A few ribbons about the dress were somewhat crumbled; she hastily endeavoured to restore them to their former original smoothness. Whilst thus occupied, a gentle sigh rose from the depth of her bosom; that sigh may have been devoted to the past.

Searchingly she now raised up the dress, and closely examined it all over with the eye of a connoisseur. It was without blemish, and with a clear and quiet conscience upon that point, she threw it across the back of a chair.

When she for this purpose brought out the straw-covered chair which had stood behind the stove, she suddenly observed a loose, very neat envelope. Anxiously she opened it, and found that it contained a most lovely wreath of red roses, entwined with silver ribbon.

Steinfort had surprised her in the most delicate manner.

Triumphantly she clapped her little hands as she spread this beautiful, tasty ornament before her delighted looks.

Quickly she took a little square box from her chest of drawers, opened its lid, and raised a looking-glass it contained. Then she carried her chair in front of it, and began to examine attentively in what manner that beautiful wreath would be the most becoming.

This was a most difficult task, for a pair of closely criticizing girl's eyes.

Put it just at the forehead?—No, for then it would cover the front too much, and Augusta happened to have a lovely shaped head. Put it at the back of the head?—No, for there it would interfere with the voluptuous freedom of those beautiful tresses. Upon the right side then?—This was not the fashion of the season, at least so she had been told not long since by a young friend who was employed in a hairdresser's-shop, and whose judgment, in a case like the present, could not be questioned. Well then, down to the temple?—yes, yes, that was the proper place after all.

Augusta fastened the wreath with a few pins for a trial, during which it had to undergo many turnings and twistings, until at last it sat right and nice, just to her liking.

She jumped up, put both arms into her sides, and standing now before her little mirror, she examined her pretty head from the right and left with every indication of pleasure and satisfaction.

Merrily snapping her fingers, she pirouetted a few times up and down the room. Her large dark eyes beamed with pleasure and joy.

It was a happy degree of levity, so harmless, so innocent, that we cannot blame the girl for it. She had forgotten the sad story which she had just told to the Lieutenant, to live entirely in the present.

Carefully she laid down the wreath by the side of the frock, and busily continued the examination of her toilette.

She next unlocked and pulled the different drawers out of her *bureau*.

A pair of open-worked cotton stockings first made their appearance.

Augusta unrolled them and laid them by the other things already selected, not without casting a hasty glance of vanity or satisfaction at her neat, well shaped little foot.

The upper drawer now produced a thin rose-coloured crape shawl, and a pair of white *glacée* gloves.

The gloves had been worn once already; a sufficient cause for close examination. At candle-light they might pass once more, if a little art was applied in restoring them.—Augusta took a piece of gum elastic, and endeavoured to remove the dark shade at the tips of the fingers. The result soon satisfied her expectations. The fingers played rather too free and loosely in the soft leather, which was the only fault she could find with the gloves on a second wearing.

A very great requisite was still wanting—white satin shoes.

Augusta opened the lowest drawer of the chest, to produce these also, but frightened, she started up—their place was empty. She then remembered that a short time previous, she had left them at the house of a friend with whom she had returned from a ball. On stopping for a little while at this friend's house, she had felt severe pains in her feet, and had left her thin shoes with her friend, who kindly loaned her a pair of loose slippers.

But what was now to be done? Time pressed, for Steinfort would return at nine o'clock; the friend with whom she had left her shoes, lived a great ways off, and most probably was not at home at present. Yet she could not go to the ball without satin shoes. These were a necessary part of her dress; Steinfort, moreover, was about to introduce her into elegant society, and she must not disgrace him by a negligent toilette.

Nothing remained for her to do, but to buy a new pair of shoes; but—a new difficulty!—she had no money.

As long as Fischergraf had been her admirer, she had learned to forget the want of money; for she never had hesitated to ask him for all she wanted, and he was ever ready to give it to her with a most liberal hand, provided he had it himself. This liberality and openness had appeared perfectly natural on both sides. But in her present position with Lieutenant Steinfort, she had learned to think otherwise. The Lieutenant made her a great many presents, but she gratefully acknowledged the fact, that he had never yet given nor offered her money. She felt within herself that the acceptance of money must lower her, and by redoubled industry, she endeavoured to earn her own bread.

Steinfort, on the opposite hand, born and bred in wealth and luxury, had never even thought of it, that she might perhaps want money; otherwise, he would easily have made, or found an opportunity of conveying it to her in a delicate and inoffensive manner.

But at the present moment, all this only had the effect of placing Augusta in the greatest embarrassment.

She considered and re-considered the matter; meanwhile the evening still advanced. To announce herself sick: to tell the real state of the case to the Lieutenant; to ask a loan from one of her female acquaintances; all these expedients she rejected. At last she resorted to a means, to which she had in former times frequently had recourse to—the pawnbroker.

Although her natural tact and good sense told her, that such a course was no longer suited to her position, as she already might consider herself as belonging to Steinfort, yet she knew not how otherwise to extricate herself from her present difficulty. With a heavy heart she looked into the drawer, wherein her snowy linen was properly folded and arranged. A part of this had to go to the pawnbrokers.

Not to lose time, she quickly selected what she wanted from this drawer, wrapped a cloth around it, and hid it under her cloak.

She hurried down the stairs as it was already growing dark, and crossed the street to her well-known neighbour, *Abraham Loebell*, the pawnbroker.

A narrow and filthy stair-case led from the street directly to the pawnbroker's office in the first story. This office was a small black looking room, with oblique windows and black doors.

The counter divided the entire length of this ill-smelling apartment. The walls all around were covered with square shelves, the repositories of the manifold objects received as pledges: clothing, linen, household utensils, books, articles of luxury, arms, statues, pictures, in short everything that might contain even a penny of intrinsic value.

A sombre looking lamp hung over the desk, and spread a dismal light over the large book of entry beneath, and over a few surrounding objects. The remaining illumination of the room was accomplished by a thin tallow candle, which was stuck into the neck of a wine bottle standing upon the counter.

Behind the desk stood Herr Abraham Loebell, a small, dried up man, with the appearance of a mummy. He wore a small black cap, a green semicircular screen was before his eye, which almost covered the haggard, brownish yellow face.

As Augusta entered, she saw him engaged in making a bargain with a tall, thin and hectic looking man, who offered to pledge two bundles of yarn.

Herr Loebell seemed not inclined to comply with the wishes of his customer, for, in a squeaking, disagreeable voice he exclaimed:

"What! five whole Thalers, *ish it* you want? —You are *shurely* a man without a *shoul*; you would make my ruin; I shall *perhapsh* give you two whole Thalers."

A deep and gloomy expression of sorrow rested on the features of the other. "I cannot do with that," he said, with a suppressed sigh, "give me four Thalers, for the yarn is surely worth more than twice the amount."

"The *plesshings* of my father! as *shure ash* you do not pay me back my *monish*, I must let the yarn be *shold* by the public auctioneer," replied the pawnbroker, as he cast the packets contemptuously upon the counter; "and ye see, if nobody buys it, I shall have to lose monish. I cannot be expected to give four Thalers for a loss."

The stranger took up the yarn again and examined it anxiously with sunken countenance, while the little Jew remained behind the counter, and closely watched the other from beneath his green paper eye-screen.

"Gracious Heaven," at last the customer exclaimed, with feverish anxiety, "I must have money; give me at least three Thalers. My good man, if you only knew what I am already doing to save my wife and child from starvation, you would not try to cut off a few more pennies from an unfortunate man. I assure you, the yarn is worth thrice the amount, which I want upon it."

The Jew again took the parcel into his hands.

"Well, if that *ish* the case," he said, "I shall be charitable. We *musht* be humane, and I have pity for your *cashe*; it touches my heart. I shall even give you *two Thalers* and fifteen *Silbergroschen*. And now, if you are *shatisfied*, you must not say no."

"Good Heavens, I can stay here no longer," answered the other, with a bitter sigh, "so give me the money."

The Jew carefully packed the yarn in a single parcel, put it upon one of the shelves, and fastened a number upon it.

"Two Thalers and half a Thaler," he began to count, "makes in six months in interest, the amount of *one Thaler, seven Silbergroschen and six Pfennige. Conshequently*, you will also receive one Thaler, sheven Silbergroschen and six Pfennige."

"How?" interrupted the other furiously, "you will take one hundred per cent. for a six month's loan, and take this usurious interest in advance?"

"If it does not *shuit* you, you can have back your yarn," replied the Jew coolly. "For every Thaler you pay two and a half Silbergroschen interest per month, invariably paid in advance for six months. Do you call that usury? Lord help you, shall I give out my good *monish* for nothing at all but charity? Must I not guarantee you against moths?"

The Jew had grown excited, and had been carried too far by his excitement; he therefore stopped quickly to rectify his error: "No, no, I don't guarantee against moths, mark that, I don't guarantee against moths; but against dust, yes, against dust, I do guarantee. And is this labour to be for nothing? Lord bless us! nobody will be pawnbroker, and if any one takes the business, shall he not have to eat his daily bread? Lord bless us! Well, will you take the *monish*?"

The poor stranger stood before the usurer pale as a corpse; the fresh disappointment had affected him most severely.

"Give me the money!" he cried in a tone of despair, followed by a few bitter curses ' not loud but deep.'

The Jew walked to his desk, dipped a pen into a very small, black looking ink-glass, and began writing the pawn-ticket. "What is the name," he inquired.

"Weaver Greif," replied the other, in a hollow tone of voice.

Augusta had hitherto remained in the background of the room, as she was anxious not to be recognized by anybody. She had been a silent witness of the whole transaction, and felt deeply affected by the evident misery she saw. The voice of the stranger had seemed familiar to her; but she could not recollect when or where she had become acquainted with it. But suddenly, on hearing the name, she remembered, that Weaver Greif had been a familiar acquaintance and visitor of her paternal house, and that she had frequently seen him afterwards in the manufactories.

With a deep and heavy sigh, the weaver pocketed the few Groschen that had remained to him after the deduction of one half for discount, and received the pawnbroker's certificate. He now turned around to leave the room. Augusta observed, that on going out he wrung his hands in deep despair; she noticed his pale, haggard and distressed features, and her warm kind heart would no longer let her remain silent.

Casting all false pride or bashfulness aside, she quickly walked towards him with a friendly greeting.

"Do you not remember me, my good *Herr Gevatter* Greif?" she began. "Are you so badly situated as to be compelled to come here? If I have heard correctly, you are married now?"

The weaver stared at the speaker and rubbed his forehead, as if trying to remember whether she had really spoken to him.

"Have you really forgotten Augusta Strass?" she continued in a friendly tone. "We were once neighbours for a long time."

The weaver continued to rub his forehead.

"Let me go," he exclaimed suddenly, "if I do not soon bring bread, my wife and children will starve at home, and this accursed usurer will have to answer for it."

At these words, as if driven by a thousand furies, the weaver rushed from the room and down the stairs.

Augusta looked after him in astonishment.

Only those who are poor themselves feel real sympathy for the poor. Only the needy know the full weight of the misfortune of poverty, and for that reason will assist the poor.

Augusta had quickly determined to leave her things with the pawnbroker, and instead of the money, to redeem and take back the poor weaver's yarn. Her former position and the observations she had made, easily enabled her to guess, that the yarn was not the property of the weaver, but had been given to him by a manufacturer to weave into cloth. She trembled for the miserable man, in case his crime should be discovered, and wished to restore the yarn into his hands before this chance could occur.

The pawnbroker, however, refused to comply with her request, as the pledge ticket was in the hands of the weaver, and as he still remained liable and bound to return the yarn upon the presentation of the certificate.

Of course it was out of Augusta's power to obtain this certificate, as she did not even know where, or in what part of the city, the residence of weaver Greif might at present be. Moreover, she had given her word to Steinfort, to be ready at the time he promised to call for her—an obligation which her heart urgently reminded her of. She therefore concluded to postpone this affair to the next day, and then to pledge one of her dresses, and to devote the proceeds to the relief

---

* *Gevatter or vetter*, angl. *Godfather*, is a term of kindness, frequently applied to neighbours and gossips, who are not actually thus related to the parties addressing them.—TRANSLATOR.

of the poor weaver. That in a case like the present, she should not at all think of Steinfort's assistance was a somewhat remarkable, but upon the whole, a natural, and not at all rare occurrence. The rich officer could not possibly have any conception of the real misery and wretchedness to which the poor weaver might be exposed, but she, who well knew, how bitter were the pangs of hunger, had the more imperative reason to give every assistance in her power.

Augusta most probably did not reason to herself in this way, for if she had done so, her love to Steinfort would have overcome all these reasonable suppositions, which as far as Steinfort was concerned, were certainly not applicable. She might be fully assured, that he would not reject her prayers or petitions, if she had asked his charitable assistance in the cause of real poverty and need. There is no doubt, however, that something like the reasoning we have referred to, unconsciously influenced her course, and by the great difference, which, as her own sad experience had convinced her, existed between the wealthy and the poor, this result was quite natural.

During the occurrences we have just related, the evening had pretty far advanced. Augusta therefore hastened to bring her business with the pawnbroker to a close, and speedily repaired to the nearest shoe store to buy the necessary pair of satin shoes. She then hurried home to begin the all-important work of her toilette.

It was certainly a long while before she was capable of banishing the image of the unfortunate weaver from her memory. She heartily reproached herself for not having prevented him from pledging the yarn, and her excited fancy already painted him entering the criminal-prison, and enduring all its horrors and degradations.

But where are the black or horrible night fancies which could not be extinguished from the imagination of a young, handsome, and lively girl of seventeen, by the immediate prospect of a ball, and of the hand of a much-loved and adored young man? Particularly when the troublesome pause intervening between the present time and the ball, could be filled up with the most interesting of all occupations, dressing for the ball.

Augusta dressed and adorned herself with the full anxiety and attention of a ball-going lady, who is aware that kind nature has not behaved like a stepmother to her, and who has fully determined, in her own little head, to make conquests of the hearts of at least half a score of fashionable admirers.

Brilliantly shone the full white neck from the tight fitting body of her dress, which displayed her fine, well-formed figure to great advantage. Her rich brown hair was smoothly parted in front, and behind it was tied up in the most admired style of plaits. Upon this dark ground shone the silver wreath, a beautiful symbol of love and pleasure.

The rose-coloured shawl was gracefully thrown around her neck; its ends were adorned with handsome fringes, which beautifully contrasted with the whiteness of her dress.

"Pretty, quite pretty," said Augusta smilingly to herself, in her usual mode of thinking aloud when alone, as she once more let all the minor auxiliaries of her dress pass in review before her modest little toilette-mirror.

Lightly she once more crossed her little room, to accustom her body to the dress, and her feet to the new satin shoes. She cast another satisfied glance at her shoes, and at those open-worked stockings, through which the brilliant natural texture of her foot and ankle shone to much advantage.

Who knows whether the judgment of old Major von Steinfort would not have been much milder if now he could have unobservedly cast a glance at the quiet little chamber of the grisette. But certainly he ought also to have heard the narrative, or rather the confession which this girl just before, urged by a simple, innate and noble sense of duty, had made to his dearly beloved son.

With military punctuality, the Lieutenant opened the door at the exact hour he had appointed. He looked upon the charming girl with eyes beaming with admiration and love. Full of hopes and pride at the victorious entrance she must certainly make on her debut among fashionable society, he led her to the carriage which was waiting at the door.

CHAPTER XLIII.

THE BALL AND THE GUESTS.

FAR distant in the street shone the brilliant illumination of the "French house."

Augusta's heart beat in high glee and delight, as the quick, rattling equipage set her down before the theatre of lively and refined entertainment.

With juvenile elasticity, she leaped from the carriage, and crossing the broad portal, hurried up the stairs to the *Belle-Etage.*

A ball is to a woman, what a fine horse is to a man; here the one shows beauty, grace, and lovelinesss, and there the sterner sex shows power, agility and strength. We therefore consider it a most silly, wrongly sentimental piece of prudery in a young maiden, ever to withdraw herself from these, the most pleasurable incidents and emotions of her early years; so it is an enervated, unmanly degree of lassitude, if the young man never takes exercise in the riding-school, the chase, or even a daily gallop to some place out of the city for exercise and recreation.

Amidst a crowd of arriving and departing guests, Steinfort and his lady entered the ante-chamber. The doorkeeper showed them politely to the wardrobes at both sides. where to lay aside their cloaks and restore their disordered toilette. After all this was accomplished, they entered the brilliantly adorned and illuminated ball-room.

Our kind and fair readers must not suppose that Augusta was so very greatly surprised or elated by this appearance of splendour, or that any thing appeared so very new and strange to her. She had become tolerably well accustomed to scenes of equal luxury and grandeur, if not as a factory girl, at least in her after life. It was a natural consequence of the very breath and air of life in a large city, to which she had been accustomed, which made her feel perhaps less embarrassed in her present position, than many a nobly born country miss would have been, who had never cast her eyes further than her father's geese could walk, and who would be embarrassed and frightened whenever she placed her foot into a city saloon.

The saloons and ball-rooms which Augusta had formerly been in the habit of visiting with Fischergraf, were precisely the same, which at other times frequently received the very *crème* of society. Steinfort was well aware of all these facts, but they were of no conseqmence to him; he desired that Augusta should become accustomed to more refined customs and manners than those of the persons with whom she had heretofore associated. For these reasons, he conducted her into a circle, which, according to a very refined term, was still somewhat mixed, yet after all, was a circle into which Augusta, without the Lieutenant's introduction, could never have hoped to find access. Here then, under his supervision, she should pass through that regular routine of studies in etiquette, which was absolutely necessary to her appearance among the *haute volée* of society.

From what we have stated, the conclusion may be drawn, that Augusta made by no means an abashed or awkward entrance, but rather passed with ease and gracefulness through the long rows of ante-chambers, towards the ball-room. Whoever had seen her floating along through those brilliant rooms, in all the bloom and freshness of her youthful beauty, would sooner have believed in impossibilities, than believed the story of her early career. Only on entering into conversation with her, and subjecting her words, pronunciation, and manners to a severe examination, a critical observer might have arrived at a supposition of the truth.

With internal joy and satisfaction, Steinfort observed the graceful appearance of his beloved girl, and came to the conclusion that it would be easy for her good, sound natural sense to accomplish all he expected of her, and to supply the deficiencies of her education.

Both now entered the large, brilliant ball-room.

It was already late, and dancing had long commenced.

The enlivening strains of a favourite Polka resounded through the saloon.

The dancing couples floated lightly over the bright, elastic floor, whilst the arrangements of the dance were carefully ordered and watched by the masters of ceremonies, dressed in black *en claque et escarpins*. They had a difficult task in keeping the joyous merriment of the dancers within the bounds of the strict rules and laws of the dance.

Here, one couple would begin dancing too soon, there another danced too long; here a little group were chatting, and forgot their turn in the dance; yonder, a few crossed out of the *terrain*, to the great annoyance of spectators. The much troubled managers had a hundred times to run up and down the room to rectify mistakes, and withal must keep an even temper, and wear a friendly smile upon their countenance. What a strange contradiction, to make the pleasure of one party, a plague to another!

Along the windows were high seats, upon which were seated the spectators. Here were mothers, aunts, guardians, duennas, and even young ladies anxious to dance, whom the changing fortune of a ball-room, had this time destined to adorn the wall. Before these passed the crowd of the heroes of the evening, the *chapeau bas*, or ball-room cap pressed under their arm, and *lorgnettes* and eye-glasses raised, seeking where the queen of the evening might be found. Occasionally, these gentlemen would, intentionally or unintentionally, push against each other, or step upon each other's toes, for the purpose of either directing the other's attention to any particular beauty who was too near to be named aloud, or for the purpose of making a handsome apology for their awkwardness in treading on a tender corn.

Around the *buffet* was a crowd of gourmands, persons with red noses and rotund figures, who preferred to please and satisfy a delicate pallate, to the enjoyment of pleasures prepared for their sight and hearing.

Around the doors and in the corners stood novices, and bashful young persons. Young students in their first year of university life, young merchants, artists, cadets, *et hic gent omnes.*—All unfortunate, modest, and diffident young men, who were continually buttoning their gloves, arranging their cravats or casting stolen glances at the mirrors, to ascertain whether their hair was still in order.

Who is there, that does not know from his own experience, that dangerous and eventful crisis of the first *ball-fever?* Those moments when from a respectful distance we cast glances towards the being whom we believe that we adore, at whose feet we would lay our hand and heart, whilst we have not even the courage to call her out of the merry circle of her fair friends, who are evidently plaguing her, because we happen occasionally to fix an intense look upon her? Those moments, when the peace and happiness of the entire evening is lost by a single glance of a pair of black eyes, and we dare not ask for the hand belonging to those eyes, from the natural fear of a sack, or of the frowning face of an elderly, respectable looking matron by their side? Those moments when the entire ball-room appears like a laughing paradise to our enchanted looks—a paradise into which we dare not penetrate, because an unfortunate bashfulness, magnetically chains us to the spot on which we stand? Reader, be candid, be kind and honest; remember the time of your own first appearances at ball-rooms, and bestow your kind sympathy to all similar sufferers which you find so plentifully around you!

Steinfort took Augusta by his arm, and for a while promenaded without any particular object through the dense, variegated and brilliant mass; now he passed by the open side-rooms, where the fathers, uncles, and patriarchs of the dancing generation were paying their devoirs to the goddess of Fortune at the card-table, and again he strolled through the middle of the saloon, where, the dance being concluded, the young people gathered in groups, laughing, chatting, and making love.

The greater part of the guests consisted of rich tradesmen, bankers, merchants, artists, civil officers, professional persons, and military men. As we said above, the company was mixed, but very respectable. There was beauty, elegance, and grace, side by side with bad taste, homeliness, and coarseness; pride and assumption by the side of modesty and humility.

Upon one of the *estrades*, opposite the large *Trumeaux*, the wealthy, vulgar, and fat *Mrs. Bierling*, the distiller's wife had taken her place; by her side was her only daughter, a marriageable girl. Both were most richly adorned: the mother was perfectly laden down with jewels. But it was easily seen in the style of dress, that it was exceedingly inconvenient to the wearers, and that the jewelry was only carried about to give token of the gold-mine at home.

Madame Bierling seemed to be dressing herself the entire evening. Now she would be arranging her collar, which would not lay downward upon her fat, heaving neck and bosom, and again her broach must be placed further to one side or the other, in order to let the light fall more advantageously upon the diamonds, or the heavy arm-rings, falsely called bracelets, were pushed higher towards the middle of her fleshy arm. The services of the splendid *trumeaux* opposite were, of course, put continually into requisition.

When the matron was done with herself, she would begin at her daughter, a quiet, simple, modest, but evidently somewhat silly girl. The mother would discover that her dress did not set straight, or that a rose in her hair had been pushed to one side, or that she ought to hold her arms in a different position.

Greatly puzzled and more annoyed, the girl obeyed her mother's whims, and more than once felt great mortification on observing, that some of their fair neighbours were noticing her mother's follies, and laughing at her.

Before *Madame and Miss Bierling*, stood *Justizrath Nathan*, a large six footer, engaged in making court to the mother, as a means of winning the daughter's hand.

He filled the air around him with the perfume of *eau de mille fleures*. Brilliant and rich rings and broaches seemed to indicate great wealth. But alas, appearances are so very deceitful! the splendour was only borrowed. He hoped to gain the daughter's hand, to use the father's gold-bags in liquidation of his immense debts.

He was busily engaged in entertaining the mamma about his intimate connexions and acquaintances among princes and dukes, else she might not fully appreciate the importance of his person.

The daughter seemed to entertain no particular objections to this connexion. It flattered her vanity to have the prospect of being called, *Frau Justizräthin*, and *Herr Nathan* was not a bad looking man. As usual she was friendly towards him. Her mother had formerly been also very kind and friendly towards him, but to day, the gentleman observed, to his no small consternation, that the venerable lady showed an unusual degree of coldness. In vain he sought to discover or surmise the cause of this strange coldness.— Poor fellow! he did not know, that his mother-in-law *in spe*, had this day learned, that he was a baptised Jew. She could not for a moment think of giving her daughter to a Jew, baptised or not; no, no, anything but that.

"I'll tell you, *Fritze*,"* she began, addressing her daughter after the Justizrath had withdrawn, "you must give up all ideas of having this man for a husband. You will have forty thousand Thalers, and with such a sum, there is no necessity of your marrying a Jew. Just wait a while, some high-born Lieutenant will yet come along; and then, just think, you may be called *gnädige Frau*."†

Frederika smiled rather stupidly. It seemed, as if she did not dislike such a prospect.

"But keep yourself straight, and hold your head up," continued Madame Bierling, in the most vulgar tone, and in her customary low Berlinian dialect. "Yonder is *Friedel's* daughter, *Hannah*, who appears to far better advantage than you, and she has not twenty thousand Grochen, while you have forty thousand Thalers.— Waiter, bring us two glasses of ice cream or Sherbet, but of the best, the highest priced you have."

Not far from this little family group, sat the bereaved widow of an artist who had died very rich. This lady was somewhat *passée*, but still rather good looking.

By her side, a formerly well known and celebrated novel writer, who, on account of the immense length and breadth of his body was usually called "the great Doctor," had taken a seat. Between this worthy couple, the little blind boy was also playing his wild pranks.

The "great Doctor," flattered himsef with the well-founded hope of shortly making the rich widow his better half. He had every reason to

---

* A vulgar abbreviation of Frederika.—TRANSLATOR.
† *Gnädige Frau*, titular address of a Lady of rank. Equivalent to "your Ladyship," in England.—TRANSLATOR.

[Unmutilated and Only Genuine Edition.]

THIERS' LIFE OF NAPOLEON,

WITH SUPERB STEEL ENGRAVINGS.

FOR SEVENTY-FIVE CENTS,

[If paid in Advance.]

W. H. COLYER having been at great expense to procure a copy of this unrivalled work, now publishes

PART I.

OF THE

HISTORY OF THE CONSULATE AND THE EMPIRE

OF

FRANCE UNDER NAPOLEON,

By M. A. THIERS,

LATE PRIME MINISTER OF FRANCE.

Wm. H. Colyer's edition of this splendid work, The Life of Napoleon, is decidedly the best in this country. It is printed on fine paper and new type, according to the design of the author, M. A. Thiers, and on comparison with other editions will be found far superior.

In Press.

THIERS' FRENCH REVOLUTION,

TO BE COMPLETED IN SIX PARTS, AT 12 1-2 CENTS EACH.

TO BE COMPLETED IN TEN NUMBERS.

THE MYSTERIES OF BERLIN,

FROM

THE PAPERS OF A BERLIN CRIMINAL OFFICER.

TRANSLATED FROM THE GERMAN.

By C. B. BURKHARDT.

With Illustrations on Steel, by P. Habelmann.

This work in Europe has been universally pronounced far superior to M. Sue's celebrated "Mysteries of Paris," and we confidantly predict. that the popularity of this translation will be without a parallel in the history of light reading.

THE

MYSTERIES

of

BERLIN.

TO BE COMPLETED

IN

TEN PARTS.

NEW YORK: WILLIAM H. COLYER, PUBLISHER.

desire such a result, as the publishers would no longer accept his voluminous novels. He had already long since passed two score years, and upon this long journey through life, had lost the imaginative fancies of his mind together with the hair of his head. Still he needed a great deal of money, for he was an immense eater, and passionately fond of eating *good* things.

The "great Doctor," entertained his "rich adored," with his last great romance, which as he said, had already been translated into nearly every known European and Asiatic language. The artist's widow listened in evident delight; she certainly knew the embarrassed situation of her *Cicisbeo*, yet she was determined to bestow her hand upon him, for she felt flattered, to be called the wife of the "great Doctor," the "better half" of the greatest of all novel writers.

The lady's brother, a rich merchant, and a jovial, somewhat sarcastic man, joined the couple.

"Tell me, my dear *Fliege*," he began addressing the novelist, "have you read *Voss's Gazette* of to-day?"

"I never read such a paper," replied the other shrugging his shoulders.

"It contains an article concerning you," continued the merchant. "*Rellholz*, the critic, has reviewed your last romance. He says, that the Government of the *Flachsenfingern* Penitentiary has decreed, that the severest punishment for offences against discipline, shall be, to compel the offender to read the whole of that romance."

"Pshaw!" exclaimed Doctor Fliege in a tone of utter contempt. "Pshaw," he repeated, as he smoothed his immense whiskers with the palms of his hands, and twisted his moustache around his first finger.

"Yet I think it must annoy you," continued his pertinacious tormenter. "Rellholz says, that they tried the first experiment with the most obstinate and unmanageable of the convicts, and that the result was entirely satisfactory. The most obstinate among them had willingly submitted to the severest discipline, rather than undergo that punishment; the lash, hunger, or solitary confinement were not to be compared to it."

"And do you think that I should be annoyed at this?" cried the great Doctor as he angrily slapped his head with his hand, thereby involuntarily pushing his entire wig to one side, "no, no, certainly not! Rellholz is a man, who understands about as much of poetry and romance, as I understand of gas manufacturing. But come, I think we should go into this side room and sup; it is too terribly hot to stay here."

The great Doctor produced his pocket-handkerchief to fan himself, then blowing, as if overcome by heat, his full cheeks and his immense body seemed to swell out to even greater proportions than usual. The conversation had evidently been very annoying to him, and several times he had made great efforts, to ascertain, what impression her brother's sarcasm had produced upon his charming widow.

On going out, Doctor Fliege, with a sarcastic smile, pointed at a couple whom he seemed to be acquainted with.

It was the rich banker *Oppenberg*, who was offering a glass of champagne to the celebrated first danseuse of the Ballet, *Demoiselle Windig*. He had, in all earnest, offered her his hand and heart, and she in all earnest, had condescended to give him hopes, of the possession of that hand. But one of the conditions of these hopes was, that he must first be made a Baron, for Demoiselle Windig considered it a well established rule, and one which she must not transgress, that celebrated dancers can only marry nobility.

Upon the strength of this principle she favoured an officer, of very ancient and noble family, who could trace his pedigree as far back as the times of Charlemagne. But in this instance, there was one very grave and important consideration—the man was poor, decidedly poor. Unquestionably she would therefore have rejected him long since, but for the prospective hope of a fat inheritance from a rich old uncle of her admirer. This was too great a consideration for the lady, who of course argued, that ancient nobility in connexion with full purses, must at all events be the most attractive qualities to the heart of a Ballet-dancer.

The Lieutenant in question, *Count Teufel von Teufelsritt** was also present at the ball, and it required all the intriguing powers of Demoiselle Windig to steer clear between the two lovers, and to prevent a collision. She had just observed, that her noble Devil, at this moment, was in a distant part of the saloon, among a swarm of his comrades, who were warmly discussing the virtues, merits and demerits of a greyhound. Dogs being one of the ruling objects of the passions of his Highness, the danseuse thought this the most available moment to pay her particular devoirs to the money bags of her favourite banker.

Count Teufel, however, for once in his life, broke off a conversation on dogs, on observing another subject requiring his attention.

With gigantic strides he crossed the room, and approached the couple, at the very moment when the danseuse was about to bring the glass to her lips.

"A short time ago, you thanked me and refused, when I offered you champagne," he said in a vexed tone of voice, "you even said you would drink none all the evening."

"That was merely a humour," replied the lady laughing merrily, "just now I really feel thirsty and inclined to drink."

The Count stared at the Banker with a fiery and furious face, whilst the danseuse emptied her glass of sparkling wine, and held it out to have it replenished.

"Will you drink some?" she asked in a pacifying tone, as she offered the glass to the Count, "here, at this side I have been drinking, it will probably taste best there."

The Count mistook this raillery for intentional satire, and grew still more furious.

* Angl. Count Devil of Devil's-ride.

11

"I do not drink with Jews," he said, insultingly, "come, Madame."

At these words, which were commandingly spoken, he offered his arm to the lady.

The long-feared explosion which she had hitherto so effectively prevented, had at last come. Demoiselle Windig knew full well, that at this moment she must choose between her admirers, must accept one and reject the other, else ruin her prospects with both. Wisely she concluded to prefer a certainty to an uncertainty; the coarse behaviour of the Count may also have influenced her choice.

She quickly drew back a step from the Count, and placed her hand within the arm of the banker. "*Allons chere Oppenberg!*" she said, as she moved away with a most lovely and artistical *pas*.

"Now, my dear Oppenberg, you will have yourself made a Baron, won't you?" she said, looking most tenderly into the face of her delighted companion.

Count Teufel von Teufelsritt stood in silence, and stared after her.

We will not fatigue our readers with a description of all the separate groups which moved about these brilliant saloons, in a similar manner. There was, as usual, a great deal of polished hypocrisy, and barefaced egotism, all covered by refined manners and splendid dresses.

Steinfort did wrong in bringing his Augusta, a frivolous, misguided, but honest and open-hearted girl upon this slippery course, to impart to her the external gloss of fine manners. He should have remembered that this gloss, without other higher qualities of education, is too apt to be dangerous to a young mind.

But even as he meant to overleap all the immense obstacles of custom, by his noble but extravagant mode of reasoning, even so he lacked, in the present instance, the necessary forethought and experience, which could alone prevent him from entangling himself and his loved girl in unforeseen difficulties.

CHAPTER XLIV.

THE END OF THE GAME.

AFTER a while the Lieutenant conducted the girl to one of the Buffets; she had been walking about, and a cup of tea would be refreshing.

Here he left her for a moment to herself, to join his comrades, who, the dance having just ended, were forming a noisy, merry group in the middle of the saloon.

He had scarcely joined them, when he was, from every side, attacked with questions about his companion, and only now he began to discover to what consequences he had exposed himself.

The beauty of the girl excited general attention. It soon was discovered that she come in Steinfort's company, without any more aged protector or protectress. As no one suspected her real character, this strange appearance could only be properly explained, by believing her to be Steinfort's acknowledged bride. No one, however, had yet heard of his betrothal.

Steinfort had never thought of all this, and his situation became most painful, as he knew not how he should best designate the girl, or how justify her presence here with him.

He finally answered briefly, that the young lady was a distant cousin from the provinces, had just visited Berlin for the first time, and had been entrusted to his care by her father, who would not arrive until late. Luckily for him, the orchestra struck up a new dance, and relieved him of the necessity of passing this dangerous examination any further.

The floor-managers approached, and the group from the centre dispersed to the sides of the saloon.

"That is a devilish pretty girl, whom Steinfort has with him here," said *Herr von Stengel*, a Lieutenant of Dragoons, to one of his comrades.

"Oh yes, certainly, she is pretty," replied the other, a tall, blonde Lieutenant of Infantry; "but these country lasses are usually very stupid. Wonder whether she has money?"

"By Jove," cried the lively *Baron von Görz*, "I don't believe at all that she is a country lass. The ladies in the provinces don't look like her. I have a little experience in this, from my last furlough."

"Yes, yes," observed a fourth, "you have been with your old aunt, and fed her lap-dogs. *Rankendorf* here, has told us pretty stories about your gentle shepherd's-life; but he excused you, by observing that you had done it all with a view to a fat inheritance."

"I believe that Rankendorf is not in his right senses," replied Görz, evidently annoyed at this sarcastic, and, as he thought, ill-timed observation: "but I tell you, the girl is not from the provinces."

"That I think very possible," said a very young Lieutenant, with a very thin voice, who had hitherto been a silent spectator. "Herr von Steinfort looked very frightened and embarrassed when he gave us this information." The little Lieutenant said these words with a most particularly smart and knowing look

"Yes, yes, that is a fact," said several others, laughing, "there is some mystery in all this."

"Such is precisely my opinion," repeated the little Lieutenant, looking even more wise than before.

"But gentlemen," began the *Rittmeister* von Bardua*, "what are you thinking of? Is not Steinfort the most virtuous, innocent, and pure young gentleman in the whole regiment, and 'without reproach,' as Knight Bayard of blessed memory?"

The noise of the orchestra drowned all further conversation, and the party separated laughingly.

Angl. Master of horse.

Steinfort had returned to Augusta, and with her had joined one of the quadrilles about to commence. In the same set was the "great Doctor," with his rich widow, who, to his great annoyance, had forced him to leave the fine supper, and obey the call of the Orchestra for a quadrille.

The music resounded, and the dancers moved through the most fashionable and artificial figures.

By her graceful ease, and natural beauty, Augusta soon attracted the attention of every one, but more particularly that of Doctor Fliege, who continually kept his eyes upon her.

Suddenly he remembered that she had been one of the grisettes whom he had been in the habit of seeing at the balls of Villa Bella, before the *Oranienburg-gate*. He had been a regular customer at this place before he began to seek the hand of the rich widow, and had even been an ardent admirer of Augusta. But as she disliked his proud, overbearing behaviour, he had always been reejcted by her.

When he saw the beautiful girl now before him in her neat and elegant ball-costume, all his former desires awoke anew. An obvious comparison with the superannuated widow by his side, might even have heightened her charms in his eyes.

He had so little command over himself, that he used every opportunity he could find in the figures of the dance, when he came near to the fair girl, or when his hand came in contact with hers, of winking, bending down to her, pressing her hand, and saying tender and flattering words in her ear. Spite of the evident displeasure of Augusta, he would not abandon these attentions, until all present were led to suppose, that he either was, or had been, upon a very intimate footing with this girl.

Steinfort was burning with rage and fury, but the laws of good breeding prevented all further explanation for the present.

The dance had scarcely been concluded, and the great Doctor had retreated into a side room to drown his sorrows in a goose-liver pasty, when a heavy judgment fell upon his devoted head.

His love-making to the handsome Augusta had not escaped the observation of the widow; she was almost beside herself with rage and jealousy, and heaped the most bitter reproaches upon the broad shoulders of her lover.

Only then, the great Doctor remembered how incautiously he had exposed himself. He feared the loss of the rich widow, and his anxiety brought heavy drops of perspiration upon his broad forehead. In vain he assured her that he had not the least pretension to this girl, that she was totally indifferent to him, and that only the circumstance of his having seen her once before, had induced him to exchange a few words with her. All explanation was useless. The widow declared herself shamefully neglected, compromised, abused and ridiculed; in short, it wanted but little of an exhibition of faintings, swoons, or fits.

In this desperate situation, the great Doctor hit upon a desperate remedy, to give to the lady of his choice the most self-evident proof, that he cared very little for the handsome young girl.

He went to the managers and told them, who and what person Augusta was, at the same time urging a serious complaint of the admission of such persons to the society of the frequenters of these balls.

The managers immediately became anxious, angry and excited, as they saw the reputation of their establishment at a risk. What judgment would the all-powerful public pronounce upon them, if it became known, that at a ball at the "French house," a ball which was honoured not alone by rich citizens, but even by high civil and military officers, a grizette had been admitted.

The necessary inquiries were immediately instituted, and it was soon discovered, that Lieutenant von Steinfort had introduced the girl.

This made the managers hesitate. It was not advisable to offend the rich Lieutenant. The great Doctor was told, that he must most probably have been mistaken, and that such a mistake might have very serious consequences.

But Doctor Fliege, remembering the threatening rich widow, who would and must be satisfied, would not admit of any mistake in his statement. He insisted upon being certain of the facts he had stated, offered to be responsible for all consequences, and threatened, if the measures proper in a case like the present were not immediately taken, that he would himself inform all the gentlemen present, what sort of society their ladies were associating with at this ball.

This menace did not miss its object upon the managers, who now began to fear the worst. Still they would go to work as gently as possible.

Lieutenant von Steinfort was called into a corner and there questioned about the name and rank of the lady he had introduced. As he could not, and would not tell a falsehood, his statements soon verified what the long Doctor had asserted. The natural consequence was, that he was requested as soon as convenient, and in perfect quiet, to leave the saloon with his companion, who was not suited for this circle.

Had Steinfort remained quiet, he might easily have avoided all exposure and noise; but with his sincere love for Augusta, and with the ideas which he entertained about her character and her innocence, he believed that she as well as himself were suffering the greatest injustice. His heart being still full of the extravagant plans and hopes which had induced him to bring her here, he could not be persuaded to abandon his views so easily.

He warmly objected to the propositions of the managers, argued and declaimed loudly about the equality of mankind, about that innocence of the heart which elevated Augusta far above all the other rich, artificial and jewel-covered ladies in the room, and in these arguments he became so loud and passionate, that he soon collected a large circle of spectators around him.

This was a most welcome opportunity for the great Doctor, who had quickly brought the widow to a seat near the scene of the dispute, and who now hoped to make his peace with her, by assisting in making the dispute more warm and interesting.

He mixed himself among the crowd that surrounded the Lieutenant, and began by making bitter reproaches to Steinfort, for having dared, regardless of the fashion and respectability of the company present, to select a grisette as his companion at a ball in the "French house."

The dispute finally grew so noisy, as to attract the attention of all present, and at last reached the ears of Augusta herself, who had previously remarked it as strange, that the Lieutenant should have been called away from her side.

She now discovered her lover in the midst of a crowd of gentlemen, observed how all were warmly disputing and arguing with him, and also that he was in a great passion, and she began to fear that one of those wild scenes might occur, which were by no means of rare occurrence in the circles she had formerly visited in Villa Bella.

Without remembering where she was at the time, she jumped up to hurry to the assistance of her lover, as was the regular habit of the ladies who frequented Villa bella.

Fearlessly she approaches the crowd of men, who noisily were surrounding the Lieutenant and the ball managers in the middle of the room, whilst the ladies in fear and terror had sought refuge in the corners and along the walls.

By this movement she exposes herself to the scandalized view of all the ladies present, and a cry of indignation at her assurance is heard from every female lip.

Augusta soon learns the cause of the dispute; the words of the Lieutenant distinctly reach her ears, as he exclaims in the greatest excitement: "I hereby declare that the young lady in question is my bride, and that I shall consider each and every word that is further spoken about her, as a personal insult, and hold the speaker responsible."

A deep murmur is heard through the room; already ominous words and sentences, such as "abominable," "barefaced," "shameless," "turn them out," &c, are becoming audible in different parts of the saloon.

Close before Lieutenant Steinfort stands the great Doctor. He has raised both arms high in the air, and exhausts his lungs in all imaginable modes of speech, which he remembers from disputing scenes in his different romances.

In her kind attentive care, Augusta now begins to fear for the life of her Carl. All her hesitation is fled, and she sees, hears, and feels nothing more but an invincible desire to penetrate the circle surrounding him, and to stand as a guarding and protecting angel by his side.

Quickly she is in the midst of the crowd.

With powerful arms breaking her way through the mass of men, she reaches the side of her lover in a few steps.

The whole company is overcome by silent astonishment at this unheard-of conduct and behaviour in a place like the "French House."

The girl, without noticing this, takes the arm of her lover.

"Come, Carl," she says quietly, "let us go home, and leave these fools to themselves."

And at these words she leads him out of the surrounding crowd and out of the saloon.

The Lieutenant had been so struck with this sudden interference of the girl, that he quietly lets her do as she likes with him, and only after leaving the room begins to collect his scattered senses.

In the saloon, however, the uproar and noise continued, even like the disturbed and storm-lashed waves of the ocean, and the quiet, calm tone of enjoyment is not again restored during the whole evening.

The widow alone presses Doctor Fliege's arm with great tenderness, and says with a delighted smile: "My dear Doctor, you have fully atoned for your error; but do not again put me to so hard a trial."

Humbly the great Doctor bows his devoted head, and respectfully pressing the forgiving hand to his lips, he kisses it most tenderly.

"Heaven is my witness," he exclaims enthusiastically, "you are great and mighty in punishing, but greater and mightier in pardoning."

CHAPTER XLV.

LOVE MAKING.

It was eleven o'clock in the forenoon.

The March snow fell in light and downy flakes upon the streets, and was here and there industriously collected by fair hands, into bowls, basins, and other vessels. The water of the snow which falls in March, is said to possess beautifying or beauty-preserving qualities.

The Frau Hofräthin Christianus was comfortably seated upon the sofa, and read the "Mysteries of Berlin," then in a course of publication by Meyer and Hoffman of Berlin. A new number had just made its appearance, which engaged her undivided attention.

Fräulein Matilda Christianus sat at the pianoforte in a charming morning dress. She played and sang:

> "My heart if I should ask thee
> What true love is, thoul't say :
> Two souls and but one impulse,
> Two wills and but one way."

This was the beautiful newly introduced song of *Parthenia*, from *Halm's* "Son of the Wilderness."

Matilda had a fresh, rich toned voice, and in the present instance endeavoured to give as much expression and feeling as possible to her song, and as much melting sentimentality as it was possible for the artful girl to introduce.

This was the Syren song, intended to entangle the heart of the rich Banker von N—, who sat by her side.

Since that memorable day, when Lieutenant von Steinfort upset the parrot cage, and broke off all further connexions with the family, and on which the Banker von N— took his place at the dinner table, Fräulein Christianus had come to the firm determination of choosing the gold bags of Mercury, instead of the laurels of Mars, for her device.

Her amiability had fully succeeded in captivating the banker. He had frequently repeated his visits, had evidently progressed in her good favours, and thus she had safely for a second time arrived at a point, at which she might daily look for a formal declaration from her lover. That she was anxious and impatient for this event, we need not repeat; experience had made her wise.

In reality she had not the least love for Banker von N—, he was even disagreeable to her; she particularly disliked the silly sentimentality of his character, which was so very opposite to the firm determination of her own.

Herr von N— was originally of Hebrew extraction, had afterwards become a Christian, and was made a Baron on account of his great riches. He was a man, as we find them only too frequent in the present age, a man without strength, energy or firmness of character.

The son of a father, who had early left him in the possession of great wealth, he had neglected all more serious occupations, and after having finished the most necessary part of his school-education, had made himself slightly acquainted with only the mechanical part of his future business. This business, however, principally rested in the hands of an old confidential and safe cashier, who had grown grey in the service of this house, and who operated and speculated with unlimited authority. He had only to be careful, to have constantly as much ready cash in hand, as was necessary for the private use of Herr von N—.

But even these necessities were exceedingly moderate in proportion to the immense wealth of Herr von N—. For his effeminate and naturally bashful nature, did not even permit him to partake of the usual excesses and extravagances of his years. The wild, dashing and juvenile habits of his acquaintances, frightened, instead of tempting him, and gradually he withdrew entirely from their society. Some thought him eccentric, others sanctified, and again others hypocritical, but all let him go his own way.

Now ennui became his greatest enemy. Ennui drove him to travelling, occasionally into society, into the opera, balls—even tempted him into a few trifling intrigues, all of course managed in the most modest and abashed silence—but he naturally lacked juvenile courage and a juvenile disposition to enjoy them. Soon Herr von N— had tasted all sorts of pleasures, but had found them all equally annoying, and now moved, or rather creeped about, resembling more an old woman, than a young man in the best of his years.

At last he had hit upon a curious alternative. He had come to the determination of trying whether he might not pass his time, with such employments as are customary among ladies. He learned sewing, knitting, embroidering, netting, tambouring, and, in fact, doing all other kinds of ladies fancy work, and finally, became passionately fond of them all.

For days together, he sat by his little work-table and sewed, and naturally began to like these amusements better as he became more and more an adept in them. But the excellence of his female labour soon became so great, that his work became celebrated throughout the city. Mothers quoted him as an example to their daughters, and gave them Herr von N—'s work for models. He soon received the honourable nickname of "Laura, the embroideress."

At the time of our story, the banker was past thirty years of age. Hitherto he had remained unmarried, because he had at least knowledge enough of his own weakness, to know, that if married, his wife must rule him. But beside this, he certainly had a desire to have a wife, as the dinner at the hotels was no longer to his taste, and as he had a prospect that his work, in female society, would progress so much better and faster.

Matilda had well considered all these circumstances, and thereupon built her plans.

Before the eyes of her admirer she never appeared but as a modest, diffident maiden, one who valued domestic manners and retired domestic life above every thing else. She seemed the most devoted of daughters, the most loving and affectionate of sisters, the most kind, self-sacrificing of friends. The noisy pleasures of society were hateful to her, balls were abominable, and she suffered herself to be long urged and entreated, before upon one occasion she could be persuaded to go to a concert in the garrison church, even in company of her mother, and her admirer, the banker.

Such modesty had excited his entire admiration and sympathy. At last he believed that he had found a woman, who, as a wife, would only live to gratify his wishes, who would ever obey him in all things, and who never would dream of assuming command. It was absolutely necessary that she should not think of the latter, for Herr von N— was well aware that he would not be capable of offering the slightest resistance to any expression of will or determination on her part.

His present attendance at the house of the worthy Christianus was the natural consequence of his usual visiting hour, which he had already for some time punctually kept. On each and every visit, he had predetermined to declare his tender passion, but on each and every occasion, his natural timidity had prevented the accomplishment of his object. Unfortunately, fear still possessed greater power over him than his will. An invincible diffidence closed his lips whenever he endeavoured to speak upon the subject; now papa Christianus would interrupt him by his entrance, again the mother of his charmer, or else the noise which the parrot made, made him too nervous. In short, our banker remained a sighing shepherd, in perfect lamb-like innocence and purity of heart, despite the encouraging looks of his adored, despite all the reproaches he still repeated to himself, whenever the cook of the hotel had oversalted the soup, or spoiled any other dish.

Matilda very nearly lost all patience; only the hope of having her trouble a thousand times repaid after the victory was gained, supported her still, and encouraged her to new attacks upon his heart. One of these attacks consisted in the above mentioned melting Adagio which she sang for him.

The banker had surprised her at the pianoforte—we know not whether accidentally, or in consequence of a shrewd calculation, or previous arrangement of her own—and had earnestly begged her to continue in her play and song.

Matilda sang the song to the end with much feeling and expression, and after the last verse, laid her hands into her lap, and her eyes sunk modestly to the ground.

She was alone with her Cicisbeo. Her mother had carefully read through the last number of the Berlin Mysteries, and had then left the room to attend to some domestic duties.

Fräulein Christianus most probably was awaiting the result of her very tender, love-breathing song. At least she did not interrupt the silence which had ensued, and only occasionally cast a stolen glance at the banker by her side.

Undoubtedly Herr von N— had again the best intentions in the world. He rubbed his hands, buttoned his coat twice from top to bottom, and unbuttoned it again from bottom to top. At last he looked fearfully and anxiously around the room, coughed twice, threw out his handkerchief, sighed, opened his lips and began: "Even in holy scripture we read—"

"Rascal, rascal," cried our well known parrot, at this most inconvenient of all moments, in so loud and shrill a voice, that Herr von N—, as if electrified, started up, and entirely lost the little composure he had with so much difficulty gained.

As we already know, this parrot was a great favourite of Matilda, but at this moment, she would have given a great deal, if she could have seen him instantly strangled before her eyes.

With great exertions, the banker endeavoured to regain his composure: "'Tis strange," he said, with a forced smile, "that the parrot should have just then interrupted me. I was actually frightened, for I was just going to tell you, that—that —we read in natural history something about the great age which parrots will attain."

This excuse, this extravagant nonsense, seemed to Matilda, even in her present serious humour, so extraordinarily ridiculous, that she quickly touched the keys of her instrument, thereby endeavouring to overcome an almost invincible desire to laugh aloud.

"This is very good," observed the banker, who was gradually recovering, "play something else, Fräulein, I am very fond of listening to music; it is not exciting, yet amuses one."

Matilda, who was still struggling between ill-humour and a convulsive desire to laugh, very gladly obeyed this request, and played all the overtures she knew of the latest and most fashionable operas.

Meanwhile Herr von N— was marching up and down the room, keeping time with the music.

After a while his glance fell upon an embroidery frame by the window, which contained a half finished, very beautiful piece of embroidery. Matilda had purchased this in one of the fashionable embroidery stores, and had put it up here for show, shrewdly calculating that her admirer's eye must be sure to observe it.

The sight of this frame awoke at once all his natural passions for embroidery and needle-work; he took up the frame and earnestly began to work. As music had now lost all its charms for him, Matilda was soon permitted to discontinue her playing.

She seated herself by his side at the window, and expressed great admiration at his excellent needle work.

"Yes, yes, Fräulein," replied Herr von N— with a delighted smile, "I flatter myself, that I understand this kind of thing. I have occupied myself a great deal with it, and thank God, I am rich enough to amuse myself in any way that pleases me."

"Why, this is really charming!" exclaimed the young lady with a delighted look.

"Oh, you should only visit me, and see my work-room," continued the banker, drawing about a yard of red Zephir worsted through his needle. "That room looks as well as the best arranged lady's boudoir; I have covered the whole floor with worked rugs, every one of which was made by own hand. I did not mind any expense for patterns, silks or worsted, for thank God, I am rich enough. In my room you will find pearl embroidery, worsted, and even some crape embroidery. What a pity, that the latter should no longer be in fashion, I had gained such perfection in its making.—Did you work this piece of embroidery yourself?"

"Oh, certainly," replied Matilda boldly, although she could not sew the most simple pattern, but had bought the work before her, which was a very beautiful and difficult piece of embroidery, of the kind which our ladies frequently buy at the magazines, and which are known by the title of "broderies commençées." According to circumstances, they require a few stitches more or less added to them, and then ladies stamp them as their own work.

"Well, this worsted work is not so bad," continued the banker, closely criticising the embroidery, "the choice of colours shows taste, and the evenness of the stitches deserves all praise. You have chosen *petit point;* did you not suppose that *gros point* would be better suited for the pattern?"

"In reality, I have already had serious thoughts about that," said the young lady, who, however, did not understand one word of all these technicalities.

"Yes," said the banker, as he quietly continued to sew, "and then instead of the Zephir, I should have chosen coarse English wool, which would have shown the strong points of the pattern to much greater advantage."

"You are right, I believe," replied Matilda. "I think my mother has some coarse English wool, and I will ask her for it, and continue the work with that."

The banker looked up in astonishment, uncertain whether these words were spoken seriously or in a joke. His face, which had become overspread with a red hue, from the downward position of his head whilst at work, looked so ridiculously serious, that Matilda had to laugh involuntarily. This laughter saved her from an exposure of her utter ignorance.

"You are a merry rogue, young lady," he said to the laughing girl, convinced that she had made the remark in fun; "but still I am in the right. When we continually practice a single subject, we must certainly acquire some knowledge of it."

"Oh, I know! yes, certainly!" began the lady again, who feared at this moment to spoil everything with her rich lover. "Your good taste is very celebrated."

"Hm! It costs me a great deal of money," continued Herr von N——, chattering. "At my house you can find embroidery frames, and netting frames, of all sizes and forms, as well as wools, worsteds, silks, and other materials of every variety. When once I am married, I shall embroider or sew with my wife for wagers, for since, thank God, I am very rich, neither of us need to do anything else. It is an extremely pleasant thing to be very rich."

This was unquestionably the beginning of a second attempt of the banker to approach the much desired object of his visit. But it seemed to have been very hard labour for him to come even so far, for he blushed deep scarlet, and quickly produced a white, richly embroidered and laced handkerchief from his pocket, which must assist him out of his present embarrassment.

"Look at this," he continued, "this embroidery and this lace is also of my work; this is very fine and difficult work, but I think you might yet learn it."

Herr von N—— actually outdid himself in boldness this morning, for, although we don't know whether intentional or otherwise, yet it was evident that this last observation again, and for a third time, pointed directly towards the object of his visit.

Matilda was perfectly ready and willing to meet him at half way, or at least to assist his modesty as far as possible. Inwardly she certainly laughed at the fool, and seemed to think: "Just wait, and let me once have you for a husband, and we will soon see about all this," but externally, she blushed and said with modest, abashed looks: "If I should once get married, I would direct my tastes and inclinations entirely after those of my husband, for such I consider to be the first duty of a good wife."

These words touched the heart of the banker to its very lowest depths. He was delighted at having found what he considered the very paragon of female perfection; he could never in this world hope to find a better wife. His bashfulness, his fear all disappeared at once; he must dare everything, attempt everything, to attain such a wife, to call such a blessing his own.

Even so the gamester, in an irresistible impulse of passion, takes his whole fortune to place it upon a single card, to cry *va banque* to the banker.

With a desperate effort Herr von N—— gathered all his mental courage. Holding the embroidery frame still in his right, and swinging the worsted needle in the left, with one mighty crash he sunk upon both his knees before the maiden.

"Fräulein," he cried with a loud voice, endeavouring to keep up his desperate courage, "Fräulein, shall we embroider together, for thank God, I am rich enough, and—"

Unfortunate fate, wretched destiny! Oh, surge-born Cythera, oh, Cupid, Psyche and all ye other heathen gods of Olympus, whose pleasure it is, mischievously to interfere in the love affairs of mortals!

At this all important moment, the room door opens, and Marianne Jobs, dressed as a servant girl, enters the apartment. At the command of her mistress she holds in her hand a tray, upon which stands a bottle of sweet wine and a little biscuit, intended for the light luncheon of the rich visitor.

Who can blame her, if at the sight of this most ridiculous and unexpected of all situations, she burst into a loud fit of laughter, a laughter which it was not in her power to stop? She hastened to dispose of her burden upon a small table which stood not far from the lovers, and to disappear as soon as possible. But the gods had willed it otherwise. Herr von N—— hastily jumps up, and his embroidery frame catches beneath the tray Marianne was carrying, which he thus hurls with its entire contents upon his own head. The bottle actually breaks against his own skull, and his head is soaked in the rich gift of Bacchus.

This was more than his warm, love-burning heart could bear

The unfortunate lover had placed his entire fortune upon a single card, this card had lost, and he must declare his love a bankrupt.

Beside himself with shame, rage, embarrassment and indignation, he picked up his hat, with a deep sigh put it upon his wine-soaked head, and rushed out of the room.

In almost the same style, Lieutenant von Steinfort had once run away.

CHAPTER XLVI.

A STORM AT THE HOFRATH'S HOUSE.

WHERE shall we find words or colouring, justly to describe the raging fury and indignation of Fräulein Christianus?

Achilles, the Grecian hero, could not have burned with more intense fury, when the divine Briseis was torn from him, than did the daughter of the Berlin Hofrath, when the rich banker had escaped her.

Yes, escaped her!—that word comprised all—perhaps for ever, at all events for the present. How long had she been anxiously looking forward to the moment of his declaration, and now when it had arrived, everything was at once ruined by the stupid and bold behaviour of a servant girl! Could not this girl have remained without? Who asked her to come in, and just at this moment interfere in the most secret affairs of her mistress.

This reasoning of the young lady will at once inform our readers that the unfortunate Marianne was again selected for a sacrifice even in this instance, although she was no more guilty at present, than at the time when she fell a sacrifice to civil justice.

The Mistress had herself sent her into the room, and she had not the necessary presence of mind or self-possession quickly to retire again—this, perhaps, was her only fault. But she had dared to laugh, that was her crime, the more so, as it offered to Fräulein Christianus a welcome opportunity of satisfying her spite and revenge.

But we still owe to our readers the explanation, how it came at all, that we find Marianne in the house of the Hofrath.

We remember, that when we last left her, a newly gained protector was leading her out of the prison yard of the Stadtvoigtei, where he had found her in a most disconsolate situation.

This benevolent, kind old man, was *Rentier Friedmeyer*, a very rich, and, what very rarely occurs together, a very good, kind and honourable man. From pure philanthropy he had become a member of nearly every benevolent association in the city, and among others, of the society for the protection and assistance of dismissed prisoners. In this latter quality he had taken pity on Marianne, and had given her to the care of this society. Hofrath Christianus happened also to be a member of this society; he was just in want of a servant girl, and in consideration of the good behaviour of Marianne, found himself induced to take her from the prison into his house.

We have no reason to suppose, that it was pure charity or philanthropy which induced the Hofrath and his family to be members of this society. The Hofrath only joined it, because he knew that the Minister would be pleased to see him do so, as the chief himself was president of it, and still held the title of "Geheime" for him in perspective. The Hofrath next thought that he would please his Excellency still more, if he would take a dismissed prisoner into his house, and thereby assist in her reform.

He certainly did not mention the very low wages which he intended to pay the unfortunate girl, who had no place to go to, nor did he mention the circumstance, that his better half had such a bad name among the servants of the neighbourhood, for her stinginess and scolding disposition, that it was always with the greatest difficulty at all, that he could replace a dismissed servant.

Marianne in reality soon had an opportunity of learning that she was not destined to enjoy rosy days in this house. She had entered the service as chambermaid, and as such, her principal duty consisted in attending to the wishes of, and waiting upon mother and daughter. Under these circumstances, she had fallen a helpless victim to the humours of both, which made her fate so much the worse, as the position of mother and daughter was one of constant strife and opposition.

Poor Marianne had nothing but heavy labour, scanty food, and seldom if ever a friendly look. But willingly and even cheerfully she bore all her misery, because at least she fared somewhat better here than at the cellar of hunchbacked Jobs. At all events she no longer saw the terrible scenes of coarse physical crime, and for scenes of mental crime, of the crime of the soul, as we might say, she lacked the necessary intelligence and education, to perceive them.

But withal this, during the short time she had stayed in the house of the Hofrath, she had innocently drawn upon herself the ill-will and displeasure of the family in the highest degree.

As we know, Marianne was a very pretty girl, and the pale, haggard appearance which the air and life of the prison had caused, soon lost itself, and health and blooming beauty returned. This, Fräulein Christianus could not pardon, for she would absolutely be the only beauty in the house.

To her great and bitter annoyance she observed that the gentlemen who visited the house, and on one occasion even the banker von N—, looked with a pleasant smile upon the beautiful girl. Unfortunately the son of the family had also pronounced a favourable judgment in this case, and had thereby aroused the anger and displeasure of his mother. This lady, as we already know, was rather indifferent to the weal or woe of her family; yet she greatly regarded the world without, and for that world's sake, she would have looked upon it as very unfortunate, if anybody had observed this young gentleman's good understanding with a servant girl. And people will talk. Perhaps that the fears of his mother were not without foundation, for the young literary Christianus had really cast sheep eyes at the pretty Marianne, but these had not even been observed by the girl.

Thus, for some time past, every thing had contributed towards drawing a new storm down upon the head of the unfortunate and unsuspecting girl, and only a fair opportunity was wanting to produce a most terrible explosion.

This opportunity had now arrived.

As soon as the banker had left the house, Matilda, in the utmost fury, rang the bell, to bring the servant girl, who had hastily left the room after the misfortune with the luncheon had occurred, back to her presence.

Marianne soon made her appearance, laden with the necessary articles to cleanse the floor of the fragments and the spots which the accident had left.

Full of fury, the young lady attacked her servant girl.

"Worthless being!" she cried, "away, away out of my sight! Oh! this impudence, who could bear it? Away, I tell you, and leave the house instantly!"

The noise soon attracted the young lady's mother, who had no sooner heard what had occurred, than she chimed in with her scolding daughter, in a perfect Xantippe style.

The Hofrath just then returned from his office, and entered the house. With a silent sigh he learned all that had occurred. For a second time he had lost the prospect of having a desirable son-in-law, and this was no joke, for his daughter was already past nineteen.

The family soon agreed that they must give to Herr von N— as much satisfaction for the awkwardness and impudence of Marianne, as was in their power. Marianne, who had again escaped by flight from the concentrated wrath of the family, was, after half an hour's consultation, for the third time, recalled to the high presence of the family trio.

The Hofrath addresssed her with all the important dignity he could muster, as follows:

"The manifold and various acts and deeds of kindness and benevolence which I and my family have bestowed on you, you have rewarded with vile ingratitude. You have proved yourself to be an unworthy, lazy, and corrupted individual. To-day you have behaved and conducted yourself towards an honourable and honoured guest of my family, in a manner which I cannot find words to designate. I shall, consequently, without any further notice, dismiss you from my service, and I now order and command you to leave and quit my premises within the space of half an hour."

Silently, Marianne left the apartment, packed her very few things together in a bundle, and left the house without knowing whither to turn her steps.

———

CHAPTER XLVII.

THE WEAVER'S FAMILY.

The hard winter was gradually drawing to a close; but even at its departure, it brought new misery upon a family who seemed to belong to that class of burden-bearers of misfortune and wretchedness, upon whom falls not even a passing ray of bright sunshine.

We hope that our readers will not grow impatient if we continue to show them only the dark sides of the picture of human society; poetry belongs to its times, and it is not the poet's fault if his time produces more of misery than of happiness. We would only awaken a sympathy for the sufferers of scenes which are of daily occurrence in the garrets and in the lowest cellars of those Hotels, whose "Belle Etage" is resplendent with the luxury and extravagance of wealth. Would that all the world remembered that in those despised caves of civilization we can find the busy, yet half-starved hands of industry, the sweat of whose brow has clothed the walls of that saloon with velvet, and the floor of it, with rich, shining carpets.

Weaver Greif was one of those unfortunate victims of civilization, who, whilst they provide for others' wealth and luxury, have themselves nothing wherewith to satisfy their own gnawing hunger.

The money which he had received for the yarn he had pledged, as may easily be supposed, did not last long, and had only served the wretched family for the momentary prolongation of their unfortunate existence. They had actually lived (if living it could be called) nearly a fortnight upon this money, and had trembled each moment with fear and apprehension, that the breach of trust which the weaver had committed in his despair, might become known to the authorities.

The last groschen of the sum had long since been sent to the apothecaries to buy some little medicine for the poor woman; and where, at this moment, was the poor man to obtain more for his wife and child?

The weaver had informed the manufacturer whose yarn he had pledged, through a fellow sufferer, that he had become sick, and that it would be impossible for him to deliver the work at the right time. Meanwhile he had succeeded in obtaining work at another manufactory, and he now laboured day and night, with almost superhuman exertion, to gain at least as much as would enable him to redeem the yarn, and escape the shame and the punishment of his crime.

He scarcely slept three or four hours per night, and in the daytime would scarcely allow himself rest enough to take the most scanty dinner; but with all this labour, he could not earn more than three thalers in a week. Of this, he must necessarily lay twenty silbergroschen, or a thaler, aside for the redemption of the yarn, and with the rest he must support himself, his sick wife, and three children. For besides the two children we know of, he had yet another daughter, nine years of age, who was not at home when we first entered his hovel.

What a life his must have been, through a very severe winter, accompanied by great scarcity and consequent high prices of fuel and provisions!

A soup made of potatoes and spiced with a spoonful of rancid lard, which, on account of its being spoiled, was sold somewhat cheaper by a neighbouring shopkeeper, was a meal, nay, a feast to this family. But even when they had boiled potatoes and a little salt, they were satisfied. Their daily food consisted in dry bread, accompanied by a draught of water, and the wretches would have been contented if they could always have obtained even that. But their miseries increased from day to day.

It was yet early morning. The weaver had again passed part of the night at his work. Fatigue had suddenly overpowered him, and he had fallen asleep upon his loom, with arms crossed over his work, and his sorrowful head resting upon them.

His sick wife lay upon her mattrass; she breathed loud and heavy. By her side slumbered her infant, and at her feet lay the boy and the girl, both very scantily covered by a few rags.

Gradually it had grown lighter; the weaver had blown out his dim lamp, highly delighted at being able to save a little oil by the prolonging days.

Fearful dreams were disturbing his slumbers. His body moved restlessly about the wooden bench.

"Mercy! oh, mercy!" he cried, in his sleep, in broken tones, "have pity—my wife—they hungered—blood—oh Heaven!"

"Jacob, Jacob, rouse yourself!" cried the wife to him from her couch, "what ails you? you are dreaming!"

"Blood—blood," again groaned the weaver.

"For Heaven's sake!" again cried the wife, "wake, wake, and rouse yourself, Jacob!—Oh that I could only reach him," she sighed, as she sunk exhausted back upon her bed.

The weaver started up.

"Thank Heaven! I was dreaming," he said, rising, looking slowly around him, and even trembling at the bare remembrance. "I dreamed that the manufacturer was here, and was about to carry me before the police on account of that yarn, and that I killed him."

"This is the consequence of your working so late. You will yet make yourself sick," observed his wife.

"Is it in my power to help it?" replied the weaver in great bitterness. "But my dream was so lively; I could feel the blood of the manufacturer trickle down my fingers, I could see it. The cause of it may possibly have been, that I had to cease working in the night, because my right hand had become too sore to work; my blood may even now stain the webb I then wove. And you know that we often dream at night of

what has happened during the day, only in different shapes."

"If dreams also presage events which are to happen," said the wife, "then I shall die soon. I have this night seen myself in a coffin. After all, that would be the best release from my sufferings."

"And I, what would become of me?" replied the weaver, with a heavy sigh. "Who would assist me in bringing up the children, or in attending to domestic affairs and house-keeping?"

"And now, my dear husband, I certainly do not assist from my sick bed! And where have we any house-keeping to do?"

"Well, you will soon get well again, my dear wife, and we must have patience until then," replied the weaver, consolingly, without feeling hope or consolation himself.—"I will now recommence my work, that we may soon redeem the yarn, and then, I am sure, we shall have at least one great trouble less. How we are to satisfy our hunger to day, I really don't know!"

Sighing, the weaver sat down to his loom, and again began the monotonous rattling of the machine.

"My spools will soon be empty," he began, after a little while; "I must awake Anne, who must sit down to the spooling wheel and prepare new ones for me."

"My dear husband," prayed the wife, "do let the poor child sleep a little longer, it is not even six o'clock yet; she was so worn out by work yesterday, and you know it was very late when she went to bed."

"What, thunder," cried the weaver with assumed severity, "am I to work myself to death alone? I cannot help her. Anne, halloo, get out of your nest and sit down to the spooling wheel."

Frightened at the well known call, the little girl raised her head and stretched her wearied limbs.

"Well, are you coming?" continued the father in a scolding voice. "You are lazy, and I have scarcely a single spool left."

"Father, I don't believe that, for Anne is not lazy," cried the boy, who also awoke, "Anne is not lazy. You are lazy, and I saw you sleep a little while ago."

"My dear father," began the girl with a crying tone of voice, "may I not lie half an hour longer? My hands are still so very sore from yesterday, and I can scarcely get up, with weakness.

These words from his children deeply touched the heart of the weaver. His assumed harshness soon made way before his bitter tears.

"My dear Anne," he said gently, "you must continue to work, else I can give you nothing to eat this day, and your mother and your brother must be hungry also."

"Don't do it, Anne," cried the little obstinate boy, "for we have to hunger at any rate."

"For shame, Anthony," said the mother faintly, "you always have bread?"

Yes, but not enough of it," answered the boy.

The little girl had risen and walked towards the spooling wheel. "Oh, how cold it is here," she began, "but now father you must first give me something to eat, else I cannot work at all?"

The weaver slowly walked towards the corner of the room, and from a box which stood on the floor, took a hard crust of brown bread, of which he gave a few mouthsful to the girl. He could not give her anything more nourishing, although he saw full well to what very great danger her health was exposed by these exertions, which were so much beyond her age and power.

"There, my child," he said, with averted looks, "only hold out this one week, and you shall not have to work so much afterwards; we shall fare somewhat better too."

The weaver had already saved so much, that he only wanted half a thaler more to make the full amount which was needed to redeem the yarn. On the next Saturday, when he hoped to have a piece of goods done, he intended to deduct that half thaler from his earnings, and redeem the yarn he had pledged. If he had only known how to keep his family from starvation meanwhile, without touching that sum.

The scene we have just described occurred on Tuesday, and Greif saw himself much nearer the accomplishment of his wishes, than he had almost dared to hope. Hitherto the fear, that the manufacturer might demand back his yarn, and on learning what he had done with it, send him to prison, had almost pressed him to the ground.

That the manufacturer might have pity or humanity enough to overlook and forgive the matter, if he would openly tell him his sad position, never even occurred to his thought. He, as well as his fellow workmen, had long accustomed themselves to look upon their master as on an inaccessible rock. They never considered him as a human being, who could be moved, whose feelings and sympathies could be aroused, but looked upon him as on a machine, which continues its unchangeable evolutions, and which mechanically annihilates all that comes into accidental opposition to its regular movement.

Greif, therefore, in his greatest troubles, could never hope that the manufacturer, if he should learn that the yarn was pledged, would be lenient on account of the poor man's misery—on the contrary, he was fully convinced, that he would immediately be imprisoned. The weaver well knew the standing phrase, which the manufacturer would use on this, as he had done on similar occasions: "I must let the law take its course. If I show myself lenient to you, I will establish a bad precedent, and the other rascals will play me the same trick."

Although Greif had formerly often wished that he might be imprisoned, because then his poor, sick wife and his starving children would be provided for, yet he was too much afraid when the actual danger approached. And in this we find a proof of the inner moral principle, which possessed not alone his breast, but those of hundreds of his companions in misery. We find hundreds of examples where these poor people even then detest crime, when, by its discovery, and by the punishment which awaits them, they can only improve their wretched condition.

In how far this assertion might be carried out, is plainly shown in a very peculiar point of our criminal code, the laws and regulations concerning begging. The experience of all courts of justice shows, that the fewest number of beggars are also thieves, although it would be natural, if instead of beggars, we would have nothing but thieves, since by a strange contradiction in our legal system, beggary is almost invariably more severely punished than theft. There is evidently no other motive in this, than the greater disgrace of the theft, which must make begging appear in a more agreeable light.

Such also was the case with Greif the weaver.

If his crime was discovered, what disadvantage would it be to him, in the end? He would be taken to prison, to a warm, airy and well lighted room, while at present he was confined to a damp, cold and dark cellar. In prison he would receive sufficient and warm food, while at present he often had to live for whole days upon a little crust of bread.

Or was he perhaps afraid of the loss of his liberty?—He was even now, worse than in a dungeon, he was chained to his loom, which he dared not leave for a moment. His children, if he went to prison, would be taken to the orphan asylum, where, compared to their present situation, they would be well fed and well clothed. His wife would be taken to a public hospital, where she would receive the best of medical attendance, of which she had none whatever at present.

What then could the weaver desire? What did he hope—what fear?

And yet he worked with superhuman industry and perseverance, to escape imprisonment. And yet he bitterly rued the criminal act he had committed, and endeavoured by all means in his power, to undo what he had done.

The fear of shame, the fear of being subjected to the horrors of a trial and imprisonment, and having once been so, of being forced to commit new crimes, this it is that urges him on to exertions.

It is of the most incalculable advantage to the welfare of society, since the great abyss which divides the upper from the lower classes, has become so deep, that even crime and its punishment may be an alleviation of their misery, that there may still be some confidence placed in the moral feelings of the lower classes.

But then it is the duty of the rich to award the proper acknowledgment to this honourable feeling of the poor, to alleviate their misery, before necessity will compel them to alleviate it by crime.

———

CHAPTER XLVIII.

IT IS EASIER FOR A CAMEL TO GO THROUGH THE EYE OF A NEEDLE, &c.

FATHER and daughter continued uninterruptedly to work for some hours.

The forenoon had somewhat advanced, still the father was steady at his loom, and the daughter at her spooling-wheel; the former had not yet eaten anything, the latter only a crust of bread.

About ten o'clock a knock was heard at the door. The postman entered the room, and delivered an unpaid city letter.

"One Groschen," said the postman politely.

"A letter for me and unpaid?" inquired the weaver, leaving his loom in astonishment.

"A letter for weaver Greif," read the other, "and I suppose you are the person."

The weaver examined the letter from every side. "It costs a Groschen," he said, "then I shall not take the letter."

"Very well," replied the carrier, "will you be kind enough to mark it, 'returned?'"

"My dear sir, I have neither pen nor ink," answered the weaver, still examining the letter.

"That is very bad!"

"My dear husband," began the sick woman from her couch, "keep the letter, it may perhaps bring us better luck. We cannot be more unfortunate than we are."

After a short pause, the weaver silently nodded assent.

He approached the bed where his wife lay, and from beneath her straw mattress he produced a dirty linen rag, which contained all his little wealth. He then took out a Groschen, and paid for the letter.

The postman withdrew.

"I hope it may be God's will, that this letter bring us better fortune," began the weaver, as he approached the window, "for we now want another Groschen more, of the amount necessary to redeem that yarn."

He opened the letter and read:

"Berlin, 15th March, 18—

"Weaver Greif is requested to deliver the yarn he has from us, or the goods manufactured therefrom, by one o'clock this day, otherwise we shall inform the Police of his fraud.

"GOTTFRIED STENDAL & CO."

The weaver had begun to read the letter in a loud tone of voice; at the second line, however, his voice faltered and refused its office; rapidly his burning eyes pursued the note, and the paper fell from his trembling hand.

This stroke fell like a thunderbolt upon his head. All his exertions, all his endeavours had been useless; in vain had he and his whole family worked and starved, disgrace and shame approached with gigantic strides.

He buried his face within his hands, and with a cry of terror, he sank upon his stool.

"Husband, what is the matter, speak, for Heaven's sake, speak," cried the woman from her couch, where she had half risen in her excitement.

The arms of the poor man fell relaxed by his side; an ashy hue overspread his features, and his head sunk back upon the bench behind him.

"Mother, oh mother, father is dying," cried the little girl, who started up in horror from her wheel, and rushed towards her father.

"Father, dear father, don't die," cried little Anthony, who was still lying on the couch. On seeing his sister weep, he also burst into a flood of tears.

Horrified, the poor woman started up. With a last exertion of all her strength, she endeavoured to leave her bed, and reach the side of her husband. Arrived at the middle of the room, however, consciousness left her mind, already exhausted and over-harrassed by the occurrences of the morning; she fell upon the damp floor in a swoon.

The redoubled cries of horror which the children uttered, who now supposed their mother dead also, restored the weaver to his senses.

With a wild, desperate stare his tall figure rose up. His eye fell upon his wife, who insensibly lay upon the floor.

"Would that she were dead," he said gloomily to himself, "then to her at least, the end of this misery would have come."

With great difficulty he raised the fainting woman, and carried her to her couch. Then he took all the money he had, picked up his ragged hat, and without noticing the children, he rushed out into the street.

He started straight towards the office of Abraham Loebell, the pawnbroker.

"A drowning man catches at straws." Greif foolishly believed that the pawnbroker would let him have the yarn, by paying him all the ready cash he possessed, and that he would trust him the balance of the debt, only half a thaler, upon his honest face. How difficult it is for a poor man, or a drowning one, to abandon hope!

The pawnbroker stood behind the counter in his little office, which we already know.

He was in a very ill humour, for he had just made the discovery, that an old customer who had been in the habit of regularly bringing a particular pledge, which was carefully packed up, and which he so regularly redeemed, that Herr Loebell frequently received it without examining the articles, had changed these articles the last time for worthless ones, and had not, of course, come to redeem them.

Herr Abraham Loebell, who in this manner lost a thaler, after he had by similar cheats gained frequently twenty, was almost beside himself at the dishonesty and worthlessness of mankind in general, and of his own customers in particular.

He moved his green eye-screen now to the

right and left, and swore that he would never again put faith in anybody.

Our poor weaver consequently came at a doubly unfortunate time.

Without being discouraged by the uncouth and coarse reception he received, he represented his position to the pawnbroker, begged him earnestly for the delivery of the yarn, and promised positively to pay the deficient half thaler by the next Saturday.

The Jew listened in perfect silence, only rubbing a large pinch of snuff into his big, red nose. He even created a hope in the breast of the poor weaver, that his prayers would be graciously listened to, nay, would perhaps be granted. But unfortunately, when Herr Loebell took such a pinch, it was an infallible forerunner of an approaching tempest.

" Ash I live !" he cried furiously, when the weaver finally stopped, " what ish that you have shaid to me ? I shall trust you a half thaler of my monish on your honest face ? What ish the worth of your honest face ? What can I get for your honest face, if I sell it ? Nothing will I believe ! No, I believe nobody ; I must see. When you bring me the monish, you shall have your yarn. Only just now an accursed Goi has cheated me of my good monish ; but I have become wise. Get the monish, and then you can come again to Abraham Loebell."

The weaver endeavoured once more to describe his unfortunate position to the pawnbroker, and he spoke most touchingly, most eloquently.

" It won't do," insisted the Jew, " in my ledger, I have no page and no column for obligations and kindness ; a bushiness ish a bushiness. Look here ; here I write down the debtor ; here I write down the pledge, and here stands the amount of monish. What shall I write down for a pledge, if I give you back the yarn ? Shall I write down your word ? If you cannot bring me the half thaler, bring me another pledge, that shall be worth half a thaler, and you can have the yarn."

" Shall I have myself, or my wife, or my children packed up and laid upon your shelf as a pledge ?" inquired the weaver bitterly ; " for besides these, I possess nothing."

" Well, then, I cannot help you," said the pawnbroker. " You are a poor man, and I am a poor man, and two poor people cannot give monish to each other. We will better let the bushiness remain as it is."

" For the sake of Heaven's mercy," cried the weaver, beside himself in despair, as he cast himself at the feet of the pawnbroker, " do for once a good deed ; save a despairing, wretched family from prison and disgrace. The yarn is not my own. Do you hear," he cried, with still louder voice, " do you hear, the yarn is not my own, but belongs to the manufacturer who demands it back of me."

" As I live," cried Herr Loebell, as he drew back in evident fright, " the Goi is getting raving. What do I care for the manufacturer ? As I hope to see the God of Abraham, I shall not give up the yarn, without the entire monish. Go way, I tell you, or I must shend for the Commisshary of Police, as you are a dangerous man."

By a retreating movement, Herr Loebell had gained the back door, and had thence quickly escaped into a sideroom, carefully looking at the further proceedings of the desperate weaver through a little sliding window.

Gnashing with rage and mortification, Greif rose to his feet. The fury which he felt at his own useless humiliation before the Jew, almost overpowered him ; but he remembered his poor wife whom he had left in a swoon, and his weeping children, and silently he crept from the pawnbroker's office.

Mechanically he took the way towards his home. What he would or should do there, he himself knew not. He walked instinctively, like an animal towards its stable—no, not as contented as an animal that scents its crib.

When he had arrived at the yard in front of his domicile, the loud crying of his children aroused him from his lethargy. Only then he remembered in what situation he had left his wife, and oppressed by fearful presentiments, he hurried down to his cellar. He rushed into his room.

" Oh father, I am so glad you have come at last," cried the little girl, " I was so much afraid, for mother looks so very pale, and that stupid boy, Anthony, continually cries, " she is dead, she is dead," and yet she keeps my little brother tight in her arms, so she cannot be dead."

The weaver, with weak, tottering steps approached the couch ; his wife was dead.

The extraordinary mental exertions of the morning, the terror of the preceding days, and finally the physical sufferings and wants to which she had so long been exposed, had cut short the thread of her existence.

Her baby was still grasped in her arms ; gently and innocently it had fallen asleep upon the corps. Thus her sad dream had been fulfilled.

With dark and gloomy looks the weaver stared upon the wasted, haggard frame of his once beautiful wife. Bitter sorrow shook the frame of the strong man, and every limb trembled convulsively ; he could not shed a relieving tear.

Immoveably he sank down upon the wooden stool by the side of the bed. " Children," he said, without losing the terrible quietness of his features, " children, your mother is dead."

After these words he sank back into a calm, silent lethargy of despair, from which even the heart-rending cries of his children, which followed his speech, were unable to awake him.

The blow had come upon him with terrible suddenness, and had benumbed all the mental powers of the poor weaver. The unfortunate man, at this moment did not live, he merely vegetated.

Suddenly another knock is heard at the door.

No one answers the knock, or invites entrance. After a short pause, the door opens without that invitation. A young, fashionably dressed man, with long blonde hair, and rather silly appearance, enters the cellar.

"Does the weaver, Jacob Greif, live here?" he inquired, with a very thin voice.

The weaver continues to stare at the corpse of his wife, without answering a word.

"I come from Messrs. Stendal & Co.," says the strange young man, as he produces his silken and perfumed pocket handkerchief, and endeavours to protect himself against the bad, damp odour of the cellar. "I wish to inquire whether the yarn, or the goods manufactured therefrom, has been delivered?"

The weaver looks at the young man, bursts into a fearful, terrible fit of laughter, and again silently fixes his gaze upon the dead body of his wife.

The stranger seemingly begins to feel uncomfortable, looks timidly around, and quickly leaves the room.

In the street, before the house, stops the splendid carriage of Herr Stendal.

The manufacturer was carelessly leaning back upon the swelling cushions of his beautiful Vienna carriage, rocking himself easily upon its elastic spring seats, whilst he slowly blew the smoke of a fragrant Havanna through his nostrils.

The fine, powerful horses stamped, and sniffed the cold winter-air, rattling their elegantly plated harness with pride and impatience.

"Well, *Herr Ahldorff*, how do things look?" he exclaimed, as he saw his clerk returning through the entry of the front house.

"I don't know, Herr Stendal, what to say to it. The weaver is sitting by the bed of his sick wife, and upon my question, he burst into a terrible laughter. Every thing appeared strange and fearful to me; I think he must have lost his senses."

"Just as I thought," said the manufacturer, taking up his large gold-headed cane and furiously striking the seat of his carriage; "I will tell you what he has done. He has lost his honesty. My dear Mr. Ahldorff, you have not yet learned, by far, how this villainous rabble is to be treated. This weaver has sold or pledged the yarn, or the Lord knows in what other manner he has made way with it. Now that the halter is at his neck, he avails himself of your inexperience, to play the madman to you. But just wait; I will soon bring him back to his senses; only please to come with me."

The manufacturer rose from his seat, and with the assistance of his clerk, he left the carriage.

He was a small man, of a rotund figure, with a broad, beardless, ordinary looking face, the coppery nose of which bore strong indications of his fondness for good wine. Before his grey, inexpressive eyes, he wore a pair of gold spectacles. In the unclean shirt-bosom which could be seen under the richly wadded overcoat of very fine cloth, an immensely large solitair might be seen, which, beside the needle, was secured around the fleshy neck by a gold chain. A many-coloured silk pocket handkerchief hung to the length of half a yard from his coat pocket.

Supporting himself on his heavy cane, Herr Stendal stamped through the front house, across the yard, and towards the dwelling of the weaver.

"Thunder, how bad it 'smells here!" he exclaimed, as both were descending the stairs; "just wait one moment."

At these words, the dainty manufacturer produced from his pocket a brilliant *tabatiere*, which a short time before had been given to him by a Prince, to whom he had presented a particularly fine fabric. After taking a pinch of Spanish snuff, he said: "Now you may open this confounded hole."

Both entered the damp cellar-room.

Immoveable the weaver still sat upon his wooden stool, staring at the corpse of his wife, as before.

At the sight of the stranger, the two children fled behind their father, and crying and weeping, hung to his arms.

"Good day, Greif," said the manufacturer, remaining standing in the door.

The weaver was silent.

"Hallo, sir vagabond; you, who passes himself for sick, don't you hear? I wish to know how matters stand; is your work or my yarn delivered at my counting-room?"

Still no answer.

"Now, may the devil take this obstinate, rascally weaver!" exclaimed Herr Stendal, furiously, as he approached closer, and roughly shook the weaver by the collar; "you scoundrel, I wish to know what has become of my yarn? Do you understand me?"

Frightened, the children looked upon the threatening man, and pressed closer to their father.

"You have pledged or sold my yarn," cried the manufacturer, shaking the weaver, still more furiously; "is it not so?"

"Silence, silence!" said the weaver, in a low tone of voice, and without looking up. "Please don't wake my wife, for she has only gone to sleep for a moment."

On hearing these words, the manufacturer directed his looks towards the bed, and recoiled in horror. The death-struggle had terribly disfigured the features of the deceased; the broken eye stared half-open, like a terrible, revengeful apparition, upon the hard-hearted usurer.

"Hm, hm," he said, quickly retreating towards his clerk, who still waited at the door, "she really is dead! How disgusting and disagreeable! Ahldorff, I don't like to see dead bodies; the smell is very offensive to me. Where is my snuff-box? Come, Ahldorff, let us go."

And both hastily left the cellar.

Arrived at the yard, Herr Stendal stopped. "Oh, I forgot; that affair about the yarn is not yet arranged. Hm! just go in and tell the weaver, that, under existing circumstances, I will give him a couple of hours longer time, and he may deliver the yarn at three o'clock. But if he fails at that hour, I will certainly inform the Police."

"My dear Mr. Stendal," began the clerk, "don't you think it would be better to let the poor devil off this time? After all, what are a few bundles of yarn to us? The poor fellow is already wretched enough."

"Hm! Harkye, Mr. Ahldorff, as long as you remain in the employ of our house, you will please to fulfil commissions that are given to you, without questions or objections. You know my principles upon these subjects: I must let the law take its course, else I shall set a bad example by my leniency, and all the other rascals will play me the same trick."

The clerk returned to the dwelling of the weaver, and delivered his commission, as he had been ordered.

His words suddenly roused the weaver from his long and terrible lethargy.

He raised up his head.

"What?" he exclaimed, despairingly wringing both his hands, "and now you would tear me from my children? Now you would give me into the hands of the police to shame and misery? Who is to bury my poor, unfortunate wife? Who will take pity on these wretched, helpless children? Are they to starve? Mercy! mercy! oh mercy! I can pay the money to redeem the pledged yarn, all but half a thaler, no, all but sixteen Silbergroschen—Mercy, oh mercy!"

The clerk shrugged his shoulders, and left the room.

A moment afterwards the carriage rattled off. Herr Stendal wanted to ride in the Thiergarden, as the oysters he had eaten the day before, did not agree with him.

CHAPTER XLIX.

HELP IN NEED.

THE weaver had remained alone. Alone with the dead body of his wife, alone with his starving children, and his despairing heart.

He raved, foamed, wept, cried even louder than his children, and then—sat down to his loom, and quietly began to work.

This was the force of habit, a terrible, fearful habit, which even vanquished all the pangs he felt within his soul.

Did he know why or wherefore he worked?— He could not know it, for in a few hours a prison must be his home. His labour was without end or aim. Yet he laboured; he seemed to have forgotten himself, his children, to have forgotten all around him, even his own position, to look upon the future with gloomy, terrible indifference, yet—*he continued to work.*

Thus man becomes a machine, and that machine works and rattles on, as long as it is wound up, feelingless, and dead to joy and sorrow.

The noisy, stormy and terrible scenes of the morning, were succeeded by a deadly silence in the weaver's dwelling.

The corpse lay untouched upon the straw mattress, still holding the life warm infant at its breast.

The boy and the girl had timidly cowed down in a corner, looking fearfully now at their dead mother, then at their father, and again upon each other.

The loom rattled, and filled the room with its creaking noisy tones. Behind it sat the weaver, sending his shuttle to and fro across the warp, and hummed in an under tone:

"Rattle, rattle, rattle,
Little wheel, now rattle,
Little wheel,
     Free and bold,
Little stick,
     Bright as gold,
I am a free weaver alone,
The king I don't envy his throne.
Rattle, rattle, rattle,
Little wheel, now rattle."

A knock is heard at the door.

"Ho ho!" cried the weaver, "they come for me quickly; come in, come in."

"Rattle, rattle, rattle,
Little wheel, now rattle,
Little wheel,
     Free and bold."

"Come in, I say," he repeated in a louder voice, as the persons without seemed to stop and hesitate.

The door opened, and Augusta Strass, leaning upon the arm of Lieutenant von Steinfort, entered the room. In her hand she carried the bundles of yarn which the weaver had pledged.

Trifling and small are often the external signs and causes which mightily determine and change the inner life of man's soul.

As soon as the weaver saw the yarn, he jumped up from his labour as if he had received an electric shock.

"My yarn is here," he cried frantically, tearing the package from the girl's hand, "my yarn is here again. I shall remain an honest man, thank Heaven. My yarn is here again! Here, take this, take all I possess."

In wild, frantic haste, he tore the little money he had saved from his pocket, and spread it upon the bench before Augusta. Then he started up again, jumped about the room, swinging the yarn like a flag over his head, while big tears of joy rolled down his face.

"Huzza! my yarn is here! I must away! quick, quick, I must away, before misfortune comes to my dwelling. Huzza! I am saved, my children are saved, all, everything is saved!"

Without stopping to ask the strangers the why or the wherefore, without even taking his coat or his hat, the weaver rushes from the room, hurrying with the yarn towards the house of the manufacturer.

Should we be astonished at this ingratitude, at the apparent egotism of this man? Certainly not. This was the egotism of honesty, which had to free itself from the stains of an involuntarily committed crime. We will not doubt the warmest gratitude of the unfortunate man; but we will not ask him to express it at the overpowering moment of his salvation.

It may serve to illustrate a beautiful trait in his character, that the disabling lethargy of mind into which he had been thrown by the most terrible of misfortunes, from which even the love for his children, or the threats of the manufacturer, only had roused him for a moment, to let him quickly relapse into deeper unconsciousness—that this lethargy, this terrible unconsciousness, was quickly vanquished by the bare possibility of *preserving his name as an honest citizen.* Spite of all his misery, spite of all his misfortunes, the weaver had awoke to fresh energy, as soon as Augusta had removed the stain from his character; the proof that he had awoke to fresh life, was to be found in the very anxiety, in the very activity with which he hastened to secure his honest name.

We repeat it: this is not an overdrawn, not even a solitary picture. Often, very often, similar ones may be found in the dark dens of misery and want, if we choose to search for them.

Weaver Greif is only another proof of what we asserted above, about the moral feeling of honour among the lower classes—a feeling which, perhaps, ere long, may become a more powerful lever of the future destinies of nations, than pride, idleness, blindness and arrogance have hitherto been willing to acknowledge.

CHAPTER L.

A GOOD DEED.

LET us avail ourselves of the time during which the weaver must necessarily be absent, to inform our readers, what fortunate circumstances those were, through which the seamstress happened to appear by the side of her lover, as a saving angel to the weaver, at the moment of his greatest need.

Accidentally, on the evening before, Lieutenant von Steinfort had found upon Augusta's worktable, the certificate of the linen she had pledged. He had reproached the girl about it, and from her had received a full and explicit confession of all the circumstances of the affair.

Steinfort felt greatly moved, and at the same time ashamed, at these disclosures. It had never occurred to him, that Augusta might probably be forced to deny herself many necessary things through a want of money; ever since childhood he himself had been so far removed from poverty, that he only knew it by name, could have no real or practical conception of its actual pangs, bitterness and misery. With the best possible intentions, he had often made Augusta presents of the most valuable articles of luxury and dress, whilst, perhaps, she went supperless to bed on the same evening.

Now, however, his vision suddenly became more clear, but at the same time the girl gained greatly in his estimation. She had thankfully received his presents, but never had complained to him of her wants; she had rather redoubled her labour to gain her own support, although she might have known perfectly well, that it only needed one word from her to Steinfort, to obtain her an easy, comfortable life.

Steinfort possessed enough delicacy of feeling not to offer her support even now, which, though it would have freed her from labour, would still have made her externally dependent on him. He only requested her to accept so much money from him as would be sufficient to redeem her pledged linen, as he explained to her that it would be a disgrace to himself, to know her to be in the hands of a shameless usurer. He determined, on the following day to accompany her to the pawnbroker's, for, by the present and former disclosures of the girl, a world had opened to his eyes, which was as surprising as it was novel to him—the world of poverty and wretchedness.

He now desired to become more acquainted with its manifold regions, partly to learn lessons therefrom, partly to find occupation for the idle time of his military life. He became daily more convinced that a great, blissful, and dignified sphere of action was open for the wealthy, if the wealthy class possessed energy and moral strength sufficient to undertake the task, instead of reducing their own existence by luxury, dissipation, and extravagance.

Perhaps the late occurrences at the "French house" may have exercised a great deal of influence, and may even have produced these views and this conviction, upon the mind of the Lieutenant. He had not further spoken with Augusta upon the occurrences of that evening, but had quietly conducted her home. On the following day, when she herself directed the conversation towards the subject, he had dismissed it briefly, as a mere matter of fun or indifference. Thus all further explanations upon that occurrence was broken off, and both kept their views and sentiments to themselves, without letting each other know anything about them.

Steinfort wished the matter to terminate thus; he felt himself too deeply excited to enter into a calm conversation on the subject, and he particularly wished to erase any disagreeable impression this occurrence might have created on the girl's mind. We cannot, for the present, pretend to say, in how far he had succeeded in this. As far as he himself was concerned, after his first momentary, confusing surprise, he began to perceive something of the great, powerful and immense social barriers which he had boldly attempted to overleap.

He began to understand that obstacles did exist, which hitherto he had not dreamed of, which he had even considered impossible, and these soon filled his noble and exalted mind with the most burning hatred against their tyranny. He declared himself not vanquished, not even intimidated or abashed, but remained firmly determined to obtain for his loved girl, an acknowledgment of that position, to which her excellent qualities entitled her. This he would attain, let it cost what it might;, but the excitement of his mind, caused him to seek for a quieting, but at the same time, strengthening element. He sought as it were, for a union between himself and the rest of mankind, for the purpose of finding in this union, strength and courage for new struggles against the hated and abhorred elements of society. He required a resting place, whence the society in which he was born to live, and with his Augusta—as he hoped—would live, would appear less contemptible to his eyes.

Such a union, such a resting place to him, seemed poverty—the suffering, the patient side of society, that side which is the only one devoid of false glimmer and hypocrisy.

Whether Steinfort was mistaken, whether his originally noble nature lacked the necessary practical experience, whether it was strong enough to oppose the almighty power of existing rules and practices, whether he did not moreover bring himself, by his ill-applied noble efforts and intentions, a sacrifice to the existing order of things, all this, we can only learn in the course of our narrative.

At present we only see how he looked upon things, what impressions the occurrences which we have witnessed made upon him, and what determinations followed these impressions—these determinations were at least noble and honourable enough to make us wish their richest success.

* * * * * *

* * * * * *

According to his intentions, Steinfort on the following morning had gone with Augusta to the pawnbroker, and had entered into a close conversation with that worthy.

Augusta had very soon arranged her little business, paid the pawnbroker, and received her linen. With a secret joy she pressed the bundle beneath her cloak ; it contained the fruits of her own industry, the products of her own needle ; she had thrown them out upon the wide world, and was rejoiced at being allowed again to carry them safely home, after having gone through so much anxiety for them.

The pawnbroker had become lively and talkative during the transaction of this business. He said, that if he had all such customers, who so soon redeemed their things again, and always paid punctually and correctly, it would be an easy and pleasant matter to conduct the business, and there might something be made by it. But he was sorry to say that such instances were of rare occurrence.

Steinfort desired to have this observation a little more explained and particularized, and the pawnbroker took this opportunity, to rail against the general dishonesty of mankind, and of his own customers in particular. As an example, he cited a certain vagabond-weaver, who had that moment left his office, and who had a few days ago, pledged a lot of yarn, which was entrusted to him by his employer. This rascal had even the assurance of coming to him and demanding it back, without repaying the "monish." The weaver, moreover, had talked very loud, in fact, had made him quite nervous by his behaviour, and would now certainly march to the prison for his swindling ; yet an honest pawnbroker was compelled to have intercourse with such persons.

Augusta's attention was hereby quickly excited, and upon her hasty inquiry, she learned that the weaver in question was no other than Greif.

In shame she confessed to herself, that the occurrences at the "French house," and her own excited state since, had totally caused her to forget that unfortunate man. The picture of the pale, haggard, despairing weaver, now rose strongly before her imagination, and urged on in her good resolves, by the immediate presence of her dear Steinfort, she soon explained all the circumstances to him. He had latterly conversed with her so frequently about poverty and its consequences, as well as its remedies, that she no longer hesitated to proffer her petition for the assistance of the poor weaver.

The Lieutenant immediately declared himself ready and willing to do the work of charity, and on depositing double its value, received the yarn even without the certificate of pledge.

The pawnbroker was now also able to designate the place where the weaver lived. He had ascertained this at the proper office, for the purpose of bringing his book in order as soon as he had learned that the weaver had pledged yarns not belonging to him. This being the case, he might momentarily expect the police to pay a visit to his office, to inquire for the yarn and the full address of the pledger.

Nothing then prevented our friends from starting immediately to the dwelling of the weaver, where, as we already know, they arrived at the moment of greatest need.

After the sudden disappearance of the weaver, Steinfort looked around, first with disgust, then with curiosity, and at last with every sign of the most intense pity.

Never had he imagined that poverty could look thus. In such terrible, gloomy black colours, even his most lively fancy had never painted it.

The dirty, patched windows, through which scarcely fell a scanty ray of light, the floor boards with their large holes, the wretched bits of furniture, consisting of the loom, bedstead, and wooden stool, the ragged straw mattrass, with a cold, bluish corpse upon it, the two emaciated children scantily covered with a few rags, who still sat shivering in a corner—all this created a most terrible impression upon his mind.

12

"For Heaven's sake, tell me," said Steinfort, half aloud, after a long pause of silent astonishment, "how is this possible? And is this place inhabited by human beings? I would not allow my horses to stay in such a place."

"This place is inhabited by human beings, or rather, to speak more intelligibly, by weavers,* who would be contented even here, if they had only enough to still their hunger. But here you behold their only, at least, their almost entire food."

At these words she pointed to the box in the corner, which still contained a part of the crust of brown bread, from which the little girl had received her breakfast.

"This poor woman, most probably has died of hunger," said Steinfort, approaching the bed, "and we, who are rich, destroy more at a single meal, throw away more, than would suffice to support such a family for eight days."

"My dear Steinfort," replied Augusta gently, "*eight weeks*, ay, and even longer they would live upon it, if necessary."

At these words she approached the children, to bring them out of their corner. But the poor wretches were so terrified, so frightened, that they only replied with silence to the kindest, the most friendly words. When Augusta took the boy by the hand, he cried aloud in fear and terror.

Steinfort found a little biscuit in his pocket, and offered it to the children; they took it, and without uttering a syllable, devoured it in the most ravenous manner.

The cries of the boy had awakened the infant, who had hitherto unobserved slumbered upon the breast of the corpse. He now began to move, and burst forth into a loud wailing. His little head sought instinctively for the mother's breast.

"Oh, how terrible!" cried Steinfort, observing the child; "my dear Augusta, at least take this young innocent babe from the fearful, pestilential neighbourhood of death."

With difficulty, the two freed the child from the firm death grasp of its mother, and laid it at the foot of the couch, where its exhaustion and weakness soon again threw it into slumbers.

Weaver Greif returned, his face still red and flushed, and the perspiration trickling down his forehead, from the over-exertion of his haste, and the greatly excited state of his mind.

"So, here I am back again," he cried, as he rushed into the room, "now I am honest; God be praised, the police no longer has any share in me! But, good Heavens," he continued, warmly taking Augusta's hand, "how shall I thank you? Look you, my dear Mam'selle, you have delivered a poor man from bitter shame, and may the good angels in heaven reward you for it. I don't think that you yourself can well spare it; but what I can repay you, that I will repay; I will work, yes, work as hard as these poor bones

will bear. Oh Heavens! I am so happy, I don't know whether to laugh or to weep. But meanwhile only take this money here. Why do you leave it there? Thank God, I am so happy!"

At these words, urged by his great mental excitement, the weaver run restlessly up and down the room, now taking Augusta's hand, again clapping his own—a touching picture of honest joy.

"You are mistaken, my good neighbour," said the girl, "you need not thank me for this assistance, but you owe it to this gentleman, who came with me."

For a moment the weaver stared at the Lieutenant, who stood before him in plain, elegant citizen's dress.

"Oh, please to pardon me, my dear sir," he said abashed, "I have not even greeted you; the joy, the pleasure, the fears—my head sometimes seems to wander—well, oh yes—to you I have to give my thanks?—But I suppose you will want my thanks still less than this young lady; such a fine, elegant gentleman, needs not the thanks of a poor, humble weaver."

At these words, he took the hand of the Lieutenant, and attempted to kiss it. With difficulty the latter withdrew it.

"Let that be, my good man," said Steinfort, in a friendly tone. "I am convinced that you are an honest man, which is worth more to me than all your thanks. Will you rather tell me what you intend to begin next?"

"What can I begin?" said the weaver, suddenly growing sad again; "I must work, work to support my children, and I would most willingly work, but this very morning I have lost my poor wife, and I must first go and endeavour to beg her an honest funeral. Perhaps, meanwhile, another of my children may starve; then I must seek to bury that, and so on, until they are all dead."

The weaver pronounced these words in tones of such bitter, hopeless despair, that Steinfort felt his very soul torn by the intense misery he witnessed.

The poor weaver really was in a most desperate situation. "I don't know what I am to begin," he said; "at home I have no bread, and if I seek it out of doors, I must leave my children alone. Now with the smallest of them, with that poor little infant, I am particularly badly off; for that needs female care and attendance. Alas, alas! and then an interment; the expenses of an interment, where am I ever to get them from?"

Steinfort could not bear to listen any longer to all this misery. Augusta's communication, as well as the entire behaviour of the man, had convinced him that he would not bestow his charity upon an unworthy person, if here he gave assistance.

"Now listen, my poor Greif," he began, "you must never lose all courage; things usually go better than you think of in your despair. I am determined to assist you. Give me the money you saved and laid upon the bench yonder, and I will keep that in remembrance of an honest man. But in return, here is for the present, the sum of one hundred thalers. Defray with this the expenses of the interment of your wife, bring your poor children somewhere to be taken care of, and then seek for yourself another and a more healthy dwelling. My fair companion here will gladly assist you in every way in her power. Then I shall expect you in a few days at my house, and we will consult together what is best to be done. You will find my address upon this card."

At these words, the Lieutenant handed the weaver two treasury notes of fifty thalers each, together with his own card, and in return put the money intended for the pawnbroker, consisting in coppers and small silver coin, into his pocket.

The weaver stood like a marble statue. Without uttering a sound, he stared alternately at the money, the Lieutenant, and Augusta. But before he could gather his senses, both had left the place.

"I thank you, my dearest Augusta," said Steinfort, after they reached the street; "I have this day become acquainted with poverty, but also with the value of wealth. Henceforth I will study poverty."

CHAPTER LI.

AN ARISTOCRATIC VERDICT.

AT the saloon of the *Café du Prince, under den Linden,* a short time after these occurrences, a splendid dinner took place.

The young *Prince Steppenfeld,* seventeen years of age, son of Prince *Andolar von Steppenfeld,* the CXXXVIII., was yesterday made Lieutenant of Steinfort's regiment, and gave a splendid *fête* to his comrades to-day.

The room was most richly decorated. An immense table run in the shape of a horse-shoe through the centre of the room, and was laden with all imaginary products of luxury and splendour. Along the walls stood blooming and rare plants and golden orange trees, which, as if by enchantment, produced a delightful spring, whilst without, bleak winter was just taking its departure.

It was towards three o'clock in the afternoon. Many of the officers of the regiment had already arrived. As it was only a short time before dinner, they stood together in groups, discussing different topics. The principal subjects of their discourse, were as usual, dogs, horses, and women.

"'Pon honour, comrade," began the young, beardless Lieutenant *von Krautgarten,* whose thin voice we have already heard once at the " French house," to another young officer of the same age, "'pon honour, last evening I was at a dinner at the house of *Commerzienrath Brandt.* He had already invited me three times before I bestowed upon him the honour of my presence. 'Tis true he has excellent wines, and moreover, it is quite amusing to court the pretty citizen girls; but the fellow seems to have lost his senses for very pride. This morning the gentleman met me ' under den Linden,' just as I walked with his Highness, our new comrade, to parade, and in his inconceivable want of tact, he addressed me perfectly familiarly, and *sans ceremonie.* Well, well, I dismissed him easy enough. I only told him, that I had no time to lose with him, and let him stand. His Highness who has a watchful eye upon the distinctions of rank, immediately observed that the man was a citizen, and asked me, how it come that I stood on such familiar footing with persons of that class? Just imagine this question! I found myself most confoundedly embarrassed. His Highness seemed to observe this, and was kind enough to remark that, most probably, I had merely run into debt with that fellow. Of course, I left the Prince upon the wrong track."

An old officer, *Count Dumritz,* who stood close by, overheard this conversation.

"Without wishing to make you any reproaches, I cannot approve of your just mentioned mode of action," he began, shaking his head. "Only a short time since, we, of the nobility, could amuse ourselves at the expense of the rich *bourgeoisie,* could allow them to regale us, nay, even court their pretty daughters. But at present, since this citizen-pride begins to doubt our good old prerogatives, we must even avoid the appearance of familiarity. There are plenty of people among these citizens, who, if we have honoured their companies with our presence, boast, behind our backs, of having done *us* the honour. At the present bad time, we must keep aloof from them as much as possible, or at least, as much as our necessities will admit. Only by such a course, which is, by not recognizing them at all, by never descending from our well-earned, well-established higher position, to their level, can we preserve to nobility that standing, which the grace of God, History, and its own renown has given to it."

"Upon the principal points, you are in the right, Count Dumritz," replied the young Lieutenant, as he unbuttoned his coat to restore a little of its natural freedom to his body; "but your views may be carried out even without relinquishing the good wine and the fair daughters of our worthy citizens. 'Pon honour, these are two things which we cannot do without. A citizen must never know exactly how to take us; to-day we must be condescending, to-morrow proud and distant. I have just found out a most charming, sweet little tradesman's daughter, whom I should be very loath to lose. Just imagine, the stupid little thing fancies that I would marry her. I could not dream of such an occurrence, 'pon honour, I couldn't. But I must court her, and why not? I don't injure my nobility by that. My worthy sire, I think, left no less than three citizen-daughters in the lurch; but he was a devil of a fellow, when young."

Count Dumritz looked upon the little beardless braggadocia in silence, shrugged his shoulders, and left him with a sigh. He felt convinced that the gradual downfall of the nobility was principally caused by these young, inexperienced sprigs, who were not capable of assuming a proper and dignified demeanour, when they came in contact with the *canaille*, but rather increased the evil by ill-timed confidence.

He approached another group of older comrades, who just seemed to have entered into a very lively conversation upon some important subject.

Baron Görz, whom we have also seen at the " French house," seemed to be the principal speaker.

" As I tell you," he said, " this seems to be a most strange and remarkable story about Steinfort. It is now generally known, that the girl whom he drags about with him everywhere, is no other than a former grisette, a seamstress, who used to be a regular guest at Villa Bella. At that time she had Fischergraf, the famous gambler, for her lover. As several of us have seen, that girl, not long since, brought him into difficulties at the ' French house,' and on that occasion he publicly declared her his bride.

" At that time, of course, every one thought that he had drank a little too much, but a few days ago, he took her to another public place, and there introduced her, immediately on his entrance as his betrothed, and that to a highly respectable family. Afterwards, I believe, *the* person got into a quarrel with a waiter, who seemed to know her, and Steinfort in some confusion, made his retreat with her. But, gentlemen, there is too much in this for a mere joke; moreover, Steinfort is always so confoundedly serious in every thing he does, that I don't believe him capable of perpetrating a joke."

" But, gentlemen," began *Captain von Tromsdorff*, with an incredulous smile, " the thing is utterly impossible. How can an officer and a gentleman forget himself so far; just let the matter drop, for it really is too ridiculous to have the appearance of reality."

At these words, Herr von Tromsdorff produced a tooth-pick from his vest-pocket, and began to pick his teeth, most probably to let his hungry stomach imagine that it was already filled. We can easily suppose that he only desired the conversation to be discontinued, to let the ensuing silence be a signal for the host to expedite the dinner. For the last quarter of an hour he had solely been occupied with dispersing the conversing groups as politely as he could. Herr von Tromsdorff was a great gourmand, and many of his comrades used to say of him, that he invariably prepared himself for a grand dinner by fasting for two days previous.

But Görz would not be interrupted even by the pitiful glances which the Captain cast at the table.

" I cannot help my impressions," he continued, " but I firmly believe that Steinfort has very serious thoughts of marrying that female. I would consider such a thing impossible in any one of us, but you know what abominable opinions he has often expressed about the existing differences of rank, and particularly about the prerogatives of nobility. One would almost have believed him to be a Jacobin."

" Hm, yes!" exclaimed Count Dumritz, " there is no telling what a Jacobin may not be capable of doing. It is shameful, it is abominable, how little these young gentlemen seem to care nowa-days for their ancient nobility."

" With the exception of Steinfort," again commenced Baron Görz, as he looked around, " we are pretty much all together. This happens just right. I will call all our comrades to our circle here, and state the case. It seems to me absolutely necessary that we should take timely steps, to prevent our corps from being compromised or disgraced in case our surmises should prove correct."

Tromsdorff heaved a heavy sigh. He believed that he had observed that the Prince was just about to give the signal for dinner.

" Well, then, if it must be so," he said, " let us hear your proposition, but be as brief as possible about it, for I find the whole affair a rather annoying one."

Baron Görz asked for the permission of their host, then clapped his hands to command attention, and began by asking leave of the honourable body of officers then and there present, to state a case in which their united honour was concerned, that they might come to a unanimous resolution upon the subject.

He repeated what he had just told to a few of his friends, and then asked the question; whether, if the foregoing was proved to be true, the honourable corps of officers would henceforth consider it agreeable to their own dignity and honour, to have and recognize Steinfort as their comrade?

The result of this speech was a universal laughter. The majority declared that Steinfort had an ordinary amour, a thing of daily occurrence among them; and that it was utterly impossible that his intentions should be of a more serious nature. A gentleman, and particularly one of such an ancient and noble family, must know perfectly well, what he owed to himself, his position and his family.

Baron Görz, however, was a most obstinate accuser. He called upon *Captain von Reitzenfeld* to testify, that he had been present, and had heard and seen Steinfort presenting the girl in question as his betrothed. That he had also seen how she hurriedly took him away, after she had attracted the attention of everybody in the room, and particularly of the ladies present, and by her very strange behaviour at once proved her very low birth, and her very low manners. Besides this, Görz referred to the very eccentric character of Steinfort, a character, easily capable of anything so extravagant as this; he then urged the importance of the subject to all the gentlemen present, and finally gained the most incredulous over to his side.

The consequence was, that he was commissioned to call Steinfort aside, and question him seriously upon the subject, but yet before they would sit down to dinner, as it would not be in accordance with the honour and dignity of a corps of officers, to receive as a comrade, or sit at table with a brother officer, who would forget himself so far, as to have earnest intentions of marrying a seamstress, a mere grisette.

Strange and wonderful people! A stranger would have believed they had all been bitten by a tarantula.

If Steinfort's intentions had been merely to seduce the girl, not one among them would have found any fault with him; it would have been perfectly immaterial, whether his victim was a grisette, a seamstress, or any other woman. If he would have taken her for a mistress, his comrades would have found this perfectly in order, nay, would even have been pleased with it, and would have admired the taste and tact of their comrade Steinfort. But to marry—actually to marry a seamstress, that was a capital offence; a man of such principles could no longer be tolerated in a circle of noblemen!

But these gentlemen were not bitten by a tarantula—the motive of their action was a different one. The devil of pride, haughtiness and selfishness had taken possession of them. The preservation of old, rusty and time-worn prejudices—prejudices upon which rested their elevated rank in society, was their object.

To these prejudices they sacrificed everything, and it was no conscientious dislike, no moral scruple—they did not know these—which armed them all against Steinfort; it was only the selfish fear, that his mode of action might in some way interfere with those rights, which they said, "the grace of God, their ancestry and history" had given them.

Without having the least presentiment of the conspiracy that was formed against him, of the storm that was about to break upon him, Steinfort entered the room a short time after the debate had closed. Accidental circumstances had detained him, and had thus caused him to arrive last at the place of meeting.

Quickly he saluted all his comrades, and crossed the saloon, to excuse himself to the Prince for his late arrival.

He received a cool reception and cool thanks; whoever could conveniently do so, kept out of his way. The young Prince evidently knew not exactly what to do, and replied to Steinfort's polite excuses, with an unintelligible murmur.

When Steinfort returned from the side of the Prince, Baron Görz approached him, took his arm and conducted him to a side room.

The whole company remained behind, in perfectly silent expectation of the result of this conversation.

After a few minutes, Steinfort with a flushed, fiery red face, rushed from the side room, and at the threshold, loud enough for all present to hear, he exclaimed: "You are a scoundrel, Görz!" Without stopping, or looking round, he rushed again out of the house.

Baron Görz followed upon his steps into the saloon, and informed his expecting comrades, that Steinfort had at once and openly declared to him, that he would marry the girl, because he loved her.

This announcement at once created a general tumult. Exclamations of astonishment, of rage, of pity and of indignation were heard throughout the room.

"'Pon honour," cried the little beardless Lieutenant, "this Steinfort is a man without any pride of birth or of ancestry. 'Pon honour, it is really scandalous!"

Count Dumritz wrung his hand in silent despair at the downfall of nobility.

Captain Tromsdorf picked his teeth still more eagerly than before.

"How annoying, that this disagreeable occurrence must just happen at my house," observed his Highness, the host.

Twenty others made different observations and ejaculations, which we cannot repeat.

"I tried to make him understand," began Görz, after the first storm had somewhat abated, "that, if such were his intentions, no officer could possibly serve in the same regiment with him; but he remarked, that this result would be immaterial to him, as he had taken his resolution, and owed to no one, an account of his private actions. I then made another friendly attempt to bring him to reason, by explaining to him, that no one among us would reproach him, if he elevated the girl to the position of his mistress, but that he must abandon the ridiculous plan of marrying her; he replied to me with the very complimentary phrase, which most of you must have heard, and rushed out of the room."

"Then it is settled, that you, gentleman, can serve no longer in the same corps with him," observed the Colonel of the regiment gravely, "and I shall so arrange it, that he will resign his commission. Upon the whole, I have cause to congratulate the corps of officers, on having been rid of so disqualified a member."

"And now, gentlemen," began the Lieutenant-Prince, "let us go to dinner, if you all please."

The verdict of this noble corps may be reduced to the following: It is an honour to a cavalier, to make a mistress of a seamstress, but it is a disgrace to him, to marry her.

CHAPTER LII.

THE CHALLENGE.

THE morning following the annoying occurrences at the *Café du Prince*, Steinfort sat in his room, absorbed in thought.

In his hand he held a small note which he had just received from the Colonel of his regiment. The Colonel referred to the scene of yesterday, and gave him the advise to resign his commission, as the corps of officers would no longer serve in the regiment with him, and as this was the only way in which he could avoid receiving his discharge against his will.

Steinfort looked upon the letter with a bitter smile. His Colonel meant him well, and had chosen his words as carefully and kindly as possible. Yet every word contained a bitter sting for Steinfort, who was very loath to resign his military position. Notwithstanding he placed his principles, and that which he believed to be right and just, higher than all earthly considerations.

His determination of marrying Augusta, was not in the least shaken, by all the disagreeable and mortifying occurrences which had taken place, though we cannot altogether deny, that all the storms which seemed to approach him, somewhat depressed his spirits.

His servant interrupted his dark reflections by the announcement, that Count Teufel of Teufelsritt, desired to speak to him. This was the same Count who at the "French-house," had been superseded in the good esteem of the lady of his love by the rich banker."

Steinfort received the Count calmly and earnestly; he knew, of course, the purport of his visit. In reality, the storm of dark occurrences had made him entirely forget, that after the scene of yesterday, a duel with Baron Görz was utterly unavoidable. But in his present state of mind, a duel for life and death, seemed rather desirable than otherwise. He thirsted for some mighty excitement; he was almost incapable of action, for a perfect apathy had befallen him, and he eagerly sought the chance which would rouse him from it.

"I can imagine the object of your visit, sir Count," he said politely, rising to meet the officer, "so you will oblige me, by being as brief as possible. Be kind enough to name time, place and weapons, and I shall be perfectly satisfied with all."

"You have rightly guessed my commission, Herr von Steinfort," replied Count Teufel, bowing politely; "but I believe, that I am only doing my duty to both parties, by first making an attempt to settle the matter amicably if possible. If you will declare, that—"

"Trouble yourself no further, sir Count, if I may beg you," said Steinfort, interrupting the cartel-bearer, in a tone of firmness and decision. "I shall refuse any, even the slightest explanation or concession. What I have said, I shall still repeat, and consequently, I look upon the duel as unavoidable. I must repeat my request, to name the necessary particulars."

"Under these circumstances," continued Count Teufel, courteously, "nothing remains for me to do, than to discharge the disagreeable duty I undertook. I, consequently, must deliver you the challenge of Baron Görz. He will fight you with pistols. He awaits you to-morrow morning at eight o'clock in the *Saatwinkel*; three bullets, distance ten paces."*

"Sir Count, I beg you to give my compliments to Baron Görz, and to inform him that I shall certainly have the honour of meeting him."

Count Teufel bowed, and withdrew as politely as he had entered.

Steinfort calmly resumed his seat, directed a few lines to Referendarius von Birkheim, requesting the latter to come to him immediately. He then lit a cigar, and calmly promenaded up and down the room.

In an instant, he again felt as manful, as energetic as ever.

The annoyances, the ordinary vexations of life had threatened to oppress him; an extraordinary excitement roused him again; this duel was to be a remedy, a means of saving him from himself.

The Referendarius von Birkheim soon made his appearance.

In a few brief words Steinfort explained the whole subject to him, and requested him to be his second.

Birkheim immediately consented, and shortly withdrew again at Steinfort's request, to make all the necessary preparations.

With the utmost quietness and calmness, Steinfort arranged his papers; wrote letters to his father, and to Augusta, provided sufficiently for the girl in case he should fall, and in the evening went to bed very early, to sleep once more as quietly as if nothing had happened.

CHAPTER LIII.

INWARD STRUGGLES.

It was quite different with Augusta.

The occurrence at the ball already had made it clear to her mind, that her supposition, that she acted wrong in continuing the existing intimacy with Steinfort, was not without good foundation. She became more and more convinced, that the elevated sphere of refined society must for ever remain closed to her.

The occurrence at the ball had by no means humbled or mortified her feelings, for she now was conscious, that after all, she was as good as any of these purse-proud, virtuous ladies, none of whom had ever been compelled to protect their innocence and virtue, against want, hunger, and misery.

The love and the respect which Steinfort paid her, had elevated her mind, and at the same time, strengthened her consciousness of being capable to become more worthy of him, by truly and faithfully returning his love. Yes, she was fully

* It is customary in Germany for the *challenger* to name time, place, weapons, &c.--TRANSLATOR.

convinced that the love she felt for him, might even succeed in making him happy, if society with all its terrors had not placed a barrier between them.

But it was even this consciousness which oppressed—which crushed her, as she possessed sufficient good sense to perceive that Steinfort would never be capable of overcoming or vanquishing the opinions and prejudices of society. A second similar occurrence at the officer's dinner, had proved this truth still more clearly to her mind.

The circumstances were as follows:

As we know, Steinfort had never again referred to the difficulties at the "French house," but had treated the matter as a trifle, without, however, being able, as he wished, to prevent Augusta from reflecting further on that subject.

A few days afterwards, he invited Augusta to go with him to the house of *Hoftraiteur* Jagor,* and dine with him there. Augusta had strenuously objected, naturally fearing that new annoyances might take place, but Steinfort had finally persuaded her to yield the point.

Both repaired to the place, and there chanced to meet a noble family with whom the Lieutenant was well acquainted. The two parties sat down at the same table, which was excellently provided, and Steinfort introduced Augusta as a young lady from the provinces, and as his betrothed bride. She was friendly and politely received. Augusta remained silent and retired, as Steinfort had recommended her, and everything seemed to go on smoothly and comfortably. The modest diffidence of the handsome young lady from the province, was even found particularly charming and amiable.

To speak plainly, the mode of action which Steinfort had assumed was in itself inconsistent. If he would introduce the girl into good society, if he believed himself possessed of sufficient courage and strength of mind to carry this through, he should also have introduced her boldly and openly, not under an assumed character. Such, certainly, had at first been his intention; but even at the ball, he already omitted it, until necessity forced the truth from him. By this inconsistency he made his own position more difficult, as he thus lost the sympathy which is always awarded to boldness and courage, and moreover, as we shall presently see, involved himself in fresh difficulties.

The party had already been seated at table for some time, the champagne corks were popping merrily, and everything assumed the appearance of hilarity, when a little ragged dealer in plaster of Paris figures, availing himself of the momentary absence of the *portier,* succeeded in entering the house and reaching the dining saloon.

The boy approached the table nearest to the door, the very same at which Steinfort and Augusta were seated, and begged the company to buy something of him. As they all dismissed him briefly, he came at last to Augusta. He had

* *Hoftraiteur,* restaurateur to the court.

scarcely observed her a little more closely, when he cried in the dialect of the lowest Berlin street boys, and in tones of utter astonishment:

"My gracious, what! Augusta, who would think of finding you here?"

This exclamation naturally created the greatest excitement among the company around the table, who alternately looked at the boy and at Augusta with utter astonishment. With a little presence of mind, it would certainly have been an easy matter to order the boy away; he would have been thrown out of doors, and the matter would have naturally been explained as a mistake of persons. But the poor, simple-hearted girl did not possess sufficient presence of mind nor power of dissemblance. Flushed with shame, fear and embarrassment, she scarcely dared to look up, and her embarrassment visibly increased, when a gentleman who sat near her, told the boy that he was mistaken, and must go away and no longer incommode the young lady. The ragged urchin saucily replied:

"What! mistaken? no, I am not. I am sure I know Augusta who lives in *Stern-street,* before the *Hamburg-gate.*"

Trembling, she sat upon her chair, until Steinfort, under the pretence of observing her sudden illness, rose and conducted her into an adjoining room. But he could not accomplish this without, of course, attracting the most general attention, and thus making matters even worse. The company now began rightly to understand the reason of Augusta's silence, and the Lieutenant, as well as the poor girl, on going out were deeply mortified by the loud laughter that followed them, and the sarcastic speeches they overheard.

In this instance again, Steinfort endeavoured gently to erase all annoying impressions from Augusta's mind, by treating this new fatality as an unimportant occurrence; but the circumstance that he brought her directly home, and then immediately left her, convinced Augusta that he was no longer master of his inner excitement. She was deeply affected by all this, and more and more determined entirely to relinquish the plan of a union with Steinfort. His interest, and indeed the peace of both parties, required that sacrifice, and she would make it.

With this intention, she had already composed a letter to her lover, in which she fully particularized the situation of things, and her own views, and then expressed the most urgent wish of breaking off their whole connexion.

But when the time arrived to send off that letter—the letter written more with tears than with ink—she thought that her heart would break.

She now was a thousand times more miserable than before her acquaintance with Steinfort, for now she had learned to understand her own position. And this is the most torturing part of the misery of these unfortunate beings, whom proud society spurns beneath its foot, because want and need, the existence, the fiendish power of which, wealth never dreamed of, had driven them to shame.

Oh, ye rich, high-born, proud and virtuous women, who have never hungered, who have never passed sleepless nights upon the hard couch of despair and misery, look into your hearts, and ask yourselves how much better than the fallen Augusta you would have remained under the same circumstances, how long your boasted virtue and purity would have bravely battled against hunger, sorrow and despair? Remember the touching, heart-rending lines of our great poet:

> "Who never eat his bread with tears,
> Who never through night's gloomy hours
> Sat by his couch and watched and wept,
> He knows ye not, ye ruling powers."

And yet, if one of these wretched creatures whom that same rank and wealth, which protected your virtue, tore to the ground—if one of these unfortunates would rise from the sink of perdition into which society has cast her, you reject her, and you spurn her back deeper into the pool of misery and crime. Beware, oh beware, ye who speak calmly: "we thank thee, oh Lord, that we are not like yonder seamstress," beware that posterity may not cry woe upon you for your pharisaic pride! Beware particularly, all ye voluptuaries, who fear not to purchase purity and innocence with your gold, and who treat him with scorn and contempt, who endeavours to atone even the thousandth part of your manifold guilt upon one of your victims!

As Augusta learned to perceive that society would not permit her to be virtuous in its circles, it became a source of intense misery to her, to have become acquainted with her own real position. She was compelled to acknowledge to herself that the same misery which for years had been her most faithful companion, would again be hers; that she would again have to suffer hunger and cold, without even daring to hope for mental consolation, without daring to expect even an acknowledgment of the innocence of her mind.

Thus it is, that the world alone throws obstacles in the returning path of honesty, virtue and righteousness!

And withal this, Augusta felt too much elevated, too much strengthened in her good resolves by the love of Steinfort, to make it possible for her to think of returning to her former wild courses. With utter disgust she rejected the very thought, and would have preferred a thousand times to die, even by her own hand.

Still, all this made it only the more difficult for her to relinquish the affection of her loved Steinfort. She certainly had written the letter, but she could not find the strength within herself to send it.

For three days, this anxious struggle continued in her mind, whilst the Lieutenant, who was occupied with his own affairs, did not come to see her. Her birds sang merrily within their cage, and the new spring unfolded the rosebuds at her window, but her brown eye remained dim and thoughtful, and the singing of her birds and the bloom of her roses passed by her without notice.

On the fourth day she stood by her window, and looked out upon the blooming, newly awakened spring, which filled her breast with warm sympathy and admiration of the soft beauties of nature.

"Kind Heaven," she cried, "forgive me! I cannot help the intensity of my love!"

And the little bits of the letter fluttered out of the window, lightly carried off by the gamboling breath of spring.

CHAPTER LIV.

BRUNE ET BLONDE.

AFTER the annoying occurrence at the house of Hofrath Christianus, Marianne had found a sleeping room with the family of a poor, but honest factory-workman, and in the same house where lived Augusta Strass.

Fortune had thus far been kind to her, as through the medium of said workman, she herself obtained employment in the calico manufactory where he was engaged. She was employed in folding calicoes, for which she received a weekly pay of one thaler and ten silbergroschen.

It would certainly have been more desirable for her, to have again gone to family service, but Hofrath Christianus had been induced by his daughter Matilda, to give her so bad a character, that she never could hope again to find service. On no earthly condition would she return to the cellar of her step-father, the hunchback, and Mrs. Rüthman, to whom, in her innocence she would have applied, she knew not where to find. Thus she blessed the accident which gave her this humble asylum, after she had hopelessly strayed about for several hours.

Marianne worked daily from six o'clock in the morning to seven in the evening, but even with all this labour, she could scarcely support herself.

As we said before, she earned about one thaler and ten silbergroschen in a week. Of this she paid ten silbergroschen for her bed, and consequently had just thirty silbergroschen for all the other necessaries of life, or in other words, not quite four silbergroschen for each day. Upon this she existed in a manner, which we cannot well designate by the name of living like a human being. She even devoted less money upon the support of her body or the purchase of food, than any of the other factory girls, as it was an absolute necessity to her, to be always dressed clean, neat and decent.

And yet she was contented. Scanty as was at present her subsistence, she at least felt herself free from the terrible scenes she had been compelled to witness in Job's cellar, from the annoyance and degradations of the prison, and from the harsh treatment she had met at the house of

Hofrath Christianus. A certain quiet, and we might say, pious resignation had befallen her, and it seemed as if she hoped for and expected nothing more from the world, but would be satisfied, if only the world would not again attack her. She had in fact, closed her account with society, and had entered into a union with herself.

Having accidently done a small favour to Augusta, she became somewhat acquainted with her, and Augusta had finally gained her favour after a most obstinate resistance. This amiable brunette was so indefatigably obliging to her, that at last she began to grow fond of her, and finally accepted the offer of Augusta, to pass the evening hours in her room. Thus these two girls became better known to each other, related their former adventures, and soon discovered, in how many points their situations were similar.

Augusta had told Marianne about her position relative to Steinfort, and had offered to request for her the assistance of that rich man. But this had been refused by the latter in the most decided manner, even with a certain degree of bitterness. Misanthropic as she had become, she would be under obligations to nobody, and particularly avoided even by any chance, meeting with the officer.

But most gladly she accepted Augusta's offer of instructing her in the sewing of fine linen, which the latter, as already intimated, was constantly practising, being too proud to live upon the gifts of Steinfort, and the latter too delicate in his feelings to force those gifts upon her. Marianne was also in hopes that by this newly-acquired talent she might be placed in a situation which would enable her to withdraw from factory work, and to live quietly and retired upon the products of her industry.

Thus, then, these two young girls were every evening—the only few hours which Marianne had for herself—together in the little room of the seamstress, the locality of which we already know well, and were continually busy at their work.

This time also, a similar object had brought them together. Marianne, although fatigued from the labour of the day, exerted herself almost beyond her strength to sew well and quick. Fatigue frequently threatened to overpower her, but still she continued on, for the great object was, ere long, to obtain that degree of expertness which would enable her to escape the slavery of the manufactory. Besides the reasons for this wish, which we have already mentioned, we might add another, namely, that she might, with her needle be able to earn two silbergroshen per week more than at the manufactory—a most important improvement, which would put her in a position to have a *warm meal* for her dinner.

She had just involuntarily nodded whilst sewing a shirt, and was in actual danger of bringing her head too near the light. Augusta observed this, and with a pitying glance at the poor, exhausted girl, she removed the light. The noise of the movement awoke poor Marianne.

"Good Heaven," she exclaimed, rousing herself, "it is very hard, very difficult for me to work to night! I am very tired."

"Certainly," replied Augusta with compassion, after standing all day behind a table and folding calicoes, you may well be exhausted in the evening. I can remember that feeling from my own experience. But you should allow me to tell Steinfort of this, for I know he would gladly assist you; it will after all only be until you have learned the quick use of your needle, and then you can support yourself."

"Never," exclaimed Marianne, greatly excited, "never. I have no longer any confidence in mankind, and will not receive any of their favours. But let that be," she continued in a more gentle tone. "I shall soon have learned enough to make fine stitched shirts, and then I shall get along much better."

"Oh certainly, my friend," replied the other, "you already sew remarkably well. I should not have thought of proposing to you to accept my support, if I did not foresee that you shall want it only for a very short time. Next Saturday, when I deliver my work, I will also bring some back for you. The fine stitching at the collars I will do for you; the remainder you can do yourself. You will then, at least, earn as much as you get now at the manufactory."

"Oh, that would be delightful," said Marianne with a grateful look, "for I can scarcely bear the life in the manufactory. All day long, I hear nothing but the most disgustingly vulgar songs, which the other work-women, who are in the same room with me, will sing; and at noon, when the workmen who print the calicoes come up stairs to the drying-room, I scarcely know where to hide my head, or where to escape their low, vulgar insults. I prefer then, even if it storms and rains, to go down to the yard, that I may not hear or see them, but even when I return, I have often to endure mockeries, scorn and insults from my own sex, which more offends me than all the rest."

"You are just repeating my own experience, my poor friend," said Augusta, looking dimly towards the light. But courage, my dear, courage," she continued more lively, "and all will yet go well. I find, that when we are in love, we have always more courage. Have you ever been in love?"

"That is a very funny question."

"Hm! I find it a very natural one, to which you would make an evasive reply," cried Augusta, fixing her sparkling brown eyes, laughingly, upon her friend; "I can't take an evasive answer. So tell me quickly, have you ever been in love?"

"Don't plague me, if you please."

"Then tell me quickly, whether you have ever been in love?"

"I do not know what love is," said Marianne, "so you must first tell me what are the symptoms of it?"

"The symptoms?" inquired the other hesitatingly, whose powers of logical definition found themselves rather severely taxed by this question, " why, why, when you cannot part with somebody."

" Well, then, I don't know what love is," replied Marianne, with an expression of sadness in her large blue eyes. " I always could easily part from all I knew of mankind, and they still more easily from me."

" My gracious !" exclaimed Augusta somewhat annoyed at her fruitless examination. " Have you never felt any particular liking for any man ?"

" Felt a liking ? Why, yes, I believe—once."

" Aha, now we shall see ! Well, then, tell me ?"

" It was when I still lived in the cellar of my stepfather," commenced Marianne, " there was one among our usual guests, whom they called cunning Schmerles, and him I liked very much for some time. Some one came to the cellar and boasted that he had stolen her alms from the pocket of a poor, blind woman ; this made Schmerles very angry ; he became quite furious, and forced the thief to return the stolen goods. I liked him very much for that deed. But in reality, even this Schmerles was a great criminal, and I believe he was caught and put into prison, and I have never seen him since."

" But tell me, my dear friend, how did you ever come among such a company of thieves and murderers ?" inquired Augusta, whose female curiosity now began to be greatly excited upon that point.

" That is a question you will ask me in vain," replied the maiden, deeply excited. " I have a dark recollection that I did not always live in that cellar. I passed my early years at a country-seat where there were many cows and horses. I also remember a very large dog, which I was allowed to ride sometimes. Afterwards I found myself in town, but how I came there I cannot remember. My step-father was always coarse and rough towards me ; my mother was almost constantly weeping. She died early, when I was still very young ; after her death, my father behaved even more brutally to me ; almost every day I received more blows and cuffs than bread. But withal this, I would never have left him if I had not been forced to do so, by the company that frequented his place. But as I could not please him in anything I did, and as I was afraid of again being arrested, and would, perhaps, be forced to appear as a witness against him, I determined to live by myself. A friend, whom I made in the prison, also advised me to do so."

The cry of the watchman, who announced ten o'clock, interrupted the conversation of the girls. That hour was always their signal to quit their work and go to bed, as Marianne had to rise early in the morning.

They kindly pressed each other's hand, and Marianne withdrew to her little chamber. Tired and wearied from the labours of the day, she sought her little hard couch.

She felt much more happy than usual this evening ; the conversation with her friend, and the prospect of being able shortly to earn her own support in a more pleasant and respectable manner, had been a soothing balm to her spirits.

Since the time when the minister of the prison had announced to her the terrible wrath of God, she had seldom, if ever, dared to pray. To-night, for the first time in a long while, she folded her hands in pious prayer, and amidst the devout feelings of her innocent heart, she sank into gentle slumbers.

CHAPTER LV.

THE SUPERVISION OF POLICE.

It might have been about midnight, when a loud knocking was heard against the door of Marianne's chamber.

Frightened, the girl started up, and with difficulty forced herself to ask a question about the origin of this nocturnal disturbance.

She received the most unexpected of all answers. She was requested to rise and admit the police, who were about to search her room.

Tremblingly she rose from her bed, covered herself as best she could in the dark, with a few clothes, and opened the door as requested.

As it was incomprehensible to her, what the police could possibly want of her, she naturally supposed that this visit must be the result of some mistake, and gradually began to recover. But a cry of intense terror escaped her lips, when by the light of the lantern she saw the *Criminal Commissary W—* and two gensd'armes standing before her.

The remembrance of that terrible morning, when the same commissary took her from Job's cellar, and treated her so harshly, came vividly back before her memory. She feared that fresh sorrows, similar to those that followed that visit, were again before her.

The Criminal Commissary announced to her with the utmost indifference, that a search of her room was about to be undertaken, to which she must quietly, and without contradiction, submit, as she stood under *the supervision of the police*, in consequence of having been on trial for stealing, and having only been provisionally discharged.

It was in vain that Marianne asked for the reason of this untimely interruption and search ; the Commissary replied in a most serious and impressive manner, that she would be informed of that hereafter.

All three of the police officers now searched through the entire appartment. Not a nook or corner remained unsearched ; but all was of no avail, the article sought for was not found. The three men consequently retired again, after having first told the girl to appear at the Police office at nine o'clock the following morning.

But the nightly disturbance was not ended with this.

The housekeepers with whom Marianne lodged had been silent spectators of the whole occurrence. After the Policemen had left the house, they immediately told the unfortunate girl that she must leave their premises early in the morning, as they could not keep a person in their house, who stood under the supervision of the Police, without great injury to their own hitherto unspotted reputation.

"Never in our lives," continued the hostess, a small, lively, talkative woman, who had been railing at poor Marianne for some time, "never yet did we come in contact with the Police. And we know this much, that having visited once, they will visit again, if we keep a suspected person beneath our roof. And all the world knows, that such visits bring neither honour nor reputation to a house."

"Such is the fact," added the husband, who always said "yes" to his wife's speeches.

Marianne sank helplessly upon her couch; her heart seemed crushed.

She felt that even her honest host and hostess mistrusted her, even believed her capable of stealing; yet could she wonder at this, after the scene that had just occurred?

Now only she began to see clearly, what a terrible judgment had been imposed upon her, by the sentence of "Police supervision?" It became terribly clear to her mind, that henceforth she must never again seek a home among persons of unblemished character, for fear of compromising them also by her own disgrace.

All and everything seemed to conspire against her.

After her maiden modesty had been outraged, and deeply wounded by her first arrest, after her religious confidence had been undermined by the ill-advised zealot of the prison, after she had been cast out from the bane of civilised society; only one last resort had remained to her, to live alone and within herself, expelled and excluded from all the world. She had already dared to hope, that here at last there might be a peace for her, if only the peace of the grave, now she was robbed even of this last hope, this last shelter, and alone and without protection, she stood in the street.

She passed the remainder of the night weeping and wringing her hands. She lost confidence in all, even in that friend to whom she had clung that night, like a drowning person to a straw. She knew not, whether that kind girl would not also cast her off, but she would not venture to approach her upon a trial.

It was a sad consolation to her, that she owed nothing to her hosts, as she had paid her lodging in advance.

At least from that side she was not annoyed, when at break of day she left her poor couch, and carrying in a small bundle all the few rags she possessed, was about to leave the humble roof which hitherto had sheltered her.

Hesitatingly she stopped for one moment, when she came to the floor below, and passed Augusta's door. All was silent within; the seamstress, happier than her friend, seemed to be sound asleep.

Marianne would not interrupt that peaceful slumber. Silently, and with a sunken forehead, she stole down the stairs, and out of the house.

The bell at the front-door rattled loudly as the door closed behind her. It sounded like a death-knell to all her future hopes.

CHAPTER LVI.

ANOTHER EXAMINATION.

HOPELESS and comfortless, Marianne strayed about through the streets of the city, where joy as well as sorrow was still invisibly buried behind the heavy, closed shutters.

It was yet too early to appear at the Police office; she had plenty of leisure to indulge in her sad thoughts and contemplations. She had almost determined to return to her friend and to seek consolation of her. But she quickly remembered that the occurrences of last night had proved that she was really an outcast, and that even her approach might bring misery to others. She loved Augusta too much for this, and preferred to withdraw from her in silence.

All her plans and hopes for the future, which her friend had excited, we may say almost forcibly, in her breast, were suddenly destroyed. Nay, her present situation was even worse than her former, for she was not only, without shelter, to-morrow she would, undoubtedly, be also without work, without support.

When, at the exact hour, she entered the Police office, all the sad recollections of her prison days awoke anew; and it was not with the feelings of satisfaction with which we usually look back upon past sorrows, nay, it was with a feeling of bitter, burning pain.

Marianne regretted that she could still feel pain or sorrow, for she had hoped, prayed and wished that she might be dead to any feeling. She walked to the room to which she had been directed, and found W—, the Criminal Commissary, who already awaited her, with his pen in hand. It made a very favourable impression upon him that she appeared so very punctual, and he therefore addressed her more kindly than it had ever been his wont.

"Child," he said, "I will now explain to you the object of our visit of last night. At the house of your former master, Hofrath Christianus, two silver spoons have been missed ever since your departure. As nobody who could possibly be suspected of a theft except yourself, had any opportunity of having access to them, suspicion naturally fell upon you. This was the cause of our visit last night, and of our search; and although the search was fruitless, I must still believe that you are the person who has stolen the spoons, and I therefore call upon you to confess the full truth upon the subject, and to tell me what you have done with them."

For a moment, Marianne was actually incapable of making any reply. The weight of these groundless accusations crushed her completely, for she now began to perceive that henceforth nothing remained for her but to go through life branded, and suspected or accused of every crime that should occur in the vicinity where she might happen to live.

In Marianne's silence, the Criminal Commissary thought that he could discover a confession of her guilt, and he therefore urged her more pressingly to confess her crime openly, and to inform him where the spoons might be found.

At last, Marianne uttered the simple answer: "Do with me, sir, just as you like; it is all the same to me."

But the Commissary was not at all satisfied with such a declaration, but threatened her with immediate imprisonment, unless she chose to give a proper reply to his questions.

The idea of being imprisoned was, in her present situation, not such a repulsive or terrible one to the unfortunate Marianne, but notwithstanding, she could not bear the thought of being positively considered a thief. She therefore once more gathered all her strength and presence of mind, and said in a calm, quiet, and resigned tone: I have stolen no spoons, sir."

The Criminal Commissary not satisfied with this, earnestly repeated his admonition to confess her crime.

" My child," he began, " I may even give you a prospect, if you will truly and penitently confess your crime, that you may escape entirely unpunished, as Herr Hofrath Christianus is well known as a very kind, humane man, and as he may not prosecute you, since the crime was only trifling, and committed by a person in his employ. Under these circumstances, it is legally in his power to pursue the matter further or not; but if you desire his leniency, you must, above all things, meet him with an open and candid confession."

Marianne remained firm to her first declaration, and the Criminal Commissary finally convinced himself, after he had uselessly lost a great deal of time, that nothing else remained for him to do but to abandon the thought of the threatened imprisonment, as he had no legal grounds for suspicion.

An useless citation or arrest, is always an annoying occurrence to a young or ambitious Police officer, as he knows perfectly well, that his energy and his capacity for office or promotion, is usually judged by his superiors by the number of criminals he has arrested or committed.

This circumstance caused the commissary before dismissing her, to examine the girl concerning her mode of living and her means of subsistence.

Marianne spoke candidly and openly about her situation. In the innocence and inexperi-ence of her heart she was incautious enough to confess, that at the present moment, she was not only without a residence, since her lodging-house keeper had thrown her out of doors, in consequence of the occurrences of last night, but that she also must fear, that she had lost her employment, since she could not go to the manufactory this morning in consequence of the present citation, and since it was customary with her employer, immediately to engage another workwoman, if one of those employed, failed to come, even for a single day.

The commissary most conscientiously wrote everything she stated into an official document. Perhaps this was done, because the authorities themselves had caused this new misfortune to the girl, and would endeavour to make reparation, or put her into employment again ? Oh no! It was rather to add to the document the very just legal decision, that Marianne must find a proper residence and means of subsistence within the space of three days, or in default thereof, would be punished for idleness and vagrancy.

The document, which closed with this decision, was placed before Marianne for signature, and then the commissary explained to her the nature of the paper she had signed.

" Now, if within three days," he continued, " you do not find a place of residence and an honest and sufficient means of support, you will be sent to the work-house; the law concerning vagrancy and habitual idleness will be put in force against you by the Criminal Court, and you may expect the punishment of the work-house for no less a term than two months."

Thus the officer thought, that he had reserved for himself, under legal enactment, the prospect of an early arrest of the poor girl, with some cer-tainty, as it was most improbable, that Marianne in the time that was allowed to her, could comply with the condition imposed upon her.

A slight movement of his head told Marianne that she was discharged and dismissed for the present.

CHAPTER LVII.

AND GIVE US OUR DAILY BREAD.

Ten minutes after this scene, Marianne stood in the same doorway, where a few months before, on her dismissal from prison, she had found a saving protector in the person of old Rentier Friedmeier. She was now just as helpless and hopeless as then, but in mind even more miserable, for she had since gained some experience, which she then did not even dream of.

When at that time she was dismissed from the prison, suspected as a criminal, she fearfully and almost hopelessly bowed down her head; but then, the world was still open to her, the great, wide world, in which she might be honest, and even appear honest, just as she liked. This, the friendly old gentleman, who had come to her assistance had told her, and had thereby aroused her to new energy. Her youth and spirits carried her through the terrors and humiliations of the prison, as she dared still look upon the world, and hope for joy and happiness.

But even the service in the house of the Hofrath had been a bitter antidote to these newly awakened hopes and feelings. These sentiments, as we have seen, then formed themselves into a perfectly silent resignation—that resignation, when love and hatred alike cease to move our breast.

But even from this calm resignation she was now aroused by the force of circumstances, by the wrong views and regulations of society, only for the purpose of being told by her civil judges, that she must hereafter be looked upon by the whole world as a criminal, that she belonged to the offended laws—which she had never offended—that peace and quiet could nowhere be found for her—that, if she had been guilty, the road to melioration was forever closed to her, and innocent, that nothing but despair could remain for her.

For who would give shelter to a person who was legally proscribed, who was continually under the vigilance of police? Who would suffer in his house a person laden with all the disgrace of such a constant supervision? With whom could she even dare to seek a shelter, to ask for a roof to cover her, except with the very rabble, where the low and vicious associated with their equals, and where she would not be mortified with the consciousness, that to-morrow, perhaps even that very night, she would again forfeit her new home, through a voluntary whim of the police?

All this wildly and confusedly passed through Marianne's mind, and before her she could see nothing but a dark, gloomy future, or again a renewel of all the terrors and horrors of a prison life.

Her whole existence appeared to her like a dim, wild dream—like a powerless struggle with mankind and circumstances, which led to no result, but brought new mortifications, taught new and still more terrible lessons to her heart.

It was nearly noon. She must hasten, if possible, to fulfil the demands of the criminal commissary; the only choice that had been left to her was to consider herself as a proscribed being among the outer world, or as a convicted criminal behind the prison walls. She chose the former, as the work-house would have inclosed both proscription and imprisonment.

She hastily repaired to the manufactory, endeavouring, above all things, to secure her work and thereby her subsistence. She could afterwards more easily find new lodgings.

It was a very long way, and when she arrived at the place, she was perfectly exhausted.

The workmen had just ceased their labour, as their dinner hour had arrived—an ill omen for Marianne, who had thus lost half a day.

Fearfully she repaired to the superintendant, to excuse herself for her absence, and at the same time to designate the cause that had compelled it.

He met her furiously. This superintendant was known as a coarse, hard-hearted man.

"So, so," he cried scornfully, "you have come at last? You may now go back where you came from; did you think that your work would wait for you? We settle very quickly with such customers as you are. So you have been before the police? For some villany, I dare say? We know these things. I have employed another woman in your place. You were too weak and lazy at any rate; we cannot keep fine ladies here. So, clear these premises, and seek for work elsewhere—march."

Saying this, the superintendant withdrew. Under the scornful laughter of some of her former fellow work-women, who had always disliked her on account of her quiet modesty, and who now rejoiced at her mishap, the poor girl left the manufactory.

But whither should she go now?

She had not tasted food since yesterday afternoon, and then a piece of bread and butter had formed her entire meal.

Her whole fortune consisted in a single groschen, which certainly was not sufficient to satisfy her raving hunger.

It was a disagreeable, cold and wet day; she had no place to go to and seek shelter, and her groschen was not even sufficient to enter a victualling cellar.

Despairingly she crossed the *Alexander-place*, and proceeded down the long *King-street*.

So many people she met, so many happy, smiling and contented faces, so much luxury and wealth—but nowhere consolation, nowhere advice or assistance for her mourning soul.

At the entrance of King-street, before the long bridge, sat a woman who sold bread. With her only and her last coin, Marianne bought a piece of bread to satisfy her raging hunger.

The portal of the castle close by gave her a shelter, under which she could take her scanty meal—a cold, comfortless place, with a sharp current of air passing through it, yet protecting her against the wet.

She had seated herself upon one of the steps of the staircase which lead to the royal apartments, thinking and darkly brooding over her sad fate. Nowhere glimmered a star upon the darkness of the night which overshadowed the gloomy path of her life. Should she not, after all, go to Jobs, or to the friend she had lately found?—She hesitated for a moment. But no, no, yonder she must live among murderers and thieves of the lowest class, and here she must sink to the ground for very shame.

Marianne may have passed several hours at this place; the sentinel was meanwhile relieved.

The new sentinel might have thought it contrary to his duty, to suffer an humbly dressed female to sit upon the steps of a royal palace.

He marched up to her, and coarsely ordered her away.

She walked off, without replying a syllable; she had at last become accustomed to be repulsed and driven away from every place.

The rain, which had threatened all the forenoon, now came down in torrents. Marianne's thin, scanty clothing was wet through. She dragged herself on as far as the entrance of the "Linden," then she could go no farther; wearied beyond her strength, and tired of life, she sank down upon one of the benches situated there, in a half swoon.

A woman who passed by the academical buildings on the opposite side of the "Linden," fixed an attentive look upon her. For a moment that woman stopped, raised her large umbrella which obstructed her view of Marianne, and then suddenly, with hasty steps crossed the street, and approached the girl. She was a large woman, dressed in a fine cloth cloak, and a large black satin bonnet.

"Good Heavens, my dear Jobs," she cried in the distance in evident delight, "how unexpectedly I chance to meet you here! but in what a condition; what ails you? how do matters stand with you? Tell me all, speak, my girl, and tell me?"

The woman who approached in this noisy manner, and with every mark of kindness and sympathy, was no other than Mrs. Rüthmann. She was for some time past, again at liberty, having been discharged, as we have already observed, for want of legal proofs.

She had by no means forgotten Marianne Jobs, but had sought for her in vain, as the situation of the latter had changed, and as she was not to be found in the cellar of the hunchbacked Jobs. After she had come to the cellar very frequently to make inquiries for the girl, the distrustful hunchback had finally grown rude to her, and she had good reasons for not instituting inquiries for Marianne at the Police. In this manner the present accidental meeting was a most wished-for occurrence.

"This is indeed a consolation," Marianne cried, "you will assist me! I am deserted by God and man; this bundle contains all I possess, and this bench is my only domicile."

"Why, this is terrible!" cried Mrs. Rüthmann in consoling indignation. "My poor child! you are as wet as a water mouse, and you tremble with cold. Most certainly, I will assist you; but first I must offer you a shelter, such is a Christian's duty. Come with me quickly; we will take a cab, as I live far from here, and on the way you can tell me your adventures."

At the corner of Charlotte-street the two women entered a vehicle, and Mrs. Rüthmann directed the cabman, to drive up Frederick-street, and then into Krausen-street, where she resided.

At the corner of Behren-street the carriage stopped for a moment, at Mrs. Rüthmann's request. She said, that she had a little business to attend to, in a large and elegant house close by.

Marianne looked up and saw a window open in the Belle-Etage of the same house. A bearded face appeared there, and directed a lorgnette upon the carriage, evidently examining its occupant great attention.

Mrs. Rüthmann soon returned, and ten minutes afterwards, the carriage stopped at a small, handsome, one story house, in Krausen-street No. 124.

CHAPTER LVIII.

THE PROCURESS.

THROUGH a low green front door, and across a narrow entry, the two women advanced to, and ascended a small staircase.

Here Mrs. Rüthmann stopped to open a room-door, and they entered a well lighted, plainly furnished chamber.

The apartment was painted grey, the furniture was plain and common, but substantial and useful. The room contained a bed with a blue cotton coverlet, opposite to which stood a sofa, covered with black, somewhat faded woolen stuff; a large arm-chair similarly covered stood by the side of the stove. Besides these things, there was a clothes-press, a table, a bureau, some chairs and a few other similar articles, all of plain beach-wood.

The room was quite cold. The large stove seemed unused to heat.

"Wait a moment, my dear child," began Mrs. Rüthmann, with an air of busy care, to Marianne, who evidently was shivering with cold, "you shall not stay in this cold room."

At these words she walked towards another door directly opposite, leading to another apartment, which was much more elegantly furnished than any one would have suspected from the appearance of the first room.

All the furniture was mahogany, and brightly polished.

A splendid, high Trumeaux graced the mirror wall. The sofa, covered with morocco, gave evidence of taste; before it stood a round table, covered with a handsome red cover. The large, handsome tent-bedstead was hung with long, snowy curtains, similar to those which adorned the windows. All the other furniture was in equally good taste and keeping.

A remarkable degree of negligence and uncleanliness seemed, however, to prevail in this room, which would cause a disagreeable contrast in the mind of a person of refined taste. Along the walls, which were covered with fine tapestry, numerous grease-spots were visible, the floor showed marks of spilled wine, the edge of the carpet was burned by a cigar, and the curtains of the bed and window, though fine and white, were hung with little care, and looked crumpled. The elegant arrangements of the room in this manner lost the appearance of neatness and refinement, and assumed a look and a style which betrayed recklessness and extravagance in the owner.

The apartment was pleasantly and comfortably warmed.

"So then," began the hostess to the girl, who was trembling with cold, this place is much better, and here you shall remain. But above all, take off those wet things, else you will become sick."

Marianne looked around the finely furnished room in utter astonishment, and could scarcely comprehend how she had come to so fine a place.

"And am I to remain here?" she inquired, at last, in astonishment; "no, no, this place is much too fine for me. Let me remain in the other room with you."

"You little fool, and why not remain here?" answered the other, in good-natured, motherly care, "would you catch your death of cold? The other room is not warmed. I don't regret any thing I do for such a sweet, good girl as you are. But hurry, my dear, hurry and take off those wet things.

"I have no others," replied the poor girl, as she sought protection against the influence of the weather and her wet clothes, by the warm stove.

"Hm! hm! cried Mrs. Rüthmann, striking her forehead with her hand, "how very stupid I am! I might have known that beforehand; but yet I can help you, even now. A friend of mine, a short time ago entrusted her daughter to my care for a few weeks, and that girl's wardrobe is still here, and I will go and bring it to you. The girl was just about your own size, and I have no doubt her clothes will fit you exactly.

Quickly Mrs. Rüthmann opened the mahogany wardrobe, and produced thence several articles of linen and ladies' dress.

Marianne at first refused to dress herself in this fine linen, but the other pressed her so motherly and kindly, that no choice remained to her.

"Did I not tell you?—everything fits you charmingly!" cried Mrs. Rüthmann, when she saw Marianne stand before her dressed in fine white under clothes; "now you need a frock; but I suppose that must be no other than this black silk dress; that is the one you must put on."

"Oh, gracious no!" exclaimed Marianne eagerly, "how could I dare to wear silk! Give me some common old frock, or a cloth, which I will wrap round me, and wait until my own dress is dry."

"No, no, my dear!" cried Mrs. Rüthmann in the same kind tone as before, "then you will after all, catch a cold. No, no, Ma'mselle, this will never do. Come here and put this on! You will soon see how pretty you will look in it."

At these words she threw the dress over the girl's head, and began busily to fasten it at the back.

"Charming!" she cried, clapping her hands, "now just look into the mirror—how elegant you look! Did I not tell you so?"

And in reality the new toilette gave the finely formed girl a most lovely, charming appearance.

"But look how bare my neck is," said Marianne, blushing to her eye-brows; "no, no, I am not used to that, and cannot remain so."

"Pshaw, pshaw! good gracious," continued the procuress, chattering, "such happens to be the fashion. What can dress-makers do? young people will have it so. But upon the whole you are right, so you may tie this neckerchief around you." At these words she gave the girl a very small gauze handkerchief, which as a covering was but little better than none at all.

"I really have my own pleasure in dressing you up so," she continued, chattering in the most friendly tone, "and I cannot bear to see your head-dress in such bad order; just look, your hair is wringing wet. Come, come, sit down, and let me have my fun. I want to see if I cannot dress your head more nicely."

Marianne was forced to take a seat before the large mirror, and in a few minutes the old woman had built a most splendid head-dress from the rich silky hair of the girl.

"Now, I will trouble you no longer," she continued, smilingly, "after you have so far complied with my will; I will now provide a little further for you, and prepare a cup of warm tea for ourselves. You will soon feel the benefit of it."

Evening had meanwhile set in. Mrs. Rüthmann lighted her lamp, and had soon set a comfortable tea-table, with all the necessary appurtenances.

Marianne felt her strength gradually restored by the pleasant warmth and the necessary food. With difficulty she prevented the hospitality of her hostess from giving her one cup of tea after another, all of them strongly mixed with rum, which Mrs. Rüthmann assured her was necessary to obviate sickness in consequence of the cold, which most probably she had taken.

At the request of Mrs. Rüthmann, Marianne related all the occurrences of her wretched life since the time she had last seen her in the prison. She was naturally willing to comply with this request, as it is ever pleasant to relate past sufferings.

The other listened most attentively, only occasionally betraying an inner excitement by a sigh or a shake of the head. But a strange liveliness overspread her faded features, when she learned that the girl at present was without a home or a shelter, and that she was moreover persecuted by the police, and threatened with the work-house.

"My dear child," she began, when Marianne had concluded, "God has been good to you. For the present you have at least found me, and you may remain with me as long as ever you like. This room is vacant, and here you will not interfere with me nor I with you."

"You remove a heavy weight from my breast," said Marianne, gladly consenting in her harmless innocence; "but I certainly must begin something, that I may not fall a burden to you."

"Well, well, we shall see about that," replied the other, "we shall see what can be done; we will quietly consult about that subject together, and we will soon form a plan of life for you. But above all, you must have rest, and try to recover from your severe sufferings."

"You really are too kind," cried Marianne, thankfully. "And to think that I could once be persuaded to believe you capable of bad intentions towards me. I must really beg your pardon for that supposition."

"What do you mean, I do not understand you?"

"One of our fellow prisoners," continued Marianne, "when I left the prison, gave me a bit of writing, wherein she warned me against you, and spoke ill of you, and I could almost have believed her."

Rage and anger overspread the face of the procuress with a scarlet hue, but soon she again recovered her self-possession.

"Who is there that could be safe against such women," she said, "but I scorn to defend myself against such a one."

"No, no," said Marianne entreatingly, "you shall not defend yourself against her, for I already deeply repent the wrong I have done you in thought."

"You shall see whether I mean it well with you," continued the other with a coaxing smile; "my young female friends have ever found a home at my house exceedingly comfortable and pleasant."

A ringing of the door-bell here interrupted the conversation of the two.

Mrs. Rüthmann quickly left the room.

It was a long while before she returned. Marianne heard her in lively under-tone conversation with a manly voice in the next room. At last she entered the room in company of a young gentleman, very fashionably and foppishly dressed, whom she introduced to Marianne, as her particular friend, *Mr. Henri.*

Marianne thought that she recognised the face which she had observed looking at her when in the carriage in *Behren-street,* from the window of the elegant house, at which Mrs. Rüthman had stopped in the afternoon, on pretence of business.

The stranger seemed perfectly at home and at his ease.

He stretched himself comfortably upon the sofa, placed his feet upon a cushioned chair, and endeavoured to enter into a conversation with the girl. This endeavour, however, was perfectly fruitless, as Marianne was too diffident, modest and restrained, to give him more than the most simple monosyllabic answers.

She felt a particular dislike towards Mr. Henri; perhaps, because late occurrences had made her even more misanthropic than before, perhaps, because he really had something repulsive in his exterior, which indicated a great degree of impudence mixed with haughtiness.

After a while, Mrs. Rüthman left the room to look after some few domestic affairs.

The gentleman availed himself of this opportunity to make closer approaches to the girl.

He drew a chair close to the one upon which she had seated herself with her knitting, and endeavoured, by trifling attentions, to establish a degree of confidence.

Marianne, by this proceeding, found herself in a disagreeable, almost fearful position. She would most gladly have fled from his importunities, if she had only known how and whither.

Yet she suffered all his silly flatteries and attentions, until the gentleman finally bowed his head and attempted to kiss her bare shoulder.

Then the rage of insulted modesty suddenly awoke in her breast. Quickly she rose from her seat, and weeping she met Mrs. Rüthmann, who was just entering the room.

"Why, why, what does this mean?" cried the old woman, apparently very angry; "young gentleman, I must beg you to leave this girl alone. You know that I won't take a joke upon some points."

Somewhat abashed, the gentleman began to look for his hat.

"The girl is as hard and inaccessible as a piece of cast steel," he cried, partly annoyed, and partly laughing; "is it such a great crime if one desires to kiss a beautiful neck? Well. well, I will exile myself for the crime I have committed. Adieu, my dear, pretty, angry child! Only permit me to come back again some time."

At these words the stranger disappeared. Mrs. Rüthmann followed him to the next room. Marianne soon heard him exclaim in a half-loud tone of voice: "devilish high, but that is the way." Soon after she heard him leave the house.

"A very wild fellow, but after all a most charming young man, and rich, rich as King Solomon," began Mrs. Rüthmann, as she returned to the room. "Don't feel so much annoyed about what he did, my dear child. We must occasionally have a little patience with these men, if they are otherwise good to us."

Without replying a word, and heaving a deep sigh, Marianne had resumed her place.

"Oh! as I was about to tell you," recommenced the procuress, "I have sent him away. You must oblige me and go to bed very early this evening, that you may rest from all the fatigues and troubles of this day. To-morrow will be another day for work."

Marianne most willingly gave her consent. She felt bodily and mentally wearied and exhausted, and rest was the only object she really desired or needed.

Mrs. Rüthmann arranged the large tent-bed in the room.

"Before you go to sleep," she said, with motherly care, "you must drink what I have prepared for you in this glass; it tastes very fine, and it is an excellent domestic remedy for all colds, and bodily or mental excitements."

[Unmutilated and Only Genuine Edition.]

THIERS' LIFE OF NAPOLEON.

WITH SUPERB STEEL ENGRAVINGS.

FOR SEVENTY-FIVE CENTS,

[If paid in Advance.]

W. H. COLYER having been at great expense to procure a copy of this unrivalled work, now publishes

PART I.

OF THE

HISTORY OF THE CONSULATE AND THE EMPIRE

OF

FRANCE UNDER NAPOLEON,

By M. A. THIERS,

LATE PRIME MINISTER OF FRANCE.

WM. H. COLYER's edition of this splendid work, The Life of Napoleon, is decidedly the best in this country. It is printed on fine paper and new type, according to the design of the author, M. A. Thiers, and on comparison with other editions will be found far superior.

In Press.

THIERS' FRENCH REVOLUTION,

TO BE COMPLETED IN SIX PARTS, AT 12 1-2 CENTS EACH.

TO BE COMPLETED IN TEN NUMBERS.

THE MYSTERIES OF BERLIN,

FROM

THE PAPERS OF A BERLIN CRIMINAL OFFICER.

TRANSLATED FROM THE GERMAN,

By C. B. BURKHARDT.

With Illustrations on Steel, by P. Habelmann.

This work in Europe has been universally pronounced far superior to M. Sue's celebrated "Mysteries of Paris," and we confidently predict that the popularity of this translation will be without a parallel in the history of light reading.

THE MYSTERIES of BERLIN.

TO BE COMPLETED

IN

TEN PARTS

NEW YORK: WILLIAM H. COLYER, PUBLISHER.

In reality, Marianne felt but very little inclination to take the domestic remedy; but the indefatigable care of her kind friend touched her heart most deeply. She could not refuse to comply with her urgent request, and unsuspiciously swallowed the draught.

With a last friendly wish of "good night," the other left the room to seek her bed also, and soon the poor, wearied Marianne fell into a deep and sound sleep.

Poor, poor maiden, there is no secure sleep for thee!

CHAPTER LIX

THE AWAKENING.

As Marianne opened her eyes on the next morning, her first glance fell upon the stranger of yesterday, who quietly reposed by her side in bed, and fixed a smiling look upon her.

With a yelling cry of despair she jumped from the bed, and undressed as she was, rushed to the front room, where Mrs. Rüthmann was just rising.

It would be a vain undertaking, were we to endeavour to describe in words the paroxysm of despair, and the misery of soul in which the poor girl found herself. Where should we find the colours to portray so much misery?

She wept, raved, cried like a maniac, tore the hair from her head, endeavoured to take her own life, until finally she sunk in a death-like swoon to the ground.

But in an instant the consciousness of her terrible fate had awakened her again; her raving and despair began anew, until a second time she sunk exhausted to the floor.

She herself knew not what had become of her. Utter unconsciousness had overpowered her, and had held all her senses captive throughout the night. But this much she understood, that a new, a terrible misfortune had befallen her, more black and more terrible than all preceding ones, and that the bitter curse of sin had been pronounced upon her whole future life.

The poor, unfortunate girl! Oh, that she had listened to the honest warning of the woman in the criminal prison! She had fallen into the hands of the most expert, the most dangerous procuress in Berlin, and a narcotic sleeping draught, offered by the hand of friendship, had assisted that fiend to rob the poor girl of the only, the holiest earthly treasure she possessed.

Mrs. Rüthmann, in the present position of things, betrayed as much keen knowledge of human nature, as she had shown herself to possess of cunning worthlessness.

She suffered the girl to rave, cry and weep as much as she liked, without offering the least consolation or contradiction. Only after physical exhaustion had overpowered Marianne, when no earnest or effective opposition could be expected

to remain in her fragile frame, she began her explanation.

"You are an ungrateful wretch," she commenced in furious indignation, "to thank me in this manner for all the motherly love and care I have bestowed upon you. What is it you would have, and what do you complain of? Here in my house you can have an elegant residence, good food, fine dresses, luxury and pleasure, in short, everything your heart can desire, and you can keep it as long as it pleases you. Does such a life bear a comparison with all the misery and wretchedness from which I have delivered you? Say, just answer me that?"

Marianne had sunk upon the sofa in apathetic exhaustion, unable to utter a sound.

"Mr. Henri loves you," continued the procuress in a more gentle tone, "and he will give you every thing you want; so it will be your own fault if you do not make hay whilst the sun shines."

Marianne still lay upon the sofa, her eyes half closed, and without a sign of life or motion.

"Above all things, you are now saved from the hands of the police, and I should think that at least would be worth an acknowledgment at your hands. Mr. Henri will support you, that is all we need to inform the police of, who will be satisfied, and not trouble you any further with questions about your residence or employment."

At these words, Marianne started wildly up. "Ha! that is just right," she exclaimed, "it is just right that you remind me of the police. Thither will I go, and see whether the authorities will not do justice to an innocent, betrayed, and ill-used creature."

"Don't I tell you," quietly answered the procuress, "that the police will be satisfied on learning that you are supported by somebody, and that they will no longer threaten you with the vagrant laws, or trouble you to prove how you support yourself; is not all this right enough?"

"No, no!" cried Marianne, almost beside herself, "it is not right enough. I shall seek my rights against you, against your shameless, terrible treatment, against the cruel manner in in which you cast a poor orphan girl entirely to perdition. I will complain against this until I am heard, and if I should lose my voice in the attempt."

"I am to understand the matter in this way, then?" inquired the other, scornfully; "my good child, don't you dare to repeat those words, else you might bitterly repent them. Do you see, I shall throw you out of doors, together with your few rags, and shall simply deny ever having come in contact with you. What can you do or prove then? You will not even have the time given to you to attempt such a proof; they will keep you, and even as they have already threatened, will send you to the work-house for vagrancy. Now you can have your choice, and take a resolution accordingly; will you remain with me, or go to the police?"

13

"Overcome, momentarily, by fresh horrors, Marianne listened to every word of this speech. Alas! the procuress was perfectly in the right. She was repulsed by the whole world, and even excluded from the benefits of the law—a law which she, the innocent victim, was destined to know only in its punishing rigour, not in its protecting and sheltering power.

But whither should she turn if the procuress withdrew her hand from her? A great part of the three days of grace given her by the police had already elapsed; her employment in the manufactory she had lost, and she could not hope to obtain a lodging-place for herself. The work-house, with all its terror, must receive her, if she would even endeavour to escape from the poisoning grasp of the procuress.

This terrible alternative suddenly rose clearly before Marianne's mind. With the rapidity of lightning, all these considerations passed before her soul? What was she to do now whither to turn? Her religious and moral power had been broken by the most unparalleled blows of fate, and now her body had only suffered equal ill usage. The last blow was but little more severe than the former ones.

We must remember that her mental innocence had long since deserted her. She had preserved it pure in the cellar of hunchbacked Jobs; but in the criminal-prison, she had lost it. Moreover, she was bodily sick, her health shaken and exhausted. This will perhaps explain why her resistance was weaker than it would have been under any other circumstances.

In a word, she was utterly annihilated.

After a long while, she said, gloomily to the procuress, who seemed watching for her prey:

"You are right, and I am in the wrong; we will remain together. Tell the police whatever you may think best."

And thus, Marianne had at last sunk down among the lowest of her sex, and the cause, the guilt of this terrible fate rested upon no one person—it rested upon the mismanagement, the contradictions and the tyranny of our social institutions.

END OF PART FOUR.

PART V.

CHAPTER LX.

NEWS OF THE JEW AND THE PRINCE.

ALTHOUGH Jobs, during a short time after his dismissal from prison, had been particularly careful, and had only admitted the most safe and trust-worthy of his acquaintances, he regained, after a while, his former security and boldness, and gradually the whole of the old company began to assemble at his cellar again.

It lies in the very nature of these frivolous beings, only to live for the next minute, indifferent to all that may happen to-morrow. At this moment the den of the hunchback seemed a pleasant retreat, a desirable place of meeting, and there they met, utterly forgetful of the police, and the late occurrence.

This peculiar feature in the character of criminals, is a mighty and powerful ally to civil order, which could scarcely ever attain its object, if the same shrewdness, care and vigilance, which distinguishes single master spirits among them, were equally shared by the great mass of criminals. In most cases it is a piece of stupidity, of incautiousness, of negligence, which strongly and strangely contrasts with the cunning and boldness, with which the previous crime had been committed, which bring the greatest criminals into the hands of justice.

As we said above, the business among the thieves in the cellar of Jobs had resumed its wonted activity, and most of the rogues sought a safe retreat in his cellar, when officers were in search of them. As a matter of course, they had to pay dear enough, with a great part of the stolen goods, for this accommodation.

On a stormy night in the early part of April, we again find very nearly the same company collected in the back cellar, which we found there in the early part of our narrative. It was a wild confused mass of thieves, robbers and worthless beings of both sexes.

A group was laying round a small cask, which stood on its end, and upon its top was a bowl of some beverage, which had been miscalled punch. Noise and wild laughter prevaded this group.

Others sat in the different corners absorbed in low, earnest conversations. The principal words which could be overheard, such as "Masematten," "Ausbaldower," "Chawrusse," &c., showed that the conversation turned upon their usual matters of business.

Blonde Augustus, and another fellow like himself, were laying in the back ground upon a bunch of straw. A female sat by their side, who received or returned their coarse caresses, in a noisy, wild and vulgar manner.

The hunchback walked in and out, bringing eatables or liquors, as they were ordered, and frequently admonishing the party to be quiet, and not arouse the neighbours with their noise. His admonitions were usually replied to with answers which sufficiently indicated the footing upon which he stood with his guests.

A sickening atmosphere prevailed through the cellar, consisting of a combination of tobacco fumes, the steam of bad liquors, the smoke of the oil-lamps, and other similar ingredients.

Among other well known faces, we also observe Eel-eye, who gloomily and quietly sat in a corner, without touching the liquor which stood before him.

His silence and gloom finally attracted the attention of the company, who was collected around the so-called punch bowl.

"What in the devil's name ails Eel-eye?" inquired the old rag-gatherer of her daughter, who, as we know, was originally the sweetheart of Eel-eye; "there he sits in that corner, just as if he was to be hung to-morrow, and leaves his schnapps untouched, as if it were mere water. Go to him, and see if you cannot rouse him, and bring him here."

For some time past a certain coolness had existed between Eel-eye and the Chonte, which coolness was by no means in favour of the cash account of the latter. She therefore gladly obeyed the request of her mother, and approached her former lover, who was sitting with his arms folded, and staring gloomily upon the ground.

"Tell me, Eel-eye," she began, "what in the devil's name ails you? you look almost as if you would begin the repentance of your sins: you will have plenty of time for that, when you grow old. Come, come and drink a glass of punch with us. My mother told me to ask you."

Eel-eye raised his head, and mechanically stared upon the speaker, like a person who has heard the sound of words, but without comprehending a particle of their meaning. He seemed entirely lost in inward meditation.

At last a deep sigh escaped his oppressed bosom. "Ah, Francisca!" he sighed, audibly enough to be heard by everybody.

This involuntary exclamation had scarcely escaped his lips, when the whole mass of guests in the cellar, burst into loud roaring peals of laughter.

The female was the first to clap her hands, and cry aloud: "Oh Jemini, Eel-eye is in love!" and the full chorus of vagabonds repeated noisily: "Eel-eye is in love!"

This noise awoke the thief from his meditations. Furiously he rose from his seat: "hold your tongues, ye vagabonds, and mind your own affairs. If one of you opens his mouth again, I will break his neck!"

Universal silence followed, for Eel-eye was a most daring fellow, whenever, as happened just then to be the case, he had been drinking. When he became angry in that state, he knew no bonds or moderation.

The rag-gatherer alone dared to walk up to him, and take his hand, as she said with a good natured grin: "don't be foolish, Eel-eye, come here to us, and drink a glass, and thus drown your blue devils. Here, *Kellerjette*, hand him a glass."

"You are right, old satan," replied Eel-eye, as he approached the company and swallowed a large glass of liquor; "come here, you girl, you may be Francisca for to-day."

And with these words he drew the girl towards him, and began to load her with wild caresses.

"The stiff Gottlieb, who had hitherto been engaged in settling some old accounts with blonde Augustus, and who had taken no notice of any of the other occurrences in the den, was just pocketing a handful of money, a balance which he had received at this settlement; he now turned round to Eel-eye:

"Harkye, Eel-eye," he began, "will you tell me, how your Masematten in the *Hotel de Paris*, with the Jew and Maulspitzer, terminated. That was a confounded scrape, and I have often wanted to ask you for the particulars; just tell us all about it now."

"Yes, yes," exclaimed blonde Augustus, and several others, "tell us all about that Masematten; the devil himself could not unravel the mystery of it. The Jew is said to have left the place; Maulspitzer, they say, has gone *verschütt*, and even you are scarcely ever to be found to give any information upon the subject."

Everybody in the cellar now pressed Eel-eye for his story, who finally agreed to comply with their wishes.

"Well, then," he began, "we had baldowert an excellent Masematten in the *Hotel de Paris*, and long Schmuel, Maulspitzer and myself, were about to *lukrire* (accomplish) it. It was in the apartments of a foreign Prince, who resided there. On the night agreed upon, we were upon our way there; I was to stand Schmiere according to agreement, whilst the other two would attempt the burglary. I did not altogether like this arrangement, for I believe that I am more handy than Maulspitzer, but he insisted upon it, and I gave way to him. The result showed that it would have been better if I had not done it.

"When we had arrived at the hotel, we immediately repaired to the carriage entrance in the side street. Our large key fitted, the door opened, and Schmuel and the Maulspitzer went to their work. I pressed into the corner of the door, that I might be enabled to keep a full view of the street, for it struck me that I had seen "white mountings" (a gensd'arme) at the end of the street.

"I had scarcely been ten minutes in this corner, when Schmuel rushed wildly out of the house, and with the cry of Lampen! Lampen! (officers) ran past me, to the street. Without looking round, I rushed after him; but I did not catch up with him, until we had reached the "*König-street*." He made no reply to my anxious questions. The Jew was perfectly beside himself; he swore, raved, tore his hair, cursed, and behaved like a maniac; with the utmost difficulty I elicited the following:

"Maulspitzer had mounted the ladder, which they had placed against a window of the first floor, and the Jew was following him step by step. The first, without great difficulty, had succeeded in breaking a window, perfectly noiselessly by means of a pitch-plaster, and had also withdrawn the inside bolts which held it. He had just entered the room, and the other was about to follow, when they heard a loud sneezing in the room, and at the same time observed a long figure moving towards the window from the neighbourhood of the stove.

"The Jew swears by all he holds dear and holy, that the figure was no other than Koftry, the body gensd'arme of the Polizeirath. In his fright, he jumps down the whole ladder, but luckily alights upon his feet, and runs off. As you may perhaps all know, he left Berlin with his wife and children on that very night, for he said he was fully convinced that Polizeirath X— wanted to catch him, and that he was only saved by the circumstance that long Koftry was forced to sneeze."

"Hm! the Jew has been a queer fellow all his life time," began blonde Augustus, in a dissatisfied tone, "but let him go, I would rather have him away. He was always sure to fish the best Masemattens out of our hand, and moreover, was coarse, rude and unsociable to us all."

The Jew had not been much mistaken in the present instance. He strongly suspected that Francisca had been a traitress. He had rightly recognised the long Koftry, that much feared and natural enemy of thieves, and of course, he could not suppose his presence to have been accidental or without a definite object. But the moment he knew that the police was actually searching for him, and upon the right scent, he considered it best immediately to change his quarters.

All these circumstances the Jew had fully communicated to Eel-eye, but the latter had not mentioned them again, as he was not desirous of letting the thieves know anything about the Equestrian.

"You are right," replied stiff Gottlieb to the last remark of blonde Augustus, "and now, since the Jew is gone, we might make a second and a more successful attempt of accomplishing this Masematten. What do you think, Eel-eye? Suppose that you, myself and blonde Augustus were to risk an attempt?"

"It would be of no use, my old friend," replied the other, "I have already thought of it, but it is too late. The Prince himself left the city a very short time after our attempt had failed. So we must of course give up all hopes of this fat job."

"Well, and the Maulspitzer?" inquired the rag-gatherer.

"Yes, yes, I had almost forgotten him," continued Eel-eye. "That is the worst, the most annoying part of the whole affair; the Maulspitzer, poor fellow, he is 'gone verschütt,' (has been caught.) They arrested him in the very room, and took him away to prison that same night. So the *portier* told me the next morning, when I, on passing by, engaged him in conversation. Further than this, I know nothing of the affair."

"Then, poor Maulspitzer is done for," observed another of the thieves present, who was remarkable for his usual quietness and the phlegmatic expression of his countenance, "he has committed the second grand larceny with forcible entry, is gone *treife verschütt*, (has been caught in the fact,) and now will be compelled to *make emmes*, (make a confession.)"

"Oh no," interrupted stiff Gottlieb, "I would not *make emmes* yet; I could find *a putz* (an excuse or defence) for him."

"Well, and what is that?"

"Perhaps you think I could not?"

"Exactly so."

"Well! I would tell them, on my examination, that the resident of the place had hired me to remove his furniture and other things silently and at midnight, as he was short of money, and wanted to leave the place without paying his house-rent."

"Stuff, Gottlieb, don't make a fool of yourself," cried the blonde Augustus, "who, in the devil's name, do you suppose would believe you? The *freier* (the person to be robbed) is a Prince, and enormously rich. Who would believe that he would try to escape paying a paltry rent?"

"Yes, yes," said Eel-eye, "it is only too true. Poor Maulspitzer will have to march to *the Larsel* (go to the penitentiary) for twenty-five years. I have already thought seriously upon it. I am half afraid that in his despair, he might make a great *emmes*, and let us all *go verschütt*, (make a general confession and betray us all.) Yes, children, that is the only thing I am afraid of. They will send him off for five and twenty years for his own burglary, of which they know, but if he confesses twenty more, he will not get any more severe punishment. This may turn out a pretty kettle of fish for us all, if he should take it into his head to get his inquisitor friendly towards himself, and you know the way to do that, is to betray as many undiscovered burglars and burglaries as he possibly can. The Lord knows where it might end."

"Pshaw! nonsense!" exclaimed the rag-gatherer, "what a stupid, useless fear that is! If he would make a great emmes, would it not be brought to daylight how the vigilant was made away with? and you know that trifle was a matter of life and death. He will be wise enough to avoid that."

"This *argumentum ad hominem* appeared very reasonable and natural to the thieves. The fear and anxiety which had begun to be felt by many of them, disappeared, and all commenced to shout, yell, sing and play as before, until they all sunk in a state of intoxication to the ground.

CHAPTER LXI.

JOBS AND THE RAG-GATHERER MAKE A COMPACT.

THE rag-gatherer was the only one who had remained sober among the whole company, although she had, perhaps, drunk more than any of them. She seemed more used to it than all the others, and spirits were like water to her.

Sitting upon a board, which was laid across a couple of buckets, she looked upon her glass with perfectly philosophical quiet and indifference, and continued to drink and replenish it, as long as she could find a drop of spirits in any of the bottles or jugs.

Gradually all around her became silent. One

after another the thieves fell asleep, and very soon their heavy breathing and snoring was the only indication of the presence of human beings in the den.

The rag-gatherer opened her glassy eyes and carefully looked around, as far as the dim light of the lamp would admit her to discern objects.

When she observed that all had fallen asleep, she rose silently from her temporary seat, and in her stocking feet she approached the straw-bed where Eel-eye lay asleep by the side of her daughter.

Listening, she bent down her head; both were fast asleep and snoring.

Gently and quietly she reached out her long bony fingers, inserted them into the breast pocket of the thief, and thence abstracted his pocket-book. With this she retreated to her seat, in order to examine its contents more closely.

Her expectations seemed but ill satisfied, for she only found three paper thalers, which she took grumblingly and with a shake of her head, and then walked back and restored the pocket-book to its place.

The whole manœuvre looked like the movements of a spectral phantom. The rag-gatherer with her long, thin and haggard figure, her ragged clothing, the loose, rough hair that hung wildly around her head, gave her the appearance of a fabulous vampyre, seeking its prey in a grave-yard.

As she had just completed her work, and was about to rise from the bent position in which she had restored the pocket-book to Eel-eye's pocket, she was interrupted by hearing, Pst! pst! called to her several times.

Frightened she looked around, and discovered the huchbacked Jobs, who stood at the entrance of the cellar, whence he had smilingly and with evident satisfaction observed her movements.

The hunchback beckoned her towards him with his finger.

"Half shares!" he cried in a whisper, as she approached him; "and I will not betray you. Come with me to the front cellar and I will tell you something; but be careful, and step softly that you may not awake any of these. There, look out, and don't step upon stiff Gottlieb, for that fellow only sleeps like a watch dog. Be careful, here lies *Kellerjette.*—Now, step softly! There, that will do, come along."

And the amiable couple left the back-den.

"Well, old woman, was it worth while to pick that rascal's pocket?" inquired the host, as he left the place with his worthy companion.

"Oh dear, no," replied the rag-gatherer discontentedly, "the scoundrel buys himself fine clothes and all sorts of nonsense, enough to make one believe he had at least hundreds in his pocket-book. To look at him, and at his behaviour, one would certainly think so. But when I came to look at it closer, I could only find two ragged thalers. There, Jobs, there is one for you; I will divide honestly with you, but you must hold your tongue and not try to create any difficulties."

"Keep your money, rag-gatherer," said Jobs, more friendly than he was ever in the habit of speaking; "I shall not betray you. But you must in return help me in another affair, which I take a great interest in; and you can make a good round sum by it."

The rag-gatherer raised her head attentively, and grinningly she winked with her eyes, thereby endeavouring to express her consent and satisfaction.

Jobs walked back through the dark passage, in order to convince himself that nobody had followed them, then he pressed the clothes-press before the opening, closed it carefully, and conducted his companion to his front store.

"Well, old woman, what say you," he began; "suppose we two take a little Schnapps together? It is rather cold to night. I have excellent Danzic Gold-water. Just look how the gold floats about in it."

At these words he held a greasy, dim looking liquor-bottle, before the oil lamp, which was still more dim.

"Why yes," replied the old woman grinningly, as a fresh desire for liquor awoke in her, "just bring it out; I have no doubt it will do me a great deal of good."

"That is right, old woman, we must take a drink, since we have to watch together. There was a time when we were young as well as others, so we will think of the time of our youthful pranks. If we were still as active as then, we would not sit this way and talk old matters over. Hi! hi! hi! What do you think, rag-gatherer? Well, old woman, here goes! to your very good health!"

During this intellectual rhapsody, the hunchback had brought two glasses from a cupboard, and placed them upon the counter. He then took a seat by the rag-gatherer, and filled both glasses with the much praised Gold-water.

The rag-gatherer took her glass with greedy, sparkling eyes, and emptied it at a draught.

"Well, old woman, is it not fine?"

"Excellent, Jobs!"

"Come, take another?"

"Certainly, why not?" said the rag-gatherer, smacking her lips.

"Now listen to me, old woman," began Jobs, after he had filled her glass again, and had then carefully removed the bottle and placed it back upon its shelf; "now listen. You come about in so very many different places; tell me, have you any idea or suspicion whereabouts Marianne may be at present."

"Well, old Jobs, I should think that you might be glad of having finally got rid of that girl; for this place, and for your business, Marianne certainly is not suited, and why should you trouble yourself further about her?"

"Don't say that; I feel a great interest in the girl."

The rag-gatherer laughed aloud.

"An interest, such as a cat feels in a mouse," she exclaimed, "don't try to make a fool of me,

Jobs. We all know perfectly well, that she is no kith or kin of yours; and if we did not know it, I would tell it you; the girl is a great deal too handsome and too good for you."

"Hm! that may all be; I don't trouble myself about beauty or goodness; but I would like to ascertain where the girl is to be found at present, and you perhaps may assist me in ascertaining that. Now speak out, will you?"

"Certainly, and why not! I am always ready when anything is to be gained by it. But what the devil made you of a sudden such a tender and careful father to the girl?"

Jobs directed his mouse grey blear eyes with a penetrating glance upon the copper coloured features of the rag-gatherer, who apparently asked this question with the greatest indifference. He guessed, however, the object of her inquiry.

"Can you keep a secret, old woman?"

"Certainly I can."

"So can I."

"Hm!" said the rag-gatherer somewhat annoyed at this answer, "then you can attend to your business alone, and not trouble me about it."

"But, old woman," recommenced the hunchback in a friendly tone, "be not foolish, and do wrong to yourself. Find the girl for me, there is money I tell you, there is much money to be made by it."

"Very well, you old sinner, but you must deal openly with me. If there is any thing to be gained by it, I am with you, but I don't want to bring the poor girl into new misery."

"You are not in your right senses," exclaimed Jobs, scratching his bushy head behind his ears; "you have drunk too much Danzic water; who the devil is speaking about misery? I will tell you the whole history, for I can never leave this accursed cellar hole, and I would rather make a confidante of you than of any of the other thieves and scoundrels that are in there. The Jew, unfortunately, who knew the whole affair, is no longer here, else he might assist me. But be silent, let us first see that no one is listening in the passage."

"Don't make a fool of yourself in your cowardice," cried the rag-gatherer. "Tell me all you have to tell me, for I would soon like to go to sleep."

"As you already know," began Jobs, after having again assured himself that no one was listening, "or at least as you say you know, Marianne is not my daughter. Before ever I was married to my wife, she had this child. The father of the girl is a very rich and noble gentleman, who is still alive. My dear departed wife lived with this gentleman at his country-seat, long before we were married, or before I knew her. She had entered into some amour with the gentlemen's yæger, and the consequence was, that on its discovery, the master drove mother and child away from his place, and both arrived here in Berlin, where they had neither friends nor home.

"Accidentally, the woman rented lodgings in the same house and upon the same floor where I then carried on my clockmaking business. She possessed a few hundred thalers, from which, for the present, she supported herself and her child. I knew this from the fact that she had once asked me for advice how she could keep her money in the most secure way. At that time, my business of clockmaking began to grow worse and worse every day, and I laid a plan of commencing tavern-keeping outside of the Hallegate. I proposed to this woman to marry her, and to establish my house with the money she had remaining.

"Situated as she then was, lonely and deserted, she gladly assented to my proposition. By a great many small obligations, I had tolerably well gained her favour; we were married, and I began my new business. But I had no good luck: my tavern would not flourish or become popular, and an accursed lawsuit which I had with a countryman, whom I cheated by selling him a sick horse, added no little to my distress, and at last, after having lost nearly all we possessed, I was glad to fly to this hole for refuge. My wife, who would never cease weeping and grieving for her gentleman, soon afterwards died, and the child remained on my hands."

"She died? Hm! she died, Jobs?" interrupted the rag-gatherer; "yes, very well, she died! Of course, how, you know best yourself. I have nothing to say about it."

"I could very easily have got rid of the child," continued the other, without taking notice of the interruption, "but that did not answer my purpose. My dear departed had communicated to me a document, or rather, I had once found it among her things, in which the father of Marianne secures to her, on the day of her marriage, or if not married, whenever she shall be twenty-two years of age, the sum of three thousand thalers. Now you see, old woman, that money I would like to finger, and then I shall give up this dog's trade here, and begin something better again.

"If I had returned the girl to her father before this, he might have taken her out of my hands, and in that way have withdrawn the whole sum of money from me; or else if the girl should have died before she had reached her twenty-second year, her father might have heard of it, and have withdrawn the sum secured to her. As it is at present, I am not prevented by any thing from offering him any other person instead of his daughter, in case the girl should happen to die. For all these reasons, you must perceive that it is of the utmost importance to me, not to remain in ignorance of the present residence of Marianne, even though it is yet a long while before we can expect to touch the money. I am not at all sorry that she is no longer with us here in the cellar, for I was constantly afraid that she might some day betray us all; unfortunately, I could never succeed in inducing her to participate in any of our secret business. But on the other hand, I must keep an eye upon her, must know where she is, that I may take her when the time comes, bring her to the old gentleman, and pocket the money."

"Oho!" exclaimed the rag-gatherer, "now I know why you were so cautious and secret. It was, because you thought I might lay a claim to part of the three thousand thalers. No, no, old friend, I am not quite so dear in my prices."

"Very well, then," said Jobs. "So you agree to assist me in finding out the residence of Marianne."

"I agree! it is a bargain! but now tell me who is the father of the girl?"

Jobs looked at her sideways with a cunning smile and wink, and said:

"You are very cunning, old woman, but I am not stupid enough to tell you all about that. I don't see why you should know it."

"You confounded old sinner!" cried the rag-gatherer with an angry and disappointed look; "but that is the way with persons who never have a good conscience. You are again afraid, that I want to get more of the money than my share, but you are mistaken. I only ask, because I am astonished, that the father himself should never have made any inquiry for his child."

"Yes, you old witch," replied Jobs with a broad grin upon his homely face, "I took good care of that. He could not well trouble himself about his child, when he did not know where the mother was to be found, and moreover he was perhaps very angry, that he should never have heard of her, who seemed to care nothing more for him."

"Oh, now I understand," observed the rag-gatherer, "no doubt, you took good care that he should not find out where they were."

"Exactly so, you old witch," said Jobs, laughing, "you see, I am not quite as stupid as I look. Before I was married to my wife, I suppose that she must have written no less than fifty letters to her gentleman, and more than twice as many after marriage; but as these letters all passed through my hand, I took them to any other place but the Post office. I may as well tell you at once," he continued, laughing at his own villany, "that I knew all about this affair of the three thousand thalers, long before ever I began my connexion with the dear departed. I wondered upon what means that woman could possibly live, since she did not work, but always remained sadly and quietly at home with her child. One morning, when she was gone out, I entered her room by means of a false key, opened her bureau and found the money and the document. If I had not found the latter, I should have quietly pocketed the ready cash, and retired. But under existing circumstances, a speculation of three thousand thalers was open for me. I threw myself in the way of this woman, forced myself into her favour, and thus I finally married her."

"Hm, you certainly did risk a great deal for the three thousand thalers; I would not undertake such a very long running account."

"Yes, yes, you may easily talk. You don't know anything about my affairs at that time. You don't know in what a tight place I then was with my clockmaking business. And besides, in the devil's name, are not three thousand thalers a sum worth working for? But at the same time, I immediately determined to assist the course of nature a little, and you know how soon I was done with my dear departed. She, at least, did not see much of my plans. That she obstinately refused to earn something in our way was a fault, which had not occurred to me beforehand. If the girl had taken to our ways, as she ought to have done, she might have made a great deal of money for me. All the fellows were constantly crazy after her.—But all this cannot be helped; and I must only be careful, that she comes back into my hands before it is too late. The worst would be, if she were to leave Berlin; she always had a desire to do so. So the wisest thing you can do, rag-gatherer, is to start out to-morrow morning, and institute a thorough search for her. You shall make a good speculation out of it, if you find her."

"Depend on it, I will hunt her up, old scoundrel. And be sure, that you cannot cheat me any more, else I will betray you."

"Pshaw!" exclaimed old Jobs, laughing, but with a displeased countenance: "I tell you, you shall have no reason to complain, upon *Lotscher-ehre*, (thieves honour.")

"Very well! but now I want to go sleep. So let me out of here, Jobs."

"Immediately, old woman."

And the compact of love and friendship was thus sealed.

CHAPTER LXII.

WHAT OCCURS IN BRAUNSDORF.

In sadness and silence Major von Steinfort walked up and down the lonely rooms of his mansion, at his country seat, Braunsdorf.

It was evening, and towards eight o'clock.

The newly awakened Spring spreads its benign influence over all nature, and the evening was balmy and delightful. Soft zephyrs fanned the burning brow of the old warrior, and upon their wings carried the rural melodies of the returning flocks to the ears of the inhabitants of the proud mansion.

The open window brought the balmy breath of Spring and the rural tones to the senses of the Major, but he heeded them not. Fond as he was of the beauties of nature, acceptable as was his honest heart to the good, true and beautiful, at present all this beauty was lost upon him.

He had this moment received another letter from his son, wherein the latter informed him, that despite all obstacles, despite all difficulties, he was fully determined to marry the girl of his choice. Just at the present moment, he considered it his most holy duty not to retract one iota of his promise, for he was convinced that he had brought the girl to a consciousness of her position, and that he would make her forever miserable, if he would not now place her physically and mentally in a better and more appropriate position. Moreover, he was fully convinced that he could not be happy without this girl, and if his father would not wish him to doubt his paternal affection, he must give his consent to this marriage.

In the first moments after reading this letter, the Major was boiling over with wrath and indignation, but as no one happened to be present upon whom he could vent his fury, his intense passion subsided gradually, and sadness, deep and bitter sorrow took the place of rage.

He considered it his imperative duty to prevent his son from committing so foolish an action as that which he seemed determined upon, and yet he hesitated again on remembering how deeply he must wound him. The experience of his own youth told him, how very difficult it was to relinquish a true attachment.

This was a passage in his own life upon which the Major never touched, not even in company of his most intimate friends; a passage which was and remained a secret to his son, and which he himself was loath to recall to memory. But he had been compelled to relinquish his passion, and had become happy after all—happy, at least as much as constantly recurring sad recollections of an unatoned wrong committed in his early youth, and which was closely connected with that dark passage of his life, permitted him to be happy.

Absorbed in the deep and earnest thoughts which were always created by these reflections, the Major, with strides which fully indicated the restlessness of his mind, walked up and down the room, loudly conversing with himself.

He had written a long and elaborate reply to his son's letter, in which he threatened him with his curse and disinheritance, if the latter should ever contract this marriage without his father's will and consent.

This letter, sealed and enveloped, lay upon the table before him, ready to be sent off.

As often as the Major passed the table, he looked sadly towards that letter, took it into his hand, and walked a few steps towards the bell-rope, to call a servant and send the epistle to the post office. But thoughtfully he always laid it down again.

"Oh, if the Prince were only here," he said with a silent sigh, "that I might have a sensible man by my side, to whom I could tell my misery, and who could advise me in this dilemma. If I look back upon my own life, I find that I have no right to act harshly and authoritatively here, and yet it must be so. The boy must not disgrace himself, for I can see it only too well, that he must make himself miserable by it. It will be useless for him to try and oppose the well established forms and regulations of society, and the hereditary distinction of rank; society would crush him. Let it cost what it may, I must endeavour to guard him against that."

The Major stood still, and looked thoughtfully out of the window over the wide luxuriant domain which stretched before his eyes. A variegated busy mass of happy rustics, who owned him as their feudal master, returning from their work, passed along; rich meadows, fine flocks and luxuriant fields lay before him; all seemed to indicate peace, comfort and plenty.

"Thunder and the devil," at last exclaimed the old soldier furiously, "and is all this to be the inheritance of a woman of that class? Should I have laboured, saved and economized, to let such a one spend it all in pride, vanity and dissipation? Thunder and the devil! the boy must have lost his senses. This madness! folly! nonsense! I know all that a heart may experience, and suffer, for I once suffered it all myself, but at least I had an eye to honesty and modesty. And yet that modesty deceived me;" he added after a pause, and in a lower and more sad tone, "appearances deceived me, and it is well that I discovered the truth, though it was a sad experience. But that same truth lies unveiled before the eyes of that boy, there is no deceptive appearance in this case, yet with his open eyes, he will be blind. Impossible! I cannot consent to this."

The Major again approached the bell-rope. But when he reached it, he again stopped and hesitated.

"I am loath to wound him so deeply and bitterly," he said hesitatingly. "I know him! my own blood runs in his veins, he is wild and impetuous. If my letter were to drive him to despair, and he were to resort to a last remedy? He might oppose me after all, or he might do himself an injury, and in either case, all would be lost."

The Major's hand had reached for the bell-rope, but again his arm relaxed and sunk down.

"I have once before been harsh and impetuous in my life," he said, "and that severity has cost me a child. Shall I now rob myself of my second, the only one that is left me? What can have become of that unfortunate woman—what of the poor girl? She would now be a full grown young woman! Hm! Can I never free myself of those sad recollections? A thousand times already have I believed them effectually banished from my heart."

Thoughtfully, the Major pressed his hand against his burning forehead.

"But no," he cried impetuously, rousing himself, "I have acted rightly. I had loved and supported a bastard. This is my merited punishment, for having deserted the strict path of established order, upon which rests society and its best regulations. I obeyed its mandates; and I afterwards became happy with the woman of my choice. And so it will be with my boy: I must then take my course; I can and dare hesitate no longer. Order rules the world, and a father must rule his son. Let him rave and be angry at his old father; his fury will come to an end, and he will then begin to understand that no one in the world meant it as well and honestly with him as this old grey-head."

The Major once more took the bell-rope to call the servant, when a shrill post-horn, which approached his mansion, interrupted him anew.

He looked out, and discovered an express rider, who was just leaping from his foaming horse.

Immediately after, his *Major-domo* entered the room, and presented a despatch, which the express had brought.

"Send this letter to my son to the post," said the Major, "and send Francis up here with lights."

"Very well, Herr Major."

And the major-domo left the room.

"Incidents are multiplying here, at my usually quiet country seat," said the Major to himself. "First, this worthless boy sets my head almost crazy, and now, they even send expresses with despatches after me. This seems to be a wild, crazy time, worse than ever I witnessed it. Thunder and the devil! when I remember my campaigns! those times were wild and crazy enough; but still there was some order and subordination, and things took their regular course. But now-a-days, a fellow becomes almost a coward in his own quiet house. I wish the devil had the whole of this accursed affair! I often wish, that they had already packed me between my last six boards."

The servant entered, and placed the bright astral lamp upon the table. He then prepared himself as usual to assist his master in undressing.

"Go down stairs, Francis," said the Major quickly, after he had cast a hasty glance at the large seal upon the envelope of the despatch, "this will do, I will ring for you when I want you again."

The despatch came from Prince Prominsky.

For some time the Major had been in anxious uncertainty about the fate of the Prince. He opened the envelope with some excitement.

The contents of the Prince's letter were the following:

"Kalisch, 14th April, 18—.

"You are aware, my dear and respected friend, in what an unexpected and unfortunate manner my last plan of securing the Jew in Berlin, failed and fell to the ground. For a moment, I then believed, that all my prospects were thereby annihilated, and I was even placed in entire uncertainty regarding the further movements of the Jew.

"At last, through our faithful ally, the Jewess, I received information, that by order of long Schmuel, the whole family had left Berlin, in the very night, and immediately after the failure of this burglary, to seek refuge in Poland. The woman then added, that her husband had afterwards retreated still farther with his family, and had crossed the Prussian frontier, as he was persecuted with handbills by the Prussian authorities, and a reward offered for his apprehension.

"At the present time, she informed me, that he was hidden in the village of *Kawno*, not far from *Kalisch*, but for the reasons above mentioned, his stay at any place was exceedingly uncertain, as he was constantly moving about to avoid the vigilance of his enemies; and that she could not definitely or with any degree of certainty, inform me where he might be gone to on the next day. Moreover, she said, that it would not be in her power to give me any farther information, in consequence of the distrustful and suspiciously attentive behaviour of her husband.

"This information induced me to leave Berlin that very night with express horses, and to send you the note, which you must have received, and wherein I promise to keep you advised of my further movements. I was fortunate enough to meet the Jewess in Kawno, and to have a secret interview with her. At this interview I learned, that the great fear of the Jew, of being taken and imprisoned, would not let him rest a single night with his family, whom he had entrusted to the care of a fellow Jew at Kawno.

"He passes every night in a subterranean cave, which is situated in the depth of the forest, and near the Prussian frontier. The Jewess has so well described to me the locality of this cave, that I can hope to find it even in a dark night, as I already made myself well acquainted with the country all round, which I explored in the disguise of a Polish peasant. If it is possible, the Jewess herself is willing to become our guide, but this is not absolutely necessary. My plan at present is to seek the Jew in his very lair, make him a prisoner, and then, provided you will still give me your kind consent—to bring him direct to your domain. When we have him there, we will endeavour to execute the plan we had formerly conceived, and force him, if possible, to confess the fate of my brother, and to inform us, where to find him.

"I do not wish, however, to have my own people employed in this expedition, as I fear they may talk about or betray the affair here or at home, and thereby might again ruin my plans. In this dilemma I have again counted upon you, and write these lines, which I shall send by express, to beg you, if possible, to come as hastily as you can to Kalisch. Bring two trust-worthy men with you come without previously speaking about or preparing for it at home, excite no attention on arriving here at Kalisch, and you may materially aid the execution of this enterprise. I am aware that I make a large demand upon your kindness, but your well and frequently proved friendship, makes me bold enough, even to urge that request.

"You know the importance of the stake, and you possess too much heart and kindness, not to understand how necessary it is for me, to obtain all the assistance of my friends, and exert all my own power and energy to arrive at the requisite result. You may count upon my eternal gratitude. God be with you!

"PROMINSKY."

P. S.—"You will find me at the Hotel of the 'Golden Lion,' but to excite no attention I travel under the incognito of *Banker Feldheim.* I have but one of my 'yaegers' with me, and have left the remainder of my servants in a little town on the Prussian frontier."   * * *

The Major was really rejoiced at the contents of this letter, which roused him from sad thoughts.

The importance of this subject gave him at the same time an excuse, for delaying his decision in his son's affair, as he now determined previously to consult with his friend, Prince Prominsky.

His preparations for the journey were soon made.

The Major had introduced an excellent system of order upon his estate. It needed but little time to have every thing prepared for the journey.

He sent for his major-domo, an old soldier, and a former companion in the wars. This was a perfectly military man, of few words, and strict notions of subordination.

"My dear Miller, to-morrow we will take a journey to Poland, and be gone a few days."

"Very well, Herr Major."

"The groom is to go with us, for we may have a business before us where a strong-fisted fellow or two may be needed."

"Very well, Herr Major."

"The letter to my son, you need not send. Keep it until my return."

"Very well, Herr Major."

"Let my small hunting carriage be at the door precisely at five o'clock in the morning. Let the coachman put my two black horses to it, and use the plain harness."

"Very well, Herr Major."

CHAPTER LXIII.

SOCIETY.

IF you would become acquainted with the very flower of Berlinian chivalry and ladyhood, you must visit the city of the Spree* in the first fair days of March or April, when the new-born bright rays of a spring sun close the mansions of the noble and wealthy, and entice the inhabitants from their brilliant saloons.

Then the gay crowd presses down from "the castle," and from both sides of the "Linden," towards the "Brandenburg-gate," whence their pilgrimage extends further down towards the "tent," or towards the "Hofyaeger."†

Fair ladies and gallant gentlemen converse friendly with each other; their pet dogs are gambolling about, and fair children play in the warm sun with their nurses.

All would present themselves to the Ruler of the new-born Nature in the paleness of their fashionable existence.

In the latter part of the summer season these promenades become deserted and vacant; watering places, summer journeys, country seats, &c., then are the attractions for the Berlin fashionable world, and the dust, heat and atmosphere of the city becomes unbearable to refined nostrils.

But in the season of the young spring, all is bright and inviting in the "Thier-garden." The most fashionable and brilliant toilettes glitter among the trees far and near; the foliage is still in its bud, and the view is not yet obstructed. Nobility in emblazoned carriages dashes along the highway, and Lieutenants in yellow, blue and green uniforms gallop among the crowd like locusts or butterflies, and thick clouds of dust ascend high into the clear spring air.

Wadding and paddings at this time become scarce, and light glacée gloves rise in price; but who cares for that? Merry, joyous spring is approaching with its flowers and its foliage, with its warm sun and its lovely evenings.

The actual crême of good society meets usually upon the shady promenade of the "Thier-garden-street." There is the place where the highest plumes wave from officers' hats, there, where most of them are seen; it is there where the nobility of the nobility, the crême de la crême is collected, and there the whole dandy-world of Berlin displays its highly polished feet.

The so-called dandies may be found in all large cities, but in Germany this *genus* has nowhere arrived to such perfection as in Berlin. Here they form a rather exclusive caste, and besides the spring promenades are mostly to be found at *Stehely's* confectionary, at the opera, and at balls.

Their appearance is always fashionable; straw-coloured gloves, cork-burned beards, pale faces, silk hats and coats with gold buttons may be looked upon as a usually infallible criterion, by which to recognize them. They have, however, lately found a more infallible criterion than the one just mentioned, namely: since the emanation of the late law, granting indulgences and priviledges to distressed debtors, their names usually appear once a month in the newspapers, in the shape of an advertisement by some tailor, wherein the *Schneider* requests them to inform him of their present address.

According to external appearances or indications, these lions of the day reside in the city for the purpose of study, or are awaiting a military commission, or perhaps fill some office at one of the courts.

But these are merely *external* appearances, which the law of custom compels them to obey, since society requires it to be so. Their inner life, their mental existence rests upon different foundations, and is not limited by the inferior boundaries of external circumstances.

A Berlin dandy knows everything; speaks about everything, and is always in the right. Thence we may learn, that that which an indif-

---

† * Berlin being situated on the river Spree, is frequently termed the "city of the Spree."—TRANSL.
† Places of public resort in the neighbourhood of Berlin.

ferent observer might call superficial, is in reality nothing else than self-confidence and self-sufficiency.

* * * * * *

It was at the hour of noon, on a fine sunny day in April, such as we have just endeavoured to describe, when Lieutenant von Steinfort and the Referendarius von Birkheim were sauntering arm in arm through the Thiergarden-promenade, amidst a large collection of the just mentioned fashionable lions.

Both seemed to be engaged in an earnest and serious conversation.

At the "Hofyaegers," one of the garden establishments for fashionable summer amusements, situated by the Thiergarden-street, they quitted the wild mass of carriages, riders, and promenaders, to take a solitary walk in the more retired "new Anlagen."*

Here are finely gravelled winding paths, through which the promenading pedestrian may comfortably pursue his way through pleasant groves and woods towards that most delightful of places, *Charlottenburg.*

These "Anlagen," are periodically enlarged and widened on different sides, and continually assist more and more in changing the Thiergarden into an immense park containing land and water scenery, and temples dedicated to Flora and Ceres. All this is very beautiful and charming, but all has also a tendency to lessen the space into which we can quietly withdraw from annoying and noisy crowds, to saunter in uninterrupted solitude, and to give audience to our own thoughts.

For what is there more delightful or refreshing for a poor, street-walking metropolitan, than to escape the crowded saloons, the busy, noisy streets, and to gather new strength, to renew his physical and mental vigour in the first bright sunrays of the virginal year? But when once gardeners are employed to smooth the paths or to plant the flowers by the roadside, we are sure to find pride, falsehood and worldliness upon our road, and the solitudes of Spring, the illusions of sweet May, are vanished.

"Thank Heaven," exclaimed Steinfort, with a sigh, as the friends found themselves alone upon the solitary promenades around the *Fasanerie,*† "that we have at last escaped this noise and turmoil. Day after day, I feel more solitary, more misanthropic in those crowds."

Steinfort carried his left arm in a sling, in consequence of a flesh wound. His adversary's ball had grazed his arm, and thus put an end to the bloodless duel.

With this duel, Steinfort intended to have removed from his mind all respect to the prejudices of his equals. He had submitted to the most unreasonable of all prejudices, he had given honourable satisfaction by a duel, from a fear of otherwise appearing as a coward. And now he thought himself the more justified in opposing all the other views and prejudices of his former companions.

It had become clear to his mind that he could no longer retain his position as an officer. One reason was, that he had daily to expect fresh quarrels and challenges, which he must accept, and thereby risk his life anew, a life which was no longer at his sole disposal; otherwise, he risked being disgraced as an officer, by non-acceptance of these constant challenges; on the other hand, and without reference to these duels, he could foresee with certainty, in consequence of the note he had received from his Colonel, that he would be dismissed by a higher authority, unless he immediately broke off all connexion with Augusta.

He had therefore applied for his discharge, and although it cost him a severe struggle to relinquish his proud military position, upon which he had looked as his inheritance ever since childhood, yet in many respects he felt happier, his mind more at ease. For he now looked upon himself as a perfectly independent man.

He no longer hoped to obtain a position for his Augusta in the higher circles of society into which he had hitherto expected to introduce her. This resignation of his claims to a certain rank in society had certainly cost him even a more severe struggle than the resignation of his military position. But here he also hoped that the pleasures and comforts of metropolitan life, the intercourse with a very few intimate and true friends, the independence secured to him by his wealth, above all, the uninterrupted society of the girl of his choice, would soon let him forget the circles and associations whose brilliant exterior no longer hid the falsehood and hollowness of its reality from his eyes.*

* * * * * *

* * * * * *

As we already know, he had written another letter to his father, for the purpose of gaining the Major's consent to his marriage.

For reasons which he could not define, this letter had hitherto remained unanswered, but he had received the intelligence, that his father had left home for some time, upon a journey. In this, he believed that he discovered an inexcusable harshness and coldness of the paternal heart, and his pride rose, and caused him to regret the humble, respectful and petitioning position which he had hitherto observed in vain. He quickly arrived at the positive determination of marrying the girl immediately, and without the paternal consent; nay, he felt the necessity of bringing the matter to such an issue as quickly as possible, partly to deliver Augusta from her doubtful and disagreeable situation, and partly to produce

---

* *Anlage.*—Properly sketch, project; but the word is frequently applied, as in the present instance, to newly projected promenades, avenues, &c.—TRANSL.
† Angl. Pheasantry.

* We purposely omit here some further meditations upon the state of society and the distinctions of rank, partly because what is said is a mere repetition of what has already been stated, and also because part of it is almost intranslatable, and at any rate of little or no interest to the readers of this edition.—TRANSL.

a state of things, which would at once and definitively preclude all further remonstrance and objection.

As we have already informed our readers, Referendarius von Birkheim had once before hinted to the Lieutenant, that there was a way of overcoming this difficulty, or rather of accomplishing the object without the paternal consent.

The plan proposed, the particulars of which we will soon learn, had hitherto been strenuously objected to by Steinfort, at least as long as he could hope to gain his father's consent by gentle means.

The late occurrences, however, had somewhat changed his views, and the object of the present promenade was simply, to converse uninterruptedly with the Referendarius about the arrangements and means necessary to the accomplishment of their plans.

CHAPTER LXIV.

THE AGREEMENT.

"WELL, I may as well tell you at once," continued Steinfort a previously commenced conversation, " that I have been to see a parson yesterday, to request him to publish the banns for my marriage. The minister, however, refused to do so, until I should have brought him the written consent of my father. I observed to him that I was my own master, perfectly independent, and that I could even live upon my own property, but he simply replied, that such were the laws, and that he must obey and dared not to act contrary to them."

" And the reverend gentleman is perfectly in the right," remarked the Referendarius, interrupting his friend ironically, " for the laws actually prohibit him from uniting you in wedlock with Augusta under the circumstances, and he dare not act contrary to law."

" Hm !" continued the Lieutenant, " so I must find that even the law is no less cruel than society ! If society had destined an unfortunate girl to disgrace, the law itself will prevent the poor victim's return to honour and position. On my soul, I would rather live among savages and Hottentots, than among such civilized society."

" Your reasoning shows that you are very angry, my good friend," replied the other calmly ; " we must have laws, that you will admit. How is the authority of governments to be supported without them ? All your rage and anger cannot alter the laws."

" But enough," replied Steinfort with a bitter sigh. " Look at the position of this affair ? Here is a girl, good and honest, a girl whom I love and who loves me in return, and whom I would marry. Society at once steps in between myself and the poor girl," and says : " we would be willing to permit you to seduce the girl, but since another has already seduced her, you cannot put yourself upon a par, or a level with him,

for you are an officer and a nobleman. Very well, in my reply, I will then cease to be an officer and a nobleman, and I shall have no more to do with you, and you will cease your interference, and let me take my own course. I come to church, to the house of God, and request the holy church to pronounce its blessing upon a union which is more pure, more holy and innocent than thousands that are closed within its walls, for no selfishness, avarice or pride urge its accomplishment, but pure attachment and holy affection. But the church replies, no, no : You have a father, go and obtain his consent, for without that we cannot allow you to become happy. And this father repulses me, inflicts upon me the disgrace, to let me beg in vain, beg like a schoolboy, without even deigning to reply to my prayer. Well, tell me, is this justice, is it right or is it law ?"

" I tell you, it is perfect justice, and a most salutary law," continued the Referendarius, in his former calm tone, " and you sigh and deservedly sigh under its oppressive weight, as long as you have not courage enough to break through its bounds. You already know my plan."

" Hm !" answered Steinfort, " it is most true, that I hitherto had not sufficient courage to become a scoundrel, and for that simple reason I have still strongly opposed your plans. And even now, I would reject that plan as firmly as ever, if I could discover any other way of getting out of this difficulty."

" I tell you there is no other," replied his legal adviser, " and for my part I do not see the wrong or injustice of such an act as cheating a stupid and oppressive law of one of her victims. You are lucky in being able to do so. It is an affair requiring a great deal of money, which fortunately or unfortunately is not in everybody's possession. But if you will agree to it, I can immediately get you a marriage-consent, which no church and no preacher in the world can possibly object to."

" I can see it very well," observed Steinfort, still hesitating, " that nothing remains for me, but to obey you ; everything else I have tried, and in every possible way. But now tell me, what are we to do, if my father should afterwards discover the steps we have taken ?"

" What are we to do ?" repeated the other laughing, " why, nothing. We let the old man do precisely as he pleases, and he will put the best face he can upon the matter, for he will find that he has no other choice. Or do you really think that he would turn against you, and deliver his own, his only son into the hands of justice ?"

" No, certainly not !"

" Well, well, then all is right, and the only question now is, whether you have money enough about you to carry it through, for I dare say it will require a sum of about five hundred thalers."

" I have money enough, and much more than necessary," observed Steinfort, " but I must tell you candidly and openly, that it comes very hard to me, to agree to this affair. I knew beforehand how the minister would receive me, and what reply he would make, for you had even informed me of it yourself, yet I did visit him, with the mere hope, that there might be a possibility of inducing him to comply. I would then have avoided the terrible alternative, which an honest man can scarcely think of choosing."

" Well, and you find no other way than the one I propose," said Birkheim, urgently, " and now you should no longer hesitate. Your own honour requires that you should put an end to this affair. You have risked, you have placed all upon the issue; your standing in society depends upon your resolution; just imagine the scorn and the mocking of all your enemies, if unexpectedly they were to learn that the old Major had put his daring boy to rights, who had the assurance of opposing the whole corps of officers. Have you any desire of being thus spoken about, or would you bring the poor, unfortunate girl into the deepest misery and wretchedness, since she is now forever compromised and well known in this affair ?"

" No, no !" cried Steinfort, whom these well conceived objections touched severely in more points than one, " no, you are right, and we must arrange the matter at once, regardless of all difficulties, and by any means at our disposal."

It may easily be perceived that the Referendarius did not act without mercenary motives, in endeavouring to overcome the Lieutenant's objections to his plans by all the cunning and persuasion in his power. It is, on the contrary, rather self-evident, that in estimating the costs of their undertaking, he considered his own trouble as not the smallest item in the affair, and worth at least the one half of the five hundred thalers.

" Then I will be with you this afternoon, at three o'clock," he continued, in a satisfied tone, " and bring the gentleman with me, whom we spoke about. In half an hour everything can be arranged, and all your wishes complied with. But be sure to have the five hundred thalers in readiness. My man is not a person we can bargain down in an affair of this kind."

After having come to this resolution, and completed a few more preliminary arrangements, the two friends again crossed the *Albrechts-hof* and returned to the Thiergarden-promenade. Slowly and leisurely they sauntered, along with the motley mass of pleasure-seekers, back to the city.

CHAPTER LXV.

THE MARRIAGE CONSENT.

PUNCTUAL to the hour, the Referendarius appeared at the house of the Lieutenant.

Accompanying him was a strange gentleman, in a fine black coat, pantaloons of the same colour, and wearing a star around his neck.

The stranger was a man of imposing figure, already somewhat advanced in years, with a slightly grey head ; his manners were those of a well-bred gentleman, and his behaviour betrayed elegance and tone.

He was an intimate gambling companion of the Referendarius ; formerly he had been a Master of Horse, and the owner of a fine estate ; at present he was only a *Chevalier d'industrie.*

With the words : " The gentlemen will please to make their own arrangements, whilst I go for a Notary," Birkheim introduced the stranger, and immediately withdrew again.

The stranger entered the room with a smiling countenance, and an easy, unembarrassed air.

" The somewhat peculiar and eccentric manner of introduction, with which our friend Birkheim has just honoured me," he began, " forces me to become my own introducer. My name is *von Schlepper*, and I am Master of Horse, not in active service."

Steinfort, who had found himself not a little embarrassed at the first entrance of the stranger, regained his self-possession by this cavalierly speech, and politely requested the Master of Horse to take a seat.

" My friend Birkheim," continued Herr von Schlepper, in the same polite and easy suavity of manner, " has informed me of the embarrassment in which you find yourself at this moment. As I have made it my established principle through life, to assist my fellow-men, whenever and wherever I can, even at a self-sacrifice, I am also ready in this instance to render you any assistance in my power.

Steinfort muttered a few unintelligible words in reply, intending thereby to express his acknowledgment of the gentlemen's kindness and magnanimity.

" No compliments, if you please, my dear Lieutenant, no expressions of gratitude," said the Master of Horse as he warmly shook the Lieutenant's hand, " a trifle like the present service is scarcely worth speaking about. I always belong to my friends ; we will soon arrange the affair to your satisfaction.

At these words the Master of Horse took off his very elegant overcoat, pulled off his gloves, and laid them together with his hat upon a corner table ; he then with an easy and graceful manner took a seat upon the sofa.

" It will perhaps be necessary," he commenced again with a smile, " that we should study and practise our parts a little beforehand ; will you permit me to make the necessary commencement of our rehearsal. Harkye, my dear son," he said suddenly, with a changed tone of voice, " I have become most terribly thirsty on the long journey which I undertook to please you ; how, if you were to offer a bottle of wine to your old, exhausted father ?"

Steinfort fully understood this hint, and felt his heart severely wounded by the impudent assumption and assurance of Herr von Schlepper ; but since he had entered into the agreement with

Birkheim thus far, he was compelled to put the best possible face upon the matter. He rung the bell for the servant, whom he had now engaged in place of his former military attendant, and gave him the necessary orders.

"If you chance to have a good cigar, my dear son," continued the pseudo father, "you would particularly oblige me with it at this moment."

Steinfort bit his lips in anger and rage: the injustice of his conduct, the wrong of which he felt, pressed heavily upon his conscience already, and now he should also learn the humiliation of seeing an unprincipled man assume paternal authority over him in consequence of his own agreement, and which that man let him feel regardless of his writhings under the infliction.

He was upon the point of dropping the whole plan, but the remembrance, that the tyranny of society and its institutions forced him to this course, nay, even entitled him, as he thought, to avail himself of such means, the regard for the girl of his heart, restrained him, and induced him silently to obey the mandates and requests of the Master of Horse.

The bottle of wine soon made its appearance, and with a quiet, pleasant air of comfort, Herr von Schlepper began to unseal it, whilst the Lieutenant sat by his side brooding over his fate, and oppressed by sad thoughts.

We do not know whether his better genius would not even now have triumphed, and have restrained him from this wrong and sinful undertaking—an undertaking by which he forfeited his hitherto unstained honour, had not his evil genius, in the form of Referendarius von Birkheim, reappeared by his side.

That worthy gentleman arrived in company of a small hunchbacked man, with an immense aquiline nose, and dressed in black, very shabby and somewhat greasy clothes.

This was *Mr. Notary Schreiber*, a man renowned throughout the neighbourhood by his pious hypocrisy and notorious avarice.

Beneath his arm the Notary carried an immense bundle of papers, and a faded, ragged silk hat covered the long bristly hair of his head.

The Referendarius informed this worthy limb of the law, that he must take a legal record of a consent of marriage; he then introduced Herr von Schlepper as Major von Steinfort, the object of whose present visit to the city was to give his consent to the marriage of his son, Lieutenant von Steinfort.

The Notary who until now had silently stood in the middle of the room, holding his package under his arm, and during Birkheim's speech had alternately looked upon one or the other of the parties as they were mentioned, now took a leather case from his pocket, produced therefrom a pair of old spectacles, which he placed upon his nose; then silently nodded his head, took a seat by the table, and began to unfold his papers.

"Herr Major von Steinfort," he finally addressed with a slow, hoarse voice, the Master of Horse who sat opposite to him, "you are then determined with the will of God, to give to your son, the Lieutenant, your *consensum paternum* to his legal connexion by marriage, and you also agree to confirm said *consensum judicialiter?*"

"In God's name," replied the Master of Horse, as he held up a glass of wine towards the light, and examined it with the eye of a connoisseur. He then quietly emptied it at a draught.

"And you do not suppose that you will regret and retract this act, but consider it in every respect an *actus bene approbatus?*"

"Yes, I fully approve of it, Herr Notary," replied the pseudo-father, as he relinquished his glass; "that, I believe, is the meaning of your Latin question."

"*Item*," continued the Notary, turning towards the Lieutenant, "this gentleman, the son, fully accepts the *paternum consensum* to an honest and lawful betrothal, according to the commands of God and man. Moreover, the Lieutenant acts according to his free, uninfluenced, and uncontrolled will, and after due and mature deliberation, and this act has not been committed *vis ac metus, dolus* or *error?*"

"Herr Notary," said the Referendarius, impatiently interrupting the current of legal Latin phrases which the other uttered, "all these questions seem to me to be superfluous; I think it would be wiser to proceed with our object and bring the act to a close."

"Not at all, if you will please excuse me," replied the small legal gentleman, "for by my oath of office, *juris jurandi officialis*, I am compelled to convince myself, that all *Paciscentes* are perfectly authorized and fully acquainted with the nature and importance of their action. I therefore must ask the Herr Lieutenant once more: *Item*, he accepts—."

"Yes, yes, certainly, my son accepts," hastily interrupted the Master of Horse, who seemed to fear, and not without reason, that the whole previous legal speech would have to be repeated.

"I accept the *consensum*," said the Lieutenant with a visibly painful effort, on receiving an encouraging wink from the Referendarius.

"Then there is only one more and a third condition necessary," recommenced the prosy Notary: "You, Herr Referendarius von Birkheim, recognize in the person here present and seen by you, the Major von Steinfort, whom you are well and sufficiently acquainted with, for the purpose of identification?"

"I recognize him," answered the Referendarius, with a firm and hasty expression.

"Then, gentlemen, we will at once proceed to the recording of the act."

The Notary now pushed his spectacles upon his forehead, mended his pen, and began to write.

It was a trying and painful moment for Steinfort, during which the Referendarius seemed quietly to enjoy his cigar, the Master of Horse was busily engaged in finishing the bottle of wine, and the ominous pen of the little legal gentleman scribbled rapidly over a sheet of paper.

If not shame, or perhaps vanity and love

for Augusta, had restrained him, the Lieutenant would, even at this moment, have cried, "hold, enough."

The Notary wrote faster than he spoke. After a short pause, he stopped, wiped his pen, took up the document he had written, and read:

"*Transacted and recorded at Berlin,*
"*21st of April,* 18—·

"At the house of Herr Lieutenant von Steinfort, in Berlin, and before the undersigned, Notary of the *Royal Kammergericht,* the following persons presented themselves, viz.:

"Herr Major von Steinfort of Braunsdorf,
"Herr Kammergericht's Referendarius von Birkheim, and
"Herr Lieutenant von Steinfort.

"Herr Major von Steinfort of Braunsdorf, declared that to the matrimonial connexion of his son, the Lieutenant von Steinfort, with ——"

The Notary stopped a moment and observed: "here I still require the full name of the honourable maiden, the bride and future wife of the Herr Lieutenant, of which you will now please to notify me."

He addressed these words to Herr von Schlepper, the supposed father, who sat nearest to him. This gentleman had been too much engaged in finishing the wine, to pay any attention, or prepare himself for an answer to this very natural question. He looked with a great deal of embarrassment towards Lieutenant von Steinfort, but the latter had again sunk in brooding abstractions, without paying any attention to, or even noticing what occurred.

Referendarius von Birkheim quickly perceived the danger, and to avoid all suspicion on the part of the Notary, he immediately exclaimed: "*Augusta Strohm.*" He believed that he remembered the name rightly.

"Augusta Strohm," repeated the pseudo-Major, quickly nodding assent. With considerable presence of mind, that honest gentleman had meanwhile been sipping at his glass, as if he had thereby been prevented from immediately replying to the question put to him.

"Augusta Strohm," repeated the Notary, with his thin, creaking voice, as he took up his pen to record the name in the document.

The triple and monotonous repetition of the name, now aroused the Lieutenant from his vagaries.

"Augusta Strass," he cried in an excited and angry tone, "not Augusta Strohm; don't write stuff and nonsense."

The Notary stopped in astonishment, and looked round at the gentlemen. "Hm, hm!" he remarked with a peculiar and doubting shake of the head, "should in a case of such importance as that of *persona* of the honourable maiden, the bride, prevail an *error in essentialibus?*"

"Not at all, my most worthy and respected sir," began the Master of Horse, who had perfectly regained his self-possession; "my friend, the Referendarius here, pronounced the name incorrectly, and I mechanically repeated his pronunciation, as I was not paying attention to the subject at the time, but was calculating in my mind, how much my son's future establishment would cost me, and which would be the best street for his residence. It is all correct; just write the name of Augusta Strass."

The Notary cast a penetrating and expressive glance at the speaker, which was not, however, observed by the others, and turned round, and wrote the name into the document. He then continued to read it:

"——matrimonial connexion of his son, the Lieutenant von Steinfort, with the spinster, Augusta Strass, of Berlin, he would give his paternal *consentum.* Herr Lieutenant von Steinfort readily and properly, after the necessary questions were asked of him, accepted said *consentum,* and both gentlemen were fully recognized and identified by the Referendarius von Birkheim, who is well known to the subscribed Notary. The present record and document was thereupon drawn, and properly signed by the two first-named gentlemen, and attested by the subscribed authorized Notary, and sealed with his seal of office."

The Notary now handed the document to the Master of Horse, Herr von Schlepper, who unhesitatingly signed the name of Major von Steinfort.

The Notary cast an examining glance upon the signature, then begged the Referendarius von Berkheim for his signature also, and closed and sealed the document.

Thus, then, by an immense and unequalled fraud and forgery, committed under his very eye, Lieutenant von Steinfort had obtained the necessary paternal consent to his marriage.

The Master of Horse embraced him, adding the following words by way of paternal blessing:

"May kind Heaven bestow upon you all its choice blessings, which your old father wishes for you, my dearest son."

Birkheim also approached him, clasped his hand, and exclaimed pathetically:

"You will be happy, and you deserve it, in marrying a beautiful, intelligent and virtuous girl!"

The Notary, for whose sake all this blasphemy and mockery was committed, at last approached, handed the document with a low bow to the Lieutenant, and wished him every possible happiness and prosperity, which was meant as a demand to liquidate the amount of fees.

The gentlemen then left. Herr von Schlepper in the most merry wine humour; Birkheim with a well-filled pocket-book, which the Lieutenant had handed him, and the Notary after casting another doubtful and penetrating glance at the worthy couple.

Steinfort had remained an inactive spectator. His head burned with fever, his brain reeled, and he scarcely knew what he was doing

CHAPTER LXVI.

THE LONG SCHMUEL AGAIN.

On the Russian frontier, not far from the village of Kawno, a dark, thick pine forest stretches deep into the country, and as far as the eye can reach nothing is seen but the dark tops of the ever green trees.

No paths nor roads penetrate its gloomy confines, and only the coal-burners and poachers ever invade its frigid solitude.

That forest, Long Schmuel had selected for his present place of refuge.

His family, as we have already learned from the letter of Prince Prominsky to Major von Steinfort, had found a residence at the village of Kawno. At present we dicover them in the public room of a low hedge-tavern of the village.

The host who is also a Jew, as we frequently find in that part of the country, is, though not himself a robber, at least intimately acquainted with all the robbers and thieves of the neighbourhood, and is ever ready and willing, for a weighty consideration, of course, to grant a safe retreat to all villains and fugitives from justice.

The room is black with mud and filth. The windows are tightly closed with wooden shutters. The entire furniture consists in a long wooden table covered with filth, and two equally dirty wooden benches.

In one corner, nearest the door, there is a small chimney, which also serves as kitchen hearth. A small fire is burning there, fed by a few pine chips, the bright flickering of which now supplies the place of a lamp. An old iron pot containing the remains of broth, which stands beside the fire, shows that the vesper meal has been cooked there only a short time before.

Upon a straw bed by the side of the fire, the three children of long Schmuel lie asleep.

Night was just approaching.

The Jewess sat by the chimney, busily mending a ragged jacket of Siegbert. By this occupation she endeavoured to overcome the oppressive anxiety and restlessness which almost overpowered her. She knew that this night would at last decide the fate of her husband, and consequently that of her children also.

She had by her communications to the Prince hastened this denouement, in the firm belief, that all would be for the best; nevertheless, she now felt frightened and anxious. Fearful doubts of the justness and propriety of her actions rose in her breast.

She was deceiving her husband, no matter for what purpose; he was the man to whom she had sworn truth and fidelity, and dared she now think of betraying him?

She was about to deprive him of his personal liberty, by a private understanding with a man, whom he considered his bitterest enemy. Her object certainly was the temporal and eternal welfare of that husband as well as of her children, at least such was her firm belief, but could she not be mistaken? Who gave her, the weak woman, the wife—who according to the precepts of that religion in which she had been educated, was bound to strict and implicit obedience to the will of her husband—a right thus forcibly to interfere in the fate of her lord and master, and to give a different direction to his entire destiny?

These and similar thoughts oppressed the mind of the Jewess, and cast her into a dark and gloomy brooding.

Forcibly directing all her attention to her sewing, she endeavoured to give herself the appearance of not taking notice of anything passing around her.

Long Schmuel himself in large and measured strides walked up and down the low room. In his hand he held a pair of loaded pistols, which he closely examined, to make sure of their being in good and perfect order.

After he had fully satisfied himself upon that point, he put the pistols into a belt which he wore underneath his caftan, and took up a heavy oaken stick, the end of which was heavily steeled.

Thus equipped, he prepared for his march towards the forest, where each evening and night he endeavoured to find among wild beasts that security which he believed he could no longer find among men.

He once more approached the couch where his children slept, spread his large hands over them in blessing, and murmured a short Hebrew prayer. His long figure then bent down over them, and he imprinted a kiss upon the forehead of each.

Thus powerful the bonds of nature, and the holy ties of blood and of language displayed themselves in this outcast robber, who had broken off all connexion, torn all the bonds which united him with society, and who lived and existed only in a constant warfare with mankind, law and order.

He quickly turned round towards the Jewess: "Good night, wife!" he said, briefly, and turned to leave the house for his haunt in the wild woods.

Her inward fear and excitement did not permit the Jewess to contain herself any longer; she started up and weeping cast her arms around his neck. Upon her lips already trembled the request, the urgent prayer, that he would not leave the village this night. She hesitated, and was upon the point of confessing all, in the deepest penitence; but the memory of her children, whose salvation from physical and moral perdition could only be hoped for by a pursuance of the course she had commenced, tnat alone restrained her. Her firm and conscientious conviction was, that in her present course she was exerting her best powers for the welfare of her husband, as well as of her children.

The great excitement and restlessness of his wife seemed to attract the attention of the Jew.

As we already know, former occurrences had even previously created a feeling of distrust against her, in his suspicious mind. Her behaviour now, might even for that reason have startled him, particularly as she run after him to the door, and in tears cast her arms around his neck.

"What is the matter with you, wife?" he asked, earnestly. "Why do you fear, hesitate and weep? Is this evening in any thing different from every other evening when I go to the forest, to my hiding-place?"

"I cannot tell, dear husband," answered the wife, "what has befallen me; but to-day I feel a fear for you, an anxiety, such as I have never felt before. If some misfortune was to happen to you?"

"How can any misfortune happen to me?" replied the Jew, firmly and quietly, "do I not stand in the sight of my God, and of the God of my forefathers, who will not suffer that a hair of my head be injured against his holy will?"

"Ah, if you could only remain here to-night! But that also has its dangers, and they are great. Farewell, then! may the Almighty guard your path."

The Jew contemplated her in silence, and with a most penetrating look, and without replying a word, walked from the house.

The Jewess fell upon her knees in earnest and devout prayer, not for the success of her plan, but for that silent resignation, which quietly and without murmur, submits to the guidance of a supreme Providence.

Noiselessly she then extinguished the fire in the chimney, wrapped a large grey cloth around her, and followed her husband out of the house.

It was a black, stormy night in April, such a night as is seen nowhere but in these northerly regions where Spring comes late, and if the stars be not favourable, comes not at all.

The stormy wind roared among the trees, and a fine, thin shower beat sharply in the face of the poor woman, as she passed silently along.

Stoutly and fearlessly she pursued her way through the deep swamp, which lay between a few scattered farm-houses along her road, now and then pursued by savage, barking dogs. After she had passed the last house, she turned away from the path, and was soon out of sight of all human dwelling-places.

Listening, she stood silent.

It was impossible to see even three paces before her. Not a star shone in the firmament; at occasional intervals, a pale ray of the moon seemed endeavouring to penetrate the heavy rain-clouds, but it was only to make the succeeding darkness appear more black.

A wild flock of owls flew shrieking above her head, and from the distant village, the barking of a few dogs was occasionally heard.

Bold, courageous, and determined as the Jewess had already shown herself in the most trying moments of her life, in her present dangerous and awful situation, she could not avoid feeling a certain fear and great anxiety.

Already she thought she had missed her course,

14

and in vain she strained her sight, to discover or recognize some point which might guide her. At last she thought she heard the rattling of a vehicle in the distance.

She listened attentively.

The noise seemed to approach her. She thought that she could discern the tramping of horses' hoofs; then she heard the cracking of a whip.

Hastily she walked towards the spot whence the noise proceeded, and now discovered a gigantic oak which stood at a cross-road, the landmark which she had before sought in vain.

Carefully she hid herself behind the immense tree.

Her acute ear had not deceived her. After a short while an open, light built vehicle approached the spot. Four men occupied it, and a fifth accompanied it on horse-back.

The new comers stopped beneath the oak, and descended from the equipage.

"Here we must await our faithful ally, the Jewess," began a well known voice, "as an almost unnecessary precaution she is coming here, to show us the right way. It is so very dark, that we might otherwise miss it after all."

"Very well, your Highness," said another equally familiar voice. "I only hope that she will not keep us waiting, for we have not much time to spare."

The Jewess heard this, and recognised the voices of Prince Prominsky and Major von Steinfort, who had come to this spot, the place of rendezvous, which had been previously agreed upon. From here they would start upon their expedition against the Jew.

The Jewess quickly left her hiding place, and showed herself to her friends.

Both gentlemen heartily shook her hand, and prepared for an immediate march.

"Your Highness will kindly excuse a poor woman," began the Jewess in a voice betraying the deep emotion she felt, "if once more I earnestly offer up my petition for the safety of my husband. Your Highness has assured me, that no harm shall be done to him in any way or manner, and I depend upon your princely word."

"Be sure of that and unconcerned, my good, honest woman," answered the Prince in great admiration of the faithfulness and attachment of the Hebrew wife, "my word is holy to me. On the contrary, all that we shall do, will be for his benefit, for I will place him in a position, to enable him to abandon his wild, vagabondizing life, and to bring up his children as honest worthy people."

"Then once more, your Highness, I thank you; from the bottom of my heart I thank you," said the Jewess more quieted.

They now determined, that the horseman, a surgeon, whom they had taken along from the neighbourhood, for cases of emergency, should take the vehicle and horses under his care, whilst the others would proceed with their undertaking.

The Jewess then took the lead, to serve as a guide.

After her followed the Major and the Prince, dressed in closely buttoned hunting coats. Both were provided with loaded fire arms as they conceived it possible, that the Jew, for his personal security, had other vagabonds and robbers with him in his lair, of whose presence he had not informed his wife.

The so-called major-domo of Herr von Steinfort, and the groom of the Prince, closed up the rear; both were provided with ropes, spades, axes and other implements, which might, according to the advice of the Jewess, become necessary at their enterprise.

Thus equipped, the small band proceeded towards the head-quarters of their enemy, through the dark rainy night, and in a state of the greatest, the most anxious excitement about the probable result of their strange adventure.

CHAPTER LXVII.

THE EXPEDITION.

THE Jewess had now perfectly recognized the localities.

Spite of the almost impenetrable darkness, she hastily proceeded on her way, and soon reached the midst of the forest, where there was no path or road to guide her steps.

She well knew all the landmarks of these woods, for in former times this wilderness had served as a place of refuge for her husband, and besides she had herself once passed a long time in this hiding place with her children and her husband.

When her husband left home that evening, we have seen her weak, doubting and hesitating in her intentions; the oft-repeated assurance and promise of the Prince had now eradicated all her doubts, and had quieted her pangs of conscience. He had frequently promised her, to protect and save the life of her husband under all circumstances, and never to deliver him into the hands of the civil authority. To make "assurance doubly sure," she had that promise again repeated to her. By these means she gained the renewed courage and strength necessary to induce her in person to conduct the Prince, the Major, and their assistants, to the lair of her husband.

We need not repeat that the Prince followed his conductress, in a state of the utmost mental excitement.

All the doubts and fears which he had felt at the *Hotel de Paris*, now returned to his anxious mind in double, or we should say, in triple measure.

Twice already had he been certain of having within his grasp, what he considered the greatest object of his life, and each time an unforeseen accident had interfered in its accomplishment. Hence, he trembled at the thought of a failure of his plans, and determined not to believe the contrary, until the positive fact of success had convinced him.

His abstracted silence had a sympathetic effec. upon his companions, who, like himself, mutely and thoughtfully proceeded through the darkness of the night. The only interruption which occasionally broke upon the universal stillness, was the stumbling of one or the other over a rock, the roots of a tree, or other obstructions in their way.

After a good half hour's walk, the little corps arrived at a clearer spot of the forest.

Here the Jewess stopped, approached the Prince, and with her finger pointed towards the outlines of a slight hill which lay a short distance before them. She then turned towards home, and in silence proceeded on her way. Her heart was too full for utterance: the approaching decision of the fate of her husband, which concerned her so much, and in which she was taking such an active part, pressed heavily upon her mind.

After the Jewess had withdrawn, the Prince beckoned to his companions again to retire with him a few steps into the dark depth of the forest. After they had gone far enough, not to betray themselves by the noise of their conversation, the Prince let the men all stand closely round him, and began to explain to them his projected mode and manner of attack.

"According to the information I have received from the Jewess," he began, "yonder little hill contains a cave, which has formerly been used by coal-burners as a shelter against inclement weather. The entrance to it is by a hole, covered with brush wood, and running in a downward direction into the hill. Only one man at a time can upon his belly creep into that hole. As you proceed further into the cave, the space widens on all sides, as well as in height, which enables several persons to find room within.

"The top of this cave, which, as you may suppose, loses in thickness at the place where the cave becomes more spacious, forms yonder hill. Our present object must be, if possible, to surprise the Jew in his sleep, or at all events to come upon him unprepared, that we may thus take him without much struggle or bloodshed. If we let him gain time to collect himself, he will, by his well known strength and ferocity, assisted by his superior knowledge of localities, and being well armed, not only defend himself to the utmost, but will even bring all our lives needlessly into danger.

"My plan, then, is the following: above all things, we must obtain an open access to him, to enable us to attack him from every side at once; for if we should simply attempt to creep into the cave, the noise of our entrance would awake him, and would bring us all into the utmost and unnecessary danger, as he has all the advantages of the light. For this reason nothing can be undertaken at the front entrance. But I think it best, and most sure, if we could cut down the top of the hill with our spades, and thus in a manner dig our way to him."

"Why, this is almost like starting a fox or

other beast from his lair," said the Major with a smile, interrupting his friend.

"It is just so, my worthy friend," replied the Prince, "only with this difference, that he whom we seek at present, not only possesses the cunning of a fox and the strength of a bear, but unites the peculiar and most dangerous qualities of half a dozen of other beasts."

"Will your Highness please to excuse me," now began Miller, the major-domo, "but having a little practical experience in matters of warfare and siege, I fear that the work you propose will be a very protracted one, and the noise which we cannot avoid making at our work must contribute to awake the Jew before the proper time."

"I have obtained all the necessary information upon that point from the Jewess," replied the Prince, "and I think that your fear will be a useless one. The front of the hill is overgrown with brushwood, and the top presents a smooth surface of light sandy ground. Our spades will penetrate that easily and without noise, and the top of the cave, which, as I have already observed, is very thin, will most probably soon fall in. If this occurs, we must use our judgment, and be guided by circumstances regarding our next movement. Besides a slight fall, when the top breaks in, no injury can occur to any of us, as the cave is not deep and the ground very soft. This fact will also keep the person of the Jew from receiving any injury by the falling sand. Now all that is necessary is that the work of digging be done as noiselessly and as speedily as possible."

"Upon that point, your Highness need have no fear," replied the major-domo, "for the groom and myself are both practical farmers, and we understand how to handle spades and shovels. The Herr Major here, our respected master, will bear testimony of that."

"Then let us go to work at once," began the Prince; "bring out the spades and the ropes, and give the latter to me. I shall only use them if the obstinacy and wildness of the Jew precludes all other means, and if he rejects our offers and persuasions."

Stepping lightly through the darkness, the men approached the cave.

"Now ascend to the top of the hill from both sides, and begin your work," said the Prince. The Major and myself will take our position near the entrance, that we may intercept the Jew if he should determine to make his escape by that passage."

This order was punctually obeyed.

The Prince and the Major placed themselves by the entrance of the cave, and drew their swords, so as to be prepared for any emergency. The two servants of the Major ascended the hill, and began to cut away the sand as quickly and as noiselessly as their instruments would permit.

It was past midnight.

In dark majestic silence the immense forest lay before them; the noiseless solitude of Nature only slightly interrupted by the occasional ocean-like roaring of the wind among the tree tops. A drizzily rain still continued to fall.

For a second the moon penetrated a black rain cloud, and cast a pale light upon this strange scene, which gained in supernatural phantom-like appearance by that dim, uncertain light.

The whole scene appeared like the wild fancy picture of a nursery tale, in which mountain imps, or other evil spirits, obeying the command of their mighty master, seek for treasures at midnight in the wilderness.

The damp weather made the task of digging more difficult, but the stout men worked arduously and indefatigably, casting the loose sand behind them to the foot of the hill, with as little noise as possible.

Without interruption they had continued their work for more than half an hour, when the spade of the groom penetrated the top, and a small lump of earth fell down upon the body of the Jew, who had remained fast asleep during the whole preceding scene.

He awoke! his eye fell upon the opening, where a grey outline of the sky was visible, and terror-struck he started up.

Attentively he listened for the proceedings outside of his lair.

The labourers, who had observed the open space they had made, and had also heard the falling of the little lump of earth, also stopped from their work, to listen in attentive expectation.

The Jew bent his head towards the opening, and placing his ear against the top of the cave, he could hear the heavy breathing of the men who were resting from their labour. The terrible certainty of being betrayed, or at all events of being discovered, burst upon his mind.

Quickly his resolution was taken.

His peculiar cunning and penetration told him, that he would not act wisely, if he endeavoured to make his escape by his usual entrance, but that rather in his present uncertainty about the number and strength of his opponents, his only possible chance of escape was in a successful surprise.

Gently he withdrew his pistols from his belt and cocked them. He then took up a wooden stool, the only article of furniture which he had ever taken to the cave, stood upon that, and pressed his broad strong back against the thin top of the cave.

Concentrating the entire strength of his gigantic body into one push, he broke through this thin top, with such a force, that the groom and major-domo tumbled to his right and left into the cave. Quickly he jumped up, and without looking around endeavoured to reach the woods. But his fate was sealed. As he rushed down the hill, to make his way through the brush wood, the trigger of one of his pistols caught in a brush. The weapon discharged with a loud report, and the thief, with a wild yell of pain and rage, fell to the ground.

Hastily the Prince and the Major approached the fallen man. The first was almost beside himself with terror, for he feared to have only obtained the dead body of the Jew as a reward for all his endeavours.

A lantern which they had brought along was quickly lighted; they were soon convinced that the Jew was still breathing. The bullet had entered the upper part of his breast at the left side, and a stream of dark blood gushed from the wound.

The major-domo, who had practised a little necessary surgery, both in his campaigns and among the rustics, endeavoured as best he could to stop the flow of blood.

The Jew had fallen into unconsciousness, and seemed not to be aware of anything that was done with him. The little party then carried him to the outskirts of the forest, after which the groom hurried off to seek the surgeon and the wagon, and to bring them to this spot.

This was very soon accomplished, and the son of Esculapius, who was provided with everything necessary, bound up the wound in a proper and scientific manner. He next examined the pulse of the Jew, and decided at once that the patient might undertake a journey, without particular risk of dangerous consequences.

Upon this professional decision, the party, as had previously been arranged, immediately proceeded on their journey to the country-seat of Major von Steinfort.

CHAPTER LXVIII.

THE PUPPET SHOW, AND WHAT OCCURS THERE.

CHARLES DE MOOR had safely murdered Amalie, (besides having murdered his own part,) the curtain dropped, and the delighted audience clapped their hands and stamped their feet in a perfect extacy of deafening applause.[*]

Charles de Moor had certainly ranted and bawled particularly loud, and his auditory would unquestionably have called him out after the performance, if that fashionable style of showing approbation had already reached this unsophisticated audience. But this public was one which still lived in pure primitive theatrical innocence, for the audience before us consisted of the patrons of the puppet-show-manager *Leidenthal*, who had on this evening presented to them a most attractive bill, including Schiller's " robbers," among other varied entertainments.

The theatre was the well known *Diana-saloon* in the *New-street*, and to reach this temple of the Muses, the spectator had to pass the lower entry of a front house, cross a little dark yard, and ascend a narrow staircase in the back building.

The critical demands of the audience were of course in just proportion with the calibre of its intellect and education, which again could be easily ascertained by the respective social position of the auditory.

In this dramatic temple then, we could find Turf-carriers, wood-sawyers, match-venders, flower-girls, wool-sorters, sand-carters, fruit-sellers, thieves, chimney-sweeps, grisettes of the very lowest class, habitual drunkards, *et hic geni omnes.*

The conversation at the end of the piece naturally turned upon the subject of the play. The critical dissertations of its merits, which of course were given in the lowest Berlinian street jargon, would have been highly entertaining to an intelligent auditor.

" Now, on my word," began an old, brown-skinned and wrinkled turf matron, whose head was adorned by a large red turban made of a cotton pocket handkerchief, " I cannot perceive why this confounded fool in the piece should kill the girl, when he might cut his stick, and run off with her, and live elsewhere in pleasure and merriment, with his sweetheart." The turf-lady who spoke thus, was looked upon as an infallible oracle among her companions, and from the strength of her fist and the rapidity of her tongue, was universally feared and respected by her associates.

" You don't understand that, aunt," replied a fair looking blonde to the turf-vender, " all this is only caused by the eternal and immortal powers of all-conquering love."

" Happy alone is the soul who feels love," says a certain *Clauren.** Ah, what dear, delightful stories that Clauren writes!

The blonde beauty sighed deeply. We may observe, *en passant*, that this lady carried on an extensive business in the match-selling line.

We also meet some well-known faces in this party.

Our friend, Maulspitzer, for instance, is seated in a corner. He is dressed unusually well, and is just explaining the plot of the piece to a friend who had arrived rather late, thereby descanting greatly on the inimitable grace with which Charles de Moor had killed Amalie.

Eel-eye and the Chonte also arrive to witness the performance; the former looked even more pale and sorrowful than he had usually looked of late, and the latter is in excellent, extravagant spirits.

As soon as Maulspitzer perceived Eel-eye, he started up, approached him, and asked him with no small degree of anxiety, whether he had safely escaped the hands of Police-officers and gens-d'armes when their masematten at the *Hôtel de Paris* came to such an unfortunate termination.

They had not seen each other since that time. This was no rare or remarkable occurrence in a city as large as Berlin, and the Maulspitzer could not well give vent before to his long prepared expressions of regret at the loss of this beautiful masematten.

---

* The play alluded to is the tragedy of " the Robbers," by Schiller, which is so very popular among the lower classes in Germany, that a version of it, has even become a standard piece for puppet-shows. —TRANSLATOR.

* A celebrated, we had almost said a notorious, concocter of German love romances. —TRANSL.

But at the present moment, it was to him of the utmost importance to relate a proper and circumstantial story to Eel-eye, and thereby explain to the latter how he escaped being arrested at the time of the burglary. He knew full well, that his arrest, which the Polizeirath X— had to undertake against his will, and only for appearance sake, was well known to all his comrades, and that it must naturally excite great astonishment among them, if they saw him again at liberty, and visiting public places in Berlin.

To explain this, and to lead the suspecting parties away from the right supposition, namely, of an understanding with the Polizeirath, he had thought it most advisable to deny *in toto* the fact of his arrest, and to call this report merely an invention of idle gossips.

"I had just crept into the window," he continued his story, "when I heard loud sneezing, and almost at the same instant, a gensd'arme rushed forward to arrest me. The Jew, who had only put his head in through the window, immediately disappeared; but I was so overcome with fright, that for a moment I knew not what to do. An instant afterwards, however, having recovered all my presence of mind, I gave the gensd'arme a hearty kick in the breast, which sent him sprawling to the floor, and I escaped by the window. It seemed too slow work for me to descend the ladder, so I took one leap, landed safely on the ground, and hurried off. Luckily, it was so dark in the room, that no one could possibly have recognized me, and thus, with the exception of a blue eye which I received, I escaped without further injury."

As we have already observed, Maulspitzer's whole story was without a foundation of truth, for Polizeirath X— had been very loath to let him escape after the failure of this attempt, as he could only hope for final success in the enterprise by keeping Maulspitzer as his secret assistant.

Eel-eye had listened attentively to the whole story, but his face expressed entire incredulity. The portier had been too particular and too explicit in telling him the circumstances of the arrest, and therefore it could not all be mere invention. But if he had really been arrested, how could Maulspitzer, who in the universal estimation of the *Chawrusse* of thieves would at least be sent for five-and-twenty years to the penitentiary, already be liberated and about the city again?"

The Eel-eye entertained very strong suspicions.

As the matter appeared to him, the intended burglary must absolutely have been betrayed to the police by a vigilant. Only one of two persons could have been the traitor: Maulspitzer or the Equestrian.

Eel-eye hesitated between the two.

Could Maulspitzer, his old, faithful comrade in many a daring theft, have become a Schlichner? That seemed almost impossible. If such was the case, Eel-eye must lose all confidence in the faith or honesty of mankind, among thieves at least there was no longer any faith or honour.

On the other hand, should he cast his suspicions upon Francisca—upon her whom he adored, loved and worshipped more and more every day, for whom he would sacrifice all he had in the world, ay, his very life, if she had asked it. Even the Jew's opinion supported him in the latter suspicion, for the Jew had told him so, and had adduced a whole string of shrewd arguments in support of that supposition.

Eel-eye knew not how to extricate himself from this dilemma, or how to find a solution to his doubts. These doubts had for a long time greatly troubled his mind, and they were the real cause of his pale and distressed appearance, and his mysterious behaviour at the cellar of the hunchback.

When Maulspitzier had closed his narrative, Eel-eye without replying a word, stared at him for some time, shrugged his shoulders, and shook his head incredulously.

His bosom was too much oppressed for utterance. He was betrayed either by love or by friendship; one appeared still more terrible than the other.

Eel-eye seemed to possess a great deal of feeling, and set high value on what he considered *his rights*. And even for this he deserves credit, when we consider the class of society among whom he moved, where every one followed the impulses of his own mind and interest, and where all was enmity and strife.

Meanwhile the theatre had disappeared from the room under the busy hands of the dramatic director and his assistants, and instead of the puppet-actors three fidlers had taken their places upon the stage, who began their ear-piercing performances. Every five minutes the so-called *Groschen-klingel* resounded, to remind the dancing gentlemen, that they had become indebted to the orchestra the amount of one silbergroschen, and that their continued dancing would soon make them liable to be called on a second time for that sum.

A wild confused noise soon filled the Diana-saloon, interrupted only by the occasional loud demonstration of those who had here and there to decide some point of honour with their fists. But this was only the usual custom in the saloon, and nobody took any particular notice of these affrays, unless the blood began to flow too freely, or the affair took a serious turn in any other way.

The only persons who marred the general enjoyment, were the two waiters, who cerberus-like, guarded the door to prevent the escape of sundry and divers consumers of Schnapps and beer, who had not yet paid their score. A large kind of *buffet* was erected in a small side room for the accommodation of the thirsty part of the company, and this was by no means the smallest part.

Amidst the general rejoicing, the blonde dealer in matches, or rather the Match Mary, under which name she is better known to us, stood silently and quietly in a corner near the orchestra. Her pousseur, a discharged journeyman hairdresser, sat at some distance from her, and stared growlingly and discontentedly upon the merry mass before him. He would gladly have joined the dance with his *Poussade* (sweetheart,) but he lacked the necessary silbergroschen.

We must here observe that the Match Mary possessed a certain degree of refinement far above the rest of her present associates. She had cultivated her intellect through the medium of one of her former lovers, who had been porter of a circulating library, and who frequently loaned her the greasy novels which passed through his hands. This higher degree of refinement was the most probable cause that she did not ask her pousseur to dance with her, and in case of a refusal, rewarding his want of gallantry or of cash by a box of the ears, here vulgarly called "*Katzenkopf*" (cats head.) She thought it more becoming to her own dignity, to let the contemptuous wretch who did not even possess a silbergroschen, feel her displeasure, by treating him with silent contempt.

Now the orchestra began to play, or to speak more properly, to scrape a Scotch waltz, a favourite dance, which in these saloons is always danced with particular wildness and extravagance, and in that respect is not unlike the dance called *Cancan* in Paris.

Eel-eye who had hitherto sat silently brooding over his troubles, now suddenly jumped up, took the Chonte who was busily engaged in conversation with the "*Kellerjette*," and began wildly to dance with her, flying like a maniac around the room. As the Chonte grew tired he cast her like a worn out tool upon a bench, rushed towards Match-Mary, and continued his wild, restless fandango with her.

Eel-eye had by this proceeding broken one of the first rules of etiquette established in this society, which rule does not permit any one to dance with a strange girl, without having first politely asked and obtained the permission of her pousseur.

The lover of the Match girl, who was already inwardly excited and angry, by the fact of not being able to dance with his sweetheart himself, now was thrown into a perfectly extravagant rage by the behaviour of Eel-eye. Furiously he rushed in among the dancers, tore the girl from Eel-eye's arm, and tossed her upon a bench, where she sunk down almost fainting.

"How dare you, you scoundrel, dance with my *poussade*, without even asking my permission?" he cried, shaking his fist in the face of his opponent—"may a thousand devils take you, you impudent villain."

In an instant a large mass of spectators were collected around the contending parties. The room resounded with the universal joyous exclamation: "Huzzah, huzzah! now we shall have a hard *keilerei*.."*

* A slang expression for fist fight.

Eel-eye in his present excited state of mind, which had only been the cause of his mad proceeding, was by no means inclined to avoid this fight. He had just caught his opponent by the throat, with a most powerful grasp had thrown him to the ground, when from every side a cry of terror was heard, accompanied with exclamations of "silence, silence, the police is coming!"

This exclamation operated with an electric effect upon the combatants. In an instant they were separated.

Eel-eye had not for an instant lost his quiet presence of mind. He was by no means anxious to come in any contact with police officers, but quickly knew how to help himself in this dilemma.

With one bound he jumped upon the stage, and crept through a hole used for the exit of ghosts into the room below. Here he met again the Chonte, who either from a natural sympathy of soul, or from a similar instinct to save herself, had conceived a similar mode of escape.

The lover of Match Mary by no means dared to interfere with his late opponent, for in the great republic of thieves, the same customs prevail as did of yore in the great Roman republic. As soon as an external enemy approaches all domestic feuds and quarrels must cease, and all unite in the general defence.

Spite of the universal cries of terror, Maulspitzer had remained quietly seated in a corner before his schnapps bottle, by which he had seated himself when he began his conversation with Eel-eye. He either believed that he had no danger to apprehend, or else he was so absorbed in the delights of his bottle, that he was no longer master of his senses.

The remaining guests had merely looked around, the music had become silenced, and universal quiet had followed the wild uproar —but only for an instant, for the next moment they all seemed to be convinced of the absolute necessity of avoiding everything that appeared like a particular personal apprehension at the sight of the police. A new attempt at liveliness and merriment was made, but this second attempt showed so much of awkwardness and inner anxiety, that it seemed as if the words of the noisiest and loudest among them, stuck in their throats, and were only uttered with the utmost difficulty.

At the very comical moment of embarrassment, when all the merry and noisy dancers stood abashed like punished schoolboys about the room, W—, the Criminal Commissary, suddenly entered the saloon. The guardian angel of thieves and villains then suddenly inspired one of the frightened scoundrels with a happy thought: "Another Scotch waltz! another Scotch! he cried, and like a storm wind the cry of "a Scotch! a Scotch!" resounded through the room. The fiddlers began to play, and the guests recommenced their dance, even as if a band of Bacchanalians had suddenly entered the room.

The Criminal-Commissary walked to the centre

of the room, looked around, and at last observed the Maulspitzer seated in a corner.

He walked towards him, and said: "Maulspitzer come out with me."

The thief obeyed silently, as he felt comparatively safe and unsuspecting; but outside the saloon, two gensd'armes awaited him, who immediately arrested him, placed him into a carriage that stood in waiting, and hurriedly drove off.

Eel-eye, from beneath the stage, had observed the Maulspitzer's departure with the Criminal-Commissary. Urged by his suspicions of the former, he quietly crept from his hiding place and followed the others, almost convinced that now he had caught the traitor in the very fact. But to his very great surprise he observed that the Maulspitzer was himself arrested and carried off by gensd'armes.

This proceeding must undoubtedly have some connexion with the unfortunate attempt at burglary in the *Hotel de Paris*. He therefore thought, that in his mind he had done foul injustice to his old and faithful friend and associate.

But he was the more positively convinced that Francisca must have been the traitress This thought filled the mind of Eel-eye with bitter sorrow. His love to her had induced him to give her his confidence, and she had rewarded him with worse than ingratitude, with absolute foul treachery.

Silently, but boiling with rage and fury, he left the noisy crowd.

Eel-eye was a worthless vagabond, a thief as all his associates, and consequently did not put much faith in what is generally termed honour and honesty. And yet it made a deep impression upon him when he found himself betrayed and deceived, where he had thought to find truth, where he had counted upon fidelity.

This was a contradiction, yet this very contradiction is an evidence, an involuntary testimony of the nobler impulses of the human heart. It is a proof of the innate goodness and virtue of man, which, like a star in a dark night, frequently shows itself the most in places, where the heart of the philanthropist might weep in hopeless despair.

CHAPTER LXIX.

MARY BERTHOLD.

THE Equestrian, meanwhile, had not lost sight of the house of Geheimerath Berthold.

Much as the better feelings of the Geheimerath struggled against it, by her cunning behaviour, her shrewd and artful manner, she exercised such an irresistible charm over him, that he had actually redeemed his former promise, and on the occasion of a fete, had introduced her to his daughter.

Francisca, who knew how to play every rôle, soon managed to gain the entire confidence of Mary.

This, however, was a comparatively easy task, since Mary, as we know, had hitherto been cut off from all society, and consequently from all intercourse, even with her own sex. She had very early lost her mother, her father had hitherto kept her in an almost cloister-like solitude, and thus she found in Francisca the first, the only being of her sex, who had met her with love or with confidence.

This attachment increased by the further influence which the Equestrian exercised over her destiny.

It can very easily be understood that a young girl, beautiful, rich, the daughter of a wealthy and respected gentleman, a man who lived in the midst of the fashionable world, whose house was often the central point at which beauty and fashion gathered, that such a girl, we say, should feel great desire to partake of the pleasures and enjoyments of the fashionable world.

This desire naturally increased with the severity with which the father refused to satisfy it, and it needed not the charming and seductive descriptions which the Referendarius made a point of giving her, to convince her that she would find more pleasure in society than between the four silent walls of her own boudoir.

And the Equestrian assisted her in the fulfilment of that desire.

She impressed the Geheimerath's mind with the opinion, that a young girl who was destined for society, must absolutely be introduced into it. She had strongly argued against the father's plan of excluding the girl from all pleasures and amusements, and had actually gained her end so far, that the Geheimerath first gave his consent for her to visit the theatre and the opera, and afterwards permitted her even to go to balls and other places of amusement. At last, he even gave soirées at his own house, to which he admitted her.

The natural consequence of these steps was, that a more intimate understanding began to grow up between the Equestrian and *Fräulein* Berthold, and this intimacy was very little lessened by the difference in years, as the former fully atoned for the want of that youth which would have equalized her with the other, by redoubled fire, energy and liveliness.

After the Geheimerath had once taken the first step, he was, as a natural consequence soon forced to take others. His manifold official duties required much of his time and attention, and he was therefore more or less compelled to leave his daughter almost entirely in the hands of the Equestrian. He endeavoured in some way to silence the pangs of his conscience, by exacting from the Equestrian a promise never to take Mary any where without his knowledge, nor to make her acquainted with any of the persons who were at all connected with the peculiar circle of associates of the Equestrian, or who frequented such parties as the one which he gave at his own house when Francisca was first introduced there. With this precaution, he believed that he had done his duty, and was anxious to quiet his conscience thereby, particularly since by his not yielding the point thus far, he thought that he would draw upon himself the displeasure of the Equestrian, which the cowardly voluptuary feared more than all else.

We must, moreover, mention a third and important cause, which contributed in a very great measure towards uniting the two friends, as it were into one mind and one soul.

Since the time when the Equestrian informed the Referendarius of the views which the Geheimerath entertained regarding the marriage of Birkheim with Mary, all attentions and approach to the girl in the presence of her father had been most studiously avoided by the Referendarius. In short, he had in round terms informed the Referendarius of his decided determination never to receive him as his son-in-law. A short time afterwards, the unfortunate lover was even requested no longer to visit the house of the Geheimerath, and the assistance which his cousin had hitherto regularly bestowed upon him, was now paid to him through a third party.

This measure seemed evidently to be caused by the Geheimerath's intentions of marrying his daughter to some other person, for a short time after, he informed her, that he would 'ere long introduce her to a young Pommeranian gentleman, in whom she might perhaps find a future bridegroom.

In all these troubles and anxieties the Equestrian remained her only confidant, and Francisca stood by the side of the love distracted girl, with ready advice and assistance in all her troubles. She gave the girl council how to behave towards her father, in order to keep him unsuspecting and kind to her; she promised, that, in case of an early arrival of the young Pommeranian—whose arrival luckily seemed to be procrastinated—she would herself use her utmost endeavours to interfere and intercede with her father, and finally—and this was a main point—after the Geheimerath had forbidden Birkheim to visit his house, with great readiness gave the lovers a secure and daily place of rendezvous in her own house. Nay, her self-sacrificing friendship went so far as to even propose to give them her house whenever they wanted a meeting, and to avoid all awkward interruptions she frequently visited the opera and concerts with the Geheimerath, or undertook small country excursions with him, whilst Mary and the Referendarius remained alone and in safety at her house.

All these circumstances and this position of things, which had gradually thus arranged itself in the course of the winter, caused a most radical change in the mind of Mary. The most intimate friendship with the Equestrian had only been a natural consequence, and since the beginning of spring, scarcely a day passed without Mary and Francisca being seen together, either upon a promenade, a ride, or at the opera.

Riding on horseback in particular became a favourite exercise with Mary.

Upon her request and with the consent of the Geheimerath, Francisca had herself become Mary's instructress in the art of horsemanship, and both ladies could now be seen nearly every day at noon gallopping the smooth roads of the Thier-garden, mounted on noble and fiery steeds.

Soon a number of gentlemen joined these fair equestrians; at first these were elderly beaux, who came with the authority and consent of the Geheimerath, but gradually younger ones, attracted by the Equestrian, rode with them also, and Birkheim would regularly find an acquaintance among the latter, who would lend him an excuse for joining the party. Thus gradually a formidable cavalcade was formed, a cavalcade excelling in bold, daring and graceful riding, and which soon attracted the attention of the whole Berlinian promenading world.

If the Geheimerath really dared now and then to think that this wild, dissipated life was not proper or desirable for his child, or if he dared to utter any objections to it, it only needed one pouting look of the Equestrian, to bring him to perfect silence. It may also easily be supposed, that amidst his own extended engagements in the city, and his own pleasures which occupied much of his time, not one half of the occurrences came under his immediate notice—certainly an additional reason, why a conscientious father should not lose sight of his child.

But one fact could not escape his observation, namely, that the health and appearance of the girl began to suffer by her wild and irregular mode of life. The blooming colour of Mary's face began to be changed into paleness and pallor, she complained of illness, headache, dizziness; her youthful loveliness was followed by a silent, melancholy manner, and she could only then again be excited to merriment and animation, when she could anew cast herself into a vortex of noisy and wild pleasures.

The Geheimerath endeavoured to direct the attention of the Equestrian to these melancholy facts, but was laughed at, for what she termed, his foolish apprehensions. From his daughter he could receive no other reply to all his questions, but that she was well, and thus he was compelled to put a good face on the matter and leave her to her fate.

Whether the Equestrian really believed the anxiety of the father to be without just cause, or whether she endeavoured to lull him into security, we cannot now decide. But this is certain, she herself did not lose sight of the exact state of Mary's health.

An impartial observer might soon have perceived the fiendish anxiety with which her large, black eyes often rested upon the face of the girl, even as if they would pierce her soul. Now and then she would ask the other, with the most unsuspecting and affectionate face, for the state of her health, and at last it actually appeared as if the positive and definite manner of her questioning presupposed a positive and definite cause of the other's illness.

Attentively she would then await the answers, the quiet and affectionate appearance of her features gradually melted away, and that demonical expression, which in eventful and exciting moments often seemed to rest upon her brow, appeared—and she again became an imposing and majestic, but fearful beauty.

If the Prince had seen her thus, the gloomy, unaccountable feeling, which often possessed him in her presence, would have changed into positive terror.

CHAPTER LXX.

THE CONVERSATION.

It was a fair Spring day, when, at the hour of noon, Francisca stood, as usual, at the window, awaiting the moment when Mary Berthold would come down the street, to take her usual promenade ride through the "Thiergarden."

The vanity of the Geheimerath which felt gratified in the fact of having his daughter appear in all the luxury and elegance which his wealth could afford, after having once suffered her to mix with the world, had been persuaded by the united prayers of Francisca and Mary to purchase a splendid and elegant carriage, which on this occasion was to be tried for the first time.

The Equestrian knew that Mary's vanity was delighted, even in expectation, at thus exciting all the envy and jealousy of her acquaintances. Much less could she comprehend the extraordinary absence of the latter to-day. It was already past noon, and the actual promenading hour of fashionable society was, drawing to a close—yet Mary came not.

To produce no delay, at least on her own part, she prepared for her departure, and descended to the lower floor, there to await the arrival of her friend.

The Equestrian had not waited long, ere the light step of a lady hastily passed by her, then turned and approached her.

It was Fräulein Christianus who came towards her, arrayed in an elegant morning dress.

She had on one occasion, some time ago, made a passing acquaintance with Fräulein Berthold, and had called with her several times on the Equestrian, to take the latter to a promenade. But for some time past, that intercourse had been interrupted. In this, the two young ladies, both real metropolitan children of the world, followed a truly Berlinian method, though it did not perhaps do much credit to their mind and soul. People meet and separate both with equal facility and indifference, as their momentary interest or the changes of a day, or of society, may dictate.

A neighbouring seat at dinner, a meeting at a social ball, establishes friendships; a little bit of jealousy, a favour shown, a beautiful or homely toilette will break it again. But still they have amused themselves sufficient for the time, in the interim.

"I have not seen you for a very long time, Fräulein Christianus," said the Equestrian, to the young lady.

"Good gracious! I only come so very rarely even to see Fräulein Berthold," replied the Hofrath's daughter, "she is so very queer, that one scarcely knows what to do with her, or what to say to her."

"Well, I could not say that."

"Ah! very well, six weeks ago, at the ball of Von Eikens, of which she must certainly have told you, she would scarcely speak to me, simply because the silver gauze of my dress looked and became my complexion so much better than the yellow stuff became hers."

"Why, you don't tell me!"

"Yes, just think, to wear yellow stuff for a ball-dress! Why, she looked like a half-ripe citron. Ha, ha, ha! I must just tell you, however, that I actually made that same joke at table, and perhaps she might have overheard it, and that crowned her anger and displeasure. But just think, my dear lady, yellow stuff for a ball-dress!"

"Yes, yes, that certainly is an unpardonable crime," replied the Equestrian, with a most sarcastic smile.

"Hm! those occurrences are of no rarity to her," continued the young, worldly, and chattering Miss, with wonderful velocity of tongue. "Why, once upon a time, she went to a dejeuner dansant, a really distingué affair, which was given by the French ambassador, and actually came in black satin shoes. How can anybody help laughing at such things? Now you see, I know perfectly well, that she thinks, because my father is only Hofrath, whilst her father is Geheimerath, that she might look down upon me, just as she pleases. But this is no reason that I should overlook her stupidities, or refrain from laughing at them; my father, I dare say, may expect daily to be made a Geheimerath, also."

"But you seemed once to have been such intimate friends?" began the Equestrian, who appeared delighted to let the charming prattler talk to her.

"Intimate?" repeated the other with astonishment, as she raised her very small hand, which was covered with the most elegant of glacé gloves, for the purpose of pushing her blonde locks, which during this animated discourse overspread her face, back to their proper places; "intimate? perhaps you never visit balls?" she added, with no slight accent of conscious superiority.

"In reality, no? I must assure you that I take no pleasure in amusements of that sort," replied Francisca with a smile.

"Oh yes!—no, no, we have never been intimate, and people of fashion do not grow intimate at balls. We are only then intimate when we impart to each other the affairs of our hearts."

"And have you never imparted these to each

other ?" inquired Francisca, who spite of her apparent indifference, suddenly seemed to grow more attentive.

"Alas! no, never. Moreover, I now have no longer any affairs of the heart," said Fräulein Christianus, with a sudden appearance of modesty. "I think that I am at liberty to inform you, that to-morrow my bethrothal with Banker von N—, will be celebrated."

"What, is it possible! and have you delayed until now to inform me of it ?"

"Well, it is a subject one does not like to trumpet about."

"I congratulate you, with all my heart."

"Thank you, thank you!"

"And do you call this, having no affairs of the heart ?"

"Certainly not! A husband is altogether a family affair, an affair of the house; the affairs of the heart then discontinue, for unless we afterwards choose to recommence them a little."

"Aha! this is your opinion! certainly you are more in the right than I thought before," answered the Equestrian in a thoughtful tone.

"But there is yet plenty of time for that in my case," continued the chattering Fräulein. "My future husband is very rich, and very amiable and kind towards me. Only look at this magnificent, fine necklace, which he brought me yesterday."

Fräulein Christianus raised her swandown boa a little, and showed the splendid piece of *Bijouterie*.

"In reality that is beautiful."

"Oh, the many pleasures I am now enjoying! Every evening, concerts, opera, or balls; I declare it is as much as I can do to keep my bridegroom from dragging me to half a dozen of places on the same evening. He is so fond of seeing me everywhere. And so you may suppose, that I have no time to think of Fräulein Berthold."

"It is true, and all this never occurred to me. —How could I be so stupid. I wonder whether Fräulein Berthold also has affairs of the heart, or even family affairs, as you are pleased to call them."

"What a question for you to ask ?" exclaimed the young lady in astonishment.

"And why, my dear ?"

"And do you not know all about it," continued the little chatterer.

"Certainly not."

"Oh, you jest!"

"No, upon honour."

"Well, well, very strange things are whispered about, and that certainly is one reason, why one cannot well visit that house."

"You don't tell me! Now you excite my attention to the utmost," cried Francisca, whose great excitement was now plainly visible in every feature.

"I really ought not to tell it to you," replied the other, "but since the whole town speaks of it—"

"Speak out then, my dear, and let me know," cried the Equestrian impetuously.

Fräulein Christianus quickly cast her eyes around on every side, to make sure that she was not overheard, then she approached Francisca:

"If—if—; but no, I cannot tell you," she cried, with a malicious smile. "I don't know what is the matter."

"You behave very strangely."

"Good Heavens! Yonder comes Fräulein Berthold herself. Don't you see her there near the corner. And she seems to be in great haste. Let her tell you herself what has happened. Adieu, I must leave you. Good Lord, how I could stand here and lose so much time in chatting; I have ten calls to make yet, to the florist, the dress-maker, and to *Arnous*, the little *modiste*. Adieu, adieu!"

And with a most graceful bow, the pretty, chattering busy-body left the Equestrian, and hurried down the street.

Francisca stared after her with a dark and gloomy look.

CHAPTER LXXI.

THE CONFESSION.

MARY BERTHOLD appeared at the other end of the street.

The quick eye of Fräulein Christianus had already discovered her at a considerable distance.

She seemed to run rather than walk. Her whole demeanour betrayed an intense excitement. The Equestrian watched her approach with the utmost interest.

"Come, my dear, come up," she cried breathlessly, when she saw the Equestrian at the door, "we must go up stairs; I have to speak to you immediately."

Without further words, and even without waiting Francisca's reply, she convulsively grasped the other's hand, and hurried up stairs with her.

She had scarcely ascended a few steps before she had to stop and hold on by the railing of the stairs. "Good God," she cried, "all is whirling round and looks black before my eyes. Just stand still for one moment."

"Excuse me for an instant, my dear Mary," said the Equestrian, who had been watching the behaviour of the girl with a most curious expression of countenance; "I will call my girl to your assistance."

"No, no, don't do that," again exclaimed Mary. "It will all go right now. Only come with me, come up quickly, for I must speak to you, I tell you."

She hurried up stairs so quickly that her companion could scarcely keep up with her.

Arrived at the room, she tossed everything off, bonnet, mantilla, &c. Fainting, she sank down upon the sofa.

This was in the small boudoir of the Equestrian.

The girl's chest heaved convulsively. She seemed to gasp for breath. Her lips were dry, her eyes dim, and her whole body trembled with feverish excitement.

For several minutes she lay breathless, unable to utter a syllable, whilst the Equestrian vainly endeavoured to give her relief by opening her dress, offering her salts, or by placing her in a more comfortable position.

How different the picture presented by this girl from that presented by the vain, proud, and dressed-up Matilda Christianus, who had just left the Equestrian, full of levity and spirits.

At last Mary seemed somewhat to recover. Her eyes again began to show animation; but they rolled wildly in her head.

"He has come! He has come!" she cried in a deep, oppressed tone of despair.

"Who has come, my dear Mary?" inquired Francisca; "collect yourself, I pray you. You are almost beside yourself. Tell me, my dear, what is the matter with you? I will assist you, advise you as much as I can."

"Assist and advise me," repeated Mary slowly, and in tones of the utmost distress. It seemed as if she had first to try and remember the meaning of these words. "Yes, if you could do that. If you could assist and advise me. But he is here, I tell you, he is here!"

"Who is here, I pray you?"

"The young gentleman from Pomerania."

"And is it nothing else?"

"It is the same whom my father intended for my husband."

"I know that."

"But whom I cannot take!" cried Mary, with great impetuosity; "no, whom I cannot, will not, have for a husband. I will drown myself sooner than marry him."

"But, my dear Mary, how very strangely you behave. Don't ruin yourself and your health, by such useless excitement. No one speaks positively of your taking him for a husband. All this matter can be arranged. Just let the young gentleman come. We shall see him and speak to him, and afterwards I will converse with your father. I am sure he cannot desire to make his child miserable."

Mary listened with the utmost attention to these consoling words. A new ray of hope seemed to appear to her, and expressed itself in her features. But soon again that ray was obscured by fresh clouds.

"This is not all I have to tell you," she began anew, in an oppressed tone, after another pause.

"Well, and what else oppresses you, my dear?"

Mary remained silent.

Deathly pallor and burning blushes overspread alternately her countenance. Her mouth seemed wanting to utter a speech, but her tongue refused to do its service. Convulsively she wrung her hands, with every expression of intense despair.

Suddenly, she started wildly up. A flood of tears bathed her cheeks. She cast herself into the embrace of the Equestrian, and hid her head in the bosom of Francisca.

"I can no longer hide it," she whispered, in scarcely audible tones, "I—I—shall become—a mother."

Although this confession could scarcely come altogether unexpected to the Equestrian, yet it seemed to create a most powerful impression upon her.

As if shocked by electricity, she shrunk back, her head fell upon her breast, and when again she raised it and looked up, it seemed as if a whole legion of fiends were revelling in her dark glance.

It was a terrible mixture of rage, hatred, sorrow, revenge, and fury, which expressed itself upon her beauteous face, and transformed her expressive features into a fearful picture of fiendish passion.

Almost involuntarily she raised her closed fist to Heaven, even as if she dared fate and Providence to the contest with her, the triumphant victress.

In silence both stood for a long while; one, the frightful picture of fury and hatred, the other of the broken lily.

The chameleon-like nature of the Equestrian even, needed the most powerful exertion to force herself back into a quiet and collected state of mind.

At last, she said: "Your situation is most distressing, my dear Mary, but by no means hopeless. At all events, the secret of your position is secure in my breast. We both need to be perfectly cool and collected, to consider what steps are next to be taken."

Mary's gushing tears almost precluded the possibility of her making an intelligible reply.

"Now you see," she said, weeping, "how terribly the arrival of my intended must afflict me. I have long since wanted to impart my secret to you; but as often as I made the attempt, the word died upon my lips. Now, however, my fear and the difficulties of my situation have forced it from me."

"Does Birkheim know of this?" inquired Francisca.

Burning blushes overspread anew the pale cheek of the girl, as she sighed "yes," in a scarce audible whisper.

"And how did he receive your confession?"

"He suffers as well as I do," continued the artless girl, "and for the present requests me to keep the matter a secret from every body. And I have hitherto followed his advice; but yesterday, when my father informed me that my intended had arrived, I thought that my heart would break. Oh, I love my Adolph with too faithful, too intense a passion; I would much rather die than ever belong to any other. And, as things stand at present," she added, casting her eyes to the ground, "that can no longer be thought of."

"Above all things, my dear," resumed Francisca, you must now be patient and collected; else you might ruin all by premature impetuosity."

"What can I do, my dearest friend?" replied Mary wiping the tears from her eyes, "I will strictly follow your advice. Our only hope at present is, that your influence over my father may obtain from him his consent to my marriage with Adolph, before we both are exposed to shame and degradation. You will certainly find immense difficulties in this, for my father is so excited against Adolph, that he will not even allow his name to be mentioned at our house.— Ah, how grateful we both would be, if in you we should find our saving and protecting angel, the origin of all our happiness."

On listening to these words, a wild fire flashed in the eyes of the Equestrian. But soon she collected herself again, and said quietly: "You know how anxious I am to serve you, but I must repeat to you, and beg of you once more, to do nothing hastily. Do not even mention Birkheim's name to your father. Listen in silence to his new plans; do not by any means offer any objections to his wishes; you must even receive your new lover friendly and kindly, and only beg your father for time, for we must have time, if we would bring the matter to the desired issue."

"Yes, oh yes," exclaimed Mary anxiously, "I will willingly do all you desire of me. Oh, I knew so well that you would give me aid and advice."

"Then we must wait," continued the Equestrian quietly, "until we find an opportune moment, when your father may be made acquainted with your wishes, or if it comes to the worst even with your situation. How and when all this can be done, we must take our time to consider."

At these closing words that fiendish smile again played around the mouth of Francisca, which was always a certain indication that the devil of revenge had full possession of her mind.

The unsuspecting girl, however, observed nothing of all this.

"I will then hasten home," she said in a consoled tone of voice, "the time for promenading is already passed, and I feel exhausted and weak. To-morrow, my dearest friend, I shall see you again."

Mary left the house.

In a tone of fiendish satisfaction the Equestrian said to herself:

"Thus far then I have advanced towards my great object. Now I only want Birkheim, who as a *cheating gamester* must run into my net. Then the last act of this drama shall commence, when all these knots shall be severed, and then, you, Herr Geheimerath, shall play the principal part."

CHAPTER LXXII.

EEL-EYE AND THE EQUESTRIAN.

ON the morning after the occurrences related in the last chapter, the Equestrian sat alone in her boudoir.

At last she was in a fair way and certain of satisfying her revenge upon the Geheimerath; in a great measure the end of her endeavours of many years was reached. But she also felt the truth of the well-established fact, that an object which has been anxiously sought after and wished for, loses in value when it is once attained. She felt this truism the more, as after all she was not fiendish enough in her nature, to overlook the warning and reproaching voice of conscience, which spoke loudly against her actions.

The picture of the innocent victim of her revenge, of the poor girl, whose youth, whose entire destiny she had ruined with coldly-calculated plans of destruction, appeared warningly before her soul. But at the same time she remembered her own life, her own wretched and ruined existence—she remembered how, after the loss of her parents, after the loss of all whom she had loved and who had been dear to her, she arrived at the little provincial town, with no friend to aid or advise her, and how there she was robbed of her sole, her only remaining treasure by her heartless seducer.

Scornfully had he cast her off among strangers, to lead a wretched, a sinful life among the vile outcasts of humanity. All the misery, all the wretchedness that had befallen her, was the natural consequence of the loss of her honour, and it was the remembrance of this which even now made her blood boil again, and she swore anew, her oft repeated vow, that she would take vengeance upon her seducer, deep and terrible vengeance, such as never had been taken by a poor, weak, deluded woman.

"Ay, I will engage in the contest for the whole of my abused sex," she cried involuntarily aloud, "and if I only can succeed in revenging the thousandth part of the bitter tears which are shed every hour, every minute, for this cold-hearted, calculating and selfish race of men Why should the champion care for the weapon which he must break? I could not well spare the girl; not upon my head, but upon that of her father the guilt may fall."

Such were the feelings, such the thoughts of the Equestrian, when suddenly, without knock or other announcement the door flew open, and Eel-eye rushed into the room.

Pale as a corpse, he sank upon his knees before her, and raising both hands to her in prayer, he exclaimed impetuously:

"Tell me, Francisca, dearest Francisca, tell me but one thing.—Have you really become a traitress to your friends? I will and must be satisfied. Speak but one word, but one syllable: Yes or no?"

Frightened for a moment by the wild, impetuous manner of the thief, Francisca had started up; but quickly she regained her self-possession, and replied with a smile:

"What a strange suspicion you have, Albert. Why do you ask me such an odd and singular question?"

"Answer me!" cried Eel-eye more wildly than before, "tell me, yes or no?"

"You are foolish!" replied Francisca in a displeased tone. "Why should I want to betray my friends? Rise from your knees and do not cry so loud, else you will alarm the whole neighbourhood. I hope that you do not believe me to be a vigilant of Police!"

"Yes or no!" again cried the thief almost beside himself, and even louder than before; "this is enough to set me crazy! Somebody has betrayed us, in the affair at the *Hotel de Paris*. I now must know who it was. My first suspicions fell upon Maulspitzer, but I have since fully convinced myself of his innocence. And now it is only you, upon whom I can fix suspicion. Woman, tell me the truth, the whole truth, or I will murder you!"

The longer Eel-eye spoke, the more his rage and fury increased. His voice seemed no longer human, it was like the ferocious incoherent bawling of a wild beast.

Spite of her personal courage and resolution, the Equestrian could not avoid a feeling of terror which crept over her.

Quickly, however, her resolution was taken. She must silence and quiet her early friend, but she could also avail herself of the opportunity of breaking off, all and any further connexion with the thieves. She well knew that her present intimacy with them, could only bring her into future difficulties, annoyances and dangers. And these had now become useless, since she was no longer able to carry out her original plan of assisting the Prince in finding his brother—the Jew as well as the Prince having left Berlin, and she knew not whither they had gone. But on the other hand it was possible, that Eel-eye might discover new means and plans to assist her, and thereby bring her to the desired end.

She therefore concluded that after all it would be her better plan, to tell her early friend the entire truth. She was so fully aware of her own powers, of the influence which her charms could exercise over him, that she not only thought that she could depend upon his secresy, but also counted upon his readiness to assist her in her endeavours to find the brother of Prince Prominsky.

"Now be quiet, Albert," she began, with the seductive smile of a syren, "and sit down calmly by my side. I will tell you all that I know, but you must not interrupt me, but listen attentively until I have finished my statement. I never betrayed you or any of your friends to the Police, that I will swear to you."

"Huzza, I knew it," cried Eel-eye, jumping up with joy and delight, "I knew that you had not betrayed me. It would have been too bad, too devilish; but now tell me all you have to tell me."

The thief seated himself quietly by the Equestrian, anxious to learn the course of the whole affair.

Francisca now openly confessed to him the reasons which had at first induced her to seek a personal acquaintance with the Jew. She also told him, that their intention had been solely to arrest Schmuel at the burglary of the *Hotel de Paris*, but not by any means to deliver him to the Police. On the contrary, their object had been to offer him a rich reward for the desired information regarding the fate of the Prince's brother. No harm was intended to be done, either to Maulspitzer, or to Eel-eye; but on the contrary, their escape would have been aided in every possible way. The police had suddenly arrived at the Hotel, and most inopportunely to the Prince, as their interference had ruined all his plans, and had induced the Jew to leave Berlin.

The other listened to this report, and doubtingly shook his head.

"This is incomprehensible," he began; "who, in Heaven's name, then, is the traitor among us?"

"You see, my dear Albert," continued the Equestrian, "how very unjust you are in your suspicions of me. But now I will make a proposition to you, which must fully convince you, that the playmate of your childhood still is your true and faithful friend.

"As you must already be aware, from the reasons I have stated, it is of the utmost importance to Prince Prominsky, to find his lost or abducted brother again. For this purpose, he immediately followed in the track of the Jew. Whether or not he will be able to attain his object, we cannot now determine. But it is very possible that even here in Berlin, among the thieves, we may obtain a clue, which would lead us to the desired end; we are most likely to find such a clue among the Polish Jews, with whom, as you have told me, Long Schmuel is very intimately connected."

"Certainly," interrupted Eel-eye, "in K— street, for instance, at the house of thick Itzig, we might learn something, for the Long Schmuel was intimate there, and even lodged there for some time."

"Very well, then," resumed the Equestrian, "suppose you were to go there and make the attempt. Should you succeed in learning any thing definite, the gratitude of the Prince would be boundless. He would furnish you with the means to emigrate to a foreign country, where you might commence an honest business, and live as an honest man, whilst here you have no other prospect, but to end your days in a prison."

This idea, which had not crossed the mind of Eel-eye for many years, and which if it had occurred to him, would have appeared like an impossibility, now seemed to make a deep impression upon his mind.

"Live as an honest man," he repeated slowly to himself. "Hm! that would be very fine, but I don't think that I would understand how to do it."

Francisca had in reality taken an interest in the fate of her former playmate, and greatly abhorred his dishonest and disreputable courses. The hope and prospect of being able to save her early friend from certain perdition, gave her delight and satisfaction, and induced her to endeavour to save him. Perhaps it was also an undefined desire which lay in the depth of her soul, to equalize in some degree, by a good and noble action, the heavy debt of guilt which was accumulating upon her conscience.

It is much more difficult to free our mind from a consciousness of moral retribution, than we are generally willing to admit. The most heartless criminal has moments at which his conscience will assert its mighty force, and will give him no rest, until it has driven him before his judge, or anticipates that judge, by forcing him to commit suicide.

"Why should you not understand how to do that which is natural to all other men," said the Equestrian, with great kindness, "that which others can do without the least trouble. Just imagine your present life, this eternal fear and anxiety, this continual danger of being taken, tried, and imprisoned by the criminal authorities; is all this to be compared to the quiet, uninterrupted happiness of a simple, safe and honest civic position? And the Prince not only is immensely rich, but he is also humane and philanthropic, and will be sure to assist you in every way, if you do so great a service for him."

The thief walked restlessly up and down the room. A new world seemed to be opened before his eyes, a new, a more happy life unfolded itself in the distance before him; yet the distance seemed so very great, that he thought it impossible ever to reach its end. Yet in his heart and soul he felt a greater longing for the attainment of that happiness, than he himself was willing to admit, or than he actually believed.

"It is true," he said to himself half aloud, "it must be very fine, to be an honest man; indeed I should like to become honest."

"Excellent, Albert," exclaimed the Equestrian, approaching him friendly, "then let us make a compact. You will assist me in searching for the Prince, and I shall assist you in becoming an honest man."

Astounded and absorbed in thought, the thief gazed in silence before him. The happy pictures of his early youth, which Francisca had once before conjured up from the bottom of his soul, when she first appeared to him at the circus, and when he recognised her so suddenly, again rose before his mind.

Again he saw the happy and peaceful dwelling of his parents; again his fancy conjured up his kind and friendly mother with her rattling bunch of keys, and his father in his morning gown and cap, stood at the cottage door watching the noisy play of the school-boys and girls during their hour of recreation.

Again he heard the barking of his father's house-dog, and the cackling of the hens; again he saw his lamb bounding over the meadow back of the garden, and again he fancied that he fished for a few trout in the mountain brook near the village. Then he remembered the time, aye, the very hour when he left all this peace and happiness and went forth into the wide world; his poor mother embraced him amidst a thousand tears, and his father placed his hands upon his head, and gave him his last blessing.—But how was it now? Those parents were dead, had gone to their honest graves long since, and their son had become a thief, a vagabond.

Involuntarily Eel-eye remembered the parable of the lost son. When a boy, he had ever been fond of reading that story, and had often begged his father to explain its biblical sense to him. And then he had always become so happy, so glad, when the lost son had returned to his home, and in his childish mind he had painted in lively colours the delights of the father and mother on the return of their lost child.

Involuntarily he repeated in his own mind, the beautiful passage which he remembered from his school-days. "I will arise and go unto my father, and will say unto him: father, I have sinned before Heaven and against thee, and am no more worthy to be called thy son," &c. A scriptural passage had not crossed his mind for many years before.

Now he himself had become the lost son, and an opportunity offered to return, if not to the paternal roof, at least unto the protecting and sheltering harbour of virtue and honesty.—And dared he hesitate?

Greatly moved, Eel-eye grasped the hand of the Equestrian: "I will obey you," he cried. "You know how much I love you. And if you were to lead me to the scaffold, I would even there follow you. I will assist you in seeking for the Prince, and I will also try and become an honest man."

CHAPTER LXXIII.

A NEW ADVENTURE.

Eel-eye had approached the window, to endeavour and master his internal emotion, which strongly expressed its intensity upon his features.

Before the house stood an old, poorly dressed woman, carrying a large willow basket upon her back, and holding a stick with an iron hook in her hand. She was busily engaged in searching through the mud of the gutter with this hook.

Thoughtfully Eel-eye looked out upon the street. At this moment the old woman raised her head, in order to toss a rag which she had just fished up upon her hook, into the basket behind. This movement caused her to look upwards, and her glance fell direct upon Eel-eye.

The woman was no other than the old rag-gatherer, who uttered an involuntary exclamation of astonishment, when she discovered her friend at the window of such an elegant dwelling.

Eel-eye hastily left the window, as it seemed not advisable, either for his own comfort or for that of Francisca to be recognised here by the old woman.

The rag-gatherer, however, could not restrain her curiosity to ascertain what the thief could possibly be doing here. Quickly she slipped into the open door, and hid herself below the stairs leading to the upper story.

The Equestrian once more instructed her newly gained associate, upon all those points, to which it was necessary that he should direct his particular attention, to enable him to be successful in his search. She had particularly directed his attention to the amulet, to the blue stone, which in fact was now the only clue to any further research. She then requested him to leave her, as she had to attend a morning rehearsal, for the performance of a new piece by the Equestrian company, which was to be produced that night.

Eel-eye convinced himself at a glance that the rag-gatherer had disappeared from the street, and then prepared to comply with the wishes of the Equestrian.

He stopped as he reached the door.

"Francisca, do you love me?"

"I like you very well, dear Albert."

"As I love you, with a warm, an intense and consuming passion, you cannot love me."

"I don't know that," answered the Equestrian, with perhaps intentional hesitation.

"But I know it!" cried the other passionately, "I know it! Oh, if you loved me as I love you——see, you are the flame and I the butterfly, who will be consumed in your fire. I know it, feel it, yet you can do with me as you please, and I must obey you."

Wildly he embraced the beautiful woman, endeavouring to imprint a kiss upon her lips.

"Be quiet, Albert, be quiet," said Francisca, pushing him back. "What have you promised me? Keep calm, quiet and collected. First find me the brother of the Prince, and then ask for your reward."

Abashed and silent, Eel-eye left the room.

Francisca followed him to the stairs to recommend once more caution and secrecy to him.

Her friend slowly descended the stairs, and without looking back, left the house.

With a mixture of excited feelings the Equestrian looked after him. Her soul was moved by sadness, hope, sorrow, regret and sympathy. She leaned over the railing of the stairs, to cast a parting glance after the friend of her youth.

On the floor below stood the rag-gatherer, staring with curiosity at the departing Eel-eye. On hearing a noise she looked up the stairs; that moment her eye met that of the Equestrian.

Amidst the burning sands of the African deserts, it occurs sometimes that the lioness, returning at night to her lair finds her cubs gone, her nest destroyed, and her lair deserted. Roaring and wild she then prowls through forests and deserts, never resting or ceasing her heart-rending roars. Suddenly she comes upon, she stands before the daring hunter who has destroyed her peace, who has robbed her of her young, and the glance of her eye threatens perdition to the pale, daring intruder.

Thus it was with these two women.

In silence they stared at each other for an instant.

Suddenly a terrible animation came into the pale face of Francisca. Her eyes flashed with the fury of a tigress. With lightning speed she pounced at a single leap down the entire stairs, and caught the rag-gatherer by the shoulder with an almost superhuman exertion of strength, shook her as if she had been a mere child, and cried in a voice that made the blood chill: "You have stolen my child from me, where is my child? Woman, get me my child back again!"

But the excitement was too great even for her strong nerves. Exhausted, she fell to the ground in a death-like swoon.

CHAPTER LXXIV.

HOW LONG SCHMUEL FARES AT PRESENT.

IN one of the back buildings of the mansion, where before we found Major von Steinfort, a quiet, and retired sick chamber had been arranged. The windows were darkened and closely barricaded, and the rays of the spring sun could with difficulty penetrate the cracks of the shutters, and throw a dim light into the room.

Upon a soft couch, but in restless excitement, we find a strong bearded figure; it is long Schmuel.

He had fallen asleep, but terrible dreams seemed to disturb his slumbers, for restlessly he was rolling from one side to the other. Large drops of perspiration stood upon his forehead, and now and then broken sounds escaped his oppressed breast.

Before his bed sat the faithful guardian of his days of sorrow, the Jewess, watching every motion of her husband with the most anxious care.

At the foot of the bed his children were seated, occasionally looking up to their mother with a silent and inquiring glance.

The Jewess was sorely troubled. The severe sickness of her husband, even according to the expressed opinion of the physician, was pronounced an exceedingly dangerous one, and his recovery certainly was involved in doubts. The Jewess, therefore, could not free her mind from the most bitter self-reproaches.

Even though her intentions towards her husband had ever been for his good, even though her conscience had been her honest guide in all her actions, still the present position of her husband had been brought about by herself.

If she had not informed the Prince of the new place of refuge of Schmuel, and if she had not afterwards even served as guide in the forest, the whole undertaking could not have been accomplished, and her present great sorrow, and the sufferings of her husband, would have been avoided. She owed obedience and faith to him whom she had sworn to love and cherish, and she had broken that faith and failed in that obedience. No matter whether she meant it for his benefit or not, the terrible consequences were before her, and the guilt rested upon her.

But there was yet another feeling which became a torture to her, and the more so, as that same feeling told her that the breach of duty and obedience with which she reproached herself, was not at all equalized or rewarded by other blessings.

We already know, that long previous at the country-seat of the Major, she had been converted to christianity.

She had become a zealous, pious and devout Christian, but at the same time had imbibed the mistaken opinion of the exclusive salvation of her own church. Consequently she feared the death of her beloved husband equally much, because his earthly loss to her was terrible, as because she thought that his eternal life in another world was greatly jeopardized by his Jewish faith.

According to her pious opinion, eternal salvation was only the reward of Christian faith. To convert him to this there was no hope, blinded and fanatic as he was with his Mosaic faith. Thus the mind of the Jewess was sorely troubled with the thought of having worked his temporal annihilation, without having advanced a single step towards his eternal salvation.

This filled her whole soul with the most bitter sorrow.

Several days had already passed whilst she was nursing the sick man, without any change having yet appeared in the condition of long Schmuel. Even the physician could not give any further opinion, except that which he had already given, and which seemed to hesitation between hope and fear.

Upon the knee of the Jewess lay a prayer-book, in which, by the dim light, she earnestly endeavoured to read, but which she fearfully hid under her apron every time when the sick man made a motion, which might indicate his awakening.

After a while he seemed to fall more firmly and quietly asleep, and the unfortunate woman sought new consolation in prayer.

Her pious care had induced her to seek for a prayer for the conversion of a sinner, and in a low tone she was reading that to herself.

She became so deeply absorbed in her religious contemplations, that she finally omitted to exercise the necessary care and attention to the state of her husband.

The Jew had awoke and began to listen to the words of his wife. At first he listened with quiet indifference, but soon he became more attentive, his features assumed an expression of firmness and of deadly hatred, and a dark fever-glow overspread his pallid cheeks. He lay there like a tiger watching his prey, his head bent forward, and his eyes nearly closed. Every fibre and muscle of his frame seemed on a strain.

At last he heard her distinctly pronounce the hateful name of the son of God, the Christian's saviour.

Raving with fury, he started up from his couch; a white foam gushed from his lips.

"A *ruech* (curse) upon thee, accursed apostate woman!" he cried madly, "would'st thou forswear the religion of thy fathers and of thy forefathers? Ha! I have not been deceived then!"

Frantically he rushed upon the unfortunate woman, grasping her throat with both of his long muscular hands, and pressing it with all his herculean power and fury.

"Die, wretch, die!" he cried, or rather roared, "die, thou traitress to the God of Israel!"

Words were no longer in the power of the madman, but he broke into the wild, unintelligible roaring of a beast, stamping the ground, and spitting into the face of his wife.

At last, exhausted, and with a curse upon his lips, he sunk to the ground, weltering in blood.

The screams of the children who believed both their parents dead, soon brought assistance to the room.

The death-like form of Schmuel was carried back to his bed, and the physician, who now, at the desire of the Prince, remained constantly at the mansion, as the life of the Jew was of too great importance, was hastily called in.

The experienced son of Esculapius doubtingly shook his head at the sight of his patient. The excitement and the subsequent loss of blood had so shaken the constitution of Schmuel, that there was no longer any hope of his survival.

The Jewess, who also had not been recalled to life and animation, until after an hour's vain labour and endeavour, was almost beside herself with sorrow and despair, on learning this distressing intelligence.

Now, a hundred times more than before, she accused herself of having been the cause of her husband's death. She found her mind torn and distracted by the most contradictory doubts. She had been converted to Christianity, and now considered it her highest duty to follow its precepts and to acknowledge her faith to the world; but at the same time, she had jeopardized the life of her husband in the very fulfilment of that duty, nay, had perhaps even murdered him.

The physician gave no prescription, but recommended perfect quiet, and the avoidance of all excitement. Even the children had to be taken away and provided for elsewhere, that they might not disturb the invalid.

But the Jewess again resumed her place by

[Unmutilated and Only Genuine Edition.]

THIERS' LIFE OF NAPOLEON,

WITH SUPERB STEEL ENGRAVINGS.

FOR SEVENTY-FIVE CENTS,

[If paid in Advance.]

W. H. COLYER having been at great expense to procure a copy of this unrivalled work, now publishes

PART I.

OF THE

HISTORY OF THE CONSULATE AND THE EMPIRE

OF

FRANCE UNDER NAPOLEON,

By M. A. THIERS,

LATE PRIME MINISTER OF FRANCE.

Wm. H. Colyer's edition of this splendid work, The Life of Napoleon, is decidedly the best in this country. It is printed on fine paper and new type, according to the design of the author, M. A. Thiers, and on comparison with other editions will be found far superior.

In Press.

THIERS' FRENCH REVOLUTION,

TO BE COMPLETED IN SIX PARTS, AT 12 1-2 CENTS EACH.

TO BE COMPLETED IN TEN NUMBERS.

THE MYSTERIES OF BERLIN,

FROM

THE PAPERS OF A BERLIN CRIMINAL OFFICER.

TRANSLATED FROM THE GERMAN.

By C. B. BURKHARDT.

With Illustrations on Steel, by P. Habelmann.

This work in Europe has been universally pronounced far superior to M. Sue's celebrated "Mysteries of Paris," and we confidantly predict that the popularity of this translation will be without a parallel in the history of light reading.

THE MYSTERIES of BERLIN.

TO BE COMPLETED

IN

TEN PARTS.

NEW YORK: WILLIAM H. COLYER, PUBLISHER.

his bedside, and nothing could induce her to leave this place even for a moment, day or night.

For two whole days the Jew lay in utter unconsciousness.

On the third day he awoke; but he had become a different man. The great loss of blood had not only weakened his body, but had also broken his mental obstinacy.

Was it perhaps the feeling of approaching death which made him so quiet and calm?

All the remembrance of the late occurrences seemed to have disappeared from his mind.

Gently he took the hand of his wife:

" Dear wife," he began in a weak tone of voice, " I feel that cold death is approaching me, and that I shall never again leave this couch. Poor, poor woman, who will take pity on thee, or care for thee and for thy children, who are despised and accursed by the world even from their very birth."

" Be quiet, my dear husband," replied the Jewess, as with difficulty she endeavoured to suppress her flowing tears, " all is not yet so bad with you. The doctor has forbidden every kind of excitement, and only by that means hopes soon to restore you again."

" The doctor?" inquired the Jew with great astonishment, as his memory seemed gradually to return to him, " do you tell me that we have a physician?"

With great exertion he raised his head a little.

" Where am I?" he asked again in a low tone, " we are not here in Kawno? Oh I remember; I was caught by the Lambden, I recollect? Were you and the children caught and arrested also? Where are our children?" he inquired more lively, rolling his eyes wildly around, and seeking them through the room.

The physician had foreseen this moment, and had instructed the Jewess to give an open and simple reply to all the questions of her husband, and to explain to him the object of his present imprisonment, as well as the cause of his illness; he had warned her, however, against letting the Jew know what part she herself had taken in his arrest, and by all means forbade her to inform her husband of her own conversion to Christianity, fearing that if he heard of this, he would again become needlessly and most dangerously excited.

This method the physician had arranged with the Prince and the Major, for the purpose of availing themselves of the few moments of consciousness which the Jew might have previous to his dissolution, to the furtherance of the plans of Prince Prominsky. For this purpose it had been especially recommended to the Jewess to urge the interest of her children above all things, and to assure her husband of the Prince's protection and care for them, provided he would in return comply with the Prince's desires.

The Jewess considered the present the most favourable moment to discharge her commission, as her husband just then, by the inquiry for his children, had shown his anxiety about them.

Schmuel listened with the utmost attention.

He fully comprehended the position of his wife, and also knew that he could only secure to them a safe and happy futurity, by complying with the important request of the Prince.

At any other time, and under any other circumstances, with his intense hatred of Christians, he would have repulsed such a request with scorn and derision; but at present, as we have already observed, the approach of death had changed his mind, and had made him kind and gentle. Perhaps also, before his departure from this world, he might have felt a silent wish to restore a much injured being to his position and wealth which he had deprived him of, and thus in a measure atone for the great and unparalleled crimes which he had committed.

After his wife had concluded, he made a long pause.

" I believe that I could die more quietly," he said at last, " if I knew that you were all provided for."

The Jewess endeavoured to dissuade him from the thoughts of death. He seemed not to heed her argument or consolation. Then the pious woman thought it her duty, to make an attempt, to do something at least towards his eternal salvation.

" Do not trouble yourself too much about our fate, my dear husband," she began, " Heaven and kind and charitable men will provide for us; but let me ask you kindly, do you ever think of your own eternal salvation?"

The Jew stared at the zealous speaker with astonishment. Already his eyes flashed again as they did two days before, when he made an attempt to strangle his wife, and the latter trembled and repented her own incautious speech. But a good genius seemed to watch over this scene; the memory of the Jew seemed again to be dimmed, and the remembrance of that occurrence to have escaped his mind.

After a momentary consideration, Schmuel said in a voice of great solemnity:

" The God of our fathers will judge this unworthy son of Israel according to his deeds. I have done much evil in the course of my life, and heavy misdeeds are oppressing my conscience; but I have also suffered great sorrows; I once saw my wife and children cast into the flames by Gojim, and I myself was led away to slavery. I then was innocent, but they thus made a criminal of me. I now with my life atone for my guilt and for my misdeeds, and therefore I hope, that the God of Abraham, Isaac and Jacob, will be a merciful judge towards me. Amen."

For a moment he was silent.

In a very weak tone of voice he continued after a pause:

" Speak no more of me, dear wife, for even now I am like a dead man, and your care only belongs to the living. But I can feel that the moments of my existence are but few, and they are numbered. Go and call the Prince Prominsky to my bedside.

In tears the Jewess left the room.

15

CHAPTER LXXV.

THE CONFESSION OF LONG SCHMUEL.

THE Prince obeyed the request to visit the Jew with that willingness, which might be expected from the ready prospect of having the great problem of his life solved at last.

A few moments afterwards he entered the sick chamber of the Jew.

Only with great difficulty could that powerful man suppress the external indications of the tremendous excitement which worked in all his features.

The Jew had, at his own request, been placed in a sitting position, and thus he awaited the arrival of his conquering enemy.

An ashy paleness overspread his lank and consumptive features, to which the long black beard lent an even more pallid appearance.

Attentively his glance rested upon the door. When the Prince crossed the threshold, his dim eyes flashed with the renewed fire of distant lightning, and involuntarily his emaciated hand closed convulsively as he laid it down upon the coverlet. At this moment his whole frame was convulsed with the coarsest fury of religious fanaticism. The Jew beheld his deadly enemy, the Christian, before him, and that Christian had vanquished him.

It could easily be seen, that it would have been a subject for ferocious delight to the sick man, if he could even now have torn Prince Prominsky to pieces, and he cursed his fate, which refuseed him that power.

But this feeling lasted only a moment.

The anticipation, the thought of a dreaded futurity, already filled his breast with the feeling of death, and even as he gradually lost all physical power of gratifying his hatred, so his mind became more calm, yielding and obedient.

Slowly the features of his face again became smooth, his closed fist relaxed and opened in its natural position, and after a pause of dark brooding, the Jew again looked upon the Prince. His features had now become calm, serious and quiet.

Prominsky had silently approached the bed, and with an expression of the most intense sorrow, he looked down upon the sick man.

Schmuel seemed to observe this movement, and it appeared that it created a most favourable impression upon his mind.

The Prince endeavoured to speak, but his internal excitement was so intense, that his voice failed him. Now was the time to decide—now he would learn, whether the last dim star of hope would change into the bright sun, which would illumine his futurity, or whether it would forever sink in darkness and gloom.

"You desire to obtain revelations of me," at last the Jew commenced in a low, but distinct tone of voice; " you desire to be made acquainted with circumstances, which are and must be of the utmost importance to yourself and to your family. It is I alone who can give you these revelations, and I will give them, if I obtain first a promise from you, which will make the hour of my death more easy."

" Ask whatever you desire !" cried the Prince passionately : " ask one-half of my wealth and you shall have it."

At this loud exclamation the patient shrunk back affrighted and trembling. His iron nerves had become weak and excitable.

"I feel it," he began in a most solemn tone of voice, " that my hours are counted. Soon I shall be gathered to my fathers, and shall be called upon to give an account at the throne of Jehovah of the few good and the many evil hours of my earthly existence. But if I would think quietly and peaceably on another world, I must first properly arrange my earthly affairs. I leave a poor deserted wife, and three helpless orphans behind me ; will your Highness promise me to provide for them, and not suffer that the crimes and sins of their father be visited upon the heads of these innocent ones."

" I will not only promise you what you request," answered the Prince warmly, " but I shall protect and care for your family as for the best and most worthy of my subjects. They shall want in nothing that is in my power to give them, as long as they will accept of it. In my own domains, I shall prepare for them a peaceful and quiet abode. This I promise you, and pledge my princely word for its fulfilment."

" Good, good," said the Jew, becoming more calm, " I thank your Highness for your promise, which I will take with me to another world. And now your Highness shall learn all that you so anxiously desire to know."

The Jew stopped a few moments as if to collect his scattered thoughts. The Prince was listening in breathless attention. Schmuel began :

" My father was the leader of a Jewish band of robbers, with whom he roved about sometimes in Russian and again in Polish wildernesses, just as their security, or the prospect of gain seemed to make one place or the other the most advisable. It was he, who about forty years ago, in a nocturnal surprise at one of your hunting castles, tore your brother from his father's arms and carried him off.

"This was done at the instigation of one of the female relations of your house, who had hired my father, under promise of great rewards, to deliver the young Prince to her alive, but to murder his Sire. In this manner she would obtain a demand upon the succession of sovereignty. At this surprise then, as you must be aware, the young Prince, your brother, was carried off. Your father was bound, and thrown into the flames to die a horrible death, but he was saved therefrom by the timely arrival of assistance, after our band had left.

" The woman who instigated my father to these deeds, had made it a condition, that my father, as a sign of having accomplished his undertaking, should bring her a large blue precious stone, which, according to her statement, your father wore around his neck. My father easily obtained that stone at the first onslaught, but when he was informed that the reigning Prince had been rescued and was saved, he feared, and not without just cause, that the lady would refuse to pay him the promised reward; moreover, it seemed to him exceedingly dangerous to be seen in the neighbourhood of the castle, after what had occurred.

"He consequently determined to keep the boy with him, for the simple purpose of sooner or later obtaining a large reward or remuneration by the possessio: of so important a person, as the heir of the sovereignty. In the same way it seemed most important and advisable to keep possession of the blue stone, as this might afterwards assist in identifying the person of the young Prince. As the child was still very small and helpless, my father brought it to a Hebrew family who were distantly related to us, to whom he told, that the boy was the son of his brother, who had very suddenly died with his wife, and had left this, his only child, in his care. At this house then, the young Prince was brought up.

"At that time I was about twelve years of age, and belonged to another band to which my father had sent me, for the purpose of inuring me to the trials and dangers of our vagabondizing mode of life. Some years afterwards, when my father felt the cold hand of death approaching him, he sent for me and related to me all these circumstances, gave me the blue stone, and informed me how and in what manner I might at a future time make that stone a source of great profit, as soon as the reigning Prince Prominsky should die, and the lady who had hired him for the foul deed should claim the succession of the sovereignty. Your Highness was not yet born at that time. Shortly after he had made these revelations to me, my father died, and I succeeded him in the command of his band. I then married, although I was still almost a youth, and soon became the happy father of two sweet, dearly beloved children."

The Jew stopped for a few moments, perhaps to revel in the remembrance of past happiness, perhaps also, deep sorrow overpowered and unmanned him.

The Prince also was silent. His looks in feverish intensity hung upon the lips of the speaker.

With a deep excited tone of voice the Jew continued :

"At that time I was unspeakably happy. We often fared rather poorly, but we had enough to live upon, obtaining money either by honest industry, or by petty thefts. I restrained my band from the committal of greater crimes with the utmost severity, although among my associates at that time, I possessed the reputation of great daring and activity. But I was not the cold blooded criminal then, which I became afterwards.

"My happiness, however, was only of short duration. An unfortunate suspicion, that my band had been guilty of robbing a church, became the excuse for a detachment of Russian boors, who surprised us, murdered nearly the whole of my band, ravished my poor wife before my very eyes, and then, together with my unfortunate children, cast her into the flames."

"Yes, sir," continued the Jew in a suppressed and trembling tone of voice, "at that moment when wounded and fettered I lay upon the ground, when the terrible cries of my wife, and the wailings of my infants reached my ears in vain, when I was compelled by brute force to witness the outrages upon these poor victims, without even being able to put an end to the terrors of my own miserable existence, at that time I severed the bonds which bound me to God and man. It was an hour in which I, a youth still in years, became an old man in icy coldness of heart. Scores of years have I passed during those minutes, yet scores of years with all the blood, sorrows and tears of my miserable existence could not atone for the terrors of them. I swore a terrible oath of revenge, and I vowed to become a cold blooded villain—a villain that would not shrink from any sin, from any crime—and I have fulfilled my vow. I know it, I feel it, that the great God of my forefathers, will now pronounce judgment upon me for that impious vow, but in his great mercy, he will also remember the day, when his hand was drawn from me, and when he would not heed the misery of his servant.

"Of the entire band, they suffered me alone to survive. They carried me off in fetters, as they hoped to force confessions from me. I could make no confessions, for I knew of nothing they accused me of—had nothing to confess. But this only excited the fury of my tormentors still more; without judgment, without trial, they carried me off to the deserts of Siberia, and there I wept and mourned for *fifteen years* of my life, amidst unspeakable miseries and persecutions. Only the solemn vow of revenge which I had taken, prevented me from putting an end to my unhappy existence.

"At last I succeeded in making my escape. I returned to Poland, had soon a new band collected under my command, and now I took the first step of revenge upon my tormentors of terrible retribution upon the destroyers of all my earthly happiness; with fire and sword I swept them all, together with the places of their dwelling, from the face of the earth.

* * * * *

At the time when we were surprised by the Russian boors, the blue stone, which my father had given to me, had also been taken from me. As the repossession of that stone was of the utmost importance to me, I caused a public announcement to be made among the prisoners, to inform them, that he, who would restore me into possession of that stone should escape with his life and liberty. This plan had the desired effect, although the present possessor of the stone had fallen at the burning of the village. But his dead body was pointed out to me, and I cut the precious relic from the neck of the corps.

My intense hatred never permitted me to think of using that stone immediately in regard to the restoration of the brother of your Highness, whom my father had abducted. No, that boy had during my imprisonment and exile, grown up in that Hebrew family, and had passed as the son of his foster parents, even as my father had requested previous to his death. With great delight I learned that he possessed great talents for the trade of thieves, and that under the guidance of his comrades he had already committed many bo'd and important crimes. It was to me a source of the most unfeigned and the greater delight and gratification, to have the son of a Prince for the companion of my days of crime and disgrace, nay, to see one, from the highest, the very first rank of these accursed Gosims, trembling with me before the lash and scourge of a beadle.

" I therefore immediately induced the Prince as well as his foster father to join my band, both became participators in my work of revenge upon the Russian boors, and both accompanied and assisted me in all my further undertakings and expeditions. Not unfrequently, these expeditions were accompanied by as much bloodshed and cruelty as I had sworn they should be, when I was still a slave in Siberia. I had now become another man, my heart thirsted for revenge, to rob, murder, and destroy, were matters of pleasure and delight to me.

" Although at first, my intentions had been nothing further than to make a robber and a murderer, such as I was, of the Prince also, and although in my great work of revenge I had disdained making a monetary gain by the denouncement of his birth, these plans gradually and in time underwent a change.

" After the death of the Prince's foster-father, I closed a most intimate friendship with a Jew, named Manasse, who like myself had become hardened by the unjust blows of fate. This friendship attained so great a degree of intimacy, that at last I made him acquainted with the whole of my secret. My friend now explained to me how great the political advantages would be, which we could gain by placing the Princely crown upon the head of our associate thief. I agreed to his proposition, and acknowledged the justness of his reasoning.

" Our first object now must be, to clear your Highness and your own descendants, (for you had meanwhile succeeded to the sovereignty,) from our path. This accomplished, we could step forward with the abducted boy, who had now grown up a powerful young man, and assisted by the precious blue stone, which would help us to identify him, claim the succession for him. Thus we would not only have gained our end in having disgraced the Princely blood and rank, by reducing one of its proudest members to one of the lowest criminals, but we also secured to ourselves the gratitude and services of the latter, by having again raised him to the rank of a Prince. That the fact of his having become a convicted criminal, would be no obstacle in his way of entering upon the prerogative of a Princely sovereignty, we were assured by certain and infallible political and diplomatic reasons, which demanded the continuance of the race of Prominsky. We were therefore assured that he would be recognised as the rightful Prince, since political hopes and objects for the future, depended on the issue.

" Now your Highness will remember," continued the Jew with a great and visible effort, " that latterly you have lost wife and daughter. That was the work of Manasse, who had bribed one of your servants at the time, by offers of immense rewards, to give them poison. A similar fate was intended for you, but the immediate discharge of that servant, and the great voyages which you undertook shortly afterwards, compelled us to delay the execution of that plan. Through Manasse I finally learned that you were in Berlin, whither I went also, after I had some time previously discarded my band, and accompanied only by your Princely brother and my family, had roamed through Germany. The burglary at your hotel was instigated by me, with the intention of then and there taking your life. The attempt failed ; pursued by the police, I fled to Poland, and there you finally succeeded in arresting me in my very lair."

Perfectly exhausted, the Jew stopped. The long narrative had taken away his last remaining strength. His chest heaved, and his throat rattled as it were with the death-rattle of exhausted physical power.

The Prince had listened breathlessly with folded hands. The terrible narrative had almost thrown him into a state of mental aberration. A glance at the sick man, however, awoke him from his abstraction, for he remembered that not a moment was to be lost

" And my brother, where is my brother at present ?" he inquired anxiously, trembling on every limb.

" At the penitentiary of Spaudau," replied the Jew almost inaudibly, " he is there known by the name of *Cunning Schmerles.*"

With a cry of the most intense terror, the Prince sank back upon the chair, whence he had risen in his excitement. He pressed both hands convulsively before his eyes, a hollow, scarcely audible groaning, escaped his heaving chest.

Suddenly he again took his hands from his face.

" It is not true," he cried in a voice of thunder, " it is a lie, a wicked, terrible, maddening lie ! You are a villain, Jew, a cheat, and even upon your death-bed you would utter a terrible, a damnable lie ! Where is the blue stone ? it is that, the stone, the stone, that I must see !"

A wild fire flashed in the eyes of the Prince. In a commanding and majestic attitude he stood before the bed of the dying man.

A slight blush, like the last flickering of an expiring light, overspread at these words the pale features of the Jew. He winked to his wife, who had hitherto sat silently in a corner, whence she could hear and observe all that was passing.

With an instructive wink he handed her his *Tephilim.** She took a sharp knife, severed the knot of this, and the blue *lapis lazuli* rolled to the feet of the Prince.

Quickly he stooped to pick it up.—All the marks were upon it; it was in reality the long lost family relic.

The Jew groaned and breathed more heavily.

"My children—children!" he whispered, with an almost inaudible sigh.

The Jewess comprehended the meaning of this request, and hastily left the room to bring her children to the death-bed of their father.

Blessing them, the Jew laid his bony hands upon the curly heads which looked with anxious eyes towards him. The poor children knew not, and could scarcely comprehend the serious catastrophe of the moment.

"I—have—your—word," stammered the Jew, turning with great difficulty towards the Prince. "Princely—honour—pity—mercy—for wife—and—child!"

Unable to utter more, he sank back upon his side—and life was extinct!—

"Children, your father is dead," said the Jewess in a voice of bitterest grief, and piously folding her hands, "pray that Almighty God may have mercy upon his soul."

Mute and dejected, Prince Prominsky stood in the midst of the weeping family. In his soul passed a terrible struggle. In silence he pressed the widow's hand, and in silence he left the chamber of death.

CHAPTER LXXVI.

A DAY AFTER THE WEDDING.

A BRILLIANT May sun shot its rays over the sea of houses of the city.

Its early brightness fell upon Lieutenant von Steinfort, who, in company of his young wife, was seated on a sofa by the breakfast-table. We find them thus in a simple, but tastefully furnished chamber.

Steinfort had attained the object of all his desires; since yesterday, Augusta was his wife, in the sight of Heaven and the world.

He now believed himself shielded against the scorn and mockery of society; nay, he persuaded himself that he was now totally indifferent to it. And withal, he was weak enough to think of repeating the attempt of introducing his Augusta into the very circles which he thus despised and undervalued. He believed and hoped that he

* A pair of narrow black leather straps with a knot of leather attached to each of them. This knot contains Hebrew prayers written on parchment, which, however. remains always closely fastened At the morning prayers it is a part of the ceremony to place these straps and knots around the forehead and arms.

must now succeed better than before, since now he would introduce his honest and lawful wife.

With this intention he spoke to Augusta, and told her, that he purposed in a few days to pay visits to some families with whom he had hitherto been on friendly terms. Among these families he particularly named that of Geheimerath Berthold.

Augusta's female tact, however, caused her to view the subject in a much more correct light than her husband.

"My dear Carl," she said, "I fear greatly, that even now you will give offence, by introducing me into society. These people will never overlook or forgive my past life, and if they treat me with contempt, you will be annoyed. Why should we seek the world? are we not enough for each other? Let us live quietly and for ourselves, and we shall be most happy and contented."

Such was the language which this sensible woman addressed to her husband, seated by his side in a charming morning dress, and looking up to him, full of intense love.

In his inmost soul, Steinfort felt that his wife was right, yet he was chained to society, and it held him captive with an iron force.

As forcibly and tenderly as he loved the woman of his choice, he could not bear even the thought of passing all his days, confined solely to her society.

There were two equally powerful motives, which drew him towards society, the force of habit and the necessity of amusement. Steinfort was honest, had acted upon his firm and honest conviction, but on the other hand, he was not morally strong enough, quietly to bear the necessary consequences of his deed.

He was one of those uncertain beings, peculiar only to modern times and to fashionable circles. These beings feel a dislike of the tyrannical prescriptions of stupid and antiquated rules, they even venture sometimes to declare war against them, for they hope to find their reward in their own breast, in the approbation of the good and noble.

But when the reverse is shown to them, when they begin to see the sacrifice they must make, and the customs they must abandon, which the force of habit has made second nature to them, then they hesitate, they retreat a slight step, and a single unimportant cause furnishes them with an excuse to overthrow the entire system, and even to retract all the good they may already have accomplished in their work of reform. Thus we often find the good, ay, the best among us, sink ingloriously to the ground or cowardly desert the banner under which they had enlisted. The spirit is willing, but the flesh is weak.

* * * * *

Urged by a similar influence, Steinfort could not abstain from forming every day new plans for the renewal of his social connexions with refined circles. At last, Augusta despite of all her reasonable objections had to yield to the wishes of her young husband, and thus they finally came to the conclusion of paying in a few days several visits to families, with whom the Lieutenant had formerly been very intimate.

The conversation on this subject which had just come to a conclusion, had somewhat annoyed the sensibilities of Steinfort, and he walked silently up and down the room.

There certainly was another matter beside the late argument which annoyed him, and put him somewhat out of humour; in itself this was perhaps a most unimportant matter, but still it was a subject, which will be another proof, how immense a power is exercised by the conventional forms and laws of society, and how very strictly each and every one should examine his own mind and heart before entering into a contest with them. They form a much more necessary ingredient of life than we are apt to believe in the more noble excitements of our enthusiasm; but when they have once disappeared altogether, then only do we miss them, and miss them bitterly.

Steinfort was aware of an existing custom, and had often observed it himself towards third parties. This custom requires all the friends of the house, to pay a regular visit to the young married couple on the day after the wedding.

No one visited him.

He knew this beforehand, for his wedding, for obvious reasons, had been celebrated with the utmost silence and secrecy; only the necessary witnesses had been present at the ceremony; Birkheim had obtained these, and Steinfort did not even remember their names.

Yet he remembered, and not without feeling secret envy and annoyance, a young married couple to whom, not long since, and in company of one half of the fashionable world, he had paid such a visit of ceremony. At that time he had laughed, and made fun of the ceremoniously and strictly prescribed cup of chocolate that was handed to him on that occasion, but to-day it was a source of bitterness and sorrow, that a custom, which he looked upon as silly and ridiculous, was not followed in his own case.

Such is mankind! and Steinfort certainly was not among the worst of men; he was a man with a warm heart, a lively feeling for every thing that was good and noble, he even placed himself as a champion, foremost in the ranks of those who advocate a social reform, but he lacked that which our time, our age is deficient of, and which consequently her sons are also deficient of—strength of character, determination, energy! Educated and nurtured in the lap of luxury and extravagance, they may feel, may discover even, what actions, what moral reforms are required by the age, but they have not the firmness of will, the courage, which dares boldly to grasp the laurel.

Steinfort was very glad, and experienced no small satisfaction, when a few hours afterwards, the Referendarius von Birkheim made his appearance, to pay the customary visit, and offer the usual congratulations on the day after the wedding, the fashionable *Lendemain*. The worldliness, politeness and external smoothness of Birkheim actually became a source of pleasure to Steinfort, and he gladly received this visit, although he really despised the man from the bottom of his soul. Still at the present moment, this very man seemed to be the only connecting link by which he believed himself still to be united with a higher sphere of society.

Birkheim behaved on this occasion as every fashionable man of the world would have done in a similar case.

He pronounced a number of nicely worded congratulations, and afterwards, presuming on his very intimate friendship with the Lieutenant, he permitted himself to make a few playful and frivolous allusions to the new state—the state of matrimony, into which Augusta had entered since yesterday.

Augusta made no replies, as she knew and felt, that Steinfort was carefully observing her, to see whether her answers would be given and worded according to his careful instructions. Yet she felt an involuntary dislike of the fashionably dressed roué before her, who had already once before created a most unfavourable impression upon her mind, when on a certain occasion, in company with Fischergraf, she had unwillingly become a guest at his house. She could not say herself, what it was, that she disliked in the man. Perhaps in the present instance it was the external, worldly formula of politeness, which the Referendarius had just now fulfilled, evidently without heart or feeling, which displeased her simple and natural taste. Every unsophisticated, simple and artless mind, which suddenly is met by these fashionable rules of cold etiquette, is usually repulsed by them, nay, their very nature gives to the simple, ingenuous mind a right to look upon them as hypocritical, even in cases where they are well meant.

After the Referendarius had, in his opinion, fully complied with all the demands of etiquette towards the young married lady, he requested the Lieutenant to withdraw with him to another room, as he wished to converse with him about some matters of business.

" My dear Steinfort," he began, as soon as this request was complied with, " I hope that the joys and pleasures of your present honey-moon, will not entirely prevent you from paying some necessary attention to the future. Above all, it will now be requisite, that we should inform your father of all that has occurred, and thus endeavour to reconcile him."

These words fell like a new weight upon Steinfort's heart.

During the last few days his mind had been so much occupied with private matters of immediate consequence, that this subject had never occurred to him, the less so, as he knew, that his father had taken a journey to Poland, and as he had not learned to what place he had gone, or when he would return. Of late, in fact, it had seemed in a measure, as if his father was no longer in existence for him.

"I should think there would be plenty of time for that," he said, after a while, in a drawling tone, to the Referendarius.

The Referendarius looked at him with a frightened appearance.

"I do not understand you," he said in an ill-humoured tone, "this admits by no means of delay, but, on the contrary, it is of the utmost importance. Until you are in possession of your father's consent, your marriage may still be annulled, and for the little cheat which we practised upon the minister, I as well as you, may be delivered into the hands of criminal justice."

Steinfort had never viewed the matter in this light, and it had still less been thus explained to him by Birkheim.

A criminal offence, then, he had committed? He had sunk down into the ranks of those, against whom the state could daily exercise its authority, and call them to an account for over-stepping the bounds of the law! This thought, to his fundamentally honest and honourable character, was terrible and distressing.

He certainly had, before this, endeavoured to philosophize, and had been strengthened in his sophistical views by Birkheim; he argued thus: If the law sanctioned the injustice of society, there was no harm in attempting an evasion; yet his mind had never been convinced of the fact that this must be accomplished by a crime.

Steinfort felt almost annihilated, and unable to form any definite resolution.

"I will undertake the task," began the Referendarius, who seemed anxious to put an end to this mysterious and troublesome uncertainty, "of writing to your father, and of informing him of your marriage. In this manner I hope soonest to prevail on him, to give his approval of what has been done, as it will be impossible for him to undo the deed without creating great eclat and excitement. You must not now give way to pusillanimity which can do you no good, but which may ruin all. Matters will certainly go well, and in all probability much better than you expect. You must, therefore, not lose courage. What, after all, remains for the old man to do? If the worst should occur, you must immediately take post horses, go to your father with your wife, and then obtain his forgiveness."

"I will leave everything to you," answered the Lieutenant, whose pangs of conscience put him into a state of the utmost excitement, "do as it may seem for the best; I feel that I lack means or words to justify the step I have taken before my father. You have greater resources, greater facilities, and more smoothness than I have, and moreover, you can mention to my father many things which would tell in my favour, but which would come to him with a very bad grace from the lips of his son."

At this moment Augusta appeared at the door, to invite the gentlemen to partake of a breakfast which was prepared in another room.

"Do not refer in the presence of my wife, to our conversation," said the Lieutenant, as they were following her, "she has not the remotest suspicion of this affair about the fraudulent marriage consent, and her belief is, that my father had given his actual and positive consent to our union."

"Oh, very well, very well," whispered Birkheim, with the appearance of a man who looks upon such things as matters of course.

Augusta had prepared a very nice and comfortable breakfast, and played the housewife in such a friendly and attentive manner, that her hearty hospitality fully atoned for her deficiencies in style and etiquette.

Steinfort seemed impressed with the same observations, for his looks rested upon the quick, light and graceful movements of his little wife, with unmistakeable satisfaction. She already began to rail at the rascally butcher who had sent such inferior meat for beef-steaks, and behaved in this respect as well as a matron who has kept house for a score of years.

"Never mind it, my dear little wife," began Steinfort with a smile, "I only hope that during the whole of our married life, we may never have a worse breakfast."

"But, my dear," replied Augusta, with a comical appearance of anger, "it is absolutely necessary that one should early commence to look to honesty, rule and order among these people. Why should not I be served for my ready cash as well as any body else, as well, in fact, as the market affords?"

Birkheim, although not in words, seemed by his actions to express an entirely different opinion from that of the young house-keeper. He eat and drank an immense quantity, and with great gusto, and only interrupted his devotions to the table in so far as seemed absolutely necessary, to pay the attentions to the hostess, which the rules of good breeding seemed to dictate.

Augusta who observed this, cast a smiling glance towards her husband, who did not, however, return it, as he had already become again absorbed in his dark and serious meditations.

"Pray, what ails you, my dear Carl?" began Augusta playfully, and gently interrupting his abstractions—"you don't eat, and seem absorbed and thoughtful."

Steinfort passed his hand across his burning forehead.

"I want for nothing, my dearest child," he said gallantly, offering his hand to his wife, "for I have you."

He now endeavoured forcibly to rouse himself from his abstractions, and actually succeeded in engaging in a very lively conversation. The excellent southern wine might have contributed its share towards driving sorrows and distress from his breast.

After they had conversed for some time about subjects and matters of little or no importance, and the breakfast being ended, Birkheim requested the Lieutenant to favour them with a song.

Excited by the spirit of the generous wine which he had drunk, and to drown remembrance,

Steinfort expressed his readiness to comply with his friend's request.

The Lieutenant possessed a fine, rich and highly cultivated tenor, and was withal a very fair musician. He took up his guitar, and sang, whilst the Referendarius joined in the chorus:

SCHILLER'S HYMN TO JOY.

Spark, from a source that gods have fed—
  Joy, Elysian child divine;
Illumed by thee, our footsteps tread,
  Holy one, thy heav'nly shrine.
Custom tears us from each other,
  And thy hand unites again;
Man in man but hails a brother
  Where'er rests thy gentle wing.

CHORUS.

Fellow myriads, far and near,
  Come and take the proferr'd kiss!
Know a power, to mortals dear,
  Rules this joyous world of his!

He whom happy fate has granted,
  Of one friend the friend to be,
He who faithful wife has wanted,
  And found her—join our jubilee:
He who but one faithful heart
  In the world can call his own!
He who cannot—let him part—
  Part from us, and weep alone.

CHORUS.

All creation owns thy sway,
  Sacred power of sympathy!
To the brighter realms of day
  Thou dost lift thy votary.

All that breathes through endless nature
Sips the nectar'd cup of joy:
Worth and vice with equal ardour
Gaily crowd her rosy way.
Love and wine, and friendship's treasures,
Joy with lavish hand bestows;
To the worm were given pleasures,
And on high the seraph glows.

CHORUS.

Millions bow with bended knee:
  Feel ye men that God is near?
Search beyond that starry sphere,
  There, there must his dwelling be.

Joy, the mainspring of the whole
  Animates the varied scene,
Moves th' eternal wheels that roll
  And impels the vast machine.
Joy breathes on blossoms—and they flower,
  Suns come forth from yonder heaven;
Joy rolls the spheres in realms afar,
  Ne'er to mortal knowledge given.

CHORUS.

Joyous as the rolling sphere
  Wanders through its path on high;
Gaily speed our short career,
  Like a chief's to victory.

Smiling sweet, in truth reflected,
  Joy the searcher's toil requites,
Virtue, lonely and dejected,
  Joy soon gladdens and delights.
High on the sunny slopes of faith
  Proudly see her banners buoy,
Lo! through shattered vaults of death
  'Mid the choral angels—Joy.

CHORUS.

Millions in distress and sorrow
  Check the tears and still the sigh,
You will know a brighter morrow,
  High above yon starry sky.

Heaven's great bounty to requite
  Is beyond our humble sphere,
Go, bring to poverty delight,
  And emulate kind Heaven's care.

Revenge and hatred must be driven
  Far from this, our gay retreat—
Here be every foe forgiven,
  Pardon every wrong await.

CHORUS.

Let all the world be peace and love,
  Forgive the trespass of thy brother;
God will judge of us above,
  E'en as we shall judge each other.

Joy sparkles for us in the bowl,
  Flights sublime does joy inspire,
To meekness melts the savage soul,
  Gives to despair—heroic fire.
Up brothers! Lo, we crown the cup,
  Gaily quaff the gen'rous wine;
Heavenward let the sound rise up!
  Praise the power that gave the vine.

CHORUS.

Praised by the angelic ring
  By stars, by tuneful seraphim,
Be the Good Spirit, the Father king,
  In heaven! This glass to *him!*

With firmness bear what fate bestows,
  Comfort tears in sinless eyes,
Keep faith alike to friends and foes,
  Man be truthful as the skies.
Manly pride show e'en to Princes;
  Buy with limb and life the prize,
Give its crown to honest merit,
  Death to all the brood of lies.

CHORUS.

Closer draw this holy ring,
  Low at truth's bright altar bow,
Swear by the stars, and by their king,
  Swear by *Him*, to keep our vow.

May tyrants soon feel freedom's powers,
  May pity still on vice await—
May hope attend life's latest hours,
  And mercy soothe the felon's fate.
Lo, the shrouded dead shall quicken;
  Brothers sing, drink and *adore;*
Be the sinner all forgiven,
  Death and Hell shall be no more.

CHORUS

Peace at life's departing hours,
  Soft repose within the tomb;
Brethren—from eternal powers
  Lenient sentence—gracious doom.

Our immortal bard's beautiful Ode to Joy being ended, Augusta approached Steinfort.

"Thank you, dearest," thank you," she said. "But my dear Carl, whilst you were singing I remembered how very ungrateful for my good fortune, the excess of my joy has made me. Only this instant have I remembered the unfortunate Marianne; what can have become of her? she was very good, kind and pious. Listen to me, Herr von Birkheim," she continued, addressing the Referendarius, "now you might confer a very great favour upon me, by assisting me in searching for that girl; I should think it would be an easy matter for you to find her. I lived for some time in the same house with her in the Rosenthaler-street. She stood under the surveillance of police, but certainly most unjustly; I never saw a more harmless and innocent girl. However, the police came one night and instituted a search for her, and in consequence of this, the people who kept the house drove her away on the following morning. Since that time I have never seen her again."

"How is this?" inquired Birkheim, growing more attentive; "will you be kind enough to relate the position of the girl, and all the circumstances more particularly?"

Augusta gladly consented to this proposition, as it gave her pleasure to speak of her protegé. "And now, my dear husband," she addressed Steinfort, when she had concluded, "could we not bring Marianne here, and let her live with us? I am so very inexperienced in housekeeping, that I need a little assistance, and Marianne is a capital housewife. At the same time, I would find a kind and confidential friend in her, and I am sure you liked her very well. Now what do you say? Shall we take her to our house?"

"I am perfectly willing, my child," replied her husband, with a smile, "provided you will promise me never to become jealous of her."

Augusta stared at him, and then seriously shook her head. She could not understand how her Carl could believe in such a possibility, and still less, how the expression he had just used, could be considered of little or no consequence in good society.

The Referendarius had quietly listened to the narrative of the young, kind-hearted woman. He knew not exactly what reply he should make to it. He knew perfectly well what had become of Marianne, and in what position she lived at present, for he was not only an old business friend of Mrs. Rüthmann, but was also a friend of Herr Henri, whose mistress Marianne had become. The latter had several times taken the Referendarius with him to see Marianne.

For these reasons, he was greatly at a loss for an answer. To confess his acquaintance with Marianne, seemed not at all advisable, and to let her become an inmate of the house of Lieutenant Steinfort, was still less desirable. The Major might accidentally learn something of her past life, and the reconciliation between father and son would thus be still more delayed and obstructed. It was a most important part of the interests of the Referendarius, and he understood his own interests full well, to prevent this by all means. His humane feelings in a case like the present, must of course become secondary, to his fears of a criminal prison.

At last he helped himself out of his dilemma by a few uncertain, hesitating and unsatisfactory answers, which gave a partial promise to comply with Augusta's wishes, but by which he intimated some doubts of his success.

Immediately afterwards he took his leave, requesting the Lieutenant to accompany him upon a little business visit which he had to make that forenoon. His real object was to induce Steinfort, not to permit the admission of Marianne to his house, on any consideration.

Arm in arm the two friends left the house.

With mixed feelings of pleasure and sadness, the young wife looked after them.

She felt as if she were not doing right in leaving her husband alone with his friend, whom she disliked; but she must let things take their course even as Providence willed it. With a soft, suppressed sigh, she rang for the servant-girl to come and clear away the remains of the breakfast.

Such was the Lendemain after the wedding.

CHAPTER LXXVII.

MISTRESSES.

At the elegant *Restaurant* of *Traiteur Zangler*, "under den Linden," at the further end of the large dining saloon, there is a small, elegantly furnished boudoir for private parties, who prefer retirement and privacy to the noise and publicity of the other rooms.

In this little room, Herr Henri, the seducer of Marianne, gave this evening a splendid supper to his friends, with the object of then and there introducing his new mistress to his friends and acquaintances.

It certainly is an evidence of the great moral degradation of fashionable society, that rich voluptuaries keep mistresses, not perhaps from motives of love or affection, but rather for show, even as they keep a blooded horse or a pack of dogs.

A new mistress is neither more or less than a new piece of furniture, which they show to their friends and comrades, and feel their vanity flattered and gratified, if their choice meets with approval or admiration.

The abandonment and degradation of a human being cannot sink lower, than when we see it thus, through the hand of pride and superciliousness, placed on a level with the brute creation or with an inanimate object.

And yet how often does this same species of degradation occur among us—in how many brilliant and splendid hotels is this terrible species of slave trade carried on, certainly more to the disgrace of the proud traders, than of their unfortunate merchandize.

＊　　＊　　＊　　＊　　＊

Herr Henri at first intended only to gratify his voluptuous animal passions upon the person of his innocent victim, not only because he admired the appearance of the girl, but also because Mrs. Rüthmann had introduced her as a pure, innocent virgin, and had demanded an immense premium for her own vile business, as procuress.

Herr Henri was one of those who only value objects which cost a great deal of money; by these means his dull, blunt and exhausted sensibilities might be excited through the hope of enjoying any amusement in an extraordinary manner and beyond that which is in the reach of any other voluptuary. To seduce a virtuous and helpless girl—helpless because by fiendish means deprived of consciousness and the use of her senses, this was a great triumph, a new chapter in the life of this enervated roué.

＊　　＊　　＊　　＊　　＊

After he had accomplished this piece of heroism and manliness to his full satisfaction, it seemed most advisable to elevate Marianne to the rank of his mistress, as his late *chère amie* had run away with one of the male corps de Ballet and as, in reality, Marianne might be considered much more handsome than any of the mistresses of his friends.

Marianne silently submitted to all. After society had expelled her—after she had been dragged through a never ending school of misery and sorrow—after she had finally by the most villanous, most fiendish scheme, been robbed of her last, her only remaining treasure, she had given up all hope of contending against fate. Moreover, she had only this last alternative remaining to her, either to fall into the hands of the police and be sent to the workhouse, or to make the best she could of her present position.

One alternative was as full of horror as the other; she suffered the latter because fate had willed it so. Her mind even in this instance had passed through all the stages of her former mental struggles. At first she raved like a maniac, then she became resigned to melancholy, and gradually she endeavoured with silent resignation to be guided by the unchangeable fate which ruled her destiny.

We have once before made the observation, that a morally and mentally strong character, would, under the same circumstances, have preferred to seek relief in suicide, but poor Marianne, to use an expressive, though somewhat homely phrase, had "become softened" to it. At last she arrived at that point when the victim endeavours to drown the voice of reproach within, by external excitements, and by a round of pleasure and dissipation. As Herr Henri readily and willingly offered his assistance to such a course, she seemed well to progress in it. At certain times, then, in Marianne's appearance and manner might already be discovered the traces of that unwomanly wildness, that mad, exalted merriment, by which those unfortunate victims of society not unfrequently deceive the observer, while they only intoxicate themselves and drown their consciousness. It is a flowery plain, but the adder is hidden beneath the flowers.

* * * * *

Thus, then, we find Marianne to day in company of Herr Henri and his friends, among whom was also our old acquaintance the Referendarius von Birkheim. The supper was nearly over, champagne flowed in streams, and had not failed to produce the usual consequences upon its votaries. Extravagant frivolity, bacchanalian wildness, and prodigality characterized these revels.

Marianne had become somewhat excited by the sparkling bowl which was continually forced upon her. Her mind was distracted. The most distressing and saddening thoughts of her hopeless situation, alternately changed with variegated pictures of pleasures and delights.

Birkheim was, or at least appeared to be, the most lively and merry of the whole party. He entertained the whole company with his anecdotes and witty sayings, perhaps because he wished to make his entertaining powers a *quid pro quo* for his invitation to a splendid and expensive feast, which his means and position did not allow him to return, or at least to return very frequently.

The remaining members of the company seemed determined on making a wild noise in chorus. The party consisted of gentlemen attached to the diplomatic corps, officers, young noblemen, civil officers, men of letters, students, artists, and other persons considered admissible into good society.

Whoever among these gentlemen was fortunate enough at the moment to possess a mistress, had brought her along. The collection of ladies, with but very few exceptions, were members of the corps de ballet, those light-footed children of pleasure, who in places and on occasions such as this one, recompense themselves for the slight neglect and contempt to which their stage utility exposes them in our days.

"Harkye, Henri," cried the Referendarius, elated by wine and excitement, "you really have fished up a most charming girl; I have often assured you, and must repeat it, that Marianne would be the only being I could love, if loving were still in fashion. But here a strange story occurs to me, which I must really tell these gentlemen.

"You must all remember Lieutenant von Steinfort; well, he had a *poussade*, a girl who formerly made some little *furore* in *Villa Bella*; now, just imagine, the man has absolutely been crazy enough to marry the grisette! What think you of that?"

A universal tumult, and expressions of wonder, mockery, anger and disgust, followed this astonishing announcement.

"Yes, yes," cried a very young, milk-bearded *attaché* of the *Flachsenfinger Legation*, with a penny trumpet voice, "yes, gentlemen, it is just so. I heard it mentioned a short time ago at the hotel of *Count Willy*, and at a dinner which the young Prince von Steppenfeld gave to the officers of Steinfort's regiment, this affair created a very disagreeable sensation. It is said that this marriage has long been a fixed idea in Herr von Steinfort's mind, and as I was told yesterday by a friend, he now has times when he is absolutely stupified and absent minded."

"Very natural," observed Herr Henri, "if he were not a madman, or had every symptom of becoming one, he could not possibly do such an action, which is disgraceful to any gentleman."

"Certainly, certainly, you are right!" agreed the whole company.

"My dear Henri, oblige us by sending to-morrow, as early as possible, the carriage of our worthy and meritorious Geheimerath H— to his house," observed the small and witty attaché, who was rewarded by universal applause for this allusion to the private lunatic asylum of the distinguished Dr. H—.

"Such is always the way of the world," said Birkheim, rubbing his hands, "whoever is the loser in the affair is sure to be laughed at. I have some very serious intentions of providing this happy young husband with a suitable decoration for his forehead. I think, at least I hope, that the conquest will not be very difficult. Yes, yes, I speak in earnest," he continued with a laugh, and nodding his head, as he met the looks of Marianne, who was staring at him with intensity : "On my honour, Henri, the longer I look at your girl the more beautiful she appears to me ! Will you permit me to kiss her once ?"

"Why not," replied the other with heavy utterance, "girls are only made for kissing ; I am not selfish enough to refuse a favour to my friends ; so don't mind me, and do it."

Birkheim needed no further encouragement to avail himself of this permission. He jumped up, hurried to the other end of the table, and endeavoured to seat himself upon Marianne's knees.

This conduct aroused all the better feelings in Marianne's breast. The words she had just heard had struck her very inmost soul. A piece of merchandize then, she had become, an article of goods which the purchaser might at pleasure transfer to another dealer in similar wares ! She at first believed to have sacrificed her honour to only one, and this already had bitterly torn her soul ; but this one bartered away, in perfect quiet and coolness, her only, her highest treasure ! This was a new disgrace which gnawed the more on her mind, since all else had seemed but a natural consequence of her unhappy fate.

This thought brought every drop of blood in her veins to boil with indignation, and with all the strength, which her newly awakened and outraged modesty lent her, she hurled the obtrusive voluptuary from her, that he staggered, and fell at full length upon the floor.

The whole company burst into a loud roar of laughter. Herr Henri felt particularly flattered by her behaviour, for he was vain enough to believe, that Marianne had thus repulsed the Referendarius simply because she loved him alone.

"Bravo, bravo, my dear child !" he cried triumphantly ; "you are a good and honest poussade, and you only wish to belong to me alone. Well, my friend, am I not to be envied ? Huzzah, to the health of my mistress ! Three cheers for her ! nay, three times three !"

The whole company burst into deafening shouts of applause, which ended in loud praises of Marianne's "conjugal fidelity," as they mockingly termed her behaviour.

The smooth, cunning Birkheim considered it most advisable to make a good face to a most disagreeable position, and to chime in with the general merriment, after he had carefully gathered up his ill-used limbs from the floor.

New libations of champagne were then indulged in by the whole company.

The wine at last had its effect.

Henri and the greater part of his guests were so deeply intoxicated, that nothing remained to the Referendarius, who alone was still sober, but late at night with the assistance of waiters and others to pack all the gentlemen and ladies into their carriages and send them home.

CHAPTER LXXVIII.

A CONVERSATION AND A PRAYER.

MARIANNE had remained behind.

She had refused to enter one of the vehicles in company with the drunken men, and preferred to seek her way to her home alone, and on foot.

Birkheim who was now also at leisure, insisted on displaying his politeness, and accompanying her home.

It was long after midnight when both walked through the solitary streets. All was silent and deserted ; they only met here and there a solitary snoring watchman, or a few dissipated young men, who were, like themselves, on their way home, and who stared at the late promenading couple, with impertinent curiosity.

For a long time, they walked in silence side by side.

Marianne seemed too much occupied with her own thoughts, to have any desire for conversation, and Birkheim, in consequence of the occurrences at the supper, felt somewhat too much embarrassed to address her.

At last Marianne interrupted the silence.

"At table you mentioned a certain Herr von Steinfort," she said hesitatingly, "who, not long since has married a—a—certain—young girl, were you telling this in a joke, or were you serious ?"

"Certainly, my dear, perfectly serious," replied the Referendarius glad to find the disagreeable silence at last interrupted. "Herr von Steinfort has very lately married this same girl, who formerly had been his sweetheart."

"Can you tell me the name of this girl ?" inquired Marianne.

"Oh yes ! Augusta Strohm ;—no, no, just wait, that confounded name has once before put me into a disagreeable embarrassment, Augusta Strass was the name, now I remember.—But why do you inquire so anxiously about these particulars," added the Referendarius, after a while, with seeming indifference, though not unintentionally.

Marianne, who had no particular reason to withhold any of the circumstances, related to him nearly the same story, which he had already heard from Augusta's lips, only with the difference that expressions of the most sincere gratitude towards Augusta were added by Marianne.

"I am very glad and delighted," she added at the close of her narrative, "that she is now so happily married. She loved Herr von Steinfort dearly, and with her whole soul ; I should like to see her very much, in the enjoyment of her new, well-merited fortune, even if our interview should only be for a moment."

At these words Marianne suppressed a gentle sigh, most probably the result of a momentary thought of her own situation.

Birkheim was silent. He had purposely endeavoured to introduce this subject of conversation, for the purpose of preventing any possible meeting between the young wife of the Lieutenant and Marianne. As far as he was able to judge of the character of the former, he was convinced that she would not again abandon the latter, or suffer her to depart from her side should they once meet.

He feared equally much. that the Lieutenant, although he had warned him, would finally yield to his wife, particularly as in the present case, the object would be, to do a work of love and charity, and philantrophically, to save an unfortunate being from perdition and ruin and misery. But Birkheim, as we have once before hinted, feared that Marianne's presence in the house of Lieutenant von Steinfort, might prove a new obstacle in the way of reconciliation with his father, if the latter, which might easily or accidentally be the case, should learn something of Marianne's former position. The personal security and safety of the Referendarius required particularly that this should not take place.

Consequently, after a pause of momentary consideration, he said :

" If I may advise you, and if you love and esteem your friend, you will not visit her. She has now left her former companions and changed her position, and her husband desires most urgently. that she should avoid all and everything that may help to remind her of it. A visit from you, therefore, might easily be the first cause of discord in their most happy honey-moon."

Marianne understood only too well all her companion was saying to her, and after all, she could not deny, that his observation was founded in a most reasonable view of her present position. Nevertheless, she felt most deeply and bitterly the pangs of being separated by the force of circumstances even from her, whose former position bore so much similarity to her own present situation.

In a tone of deep resignation, she replied ; " I feel, sir, I feel, that on the whole you are in the right, and consequently I shall not endeavour to meet my former friend."

" You have taken an excellent resolution," replied Birkheim, to make more certain of the attainment of his object, " for you would certainly be very much distressed, if you found that by your incautiousness, you had darkened a single bright ray of fortune to a poor girl who has suffered so much previous misery."

" No, no," cried Marianne, deeply moved by these words, " I will promise you that I shall not seek an interview."

During this conversation both had arrived at the door of Marianne's lodgings, and as the Referendarius, after the last assurance, believed that he had attained his object, he had no longer any occasion to withhold his wearied body from the necessary comfort of a bed.

Perfectly quieted upon the point which had previously annoyed him, he took his leave, walked quickly down the *Markgrafen-street*, over the *Gensd'armes-market*, down *Charlotte-street*, and arrived at his house in *Behren-street*.

The bright moon protruded her pale silvery rays through the dark firmament. Her course remains the same through thousands and tens of thousands of years. With unchangeable clearness and purity she rises and sets again, above the dark tumults and revolutions among pigmy mankind below !

Marianne also had arrived at her solitary chamber, and the whole weight and burden of her terrible situation, suddenly fell with new and immense weight upon her breast.

We have already told our readers, how, partly by a falsity of arguments, the consequence of her own unfortunate position, partly by the power of necessity and habit, she had endeavoured to reconcile herself to a position into which stern fate had forced her. The inexhaustible arguments of Mrs. Rüthmann, who alternately used gentle and severe means to enforce her obedience, might also have contributed in no small measure, towards silencing and incapacitating the force of her moral resistance to the wild and intoxicating pleasures of her present course of life.

She was a *femme entretenue*, and as such dependent upon the favour and mercy of Herr Henri, but expelled and rejected from all respectable and virtuous society.

All this she knew, was compelled to know. Yet her position towards Herr Henri had hitherto retained the appearance of exclusiveness. She had sacrificed herself, or rather been forced to do so, to Herr Henri alone, and she might even believe, that he in return would be true and faithful only to her, and this consciousness, which even in society, and before God and man, is considered as the holiest and dearest bond of matrimony, might have served for the purpose of being a very weak consolation to her own mind, for her public disgrace. After all, the world was greatly mistaken if it looked upon her as a public wanton. She was the victim of a single man, sacrificed to only *one*, partly through money, partly by the force of circumstances, and would have repulsed any other man who should have dared to approach her with disrespectful propositions.

The reader may look upon this as sophistical reasoning, and in a strictly moral view, the reader will not be in the wrong. Yet Marianne clung even to this reasoning, as a drowning person will cling to a straw, and it argues well for her moral and mental strength, that she even felt a desire to cling to such a straw, instead of sinking idly and carelessly into the pool of vice, vulgarity and perdition.

But this evening had destroyed her illusion. Those terrible, cruel words with which her seducer had offered her to the Referendarius, like a piece of merchandize, still rung in her ears. She was then really looked upon as the common property of all roués, and the man upon whom she depended, as by whose vice and villainy she had fallen his victim, even he, with the mocking laugh of infernal levity, cast her to the abyss of endless perdition.

Marianne now felt more than ever that she had sunk into a depth of human misery, whence a release by her own powers or moral strength in future would be impossible. The Referendarius was in the right; she could and dared never think of seeking access to the house of her most happy friend.

With what mien, what front, could she, the fallen one, appear before her who had risen to purity? How could she plead an excuse, which would not at the same time become an accusation? Despair now took possession of her distracted mind; *now* only she thought of putting an end to her miserable existence by her own hand. Only a small remnant of religious conviction, at this moment prevented her from accomplishing that deed. Her miseries certainly were great enough to have overcome all cowardice which might at first have restrained her.

Weeping she cast herself fully dressed upon her couch, praying to God from her inmost soul, to let her die,

The consoler of all sufferers, the mild God of dreams, at last put an end to that honestly meant prayer, and Marianne fell asleep.

CHAPTER LXXIX.

THE DISCOVERY.

THE exhaustion of the preceding day had been so great, that Marianne slept until towards noon.

The chimes of the bells, calling worshipers to the house of God, awoke her from a slumber which was more stunning than refreshing.

It was Sabbath morning, and sadly she arose from her couch.

She felt in her mind a most irresistible desire to visit the house of God. But dared she, who belonged to the children of perdition, dared she enter the temple of the Lord? And yet she would so gladly have gone, would so earnestly have endeavoured to find hope, consolation and a balm for the pangs of her soul.

For a moment, she hesitated in undecisive consideration, then with a voice of thunder the sentence of condemnation which the minister of the prison had pronounced upon her, once more resounded in her ear. Even then, when she was still innocent, the wrath of God had been announced to her, how could she now, since she had really fallen and was guilty, dare to hope for mercy and pity in his sight? With what conscience dared she at the holy temple of the Lord, pray to the Almighty for the forgiveness of her sins and iniquities, when she dared not even think of abandoning this same sinful course of life, without also falling into the hands of offended, so-called justice, and being punished with the work-house.

She saw no hope, no salvation! It was the clergy and police alike, who placed themselves between her and the church; the one opposed her from an honest but misconceived sense of clerical duty, the other for the preservation of civic order; the one urged on by fanatical zeal, the other by a harsh and unjust proscription of the law.

She approached the window, and with dim and tearful glances looked down upon the happy multitudes, who with pious and quiet Sabbath faces, carrying nicely gilt prayer and hymn books under their arms, were wending their way towards the house of God.

Here was a plain, honest mechanic, in a long frock coat, by the side of his rotund better half, who wore a high cap with dashing ribbons on her head; here again was the young, handsome maiden, dressed in all the best her wardrobe and toilette afforded, modestly pursuing her way, or casting a hasty glance to one side or the other, fearing or expecting some company; yonder was the rich tradesman or merchant, an imposing figure, somewhat *em bon point*, adorned with chains and rings, the rich gifts of Mercury, and his serious features laid in devout yet proud wrinkles; at last came the mass of noisy youth, with the ruling pedagogue, who in vain endeavoured to preserve silence and order among his unruly flock.

Amidst the different groups of more humble pedestrians, there rolled here and there a splendid emblazoned carriage of proud nobility, taking its haughty owner in all pride and vanity to church. It had lately become fashionable to attend divine service, and all that lives and moves in society must bow and obey the mandates of fashion. But these people in silks and velvets and dashing equipages looked wearied and annoyed at their present errand; they would have much preferred if a ball, a *dinner*, or a *dejeuner a la fourgette* had called them from their homes.

In this manner, then, to-day as on every other Sunday, the streets of the metropolis were thronged—terrestrial interests gave way to heavenly ones. For one morning at least, not the spirit of trade and traffic, of ambition or vanity moved the masses, it was that spirit, who in an involuntary shudder, even moves sometimes the coarsest and most depraved mind, to bow down and pay homage to the great ruler of the universe.

The young wife of Lieutenant von Steinfort also desired to go to church. She felt the necessity, the pious desire to offer up her thanks at the throne of her Maker, for the great unmerited fortune with which he had blessed her. Her husband willingly accompanied her.

Intending to go to the Bohemian church, their road led them past Marianne's house. Accidently Augusta looked up, and discovered the former at the very moment when she wiped the fast flowing tears from her eyes. Marianne had noticed the glance, and hastily left the window; but Augusta had recognized her, and this single glance sufficed to enlighten her, to tell her the whole position of the girl. The situation of the house, Marianne's dress, the rich draperies at the window, the other's tears, all this told her in an instant, that her unfortunate friend had sunk to that abyss, whence her own good genius had just delivered her. As she was well acquainted with Marianne's position, she very naturally guessed, that the same fate beneath whose influence she herself had once fallen, the vain struggle with material misery, had also wrecked her poor friend.

Augusta reproached herself most bitterly, for not having in her own fortunate position paid more attention to the fate of her poor friend. But even this very morning she had thought of her, and had been greatly troubled about her, as she could not ascertain her present position. As usual, she had communicated these thoughts to her husband, and had earnestly entreated him to institute a search for the girl, as she was convinced that the other must be in great misery, which she desired to alleviate.

Steinfort, who through Birkheim was already fully acquainted with the present position of Marianne, had become somewhat embarrassed by this request. He could scarcely think of refusing the prayer of his much loved wife, as it was a new proof of her innate goodness of heart, and yet it seemed not advisable to receive a friend of his wife, a witness of her former course of life, under his very roof. With regard to Augusta, love had urged him on to the step he had taken, but even in this respect he looked upon his future life in a mistaken light, for he hoped that by marrying Augusta he would draw a curtain over the past, which no one should have the audacity to raise. But now, that wife herself requested him to receive a witness of her former disgrace, and one who at the very moment had herself fallen into the same abyss of disgrace.

This was the only point which he would not grant; to save Marianne from shame and perdition, to place her in an independent and honest position, he was ready and willing. He would have done this immediately after hearing the communication of the Referendarius, if he had only known how to keep it secret from his wife, or if he had been certain that Augusta would not insist on giving Marianne an asylum in her own house. Meanwhile he had taken to the usual evasion, natural to all characters who lack firmness of purpose, he had given her an answer satisfactory for the moment, but *non committal* for the future.

It was somewhat remarkable, that he should not at once have told his determination to his wife, and informed her of the present situation of Marianne. But it may be possible, that he was restrained from doing this, by a certain consciousness of his own weakness, perhaps also by the fear of wounding the feelings of his wife by the reference which must naturally be made to her own former position. As plausible, however, as these considerations were in themselves, he might probably have forwarded his own objects much more, by openness and candour. For we must here observe, that Augusta's intentions of giving relief and assistance to her unfortunate friend, through the momentary and accidental discovery she had just made, became firm and determined; nevertheless she hesitated to make her husband acquainted with her new discovery. She felt herself fully justified in requesting her husband to give roof, shelter, and food to the starving but innocent Marianne, but whether to ask the same favours for the fallen, the guilty Marianne, that she knew not.

She certainly could discover no reason, which seemed sufficient for such a course of conduct, yet she felt herself restrained by an inexplicable hesitation. Evidently, however, she was guided by the same reasons which guided her husband's course, though the reasons were very different in their appearance. She felt an indistinct fear, that in his eyes, she would herself appear, to view a great guilt, one to which she herself had once fallen a victim, and which he had kindly overlooked in her, to view this, we say, more leniently, than she should do if mentally pure, or than in reality she did.

Upon the whole, it cannot be denied that the tender consideration, which Steinfort felt for his wife as well as she for him, did honour to both their heads and hearts.

It was an evidence of that intense and deep felt love which ruled this couple, and by which each felt induced, anxiously to avoid all and everything, which in any manner could give cause to misunderstandings, and to consequent sorrows and troubles.

The result of this at the present moment was, that Augusta silently passed the window of her friend, without stopping to offer a helping hand. She consoled herself, however, with the proverb, that "postponed is not abandoned," and that upon further consideration, she would certainly find ways and means to save her unfortunate friend from misery and perdition, or even to see her yet a guest at her own house. At this thought she nodded saucily with her little head, as if to say, "just wait, I would be but a poor daughter of Eve, if I could do less with my husband, than any other young and well-loved wife."

Steinfort had accidentally looked in an opposite direction, and had taken no notice of the whole occurrence. They continued on their way to church without delay.

END OF PART FIFTH.

———

PART SIXTH.

CHAPTER LXXX.

DECISIVE DETERMINATIONS.

A FEW days after these occurrences, the light hunting carriage of Major von Steinfort, stopped before the *Hotel de Paris.*

Prince Prominsky and the Major alighted from it, and in silence passed through the throng of bowing attendants towards the rooms, which had been retained for them.

Here also, even after they were left to themselves, they continued for a long time in this painful silence, each seeming to be particularly occupied with unpacking and arranging small matters. It appeared as if both were endeavouring to find an excuse, for withdrawing from further conversation and consultation.

After having remained for some time at the country seat of the Major, they finally had determined to come to the city and take steps in those important affairs, which must decide the fate of their families, and which might be attended with results either very fortunate or incalculably unfortunate.

This feeling, or rather this consciousness, when they passed the *Brandenburg-gate* seemed to have taken entire possession of their minds, and to have placed them both in a humour, in which neither dared to think of interrupting the other.

The Major, without having the least intimation of those steps, which his son had lately taken, knowing neither of his solicited discharge from his regiment, nor of his actual marriage, had fully determined in his own mind to put a definite end to this disagreeable affair.

He looked upon the plans and determinations of his son, as youthful, foolish, and romantic vagaries, which must be put an end to, by the mature experience of the father. This he would do if possible, by gentle means, but if those failed, and it came to the worst, he would exercise his paternal authority even to the utmost extent of severity.

In order to carry this object through as easily and gently as possible, the Major had so arranged with the Prince, that the latter should take the necessary preliminary steps. He should see the Lieutenant, endeavour by a course of sensible reasoning to convince him of the unpracticability of his intentions, and finally to inform him of the decided determination of his father. The Major, whose sound, honest practical good sense was far removed from any extravagant, reforming and ultra-philanthropical mode of thought, would rather let things come to the very worst, than give his consent. The thought of a seduced, disgraced and dishonoured daughter-in-law, became hellish torture to him, and the more he considered upon it, the more he brooded over it, the more it tormented him.

Although he had in a very great measure freed himself from the prejudice of rank, although it was perfectly indifferent to him whether his son married a girl of humble birth, or one, who was his equal in rank, and although he was even proud at having himself overcome prejudices of birth, and at having adopted these liberal principles, yet in consequence of all this, he insisted only the more obstinately, upon what he called old fashioned citizen's honesty, truth and worth. He always felt an insurmountable disgust at all the revolutionizing, experimentalizing theories of our times; he avoided and hated these struggles, which, as they always have done, must throw the world into confusion, these theories, which, even when they are good and plausible, are never understood by the million, and he preferred to ensconce himself, behind his more limited, perhaps even more illiberal, old fashioned theory, which at least had the advantage of resting on a more firm foundation.

Thus he looked upon his son only as a victim of this spirit of innovation, from which he considered himself bound to save him for the sake of his mental and bodily welfare. He certainly could not deny to himself that he must meet with great and powerful opposition, that it would perhaps be a struggle of life and death, in which the welfare of his only and last child was at stake; and it was this thought that filled the heart of the old warrior with sorrow and sadness. But he conscientiously believed that he could not avoid this struggle, unless he would suffer his only son to go to perdition by his unfortunate youthful folly.

In a similar way, we can account for the sad, monosyllabic manner of the Prince.

Ever since the very moment, when he believed that he had found the first, certain trace of his long lost brother, he had had a dark and unaccountable presentiment, that he would find him again only as a criminal. This presentiment had daily become more confirmed, but had never for a moment altered his determination. Now, however, his long fear had become a certainty; his much sought, bitterly-regretted brother, was one of the most notorious of robbers, and was an inmate of a penitentiary! But the disregard of this very circumstance, which, as long as it was enveloped in doubt, suspicion, presentiment and anxiety, could never make him hesitate for an instant in his endeavours, now, that the terrible truth lay in the most glaring light before his eyes, seemed to him almost like a breach of every duty he owed to the world, to morality and to his own honour.

His brother, the head and chief of one of the oldest and most noble families in the empire, according to Russian laws the rightful master of thousands of subjects, was the associate of the lowest criminals, lay now disgraced in a state prison, perhaps at this very moment writhed beneath the lash of the beadle. And such a brother he should recognize, should liberate from his chains, should elevate him to the command over all these thousands of honest and industrious men! Had he a right to do so? Dared he to set aside the human rights of thousands, to give the right of legitimacy to the one? How, if this brother chose to remain a villain, a criminal, or a murderer? How, if in his terrible and vicious course of life he had already become so hardened, that he would only change into a tyrant from being a slave to vice? How if he continued to rob and murder—which he could do now without so much fear of punishment? And, to say the least, what disgrace, what shame, would he be the means of bringing upon distant relatives of his family, if this affair ever came to their knowledge, a consequence almost impossible to be avoided! A race which had reigned and existed spotless through centuries, would forever sink into disgrace!—

But on the other hand, a strict sense of justice possessed the soul of the Prince, and that, supported by the voice of blood-relationship, demanded that he should reinstate his brother, his unfortunate orphan brother, who, by villany unheard of and unequalled in the world, had been cheated of youth and honesty, out of his hereditary rights and privileges. It was not the fault of that unfortunate victim, that in his earliest youth he was cast out among thieves and murderers, had even become the apprentice of the greatest among them, and thus had himself become a criminal! Could he be expected or supposed to possess that supernatural moral power which would have been requisite to tear himself out of this pool of vice and shame? And after all, wherein consisted his, the Prince's right to examine and weigh all these reasons so closely? Was he appointed the judge of his brother? Was his duty any other than to reinstate him in his possession as soon as it would be in his power? Must not he himself appear dishonest, appear a swindler, if not before the eyes of the world, at least before his own conscience, if he even for a single hour beyond the absolutely necessary time retained unjust possession of the sovereignty? No, it was rather his duty to act immediately, to do full justice! If afterwards his brother, as master and Prince, should offend against law and justice, law and justice might punish him for it, and it was not his, the present Prince's fault, if that law and justice should prove insufficient or too weak for the purpose.

These doubts, these contradictory motives and arguments filled the manly and honest mind of the Prince with disquiet and anxiety. The matter was of such importance, his determination, no matter which way he resolved, of such incalculably great consequences, that we can forgive his doubt and hesitation even to this usually firm and determined man.

There seemed to be but very little difficulty in the way of obtaining his brother's liberation, as he might soon hope to obtain that through the favour of the King, who personally knew him and was ever most gracious to him. But should he apply for it or not?

At last the Prince definitely returned to his original intention and resolution which he had repeatedly taken before, and which certainly fully agreed with the mode of action he had hitherto pursued, and which he felt convinced was supported by the best reasoning.

He was first to break the mutual silence.

"I shall remain firm to the determinations which I have already informed you of, my worthy friend," he said. "It is certainly a most distressing fate, to find a dear long lost brother an inmate of a penitentiary, and it was this conviction which affected me so cruelly on learning the terrible intelligence. Even now I feel the most distressing anxiety in consequence, but my peace of conscience can only be obtained at this price—I must act thus. I will consequently this very day wait on his Excellency, the Prime Minister, will inform him of my history, will place the proofs of my brother's identity into his hands, and will request him to obtain me an audience with his Majesty, the King. We can then count with some certainty upon his obtaining an early pardon."

"You already know my doubts and objections, Highness," replied the other, "which I have already expressed to you, in the most heartfelt sympathy with your fate; nothing remains for me to do, than again recommend these objections to your most serious consideration. You will put a blemish on the fair fame of a family, which has existed for centuries without a spot on its escutcheon, and you will put the fate of thousands of your subjects who love and venerate you as a father, into the hands of one—of only one man, who will probably make them all miserable. Certainly you must also take into consideration, that the individual in question is one, who, no matter what has been his unfortunate career, has the blood of your noble family flowing in his veins."

"I will most candidly confess to you, my dearest friend," said the Prince, warmly pressing the hand of the Major, "that these doubts have occupied my entire mind on our journey hither, and that even now they have disturbed me again. But I must end them, must decide as I have done. I know now what the commands of my conscience are, and it would cost me the peace and quiet of my entire future life did I not obey its mandates. Let us, therefore, look upon this matter as settled and decided."

"Very well!" replied the old warrior, warmly returning the pressure of the hand, "be it even as you like, Highness; you must best know yourself what course to pursue. But for similar reasons I must keep to my original intentions. I have quietly considered all you have said in favour of my boy, and I shall remain firm to my first determination. If he does not quietly submit, he shall leave Berlin, and in less than eight days he shall be on his journey, to serve one or two years in a regiment abroad, at Algiers or elsewhere. Just let him hear a few blue beans whistle about his ears, and these love and romance stories will soon quit his head; I know these things."

" Certainly !" answered the Prince with some hesitation, "our compact then is mutual. I must agree with you, if you will have it so, and must, moreover, endeavour to make my apologies for having hitherto occupied my own and your time solely with my own affairs. But the interest I take in your affairs is not diminished thereby. Our first arrangement must still be valid : you must give me one or two day's leisure to obtain all the necessary information concerning the actual position of your son's affairs, and until that is accomplished, you must not take a step in the matter. Your warm temper and impetuosity might otherwise easily spoil the whole affair. You agree to this ?"

" Upon my word !" exclaimed the Major, after he had given his promise for the fulfillment of the latter clause, " I don't believe that my old father, would have stood upon half the ceremony with me, when I was still a milkbearded boy. No, no, he was as stiff and inflexible as the tail he wore to his wig. However, be it so, for I suppose you are in the right."

" Permit me, now, to retire to my room, that I may address a few words to the minister," said the Prince, closing the conversation, and retiring towards the door, " as soon as that is done, I shall again be at your service. We have yet a great many things to speak about."

CHAPTER LXXXI.

AN UNEXPECTED OCCURRENCE.

AFTER the Prince had left the room, the Major approached the table upon which a number of journals and morning papers had been spread out.

He took up the *Voss*-Gazette, endeavouring to read a few paragraphs and disperse the annoying thoughts which still crowded his mind.

Without stopping to read the dry, heavy and stupid matter contained in the principal paper—without even glancing at the lengthy political leader—he took up a Supplement, in which the articles headed " communicated," had often before now, served to amuse him in a leisure hour.

The Supplement of to day was most particularly rich and racy.

Here one inquired " most respectfully," why the gutters in a certain street should smell so abominably ? There, another " wanted to know why the gas lamps were not lit, when moonshine stood in the almanac but not on the horizon ?" A third, in this same, somewhat hackneyed way, endeavoured to find a wife with twenty thousand Thalers, as his own acquaintance with ladies of such qualifications was rather limited. A fourth, wanted to know why the City Council and board of Aldermen, should have expressed a dislike to the publication of their pro-

ceedings, since it was well known, or had been asserted, that the entire board of the Common Council and Aldermen, consisted of Radicals. A fifth desired to have it explained, why it was, that neither himself, nor any of his friends, had ever drawn a prize in the " Carriage lottery," as they took every month sixty or more chances. He therefore declared the " Carriage-lottery," as one of the most dangerous undertakings, and advised all holders of chances to tear them up, and thus endeavour to break the proprietors. Next followed an immense mass of unintelligible and hieroglyphical replies and announcements concerning private affairs, meetings, rendezvous, all only intended for the eye of one party, and consequently of no interest to the Major, who threw the paper down again.

He took up the second Supplement. He had scarcely read a few lines, when he stopped with an involuntary exclamation of surprise, looked once more closely at it, and with the utmost haste rushed from the door.

Quickly he reached the room of the Prince.

"Oh your Highness !" he cried as he crossed the threshold, " read, I pray you, read what I have just found in this paper. This certainly is a new and remarkable occurrence."

The Prince took the paper which the other had brought, and with a voice that grew more trembling and uncertain as he proceeded, he read as follows:

" STECKBRIEF."*

" The Jewish burglar, F. Schmerles, who has been sentenced for five and twenty years at hard labour, consequently of a great number of forcible burglaries, thefts and other crimes against the public peace and the security of private property, and who has repeatedly on previous occasions been tried and condemned, has found an opportunity, by means of forcibly breaking through the outer walls of his cell and the prison, to escape from the state penitentiary at Spandau.

" All civil and military authorities at home or abroad are hereby officially requested to pay most especial and particularly watchful attention, to this Schmerles who is hereafter described. Said Schmerles is known as a most cunning, notorious and adroit criminal ; and is a most dangerous foe to the public, peace and the security of property.

" If he is found, all, and any authorities in his Majesty's dominions, and all authorities abroad on friendly terms and relations with this government, are requested to arrest him, to have him transported here in chains, together with all the moneys, papers or other effects that may be found about his person, and to deliver him to the expedition office of the Spandau penitentiary.

" In return we secure the immediate repayment of all and any expenses thereby incurred,

---

* *Steckbrief*, official proclamation or advertisement to civic authorities at home and abroad to arrest fugitives from justice therein described. TRANSLATOR.

and to all such authorities out of this kingdom, we proffer our own attention in return."

Spandau, the fourth of May, 18—.

The board of Supervision
of the Royal Penitentiary.

DESCRIPTION OF THE PERSON.

"The Jewish burglar F. Schmerles is about forty years of age, a Polander by birth, of the Jewish persuasion, and is five feet six inches in height.

"He has black, curly hair and eye brows, a high, open forehead, dark eyes, an aquiline nose, well proportioned mouth, black and large whiskers and an oval face.

"His dress cannot at present be described, as he found an opportunity to exchange the dress of the convicts of this prison for some other, leaving his prison dress outside of the outer prison wall.

"No particular marks upon his person.

Prince Prominsky read to the end of this "Steckbrief" with the utmost excitement. He had began to read it aloud, but his voice died away long before he had reached the end.

It may easily be understood, that it made a deep and terrible impression upon the mind of this highborn Prince, to see his brother pursued even as the lowest of criminals, to see him thus advertised, *him*, whom he thought to elevate to the sovereignty over thousands. So much wealth, rank, honour, splendour and power, in the *same* hand with so much crime and disgrace! What were all his reasonings, all his fancy pictures of reform and honesty, compared to this terrible blow of positive, self-evident certainty.

And add to all this, the new difficulty, the new terror, of once more seeing every hope of finding him lost, or removed to a far, and uncertain, distance. Schmerles might endeavour quickly to escape across the frontier, to seek temporal safety in another country, the authorities were bound to pursue him, his life even stood in hourly and most imminent danger, whilst here was his brother, waiting with a heart full of love, holding a Princely crown in his hand, endeavouring in vain to restore him. This blow was too much; like fevery chills, it shook the frame of the firm and powerful man, and he trembled in every limb.

Prominsky dropped the paper upon the table, and sunk back into the chair, whence he had risen in the intense excitement of the moment.

After a few minutes of close consideration, he was himself again. He became convinced that he must endeavour forcibly to shake off even this blow of fate, and his noble nature had strength and power of will sufficient not to desert him, even in these most trying, most terrible moments of his existence.

The quiet, manly and imposing calmness, which characterized his entire being, was quickly restored by a powerful effort. Firmly, and in a tone of decision he said to Major von Steinfort:

"I think the escape of my brother from the penitentiary can only be favourable to my plans. As I know what name I have to seek him by, I hope that I will ere long succeed in finding him. Then I will take him to my dominions, where no one knows him, or knows aught about his former life. All eclat must for the present be avoided, and after I myself have learned to know him somewhat better, I can easily consult with him, what steps would then best be taken. Under this supposition, I will at least delay my visit to the minister for the present. If meanwhile, my plan of finding him privately should fail, I have still the last, certainly more noisy and public remedy, remaining to me, namely, to obtain for him the King's pardon. I can then issue the Royal proclamation in the public papers, which will almost certainly bring him to me."

Spite of the deep and intense sorrow of soul which expressed itself in his fine manly features, the Prince had made this declaration with so much quiet and calmness, that the Major felt deeply moved by it. It was the true nobility of nature and of soul, which at this moment was enthroned upon the forehead of the high-minded Prince.

"I admire you in all your noble resolutions," said the Major, deeply moved; "but permit me one question, Highness. I hope you will not yourself penetrate the dens and hiding places of thieves and robbers to institute your search?"

"And why not?" replied Prince Prominsky, his eye sparkling brilliantly, "if I only knew that such a course would help me any thing! But, my worthy friend, do not fear; how could I, unacquainted with the manners, language and habits of these people, hope for success in such an undertaking? Luckily, I have another resource, another assistant in my enterprise, whom I will seek immediately. Do me the favour to await me here; I hope to return very shortly."

At these words the Prince took up his hat, pressed the hand of his friend, and left the hotel.

CHAPTER LXXXII.

THE DENUNCIATION.

THE course of our narrative brings us once more back to the Equestrian.

We find her at her residence, again absorbed in deep and serious thoughts.

Her great object had been attained. The Geheimerath had been punished in his own daughter —punished even in the same manner as he had once destroyed Francisca's existence, her future life. Only one thing remained to be done, in order fully to accomplish the great work of revenge, and this was, to deliver a dishonest criminal to his well merited punishment, in order to make it impossible for the Geheimerath to equalize Mary's indiscretion and his own disgrace, by giving his daughter as a wife to the Referendarius. Birkheim must be delivered into the hands of punishing justice, must be sent to a prison.

For this purpose, Francisca had determined, now to avail herself of her knowledge of his mode of life and means of existence. She would now denounce him to the police, as a false player, a professional gambler, and thus deliver him into the hands of justice.

She was already seated at her writing table, for the purpose of informing the authorities over her own signature of the ways and means by which Herr von Birkheim kept up appearances.

In this situation we find her now in the large front room belonging to her house.

A certain want of resolution, of positive determination is plainly visible in her pale, expressive features, which only too strongly bore the marks of the struggles of internal passion.

A white sheet of paper, pen and ink are lying before her.

Already she had three times taken up the pen, already three times had dipped it into ink, and equally often put it to the paper, but each time she had laid it down again without using it.

Evidently she hesitated in the execution of her determination. It had long been decided upon; she had hitherto only waited for that declaration of Mary, which she had just received, to execute her intentions, and now when the moment for action had actually arrived, her very heart and soul rebelled against the thought of becoming a denouncer.

The Equestrian could not understand her own present state of mind, for never before had it occurred to her, or had she even dreamed, that a want of determination of this kind and just at such a time should overcome her.

And in reality it was peculiar, it was wonderful!

With the most firm, iron determination had she hitherto pursued all her plans. The wild natures of the thieves had become subject to her will, the Geheimerath even she knew by an unequalled power of self-command to chain for months at her feet, an innocent girl she could coldly select and sacrifice as a victim to her revenge, as long as the object only was, to let a thoroughly bad man fall a victim to well merited revenge—and now she was undetermined, now she hesitated.

But this is only another evidence, how deeply in an impure intriguing breast a horror of betrayal and denouncing to authorities is usually seated. It seemed low, disgraceful and dishonourable to the Equestrian to make, as it were, a covert attack upon the Referendarius, to deliver him defencelessly to the powers of the law. It is evidently the secrecy, treachery and cowardice of a denouncement, which usually fills honourable minds with horror of it, and which also restrained the Equestrian. She was a fearless, bold woman, she dared everything because she sought revenge upon the betrayer, the destroyer of her harmless youth, but for these same reasons, she disdained the sneaking, watching and creeping villainy of a spy. She played a game in disguise, under false colours with the Geheimerath, but then she played it herself, upon her own risk and danger, and she could lose and miss all—the other could possibly penetrate her motives, and he was at liberty to resist, perhaps to vanquish her.

But such was not the case in the present instance, where disgraceful betrayal, and denouncement would bring the certain powers of public justice upon the defenceless victim, and where that victim must helplessly sink beneath the irresistible blow. It was this kind of reasoning which the Equestrian held with herself, it was this she felt, and which turned the arrow of self-reproach against her own conscience, even though she endeavoured to quiet its sting, by reminding herself of the fact that the Referendarius was a villain.

*   *   *   *   *

Nevertheless, she saw the necessity of silencing these inward scruples, if otherwise she would crown her great work of revenge. She felt that she must sacrifice him, and yield to the pressure of external circumstances.

Again she took up the pen to finish the work she had commenced, when—a most opportune interruption—her maid entered and announced a strange gentleman, who desired a conversation with her, without being willing to give his name or rank.

Francisca quickly rose from her seat, and nodded assent to this request.

A minute afterwards Prince Prominsky stood before her.

A tremor of joyous emotion shook the frame of Francisca, when suddenly, and so unexpectedly she saw him appear before her, him—she scarcely dared to confess it to herself—whom she already received with the full fire and love of her affectionate and warm soul.

The Prince also seemed not without difficulty to master a slight embarrassment, which was evidently increased by the visible confusion of Francisca.

In a second, however, the man of the world had overcome this weakness and again recovered his full presence of mind. He gave the blushing woman time to recover her equanimity, whilst in an easy tone of politeness, he begged her to excuse his sudden and unceremonious appearance, by the urgency of his business.

Abashed, the eye of Francisca had sought the ground; slowly only, she gradually dared to raise her dark lashes, and to rest her looks upon the tall, commanding figure of the handsome man.

"An accident, which even to this day is inexplicable to me," he began, "initiated you into the most private affairs and secrets of my family. Under those circumstances you have so far offered me a helping hand, given me your aid, and at the same time have shown such a deep interest in in my fate, that it leads me to hope that in the request I am about to make, and wherein I need it more than ever, you will not refuse me your assistance."

The Prince stopped as if awaiting the consent of the Equestrian, but the latter was only able to reply by a silent bow, whilst at the same time, by a wink she invited the Prince to seat himself, pointing to an easy chair by her side.

"Above all things," continued Prominsky, as he accepted the invitation with an easy grace, "you must permit me to inform you how all my affairs are situated at present."

After the Prince had related to her the flight of long Schmuel, his subsequent capture, sickness and death, all of which our reader is already acquainted with, he continued :

"I know that I can fully and entirely confide in your discretion. Although, for my part, I am far from feeling any desire or wish to interfere or inquire into your private affairs, I must yet take it for granted, that in some way or another, you are in connexion with persons who either already know my brother, or can easily make his acquaintance, and thus materially assist me in finding him. May I count upon your kind assistance in this respect? All I would require you to do, is to put me into communication with those persons, unless indeed, you should undertake the mediation yourself, and assist me in obtaining the great object of my wishes."

In a quick and lively tone, Francisca replied : "Your Highness may believe my words, when I assure you, that without compromising third parties in a most sensible, dangerous and unwarrantable manner, it is for the present impossible for me to give you a further insight into my own affairs. But I will give your Highness the assurance, that it shall immediately be made my highest, most important duty to discover the hiding place of your brother, and if he still remains within the walls of this city, I don't doubt for a single moment, that I shall be fully successful."

"You give balm and consolation to my distracted mind," said the Prince, in a gentle, melting tone of voice. "I have a most inexplicable confidence in your activity, and doubt not that you will fully succeed in the great accomplishment of my most ardent wishes. Then grant me only one more request, and inform me how and by what means, I shall be able to thank you for the great and generous interest you take in my welfare?"

Francisca cast a hasty glance upon the Prince, as if endeavouring to make a reply, but she seemed to suppress the words upon her lips and remained silent.

"That, which, when last I spoke to you, I treated as a reasonable supposition, has now become a firmly established fact," continued the Prince. "By the information you gave me then, you saved my life at the *Hotel de Paris*, which the Jew hoped to deprive me of at the time of the burglary. I already thank you for my own existence, and I doubt not, that I may soon have to thank you for that of my brother; should the noble and wealthy Princes von Prominsky really be too poor, to show their gratitude to their mysterious benefactress ?"

Partly playfully, and partly in earnest, the Prince at these words took the fair hand of Francisca which hung idly by her side and pressed it to his lips.

"Tell me, dearest Francisca," he repeated in entreating tones, "is Prince Stephan von Prominsky really too poor for this proud heart.—You are still silent?—Do you esteem me so very little ?"

Slowly Francisca raised her liquid eyes, in which the bright rays of love were softly melting by the consciousness of unmerited reproach at this hard question. Involuntarily she bent her beautiful head towards this much adored man, and a large, pearly tear, trickled down her velvet cheek.

Ardently, and urged by the very fulness of his heart, the Prince drew the beauteous woman towards his breast, and imprinted a long and ardent kiss upon her lips. Suddenly, however, she seemed to awake from a dream. With a heart-rending cry she endeavoured to free herself from the arms of the man. Gently he replaced her upon her seat, and with a hasty step left the room.

Deeply and sadly moved, Francisca's looks followed him, then she turned to her writing desk and hastily tore the letter she had commenced.

"The work of revenge must terminate," she said, "where the work of love commences."

CHAPTER LXXXIII.

A ROGUE IN DIFFICULTIES.

THE entire Berlinian world of thieves and scoundrels was in a state of the most intense excitement.

The unexpected arrest of Maulspitzer had created this great alarm.

The usual places of rendezvous of this gentry, the cellar of hunchbacked Jobs, the puppet-show at Leidenthal's, the *golden Mops*, the *broken Schmortopf*,*—all these and other localities were lonely and deserted. Each villain avoided the other.

When two of the usually most intimate scoundrels now met in the street, they would quietly pass each other in great apparent haste and without exchanging a word.

Whence this strange and peculiar position of things ?—Was it anything so unusual that a thief should be arrested ? Did not the same fate await them all in a greater or lesser degree? had it not already frequently overtaken them, and had they not all escaped with more or less injury ? Or perhaps, did they all take such a very great and intense interest in the fate of the sand-carter, or

*Names of low places of resort. "Golden Mops," is golden Pug-dog, "broken Schmortopf," broken Lard pitcher.

were they able by these signs of intense regret, sorrow and distress, to modify or relieve his doom?

But the affair had quite a different foundation.

The most varied and contradictory reports circulated in the world of scoundrels. Among other things, it was reported that Maulspitzer had made *a great emmes*, (a general confession) the greatest indeed that had ever yet been made.

Every one who had a bad conscience—and they all had *very bad* ones—feared by the confessions of the arrested criminal, to be mixed up in investigations, and perhaps to be led towards the end of his most glorious career.

The thieves in their apprehensions, were supported by their experience and their knowledge of these affairs.

A great emmes, made by one of the *Matadore** of thieves, is an occurrence which makes them all tremble, and which frequently descends upon them like a thunder-bolt from an unclouded sky. A cunning and acute scoundrel is not easily brought to confession; in the very face of the most positive testimony, he will deny every thing most obstinately, and will never hesitate to resort to the most silly, senseless and most ridiculous excuses, often consisting in the most improbable sillily invented stories.

In consequence of this, extraordinary punishment which is very frequently inflicted, still remains an important resource whenever it does occur, as this extraordinary punishment must answer in place of the regular and more severe punishment, which cannot take place without full and sufficient proof of guilt.

And this perhaps may be the reason, that, spite of all the attacks of the learned, our courts of justice still persevere in a mode of punishment, which, in reality, is a contradiction in itself, since the accused must be either guilty or innocent, and in the first instance must be fully punished, in the latter must be entirely discharged. However this may be, in all the numerous cases in which the extraordinary punishment has been the doom of the prisoner, the cunning of the accused party usually has gained a victory, and just as little as the prisoner would think of confessing himself guilty, just as little, we say, can he ever think of betraying his comrades.

Occasionally, however, it occurs—and the very greatest of criminals have such moments—that their lying qualities will no longer support them. Whether this be caused by the superior talent of the examining officer, or by the awakened voice of conscience, or whether it be a physical phenomenon which causes the power of individual resistance to civil authority suddenly to disappear, in short the obstinacy seems broken, and all the channels of an entire and open confession are suddenly thrown open. The most intricate, terrible, and before inexplicable cases are thus brought to light, even when the judge does not demand such explanation, or having no

* Chiefs or particularly notorious thieves.

suspicion of these facts, does not even allude to them.

It is in reality a great proof of the all-victorious element of truth, that it should assault the guilty one, and as it were, force from him all which hitherto he had kept closely locked in his own bosom, spite of rewards offered, spite of the most severe investigations. It certainly is only a moment, which disappears again with the very excitement which bore it, and which not unfrequently induces the criminal, even after making the confession, to recall and deny it again; yet these disclosures, as far, at least, as third parties are concerned, are almost invariably found correct on further investigation.

This circumstance, which must have a deeper psychological cause than we can discover at the surface, is of much more importance to the police and to the administration of justice, than the best regulated system of police and the sharpest eye of her secret and open officers and agents.

But the thieves also know this danger, and fear it as the greatest misfortune that can happen to them. Long buried and forgotten murders, incendiarisms, burglaries, robberies and every other species of crime which have long been forgotten even by the authorities are then suddenly brought to light, and being once thus exposed, the avenging hand of justice suddenly reaches the criminal who had long since been lulled into security.

Such was the nature of the dangers which now seemed to threaten all the Berlinian robbers, and it was this which made them all afraid. The more indistinct, gloomy and dark these reports appeared, the more painful became their fears. A heavy, oppressive cloud seemed to overshadow the horizon of every rogue. No one could speak of anything with certainty, no one could name authority. All spoke merely from hearsay, yet all lived in constant trouble and tribulation, uncertain of their fate of the very next moment.

Eel-eye had also heard some of these reports.

He had only too much reason to be careful of his personal safety, for he had been a participator of many, very many of Maulspitzer's massemattens, and certainly could not have the least hope of escaping unscathed if Maulspitzer had made a general confession. At the same time, it was of the utmost importance to him, just at this particular time to remain at liberty, for the prospect of a future existence, which the Equestrian had opened before his eyes, had made no slight impression upon his heart.

The realization of this prospect, however, depended upon his co-operation in restoring his long lost brother to the Prince. Who that brother was, and that he was most probably in Berlin, Franzisca had already informed him. But then it was absolutely necessary to the attainment of his object, that he should visit the very district, and the very places at which, if the confessions of the Maulspitzer had really taken place, he must expect to find the police most carefully searching and upon the watch for him.

It consequently was of the utmost importance

to Eel-eye, to ascertain precisely how matters and things stood with Maulspitzer, and whether or not he had made any confessions. Then only he could determine what course he would have to pursue in order to find Schmerles, without absolute danger of running direct into the arms of an arrest.

Great and intense was the passion which Eel-eye felt for the Equestrian, but the greater in consequence was his desire to serve and effectually assist her in the execution of her plans. Yet all this impressed him the more with the necessity of proceeding in his work with the utmost caution.

Moreover, it was his earnest wish to abandon his thieves life, and, if possible, to become an honest member of society. Should he run the risk upon his very way to reform, to fall into the hands of the police?—If that should occur—and he felt this keenly—his reform, his restoration to society was postponed for a long time, perhaps forever.

Above all, in his present distressed situation he could not well dispense with the assistance of the Prince, and whether he would ever afterwards find another opportunity to meet that assistance, was, to say the least, a matter involved in great doubt and uncertainty.

But how was it possible for him to obtain the necessary information concerning the fate and confessions of Maulspitzer?

Eel-eye considered long and deeply upon this. He formed half a dozen of plans and rejected them all again; not one of them seemed feasible, yet his time pressed more and more.

At last he thought he had hit upon the proper course.

CHAPTER LXXXIV.

A DARING ENTERPRISE.

THE river Spree, as it is well known, runs through the entire length of the city of Berlin.

The parts of the town situated along its shores, though they cannot in all instances be called the most beautiful, are certainly among the most interesting and original.

The life upon the river itself is active, busy and thriving, and though it presents but a dim and weak counterfeit, yet it does present something of the picture of the ports of commercial cities.

We certainly cannot find men of war in this port, nor shall we find them, even if the *Amazon* should ever be blessed with a greater progeny than there is at present any hope for. We do not even see merchant vessels, either of the first or second class, nor yet of the third, but only the small long *Spree* and *Oder* boats, and at the utmost a small steamer, which looks ashamed and abashed at its own existence here, as its wheels rush through the dark muddy waves.

But withal, these navigators of the Spree form a nation by themselves, and look upon the land and its inhabitants with the same contempt as old sea captains are wont to do. For the most part, these watermen with their wives and children never live in any other habitation summer or winter, than in the narrow cabin of their boat. Their occupation consists in the transportation of provisions, grain, fruit, potatoes, flour, and of fuel, such as wood, turf, coal or materials for building, or feed, straw, hay and whatever other necessaries of life are received in the city, from the country above and below.

Upon the whole, these people form a peaceable, good natured race, which braves storm, wind and weather—but they are mostly coarse, insolent and very selfish. The disputes and wars of words which frequently arise, when now and then their respective vessels run foul of each other, or when the wharf-master has a difference with them, or when a dispute arises with the purchasers of their merchandize, are no less classic than the renowned disputes of the Grecian and Trojan heroes at the ten years siege, and often are a subject of great amusement to the not over refined or delicate ears of the Berlinians.

The life *by the side* of the water in its ever changing peculiar formation, stands in worthy juxtaposition with the life *upon* the water.

It is partly among the many manufactories and the numerous labourers there employed, which give this scene a most lively appearance, partly the large bathing institutions, partly the wharfs at which the above mentioned boats discharge their cargoes, and the natural frequenters of these wharfs, such as stevedores, labourers, carmen, turf-women, fishmongers, &c., and finally among the numerous schnapps and beer-shops, as for instance at the *Schiffbauerdamm*,* where the ever active police has to quiet many conflicts and settle many disputes. A more elevated sense for beauty may also find gratification among the scenes along the Spree, as for instance, at the castle, the museum, the cathedral and other most beautiful sights and picturesque views, which may easily be found by following the manifold windings of the stream.

In short, we believe that a stranger who would embark somewhere on the Upper-Spree, and follows the stream its entire length through the town as far as the *Unterbaum* or the " Tents," will not regret the journey. He will at least learn that Berlin contains a third element, which is neither to be compared to the hightoned character of the *Linden* or the *Wilhelms-street*, nor yet to the city life of the busy and commercial *König-street*.

But we must return from our digression, which we hope our readers will pardon us, as the subject thereof belongs to the Mysteries of Berlin, although not directly to the progress of our story. We were led to it by the circumstance that the

---

* The *Amazon* is the name of the *only* Prussian vessel of war.

* Wharf for ship builders.

next event, with which we must now immediately acquaint our readers, occurred upon the river Spree.

Among the other streets, which, in the heart of the city, run along the shore of the river, there is one, which, as well as the whole district in which it is situated, bears the name of " *Neuköln am Wasser.*"*

That this district is one of the oldest in the capital, may easily be perceived by the peculiar construction of the houses, the small *façades*, the narrow and low entrances, the old fashioned gothic gable ends, and other similar signs of the olden time.

Said street even on the opposite, the land-side has a similar antiquated appearance, at least as far as it is not interrupted and changed by the new buildings and other modern improvements which annually take place here. On the water-side we find the high levees and the breastwork, which divides the Spree from the street—a measure of security.

If from this place we cast a look across the dark surface of the water, we discover on the opposite shore a row of smoky, black and dingy houses, which, together with out buildings, yards, stables, &c., all lay close to the water. Amidst these various buildings, we can also discover a grey, plain, and somewhat dilapidated wall, which, forming the outer barrier of the wing of a large building, also leans over into the water. The very small, gloomy windows, barricaded with iron railings, easily betray the nature of the large gloomy building—it is a part of the Berlin S*tadtvogtei-prison.*

It was a very dark night in May, when a solitary man might be seen carefully and cautiously walking up and down that part of the above named street, which, *par excellence*, is called "*on the Fisher-bridge,*" and which is situated directly opposite to the prison.

He was dressed in a light frock coat, buttoned tightly across the breast, wore a small dark cap upon his head, and carried a strong, broad bludgeon of considerable length in his hand.

Several times he walked up and down by the breastwork, whilst he frequently cast searching glances to the right and to the left, to convince himself that he was not observed or watched by any body.

The hour of midnight was past; only a few late wanderers loitered still about the street.

When the solitary stranger believed himself entirely unobserved, he suddenly approached the breastwork, with great ease and activity swung himself over it, and jumped down upon a wash-bench which floated on the water near the shore.

Here he stopped for a moment and listened: then he laid himself flat upon the bench, crept to its furthest end, and produced a small iron crowbar from his pocket. With this he loosened the padlock and chain by which a small boat had been fastened to the wash-bench.

* **Angl.** New-Cologne by the water.

Having accomplished all this as noiselessly as possible, he drew the boat sideways to the bench, and then, without rising or making the least noise, rolled into it himself.

After he had for some time laid silently and listening in the bottom of his boat, he rose a little from his reclining position, and, using his broad bludgeon as an oar, directed the course of the boat towards the opposite shore.

Near that shore, there is a row of strong pillars which rise from the water to the height of about eight or ten feet. These are placed there to prevent boats from running against the bulwark.

To one of these pillars, and as near as possible to the prison-buildings, the stranger fastened his vessel, and then again resumed his former position at the bottom of the boat.

At first in a low tone, but gradually louder, and at short intervals, he now began to whistle a peculiar strain. It lasted a long time, before this whistling seemed to attract the desired attention, and not unfrequently the whistler uttered a suppressed malediction at the ill success of his efforts. At last from one of the upper stories a similar and very low strain was heard in reply.

The man in the boat remained immoveable and silent.

After a little while, the window whence the signal had been responded to, was opened, a head bent down towards the water, and a low but distinct voice said :

" With whom do you wish to *dibber* (to converse) ?"

" Syrupsnose, is that you ?" inquired the stranger below, by way of an answer.

" Certainly it is," was the reply heard from above, " but in the devil's name, Eel-eye, how do you come here ? What do you want ? Thunder, but you are ever a bold, daring fellow."

As this side of the prison run towards the water, and as this circumstance almost effectually seemed to preclude the possibility of a communication from without, the windows here were not closed by the usual tin boxes. This consequently greatly facilitated the conversation between the two.

" I must speak to Maulspitzer," replied Eel-eye, for the daring stranger was no other, " whose cell is said to be here, somewhere near the water."

" Maulspitzer is no longer here," rejoined Syrupsnose, " he has been sent to the *Riesenburg.* But be very careful of him, for I think you might be much better employed, than thus to bring your neck into danger. He had become a *Slichner*, (spy) but now he has made *great Emmes*, (general confession,) and has *whistled upon all his Chawairem* (betrayed his comrades)."

" What ?" exclaimed Eel-eye in astonishment, " and do you also know of this infernal affair about this *great Emmes*, which has put us all into such a state of consternation ?—But he can not have become a Slichner, that is impossible ; for I myself saw him, when he was arrested."

"And yet it is true," answered Syrupsnose, "for he was confined here in the same cell with me, and I know the whole story. Just listen and I will tell you, how it all occurred."

The imprisoned rogue, endeavoured as far as possible to protrude his head through the iron bars of his window, while Eel-eye raised his head to listen attentively: the other began:

"The Maulspitzer was Vigilant for the *Dicken* (nickname of Polizeirath X—) and by his assistance, the latter had very nearly caught long Schmuel in the *Hôtel de Paris.* The Criminal Commissary W—, was no little annoyed at this, for he greatly envied the Polizierath the possession of so good a vigilant. He therefore sought an excuse, of at least making Maulspitzer useless to the other, since he could not possess him himself.

"He instituted a search in Maulspitzer's sleeping place, where he found *Klamones,* (a bunch of false keys,) and upon the strength of this, he let him go *verschütt* (arrested him) in the Diana saloon, and accused him of a burglary at the house of some Geheimerath. I believe that was the same Masematten in which you had a *Hellig* (share,) while just Maulspitzer himself was refused to participate in it by long Schmuel. *Double Pech* (double misfortune) for Maulspitzer! But to continue my story.

"Maulspitzer was locked up with me in the same number, and had been confined about three days, when suddenly in the night he became *meschugge* (crazy.) The devil only knows what was the cause of it. Whether it preyed so very severely upon his mind, that they should have imprisoned him, although he had become a vigilant—I cannot tell. It is certain however, that the fellow was already half crazy when he was brought here. One night we lay very quietly upon our straw sacks, when suddenly he jumped up like a raving maniac, and bawled with the utmost power of his lungs:

"'Help, help, the schlappe Anthony is coming! He wants to put me under the ice!' We all—there were three more of us in the same cell—started upon our feet, endeavoured to pacify him, or at least to make him keep silent, but the fellow cried more lustily than ever, until we all shuddered with very fright: 'Schlappe Anthony is strangling me! he is killing me!' We now knew no longer what to do with him; he must have dreamed something. We were just upon the point of taking hold and forcibly silencing him by tying up his mouth, for he increased his noise at a wonderful rate, when we heard the keys rattle in the lock, the door opened and the thick Wiechmann entered with a lantern in his hand. No sooner does Maulspitzer see the light, than he rushes upon Wiechmann with the cry: 'there he is already and wants to push me under the ice, where I put him. Oh help, help!'

"I tell you, Eel-eye, in the whole course of my life, I have never experienced such a scene. Cold perspiration stood in heavy drops upon my forehead. The thick turnkey, who no doubt scented the game, took him immediately away with him, and brought him to the parson, whom he awoke in the middle of the night. The parson then, of course, knocked him perfectly flat at once, and the next morning a great Emmes was brought to light, greater than any you have ever heard of before. The parson was smart and cunning enough, to keep the fellow with him, until the long Criminalrath had been sent for, who quickly took down everything in black and white.

"Only towards noon, the rascal was brought back to our cell, and then he looked as if he had laid in his grave for ten years. We very easily elicited from him everything I have told you; he was so very soft, so perfectly melted, that I think the Criminalrath scarcely needed to examine him. In the afternoon he was taken away, and since then he is imprisoned in the Riesenburg. God only knows, what other new Emmes he may have made there. But I am sure that he has *also whistled* upon you, (betrayed you;) I am certain of that. So you must be very careful."

"The story then is correct," said Eel-eye with a shake of his head, as the other had closed his report, "and now everything explains itself to me. The fellow murdered a Vigilant, and then turned Vigilant himself. That must have preyed upon his mind. It is all over with him. He has talked his own head off his shoulders. Well the fellow is a scoundrel, and has not deserved anything better than the gallows on all of us, but notwithstanding all, I now pity him The executioner is a rough customer."

Eel-eye had scarcely given vent to these philosophical expressions, when the sentinel, who stands upon the bulwark, and who had hitherto paid not the least attention to what was passing below, exclaimed in a voice that struck terror to the souls of the thieves: "Who goes there?" At the same time, the soldier approached close to the waters edge, levelled his musket at the boat, and cried; "Let no one move or I shoot him down."

Quick as lightning, Eel-eye started up, determined by an active movement to get beyond the range of the musket. Spite of the darkness of the night, however, the soldier must have discovered the outline of his figure, or at least must have heard the noise of his movement and therefrom have suspected that the other was disobeying his mandate. With a loud report the musket was discharged, the ball whistled close past the other's ears, and struck the water within a few inches of his head.

But suddenly Eel-eye found himself in even a more dangerous predicament, than the one from which he had just escaped. In vain he endeavoured to find his oar, or rather his substitute for an oar; in his haste, or while he endeavoured to fasten the boat, this must have fallen into the water.

In this new difficulty, without for an instant

losing his presence of mind, he threw himself back lengthways into the bottom of the boat as quickly as he had risen from it. He entertained a hope, that the sentinel, if he heard no further noise in consequence of his shot, would naturally believe that he had made a mistake, return to his post, or at all events, would await the break of day.

But even in this hope he was deceived. The shot had been heard by the sentinels and the prison turnkeys who were on guard within the yard. Hastily these men opened a little door which led to the water; at the request of the sentinel, they entered a boat laying there for this purpose, and rowed towards the vessel wherein Eel-eye was hidden.

Now this bold thief found himself in the utmost danger. He heard the approach of his pursuers, who were scarcely a moderate hundred yards distant from him. Without an oar, he could not even make an attempt, which by his personal strength or his agility might have still rendered his flight successful. Only one hope of safety remained to him, and he daringly determined to avail himself of this as a last resource.

He quickly rolled the whole length of his body to the opposite side of the boat, pressed the vessel down as close as possible to the surface of the water, and then without the least noise, shot down into the depth of the river.

After he had swum a considerable distance under the water towards New-Köln, he again rose to the surface, to look round for his pursuers.

With pleasure he discovered them about twenty yards behind him, stopping by the side of his boat, undetermined which way to direct their pursuit. He bravely continued to swim, and had soon reached the wash bench, which he gently climbed upon, without being discovered by any one. Without rising to his feet he succeeded in crawling along to the breast-work, in the shade of which he intended to rise up, and swinging himself over the barriers as before, to reach the street.

He was just upon the point of executing this manœuvre, which would have crowned his efforts, when a new difficulty arose which threatened to deprive him of the reward of all his struggles.

Just behind him he heard the signal whistle of the watchman of the Stadtvogtei-prison, a sign to all other watchmen and night police that somebody was being pursued, and soon this call was responded to by similar signals from the streets.

Under these circumstances he dared not return to the street; it was equally dangerous to remain where he was, as he could not hope to find security in his present asylum. All the watchmen of the district were now on the alert, and a part of them searched already along the shore and through the breastwork.

Eel-eye had no time for consideration. Quick as thought he slipped back into the water, and descending the stream, he swam under the next bridge. Here he clung to a pillar, at the same time hiding his body up to his neck under water.

The fear and anxiety which he had to suffer were not little.

Twice his pursuers passed close by him with their boat, and once they even stopped and commenced a confidential conversation with the watchman who walked upon the bridge, expressing their astonishment at the strange and unaccountable disappearance of the fugitive. He might, from the very close vicinity of the speakers, have himself joined their conversation. However, he remained motionless until his enemies had passed him, whilst he sunk his head up to his nostrils in the water, and thus he once more gained his liberty.

Finally the noise subsided.

His pursuers desisted from further persecution, which seemed useless according to their views, and then retired to their usual places.

Now Eel-eye might dare to leave his hiding place at last. He swam as far as a staircase which led out of the water, the location of which he had previously ascertained, and thus unattacked and unmolested he reached the street.

But even then he could not consider himself entirely safe, or free from pursuit.

Whither now should he direct his steps? His entire body was stiff and every limb chilled with wet and cold, and through the superhuman exertions and indefatigable energy which he had shown, he was perfectly exhausted and scarcely able to support himself upon his feet. Every moment he was in the utmost danger of sinking to the ground, yet he dared not venture to seek a place of rest anywhere in the neighbourhood.

With difficulty he dragged himself along the street, without daring to stop even for a single moment, from fear of exciting the attention of a watchman by his very peculiar and suspicious appearance.

At last, amidst difficulties, anxieties and hairbreadth escapes of all kinds, he reached the "*Schlossfreiheit.*"*

Here an elegant, dashing carriage, provided with two bright burning lanterns rattled past him. The seat behind, intended for the footman, was vacant.

Without hesitation, or without even a moment's consideration, Eel-eye mounted that seat, partly from a desire of moving onward, and partly from the hope of finding a night's quarter in the carriage itself, when the owners should have left it.

To his utter astonishment the vehicle stopped before the house of the Equestrian; still more was he astonished on seeing Francisca herself descend from it. She had just returned, and returned rather late from a soirée at the house of her friend, the Geheimerath.

Quickly he descended from his seat, approached the coach door just as Francisca was about leaving the coach and entering the house

* A certain locality in Berlin

"Francisca," he exclaimed in a hasty whisper, "save me, save me, I am pursued."

A glance at the personal appearance of the friend of her youth, soon told the Equestrian all the rest. Without expressing any fright, wonder or astonishment, she silently nodded her head.

The thief followed her into the house, and the maid closed the protecting door behind both.

CHAPTER LXXXV.

FAMILY SCENES AT HOFRATH CHRISTIANUS' HOUSE.

THIS day was a highly important one in the house of Hofrath Christianus.

The marriage of Fräulein Matilda with the Banker von N—— was to be celebrated very shortly. Matilda had so far prevailed upon her admirer, that he had agreed to close a marriage contract, wherein a very large income to herself for life was stipulated, in the case of her widowhood without children. We may naturally suppose that she entertained an opinion, that Herr von N—, blessed in connubial felicity and by her side, would not live to a very great age.

To-day then, this marriage contract was to be closed, and for this purpose we find the whole family collected.

The pious, hypocritical and avaricious Notary Schreiber, whom we have once before had occasion to introduce to our readers, is seated at a writing table, behind the gigantic, black wooden inkstand of the Hofrath. He had drawn up the necessary legal document to the perfect satisfaction of all parties, and in his disagreeable screeching voice had just read it aloud.

He was upon the point of manœuvering his body backwards out of the door, amidst bows and a mass of unintelligible, complimentary, Latin-German phrases, when the servant announced Major von Steinfort.

Quickly the Notary resumed his seat, opened and spread his documents before him, as if searching for an error therein, or as if to insert some necessary remark previously omitted.

The Major had considered it his duty to pay this visit to his old friend, to convince the latter, that neither himself nor his unchangeable friendship, but only and alone his reprobate son, had been the cause of the non-fulfilment of their long arranged plan of family connexion.

During the first formalities of greeting, shaking hands, &c., the Notary fixed a searching glance upon Major von Steinfort, shook his little head almost imperceptibly, and murmured a few unintelligible words into his unshaven beard. Then he quickly and noiselessly withdrew from the room.

Herr von N— was immediately after introduced to the Major, as the declared bridegroom, and future husband of the young Fräulein.

The old warrior seemed not to have anticipated such an introduction, and only with great difficulty overcame a certain embarrassment, which showed itself on his browned features. But as he, as well as Hofrath Christianus might have considered all allusions to former occurrences ill timed and in bad taste, they finally entered into an easy and indifferent conversation about the state of the weather, political movements, stock gambling, temperance societies, railroads, &c.

A mischievous demon, however, interrupted this artificial quietude.

Matilda was already well aware of the marriage of Lieutenant von Steinfort, and felt deeply annoyed and injured by it. She easily persuaded herself, that it could only have been the present young wife of Herr von Steinfort who had robbed her of the hand of the handsome and wealthy young officer. And this woman not only belonged in a position, far, far below her own rank in society, but was even a fallen, abandoned, dishonoured being! And with all this, Lieutenant von Steinfort had preferred such a wretch to herself.

Excited by the remembrance of all this, and at the same time elated by her present success and good fortune, the Fräulein would not let an opportunity for spiteful revenge escape her.

Maliciously and indelicately enough, she addressed the Major with an inquiry after the health and welfare of his son.

The old Major glanced at the bold speaker with a displeased look, and without making any reply, endeavoured to change the subject of conversation.

Perhaps at this same moment, the father might have felt within his inmost heart, the first excuse for his son's refusal to make the daughter of the Hofrath his bride. Spite of the rude and rough exterior which he frequently showed, the Major had a deep and acute sensitiveness of womanly delicacy and lady like behaviour.

Fräulein Christianus, however, was not so easily baffled in her malicious intentions. She repeated the question, whilst she added ironically:

"And how fares your worthy and beauteous daughter-in-law ?"

This question had merely been asked for the purpose of embarrassing the Major, and of wounding his feelings. For the honour of the young lady we must admit, that she did not know how deep a wound she was inflicting on an already sore and oppressed heart. She certainly pre-supposed, beyond a doubt, that the Major knew of his son's marriage and had given his consent to it. And it might very easily be the case, that it was this pre-supposition which excited her anger and displeasure even against the grey head of the aged father.

The Major sat before her as if thunderstruck. With lightning speed all the late letters of his son passed before his mind's eye, and suddenly combined into a cue, which disclosed to him the most terrible truth. Yet he would not abandon hope, and he even now believed, that his ears had deceived him, in regard to the young lady's question. With a shaky, trembling and anxious voice, he inquired:

"About whom did you ask, Fräulein?"

"Why, about your young daughter in law," repeated the malicious girl, "I have heard a great deal said about the many amiable, kind, good natured and delightful qualities she possesses, and you must therefore excuse a little curiosity on my part."

This was too much for the old man. He could not comprehend the terrible import of this speech. Without replying a word he stared upon vacancy. His mind was confused, almost deranged.

Matilda, who quickly observed that her arrow had not missed its mark—though, as we said above, she had no conception of the depth of the wound—enjoyed with real malicious pleasure, the misery of the old man, which was plainly enough expressed upon his every feature. She was certain that she had at least revenged herself upon the father of her faithless lover, and through him upon his son.

The old Hofrath Christianus felt more humanely for his old friend.

To put an end to this painful scene, he took the Major by the arm, and lead him into his private library, telling the company present, that he had to speak upon matters of business with his friend.

The latter followed mechanically.

The rest of the company looked at each other with expressions of wonder, doubt and astonishment. The banker von N— had really been frightened by the silent stare of the Major.

"My Heavens! dearest Matilda," he exclaimed as he wiped the perspiration from his forehead with a scented silk handkerchief, "dearest Matilda, I hope this wild old man will not prepare some terrible scene for us! He made such a furious, horrible face; I really was almost afraid of him."

"Pshaw!" cried young Christianus, the young aspirant to literary fame, as he measured his future brother-in-law, with a look, which meant to express the deepest scorn and contempt: "who would be afraid?"

"But, but! my dear Adolph," answered Herr von N— anxiously, "you may easily talk. Don't you know then, as literatus and author, that we have plenty of examples, where old and wounded soldiers, invalids and others, frequently are attacked by a certain battle mania, in which state they kill, murder and butcher every body round them? Now it is said, that these symptoms frequently occur when old wounds break out afresh. There is certainly plenty of cause here, in the case of the old Major."

"As a man of letters and an author, I must totally disagree with your views," said the young gentleman with easy and contemptuous indifference. "We of the liberal party, know not the meaning of the word fear."

Fräulein Christianus, seemed not a little vexed and annoyed at the haughty and contemptuous manner which her brother assumed towards her betrothed, and seemed determined upon her revenge.

"Tell me, Adolph," she began, "what do you mean by a liberal author, as you call yourself every moment. I believe that a liberal author must be one of that kind of men, who talk about every thing, and understand nothing!"

We regret exceedingly, that we shall not be able to furnish to our readers the most exciting debate, about the actual position, the merits and demerits of so-called liberal authors, which between two children of a Hofrath of the ministerial cabinet would unquestionably have become highly interesting. But at this very moment a great noise and tumult was heard issuing from the so-called library of the Hofrath, and this noise for an instant silenced the contending parties as well as all others in the room.

Above the tumult, the voice of the Major could be heard, exclaiming in a tone of intense excitement and frantic wildness:

"I will renounce the boy together with his confounded wench; I will murder them both!"

The door flew open, and the Major rushed through the room, and out of the house, without paying the least attention to any person around him.

Herr Banker von N—, at the stormy entrance of the Major, had fearfully retreated to a distant corner, and as an additional security had drawn a large *fauteuil* before him.

After the furious old man had disappeared, he carefully advanced from his corner, and addressed the young literary gentleman in a tone of triumph.

"Well sir, was I not in the right after all? Would not this Major have murdered every body, who would have crossed his path? There is little doubt now, but that an old wound, probably in his head, is broken open afresh. He is a wild man, and I really have a kind of fear of him."

Matilda saw no occasion for informing her betrothed of the actual cause of the great excitement of Major von Steinfort; perhaps she was somewhat afraid, that in making such a disclosure, she would have to expose more of her own past adventures, than was exactly suited to her present plans. Moreover she herself knew only half of what had put the old warrior into such a mad fury, as she believed that her own inquiries had been the sole cause.

She therefore contented herself with merely observing, that the Major was a very old friend of her father's, whose eccentricities they had all long since become accustomed to, and that they scarce noticed an occasional freak of this kind.

"But, my dearest Fräulein, my adored Matilda," whispered the Banker, still trembling, "these are very dangerous eccentricities I think, and they may even some day put your own dear and valuable life into danger. I shudder at the very thought. Why don't they lock up a man so dangerous as he is? I pray you, my dear father-in law and Hofrath, please tell me and quiet my fears; I hope this dangerous man will not be apt to return here very shortly?"

"Certainly not," replied Matilda, with a smiling countenance, "I believe that you may make yourself perfectly easy on that point, for I do not think that he will ever come back."

The fears of the Banker were at last, and with no little difficulty quieted, and he took his leave, with the remark, that his time did not permit him to remain any longer, as he must yet do a great piece of embroidery on the bridal veil, which his most adored Matilda should receive on her bridal morning from his own ingenious hand. He pledged himself to make it one of the most elaborate pieces of embroidery and lace work, ever produced by the hand of man.

Matilda looked after the silly, imbecile dotard with a look of triumph, whilst she said to herself:

"Just wait, and let me once have you for a husband. I will soon teach you to embroider."

CHAPTER LXXXVI.

CHARACTER OF A GRISETTE.

FOR many days afterwards the young wife of Herr von Steinfort could not free her mind from the remembrance of her unfortunate friend Marianne. She continually saw the pale, tearful picture of the poor girl floating before her, and was constantly occupied with plans of changing her destiny.

At last she believed that she had found a way; she certainly by adopting this, would have to deceive her husband for a moment, yet she believed that her noble object would be sufficient to justify her in his eyes, if afterwards she confessed all openly to him.

Quickly she repaired to her friend, whom she found alone and absorbed in sad thoughts, in her room.

We already know the circumstance, which at the supper, "under den Linden," had excited all the better feelings and emotions of Marianne anew. The thought of having become a piece of merchandize or a mere animal, destined only to satisfy the base desires of any or every voluptuary—that thought gnawed bitterly upon her soul.

It was already horrible enough to have fallen the victim of one, without love, without affection; to have fallen thus merely through fraud, through deceit and villany, through the terrible force of circumstances; but it was almost beyond belief, it was sufficient to madden her, to have thus become *common* property in every sense of the word. Despairingly the wretch wrung her hands, clinging still more desperately to the last, the only hope of escape that remained to her— suicide.

Augusta covered her with caresses and kindness, despite the cold and reserved reception with which Marianne at first endeavoured to repel her affection.

"Do not repulse me, dearest Marianne," she said kindly, and in a supplicating tone, "I can guess every thing. You can only gradually become acquainted with all the horrors, the terrors of your present unfortunate position, and believe me, the longer you remain in it, the more your eyes will be opened to all its manifold terrors. Therefore I will and must save you. To-morrow you must no longer reside in this house of sin and shame. You shall find an asylum in my house, since I have been fortunate enough to find you, even against your will."

Marianne disbelievingly shook her head.

"I will just inform you how I intend to arrange it all," continued Augusta, urgently and kindly. "You shall receive no benefits at my hands, as I well know the noble pride, with which before now, you have refused them. I will, however, give you opportunities, of working and earning all that which I intend to give you. I will employ you, and you must accept remuneration. I am very young and inexperienced in all housekeeping affairs, and absolutely need support and assistance, if I would not fall a sacrifice to the swindling and cheating of my people. In your former position, you have gathered a store of knowledge and experience, which might be of the utmost use to me. Consequently, all I desire is, that you come to my house to-morrow, as if in search of a situation, and I will give you one."

Marianne seemed to gather a little more confidence on hearing this proposition, although it was the curse of vice which also almost deprived her of the courage for virtue. After having silently considered the *pros* and *cons* for a long while, she at last inquired:

"But will your husband be perfectly satisfied with this, if he should be informed of my former history and of my present fate."

"Why, my dear," replied Augusta hesitatingly, "for the present it is not necessary that he should know anything about it, and by and by I shall find an opportunity of informing him in a gentle and quiet manner of every thing."

"No," answered Marianne firmly, "then you will please excuse me, if I do not accept of your kind offer. That would be a deception, and no deception shall through my fault obscure the bright horizon of your well merited connubial happiness.—Leave me to my fate," she added with a deep sigh, "no hope is left for such as I."

In vain Augusta tried every means to change the resolution of her friend.

"Do not call me obstinate or ungrateful, "continued the poor girl; "God in heaven knows that there is no person in this world, whom I would rather thank for happiness than you. But would you have, that if matters should come to the worst, the reproach of having destroyed the matrimonial happiness of a dear friend, should rest upon my conscience? And at the best, would not the thought of having practised falsehood and deception towards an excellent and noble man, be constantly oppressive to you and me?"

Ashamed and abashed, Augusta had to acknowledge that her unfortunate friend was in the right. She could not help admiring the noble grandeur of the despairing girl, who would reject a saving hand, because its acceptance seemed not in accordance with her views of truth and justice. But the more she admired this, the greater became the interest she felt for her, and the more firm became her determination to assist her under any circumstances.

This resolution was only the more strongly confirmed, when, in the course of conversation, Augusta learned by what immense, unheard-of and terrible villany and fraud, the poor girl had been hurled down, from the proud consciousness of innocence and purity, among the lowest, the most depraved of her sex.

It certainly may occur very rarely, that we find so much unmerited misery and at the same time so much honest and uncorrupted virtue in the same heart, as we find here with Marianne. Yet these cases are more frequent and more elevated and strongly marked, than pharisaean haughtiness and self-sufficiency is willing to admit.

It is one of the greatest falsehoods of our deceitful, and so called refined culture, to consider those fallen and despised children of society invariably as irretrievably lost creatures; not rarely their minds are the domicile of strength in virtue, of morality, and of resignation, which are, as it were, only veiled in vice, and which, upon the removal of that veil, appear with surprising purity and primeval strength before the eyes of the observer.

That principle only is as false as it is prevalent in our age, which teaches us to believe that ascetic mortifications, and hypocritical eye-worship can destroy that veil of vice, which often covers purity of heart.

A humane and kind word, kindly and humanely spoken to the heart,—that only is the secret of salvation, as it has been taught to us by reason, and as it has been revealed to us, in the holy books of the old, and of the new testament.

Augusta left the Grisette, more than ever impressed with the true worth of her heart.

CHAPTER LXXXVII.

FAMILY LIFE.

In the intensity of his excitement, the Major had forgotten the promise which he had given to the Prince, namely that he would not endeavour to have an interview with his son.

Without a moment's delay or consideration he hurried to his son's former residence, thence to his present house, which had been indicated to him.

This change of residence of the Lieutenant, of which the Major had not heard before, was only another confirmation of the terrible truth of that which had been told to him, but which he still was inclined to doubt.

High and wildly beat the heart of the old warrior, as with flashing eyes and furious appearance he rushed through the streets of the city, and was only here and there detained by rushing against or coming in contact with a peaceful citizen.

He never stopped to look round or even apologize for running over persons, until he had reached the ominous house.

The young couple sat side by side in affectionate confidence upon the sofa.

This very morning the first cloud had slightly overspread the springlike horizon of their wedded love, and now more brilliantly and brightly than ever, the sun shone down upon their mutual happiness.

Augusta had, through the intensity of sympathy which she felt for Marianne, been urged, as no other way or means seemed to remain to her, once more to speak to her husband, and to request him to take Marianne to the house. She had moreover added, that she had accidentally learned, that Marianne lived in the utmost distress and poverty, and that she was actually exposed to starvation. As Steinfort—which Augusta was not aware of—had through Birkheim been informed of the entire position of Marianne, he inquired rather more particularly into minor circumstances, than he would otherwise have done, and he soon elicited from his wife the confession, that she had herself been to visit her friend, and was fully acquainted with all her circumstances and mode of life.

Enraged at these attempts of his wife to deceive him, though for a noble object, he had reproached her with the injustice of such a course in very severe terms, and had even threatened her with the loss of his love.

Augusta quickly comprehended the full extent of her fault, but at the same time openly confessed, that Marianne had already told her of the same wrong, and had firmly refused to enter into the plan which she had proposed to her, and which only could succeed by a deception practised upon the Lieutenant.

This noble-mindedness of the Grisette gave Steinfort no small cause for admiration, and he appreciated it equally well as he appreciated the open unrestrained candour of his wife. Moreover in his inmost heart, he approved of a sympathy and a kindness, which were sure tokens of Augusta's innate goodness of heart. Finally he said to himself, that his wife might believe in the end, that he was ashamed of her also, if he refused to extend his aid, to serve an unfortunate wretch, who found herself in a similar situation to that in which he had himself first found his wife, and whose circumstances, as Augusta well knew, he was now fully acquainted with.

These considerations, which could not but reflect honour and credit upon the character of Herr von Steinfort, had determined him to act contrary to the propositions of the Referendarius, and to permit his wife to introduce Marianne to his house. Augusta had that very forenoon availed herself of that permission, and had hurried to the lodgings of her friend, to be herself the bearer of Steinfort's invitation.

Gladly Marianne had now consented, and amidst flowing tears of gratitude she had promised, even that very day to remove to the house of the Lieutenant.

Augusta had just described to her husband the scene of their meeting, and was indefatigable in her accurate relation of the most trifling, minor particulars of this interesting meeting.

Smilingly the Lieutenant listened to this animated narrative, for he felt and sympathized with the purity of two naturally noble minds, as it appeared before him in two *fallen* maidens. He rejoiced at having overleaped the barriers, freed himself from the trammels of society.

"Oh my dear Carl," said his affectionate wife with sparkling eyes, "You cannot conceive how happy I feel, at the thought of being now enabled to do some good and to assist my unfortunate fellow creatures. For this pleasure, I must thank you alone! Oh that it were in my power to reward you with all the love and affection of my poor heart."

"And so you can, my dearest little wife," replied the Lieutenant returning the caresses of his wife with equal ardour and warmth. "Henceforth we will live far away from this wicked world and its pride. Are we not enough for each other?"

"Certainly, my Carl," answered Augusta, "we are, and I thank Heaven, that you have taken such a resolution. I only obeyed your decided request on the morning after our wedding, when, being a new married couple, you proposed that we should pay the customary visits to families with whom you were acquainted. You have seen how coldly and superciliously those people received us, and how unfriendly and impolitely they dismissed us. All these mortifications and annoyances I have felt with you and felt them thousand fold, and would gladly have avoided them, but you would not permit me."

"Yes, yes, you were in the right," rejoined Steinfort, with a suppressed sigh. "I see it will not do. The world will not be taught, will not be reformed by a single voice. But let that be; I have had to pay for my apprenticeship, and know what I have learned."

"But then you must not appear sad in consequence, my dear Carl," said Augusta, in a coaxing tone, "else it will ever appear as a silent reproach to me."

"No, no, dearest," answered her husband, "I would not for worlds reproach thee. Let us change the subject; let us speak of more pleasant things, of our plans for the future, which seem to look bright and flattering."

"Oh dear yes, I should think so," cried Augusta, clapping her hands with joy.

"Next month, I think, the season will be far enough advanced to start upon our journey to Italy. That will help us to pass the time pleasantly enough. Through the winter we will remain in Paris, and there we can have time to consider upon our further movements."

"Oh, Italy must be such a delightful country," said Augusta. "Tell me, dearest Carl, is it true, what people tell me, that oranges, pineapples and lemons there grow by the road-side, even as apples and pears grow here?"

"Certainly!" replied the Lieutenant, smiling at the naivete of the question, "and those beautiful Italian ladies, of whom you here only see a very few indifferent copies at the *Königstadt* Theatre, they all run at large there in the streets."

"Oh Carl, now you are making fun of me," said the little wife pouting, with an inimitably charming grace, "and it is *right wrong* of you, since I am very ready and willing to learn."

"Right wrong?"* repeated Steinfort, laughing and amused, as he felt himself momentarily growing more happy in the possession of so charming a little wife, and became extravagant and wild in his humour. "Right wrong! Charming! Where did you learn this right wrong mode of speech?"

"Oh Carl, I declare I shall not speak to you any more."

"Don't be angry, little woman."

"But you won't plague me any more?"

"Certainly not."

"Then you may have a kiss."

Full of warmest affection, the Lieutenant embraced his wife.

"Now listen, Carl, to what I was about to tell you this morning," continued Augusta after a pause, as she seated herself upon her husband's knees, and put her arm around his neck— "—ah, this morning?—Carl, are you quite sure that you have forgiven me every thing, and that you think no more of my attempt at deception and falsehood? You shall see that it will never occur again."

"I think no longer about it, my dear wife, so let the matter rest.

"Oh you good, dear kind soul.—But then, what I was about to say; before we start upon our journey we must first see your father? You see, I have not even thanked him yet for having accepted me as his daughter-in-law, and certainly he has done it most kindly, and without ever having even seen me. But you know perfectly well that I cannot get along with letter-writing. Let us therefore go and visit him very shortly. I should be so delighted to become personally acquainted with the dear, good old man, and I should so like to thank him from the bottom of my heart for the son which he has given to me."

"For the present, as you know he is absent from home," said the Lieutenant in a suppressed tone of voice.

"But as soon as he returns home we shall

---

* It is impossible to convey the ludicrous mistake of the wording of this sentence into English. TRANSLATOR.

visit him, not so, my dear Carl ? I am most curious to know whether he looks as I imagine him."

"And how do you fancy that he looks?" inquired Steinfort, abstractedly.

"Well I fancy a large figure, as large as yourself, but broader across the chest, and more corpulent in body. His features are browned, full of wrinkles, but mild and venerable. Thick white hair covers his head, and a grey warrior-like moustache covers his upper lip. Beneath two heavy, bushy eyebrows, shine a pair of large, but lively and fiery eyes. He walks straight and proudly in a soldier-like, but rather stiff manner, and——"

"Good Heaven, here he is himself !"

CHAPTER LXXXVIII.

A TERRIBLE CHANGE.

NOISILY the door was torn open.

Pushing the servant who had preceded him ruthlessly aside, the Major suddenly entered the room.

A terrible silence followed his entrance.

With wildly staring eyes, the old nobleman looked alternately at his son, and at his son's wife.

Despite of all signs and indications he might still have entertained some silent doubts of the truth of what had been communicated to him. He could not believe it to be true; could not believe that such an outrage should have been committed by his only, his dearly loved son. All his paternal feelings revolted against such a belief.

Now he discovered them both in a moment of the most tender, affectionate happiness. She, the wanton, was seated upon the knees of his son. All his paternal affection and anxiety revolted in his breast. His own senses fully convinced him, and incontrovertibly attested the terrible truth.

The words died away upon his lips.

The Lieutenant also was mute.

At the first moment he indulged in a sweet deceptive hope, that his father had come in consequence of a communication received from Birkheim, and that he had come to proclaim his pardon to his son. In this delusive hope, he had risen at the first entrance of his parent, and had hurried to meet him. Half way across the room, however, he stopped hesitating and frightened, for the serious, wild features of the Major soon told him, that other emotions than those of pardon and forgiveness excited the breast of the old soldier.

His hesitation had a magnetic influence upon Augusta, to whom the whole scene appeared a mysterious riddle, and who seemed chained to the seat she occupied.

The son was the first to recover his presence of mind.

With the exclamation of, "My father, my dearest father!" he cast himself upon the neck of the old Major.

When Augusta perceived this, she rose, and hurried towards him to be included in the embrace.

Then Major von Steinfort awoke in all his fury.

The contact with this dishonoured creature, who, according to his mode of thinking, had lured his son into her nets, and had induced him to tear all the bonds of nature by a fearful, terrible and outrageous deed, all this excited him to an unnatural, a frightful degree of fury.

With raving, frantic impetuosity he tore himself from the embrace of his son. Then he grasped the woman's arm, and with the terrible words, "do not dare to touch me, dishonest, wretched wanton, on whom I bestow my curse instead of my blessing," he hurled her far from him, across the entire length of the room.

Augusta struck her head against the sharp corner of a piece of furniture, and sank backwards to the ground. A large stream of blood rushed over her forehead; her senses forsook her.

When the Lieutenant observed this occurrence, which had taken place with the speed of lightning, so quick indeed, that he could not prevent it, he suddenly felt every bond broken, which had hitherto bound him to his father. Poisonous claws seemed to tear his heart; he felt as if he had no longer a father in this world.

He rushed towards his wife, raised her from the ground, and in vain, amidst tears, words and kisses endeavoured to restore her to life.

The Major again stood motionless and abstracted at the door, even as he had stood there before.

After a few moments Augusta opened her eyes Her first look fell upon the Major.

Terribly frightened she shrunk back, and cried in a fearful tone :

"For Heaven's sake, Carl, protect me, for he will murder me."

And again her senses forsook her.

The Lieutenant shook and trembled in every limb, and a cold perspiration trickled down his forehead.

With a quiet of despair he placed the fainting woman upon a sofa, then turned to his father and said in a terrible tone of determination :

"Herr Major von Steinfort, henceforth you no longer have a son. You yourself have, of your own accord, torn the ties which have hitherto bound us to each other. My wife alone still remains to me. You see how the sight of you affects her, and I must request you to leave my house."

Without replying a syllable, the Major turned and left the room.

Amidst the most anxious fear, Steinfort busied himself with the restoration of his wife from her death-like swoon.

He carried her to a bed, and endeavoured to wipe away the blood from her forehead, but still it only streamed the more from the open gash of the wound. A high fever shook all her limbs, and she began to speak confusedly. Her pulse beat very weak and low.

At that moment, like a saving angel, Marianne appeared at the door.

Without entering into further explanation, he said to her very briefly :

"Watch over my unfortunate wife, until I return with a surgeon, and do not leave her for an instant."

He hurried from the room.

Marianne astonished and frightened to death, seated herself silently by the side of her pale and bleeding friend, and looked in the most anxious expectation for the speedy return of the Lieutenant, and the solution of the riddle.

CHAPTER LXXXIX.

HOW JOBS AND A FEW OTHERS COME TO AN END.

In the dark room of his cellar sat Jobs, the hunchbacked host of all the Berlinian thieves, absorbed in deep thought.

For a long time past, none of his former guests or associates had showed themselves about his premises. The cellar was lonely and deserted.

"I cannot comprehend," he said to himself, "what can possibly be the matter, that none of these scoundrels show their faces here. It seems as if I was no longer in existence. Hm! What can it be? Perhaps the rascals have found better quarters, and now the thieves are ungrateful enough to desert me. What immoral, worthless villains they are, without any faith or honour!—If they only had paid their debts to me! But not one of them thought of such a thing—no, not they! There is that dashing, elegant rascal, the Eel-eye—he still owes me a matter of ten Thalers. I certainly might be satisfied with five, and even then I would have quadruple payment, but, confound him, I don't see even one."

Very ill-humouredly, he raised his little greasy cap and scratched his bald head for some time.

"Thunder and the devil! They certainly cannot all together have gone *verschütt?*" he suddenly continued his soliloquy, as he shrunk together and trembled with fright at his own words. "A pretty piece of business that would be. But no, no, that is impossible, else I certainly would have heard of it before this."

Whilst Jobs was absorbed in these and similar thoughts, he suddenly heard the door bell of his cellar rattling, and foot-steps entering.

Under the influence of his present fearful state of mind, this noise frightened him not a little, and shaking in every nerve he started up. Tremblingly he entered his front shop, but was soon collected again, when the grinning haggard countenance of the rag-gatherer met his view.

Every one of her movements seemed to indicate fear and great mental excitement.

"Thank Heaven Jobs, that you are still here," she began, "I had very little hope of finding you left behind."

"Why, where should I be?" inquired the hunchback with great apparent astonishment, while fear and anxiety were only too plainly visible on his features.

"Where should you be? What a question! Why in the *Twise*, (prison) my good old Jobs," continued the old woman with a grin.

Jobs stared at her with a look of stupefaction.

"Oho! then you are not yet acquainted with your fortune? Well then, I will tell you what you may have to expect; but first give me a glass of Danzic Gold-water, else I cannot speak a word."

Speedily Jobs complied with the old woman's wish.

"Well then, now listen. Maulspitzer, you know, has *gone verschütt*, (been caught) has made a great *Emmes* (general confession) and has *slichnet* upon us all (betrayed us all.) This we knew all along, and for this reason no one came near your place. Three days ago, however, the police at one and the same time came to the *broken Schmortopf*, the *golden Mops* and to the *Diana-saloon*, and made the whole *Chawrusse verschütt* (arrested the whole company.) The stiff Gottlieb, blonde Augustus, lame Joseph, the Syrups-nose, the Crow-foot, the Match-Mary, the Slop-Lisa, the Kellerjette,—yes, yes, and even my own flesh and blood, the poor Chonte, all, all are in prison. Only myself, and one or two others are yet at large. To-day or to-morrow at furthest, they will come here to take you away. Two of the arrested parties have already whistled on you ; (betrayed you) I believe it was Kellerjette and Crow-foot."

The serious and anxious face of the Hunchback elongated perceptibly and became as pale as the whitewashed walls.

"Oh what a poor, unfortunate man I am," he cried, wringing his hands, "I certainly shall be able to prove my innocence and honesty, but most probably they will take the word of these thieves before mine, and not believe me after all. And then my hard earned savings of many a year, all that I have honestly gathered, what will become of it? They will take it and I shall be ruined, I shall be lost!"

"Don't bawl and cry like an infernal ass," exclaimed the old woman angrily, "You see that my intentions towards you are honest, otherwise I would not have come here, and ran the risk of going verschütt with you. Only put everything of *treife Sore* (stolen property) which you have here into a *good Kabore* (safe hiding place ;) I will assist you. If they don't make you *treife verschütt*, (find you in the possession of stolen goods) you can still putz you (plead yourself) out of it, and they can give you no *Knas* (punishment.)

Jobs quickly perceived the truth and practicability of this proposition.

"But where am I to lay this Kabore?" he inquired hesitatingly ; "the Maulspitzer must

[Unmutilated and Only Genuine Edition.]

THIERS' LIFE OF NAPOLEON,

WITH SUPERB STEEL ENGRAVINGS,

FOR SEVENTY-FIVE CENTS,

[If paid in Advance.]

W. H. COLYER having been at great expense to procure a copy of this unrivalled work, now publishes

PART I.

OF THE

HISTORY OF THE CONSULATE AND THE EMPIRE

OF

FRANCE UNDER NAPOLEON,

By M. A. THIERS,

LATE PRIME MINISTER OF FRANCE

WM. H. COLYER's edition of this splendid work, The Life of Napoleon, is decidedly the best in this country. It is printed on fine paper and new type, according to the design of the author, M. A. Thiers, and on comparison with other editions will be found far superior.

In Press.

THIERS' FRENCH REVOLUTION,

TO BE COMPLETED IN SIX PARTS, AT 12 1-2 CENTS EACH.

TO BE COMPLETED IN TEN NUMBERS.

THE MYSTERIES OF BERLIN,

FROM

THE PAPERS OF A BERLIN CRIMINAL OFFICER,

TRANSLATED FROM THE GERMAN

By C. B. BURKHARDT.

With Illustrations on Steel, by P. Habelmann.

This work in Europe has been universally pronounced far superior to M. Sue's celebrated "Mysteries of Paris," and we confidently predict that the popularity of this translation will be without a parallel in the history of light reading.

THE MYSTERIES of BERLIN.

TO BE COMPLETED

IN

TEN PARTS.

NEW YORK: WILLIAM H. COLYER, PUBLISHER.

certainly have *slichnct* the whole of our secret retreat here. But stop, now I remember a place, which is very good for the purpose."

Jobs thoughtfully put his finger to his nose.

"Yes, yes, that will do. Very well, now you better hurry and get away from this place; the *Lambden* (Police officer) might come and find you here."

"No, no," replied the rag-gatherer saucily, "I will remain here, and help you to put the things to Kabore. You old rascal perhaps you are again disinclined to confide in me? is this the reward for my care in cautioning you? Lookye, now you must trust me, and I will know where you put the Kabore. I shall not go away from here."

Jobs was thus placed between two fires.

The police might at any moment come upon him, and take him unprepared and by surprise, for that the story of the rag-gatherer was fully correct, or at least had a very good foundation, he knew from different other minor signs and indications, all of which now appeared suddenly clear and explained before his eyes. But nevertheless and for very good reasons, which our readers will easily comprehend, he would not let the rag-gatherer know the exact place of his Kabore.

"Now hurry and bustle about, you lazy old camel," recommenced the rag-gatherer. "But another thing, whilst I think of it; I know now, where Marianne is to be found, and if you hesitate much longer in this present business, I shall go to her, and reveal to her the whole secret of her history, whilst you may lay and rot in the *Twise.*"

In this instance, the rag-gatherer told a falsehood, for all her endeavours to find Marianne had hitherto been fruitless; but the old woman's hint induced Jobs to yield the point to her. Moreover, the police at the present moment was a much more dangerous enemy to him, than the greedy, avaricious hand of his accomplice.

He therefore entered the back room with her, and there, from every nook and corner of the den, gathered the most varied and manifold articles. Watches, clocks, spoons, articles of dress, dry goods, melted gold and silver, and a thousand other articles of various kinds, which during the course of his house keeping he had obtained by fair or foul means from the thieves who were his guests. Every thing was carefully put away into a large sack.

Now he suddenly stopped an instant as if considering about something. Then he approached a small closet in the wall, unlocked it leisurely, and thence took a paper which he carefully and hesitatingly examined.

It was the document which had been drawn by Marianne's father.

With the eyes of a hawk, the rag-gatherer who had been standing behind Jobs, had followed every one of his movements. Finding that no other hiding place remained for him, he was just upon the point of putting this important paper

into the sack, when like a tigress she rushed upon him.

Availing herself of his stooping position, she caught his coat collar with her hook, and with a powerful pull, hurled him to the floor. Before the other, who was absolutely stunned by the suddenness of this attack, could gain time to recover from his surprise, the paper had been torn from his hand, and the quick and active old woman had fled with it from the room, and out of the cellar.

Furiously Jobs rose from the floor, and started in pursuit of the robber of his long cherished treasure.

As he had reached the top of the stairs which lead down to his cellar, he just caught a glimpse of the rag-gatherer's dress as she disappeared around the next corner.

But at this very moment, the much feared Police-officers, who had approached from the other side, stood also before him.

They found and arrested him, with all his stolen goods, which seemed all to have been arranged and prepared for their reception, and delivered him to the proper authorities.

A short time afterwards, the authorities awarded the proper punishment according to law, to him and all his associates.

Dozens and dozens of sentences were passed upon this gang, and the prisons and penitentiaries received an immense number of new recruits. For months nothing was spoken of, but the great number of criminal examinations.

Maulspitzer was executed.

CHAPTER XC.

A SCENE AT AN HOTEL.

A GREAT concourse of richly liveried servants was seen standing about noon before the door of the *Hôtel de Páris*, seemingly engaged at nothing more important than having the warm spring sun shine upon them.

Most of them joined to this occupation, that of smoking cigars and conversing about the newest political and city occurrences.

Every Berlinian is acquainted with such little scenes.

Nothing can compare with the dignity of these gentlemen of the whip and brush, as they thus stand in a circle around the *portiers*. The past and the future is penetrated by their acute wits, whilst they still recur with mysterious and knowing miens to the *chronique scandaleuse* of the different guests then lodging at the Hotel.

Absorbed in thought and without participating in the general amusement, the new Yaeger of Prince Prominsky stood at a little distance from the crowd, not without, however, escaping the mocking and scornful observations of his colleagues.

"He seems to be a fine gentleman," observed

the head waiter, "who does not wish to hold communion with us, yet I'll lay a wager that the Prince picked him up somewhere in the street."

"Nothing is more likely," confirmed the hair-dresser of the hotel. "Only look at the fellow's head. Before his departure, the Prince had not such a fright in his retinue."

A little impudent jockey approached the object of these criticisms, and exclaimed:

"He, Herr Body-yaeger! Will you gracious-ly condescend to communicate to us, what great state secrets you are meditating upon? We should like to profit somewhat by your great wisdom."

The other by this address seemed suddenly aroused from his dreams, looked scornfully upon the boyish face of the jockey, and replied:

"No state secret, my boy, yet a mystery to all the world. In vain I was endeavouring to guess the object of the Almighty, in sending you into this world."

By this repartee, the yaeger gained the laugh-ers over to his side, and the jockey now became the target at which their jokes were aimed. But the other again left the group, and once more became absorbed in his reveries.

After a pause the scene underwent another change.

An old woman clad in rags, carrying a basket and a hook, stopped before the door of the hotel to explore the mud of the gutter. To the loung-ing crowd, this was a most welcome excuse to give another direction to the current of their wit, and her appearance gave a new impulse to their conversation. It was evident that it gave more than ordinary pleasure to the mocking rascals, to make the unhappy woman and her miserable occupation, the object of their jokes and witti-cisms.

"How many Louisd'ors have you found to-day already, old she-dragon?" asked the *portier* who stood nearest to her.

"I suppose you don't need a Government-licence for your business?" continued the butler.

"Is there much competition?" observed the above mentioned little jockey.

"Why certainly," answered the hair-dresser, who was generally considered a great wit, "much is done here in rags."

"Ha, ha, ha!" laughed the whole chorus, "the old hag makes fortunes in rags."

The object of their witticisms, however, did not remain much in their debt for answers.

"Hark'ye, Mister *portier*," she said, "if you have Louisd'ors to throw away, I am sure to find them. Only let me see you throw them away, sir. Yes, yes, they are not so easy to throw away."

"Well come, old hag," cried the butler, "I will throw away a louisd'or, let us see whether you will find it."

The speaker was extravagant enough after these words to throw some copper coin into the mud, which to the universal and general amuse-ment of the company, the old woman picked out with her hands.

In doing this, however, she several times cast strange glances at the yaeger, who was calmly and unconcernedly standing aside.

She slightly and doubtingly shook her head, as if something extraordinary and incredible had entered her mind. At last she seemed to have come to a positive conclusion of her uncertainty and suspicion or at least seemed resolved quickly to make sure of something.

She raised herself, walked up to the silent man, and bowing low asked him for an alms.

"Please to give me also some charity, my handsome sir, and I will pray that you may soon obtain your love," she said with a sharp intonation.

The yaeger turned pale when he saw the old woman standing before him, but soon he recover-ed himself, put his hand into his pocket and gave her some coin.

The old woman thankfully accepted it, and on going away, whispered to the giver: "Your false beard is very becoming to you, Eel-eye; the rag-gatherer will not betray you; but to-night, at midnight, I shall expect you in *Müller-street*, at the corner of the Schnapps laden."

And at these words the old woman withdrew.

It really was the rag-gatherer, who despite of his present disguise, had easily recognised her former companion.

Eel-eye was disagreeably affected by this inter-view, for gloomily he looked after her as she hurried along the street.

At the desire of Francisca the Prince had taken him into his service, to secure him against the prosecutions of the police. Eel-eye's services at the present time were naturally of very great importance to him, as through him alone, he could hope for the fulfilment of his most ardent wish, namely, that of obtaining possession of the person of his brother, without further danger and eclat. And above all, the thief had really come to the firm resolution of abandoning his dis-honest, miserable course of life, and by honesty and industry to atone in some measure for his crimes against society, which had been caused originally rather by levity and frivolousness, than by any real malicious disposition. Like many others, he had only lacked a saving hand to draw him out of the abyss. This hand had now presented itself, and he would not repel it.

Eel-eye made a really fine appearance in the livery of the Prince, and he had very little fear that he should be recognised by any one, as his former companions had nearly all been arrested; in regard to the police he certainly seemed to be safe from every discovery, partly through his situation in the Prince's retinue, and partly through his external change, wherein especially the false beard added no little to his disguise.

His position and his future prospect especially, had occupied his mind in his late thoughtful mood in front of the hotel, and had kept him from the noisy crowd of his colleagues, to join whose company prudence and self-preservation would otherwise have induced him.

He thought of Francisca, whom he now loved only the more ardently, as it had been she, who opened to him a prospect of becoming reconciled with the past. He thought upon plans by which he might perhaps soon succeed in accomplishing the wishes of the Prince, and in such a manner as would ensure to him certain claims upon his thankfulness.

Then he would be certain of finding a position in society, which in some way would suit his inclinations and his abilities, and certainly a good school education which he had received and not neglected, seemed to justify such expectations. Yes, his wishes and hopes even rose so high, that under these suppositions, he did not consider it an impossibility, that Francisca might still become his own. She had certainly not returned to him any mark of inclination, but there seems nothing impossible to a loving heart, strong with hope, especially when that heart and mind is strengthened by youthful courage and youthful freshness.

From these peaceful and pleasant dreams, the disgusting face of a former companion of his crimes must certainly have roused Eel-eye in a most disagreeable manner. But on more mature and closer consideration, he found that even this circumstance might become available to his purpose, if he only had luck and ingenuity sufficient to use it.

"How often have I known and had to learn, how to struggle with and conquer the greatest obstacles," said Eel-eye to himself, "when it was only for the attainment of dishonest, thievish purposes; should my strength and energy fail me now, when my object is to enter among honest and peaceful citizens of the country and to procure for myself a quiet and peaceful future."

CHAPTER XCI.

AN EXTRAORDINARY STORY.

THE carriage of Prince Prominsky driving quickly up to the hotel, dispersed the servants and reminded the dreaming Eel-eye of his duty.

He hastily stepped up to it and opened the door of the carriage. Major von Steinfort leaped out, and without pausing, hurried up to the apartments of the Prince.

This latter had been eagerly expecting him for some hours.

The Major was in the greatest excitement. Impetuously and wildly, he rushed into the room, and exhausted, threw himself upon the sofa. It was a long time before he recovered himself so far, as to be able to begin a reasonable and connected conversation.

Finally he exclaimed, "I am a lost man! all combines against me! It is not enough that my son has heaped eternal shame upon my gray head, I must even bear it without the power of resistance."

Overcome by the intensity of his excitement, he stopped, while the Prince compassionately approached him, and in silence seemed to wait for further explanation.

After a short pause, the Major again exclaimed in the most heart-rending tones: "Oh, that lawyer unfortunately is too entirely in the right! I must be silent, if I would not wish to place my own name on the pillory, to brand my own family, and to deliver my own child into the hands of justice."

"Collect yourself, my dear friend," said the Prince, consolingly, taking the hand of the aggrieved father, "and communicate minutely the cause of your grief to me. What has happened to you? I should almost think, that after what you had met with already, nothing more terrible could fall upon you."

"So I thought myself," said the Major, interrupting the Prince, and sadly nodding his assent to this assertion, "still there is yet greater sorrow in store for me."

"Speak then, I pray you speak. I will help, advise, assist, or at least carry an equal burden of your pain with you. I am in a position very much like your own; I fully understand what must be your feelings at the behaviour of your son."

The Major pressed both his hands to his head and stared before him, as if he was gathering thoughts for his communication.

"My head sometimes becomes perfectly benumbed and heavy," he said, "you must have compassion with an old man.—The lawyer S—, the same whose advice in the matter I sought on the very day after the occurrence of the affair, has just made communications to me, from which I learn that it is impossible to declare the marriage of my son void, although it has been contracted without my paternal consent. My hair rises on my head, when I remember what I was obliged to hear. Listen then.

"This marriage has been closed in conformity to a legal consent, which it is said, had been given by me before a public notary! When at this communication I started up, and declared the whole affair to be a most villanous piece of knavery, the lawyer with terrible and calm quietness explained to me, that under such circumstances he must decidedly advise me, to abstain from all legal proceedings. According to the appearance of the documents, my son himself was connected with the vagabonds in the committal of the forgery; if a suit for separation were commenced, the authorities must become acquainted with the fact, must *ex officio* commence a criminal proceeding against him, and finish by sentencing him to prison. Do you see, your Highness, this it is, that I had not expected to hear. A cheat, a knave, a swindler and a forger—is my son."

The Major was silent, whilst two large tears trickled down his brown and wrinkled cheeks, giving the heart-rending sight of a weeping old man.

"The lawyer is right," he continued, after a moment of peaceful thoughtfulness, "I must abstain from all legal proceedings, I must even conceal the wound of my heart from the world, that this fraud and forgery may not become known, and the last of the Steinforts bend beneath the lash of a prison beadle. And yet, how shall I bear it, to be compelled to recognise a villain as my son, ay, and to see this son married to a disreputable, dishonest wench! What will people think of me, if they believe that I had really given my consent to such a union? The only hope to save my honour, is lost, is gone! Whichever way I look, I see nothing but shame, disgrace and scorn. O Lord, Thou punishest me severely through my only child!"

Despairingly the Major wrung his hands, while the Prince stared gloomily and in silence before him.

"I must believe that in this fate, a higher Nemesis exercises her revenge," commenced the Major anew, "at least this is the only manner, although it is without consolation to me, in which, during these bitter sorrows, I can support within my own mind the belief in divine justice. If this blow had fallen upon me wholly unmerited or innocent, then I should believe that hellish demons, not divine love and providence ruled the world."

During this sad and gloomily mysterious speech, the Prince looked with inquiring glances at the speaker.

"You do not understand me," said the Major, who might have observed these glances, "for I allude to an event of my life which I wished to have forever buried within my breast, and which, without exception, I have never mentioned to living being. But the sorrow of this hour brings back from oblivion long vanished figures before my mind's eye, and the communication of these circumstances, will perhaps relieve my oppressed heart. Let me speak, I know that I can confide in you."

Silently the Prince pressed the Major's hand.

"It is now many years ago," commenced the latter, "when I also was a young man, when my fiery blood rolled wildly through my veins, and when I was fond of disregarding that which I considered prejudice and pride of ancestry, particularly if it opposed any of my momentary inclinations and wishes. My father died early. I undertook the management on my dominions, and became my own master, at least as far as I was not impeded in the exercise of my will by my harsh and domineering mother.

"There was a house-keeper on our domain, a fresh, gay, obliging creature, who soon made a deep impression upon me. I became enamoured of this girl with the whole passion of my age, and young and good looking as I was, my attentions were not destined to be long disregarded by her. Our connexion daily became closer and more intimate, and finally it bore its consequences. I

will not attempt to describe the anger and fury of my mother; only with great difficulty I succeeded in saving the unfortunate girl from personal injury and maltreatment, and secretly to bring her to a place of security, there to await her accouchement. She gave birth to a daughter, who at baptism received the name of Caroline.

"It made a deep and lasting impression upon me, when I held the new-born child in my arms; the innocent babe, who in its own helpless condition, together with its equally helpless mother, looked for support only to me. I took great care that both should never be in want of any thing, and when, soon afterwards, my mother departed this life, I took them back to the domain, and had lodgings arranged for them at the house of the gardener in the park of my castle. In the beginning my servants seemed to be grumbling about this, and suspecting something, but on the other hand, it may have pleased them that I took so good care of the helpless, and upon the whole I did not care particularly for their opinion.

"I still loved the girl most dearly; what, however, would be the result of this love, I scarcely knew myself, and suffered matters to take their own course.

"I cannot deny that now and then, a thought came to my mind of legitimating my child by actual marriage with its mother, but I was prevented from doing this, partly by a certain respect for the memory of my own mother, who I believe would have turned around in her grave; partly by an inexplicable fear, which afterwards was explained only too well.

"Thus a whole year had passed. Caroline grew up to be a sweet child with blonde locks, and gave me much real joy and pleasure, when suddenly an occurrence took place, which brought with it the most important consequences for the whole of my future life."

The Major jumped up and paced through the room in great agitation, then he resumed his former seat and continued his story.

"One day while undressing me, my servant told me with such a mysterious accentuation, as to be certain to attract my attention, that my yaeger very often, and late in the evening could be seen going into the park, whence he would not return again until towards morning. I answered him that this was in accordance with my positive orders, as I was desirous of catching the person or persons who were constantly in the habit of stealing my wood, and then indifferently broke off the conversation. But I felt not the same indifference within me; the observation had thrown a faggot into my heart, which was burning and raging within me with all the fiery pangs of passion and jealousy. I could only remember the gardener's house and my faithless inamorata.

"Being unable to sleep I rose from my bed at a late hour of the night, quickly dressed myself, armed myself with a hunting-sabre and silently crept through the garden saloon into the park. Unobserved I approached the gardener's house;

there was still a light burning within. I stepped nearer and saw the faithless woman sitting on the sofa in the tender embraces of her lover. In their fancied daring security they had not even thought it necessary to take the precaution of closing the window-shutters.

"Yes, your Highness, years of pain, and sorrow and trouble have since elapsed; I have fought through many a hard battle, I have traversed seas, and yet, even at this moment, I feel again all the pangs, the terrors of that dreadful scene. For an instant my convulsed limbs seemed to refuse their office, I was fixed to the spot by the intensity of my fury; the next instant, however, with frantic madness and a drawn weapon in my hand I rushed through the open house door into the room. As soon as the yaeger saw me, he started with an exclamation of fright, tore open a window, and jumped through it into the park. I followed him in the same way. Running for his life, he rushed through the park, whilst I followed close upon his heels: at the other end he cast himself into a river, swam through it and escaped safely in the wood on the other side, whither I had indefatigably pursued him. This chase saved the life of the faithless girl, for I would have killed both if I could have had them together.

"I returned to my bed chamber, and passed a terrible night. On the next morning I ordered the butler to drive mother and child away from the domain, and both went without even making an attempt to reconcile me. Such an attempt would certainly have been vain, for my fury knew no bounds.

"I had been deceived, betrayed, in the most awful manner! How often had my mother told me, that it would never do good to relinquish the prerogatives of rank, that the vulgar and common was fit only to associate with the vulgar and the common, and that every transgression, every breach through the natural boundaries acknowledged by society, is sure to be punished through itself. I never would believe the words of my mother, and in my very heart I perhaps even smiled at her antiquated opinions, and now I had to learn, and by a most terrible lesson, to comprehend the justice of her maxims. I may well say that from that terrible, fearful night, an entire revolution took place within me. All the means and arguments, which in after times I opposed to the wishes and inclinations of my son, were then instilled in my mind, and they have been daily confirmed, during a long and checkered course of life. I care not much for rank and nobility, but above all I look for virtue, honesty, veracity, respect and obedience to the rules and orders, which nature itself has created in the animal as well as vegetable world, and consequently also among mankind.

"With the same degree of frivolousness and levity, with which the mother of my child once sacrificed herself voluntarily to me, to whom she could never hope justly to belong, with the same frivolousness, the same levity, she afterwards gave herself up to another; such a result I ought to have expected, to have foreseen. That, which I overlooked in a certain degree, my son however has overlooked in a thousand fold stronger degree, for instead of a seemingly pure, and undefiled girl, he dealt with an acknowledged and well known wanton—and with a heavy heart, a soul overburdened with sorrow, I must tell your Highness, that he will reap what he himself has sown by his own treachery. But I am coming to the end.

"The life on my domain became disgusting to me, I wished to seek relief from a troubled soul in a life of danger and activity. Thereupon I joined the military, and as soon as practicable married a young lady of my own rank, the mother of my son. Upon the whole I had lived a happy life with her and I would have been happier still, if not occasionally a recollection of the past had risen within my breast. But if in the beginning these remembrances filled me always with bitterness against a treacherous being, in after years, when my blood had become more cool and calm, I have often been obliged to reproach myself for having entirely withdrawn a helping hand from my child, which, as I believe to this day—for then its mother was yet faithful and pure—is my own flesh and has my own blood in its veins. I never afterwards heard anything of the rejected mother and her child. During the first years when the slightest contact with her or allusion to this point would have been painful to me, this reserve was rather pleasant to me; at a later epoch it filled me with fresh bitterness against the mother of my child, whom I must believe so obdurate, as perhaps even to think herself injured by me, instead of endeavouring to implore my forgiveness; finally her silence began to fill me with anxiety about her fate, the desire to regain my daughter became stronger every day, and then I took many steps to bring her back to me.

"But all has been in vain; personal researches, advertisements to the point in the public papers, which she alone would have understood, all has been of no avail, and one circumstance especially strengthens me in this belief, that mother and daughter have long since left this world, perhaps in need and misery. For at the time when my daughter was born, I endeavoured to sweeten to the mother the sorrow of a solitary sick bed, by securing immediately in certain ways the future destiny of her child I gave her securities for several thousand Thalers, which I promised to pay on the day of the child's marriage, or at the latest, on its twenty second birth day. This document, the mother took away with her, but it has never yet been presented to me. If I even should suppose that the girl has never entered into the matrimonial state, and if I consider that it is yet nearly a whole year, to the end of this term—for she must now be twenty one, being two years older than Carl, who has just closed his nineteenth year—still it is highly probable, that for the sake of the money alone, this communication with me would ere now have been renewed. Consequently as I said before, no other reasonable supposition remains to me, but that mother and child are dead, and supposing such to be the case, in regard to the latter, I can in no way free my mind from the accusation of harshness, cruelty and want of consideration, and in my present hard fate, I find a just and severe punishment for it. Who knows, whether by the side of this forlorn son, I might not in that girl have retained a loving and kind daughter."

The Major closed his narrative in great exhaustion.

"But the document ought certainly to have been sent back to you, by other persons, if your promise had been annulled by the death of the child and the mother," observed the Prince, who had listened very attentively.

"And why so?" answered the Major, "who can know what has become of that paper? It might easily have been lost."

Both were silent, equally oppressed by the weight of their feelings and unable to come to a fixed resolution, or to continue a farther conversation.

CHAPTER XCII.

THE SICK CHAMBER.

DEEP silence reigned during the morning hour in the sick-chamber of the painfully suffering Frau von Steinfort.

Pale as a broken lily, the unfortunate woman lay in holy, resigned suffering upon her couch. Her beautiful eyes were firmly closed.

The occurrence with Major von Steinfort had so cruelly attacked her already excited and weak constitution, that a nervous fever was the next consequence. She had suffered terribly during the last few days and the character of the malady soon had assumed such a change, that the greatest medical men who had been called in, had declared their science insufficient to preserve her life.

Marianne knelt by the bed side of her friend absorbed in deep and ardent prayer for her recovery.

Steinfort had seated himself by the side of his wife. Bent forward, with his left hand beneath the head of the invalid, he seemed eager to anticipate her slightest unexpressed wishes. Deep, heartfelt grief was expressed in all his features.

Augusta seemed to have fallen asleep upon the hand of her husband. The heavings of her breath passed scarcely audible through the quiet chamber.

When she opened her eyes, her glance fell upon the praying Marianne.

"You pray, my dearest Marianne?" she asked in a feeble voice, "but not I hope for my recovery. Let me die quietly. I heartily wish to be called away from this world, where I have only become a burden to all."

She looked at her husband, down whose cheek at these words, gushed an involuntary tear.

"Do not weep my dearest Carl," she continued, "the curse of my existence has also fallen upon you, and only by my death can it be taken from you. You will then certainly be happier. I am satisfied, contented, with the end of my unfortunate existence, grant me at least this satisfaction."

Marianne was silent, for she felt that Augusta spoke a truth, to which nothing could be opposed.

Steinfort, however, felt deeply affected by these mild words of the sufferer.

"No," he cried beside himself, "you must, you shall not die. My life is poor, deserted and lonely as an orphan's without you. Let my father's curse rest upon us, let the whole world reject and despise me, you are to me more than all, you are my world."

Augusta listened with emotions of happiness to the passionate words of her husband, which gave to her the assurance of his undivided love. Then she became more serious and replied:

"No, Carl, it must not be thus. Consider what great wrong against your father, you have been guilty of, have burdened upon your conscience. It does not belong to me, to pronounce judgment upon it, for you did so from pure love to me: but I may be rejoiced, when that injustice will be atoned for, that wrong, which will never bring blessing upon our union. My death will reconcile you with your father and with the world, and therefore I see its approach quietly and even with a happy feeling. I know, that even afterwards you will not forget your Augusta, and there comes a time when we will all meet again. See, such is my belief, such my faith and the assurance, to which I cling."

"Amen," added Marianne in a low tone; she had risen from the floor and stood now at the side of the bed, with her eyes swimming in tears.

"O gracious God!" exclaimed Steinfort, beside himself. "Oh man, man, is it possible that thy folly can trample so much virtue, so much real kindness beneath thy feet! Yes, I have acted wrong, and now in my inmost heart I atone for it; but what else drove me to it, but the perverseness, the shortsightedness and the narrow-mindedness of society!"

"Dear Carl," responded Augusta with heavenly self-denial, "men cannot all be angels. They have their faults and their virtues; take the one with the other. You have views and feelings in which the majority does not participate; yield to it or inclose within your breast what you feel, and you will be happier. There is no judge between you and mankind, you must submit and learn how to conquer your rash impulses."

"No," exclaimed Steinfort firmly, "that I can not. Rather will I perish in the honest struggle."

During this conversation, Prince Prominsky was announced, who anxiously desired to speak to Herr von Steinfort.

The Lieutenant was just about to refuse his

admission, with the excuse, that the sickness of his wife rendered it impossible for him to receive visitors, when Augusta who had heard the announcement, interrupted her husband.

"Do not refuse to receive the noble friend of your father," she said, "he comes to meet my most ardent wishes. Ask him to come to me for a few minutes, I have something particular to speak with him."

Steinfort could raise no objections to this request, and hurried out, to conduct the Prince, who immediately consented, into the chamber of the invalid.

Marianne left the room, as a just and refined feeling of delicacy told her, that she might perhaps be an obstacle there.

A deep emotion overcame the Prince when he observed the pale face of the sufferer. He seemed to feel, that before him was not one of those outcast, hopelessly lost creatures who are entirely fallen to perdition, but at the utmost, only a victim of misery, seduction or the tyranny of our social system. As the heart of the Prince did not entertain any of the high aristocratic prejudices, and as a certain romantic inclination in his breast attracted him to all that betrayed an extraordinary character, his compassion increased in proportion.

"You have desired to speak to me, Frau von Steinfort," he said in a gentle tone of voice. "You see me ready to fulfill every one of your wishes."

A slight smile of satisfaction passed during these words over the face of the invalid, which added a material and charming beauty to her pale features. It was a silent satisfaction to her, by the mention of her name, to see her present rank and position recognised and acknowledged by the noble, high-born man. Reader, do not blame this really womanly feature; it was a pure, gentle, human smile, purchased at super human sacrifices.

"I knew it," she said, after having for a moment attentively looked at the Prince, "I knew that your Highness would not refuse the request of a dying person. I feel my end approaching with rapid strides, and I have only one wish left on this earth. I would like to implore the pardon of the father of my Carl, for the grief, the sorrow, which, unconsciously, I have caused him. Your Highness may materially assist me in the accomplishment of this desire, if by your influence you can determine the Major to come to my sick bed, if only for a few moments. With life every account will be closed, every debt paid. If he sees me die, he will pardon me and his son, and thus change my last bitter hour of death, to one of quiet and resigned dissolution.'

"Your Highness cannot understand or conceive half of the high-mindedness of this pure and serene soul," interrupted the Lieutenant, "I must inform you, that she had not the least suspicion of the ways and means by which I procured for myself the necessary consent for the marriage. She would never have agreed to it,

unless I assured her, that my father had given his free and voluntary consent. Only a few moments before he came here, and that terrible scene ensued, she mentioned him with the tenderest love and affection, and pressed me to procure to her his personal acquaintance. Tell this to my father, and please to add thereto, that, at the particular, expressed desire of my wife, I also am willing to extend to him my hand in reconciliation."

With the deepest emotion painted in every feature, the Prince gave his hand to the invalid, and promised to do every thing in his power towards the accomplishment of her wish.

"I was about to make to you other offers and proposals in the name of your father," he said on leaving to the Lieutenant who accompanied him to the door, "but as I see, these are now useless. Where a greater judge interferes, human action and human wisdom must vanish. God will guide all for the best."

At the lower floor of the house Eel-eye was waiting for the Prince. He had followed him hither, as he had important communications to make to him.

"Sir Prince," he exclaimed, even while the other was yet descending the stairs, "I have found him; soon you shall have your brother."

Prominsky listened attentively; his breast heaved in eager expectation.

"Then let the coachman immediately drive home," he ordered; "then you shall give me more detailed information."

Quickly the Prince hurried to his carriage. Eel-eye commanded "*Hôtel de Paris!*" mounted his servant's seat and the carriage drove rapidly away.

CHAPTER XCIII.

EEL-EYE'S COMMUNICATION.

"WELL, how is it?" inquired the Prince, full of impatient expectation, of his body-yaeger who was standing before him. "Tell me, but be quick and brief."

"Your Highness knew," began Eel-eye, "that I had a meeting last night with the old woman whom we call the rag-gatherer. She wanted to make the proposition to me, in company with her, to commit a theft upon you, presupposing that only with that object, I had entered your service. At first I objected, telling her that I intended to become honest; she laughed at the idea, and intimated that by such an excuse I could not turn her away; she told me, that she had recognised me and claimed now her share of the *masematten*—I beg your pardon, Highness—of the robbery, I should say, which she believed had now been prepared by me. But when I firmly insisted upon my declaration, she plainly told me, that she would in no way agree to that, and that she would betray me to the police if I did not agree to her proposal. I now began to listen more willingly to her words, but told her that we must have still another companion, as I could not possibly take an active part, in consideration of the dangers of discovery to which I exposed myself. This seemed reasonable and comprehensive to the rag-gatherer; but the question now was, where to get a companion, as most of our company had been arrested and others had fled.—First, I seemed to think seriously about this difficulty for a long time, and then I told her, that I well knew one if it could only be ascertained where he could now be found, namely, cunning Schmerles. I told her that I knew he had recently escaped from the prison of Spandau —good Heaven, your Highness will pardon me for this remark by which I caused grief, which certainly was not my intention—your—"

"Go on, go on," exclaimed the Prince passionately, having turned visibly pale at the last remark of Eel-eye's, "do not dwell too long upon trifling particulars foreign to the subject."

"The rag-gatherer," continued the other, "looked sharply at me, but I endeavoured to appear wholly unconcerned and seemed not to observe her glance. Then she agreed to my proposition, and told me, that she well knew the present whereabouts of Schmerles, and that she would engage him for our companion in this enterprise. I now made a number of inquiries, but she seemed disinclined to enter upon any further particulars, and only promised to bring him along with her in the next night to Müller-street, or to any other secure place which I might indicate, when we all three could consult about the further necessary preliminaries. Not to arouse her suspicion, I had to declare myself satisfied with this; and indeed it seems fully satisfactory, for I have already laid a plan for our further proceedings."

Eel-eye was silent, perhaps in the expectation that the Prince would ask him to give some further explanation, and probably to see what impression his information would make upon the Prince, who he seemed to expect would receive the news with great joy.

But the Prince was sunk into the deepest silence. The communication of his body yaeger seemed rather to have made a serious than a joyous impression upon his mind.

"It is horrible," he said after a few seconds, as if speaking to himself, "to think of robbing and stealing from one's own brother, and yet I cannot reproach him for doing so!"

The sound of his own voice reminded the Prince of where he was, and what he was doing. He seemed to awake from a deep, and heavy dream.

"I thank you for your carefulness," he said, heartily shaking Eel-eye's hand, "I think I shall be able to reward you. Come back to me within an hour, then I will hear more of you, and communicate to you my will, but at present, I must attend to another, and most urgent business."

"Another subject, your Highness," said Eel-eye, going towards the door, "Marianne Jobs, whom you inquired for of me, is at the house of Lieutenant von Steinfort, I believe, as a servant, housekeeper, or something of that kind. When I was waiting there for your Highness, I saw her crossing the passage; luckily she did not recognise me. How she came into that house I cannot imagine, but it certainly has been most fortunate for her, for this was perhaps the only way by which she could escape an arrest and imprisonment, which has been the fate of her father, and most all of my former companions."

Eel-eye left the room.

The Prince proceeded to the chamber of the Major, to fulfil the request of the dying Augusta, whose pale suffering image was still floating before his eyes.

He could only expect to find a most obstinate opponent in the old warrior, knowing the aversion which he felt to his daughter-in-law, although he did not doubt, in the least, that the same feelings would take possession of the Major's breast, which he himself had experienced, whenever the Major should approach the sick bed of Augusta.

A principal point was, that contrary to the Major's opinion, Augusta had not enticed the Lieutenant into this marriage, but, on the contrary, had been persuaded to it by him. From this fact, the Prince intended to draw the greatest advantage for the furtherance of the object of his message.

The Major had been eagerly expecting the Prince. He had desired his friend to endeavour and bring his son in his name to the resolution quietly and peaceably to separate from his wife, and to tell him that on his refusal, the *curse of his father* would await him. Tremblingly he awaited the answer.

CHAPTER XCIV.

SCHMERLES APPEARS AGAIN.

BETWEEN Berlin and the village *Moabit*, on the right bank of the Spree, lies a vast sandy desert. a very Sahara. All the sand which the people of the metropolis strew into each others eyes, might be taken from this place, yet there would never be any scarcity.

The last houses of the suburbs before the new gate, reach far into this desert. Where they cease, a low plain commences, only here and there, and rarely interrupted by little hills, upon which hardly a crippled willow can manage to grow. No grass, no flower, no vegetable nor shrub changes the gloomy monotony of this region.

It is midnight.

Black darkness covers the earth. For moments only the narrow sickle of the moon passes through the thickly clouded sky, to throw its feeble light upon two figures, who are standing on one of the above-mentioned hills. It is Schmerles and the rag-gatherer. Both engaged in a low, frequently interrupted conversation. All the time, they look eagerly and cautiously all around.

From the distance the feeble knell of a town clock is heard across the fields.

"Listen, old woman," said Schmerles, in a dissatisfied tone, "in Moabit, the clock strikes twelve already, and Eel-eye is not here yet. What does that mean?"

"It means nothing at all," replied the rag-gatherer. "I should think you knew Eel-eye well enough; he does not stay away when a good masematten is to be made."

"But are you sure, that we are right here?" asked Schmerles, with equal concern.

"O yes! Eel-eye has carefully described the place to me. Upon the middle hill, at the right side, and back of the black-thorn bushes. We certainly have been here often enough before! Our best masematten have been arranged here. Only be perfectly quiet; the poor boy sits now with his Prince, and cannot get away so easy; he told me at the time, that he would perhaps not be very punctual."

"What kind of a Prince is it?" asked Schmerles.

"How should I know! He has come from Poland or Siberia, or Italy, or from some country thereabouts. This much at least I know, that he is said to have immense wealth. It is a perfect masterpiece of Eel-eye, to have established himself thus in his house. We shall do a great business there."

"Old woman, if I knew that the Prince was from Poland, I would leave the masematten to you alone."

"Pshaw, are you crazy man? Have you become converted and grown pious and godly at Spandau?" asked the rag-gatherer, scornfully.

"The devil I have! turned pious, indeed!" replied the other, "there is little occasion or chance for that in Spandau; but if the Prince is a Pole, then he is my countryman, and I do not like to rob a countryman, when he is abroad."

"Ridiculous fool!" murmured the rag-gatherer between her teeth.

"Did you say something?"

"I merely observed that Eel-eye would be able to give more definite information concerning the Prince. Hark, I believe there he comes. I will just go down the hill, and see whether I can discover him."

"You do not stir from this place!" cried Schmerles, violently pulling the old woman by the arm, at the same time showing a long knife, "if you dare to move, I will kill you. Did I for this at the risk of my life, break through walls, and swim through rivers, that in the end, I should be betrayed even by one of you? No! thunder! I would rather strangle every one of you."

"Don't be crazy," replied the rag-gatherer, half-frightened, yet half saucily, "what in the world are you thinking about?"

"Upon my soul," continued Schmerles, still raving most furiously, "if hunger did not compel me, I would not hold intercourse with any one of you. Since the Maulspitzer has turned a Slichner, one is no longer safe with any of you. You are all mean, ragged vagabonds; it is a shame to have any thing to do with you. As sure as God is my judge, I would rather bite off my tongue and throw it into the face of a *Lambden*, than be guilty of betraying a single honest Gannew (thief.)"

"You might have rejected my proposition," replied the rag-gatherer, evidently hurt in a tender point by these words, "I did not force you to participate in it."

"*Force me?*" cried Schmerles, laughing disdainfully, "no you did not force me, certainly you did not! But want forced me, the most dreadful famine and starvation was consuming my body. For the three days since I met you in the *Kirsch-allee*, (cherry-alley) and where in pity you gave me your bread, I have tasted no food. I have passed days and nights in the thickest part of the *Jungfernhaide*, without daring to leave it, and have with maddening anxiety waited for this hour.—Why did you not bring something to eat with you, woman?"

"Because I had nothing myself," was the answer, "I no longer dare to enter a store or shop, for since your escape the accursed vigilants have become perfect devils. But I have told Eel-eye to bring provisions with him."

"Well then I wish that he might come soon," said Schmerles, "I am almost fainting with weakness."

"He is here already," suddenly said a loud voice behind them.

Frightened, both looked around. Eel-eye stood there, although his arrival had not been observed.

"It is well for you that I am not a Lambden or a Slichner," he exclaimed gaily, "or I could very easily have arrested you both."

"Yes, yes," answered the rag-gatherer, "I believe you. If the Lambden could do what thieves can do, we would soon all go to the devil."

"Stuff and nonsense," cried Schmerles impatiently, tormented by the most raving hunger, "have you brought any thing to eat with you?"

In the place of any answer, Eel-eye produced from beneath his cloak a large parcel wrapped up in paper, threw his cloak upon the ground and the paper upon it.

Without losing a single word, Schmerles and the rag-gatherer threw themselves upon it, tore the paper open, and with ravenous greediness devoured the eatables they found there.

Eel-eye observed them silently, and with a countenance, upon which at the same time a smile, and the deepest compassion were expressed.

"Upon my word, Eel-eye," said Schmerles, after the first wants of hunger were satisfied, "I thank you for my life. I could no longer have borne it; such fasting is more than even a wolf's nature could stand."

"We shall find a time when we shall settle

with each other, and when I may require a service in return," answered Eel-eye, hastily shaking the hand of the speaker, "above all, let me welcome you to liberty. You have accomplished a master piece at Spandau, they will long think of it."

"Yes," said Schmerles, drawing a heavy breath, even at the recollection, "it has cost superhuman labour. But what would not a man do to gain his liberty. Look at the tips of these fingers; these have attacked a wall of six feet thickness. I often had no little trouble to lick the blood from my fingers' ends, that it might not create observation.—But what is the use of chatting here; how is it about this masematten? I must have money, that I may get away from this place as soon as possible. In the Jungfernhaide I cannot live long, and into the city I dare not venture."

"With the masematten all is right!" answered Eel-eye, "but we can not act, or commence any operations for two hours yet. The Prince never goes to sleep before one o'clock, and it is only just past midnight. I have then planned it so, that the old woman should stand *Schmiere* in the street, whilst you from the yard can ascend into the window. I have prepared a ladder and will designate to you all the particulars more minutely and moreover have a care, that the Prince does not awake or gets attentive."

"One more question," cried Schmerles interrupting the other, "is the Prince a Polander?"

Immediately after the question, Eel-eye felt a slight pinch from the rag-gatherer, who at the same time made an almost imperceptible signal to him, to answer the question in the negative.

He readily obeyed, without considering what the possible motive of the question might be, as he was satisfied that the rag-gatherer had agreed to his plans, and as he presupposed, that the answer she desired him to give, was necessary to the attainment of his object.

"Then all is right," resumed Schmerles, "and my conscience will not be troubled by the same scruples, as if he had been my countryman."

Eel-eye who now began to understand the reason of Schmerles' first question, was well pleased that he obeyed the hint of the rag-gatherer. This trait in the character of Schmerles made a deep and most favourable impression upon him, and he determined at the earliest opportunity to delight the heart of the Prince, by telling him of it.

"And now, since we have to be patient, and remain idle for a few hours longer," said Eel-eye, "I have stolen a few bottles of very fine wine from the cellar of the Prince. These will meanwhile help us to spend the time pleasantly."

All three seated themselves upon the ground.

Eel-eye produced his wine, and pledged the others in a glass of sparkling grape juice.

"You ought to relate to us the story of your escape," began Eel-eye, "for I am really anxious to hear how you managed to escape even from Spandau."

Schmerles, whose good humour and confidence had been restored by the generous wine, declared his readiness to comply with their request, and began his narrative as follows:

"You all must remember, or at least must all have heard of it at the time, how I became *verschütt* through the treachery of the hostess of the green Elephant—devil take that woman, but she shall yet pay me for it. My arrest occurred under such unfortunate circumstances, that I could not for a moment entertain a doubt of being sent off for about twenty-five years or so. I suppose I need not tell you, that I did not turn *Slichner* (traitor) in consequence.

"Well, after a detention for examination of about three months, the proceedings were peremptorily closed, I was immediately carried 'over the mountain,' (to Spandau,) where I afterwards was made acquainted with my sentence of hard labour for twenty-five years. How I felt on receiving this sentence, you can easily imagine; I received a few iron *manchettes*, (handcuffs) and for the present, that is for six months as I was informed, was put into *Cachot* (solitary confinement,) for the purpose of bringing me to repentance and acknowledgment of my sins. As a natural consequence of this solitude I very soon became repentant and prepared for Heaven. I discovered that I had, by my wicked life placed myself on the brink of an abyss of eternal perdition, and on the third day already demanded a prayer and hymn book. In the course of two months I had safely prayed myself out of Cachot and irons, and was comfortably seated in the large working-room. My conversion evidently progressed very fast, but I must tell you, that even in the Stadt-vogtei, I had applied to the prison-minister and from him received instructions in piety."

Schmerles now took a hearty draught at the bottle and then continued:

"From the moment of my arrest, I naturally had but one thought, but one object in view—my escape. But how to accomplish it? I did not dare to make an attempt at this in company with others from fear of treachery, and alone I knew not how to go about it. I could see but one possible way of accomplishing any thing, namely by getting on the sick list, and being sent to the hospital; but then I was as sound as a fish At last I endeavoured to help myself.

"One day, when I was passing my time in turning the wool-carding machine—you know that beautiful employment, rag-gatherer—I made a very adroit slip, which brought my foot within the wheel, which severely sprained my ankle, of course without doing me any further injury. My plan succeeded; I was brought to the hospital, and the chains were taken from me. A bible, a prayer and hymn book had also to accompany me to my sick bed, as by these I expected to gain some material advantages.

"The Cachot for sick persons, or rather that part of the prison hospital lies by the side of the water, and I must endeavour to have myself brought there, in order to be alone and succeed in making my escape. Consequently, three days afterwards I sent for the parson, and when alone with him, I told him, that filled with the Grace of the Lord, I had almost arrived at the determination of being baptised, and that my heart and soul required that moral and mental change ; but in order to let this good resolution ripen within my breast, I needed solitude and quiet, as the presence of the other prisoners continually interrupted me in my pious meditations.

" This had the desired effect, and on the very same day I was brought to the place where I longed to be. I had scarcely been left to myself, when I subjected the whole place to the strictest examination. But my courage soon began to fail, when notwithstanding the closest search, I could not find a single particle of iron, which I could have taken away without being observed. At last, after three days vain search, I discovered a nail beneath my bedstead. This nail was driven deep into the wood, but I did not despair. On the next morning, when the Doctor visited me, I placed a bottle of oil, which he had left me to rub my foot with, in such a manner before my bed, that he must step upon it, and break it on approaching my bed. The fragments lay on the floor for some time, and before the attendant came to clear them away, I had secured a piece and hidden it in my bed.

" With this bit of glass I soon dug the nail out of the wood, and now I was in possession of a treasure, wherewith I could begin my work. I ground the nail against the wall until it had an edge like a chisel and then spent three weeks in indefatigable labor, day and night to break one of the iron bars from the window sill. When my foot was sufficiently healed to enable me to leave the hospital and it was announced to me, that on the next morning I would be removed, my work was just completed. The night before, I prepared for my flight.

" By means of a rope which I twisted together from the straw of my mattress, I descended from the window, dropped lightly into the water, and swam to the opposite shore. I was now free, but in my convict's dress ; at any and every price I must get clothing before the morning dawned. I took again to the water and swam back. The Clothing-room,* as you perhaps may know, lies directly below the Hospital-Cachot, and is not secured with strong shutters as the water beneath is considered sufficient protection. With much difficulty I succeeded in gaining access to this room, and I quickly gathered up a bundle of clothing. With these, I again descended into the water, gained the opposite shore, changed my dress, hurried off and reached this place in safety."

" You are, and ever will be, all our master," cried Eel-eye laughing, when Schmerles had concluded his story ; " drink ! Another toast : Your health and liberty !"

* A place where the dress of the prisoner on his arrival is deposited to be returned to him on liberation.

The bottles circulated very freely, and were soon emptied. Eel-eye only touched them with his lips, without drinking, which however, was not observed by his companions in the darkness of the night ; but the rations which came to his companions were only the greater in consequence.

" Thunder and the devil !" suddenly cried Schmerles, " this will be a very bad affair with this Masematten, for my head is suddenly getting so heavy, that I am afraid I have drunk too much of this wine."

" And I too," said the rag-gatherer, scarcely able to speak, as she endeavoured to rise, but immediately had to sit down again.

Both only spoke a few more incoherent and unintelligible sentences, and overpowered by sleep sank to the ground.

The wine had contained a strong sleeping draught.

Eel-eye remained quietly seated for a while longer, whilst his eyes were fixed in close observation on his companions. When he had arrived at the positive conviction that both had fallen soundly asleep, he arose, and quickly hurried to a little hill which lay in the distance. Immediately after, he returned in company of a tall, stately man, closely wrapped in a cloak.

Eel-eye conducted the stranger close to Schmerles, the cloak fell from his shoulders and—the Prince bent over his sleeping brother.

In deep silence he stared upon the sleeping form of the latter, seeking in vain to penetrate the darkness of the night and to discover the features of his brother.

Our pen is too weak even for the attempt to portray the feelings and emotions which, with the rapidity of thought, passed through the breast of this noble man. Joy at the ultimate success of a plan which had absorbed all his energies for years, delight at having again found his much loved brother, deep and bitter sorrow at the present position of the latter, fear and hope of the events which the next few days might produce, resolutions to guide these events, to break his position to his brother in the kindest, mildest possible manner—such may have been the sentiments, which for a few minutes filled the heart of the Prince.

Silently he stood there, surrounded by the deep silence of a midnight desert, silently he sunk upon his knees to offer his prayer and the sacrifice of his heart to the ruler of the world.

Eel-eye had withdrawn a few paces, paying an humble tribute to the emotions of the Prince, by keeping at a respectful distance.

Involuntarily he now followed the example of his master, involuntarily his lips began to move, and his heart filled with the first feeling and presentiment of a better and brighter future.

The Prince arose from the ground, turned around and commanded: " get the carriage !"

Eel-eye again disappeared behind the hill, and soon returned with a close carriage, accompanied by a single saddle horse.

Without delay, Schmerles and the rag-gatherer were placed into this carriage, which was carefully and securely closed from every side.

Eel-eye mounted the coachman's box, the Prince took to the saddle horse, and thus the party proceeded towards the city.

To avoid attracting any attention, they did not proceed towards the *Hôtel de Paris*, but towards a solitary, unfrequented street in the *König-stadt* on the other side of *Alexander-place*, where, at the command of the Prince, Eel-eye had rented a house for the purpose.

It was about three o'clock in the morning when the little caravan arrived in this place, and placed the sleeping couple securely into rooms.

Only when all this was accomplished did the Prince begin to feel quieted, as up to this moment, he had still been in fear that another accident might once more deprive him of the person of his long sought brother.

The intense excitement of his heart gradually diminished, and hot tears flowed freely from his burning eyes. The strong, powerful and noble man was not ashamed of these tears.

CHAPTER XCV.

TRIUMPH OF BROTHERLY LOVE.

FULL of fear, love and anxiety, the Prince had since daylight looked for the awakening of his brother.

The excitement of the occurrence did not permit him to rest. He endeavoured for a few hours to lay himself down undressed upon a couch, but soon he started up again, chased up and down the room by the intense and wild mental excitement under which he laboured.

Again and again hesitations and doubts about the justness of the course he was pursuing troubled his distracted mind.

The rank of Prince belonged to his brother, and wrongfully, and by fiendish, unparalleled malice had he lost it; but then this same brother, what had he become?—A man, morally lower than the lowest of his subjects! a criminal, an outcast of humanity! And this man was to be elevated, to be raised above all others!

The Prince folded his hands in warm and ardent prayer, beseeching a higher power for a blessing upon his deeds and actions.

Impatience at last drove him into the room, which had, for the time being been assigned to his brother.

The Prince had made it the duty of Eel-eye to have the dirty, ragged and uncomfortable clothing which Schmerles had secured on his escape, exchanged for another and more comfortable dress, at least for one which was suitable to his present rank and position.

In a comfortable, and rather elegant morning-dress, lay the much feared and cunning robber upon a soft sofa. The homely, wild beard, and the long, uncombed hair had disappeared beneath the expert hand of Eel-eye, and this metamorphosis had such a remarkable effect, that the Prince stopped in silent hesitation and astonishment at the door.

Despite of the paleness and haggardness which a long prison life had produced upon the features of the sleeping man, the originally noble and aristocratic features were now fully perceptible, and not to be mistaken.

Schmerles was a few years older than the Prince; he might be about forty years of age. But the filth and the rags which had been the natural consequences of the mode of life he had hitherto led, these had caused him to appear much older. Now the beholder would recognize a well formed man, of by no means repulsive exterior, and in the very strength of manhood.

The large aquiline nose and the arched forehead — inherited family marks of the Princes Prominsky — these spoke in kindly and familiar tones to the eye of the beholder, and served to verify the voice within which told him that his brother, his own dearly beloved brother lay before him. It was a strange humour of accident that these same family traits of his features, had also before served, to put the Hebrew descent of the robber beyond a doubt. Another proof how easily our weak, prejudiced human observations may deceive us.

The Prince seated himself by the couch of the sleeping man, and in almost voluptuous delight, enjoyed the hitherto unknown pleasures of family affections and brotherly love.

Gently he took the right hand of his brother which hung by the side of the bed, within both his hands, and with eyes dimmed by tears, he contemplated the haggard, pale and distressed appearance which superhuman sufferings had produced upon that brother. The skin of his hand, in consequence of the immense labour used in making his escape from the prison had burst open, all his finger nails were deeply torn, and congealed blood was collected beneath them.

"Poor boy," sighed the Prince shaking his head, "all these tortures you might have escaped, for in a very few days I would have obtained liberty for you."

With anxious care he laid the arm of the sleeping man back across his breast. The latter already commenced, restlessly to move up and down and seemed to struggle with an approaching awakening.

The effect of the sleeping potion seemed in reality about to lose its power. The sleeping man stretched himself out at full length, as if to shake off the iron bands of sleep.

The Prince could scarcely draw his breath from the strong effects of his internal excitement.

Finally the closed eyes opened themselves, stared wildly around at the strange and novel objects which surrounded him, but quickly closed again, evidently believing themselves to be the captive slaves of a mocking dream.

Then a mighty and urgent feeling overpowered

the Prince; he forgot the wisdom and the caution which made a quiet, slow and deliberate revelation necessary. With a loud and joyous exclamation he cast himself upon his knees before the half awakened man.

"My brother," he cried, "Iwan, my dearest brother, have I found thee again?"

This loud exclamation fully awoke the other. Without understanding the words, the sound of which struck terror to his ear, he started with a mighty leap from his bed.

"Ho! where am I? Where am I? Where am I?"

Without looking around, and with an instinctive desire of self-preservation and liberty he rushed toward the door.

Precaution had been taken to lock it.

He hurried thence to the window.

It was too high for him to make his escape by.

All this was the work of a moment. Like a furious animal in a cage, the frantic imprisoned robber rushed about the room, from the door to the window, and from the window to the door.

Frightened and irresolute, the Prince looked upon this mad behaviour; he felt that he had acted hastily, but knew not, what was now to be done.

When Schmerles found all his attempts at flight frustrated, he recovered his presence of mind. With a look of burning fury he measured the Prince.

"Where am I?" he cried once more; "do you keep me a prisoner here?"

Quickly his hand sought his vest pocket as if endeavouring to find a knife or some other weapon.

Now only he observed that the clothing he wore was different from the dress in which he escaped.

In astonishment he examined the fine texture of the garments he had on, slowly he looked around the room, and only now he seemed to observe the comfortable and elegant arrangements of the apartment.

Seemingly stupified he rubbed his forehead with both his hands.

"Good Heavens, where am I," he cried again for the fifth or sixth time. "This is no prison, this is no prisoner's or convict's dress! Who brought me hither? Where was I? Where am I? Did not the Lampen have me imprisoned at Spandau?"

The frantic fury, the velocity, the impetuosity of manner with which all this was incoherently uttered, prevented the Prince from giving any answer whatever, even if the excited feelings of his breast had allowed him to speak.

He experienced bitter and burning pains at this wild unnatural behaviour, which presented so true an impress of a being ejected and cast out of the pale of civilized society.

Incapable of looking longer at this horrible tragedy he approached the table and rang a little bell that stood thereon.

Upon this preconcerted signal, the door opened and Eel-eye entered the room.

As soon as the self-conceited prisoner saw the latter, he hesitated a moment; but suddenly he seemed to recollect himself.

"Villian! traitor! scoundrel! slichner!" he cried in the utmost fury, "whither have you brought me? Yes, yes, every thing is clear to me now. Your wine has made me drunk. By your infernal mascmatten you have enticed me for the purpose of imprisoning me here. Man confess, confess what you have done with me, or I will strangle you."

In blind fury he rushed on his former companion and would most probably have murdered or seriously injured him, had not the Prince stepped in between the two.

"Iwan!" he said with dignity, "why do you rave thus? will you not at least give us a hearing? You are not a prisoner, you are free, and you soon will be a mighty and powerful man."

The earnest, severe, half commanding, yet half sorrowful tone of these words, made a fresh and peculiar impression upon the wild uncontrolable nature of the robber. He hesitated, became silent, and now for the first time, looked at the figure of the Prince, with distrustful, yet astonished glances.

"Albert," began the Prince, unable to continue this exciting conversation, "Albert, explain to my brother, why he has been brought here."

Eel-eye put his face into the most comical wrinkles. The easy confidence and fellowship towards his colleague and comrade of many past years of crime, struggled with the respect and veneration, which he believed that he owed to the new, elevated and aristocratic position of the late robber.

"I—I—You—" he began hesitatingly.

"Speak out, Albert, speak briefly, even as you may feel," said the Prince with a sigh, which expressed or contained much more than he could possibly believe himself.

"Well then, Schmerles," said the other, trying to screw his courage to the sticking point, "I will once more, and for the last time address you by that name. Schmerles is a name, which does not belong to you, and I trust that henceforth you will no longer be called thus, or be a robber."

Eel-eye again hesitated, for his speech did not yet seem to flow. It might have appeared remarkable even to himself. At all events he could not continue his speech in his usual flowing and easy style.

Who is there, that would dare to dive into the depths of the human heart, to ascertain all that in this moment moved the soul of the speaker? Was it surprise, joy at the fortune of his former boon companion, sorrow and regret at losing an old, well-tried and faithful comrade, or was it a silent sorrow at not possessing similar fortune? We cannot tell.

Eel-eye again raised his voice, and in an almost overloud tone he exclaimed:

"Schmerles, you are a Polish Prince! In your early youth, you were stolen from your parents, and you were brought up among Hebrew thieves. His Highness yonder, Prince Prominsky is your brother, who, after years of anxious search, has at last found you, and is now ready and willing to restore you to your rank and to your possessions. For this reason we have put you into an artificial sleep, and have brought you here. And now you know every thing."

Eel-eye was silent, and a flaming blush covered his entire face.

Schmerles looked at him slowly and quietly from head to foot, looked in a similar manner at the Prince, then in astonishment felt all over, and looked at his own body, and finally burst into a fit of laughter, which made the strong nerves of the two men tremble like aspen.

This was no human laughter.

"Eel-eye," he cried in tones of bitterest scorn, "Eel-eye, this is a splendid story; tell another such, just one more like it!" and again he burst into frantic laughter. Then becoming more serious, he said:

"Miserable, stupid boy! These are nursery tales to put children to sleep. Speak out like a man and confess that you have also become a Slickner like Maulspitzer, and that the Lampen will soon come to take me away. Why this mockery? Don't you see that I am helpless and given into your hands? Oh, my presentiment! Why did I trust that accursed old woman?"

He stopped for an instant pressing both fists tightly clenched before his eyes.

The Prince again made a powerful effort to regain his self-possession. He felt within himself, that he must put an end to this scene, lest his courage should even now forsake him.

"Iwan," he began, taking his brother by the hand, "sit down here, and listen quietly to what I have to say, and I will explain every thing to you."

Almost against his will, and certainly against his inclination, the other obeyed this demand, exhausted by his own exertions and wonderfully affected by the influence which the firm will of the Prince always exercised over his own subjects.

The Prince now related to his brother in a gentle, quiet, affectionately earnest tone, what had been his fortunes past and present.

He recommenced at his brother's early youth upon their paternal castle, and repeated, partly from his own knowledge, and partly from the communications of the Jew, all of the after occurrences of the lives of the Prominskys. Then he informed him, by what means, by what stratagems he had again gained possession of his person, and what a bright and glorious future was before him. In conclusion, he referred to the testimony of the Jewess, amd to the possession of the blue *lapis lazuli*, which the dying Schmuel had delivered into the hands of the rightful owner.

After the relation of this plain, romantic, yet closely connected and highly probable narrative, Schmerles again relapsed into deep thought.

He, the robber, the vagabond, the convict, should be a rich and noble Prince?

He, who yesterday was almost famished in a wilderness, should now revel in brilliancy and wealth?

He, who fled the sight of man, because the very lowest of the human race, might put his hand upon him, arrest him, and gain a certain reward, he should become the independent, the authorised ruler of thousands?

There was a maddening, a distracting thought in all this, and perhaps it was only natural, that a man, who had hitherto only believed himself a wretch and an outcast, should believe himself in a mad and unreal dream.

If any one had told him that he must return to his dark dungeon, that he must once more, and in a thousand fold greater degree undergo all the terrors, humiliations and sorrows which he had undergone—he would have believed and comprehended all that. But of fortune, of power, of *Princely* might and splendour—no, of these the wretched robber could not dream.

Schmerles—or rather Iwan, as we shall henceforth have to call him, remembered dark and distant dreams and fancies of his earliest youth, which seemed to harmonise perfectly with the narrative of the Prince; he remembered perfectly of having heard the blue stone spoken of, as serving to the identification of some Prince, and he moreover became fully aware that the Prince could only have learned all the subjects touched upon in his narrative, from Long Schmuel—but nevertheless, it was impossible for him to believe in an occurrence which his power of comprehension declared as absolutely impossible.

After all, the surrounding circumstances, his change of dress, and all other minor particulars had fully convinced him that they had no evil intentions towards him, least of all would deliver him to the authorities, and he now sought refuge in the supposition, that an exchange of person had caused all this mistake.

In this he firmly insisted, and neither the Prince with a heart overflowing with brotherly affection, nor Eel-eye with all his homely and matter of fact arguments, remonstrances and importunities, to which their past intimacy entitled him in this present difficulty, could take this conviction from his mind or convince him of his great fortune.

Eel-eye at last remembered that the former robber had always entertained the greatest veneration, respect and attachment for the Jewess, and had always willingly obeyed her councils and advice. He therefore made a proposition, to call in the testimony of the latter, and to prove thereby, that according to the declaration of her deceased husband, Iwan was that person, whose identity and whose princely rank could be proved by that precious stone.

Of course the latter could have no objection to this mode of settling the question, but he was fully convinced beforehand, that the decision of the Jewess would be in favour of his own firm opinion. Nothing could induce him to avail himself of the kindness of the Prince, or to look upon himself in the light of his Highness's brother.

Strange as it may appear, that this man, who amidst a thousand dangers, and with the most daring intrepidity, had often been capable of possessing himself of strange, often valueless property, should now refuse the acceptance of freely offered treasures, yet this very fact contains a most terrible proof, that necessity and misery may become as habitual and familiar to man, as joy, plenty and luxury.

There is not the least doubt of this one fact: Iwan feared his great fortune, and found it oppressive and tiresome to his acquired habits.

No choice remained to the Prince. He had to submit to the obstinate will of his brother, and quietly await, whether the abashed retiracy of the latter would give way before the decision and the arguments of the Jewess, who had first to be brought from Braunsdorf.

But if the Prince by this reserve of his brother, which rejected his kindness and his love, felt slighted and painfully affected for the moment, we cannot deny, that his pity and attachment to Iwan were in no small measure increased by this circumstance. He said to himself, that it must have been *sheer despair*, which in his brother's mind had destroyed even the belief in the presence of fortune or happiness.

CHAPTER XCVI.

FATAL MEETING OF SUNDRY WORTHIES.

WE must now proceed twenty-four hours with the occurrences of our story.

It was almost noon, yet our old acquaintance, the Referendarius von Birkheim had only just left his bed, for he had once again, in his usual way, remained at the gaming table until late at night.

He felt uncomfortable and sickly; the hackneyed phrases and standard expressions of the gambling table still sounded in his ears; ill humour made him perfectly unbearable.

His rooms had that appearance which is rather the stereotyped one of fashionable garçons rooms after a night of dissipation; wild and confused disorder reigned every where.

The fashionably made dress coat, hung upon the back of a chair in the middle of the room, and over it the finely embroidered and elegant vest was carelessly thrown.

Upon the bureau lay brushes, combs, cologne bottles and pomatum boxes, the memorials of the toilette of last evening. The open drawers of the different bureaus and cloth presses presented many and various, selected and rejected cravats, shirts, kid gloves and embroidered handkerchiefs.

The hat together with a pair of well worn gloves stood upon the table, elegant inexpressibles containing a pair of fashionable glazed boots, lay on the floor.

Every thing indicated, that Birkheim had spent last night at one of those gaming parties of the fashionable world, which are distinguished from ordinary circles by this difference, that gold pieces, instead of Thalers, are played for, and that disputes are settled with pistols not with fists.

The only animated object, visible amidst the fashionable chaos we have just endeavoured to describe, was stretched at full length upon a sofa, and appeared anything but what we have just called him—animated.

A velvet morning gown of a violet colour and handsome appearance covered his well fed body, his feet were enclosed in red morocco morning-boots and around the chin a red pocket handkerchief was tied, which was intended to keep the whiskers back in their proper place. The hair hung loosely around his head in undressed and uncurled liberty and the ashy pale face shone like a full moon beneath them.

Herr von Birkheim held in his hand a cigar, which he continually relighted at the wax candle which stood before him, whilst it extinguished as often again, for want of his smoking. While endeavouring to smoke, and with a lengthened and most sour face, he drank in small draughts a cup of black coffee, and every time he took a taste he replaced the cup upon the table, with a disconcerted sneer.

Every now and then, he looked at the blank scraped nails of his fat fingers, yawned once or twice, until he relapsed into his former lethargy, and then thoughtlessly stared after the clouds of his cigar smoke.

Annoyed and ill-humoured, he finally threw the cigar towards the door, which opened at the same moment, and by the accidental contact of door and cigar, threw a perfect shower of ashes and fire, upon the head of Herr von Schlepper, who entered at the same moment.

"Phew!" he exclaimed as he entered the room.

"I beg ten thousand pardons, Herr Baron," cried Birkheim partly amused at this accident, and somewhat annoyed at a visit which interrupted his quiet, lazy solitude.

"It is of no earthly consequence, my dearest Assessor," replied the Master-of-Horse obligingly, as he took his pocket handkerchief to dust the ashes from his clothes, "don't mention it, my friend. I have come to visit you upon a little business, and will not incommode you very long."

"I am entirely at your service," replied Birkheim, with a countenance which plainly indicated that he spoke an untruth. "May I beg you to be seated?"

"You must have observed, my worthy Assessor," began the *ci devant* Master-of-Horse, "that last night I was entirely fleeced, plucked to the last penny. I have even had the happiness of seeing a part of my ready cash, find its way into your treasury. Now since I have yet a small demand upon you, from the last star engagement which I played, and when I performed the part of Major von Steinfort in such an unsurpassed and most excellent manner, I must take the liberty, to request of you the settlement of that trifle—I think it is just ten Louisd'ors."

Birkheim had been particularly fortunate at play on the night previous; he had won a great deal of money, and consequently had a well-filled purse. Moreover the debt of Herr von Schlepper might be called a debt of honour. He consequently hastened immediately to satisfy this demand, although his creditors usually could not complain of too great a readiness on his part to settle their accounts.

The immediate compliance and fulfilment of his wishes, put Herr von Schlepper in the best imaginable humour.

"Eh bien then, this business is settled," he said, pocketing the gold pieces with an air of exceeding comfort, "now I have another affair to propose, at which you can soon get back this amount of gold and much more.—But—really, my dear sir—you smoke with such remarkable grace, may I beg for a cigar?"

Herr von Schlepper, as was well known, never smoked cigars but at the expense of his friends. Birkheim consequently with an ironical expression of face, offered him an assortment of three or four, from which he selected and lighted one, whilst he let the others imperceptibly glide into his pocket.

"Well, as I was about to tell you," continued Herr von Schlepper, as he blew the smoke in fanciful rings from his mouth, "you know my dear Assessor, that the rich *Count of Sowaloff*, who as every body knows is very fond of *setting one*, (of playing at Faro,) has just arrived from St. Petersburg, and has taken rooms at the *Hotel de Paris.* I shall go and dine there to-day, and endeavour to make his acquaintance. If we can succeed in bringing him into our yarn, he will be a capital *Freir* (a person who is to be cheated at Faro.) How, if I were to introduce the noble Count to you? You might give a *dejeuner* and the matter would be settled at once."

Birkheim gladly and readily assented to this proposition, as it opened a prospect for great profits.

"The old gaming party, which Count Sowaloff formerly frequented here," continued Schlepper, "is broken up since the death, I mean the bankruptcy of Prince Seeburg. Now our only object is to be the very first in getting hold of this Count, for you may easily imagine, that there are gamesters enough, who are making chase for him; but whoever happens to be first in the field, is sure to gain the battle."

At this moment the door was hastily and noisily thrown open, and Fischergraf, retaining his hat upon his head, entered the room, to make up a worthy trio.

"Aha, good morning, my little Assessor," he cried as usual in a tone as if he were calling to some person in the street from the third story of a house, "ah, and do I find you here also, my old friend Schlepper—charming, charming. Well gentlemen, how goes the world, what are you doing? Give me a cigar, Birkheim."

The two gentlemen on the entrance of Fischergraf, looked at each other with rather dissatisfied faces; the patronizing, familiar tone of the latter disconcerted them still more, as it was highly probable that neither of them liked the other to know aught of his intimacy with the Plebeian.

The latter, however, took not the least notice of the coolness with which he was received. He drew up a chair, placed his feet across the table, and began playing with his walking switch. Then he continued in the same loud tone as he had commenced:

"Ha, ha, ha! My little Assessor I have already heard all about it. You have had an *immense pig* (remarkable great luck) last night. He was rather green! 'He was naked and you took him in,' as the oyster said to the man who swallowed it. Ha, ha, ha, well, well! that is all right, it must go thus, as the man said, who was run over by a locomotive. You are the aptest pupil I have. Hammer the fellows together like old iron! these aristocratic blockheads are always the best Freirs.—Well friend Schlepper, how goes it, what are you driving at? How do you get along?—But, about what I came to tell you," he continued without awaiting any answer, "that rich Russian, Count Sowaloff, happened to fall in with me last night at the Hotel Trick-track, (a well-known gambling-house,) and I worked him well. I swear he will remember me for some time."

The two gentlemen looked at each other still more disconcertedly.

"Then Count Sowaloff has in reality been to the Hotel Trick-track already?" at last inquired Schlepper with a dissappointed air.

"I should say he had! I tell you he was there and considerably larger than life! Towards the end we had quite a nice general fight. The Russian asserted that he had been cheated and the other Russians present stuck to his side. But our party stuck well together. Thunder and—"

The word rested upon his lips, for just at this moment another knock was heard at the door. The Referendarius quickly replied with a " walk in," when a small strong built man with blonde hair, and a full, round, smiling face, crossed the threshold.

"The devil," murmured Fischergraf in his beard, as he quickly withdrew his legs from the table, and discontinued rocking his chair to and fro. He was the only one who seemed to have recognised the new comer.

"Have I the honour of seeing Herr Kammergericht Referendarius von Birkheim before me?" the stranger began most politely, as he approached Birkheim, whom he easily recognized as the master of the house by the negligence of his dress.

"At your service, sir," replied Birkheim, equally polite, "may I beg you to be seated. With whom have I the honour of conversing ?"

" Permit me to tell you this afterwards," replied the stranger with a smile, as he took a seat. "Why, look here! here is Herr Fischergraf also," he continued, as he quickly turned to the latter; " we two know each other. Is it a habit with you to keep your hat on your head in gentlemen's rooms, or have you turned Quaker. I should think it no more than proper if you were to take it off."

To the greatest astonishment of the other two, Fischergraf only murmured an unintelligible reply, in a low, humble tone, which was meant as an excuse, and placed his hat aside.

" If I am not greatly mistaken," continued the little, quick, talkative man, suddenly addressing the third party present, " you are Herr von Schlepper, formerly Master of Horse, now living as a private gentleman ?"

Schlepper stared at the stranger in great surprise; his own, and Birkheim's astonishment continued to increase.

" I don't know that I have ever had the honour—," stammered the Master of Horse, who began to feel extremely uncomfortable.

"Oh yes, yes, certainly!" cried the stranger, " at least I have the pleasure of knowing you well, as you perceive. You seem to have no memory for your friends. Well, well, I will soon bring myself back to your memory."

At this remark, Fischergraf once more murmured a few unintelligible words.

" Did you make any remark, my worthy friend ?" inquired the mysterious stranger, with the same stereotyped smile as before.

"Oh no, no—I merely—observed—I thought —and—," stammered Fischergraf, in great confusion.

In the most easy, friendly and indifferent manner in the world, the stranger continued the conversation for a few minutes. Then he rose, approached the window, looked out, made a few quiet remarks upon the state of the weather, and returned to his seat.

Immediately after, the door again opened, and Mr. Schreiber, our old acquaintance the Notary, entered the room.

Birkheim and Schlepper, at the sight of him, turned deadly pale.

The latter now looked closely at the other stranger, and with a suppressed curse, struck his forehead. He seemed just to remember that the stranger had a very good reason to know him.

The hitherto unknown little man suddenly rose from his seat, and assumed a most serious, authoritive expression of face.

" Herr Notary," he began, addressing the latter, " do you know these two gentlemen whom you see before you here ?"

" Certainly," replied the little busibody, " Herr Referendarius von Birkheim has been personally and officially known to me for many years past —the other person has been introduced to me as Herr Major von Steinfort, by Herr Referendarius von Birkheim."

"Gentlemen," now began the stranger, addressing the two persons just named, who stood in silence, and seemed perfectly electrified by surprise, "gentlemen, I am Polizeirath X—. Your arrest has become my absolute duty, as Herr Referendarius von Birkheim, being a legal man, must of course know. I must, therefore, request you, without further resistance, and without attracting, for your own sakes, more than necessary attention in the neighbourhood, to follow me at once."

Schlepper now seemed perfectly to remember his former acquaintance with the stranger, and perhaps with regard to this, to consider all delay and remonstrance perfectly superfluous. At least, he immediately prepared himself to obey the request of the Polizeirath.

Birkheim was silent; he seemed perfectly annihilated, and unable to utter a word. At last he began in the tone of a most humble petitioner:

"Herr Polizeirath, I pray and beseech you, save me, and do not arrest me here. You will ruin me and all my future prospects. I will give you my most sacred word of honour, that I will not leave Berlin, and you certainly can be satisfied with that."

"Herr von Birkheim," replied the Polizeirath coldly, " your arrest is legally proscribed to me, and you, as a Jurist, ought certainly to know that best. I must, therefore, request you to cause me no unnecessary trouble or delay."

"And you, my worthy friend," said the Polizeirath sarcastically to Fischergraf, whom he addressed with rather more cordiality than the others, perhaps from a regard to his lower position, perhaps also, because he had more frequently come in contact with him, "you will perhaps also do me the favour to accompany me. Your arrest is for a certain gambling affair which occurred in the so-called Hotel Trick-track, and for which you were this morning denounced at my office. It was my original intention not to arrest you until to-morrow, but this happy accidental meeting, will save me that trouble."

Fischergraf followed with the same readiness as Schlepper.

" Allons, gentlemen, a little quicker if I may request," said the Polizeirath in a commanding tone, " I have more business to attend to this forenoon. My carriage waits for you at the door."

The gentlemen entered the vehicle.

" First to the *Hausvogtei-prison*, then to the *Stadtvogtei*," sounded the order of Polizeirath X— to his coachman, as he followed his prisoners into the carriage.

The coachman cracked his whip, and quickly they rattled down the street.

"Hm, hm! I thought at the time that every thing was not correct about this affair," said Notary Schreiber to himself, as he slowly followed the carriage; " a long official life lets one almost to scent these fellows. Real gallows birds upon my word. But, *fiat justitia et pereat mundus*."

18

CHAPTER XCVII.

RECONCILIATION AND DEATH.

At the time of the occurrences which we have related in our last chapter, we discover father and son once more together by the death-bed of the young Frau von Steinfort.

The arguments of Prince Prominsky had already in some measure had the effect of softening the heart of the father, when at an early hour of the morning an humble and reconciling letter of the Lieutenant came to hand, which the latter had written at the most urgent request of his wife. In this he again expressed the sincere wish of the poor dying woman, at least once more before her dissolution, which was already close at hand, to see the face of her father-in-law. The expressions of repentance, of deep regret and sorrow which were visible in every line of the letter, vanquished at last the obstinacy of the father, and he determined to go.

The scene at the sick chamber was most exciting and deeply affecting, yet the physicians had urged no objection to it, since they unanimously agreed, that there could be no hope of protracting the life of the invalid much longer. All that remained to medical science to do, was to endeavour to sustain her departing pulsation as long as possible, and to make the moment of dissolution as void of pain, and as easy, as human skill could make it.

Augusta had at her own request been removed with her bed nearer to the window, that she might once more enjoy the view of her little garden. All nature seemed clad in bloom, in its bright summer holiday dress.

When the Major entered the room she raised herself feebly, and with half-broken eyes endeavoured to look upon him. Piteously she reached out both hands:

"Pardon, pardon!" she cried in feeble tones, "pardon for all the sufferings and sorrows which I have innocently caused you, which I never intended!"

When the old warrior recognized the pale, gentle sufferer, when he saw her in angelic mildness laying upon her couch of death, his anger disappeared. Deeply moved he stood by the side of her bed, and gently laying his hand upon her head, he said in a trembling voice:

"May the blessing of almighty God rest upon thee, my daughter, and may every thing be forgotten and forgiven."

A sudden and slight blush at these words overspread the pale features of Augusta—she was at this moment wonderfully, supernaturally beautiful.

"Thanks, father, thanks!" she exclaimed, "a thousand thanks for your love and kindness! Only one word more, and I shall die happy and contented.—Come, Carl," she said, turning to her husband, whose hand she took within her own and then placed it into that of his father, as she continued:

"My life separated you, but my death shall re-unite you."

Slowly she sunk back upon her pillow, fixing her half closed eyes with a look of the most intense and warm affection upon father and son, who rested in ardent embrace.

"I have acted rashly, Carl," said the Major in a voice of deep sorrow, "forgive your old father, who thought he was doing all for the best."

"Father, dearest father, do not speak thus!" exclaimed the son, "it will break my heart. My fate is deserved—deserved by my unmanly weakness and by my criminal action. But I will again become what I have been, your faithful and obedient son."

Heavenly satisfaction was painted upon the features of Augusta as she listened to this affectionate dialogue. She was already dying. Once more, however, the lamp of her life flashed up with a bright glimmer; quickly she raised herself from her couch.

"Now I am contented and satisfied," she exclaimed; "I have your forgiveness, you both are reunited, and the ruler of the universe will be a lenient judge towards me. Thanks—dearest Carl—for all the love—and truth—and affection—which made life blissful to me—we shall—meet—again—above—"

She gently sank back to her pillow, and her once beautiful eyes broke; gently and without pain, she had glided from this world to the brighter regions of a better one.

In inexpressible sorrow her husband cast himself upon the corpse.

He kissed the pale lips, he raved, tore his hair, was about to take his life, and implored the departed spirit of his wife to take him with her to another world.

Marianne also had gently crept into the room, and had seated herself by the side of the bed upon the floor. There she sat in silence and shed sincere and bitter tears. She had lost the only friend, the only sympathizing soul which this joyless world had ever had for her, the only one who had ever understood her. Now she was again deserted, had once more become an orphan as before.

The Major stood immoveable and in silence. His conscience seemed to reproach him most bitterly.

The religious fanaticism of Marianne's mind, which had of late regained much of its original strength, as she believed that now, more than ever she discovered the hand of God guiding her path, that fanaticism was the first to strengthen her again. Nay, in this she found strength and courage enough even to give consolation to the two men before her.

"Do not blaspheme, Herr von Steinfort," she said, addressing the Lieutenant, who in his despair was railing against human laws and divine Providence. "God, as we are taught by divine revelation, punishes those he loves. Heaven has subjected us to this severe trial, but only when we endure it patiently, and never murmur against the will of an almighty and kind father, can we hope to be victorious in the end. Let us therefore bow to his will in gentle submission, for he guides every thing for the best."

The Major looked at the plain, simple girl who spoke at this moment so enthusiastically, so inspired as it were, and opened his eyes wide in astonishment.

"You are right, my dear girl," he said, as he gently pressed her hand, " let us bear patiently all that the Lord may inflict upon us. And at the end of time, may he be a kind and lenient judge to us all."

The son would not listen to these mild and pious words of consolation. In wild, passionate speech, he again and again implored the eternal powers for his death, until exhausted and worn out, he relapsed into silent vacuity.

Amidst the confusion of this heart-rending scene, the house had been left entirely unguarded; every door stood wide open. Thus it happened that Polizeirath X—— could unobservedly enter the house, and become a silent spectator of this sorrowful scene.

With what object he had come, we need not repeat to our readers. But for the first time, during a long and efficient official career he felt his heart tremble in the discharge of his duty.

He could scarcely force himself to the necessity, of tearing the bereaved and despairing husband away from the corpse of his wife, and of taking him thence to a prison. Such a course seemed too inhuman even to the policeman's stony heart.

Hesitatingly he stood at the door and looked upon the mournful picture before him.

"No, no!" he said to himself, "I cannot become a barbarian, be the consequences what they may."

And with these words, as noiselessly as he had entered he withdrew unobserved to the front rooms whence he had just come.

But here the consciousness of official duty again awoke in his mind; the responsible office he held alone appeared before his eyes, and in the back ground there might still have lurked the innate and instinctive passion of making arrests.

He considered how easily it might happen that the Lieutenant should learn of the arrest of Referendarius von Birkheim, and how much more likely it was, that he would now be inclined to take immediate measures to make his escape, since the ties which had hitherto bound him, would now bind him no longer.

This thought alone excited the whole mind of the officer, for it would have been without a parallel in the annal of the police administration of Berlin, that an arrestant should have escaped so great and distinguished an officer as Polizeirath X——.

Herr X—— stood as it were, upon burning coals, his humane feelings, excited to pity at the sight of a corpse which was scarcely cold, at the sight of a disconsolate husband, and of a grey headed father, struggled against his innate passion of making arrests, and against a consciousness of severe official duty. The arrest must be made, his duty must be obeyed, and the only question was how to do it in the mildest possible way.

At last, accident came to the assistance of the hesitating officer of the law.

A servant of Lieutenant von Steinfort entered the room, to carry a bottle of medicine, which had even as late as this been prepared, into the sick-chamber of the dead woman; the Polizeirath requested this man to inform his master that a stranger wished to speak to him immediately, and upon urgent business.

Mechanically Steinfort obeyed the request; he was so deeply absorbed in his sorrow, that he never even thought of sending away the importunate visiter who had called at such an improper time.

Polizeirath X—— introduced himself to him in the front room, and in the most lenient, earnest, and measured terms he told him that he was under the disagreeable necessity of arresting him.

At this introduction of Polizeirath X—— Steinfort shrunk back convulsed, his eye assumed so will and fearful an expression, that the man of Justice suddenly stopped apprehensively. The Lieutenant, however, quickly recovered his presence of mind, and politely requested the Polizeirath to continue his communication. A determined and desperate quietness suddenly seemed to overspread his features.

When X—— had concluded his speech, both remained silent for some time. It was a solemn, serious pause, which even the Polizeirath dared not to interrupt.

Earnestly he then said:

"Herr Polizeirath, I appreciate the kindness and consideration which you have shown towards me, and I thank you for it. The commands of your duty, you were bound to obey. I know that the laws of my country can claim me, and now the blow falls upon me with much less severity, than it would have done an hour ago. Permit me only to take one more, and the last farewell from the corpse of my wife, then I shall immediately be at your service. I will pledge you my word of honour, that I will make no attempt at flight."

The Polizeirath readily assented to this reasonable request, and Steinfort returned to the death-chamber of his wife.

With a determined face, he returned to the bed-side of his dead wife, gently closed her broken eyes, and impressed a last ardent kiss upon the cold forehead of Augusta.

"We were not suited for this cold, unfeeling world," he said, looking sadly down upon her, whose sufferings were past, " our hearts have only brought us into opposition, and into contact with the established, yet bad usages of society. This was a fault for which we had to atone, before we dared to hope for a new and happy asylum."

After these words he turned to the Major.

" Dearest father," he began, " I have acted

against the laws of honour, and I alone must give atonement to these laws. Your love, your kind affection, may facilitate that bitter journey by your forgiveness, in this hour of sorrow and misery, do not refuse me your blessing."

At these words he kneeled at the feet of the venerable old man.

The latter could only partly understand the meaning of those words.

"The future will equalize everything," he began, as in ardent prayer, he spread his hands over the head of his kneeling son; "may the blessing of your father from this day henceforth, make you again his only and faithful son, and may the peace and blessing of the Lord rest upon us all for ever."

As if newly strengthened, the son arose, and with firm steps, he entered a side room.

A minute afterwards, the report of a pistol was heard in that room.

They burst the door open, and all rushed in.

The body of Steinfort enveloped in a cloud of smoke, rolled about the floor. With a firm and sure hand, he had sent a bullet through his heart.

With the fearful cry of terror: "My son, my son! I have murdered him!" the distracted father threw himself upon the corpse of his son.

"Drive directly home," said X— to his coachman, in very ill humour, as he entered his carriage alone: "I shall remember it," he said to himself, grumbling most discontentedly, "that I must never suffer an arrestant to take leave of any body, not even when he has pledged his word of honour. To day I have for the first time in my life been cheated out of a prisoner."

* * * * * * *
* * * * * * *

A few days after the above scene, two simple black coffins were seen being moved down the broad *Louisen*-street, and out of the New-gate.

The people in the street told each other, that this was a suicide, and his sweetheart, whose end had come at the same time. The suicide was a noble and rich Count, while the other, for whom he died, was only a girl of the town. The Count had been on the point of marrying her, when she became faithless to him. Then he had strangled her, and blown his own brains out. This, they said, was about the purport of that terrible story which any one might read most beautifully, and eloquently described in the " *Beobachter an der Spree*,"* under the head of " crimes and casualties."

A simple black carriage followed these coffins. The carriage contained but a single old man, with silvery head, and most sad and deeply distressed looks.

Behind this carriage, and on foot walked a simple, and cleanly dressed citizen, leading a boy on one side, and a girl on the other, by the hand.

This man was weaver Greif, whom the Lieutenant had once saved from starvation, and who now offered his last token of gratitude to his benefactor.

* A daily Berlin Newspaper.

CHAPTER XCVIII.

A NEW CATASTROPHE IS PREPARING.

In the quick and hurried succession of the late occurrences, the Equestrian had almost forcibly had to repress a remembrance, which lately had obtruded itself upon her heart and mind, more strong and forcibly than for many years previous. It was the remembrance of the fruit of her first fall, of that child of sorrow, which she had borne amidst want and misery, only to see it soon after torn from her arms.

The sudden and most affecting meeting with the rag-gatherer, who had once been the mediatress of that affair which lead to the loss of her child, this meeting, had again torn open old and long closed wounds, and had awakened maternal longing and maternal anxieties anew. But her heart longed in vain, for the rag-gatherer, who really was humane enough to assist in carrying the fainting Francisca back to her room and to await her awakening, could give no new or further clue to this mystery. We already know from the former narratives of both ladies, in what manner the child had been taken from its mother, and this was all either of them knew about the matter; yet these facts were by no means sufficient to throw any further light upon its mysterious disappearance.

Francisca had made the old woman a small trifling present, and had dismissed her without further remark. It had been too exciting to her, to see a being before her eyes, who would hourly remind her of the loss of her dearest treasure, and without any hope of recovering it.

But this absence of all hope only tended to increase the bitter sorrow she felt. Momentarily and hourly the past would appear before her eyes, and the present would only seem a horrible dream. For all the unspeakable sorrows of many months, for all the bitter pangs of that terrible hour, nothing had remained to her but the fearful consciousness of deserving the name of *a fallen, yet childless mother*.

Whither was she gone, that daughter of tears and bitterness, to what wants, cruelties and sorrows might she not be exposed, that girl who once had drawn its first source of life from this burning, high beating bosom?

We scarcely need to repeat it, that as a natural consequence of these sad and bitter remembrances, Francisca's hatred of Geheimerath Berthold, the origin of all her misery, received fresh nourishment. It was he who had prepared all this sorrow and misery for her, whilst at the same time he had most villanously robbed her of her dearest treasure. It was he, who had cast her off to misery, wretchedness, and want, while he dissipated in wealth, extravagance, and luxury. His luxurious fortune gnawed with fiend like fangs at her breast—she would seek revenge for her crushed existence.

Once more we find her alone in her Boudoir. The longing desire to see her child, shook the heart of the firm and resolute woman, till she was weak and helpless, as a fragile reed. She endeavoured to strengthen herself in her very feelings and desires of certain revenge, which seemed to have just been made doubly sure, by the late confessions of Mary.

All that remained for her to do, was to deliver the Referendarius to his judge, in order to make sure of annihilating the Geheimerath. How to accomplish this, she still was in doubt, and again considered upon it, as she could not yet make up her mind to become a denouncer. She knew not that the strong arm of Justice had already anticipated her, and that the victim which she had intended to sacrifice, had already fallen beneath the just consequences of his misdeeds.

"Yet withal," she said to herself, as the cold and rigid expression of her marble features gradually relaxed, and became mild and mournful, "if any one were to bring back my child to me, I believe, that even now I could relinquish all my long cherished plans of revenge, nay, even sue for forgiveness of him, who has poisoned all my days. Alas there is no hope but for revenge! Oh! a, happy mother must know more of bliss, more of real happiness, than a human mind can conceive!"

Geheimerath Berthold was announced.

The old coxcomb entered the room, in all the extravagant, and disgusting pomp of a beau of twenty.

On the day before, a slight dispute had occurred between him and the Equestrian; the origin of this difference was apparently trifling, but the real cause lay somewhat deeper; it was, that he began to feel most uncomfortable in the nets of Francisca, who despite all the affection and devotion shown by him, firmly continued to refuse the long promised reward of his love and constancy.

But withal this, the sensual desires of the old voluptuary, were so strongly predominant, that he could not gain sufficient courage, to throw off the chains, which so severely oppressed him. The coldness of Francisca had become more and more unbearable every hour, and he hastened to take on his part at least, all the necessary steps to reconciliation.

"Good morning, sweet leaf of my heart," he began with an affectation of boyishness, "I have just passed a silk magazine, dearest, and seeing this very pretty trifle I could not resist buying it for you, and here have I brought it myself. I hope you will not be offended?"

"Herr Geheimerath!" said Francisca with an abashed, modest look, and with that gentle reproach in her tone which she knew always penetrated the heart of her lover.

The Geheimerath opened a parcel, which, enveloped in paper, he carried under his arm, and spread a most splendid, costly *crêpe de chine* shawl, with magnificent embroidered garlands, before the dazzled eyes of the Equestrian.

"Oh how beautiful!" exclaimed Francisca, examining the shawl, with a well feigned expression of childish joy, "and is all this splendid shawl to be mine?"

"Certainly, it is thine, dearest, fairest creature," replied her antiquated lover, "and I will give you much more than this, if you will only cease tormenting me with your proud coldness."

Abashed and modest, Francisca sunk her eye to the ground.

"See, Francisca," continued the Geheimerath, "for months past I already suffer in your chains. I love you—no, I adore you, I worship you. But you torture me with your humours, you merely show me some signs of your love, and then refuse it again, to make me only the more ardent for its attainment."

"You certainly cannot blame me for my refusal," answered Francisca with lively anxiety. "I would not like to lose your love, and all the world knows that the faith of men only reaches as far as their unfulfilled wishes."

"Cruel, cruel fair one!" said Berthold with a sigh, "thus to torture me, and to let silent and unfulfilled desires consume me. No Francisca, even if you were right with all the world beside, towards me alone you commit a bitter wrong by your doubts. Ask as the prize of your love whatever you like, and if it is within my power, I will grant it."

"Well then, I must ask you to leave me," cried the other, in proud and haughty disdain.

"Francisca!" exclaimed the Geheimerath, almost beside himself, half entreating and half in anger, "why do you torture me thus. Do not drive me to despair. Quench the flame, the fire which you have kindled before it consumes me. I suffer more than mortal can imagine, more than words can express!"

An unholy fire at these words shone from his greedy, voluptuous eyes. He drew the beauteous woman towards him, and covered her snowy, swanlike neck with wild and ardent kisses, whilst he held her in his embrace with all the strength of his enervated system.

With graceful coquetry the wily Francisca withdrew from the grasp of her importunate admirer, only increasing in a ten fold degree the tortures of the refusal to her victim, by the very charming grace of her movement.

"Perhaps," she said in a gentle, scarce audible tone, "I may soon belong to you entirely, much more entire than you may wish."

A bitter, mocking scorn lay in these words, but the lovesick voluptuary gladly grasped at them as an assurance of his fairest hopes.

"Heavenly woman!" he exclaimed, almost frantic with sensual desires, throwing himself upon his knees before the beauteous woman, "oh that you spake the truth."

With indignation and disgust, Francisca looked upon the hoary head of the kneeling dotard.

At this moment the door opened, and Mary Berthold, whose intimate friendship with the Equestrian had long since made ceremonious announcements superfluous, entered the room.

Somewhat abashed and embarrassed, the Geheimerath rose from his kneeling position, endeavouring with both hands to obliterate the traces of kneeling from his cloth pantaloons.

Mary seemed not to observe the embarrassment of her father, for she herself seemed but little less embarrassed and excited than her parent.

"I am glad, dearest father, that I find you here," she cried in great haste, "I thought it possible and therefore came here. At this moment, this letter arrived at our house for you, with the most urgent request that it might immediately be delivered to you, as it was of the utmost importance. If I am not mistaken in the hand writing, it is that of Birkheim."

The Geheimerath examined the letter from every side, with curiosity, shook his head and at last broke the seal and read it.

"Good! then the vagabond has his just reward at last!" he cried furiously, when he had read to the end: "I will know nothing more of him. If his life has been criminal, let his death be so also. I care nothing for him or his fate."

Francisca and Mary stared at the Geheimerath in astonishment; they did not comprehend the meaning of those words.

Mary was almost beside herself with terror and internal fear.

At last the Equestrian inquired for the cause of this sudden displeasure.

"There, read for yourself," replied the Geheimerath, "why should I once again have the annoyance and anger it will cause me." At these words he handed the letter to the Equestrian.

Fearfully Mary looked over the shoulders of her friend at the paper.

The letter was in reality from Birkheim. In cowardly fear and repentance, he confessed to the Geheimerath the whole transaction of fraud and forgery at which he had assisted, and ardently prayed that the Geheimerath might use his influence to obtain a pardon for him.

"I shall do nothing of the kind," continued the Geheimerath still furiously, "why should I intercede for this worthless scamp? Give security for him perhaps, to get him out of prison, and let him escape at my expense? I shall know him no longer, and shall never again trouble myself about him."

At this burst of fury, Mary's consciousness almost forsook her. It seemed as if those words had for ever annihilated her dearest hopes.

She cast her looks upon Francisca. The latter with cool indifference looked another way.

For a long time the unfortunate girl could not find expressions for her feelings. At last, however, the intensity of those feelings overcame her, and weeping she cast herself around the neck of her father.

"Father," she cried frantically, "father, save him, for Heaven's sake save him! I love him, and cannot exist without him."

"Are you mad?" exclaimed the Geheimerath furiously. "Have I not once or twice before, told you my opinion of this silly, childish attachment? Never again name that villain to me; the just laws of his country will send the forger to his well merited prison."

That sentence struck dread horror to the soul of the unhappy girl.

Pale as death she cast herself at the feet of the Geheimerath, and wringing her hands, she cried in tones of the most bitter despair: "Then at least have mercy upon your child, which will come to shame and hopeless disgrace—I shall become a mother! Birkheim is the father of the young life, which I bear beneath my bosom."

Horror-struck, the Geheimerath wrung his hands, whilst Francisca's eyes hung upon every one of his features with the intense and fearful malice of a fiend.

But soon Berthold recovered his equanimity. Icy, gravelike coldness began to overspread his entire face, and casting one look of deep contempt upon his kneeling daughter, he said:

"Go then, go, worthless wanton! go and marry your paramour, but hasten, else he may be sent to the penitentiary before you are united."

He then quietly turned to the Equestrian.

"Adieu, dearest Francisca," he continued, "please to pardon my departure for the present, but scenes like these are in reality extremely uncomfortable."

He took up his hat, and hastily left the room.

With a wild and frantic glance, Mary stared after her departing parent.

"Do you know of any other hope, Francisca?" she inquired in anxious, convulsive excitement.

In silence the other shook her head.

"Farewell then, farewell for ever!" cried Mary, and without listening to the anxious voice of her friend, she rushed in wild fury from the house.

Attentively the Equestrian looked after father and daughter.

"How was this?" she asked herself in astonishment. "A communication, which I thought would annihilate him, he receives with perfect coldness, with indifference?—Can it be possible that even in this I am mistaken! Can it be possible that all the tenderness for his child has been assumed, and that her great misery will have no effect upon him. Then all my endeavours would have been in vain. In vain would I have sacrificed the innocent girl, and in vain would a lucky accident, have brought that frivolous, dissipated vagabond, Birkheim into the hands of avenging justice even without my co-operation, though perfectly according to my desire.—But why do I hesitate?" she continued with greater assurance and determination, "one annihilating and principal master blow yet remains to me: he shall learn who it was that prepared this disgrace for him! This must be done immediately: then my task will be accomplished, and then—I would wish—to die. Perhaps, however—I would live and love," she added with a deep sigh and a glance at the bust of Apollo.

CHAPTER XCIX.

TERRIBLE DISCLOSURES.

WITH a sad and troubled countenance, Geheimerath Berthold sat on the following morning in his library.

The necessary companion of his morning hours even, his favourite meerschaum, was to-day left deserted and hung unsmoked on its hook.

Several papers were spread open before him, and in blind haste he searched through them. There were letters, legal acts and other documents. A small wooden box with a strong lock stood also there.

Several times he read through a very long report, to which all the other documents seemed to refer, opened the little box, looked into it, locked it again—in short, he gave every external indication of a man at issue with himself, regarding an important resolution he was about taking.

"What shall I do?" he said at last in impatient soliloquy. "I would willingly have covered over every thing with the mantle of love, for I shall be derided and laughed at. My late amiable wife, Heaven rest her soul, or the devil take her, just as he pleases, independent of all this, never enjoyed too fair a fame among the city gossips. But if I remain silent, what am I to do with this reprobate, wretched girl? I cannot even in honour and decency give her that dissipated, dishonest vagabond for a husband, for a number of years in prison is his almost certain doom.—What then, am I to do? I, a *Royal Geheimerath*, (Privy Councillor) am without advice or council in my own difficulties."

His internal fear caused the Geheimerath to become humorous; but it was only the humour of fear.

This man belonged to a class of saints peculiar to our times.

With insolent levity he had crushed numberless innocent flowers that lay upon his path of life. With triumphant pride he had pointed at those terrible victories which he had gained over female virtue and modesty, and had boasted no little of the unenviable reputation, of being considered the greatest *roué* in the capital.

It had never once occurred to his mind that there might be disgrace in this, that he might be despised for it. But now, when the matter changed and took another aspect, now when retribution came upon him through his own daughter, he became pusillanimous; now he found his honour deeply injured, and would perhaps have given all his wealth if he could only have saved his reputation in the eyes of the world. But was it on his own account that his conscience pricked him? was it the remembrance of his own past misdeeds that now troubled his mind? We believe not! He was so entirely lost and absorbed in sensual, sinful longings, low dissipation had so absolutely superceded all nobler feelings, that he perhaps never thought of his own misdeeds.

There is very little doubt, but that this step of human depravity is the lowest, because the God-like within the human soul has already degenerated into the mere animal, yet we are sorry to write it, society at present offers not a few, whom we may consider fac similes of our Geheimerath.

Whilst he was thus absorbed in thought, he was interrupted by the Equestrian, who, according to her prerogative, had entered the room unannounced.

A bright ray of sunshine overspread his darkened looks, for what else could bring his lady love at this early hour of the morning to him, but an impulse of love? Yes, yesterday he must have completed his conquest of her heart by the *crêpe-de-Chine* shawl; there was no earthly doubt, but that she had been impelled by affection to come thus early and thank him for it. At last then, the hour had arrived, when she would entirely be his own, belong to him, even more than he could hope for—had she not said so?

With a countenance burning, red, and flushed with intense passion, the roué rushed towards the beauteous woman. His senses thirsted madly with wild love and passion.

"My delight, my love, my life!" he exclaimed, as he forcibly pressed his hot, withered and parched lips upon her rosy mouth.

With silent and stern dignity, the majestic woman repulsed the ardent attacks of the enamoured old man, and only now he observed, that the wonderful change which had taken place, was not confined to her face or her manner.

Instead of the splendid and costly silk dresses, in which his extravagant liberality used formerly to dress her, she was now only clad in a simple black mourning dress. Around her neck she wore a silk neckerchief of black colour, which closely concealed the voluptuous neck, and, being brought around the body, beneath the arms, was tied in a knot at the back. The rich mass of locks upon her head had been combed down into simple modest braids, and the voluptuous long hair at the back of her head, was adorned by a small bow of black satin ribbon.

In this sombre frame, her pale features, which had now assumed that unmoveable rigidness, which we know they were so capable of, became gloomy and ghastly in appearance. Only the large, brilliant black eyes still betrayed the existence of life in this marble statue.

The Geheimerath shrunk back affrighted before this dread-inspiring, fearful figure.

"What means all this, Francisca?" he inquired, shaking with uneasiness, yet forcing himself to appear merry. "Did you wish to give me amusement, by this strange masquerade?"

Like the ray of lightning which passes through a dark cloud, so a flash of anger passed across her marble features.

"Amusement?" she repeated, laughing in terrible derision, "amusement? No! This is fearful reality." And suddenly changing her tone to stern seriousness, she said: "This mourning has more causes than one; it is first for my unfortunate friend Mary, whom you yesterday drove from your presence with such hardhearted coldness."

"Speak not of that!" cried Berthold, half in prayer, half commanding, "I will hear no more of that spoiled, unworthy wanton. Last evening I sent her out of my sight, and with sufficient severity, I hope."

Francisca's majestic figure seemed to increase in height.

"Speak not of it!" she repeated passionately, "I not to speak of it? No sir, I will not be silent. Has the poor girl committed this once, a greater crime, than the one you have been guilty of hundreds of times towards my poor sex? or is she aught else, than one of those victims, the like of whom, you have seen twenty times prostrate at your feet, whilst you spurned them with cold contempt? And why are you now enraged at her?"

Berthold seemed to find this language unbecoming even from the lips of a woman whom he adored, for although he experienced no regret for the past, yet in common with all other voluptuaries, he felt a cowardly fear of hearing a remembrance of the past recalled.

"Francisca, once more," he said with firmness and decision, "I do not wish to hear you speak of those things. How are you justified in speaking to me thus?"

"How am I justified, sir?" suddenly exclaimed Francisca, who now suddenly assumed a tone of voice which the Geheimerath had never noticed of her before, and which sounded to his terror-struck ears, like the voice of an avenging angel on the last day of judgment, "how am I justified? My *disgraced and annihilated* youth, my *lost honour* justifies me. Look upon me! Do you now recognize me? Have passions, the miseries of life, and the thirst for revenge, really put an impress upon me, which would veil the truth even from the seducer? If so, look upon this miniature, and you may comprehend why I appear thus in mourning before you!"

At these words the Equestrian produced the well known portrait which the Geheimerath in former years had had painted of her, from her pocket, and held it before his eyes. Upon this miniature she was dressed precisely as she appeared to-day.

Thunderstruck the pale, hoary sinner started back, casting a quick, comparing look upon the picture and upon the features of Francisca. A fearful and terrible presentiment seemed to rise in his mind; he was incapable of replying a single word.

"Do you recognize me now?" continued Francisca in the same tone of voice. "Yes sir, yes, I, your own, your adored Francisca, I am the original of that portrait; I am that harmless, innocent and guileless girl, whom you once robbed of her last, her only treasure, her innocence. Do you

remember these sable clothes in which I then mourned the loss of my parents, and soon after the loss of my aunt also, at whose grave you swore eternal truth, fidelity and help to me, the helpless maiden?—How have you fulfilled that vow? With the power of police you drove me from the gates of the town of B—, after you had disgraced me, robbed me of my virgin honour. At that time you were an unknown Assessor, to-day you are a high and important officer of the state; but for that very reason my thirst for revenge is the more burning, and since at last, after long years, the hour of revenge has arrived, you now see me clad in its colours."

With all his powers the Geheimerath had endeavoured to gain some composure, which seemed to have entirely deserted him before the furious, yet majestic and commanding woman. At last he hit upon an outlet, which he availed himself of as soon as Francisca stopped for a moment to regain her breath, after her passionate speech.

"I greatly fear that your mind wanders," he said in a cold, yet cowardly quiet tone of voice, "for I cannot remember any thing of your adventures in B—. But the portrait which you hold in your hand belongs to me, and was stolen from me. I now demand of you to let me know how it came into your possession, unless you really should wish me to deliver you as the thief to the criminal courts."

Francisca was silent, for she seemed to have expected any other answer sooner than this from the thoroughly chilled and hardened roué. But her eye-brows contracted darkly, her eyes flashed fury, and a bitter contempt, beneath which the eyes of the Geheimerath quailed, played around her mouth. She seemed to feel, that she was upon the point of resigning all and every thing which nature had given to her person of womanhood and womanly qualities. With a herculean effort she returned back to the bounds of becomingness.

"Miserable wretch!" she exclaimed, "where is the tribunal which will award me right and justice for the theft you have committed upon me? which will recompense me for the unspeakable disgrace of long years?—Show me such a tribunal, and I will account to you before your courts and judges for the possession of the picture in my hand!"

With icy coldness she then continued:

"But I do not wish to become excited; I do not wish to embitter the enjoyment which this hour will give me for the pangs of years. Listen, Herr Geheimerath, for I have a long story to tell you.

"You know now, that I was once that modest, artless and inexperienced girl, to whom you promised to unite yourself at the altar, and whom you villanously deceived. I will not repeat all that I have suffered, but I will tell you, that only the thought, the hope of finding you again and of taking terrible revenge upon you, still supported me. Year after year have I sought for you in vain, until at last I found you, surrounded by fortune and luxury. I endeavoured to approach you; fortune or accident favoured me, and my charms, for a second time, enslaved you.

"You remember how often you have winced at my feet, and what tortures of love you have suffered. Often, when you thus languished, I felt a silent desire to stand up openly before you, to disclose every thing to you, and to luxuriate on your pale horror. But that revenge was too trifling for me; mine must be greater. You have a daughter. Disguise it as you may, I know that she is the only hope of your life, the pride of your old age; often enough have you confessed this to me in warm enthusiasm. That girl I sought out for my victim; in that daughter I would annihilate your hopes, even as you once annihilated mine.

"That maiden is now dishonoured, and this is *my* work! I have favoured the intercourse between Mary and her worthless lover, I, by wise and cunning counsels, have produced the consequences of this connexion, and I have done it only, because I knew that Birkheim was a swindler, and ripe for a prison. In this latter fact lay the certainty, that even your paternal consent to the match, would never be able to hide the disgrace and dishonour of your child from the world. I myself would have delivered her seducer to the hand of avenging justice as a false player, but fate anticipated my intentions, and saved me from becoming a denounceress.

"Now you see, sir, to accomplish this work, I entered your house; to accomplish it, I have compelled you to introduce your daughter to me, and for the same purpose have I excited your anger against the Referendarius, his hatred against you—and now tell me, was the work of revenge, worthy of Francisca? *Your only daughter is disgraced by a common swindler!*"

The Equestrian stopped, and with the looks of a tigress, watched for the result and effect of her communication upon the face of the Geheimerath.

But instead of the entire, and hopeless despair which she anticipated, she found him perfectly calm and collected. Slowly he walked up and down the room, stood quietly for a moment at the window, whistled carelessly, and finally approached her again. With a certain fiendish contempt he looked upon her excited, passionate appearance. He had evidently been weighing an important subject in his own mind.

"Your frankness deserves my thanks," he said with scornful sympathy; "but you have taken great pains, and worked very long, to gain nothing in the end. Your arrows have all passed harmlessly over my head. The subject might have remained for ever a secret, at least such was my intention, but I now feel the necessity of rewarding your open hearted candour, by a similarly candid confession. Know then, that Mary is not my daughter, although even I have believed her to be such until very lately, but that she is a bastard, who does not belong to me, and whom

I would immediately have removed from my house if appearances, and pity for the situation of the poor girl had not restrained me."

"How is that!" cried Francisca, trembling, and scarcely able to support herself.

"You shall learn every thing, my dear, my most adored," began the Geheimerath, who was gradually recovering his presence of mind and seemed determined upon fearful retribution; only be patient, and you shall soon see, that I will even exceed you in the candour of my confession. Perhaps you can remember, that a few weeks ago, Herr von Birkheim, your most worthy partner, called me away from your house, and informed me that a stranger anxiously wished to speak to me. That stranger came from Italy, and brought letters and documents with him, which fully explain all that was before mysterious.

"Immediately after I had known you in B—, and after you had disappeared from that town, I took leave of absence, since that affair with you, had created a rather disagreeable sensation. I travelled direct to Rome, and there soon became acquainted with the daughter of a former Roman nobleman, who was then engaged to be married to a chevalier. I became most intimately acquainted with this lady, and consequently got embroiled in a duel with her betrothed, whom I wounded mortally, and was compelled in the utmost haste to fly to Germany.

"The Italian lady, in company with a Duenna, accompanied me, and we all safely reached Berlin. The lady, however, was not at all satisfied with being considered my mistress, but was determined to become my wife. To attain this object, every art of female intrigue and ingenuity was applied both by herself and by her companion, and finally they even persuaded me, that my Italian mistress was in hopes of shortly becoming a mother. I had very often expressed my great fondness of children, and the cunning intriguing woman rightly concluded, that, should she ever become the mother of my child, she might soon urge well founded claims upon my hand.

"For the purpose of entirely and successfully carrying out this plan, they managed so, by further intrigues, which I cannot all explain to you now, that I had necessarily to be almost six months absent from Berlin. During this absence I received intelligence of the confinement of my mistress, and on my return I found myself the father of a fine, healthy and good looking girl.

"This girl is Mary, and the mother, by her fraud actually attained her object and became my wife. My matrimonial life with this woman, who was frivolous, vicious and tyrannical, was by no means a pleasant one; luckily for both of us, she died before we had been married very long. Her companion, the duenna of whom I have spoken, returned to Italy, and died at Rome some few months ago. Upon her death-bed she confessed her crimes, and delivered all the letters, vouchers and other documents necessary to prove the case to her father confessor, with the request of forwarding them to me immediately.

"By these documents, as well as by her last confession it is clearly proved, that Mary is the natural child of a poor unfortunate girl, of whom sixteen years ago, through the agency of an old woman who sold matches in the streets, she bought it for considerable sums of money, and gave it to my late wife, who died and took the falsehood unconfessed into the grave with her. They have even sent to me from Italy the strange little shirt which the child wore when they obtained it.

"I have never exposed any of these facts, but carefully concealed them all in my breast. I would have continued to keep Mary and consider her as my child, if only for the sake of the world. I was certain not to expose it even for my own sake, since my wife, as I have also learned very lately, was not the daughter of a nobleman, but was a common wanton, whose entire history I would wisely have concealed for ever. But now, since this girl also has prepared to disgrace me, I must even submit to the small annoyance of declaring myself deceived by my wife. I shall drive the girl from my house, and leave her to you alone to continue and complete your work of revenge upon her in any manner you may think fit."

In fear and trembling Francisca had listened to this narrative. She dared not to draw her breath from fear of losing a single word; but her face became paler and paler, the longer the Geheimerath spoke to her.

When he had finished, she exclaimed in feverish anxiety: "the shirt, show me that little shirt!"

With immoveable calmness the Geheimerath handed her the little wooden box. Anxiously she tore it open, produced the little garment, looked at the mark, and with a fierce yell and a voice of the most intense terror, she exclaimed: "Almighty and just God! Mary was my own daughter!" Her senses forsook her, and she sank to the ground.

This cry of intense despair even penetrated the soul of the Geheimerath; overcome by gloomy horror he stood before the prostrate woman.

But her despair was too intense to permit her to remain long in a swoon.

After a few seconds, she again started up from the floor.

"Mary was my daughter!" she repeated with the same cry of despair. "She was our child! mine and yours: she was the fruit of your villanous betrayal; here in Berlin I was confined, and it was in an humble, low attic-chamber, inhabited by an old woman who sold matches. My child was on the point of starvation, and I parted with it to a couple of Italian ladies, who shortly afterwards disappeared. That little shirt yonder, I made for the child from one of my own, and it still bears my mark."

At this moment a servant of the Geheimerath entered the room looking greatly disturbed, and brought a note, which that morning had been found in the room of the young lady, who herself had not been seen for several hours.

The servant withdrew, and with a trembling hand the Geheimerath opened the letter.

It contained the following words:

"My dearest father!

"Life has become a burden to me, forgive me if I throw it off. I cannot do otherwise! When you receive this letter, your daughter already stands before the Judge of the universe. There she will pray for you.

"MARY."

Without speaking a word, the Geheimerath handed the note to the Equestrian.

His features had become ashy grey, his eyes stared phantom-like upon vacancy, and his hair seemed to rise.

The Equestrian read, and then burst into terrible, loud, yelling peals of laughter.

The blow had fallen too severely upon her, and too sudden. The unfortunate woman had lost her reason.

"This invitation to come to the Prince's ball, comes much too early for me!" she cried with a merry laugh, "I have not yet finished my wreath, my wreath of white roses. Oh, how beautiful that will be! how handsome I shall look in it! Only see, Carl, how pretty!"

At these words she twisted the little baby shirt into a coil and put it upon her head. Then she pushed table and chairs aside, stopped before the large *Trumeaux*, and with wild and frantic passion endeavoured to dance a few lively *pas*.

Suddenly she stopped again.

"Listen Carl, Mary is calling," she said in the low, hoarsely whispering tones of madness, "she too wants to go to the ball with us, and I have left her all alone. She is simple and innocent, and she will be seduced. Hark, hark! Yes, yes, my child, I will come presently, I come, I come. Adieu Carl, dear Carl, adieu star of my soul, adieu!"

And at these words with a merry, playful movement she danced out of the door.

Despairingly the Geheimerath looked after her.

His face had assumed a fearful, terrible, deadly stare. His eyes were deeply sunk into their sockets, the fanciful grey locks hung in long strings around the ashy pale face, and his upper teeth had bitten into the lower lip, until the blood trickled down drop by drop.

He seemed to observe nothing that passed.

"Retribution," he exclaimed in a low, inaudible tone, "retribution, at last you also overtake me! Hu! hu! how it tears and burns in my inmost heart.—Almighty and great Heaven!" he suddenly exclaimed, yelling aloud, "do not desert me, this torture is death!"

*   *   *   *

When, towards noon, the servant entered the room, to inquire for his master's orders for the day, he found the dead body of the Geheimerath hanging by the cross railing of the window. He had hanged himself with his pocket handkerchief. His eyes had turned black, and his tongue hung far out of his opened mouth.

* * * *

Mary in reality had been the daughter of the Geheimerath and the Equestrian. The caution and carefulness with which the fraud upon the Geheimerath had been accomplished, had rendered it impossible to discover the cheat before this terrible catastrophe.

The only circumstance which could possibly have led to suspicion was this, that Mary must have already been several weeks old, as she really was, when the Italian ladies could possibly, according to the natural course of things, advise the Geheimerath of her birth. This, with the inexperience of the Geheimerath was very easily hidden, as his return had, by the cunning machinations of the woman, been so delayed that his own child must be a few weeks old, when the discovery of difference of age was as good as impossible.

CHAPTER C.

RENEWED TERRORS.

PRINCE PROMINSKY was walking up and down in his room, in a state of the utmost excitement.

"And will she not confess, whence she has obtained that document?" he inquired of the yaeger, who stood before him, as he pointed to an official document that lay upon the table.

"Before me, at least, she is silent," replied Eeleye, or rather, to call him by his proper name, which he had again assumed, *Albert Walther*, "I have no doubt, however, but that gold will loosen her tongue, and that she herself is only waiting for the offer of a large reward."

"But how comes it, that since the occurrence of the late events, this document has never been spoken of before?" continued the Prince.

"Oh yes," replied the other smiling, "a great deal has been spoken about it. At the command of your Highness, the ragged, dirty clothes were taken off the old woman during her sleep, and clean ones put on her instead. To create no suspicions, I immediately locked up those rags, without examining them any further. As soon afterwards as she awoke, and in some measure had recovered her senses and observed the change which had taken place in her appearance, then the noise immediately began. The old woman attacked Frederic very severely, as she asserted, that the latter had stolen the document from her, and for that reason held her a prisoner.

"Frederic, however, had orders not to enter into any conversation with her, and as you are aware, he knew not that she had ever worn any other clothes, and still less, that anything had been hidden in them. Thus then, the affair remained as it was, until I had returned from Braunsdorf, at which place, as your Highness knows, I was detained a few days longer with domestic arrangements.

"This morning then, I entered the room of our prisoner for the first time, and I certainly had a great deal of trouble to guard my face against the attacks of her claws. She fell upon me like a furious wild cat, and demanded the return of the document. I knew not what she could possibly mean by this, but on searching her clothes, I happened to find this document. The signature appeared remarkable to me, on account of its similarity to that of Major von Steinfort, and for that reason, I thought it my duty to inform you of the whole affair. By your command, I immediately examined the old woman closely, concerning the origin of the document; but as I told you before, she persists in the most obstinate silence."

"I must tell you, Walther," continued the Prince, "that the signature to this document, is in reality none other, than that of Major von Steinfort, and you would do as high and important a service to that gentleman, as you have done to me, if in case that the girl herein mentioned, who really is his daughter, should be still alive, you could by some means bring her back to his arms. This would be the only means by which we might renew the existence and animation of my worthy friend, who, since the death of his son, has fallen into deep and absorbed melancholy.

"But stop!—a terrible thought here crosses my mind; the rag-gatherer, as you tell me, has a daughter, who is at this present moment, the inmate of a prison; is it possible that this be the girl in whose favour the Major originally drew that document? This certainly would be new and redoubled terror!"

"No, no," replied Walther, "that is impossible; I have long been well acquainted with the rag-gatherer, and more than well acquainted with her daughter. The old woman has led a wild, infamous and lawless life from her childhood, and her child dates its origin from a house of ill fame. Moreover, this document has not been in her possession above a very few weeks, and she has no doubt stolen it."

"This quiets my anxiety in some measure," resumed the Prince, but the old woman must confess, be it by force or by kind means; too much is depending upon that. Consider upon the best means of doing this very quickly. But now accompany me; we will proceed to the house of weaver Greif, who lives before the New-gate. Major von Steinfort has requested this of me, as among the papers of his son, plans for securing the future welfare of that man and his family have been found, which the Major considers an inheritance from his son, and conceives it to be his duty to carry them out."

"Ah, your Highness," began Walther, in evident embarrassment, "I have another subject at heart, if you will kindly permit me to reveal it to you."

"Well Albert, what is it?" inquired the Prince

kindly, " I am under so many and great obligations to you, that I cannot easily refuse you any reasonable request."

Albert's embarrassment increased so evidently, when it came to the point of speaking, that the Prince could not keep from smiling at him.

" Well," he began, " tell me what it is. Why, you are blushing like an innocent maiden of sixteen !"

Walther rubbed his hands, rested upon his right foot, then upon the left, scratched his head, and finally said in comical haste:

" Yes, yes, your Highness, if I were an innocent girl of sixteen, I would have less cause for embarrassment than at present, for then my bashfulness would be becoming and in character while in an old sinner like myself it must appear ridiculous enough. But I may as well ease my heart, and speak it out at once; I am mortally in love with a girl."

" Well, well, is it possible ?" answered the Prince, with an ironical smile, " and now, I suppose, you are *mortally* anxious to marry said girl, and anxious that I should build you a cottage and give you a start towards house-keeping. Well I will be faithful to my promise to you— or rather, my brother will keep my promise now. As soon as we are returned to our dominions, you shall travel through them and select a chief-forrester's place, wherever you like to have it best."

" No, no, your Highness," replied the other, who had been listening with great impatience, " I don't mean any thing of that kind. I already know perfectly well, that your Highness will plenteously provide for me, and I could never dare to doubt the fulfilment of your promises. But my request was of an entirely different nature."

" Well, speak out then."

" The girl whom I love," said Albert, " knows me, and every circumstance of my life since childhood, and I know that she wishes me well; but then she is proud and haughty, and evades the question whenever I want to speak seriously to her. Most possibly she does not like my external position. I have consequently come to the conclusion, that it would flatter her vanity and self-love, if so illustrious a person as your Highness would intercede and speak a good word for me, by telling the girl that you intended to provide a respectable living for me."

" This is, in other words, that you desire me to court the girl for you, to become a match maker ?" said the Prince with his former ironical expression.

" Why, if you please to call it by that name, yes !" replied Walther.

" It is a disagreeable and generally thankless undertaking," replied Prince Prominsky with a smile. " Above all things what is the name of the woman who is so happy as to have gained your affections ?"

" She once was my playmate, the companion of my early childhood," replied the other, gath- ering courage, " and your Highness knows her; it is Francisca, the Equestrian."

Involuntarily the Prince shrunk back in affright, and a slight blush mantled on his face.

" Francisca ?" he inquired in a drawled tone— " and is she the woman of your choice, whom you would marry ?"

" Yes, your Highness."

" But she does not love you."

" I think she does."

" No, on my word she does not, I tell you no, she does not love you !" exclaimed the Prince, with so eager an anxiety, that the yaeger stared at him in astonishment.

The Prince observed this, and endeavoured to compose himself.

" I simply mean," he replied, and a sad bitter expression played about his noble features, " I simply mean, that she cannot love at all, that she owns a heart cold as marble."

" No, no, your Highness, you mistake her," cried Walther with much warmth: " her's is a warm, fiery, passionate heart, but one which has been terribly abused by the world, and around the outside of which, a hard, impregnable, adamantine covering has formed itself."

" Well, well," replied the Prince, who evidently endeavoured to break off the conversation, " we will speak about this matter at some other time. Meanwhile," he continued with a suppressed sigh, as he offered his hand to the yaeger, " be fully convinced that I shall not forget the great services you have rendered me, and that I shall endeavour to reward them whenever and wherever I can. But now come along, for I am in a hurry."

Without further delay both emerged into the street, and started upon the proposed visit.

Their way led them after a long march through the *Augustus-street*, where an extraordinary concourse of people attracted their attention.

In this street is situated a long one story house, which has a little turret on top, and is consequently usually called by the Berlinians " *the Thürmchen* " (the little turret.) In the yard of this house, we can discover another small house, also built of only a single story, consisting of a narrow entrance and hall, which leads to two small rooms to the right and left.

This house is the Berlinian *Morgue*, (dead house.)

Hither all dead bodies which are found are usually conveyed, unless they are immediately or previously reclaimed by relatives, which in a large city like Berlin does not often occur. The number of persons, who in Berlin lose their lives by accidents or suicides and are found in the Spree, in the public canals and elsewhere, is frequently not inconsiderable, and this little turret is constantly filled by visiters or persons in search of missing friends.

On this occasion, as we observed above, a most extraordinary concourse of people had gathered at this place. The Prince and Eel-eye observed a great number of persons who arrived and went away again, and with every mark of deep regret, spoke of a most affecting sight which might to day be seen in the interior of the Morgue.

They spoke of two female bodies which had that morning been brought in, the one of which seemed to have been a beautiful woman, but no longer very young, whilst the other seemed a fair maiden still in her teens. The perfect symmetry of both figures, and the fine expression of their pale features were the theme of universal admiration.

Driven by an inexplicable degree of curiosity, the Prince desired to witness this spectacle himself, and with his companion, followed the mass to the interior of the house.

The room to the left of the hall above mentioned, served for the exposure of dead bodies. This room is perfectly empty and vacant, with the exception of a wooden reclining berth, such as may be usually found in guard-rooms. Upon these boards the dead bodies that have been found are laid, are divested of dress, in order to enable friends or relatives to recognize them by marks, scars, &c., and if they chance to be thus recognized and reclaimed, the full and punctual description of the affair is recorded by the proper officer.

Towards this room the Prince and Eel-eye proceeded.

With a simultaneous cry of terror, both shrunk back, at the first glance they cast inside of the room. Francisca's dead body lay before them, and by her side that of Mary Berthold, who was also known to both, though not intimately to either.

Death had cast a gentle and placid expression over the pale features. There they lay, the one not unlike the broken lily, the other like the pale reflection of a winter's moon; their faces no longer betrayed the late wild struggles of their hearts.

Sad, painful thought. A cruel fate had separated mother and daughter even from the cradle through their whole lives, but that fate permitted them to lie side by side upon the bier of the suicide.

Unable to utter a word, in mute silent horror, the two men withdrew from the room. They both believed themselves to be under the influence of some horrible dream, the purport of which they could not comprehend. But in vain they endeavoured to free their minds from the oppressive fetters by which that dream chained them.

CHAPTER CI.

FIRST RAY OF SUNSHINE.

SEVERAL days had passed.

In dark, sad brooding, Walther was moving about his master's place; he ate, drank, worked as he was commanded, but took no further share or interest in any thing that passed around him.

The Prince also was so sadly affected, so deeply cast down by the late occurrences, that it re-

quired some time to regain his evenness of temper even in some measure. Only now it became clear to him, how deep and intense had been the interest he had felt in that mysterious woman, who despite of many hardened, cold and selfish traits of character, despite her malicious scheming, often had displayed a noble germ of innate goodness, and had sufficiently shown, that she also had only been one of the many victims who daily fall a sacrifice to the present ill-judged and unfortunate position of society.

The Prince had inquired more closely into the probable causes of her madness and death, and in regard to the internal causes which brought about this terrible denouement, he had arrived at pretty correct conclusions. He had learned positively that the unfortunate woman had become a maniac, and in her madness had taken her own life. Phantastically attired, she had one day at noon walked to the castle bridge, apparently peaceable and collected, and here to the terror of all around her, and with almost superhuman strength and agility she had precipitated herself over the broad granite wall into the stream below.

These sad occurrences only increased the interest of the Prince, who had ever been most deeply affected by the peculiarities of this wonderful woman—certainly without having any presentiment, of how deeply he was loved in that proud, wounded heart.

But all this only convinced him the more, how deeply he himself had loved that unfortunate victim.

The Prince longed to be absent from the great capital, for the sea of houses seemed to crush him with its weight. His brother, who, after the definite declarations of the Jewess, had finally, though still with reluctance and resistance, been convinced of the brilliancy of his fortune, shared this desire with him. After a long and necessary consultation, and with the consent of the Major, it was finally determined to retire to the country seat of the latter, and there to spend some time together, prior to the departure of the two Princes for Poland.

The Major was satisfied with every thing; since the death of his son, he had lived in the house of the latter, where Marianne was his only companion, who endeavoured in vain to raise his drooping spirit with all the consolation which her simple, devout and religious mind could give. He looked upon his sorrow as the visitation of God, as a just punishment for his prior treatment of his cast off and rejected daughter, and with this idea he had abandoned the world and all its joys. The strong, manly, energetic and almost blustering old warrior, had suddenly become a weak, dejected and meek old man.

Before leaving the capital, however, the Prince considered it his duty, if possible, to obtain an explanation of one other circumstance; this was the question, of how the rag-gatherer had obtained the document which Major von Steinfort had drawn in favour of his daughter, and whether that same old woman might not also be able to give a clue to the whereabouts of the child. The Prince had not intimated any thing of this affair to the Major, as he would not throw him into a fresh, and in all probability useless state of excitement; moreover, his own sadness and sorrow at the death of the Equestrian had too much absorbed his mind during the last few days. He now determined to undertake the matter with more earnestness.

The rag-gatherer had obstinately refused to give any information whatever, and had even rejected the promise of rich rewards—evidently because she hoped to obtain the full amount promised in the document, namely, three thousand Thalers. Hitherto the Prince would not agree to promise her such a heavy amount, as there was every probability, that the child in question was long since dead and forgotten. And although the rag-gatherer threw out certain and definite hints, that it would be in her power to give positive information concerning the child, the Prince could not help remembering that he was dealing with a most artful and cunning thief, who would not hesitate to resort to any intrigue for the purpose of obtaining money. Walther himself had warned his master of her.

The Prince finally determined to avail himself of a certain means, which he had hitherto been loath to resort to, since a certain and rather laudable feeling of Walther's struggled against it. It was namely, his intention, if the rag-gatherer should persist in her constant refusal of confession, to threaten her with a criminal accusation by Walther, who, as she must be aware, by such an accusation, would secure himself, by turning state's evidence, from a punishment of his own past crimes.

Against such a course Walther had hitherto most strenuously objected, as we observed above, from a consideration of his former position, yet the Prince had finally prevailed upon him, by using as an argument, that in this case the happiness or misery of a noble and honourable man, was placed in juxtaposition with the sordid greediness and selfishness of an incorrigible criminal, and that a mere threat would be as good as an action, since it was highly probable that a threat would be quite sufficient for their purpose.

Walther finally yielded to this reasoning.

When the rag-gatherer in this manner found herself cornered, as from one side she saw herself threatened with the police and the workhouse, whilst from the other she saw the most pleasant prospect of receiving a good reward with which she would also regain her liberty, she at last yielded to their wishes and confessed every thing she knew.

Thus it came to light, what is already known to our readers, namely, that the document was in favour of Marianne Jobs, the step daughter of the former cellar-keeper, who now in the immediate vicinity of her real father retained her former position of housekeeper.

The Prince was most deeply affected on learn-
ing this news; however, he remembered the letters, which the Jewess had once written to Major von Steinfort, and in which she had referred to the extraordinary character of this girl. These letters, which the Major had shown to him at the Masquerade, and which again were stolen from him at the Circus, by the present Prince Iwan, and were afterwards returned by Francisca to Prominsky, these letters, now became most important documents, whereby to judge an unfortunate woman, and to assist in installing her into her rights.

With all these necessary documents in his pocket, the Prince hurried immediately to the Major.

As usual, he found him in a little garden which had belonged to the new domicile of his children. Here the unfortunate old man used to sit amidst the beds of flowers and vegetables, which his son had laid out with his own hands, a short time before his marriage, for the purpose of preparing a surprise for his young wife. Sadly and absorbed in thought he stared upon the plants and flowers, which the warm June sun had drawn from the mother earth, and which mocked his sadness and sorrow in a thousand merry buds and flowers.

It was the warm afternoon of a fair summer-day, when Prince Prominsky crossed with hasty step the white gravel walks of the little garden.

The sun shone brilliantly down upon the rich luxurious green of leaves, and upon the many coloured blossoms and flowers which impregnated the air with their luxurious scent. The Major was seated in the arbour, which adorned the background, his arm rested upon the garden-table, and his sorrowful head was supported by his hand.

He was absorbed in deep and sad thoughts. The long, grey eye-lashes were dimmed and wet, for a bitter tear had just trickled down that rugged cheek.

"You are again so sad, my dear friend !" said the Prince gently, as he remembered that he must be very careful to avoid too sudden a communication of his joyful intelligence.

"I have no reason to be joyous," replied the Major with a deep sigh.

"You have lost what can never be replaced," said the Prince, "but nevertheless you should not abandon hope, or otherwise you may also lose the courage of life."

"And who tells you that I still possess any courage of life ?"

"The fact of your existence. You would not live without the courage of life."

"Certainly !" replied the Major. "But my life in reality is no life ; I only vegetate."

"I observe it," replied the Prince who had closely watched the manner of the speaker, "you must be assisted by a powerful medicine, by one which will strongly excite the lamed powers of your existence. I have such a medicine in preparation for you, and I offer it to you without hesitation, as I consider your physical nature sufficiently strong to endure its effect. Is this known to you?"

At these words the Prince produced from his pocket, the document which the Major had drawn for his daughter, and spread it open upon the table.

The Major cast only a slight passing glance upon the paper; but his eye was suddenly fixed upon it. A deep and all-powerful emotion portrayed itself in his every feature; his pale lips quivered, and every one of his iron nerves trembled:

"Great Heaven!" he cried passionately, "what is this? How comes this paper into your hands?"

He looked into the face of the Prince with an intensity, as if he would read the words even before his lips had uttered them.

"I come by it, strangely enough," answered Prince Prominsky. "Albert has found it among the things belonging to the old woman who fell into our hands at the same time with my brother. She professes to have stolen it from another thief, without exactly knowing where the latter remains at present, or how he obtained possession of this paper."

The intense excitement in the features of the Major, relaxed as quickly as it had appeared.

"Then this paper is of no earthly value," he said in a sorrowful tone. "Apart from the unfortunate child, this can no longer serve as a cue whereby to find my daughter. And upon the whole, who knows how many persons may already have owned this paper. As I told you once before, mother and child are both long since dead. Let the matter rest."

The features of the Major showed plainly that these hopeless words were not spoken from his heart. With unmistakeable interest, his looks hung upon the lines, which many years ago had flown from his pen. His whole past life seemed to be legible in those letters.

"Two and twenty years," he began half aloud, as his finger pointed to the corresponding words in the document. "That long term even is nearly at its close. I would give thrice three thousand Thalers—ay, my entire fortune would I willingly give, if my child would offer me that paper on that day. But, no, no! All, all is past!" he added bitterly.

"Not quite all, my worthy friend," exclaimed the Prince encouragingly. "At present you have at least gained a starting point, which the kindness of fortune has most wonderfully and unexpectedly given to you, and to which for the present you may cling with some prospect of success. As well as I have found my brother after some difficulties, you may also be able to find your daughter. Let us now change our respective parts; you have lately helped me to search, and now I will help you."

The Major sadly shook his head.

"I have yet another piece of news," began the Prince, changing the subject, "which may not be without interest to you. Your pocket-book, which, as you may perhaps remember was once stolen from you at the Circus, has been restored to me again. Francisca, the Equestrian, gave it to me some time since, and I have hitherto forgotten to restore it to you."

Mechanically the Major took the proffered pocket-book.

"How did the Equestrian obtain possession of it?" he inquired in a tone of indifference, as he opened the *Portefeuil*.

"That I do not know," answered the Prince in a most uncertain tone of voice; "this wonderful woman, has evidently had connexions with the highest as well as the very lowest and most degraded classes of society, and the latter have assisted me most materially in the recovery of my brother. Most probably it has been by these means, that she gained possession of this pocket-book; despite of my many inquiries, she most studiously avoided giving me any information on that point, until it has now become impossible. Examine these papers," he recommenced, addressing the Major after a short pause, when he observed, that the latter had, among other things from the pocket-book, also spread the letters of the Jewess before him, "I am very confident you will find every thing there."

The Major obeyed this request mechanically, as his mind was evidently occupied with entirely different matters.

The Prince, who seemed to observe this, carelessly took up one of the letters and hastily glanced over it.

"*Apropos*," he exclaimed after a few seconds, "here I first find the name of Marianne Jobs, whom this Jewess recommends to us in her letters with such eager anxiety—I believe it was in the third of those letters?—yes, yes, here, just please to read it. Do you know that this same Marianne Jobs is now an inmate of this house? Upon my honour, fate is more careful of our protegê than we are ourselves, for we had forgotten all about this unfortunate girl."

"What! My Marianne? is it possible that she could be Marianne Jobs?" inquired the Major with newly excited attention, as he took up the letter of the Jewess. "No, no, I certainly did not know that! Let me see, what was it the Jewess then wrote about her?"

"'—and this girl is an angel of innocence and love. Never have I seen so pure and noble a heart, never so pious and innocent a mind, united to such determination and strength,'" he read aloud. "Yes, yes that is right."

"It is true, my dear friend," he continued, after he had read the letter to the end, and had folded it up again, "it is true, that kind Providence has sent a real blessing to me in the person of this girl. She is the only consolation that has remained to me in these bitter days of sorrow and tribulation, and I have serious intentions of keeping her by my side and never parting with her again. All that the Jewess then told me of her, in those warm enthusiastic words, I find true to the letter, and much more than true.

"A few days ago I prevailed upon her to tell me the whole history of her life, and I must confess to you that my heart would have bled at her recital, had not its own deep wounds already exhausted its blood. After indescribable miseries, that poor girl, like thousands of others in this demoralized, wicked city, at length, by means of fiendish, inhuman fraud and malice, fell a victim of the seducer; my son, at the urgent request of his wife, who was her friend, took her from the house of a vile procuress to his own.

"You know, my friend, what my opinions on those points formerly were; but my late experience has changed my mode of thinking. I no longer reproach my son for his charity or philanthropy, but on the contrary, I implore Heaven's choicest blessings upon his memory. Where we can find so much purity of mind, so much real piety, so much true Christianity, and such true penitence as we find in this girl, and which she preserved even after her gloomy and unfortunate life, there a grain of unalloyed gold must have lain at the foundation. She has not only reconciled me to the memory of my dear departed children, but has united me to the whole class of unfortunates to whom she belongs.

"You should have heard, my dear friend, the narrative of her life, which bore the pure love of plain unvarnished truth upon its front, how she accused herself where she might have cast a curse upon society and its institutions, how she accused herself of faithlessness to her God, when the minister of the church had shaken her faith by his wild fanaticism, and how, finally, in her indescribable modesty, she endeavoured to find an excuse for them all, only to appear guilty herself. You should have seen the heavenly, the angelic mildness with which she took the part of her sainted friend and of my own son against me, the hard hearted father, and then only, you would have begun to understand with me the words of our Saviour, 'there is more joy in Heaven over one sinner that repenteth, than over ninety and nine just persons who need no repentance.'

"On my honour, Highness, the tears, which repentance pressed from her simple heart, fell like burning fire upon my soul, and I cried woe, thrice woe, upon that society, which in pride, haughtiness, and the luxury and extravagance of their wealth spurns such minds and crushes them beneath its feet.

"The great, nay, highest problem which the history of the future has yet to solve, *is to place beyond men's power to commit that species of civilized suicide, which is daily committed under the protection and authority of the laws.* No blood flows at these murders, but millions of tears are shed, and those tears will generate the curse of coming generations!"

The Major had spoken this in great enthusiasm; his eyes sparkled, and his dejected, mute depression had entirely left him.

The Prince had attentively listened to him, and the deepest sympathy was expressed in his fine, manly features.

"And now, if fate would take you at your word?" he inquired, "and if Providence were to bring back your child to your arms, even as Marianne is now, even as that girl stands before you, would you still open your paternal arms to receive her?"

"Ay," replied the Major solemnly, "ay, I would. I would endeavour to atone to her, for all the wrong society has done her; and more than this, I could believe that I myself was atoning for my obstinacy and hard heartedness of my former years, and I would even dare to hope for more quiet and peaceable hours on the evening of my life."

"Then trust in God," said the Prince, "for I tell you, your wishes shall be gratified."

The words were pronounced in such a decided, firm and confident tone, that the Major in the utmost astonishment stared upon the Prince's face, which looked at him with an expression of mild earnestness.

A blessed presentiment seemed to rise in his bosom.

"Highness, explain yourself," he cried with a trembling voice, "you speak strangely! This document in your hands—your tone of confidence!—Our late conversation!—No, no, I am not mistaken—you know much more than you choose to tell me. I entreat you, I beg of you, put not a weakened old man to this torture of soul and mind! Tell me all you know."

The Prince discovered, that longer delay might operate more dangerously, than a sudden surprise. Moreover the Major seemed with certainty to anticipate all that was to follow.

"Yes," began the Prince, "my dear and sorrowing friends I have news for you. Your daughter is alive, and in a few minutes she will rest at your heart."

Like seraphic tones, these words resounded in the ears of the exhausted old man; his lips remained silent, but the devout prayer of the heart ascended inaudibly to the throne of the King of Kings.

Ten minutes afterwards, Marianne rested in his arms, and a joy holy and elevated as the raptures of Paradise descended upon their heads; and the tears that bespeak a heart overflowing with happiness, flowed calmly and sweetly as the tide of a summer brook.

CHAPTER CII.

RURAL RETIREMENT.

ONCE more we find all the persons of our narrative, who had safely reached the haven of happiness, after passing the wild whirlpools of adversity and misfortune, in a quiet, social circle at Braunsdorf, about the middle of the summer of 18—.

Here is Major von Steinfort and his daughter Marianne, Prince Prominsky and his brother

Iwan, the Jewess and her children, and last not least, Albert Walther.

All had carried off deep and sore wounds from the thorny path of their life, and it needed the healing balm of time, to make them less sensible to the first intense pains.

Here Prince Iwan Prominsky gradually, and by slow degrees succeeded in becoming accustomed to his new station and dignity, and finally to look upon it as his real hereditary right. But the more he gradually began to perceive and understand, what great sacrifices his brother had made for him, nay, what immense and unparalleled personal exertions had been necessary, even to enable the latter to bring so great a sacrifice to what he considered his duty, the more his love and warm affection for this wonderful man increased.

Iwan had retained in his inmost heart better feelings and sentiments, than could have been expected from the education he had received, and from the associations which had been forced upon him. The nobler part of his nature now awoke in all its might, and as this necessarily led him to repentance of his past life, he endeavoured by perfect and unquestioning submission and obedience to his brother, to show the first fruits of the mental reform which his change of condition had wrought.

We need not tell our readers, who already know him so well, that the former only used his influence in the most noble manner, by making his brother acquainted with his new and high duties; by standing at all times at his side with word and deed, representing as it were the kind and gentle tutor, who is endeavouring to restore a lost, neglected and abandoned heart to the bosom of human society. Since the catastrophe of the Equestrian, the mild serenity of the Prince had even appeared more predominant than usual in his character, and in the fulfilment of all the duties he owed to his now dearly beloved brother, he sought consolation for his sore heart.

Major von Steinfort still deeply mourned the loss of his only son and his daughter-in-law, yet, even as he had said himself, the blessing of God had fallen down upon him, in the person of his newly found daughter. The veracity of the statement of the rag-gatherer, who only repeated the original statement of Jobs, the hunchbacked cellar-host, was easily proved, partly by the existence of the document, and partly by the communications which Marianne was enabled to make about her mother, which soon convinced the Major, that Marianne's mother could have been no other than the woman of his early love.

He consequently did not for a moment hesitate to acknowledge the girl publicly and solemnly as his daughter, to legitimatize her, and thereby to give her the rank of a noble *Fraülein*, and of the descendant of an ancient and renowned family. The girl, however, in thought and feeling continued to look upon herself, even in a similar light as Iwan continued to look upon himself. She could never forget what she had been,

though innocently, and endeavoured on her part, by gratitude and repentance, and by the most childlike attention to every wish of the Major, to atone for the errors of her past life.

Day after day, the old man took her more closely to his heart, and transferred all the love he had entertained for his lamented son, to his newly found daughter. He delighted in hearing her tell of his daughter-in-law, whom he had unfortunately so little known, and with sad joy listened to hear her daily repeat the praise of his beloved son.

Amidst the papers of the latter, he had found the carefully digested plan of an institute, a society, for the promotion of morality, industry and respectability among the lower working classes. This idea, which concerned one of the most important interests of the time, he determined to carry out with the utmost care and conscientiousness, and to devote to it the entire independent fortune of his son. By this arrangement, in which it was especially intended to have all the offices of directors, secretary, &c. filled by members of the working class, weaver Greif was to fill the office of managing director. This office had already been assigned to him by the Lieutenant, who by personal consultation and examination, had convinced himself of his ability to fill that office.

It is certain, that in this manner, the Major erected for his son the fairest monument, which at the same time was a proof, that the latter had not uselessly conceived the plan of studying poverty.

With intense attachment Albert Walther clung to his new master, whom he had to thank for his reform, and for being again received in the pale of civilized society. The terrible death of the Equestrian, the cause of which still remained an unsolved mystery to him, filled his heart with bitter pangs of sorrow. He fulfilled the duties of his new station with attention and fidelity, and waited for time to bring the necessary balm to his wounds.

The Jewess also, who, notwithstanding his vicious and criminal mode of life, had most ardently loved her husband, deeply deplored and mourned his loss. She felt her bereavement the more bitterly, as it was a long time before she could free her mind from the accusation of having been the cause of her husband's imprisonment and death. Only the thought upon her children consoled her, and quieted her stings of conscience and self-reproach. Together with those children, she now publicly became a christian, and endeavoured by maternal precept and example, to eradicate the bad impression which early instructions from their father might have made upon their youthful minds. Fortunately the hearts of these children were yet tender and flexible enough to be capable of receiving new impressions, and the endeavours of the mother seemed about to be crowned with the most perfect success.

We must particularly refer to the present position of Fräulein von Steinfort, (our old friend

19

Marianne) and Prince Iwan Prominsky, who, having always been friends in former times, now suddenly meet again in entirely changed circumstances. They delicately avoided referring to their past position, as each was afraid to touch a chord which might still reverberate sorely upon the other's heart. Nevertheless they were heartily rejoiced at meeting again, and soon showed that their temporal separation, had not had the effect of obliterating a mutual interest, which each might have felt for the other in some measure before.

On the contrary, it rather seemed that their present acquaintance would ripen into a more intimate attachment than before, and it even appeared that this position of things was not only pleasant and desirable to Major von Steinfort, but also to Prince Prominsky. This much at least was certain, that these two gentlemen often had long and earnest conversations, wherein an unseen listener might continually have heard the names of Iwan and Marianne, or rather *Caroline*, as the young lady had been originally called, and which name had now again been given to her.

We must also observe, that the latter or Iwan, if they accidentally sought each other with their looks—an accident by no means of rare occurrence—invariably found the eyes of both of the other gentlemen upon them, and mutual confusion was the almost unavoidable consequence.

Thus passed several months in rural retirement, when a plan was conceived, which was destined to give another and most decisive direction to the future welfare of this little society.

———:

CHAPTER CIII.

EMIGRATION.

THE summer was already declining, and the yellow leaves of autumn began to make their appearance.

The two Princes Prominsky were one afternoon returning from the chase, at which, in company of Walther, they had amused themselves, in the fine old forests of the Major's domain.

"My dear Stephan," began Iwan, addressing his brother, "for some time past one single thought, which I necessarily must communicate to you, has occupied my mind. The moment when we must bid farewell to our present kind and hospitable host, and must return to our dominions in Poland, is near at hand. I am then to become the legitimate Prince, and take the government of my boors in my own hand. The nearer this time approached, the more fearful I was of the consequence, and I have now become fully convinced that it will never do. I am willing to believe, since you tell me so, that there will be no obstacles in the way of the acknowledgement of my legitimacy; but allow me to ask you, how am I to appear among the nobles of my rank? I lack the accomplishments, the ease of intercourse, knowledge of circumstances and etiquette, and Heaven knows what else.

"Yet perhaps these deficiencies are the least; but soon people will begin to inquire: whence does this Iwan, this new Sovereign come? Where has he been all his lifetime? And what is then to be done? Will you tell people the truth? That will never do, for in that case it will soon come to the ears of my subjects, and the former as well as the latter would make life a heavy burden to me, and besides all this, my government would yield the worst possible fruits.

"But even supposing you were not to tell them the truth of my former history, what can you tell them, and how can you protect any untrue explanations against the discovery of the truth? Am I to be constantly exposed to the danger, of being some time or other, perhaps at some most brilliant and public occasion, recognized as the thief Schmerles, of being called to account by my neighbours and equals in rank for the imposition practised upon them, and of being in shame and disgrace expelled from their society?

"Let me finish, dearest Stephan," he continued, as he observed that his brother was on the point of interrupting him, "for I am not yet done. I may as well confess to you," he said with a smile, "a circumstance which you may probably have known long since. Marianne, or rather Fraülein Steinfort and myself have renewed our old acquaintance, and this time with a more sincere attachment. I love that girl dearly, my love is returned, and I desire to marry her. I know that neither you, nor the Major will entertain any objections to this; but every thing that I have told you of my own individuality, may also apply to her. And now consider if the people of our Sovereignty should learn, in what condition you found not alone my own, but the nobility of my wife.

"Both of us would hopelessly have to fall beneath the hatred and derision of half the country, and even though I might be able to bear this as far as I myself am concerned, I dare not risk it, since another, and a most dear person would suffer by it. From all these reasons you must perceive that I am not formed for a position, in which one must be educated to be able to live in it. As a conclusion to this very long speech, I must consequently make another proposition to you: You will pay me a sufficient sum of money, the Major will do the same by Marianne, and we will marry and emigrate to America. Then you take and keep our dominions and your rank of Sovereign."

Stephan sunk into silence when Iwan had concluded, and without speaking a word, the two brothers walked for some time side by side.

Prince Prominsky soon saw the truth and rationality of his brothers reasoning. He had never in fact denied them to his own mind, but had partly suppressed them, and partly he had hoped, that many things might be repressed and changed, until finally he came to the definite conviction, that his brother not only wanted much to make him a proper person for a Sovereign, but that at his advanced age, there was little or no hope of his making up for lost time.

Besides all this, he had the sad example of Lieutenant von Steinfort right before his eyes, which could teach him all the dangers of impetuosity and want of care. And moreover, despite of his endeavours, he could not forget in his love for his subjects, that the government of his brother could not possibly lead to happy or blessed results, if the dark spots which rested upon his mental and moral qualifications should come to the knowledge of his subjects. He must reasonably entertain the utmost fear, that scenes might occur, calculated, again to harden the mind of his brother, and all this he must absolutely endeavour to avoid, since he himself had ever been a kind, good and charitable ruler of his subjects, who in many respects were without protection against their Sovereign; since by the principles of feudal serfdom, they were but little better than the slaves of their master. But on the other hand, he would have to separate from his dearly beloved, and newly found brother, if he should agree to that brother's proposition, and this thought was equally unbearable to him.

At last he replied:

"I cannot deny the truth and correctness of your reasoning, my dear Iwan, and in fact, the same apprehensions have long since occupied my mind; but I believe, that I can offer an amendment and improvement to your plan; how, if I also were to emigrate to America with you?"

"Ah, if you would do that," replied the latter, "you would make me so very happy; I was upon the point of asking it of you, but would not do so, as I did not know, whether you would like to relinquish your rank in Russia."

"My dearest brother," replied Prince Stephan, seriously, "you might easily have learned ere now, what are my opinions in regard to this. I only esteem the *man* and his personal merit, not the merit and nobility inherited at his birth. Come, it is a bargain! together we will emigrate to free and happy North America."

And thus the treaty was concluded.

Major von Steinfort readily gave his consent to the marriage of his daughter and Prince Iwan. Blushingly she confessed to her father, that she hoped again to become happy by the side of her admirer, and Prince Prominsky declared that he would never refer to or think of her past life, since his own was not only equally black, but much more criminal. The old gentleman had long since foreseen this result of the renewed acquaintance of Marianne and Iwan, and had already come to this conclusion with Prince Stephan, before the young couple had openly confessed their attachment.

And now when the plan of emigration was brought upon the tapis, the old warrior declared stoutly, that he would never again be separated from his children, but if they emigrated, he would bear them company.

Of course our readers must easily understand, that Walther and the Jewess with her children could not be left behind.

It was then finally concluded to emigrate all together, and to seek a new and peaceful fatherland in the western hemisphere.

The Major found an opportunity of selling Braunsdorf in the course of the autumn of the current year, after which, all the persons above named retired to Poland to the hereditary castle of the Princes Prominsky.

Here the nuptials of Iwan and Marianne were celebrated, and the winter was passed in quiet and happy retirement.

Early the following spring, Prince Stephan Prominsky issued a solemn proclamation, wherein he gave liberty to all his serfs and feudal subjects; he also made many and large donations of his landed property, and declared the rest transferred by legal sale to the crown.

This was the last sovereign act of the Princes Prominsky upon that territory, which for centuries had felt their prowess and influence; Poland no longer owned the noble race of the Prominskys, which had even seen kings chosen from the glorious line of their ancestry.

* * * * *

* * * * *

In the month of June of the current year, and in the harbour of the free Hanseat-town of Hamburg, the fine brig Catharine, Captain Elsner, spread her canvass, and with a fair wind started upon her voyage to New York.

On her deck stood our friends, waving their handkerchiefs and bidding a last farewell to their dear fatherland. They were accompanied by a considerable number of farmers, mechanics and others from the former domains of the Major and Prince Prominsky, who were determined to remain with their old masters, and together with them to found a new colony in the far west. God speed them.

THE END.

[Unmutilated and Only Genuine Edition.]

THIERS' LIFE OF NAPOLEON,

WITH SUPERB STEEL ENGRAVINGS.

FOR SEVENTY-FIVE CENTS,

[If paid in Advance.]

W. H. COLYER having been at great expense to procure a copy of this unrivalled work, now publishes

PART I.

OF THE

HISTORY OF THE CONSULATE AND THE EMPIRE

OF

FRANCE UNDER NAPOLEON,

By M. A. THIERS,

LATE PRIME MINISTER OF FRANCE.

WM. H. COLYER's edition of this splendid work, The Life of Napoleon, is decidedly the best in this country. It is printed on fine paper and new type, according to the design of the author, M. A. Thiers, and on comparison with other editions will be found far superior.

In Press.

THIERS' FRENCH REVOLUTION,

TO BE COMPLETED IN SIX PARTS, AT 12 1-2 CENTS EACH.

TO BE COMPLETED IN TEN NUMBERS.

THE MYSTERIES OF BERLIN,

FROM

THE PAPERS OF A BERLIN CRIMINAL OFFICER,

TRANSLATED FROM THE GERMAN

By C. B. BURKHARDT.

With Illustrations on Steel, by P. Habelmann.

This work in Europe has been universally pronounced far superior to M. Sue's celebrated "Mysteries of Paris," and we confidently predict. that the popularity of this translation will be without a parallel in the history of light reading.

www.ingramcontent.com/pod-product-compliance
Lightning Source LLC
Chambersburg PA
CBHW080819020726
47501CB00009B/2342